ROYAL POINCIANA

ROYAL POINCIANA

A novel of old Palm Beach and New York

Thea Coy Douglass

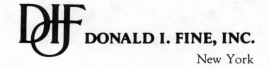

DONALD I. FINE, INC.
New York

Library of Congress Catalog Card Number: 1-55611-048-0

ISBN: 87-81426

Library of Congress Cataloging-in-Publication Data

Douglass, Thea Coy.
   Royal Poinciana : a novel of old Palm Beach and
New york.

   I. Title.
PS3554.0845R69   1987   813'.54   87-81426
ISBN 1–55611–048–0 (alk. paper)

Manufactured in the United States of America

10 9 8 7 6 5 4 3 2 1

Photograph appearing on the half-title page is used with the permission of the
Historical Society Palm Beach County.

To C. E. R.,
a counselor of rare prudence,
and D. I. F.,
a bookman of discernment and tenacity.

$\mathcal{A}$ very rich man with a driving dream can prove an awesome antago-
nist. Even nature herself can be tamed, transfigured and bent to
the will of a man who commands armies to carry out his wishes. Henry
Morrison Flagler was such a man. While it was true that cold weather
exceedingly displeased him, other factors contributed more heavily to the
fulfillment of Flagler's mightiest handiwork—transformation of the eastern coast of Florida from an unpassable boggy wilderness to a tropical
playland for the wintering rich.

Flagler had won his fortune as a partner of John D. Rockefeller in the
Standard Oil Company, but there had not been satisfaction enough for
him in this achievement, an amalgam of dynamism and ruthlessness.
Something beyond self-service, and beyond his loathing of wintry
weather, drove him to cultivate the commercial flowering of the great
peninsula. No obstacle withstood his will and his purse. Jungles were
felled, marshes were filled, creeks and rivers and bays and the ocean itself
were bridged at his command, railroad lines and depots imbedded in
sand, problematical land titles and official cooperation purchased and a
personal empire spread ever-southward before the wave of his not entirely
benign hand.

Destinations were needed, of course, if Flagler's golden coast were to
flourish, so he ordered the creation of a necklace of grand hotels along
the steadily lengthening projection of his hubris. The first was the Ponce
de Leon in St. Augustine, devised for him by prominent New York
architects. It was a splendid structure, summoning visions of Old España,
from its massive dome upheld by huge oak pillars and its medieval towers
that shadowed the Atlantic, down to the heavy metal door knobs patterned like seashells from the Mediterranean deep. Not long after, he
built another hotel north of Daytona with an entire eighteen-hole golf
course attached. But his vastest pleasure palace was erected on the eastern
shore of Lake Worth, a misnomer for a long, emerald-lined ocean inlet
two-thirds down the peninsula. Here, upon the sandy shoestring of land
called Palm Beach, between the ocean glitter to its east and the lakeside
lushness to the west, Henry Flagler began building in 1892 the largest
resort hotel the world had ever seen.

Painted bright yellow with white trim and green shutters, the Royal Poinciana's six sprawling floors contained, by the time they were completed, nearly twelve hundred rooms and offered the latest conveniences of science and technology—glass-shaded electric light fixtures, telephones in every room and modern plumbing. Servicing its hundred-foot-wide lobby rotunda, three miles of corridors, thirty-two acres of fragrant grounds and three dining rooms (one for the guests, a second for their children, a third for their servants) was a work force that grew to sixteen hundred at the height of the ten-week season.

Among the ranking members of the Royal Poinciana's staff was the head housekeeper, whose responsibilities for maintaining the hotel's standard of spotless luxury were such that her compensation included a three-room suite of her own. At the beginning of the 1896–97 season, this important position was filled by Madeleine Memory, a woman of exemplary efficiency and subdued temperament, except when occasionally aroused by the inexpertness of her underlings. Mrs. Memory was never seen in clothing other than the black accouterments of mourning, her personal uniform. This dark costuming, and the singlemindedness with which she performed her duties, had the effect of diverting attention from her physical appearance. For, despite her more than twenty years as a working woman, with their inevitably coarsening toll on her form and features, Mrs. Memory was by no means devoid of the bloom of life. She did her best, however, to cloak the attractive aspects of her person that, in a less discreet woman of her station, might have invited intrusions upon her professional activity as well as her treasured privacy.

ONE

℘he train whistle startled her, causing the keys hanging from the chain around her right index finger to jangle uneasily. As if by reflex, she pulled her finger palmward, circling the keys within her hand. No disorderly sound was to disturb the peace or delicate constitutions of the guests. Her soundless pace quickened. If the whistle was plainly audible, the train had to be in at West Palm; all should be in readiness.

She drew the list of room assignments for arriving guests from the pocket of her black skirt. Rooms 318, 325 and 351 were impeccable. Only two left to check. Yes, the new chambermaid might work out. But could she sustain her performance? Any girl could do a few rooms right. The trick was to keep on doing it after fatigue and disinterest had set in; competence had to become automatic.

Murmurs and even an occasional giggle sifted out through the closed doors as she hurried through the hallway. Guests were entitled to their mirth, she supposed, considering how much they were paying for the privilege. Imagine: a hundred *a day* for the suites, and even the smallest rooms went for thirty-five—more than two months' salary for a New York chambermaid! But these people could afford it; indeed, they gloried in their ability to overpay for the world's goods, insisting only on extreme deference in return.

As she stepped into Room 374 from the dim hallway, the brightness within momentarily assaulted her. The perfection of the green and white color scheme soothed her at once. At first she had thought the combination, which Mr. Flagler himself was said to have mandated for most of the rooms, to be tedious, but lately she had changed her mind: green for life and growth and renewal, white for purity and cleanliness and health. It was all thoroughly refreshing and restorative, especially when set

9

against the pure azure and golden sunlight that filled the windows.

Expertly she scanned the room. The white wicker furniture was all in its assigned place. The windowpanes sparkled, the sills were immaculate, the bedspreads were pristine and cream-smooth and the green floor-matting betrayed no imbedded debris. Only the complimentary basket of fruit awaiting the new guests struck a discordant note. What was it doing on the desk, where it interrupted the view through the window? The fruit belonged on top of the dresser, where it took on an arranged prettiness that bespoke the bounty of nature in that latitude. She placed the basket to the left side of the chest top, taking pains to see that the dresser scarf hung symetrically. And the curtains, she saw now, were a trifle too full. She adjusted the folds so they no longer appeared to be supported from below by a crinoline.

In the bathroom the towels were crisp and white and folded properly on their holders. The porcelain surfaces gleamed. She ran a finger across the bottom of the tub and came away with a powdery film. Plainly, the new girl had scrubbed it; now if only she could learn to rinse it out till the last traces of the cleanser vanished. Back in the bedroom, she cast one last look around. Her eye fixed on a single tiny white mote that had settled upon the base of the telephone. Mrs. Memory blew it away and departed. The new maid might do quite nicely.

Imagining the hubbub about to explode in the lobby with the imminent arrival of the morning's trainload of guests, she sped around the corner to Room 398. The door was ajar. Her sixth sense told her all was not well within. She pushed through the doorway. A pile of used linen sat on one of the chairs while the beds, stripped to their mattresses, looked skeletal and forlorn. This would never do. Rooms at the Royal Poinciana were to be fully ready to receive their exalted occupants—and not just seconds before their arrival. Where *was* the new girl?

She pivoted about, preparing to summon the delinquent from whatever corridor recess was hiding her, when a heavy thump and an exclamatory "Hey!" in an unmistakably male voice sounded in the hallway just outside the room. She hurried out to investigate.

A man in a striped linen blazer sat sprawled on the floor, legs splayed on the matting in front of him, his straw boater still rolling down the hall in a lazy spiral. Behind him the new chambermaid, lace cap askew, strands of sandy hair descending from their topknot, stood rigidly, her wide eyes terror-filled, with one hand pressed against her mouth, the other clutching the handle of a basket that was hanging empty over a large heap of white linens surrounding her on the floor.

The maid could wait; guests must be served. "Are you hurt, sir?" Mrs.

Memory asked the gentleman, bending over him. "May I be of assist-ance?"

For a moment the felled victim said nothing, and she worried he had been severely stunned. But then he came to life. "No, I'm fine—just fine," he said. He raised and lowered his jaw tentatively, as if testing to see if it was still adequately hinged. "Right as rain," he said, next waggling his head from side to side to assure himself further of the claim. "Nothing seems to be broken." He began to pull his feet toward him.

She introduced herself, identified her position on the staff and ex-tended a hand toward him. "May I help you up?"

"Very kind of you, I'm sure," he said, tucking one knee underneath him and setting his weight on it gingerly, "but I can manage." He climbed to his feet and began brushing himself off, seeming more troubled by the indignity of the episode than by any bodily damage. He had just stepped out of his room, he explained, swiveling his head to indicate the door to 396, and had been bending over to lock the door when the chambermaid, her vision obviously impaired by the basket of linens, piled directly into him. "Knocked me off my pins like a locomotive." It sounded more anecdotal than accusatory as he recounted the run-in. A slender chap of perhaps thirty, he seemed rather better natured than most of the guests.

Mrs. Memory apologized for her chambermaid, who, at this recogni-tion of her existence, let out a quiet sob but remained posed in horrified rigidity.

The gentleman took a series of long-legged strides to retrieve his straw hat, which he slapped on jauntily, then gave a two-fingered wave over his head as he turned the corner in remarkably unperturbed departure.

As soon as he had disappeared a low wail erupted from the chamber-maid. "Quiet," Mrs. Memory said. "Help me pick these things up—the new people will be arriving any moment."

They tossed the linens into the basket willy-nilly. At the bottom of the pile the housekeeper came upon two playing cards that apparently had been dislodged on impact from somewhere on the gentleman guest's person. She slipped the cards into her pocket and hurriedly shoveled the maid and the linens inside Room 398, closing the door firmly behind them. At the sound of the latch engaging, the new maid whirled around, her face still ashen, and held the basket in front of her like a shield.

"What is your name?"

"R-R-Ruby Lee, ma'am."

"Do you have a surname as well?"

Short and scrawny with a long thin face and an almost lipless mouth, the girl seemed no more than sixteen. "Ma'am?"

"Ruby Lee what?"

"Eustis, ma'am."

"Be quick then, Ruby Lee Eustis—clean the bathroom while I make up the beds. There's no time to lose."

"Oh, I done all the cleanin' before. All's needed here is the beds and fixin' the towels up proper."

"Well, then, get on with it."

The girl's eyes widened. "Ain't you goin' to give me the sack?"

"Everyone is entitled to one mistake, Miss Eustis—and you've just made yours. See to it there are no more."

"Oh, yes, ma'am," said Ruby Lee, scarcely able to believe her good fortune. "There won't be none." She set down the basket on the floor, reached for a sheet from the pile and then hesitated. "Should we use these here sheets, ma'am? They might'a got dirty from the floor—"

Damnation. The girl was right—under normal circumstances. But it would require precious minutes to fetch fresh sheets from the far end of the corridor, which even now was beginning to sound with the clatter of bellmen arriving with luggage. Mrs. Memory peered closely at the sheets. "These will have to do."

The girl sprang into action. The two of them worked smoothly together, wasting no motion. Ruby Lee managed especially well the tricky business of achieving a French bolster effect with the pillows, chopping them in half with a single swipe from elbow to palm and tucking them under the bedspread smartly. She was a very good worker despite her unprepossessing appearance. "All right, miss—finish up with the towels."

"Yes, ma'am—and thank you, ma'am." She bobbed a quick curtsy, like a cork pulled underwater and released abruptly, her motion jostling the just-made bed. She smoothed the spot and fled while her luck still held.

Gently closing the door behind her, Mrs. Memory tried to replace the ring of passkeys in her pocket but found it clogged by the two playing cards that had been loosed from the fallen gentleman's possession. She studied the pair of pasteboards. A jack of clubs and a queen of diamonds. Turning them over, she noticed that they were from different decks. How odd. And why would a gentleman leave his room with playing cards on him when the hotel provided them in the game rooms? No satisfactory answers rushed to mind, but then she reminded herself, as she had long since discovered, that there was no accounting for the quirks—and worse—of the idle rich. Or the doubtful character of their attentive consorts . . . like the pretty Yale boy whom she had taken, in her innocence, for a sterling sort and given herself to wholly and paid the dear price. But that had been in another life, which seemed disconnected from this one, with all its manifold indignities. She must not complain, though, seeing that there were so many far worse off than she—and, at any rate, there was nobody for her to complain to.

The incoming guests, many still wearing their dark, heavy clothes from the north, thronged the lobby in a festive mood after having been sere-naded to a fare-thee-well from the train platform to the lobby by the hotel orchestra. They exchanged shrieks of recognition with pastel-clad friends who had clustered in the rotunda to greet them, causing a nearly impassa-ble logjam of humanity, white and black, as blue-uniformed bellmen, their fixedly smiling teeth as shiny against their dark faces as the brass buttons on their liveries, staggered under remarkable quantities of luggage.

Skirting the lobby bedlam, Mrs. Memory descended to the retail shops lining the ground-floor arcade and renewed her rounds. Maintenance of the shops' interiors was the responsibility of the individual owners, of course, but their facades and entranceways fell under the hotel's supervi-sion. She took out a folded envelope and pencil from her pocket and noted the imperfections as she glided by each shop.

A paint chip the size of a silver dollar was missing from the haber-dasher's front door, and the floor matting was almost worn through in front of the apothecary—how had she missed spotting that earlier? Proba-bly the heavy tread of ever-increasing numbers of guests in the past few days had hastened its deterioration. The milliner's sign needed tighten-ing, and the curtain screening the hairdresser's front window was unac-countably soiled in several places. She would have a word with her after lunch. No one had yet bought the pretty opal bracelet in the jeweler's window, she noticed, but did not doubt that it would soon adorn a guest's dainty wrist.

The sign in the travel agent's window further distracted her. It invited the guests on an excursion to a Seminole village and the thrilling discov-ery of ancient tribal rituals. She herself would relish such an adventure. Perhaps on her day off. But how? Not accompanying the guests, certainly; fraternization with them by the hotel officers was not permitted. And she could not make a trek of it with her peers—Miss Sanderson, say, who, as Mrs. Memory's assistant, was of course on duty when Mrs. Memory was not. She had little in common, moreover, with the wives of the married officers. The only one with whom she had exchanged more than pleasantries—Mr. Stokes-Vecchio's dumpling-shaped spouse, over Thanksgiving dinner to which she had invited Mrs. Memory at their stuccoed house in St. Augustine on her way to Palm Beach—chose to remain at home during the hotel season so that her husband would not be distracted from his heavy responsibilities as general manager. And since she had no suitable male friend with whom to attend the Indian rituals and she could hardly go unaccompanied, her sightseeing would have to be postponed for other times and other places.

Her brief reverie was broken by the sudden discovery of a small work of vandalism to the white wood paneling alongside the notions shop. Someone, probably someone small and male, had carved the initials P.E.B. in letters about an inch high and sufficiently deep for the tannish wood beneath to be revealed. It looked like the handiwork of a pocket-knife, perhaps pearl-handled if possessed by one of the pampered darlings of the clientele. She would advise Mr. Jenkin, the hotel engineer, over lunch, so that the blemish might be promptly repaired. But what about the child? Should he escape scot-free? Surely the youth would be improved by accountability for his crime, small as it was.

She slipped behind the main desk and consulted the registry before Mr. Walters noticed her and had time to offer his unsavory services. The chief desk clerk made a practice of confiding some choice morsel of gossip to her about any guest whose name or room assignment she had occasion to obtain. This thoroughly distasteful trait appeared to bolster Mr. Walters' fragile self-esteem, so she would merely murmur an acknowledgment on hearing his latest revelation, but she steadfastly refused to trade with him in kind. Swiftly now, she ran her finger down the alphabetically arranged guest list at the front of the large book, searching out P.E.B., the knife wielder. It was a matter of no great detective work: Barton, M/M Alfred; Basset, Mr. C.; Bates, Mr. William M. and Miss Elspeth; Bennett, M/M Judson II; Benson, M/M Phillip Edward, Miss Anne and Master Phillip, Jr.—ah, the little villain himself. Rooms 538 and 539, she noted on the front of her folded envelope.

The policy question of responsibility for the cost of repairing the damage she had intended to raise briefly at lunch with Mr. Stokes-Vecchio, but on her arrival in the first officers' dining room she found Mr. Krause, the assistant manager, seated in his place and waiting for her—a shade testily, she sensed; all the others were already on hand. Was anything wrong with Stokes-Vecchio? Or had the porcine Krause been elevated to his post because of some horrid malfeasance? The possibility was too gloomy to consider. That it was groundless was proved a moment after the assistant chief of staff had pronounced grace and vacated Stokes-Vecchio's place for his own regular chair. Apparently the Lord was to be addressed from the head chair only.

Stokes-Vecchio, it turned out, was off conferring with Mr. Flagler that noon hour, so she directed her inquiry about vandalism to Mr. Krause, who looked up in surprise from his plate of cold spiced ham awash in a treacly orange sauce. "Can there be any doubt in your mind, Mrs. Memory?" he asked, patting the moisture from his tiny but active lips.

"If there were not," she said, "I would not have asked."

Krause inquired into the details of the little woodcarver resident in either Room 538 or 539, then advised that Mr. Flagler himself had laid down the policy in such cases: the guests in question were to be held entirely responsible. "How could it be otherwise?"

"I thought perhaps that their room tariffs were sufficient for management to absorb the cost of the repair rather than confronting the wrong-doers and possibly earning their enmity."

"It is the principle of the thing, madam," Krause said. "That is the trouble with women—even the best of them. They are inclined to sacrifice principle for practicality."

"Perhaps their burdens in life sometimes dictate that choice, Mr. Krause."

He readdressed his luncheon plate. "I was not aware that men were unburdened by life," said the assistant manager, attacking a fresh sector of his ham filet.

"I for one think Mr. Flagler's policy is both practical *and* principled," said Mr. Burdette, the gray-clad finance manager of the hotel. "He who causes the damage pays for it—what could be simpler, cleaner or more ethically correct?" Everything about Mr. Burdette was gray: his gabardine suit, his plastered-down hair, his pinpoint eyes that glittered at her through steel-rimmed frames. His expression of dour intensity rarely varied, and she had never seen him smile; if he had any teeth at all, he had yet to reveal them to her.

"I understand all that and approve," said Mrs. Memory, "but I myself would favor considering each case on its merits. In the present one, for instance, I should think that a modest reprimand from the hotel—which might inspire a firmer one to the boy from his parents—would be better business in the long run than merely billing the family."

"With all due respect, madam," said Burdette, "the business considerations fall outside your department."

"Quite," said Krause, pat-patting his bowed lips in farewell to the ham.

"I'm just wondering," put in Mr. Bedient, the small, bald cherub who served as head groundskeeper, "if it might not be preferable for Mrs. Memory to couch her discussion with the family in terms of an inquiry rather than an accusation—"

"I fully intend to. My question had to do with the consequences if the boy's guilt was conceded."

"Now you know," said Krause. His usual haughtiness seemed doubled in the absence of the general manager.

Dear Mr. Benson, she wrote that afternoon under the management's letterhead, *I shall be grateful if you would oblige me by coming to my office tomorrow morning between nine and ten o'clock about a matter that I fear requires your attention. Mr. Walters, at the front desk, will direct you. Very truly yours, M. Memory, Housekeeper (Mrs. R. Memory).* She paused after rereading it, decided that "fear" was rather too prejudicial and softened it to "believe may require" in a second rendering of the note. Yes, that was just right.

Then she withdrew another sheet from her desk drawer and addressed it to the occupant of Room 396, who Mr. Walters had advised her by the house telephone was named Loring, Mr. H. St. J. *Dear Mr. Loring: Permit me to return these pieces of property that were inadvertantly lost during your hallway misadventure this morning.* She fingered the two playing cards for a moment, recalling the incident and appreciating the good temper with which he had responded to it, then added *Good luck* before signing her name and sealing the note and cards in an envelope that she dispatched to the front desk along with the one to Mr. Benson. For an instant she mused whether Mr. H. St. J. Loring, with his odd reserve of gaming cards, might not be rather more of a cutup than Master Benson, Jr.

The fire had been out for more than half an hour by the time she was summoned to assess the damage. It was not much of a blaze—a misplaced cigar had lighted a chair cushion in cardroom #3—but any disfigurement to a place devoted to the pleasure of the exceedingly rich was an assault on the sensibilities of the clientele and required immediate repair. There was only one occupied table in the room when she arrived to inspect it; less hardy players had abandoned it when the fire began. "Give it up, Pudge," one of the four participants called out. "You're bluffing again."

"Am not," said the accused. "Laddie's the one."

There was a playful, even raffish quality about their contest, as if the outcome were entirely secondary to its goodfellowship. "Hey, boy!" one of the men called out to the gray-headed bellman standing on duty against the far wall. "Get us another round before we die of thirst. Put it on the bill for Room 245." Off the black oldtimer scurried; shuffling did not meet the Royal Poinciana's standard of service.

As unobtrusively as possible and with averted eyes, Mrs. Memory edged around the players. There was a slippery feel to the carpeting in spots, doubtless from the sloshed water used to put out the fire, but hardly any other evidence of the incident. The burned chair was nowhere in view, but a streak of soot ran from the white wainscoting at the base of the wall, against where the victimized chair had stood, right up the wallpaper almost to the ceiling. She would have to oversee the repair to make sure Mr. Jenkin's men matched the pattern—stylized pineapples enmeshed in intricate scrollwork—quite precisely. After dinner she would return to determine whether the carpeting ought to be removed to speed its drying; even a whiff of mildew could not be risked.

As she turned away from the wall stain, her acute eye was caught by a certain listless quality to the fronds of the miniature palm tree in a nearby jardinière. Her glance skipped to a second one a dozen feet away; it, too, drooped disconsolately. Had they been scorched by the fire? She moved closer to inspect. There was a fine line of brown edging inward along the tips. She inserted a finger in the potting soil. It was gray and hard. The palms were suffering from neglect, not smoke inhalation. It was true there were hundreds of potted plants in the hotel that required regular watering, but once the standard of maintenance was not honored everywhere, the neglect might spread like contagion. The job must be done correctly, and there were enough bodies to do it. She would have a firm word with Miss Sanderson later in the—

"Harry, you old son-of-a-bitch!"

The expletive snapped her head around toward the gaming table. From her present angle she could see the target of the invocation, whose back had been toward her when she entered the room: the previously prone Mr. H. St. J. Loring, now smartly done up in hound's-tooth. Obviously he had made a full recovery. Cards seemed to be his favorite pastime. Their eyes met for only an instant, yet in it she thought she saw his left eyelid drop in a wink of recognition. But it could hardly be possible. Their earlier encounter had been in a dim hallway and under circumstances in which he had scarcely glanced at her.

As she neared the doorway, the bellman returned with the fresh drinks for the players amid huzzahs and genial roistering. During it she took a step nearer their table and almost surreptitiously sampled the soil in the sole remaining pot, which stood a yard or so to the left and rear of Mr. Loring. The soil, to her surprise, was soggy and quite cold. How could that be? Angling off to the right of the card players, she hugged the wall and appeared to immerse herself in the serenity of the woodland scene depicted on it in a mezzotint. The intervening fronds of one of the potted palms further hid her from the awareness of the players. Out of the corner of her eye she watched as Loring gently tilted his chair back from the table, his left arm looped behind its backrest and holding his iced drink while his right hand held the cards. As the others chided and feinted one another, Loring, with a smile fixed in place and an occasional burst of taunting of his own, tipped a small portion of his drink into the potted palm behind him with an artful backhand twist of his dangling arm. It was so brief a motion that she would not have noticed it if she had not been spying the scene closely.

That was one mystery solved. But it immediately inspired another. *Why* was Loring watering the palm? Could he be a teetotaler who was only pretending to share in the merriment? He did not exactly seem the abstemious type, though; she took him for a gay blade—he was unattached, according to the hotel room registry, meaning he was either a bachelor or indulging in a respite from his marriage—of the most feckless sort. As this puzzling quality about the man was engaging her Loring glanced directly at her, seeming to know that she had been watching. And this time there was no mistaking it—the man definitely winked at her. Her body straightened slowly and turned away with all the dignity at her command, and as quickly as she dared she left the players to their revels.

Her breakfast the next morning was disrupted by a message that a member of the groundskeeping crew was waiting for her in the service yard. Perhaps there was some mistake, she told the waiter, and the message had been intended for Mr. Bedient. "No, ma'am," said the waiter, "he say you."

Annoyed that her lukewarm oatmeal would likely congeal in her absence but responsive to her duty, she moved down the main kitchen hallway, past the great clangor of pots and the pervasive aroma of sizzling bacon as the small army of cooks, waiters, busboys and bottlewashers bustled to prepare breakfast for the guests. The groundskeeper, in a soiled white shirt and rumpled brown trousers, doffed his cap in appreciation of her prompt response and gravely invited her to follow him. In a far corner of the littered yard, through which she navigated carefully lest one of the jagged work implements snare her skirt, he directed her attention to a small mound of white painted porcelain shards that were unidentifiable until he lifted a sample for her to inspect. They were the remains, she recognized, of the chamber pots that had been made especially for the

Royal Poinciana and normally resided inside the night table beside each guest's bed, largely as an emergency measure in the event of a malfunction by the hotel's newfangled plumbing.

"I found 'em on the beach," the workman said. "There's a whole sackful." His callused palm also revealed a collection of small brass cylinders that he had found on further search a hundred yards or so from the shattered chamber pots. The metal objects she did not recognize. "Bullet cartridges, ma'am. I thought maybe you should know about it."

"Yes, thank you."

Why in creation would somebody, or somebodies, want to reduce the pots to smithereens? To be sure, purists might consider the gold stripe around their top and the palm-tree adornment of their interior *un peu de trop,* but that was no reason to destroy them. Likely it was a prank, she decided, not an aesthetic judgment rendered against the pots, and probably a number of guests were involved since there was only one pot assigned per room, and, from the looks of the shattered remains, half a dozen or more pots had been sacrificed to the asinine whims of the perpetrators.

The sheer willfulness of the destruction infuriated her, and she was determined to discover the guilty parties and, under the Flaglerian rule of accountability, make them pay. But how to find them? She could hardly search through every room to find which ones were missing their chamber pots. No. But she had a whole staff at her disposal with legitimate access each day to every room in the hotel. Before an hour was out, she distributed notices to all the linen-supply rooms, asking the maids to compile a list of every room missing its pot. Madeleine Memory would not be trifled with this way, no matter how *distingué* the clientele.

Within twenty-four hours she had her list. Seven of the rooms had been depotted. She was not pleased, or surprised, to note that Room 396 was among them. Still another black mark against the jaunty Mr. Loring. To his fondness for gambling, winking and drinking (or studied avoidance thereof) now had to be added wanton destruction of property. But what, after all, could she expect of such an individual? Or of the people in his set? They had all no doubt been indulgently raised by wealthy parents who likely allotted them plump allowances and placed few if any curbs on their behavior. Did any of them do anything useful with their lives? Poor or rich, a hooligan was a hooligan; the only difference was that the rich were able to buy dispensations for their offenses.

She composed brisk notes to the offenders, advising them that the cost of the porcelain items in question would be added to their bills and that she hoped such incidents would not recur. The following morning she received a note in response:

> My dear Mrs. Memory,
>
> Your most recent letter, and the reason for your having sent it, fill me with a deep sense of embarrassment. I have nothing adequate to offer by way of excusing my behavior, but I hope you will allow me the opportunity to try to make amends.
>
> I would be grateful if you would condescend to join me for tea in the Cocoanut Grove this Friday at 4:30. The table will be reserved in my name, and I shall await your arrival there.
>
> With every sincere apology,
>
> Harrison St. John Loring

What an extraordinary cheeky fellow. But at least he showed a tinge of remorse. Perhaps a conscience lurked somewhere beneath that well-groomed exterior. Why seek a meeting with her, though? It seemed an excessive gesture of contrition on his part. There was, moreover, Mr. Stokes-Vecchio's rule against staff fraternization with the guests. She would write back declining Mr. Loring's invitation.

But she did not. There was something—something somehow saving—about the chap, although she could not think precisely what it was. And anyway, the antifraternization rule was well known to apply mainly to any latent tendency to promiscuity among the chambermaids, not to senior staff. Did not the general manager himself sometimes accept invitations to join guests at their tables in the dining room? Besides, she had yearned to take tea like a lady in the grove behind the hotel.

The great man's private rail car, a tasteful maroon with the name "Alicia" gold-lettered on its sides, sat on a shaded siding a few hundred feet away from the herd of others belonging to guests who were able to afford that grand mode of travel. The difference was that Henry Flagler remained aboard his miniature palace on wheels while the other owners camped at his hotel and ceded their traveling quarters to the servants who had accompanied them south.

Mrs. Memory's appointment was scheduled for two-forty-five, shortly after she went off duty. It was important, Mr. Stokes-Vecchio had stressed, that the proprietor's presence in no way interrupt the hotel routine. She boarded precisely at the designated moment, her head held high, her eyes watchful that a wayward step should not unbalance her;

nobody was there to assist her. The car's interior surfaces of mahogany, cherrywood, brass and leather all seemed to glow with an equal luster. Despite the heat of the day it felt cool inside, thanks to the noiseless flutter of the ceiling fans and the open windows, which she noticed were fitted out with custom-made wire screens.

Mr. Flagler was receiving in the sitting room, where he stood in a small semicircle with Messrs. Stokes-Vecchio and Krause; the Reverend Mr. Reynolds, Mr. Flagler's spiritual advisor, who was to remain at the Royal Poinciana for the rest of the season; and Dr. McBride of St. Augustine, the supervisor of Mr. Flagler's Florida enterprises. The tycoon himself was taller, leaner and softer-voiced than she had imagined, his hair and mustache rather whiter and fuller, his posture more erect, considering that he was now in his sixty-seventh year. Only his pale blue eyes showed age and wear; they struck her as clouded and distant as he turned to meet hers.

"Mr. Stokes-Vecchio here advises me you're off to a fine start with us, Mrs. Memory," Flagler said. "I'm pleased to hear of it."

"Mr. Stokes-Vecchio is very kind, sir."

"Not always, Mrs. Memory—and not undeservedly. His obligation toward me is to be candid in evaluating the staff. He says you've had extensive training in New York. Where in particular?"

"At several establishments. Most recently I was—"

"Do you know the Savoy-Knickerbocker? I'm there quite a bit now."

"Not from personal experience. But I'm told—"

"The staff seems lackluster, frankly, although they're discreet enough. I suspect they could use your gifts, Mrs. Memory."

"Thank you, sir."

"Are you adequately staffed here? I want our guests to be as comfortable as humanly possible. They come a long way to enjoy our hospitality."

Her eyes moved a fraction to the right to determine Stokes-Vecchio's attentiveness. "I—should say so, sir."

Flagler had detected her hesitation. "Oh, don't fret about Anthony here. He's promised me there'll be no reprisals for honesty. When I meet with the senior staff at any of my establishments, Mrs. Memory, I ask only for their utmost candor."

"I quite understand, sir. In frankness, then, I cannot yet fully vouch for the caliber of my staff. It is rather harder to enlist experienced help in this region. But I have a full complement of girls at my disposal, certainly—training them properly is up to me. If there should prove to be any shortcomings in the housekeeping standards, the responsibility will be fully mine."

His mouth stretched outward a bit in his closest approximation of a smile. "Well said, madam. Your efforts toward helping us create the finest resort in the world will be greatly appreciated." There was not a hint of a wrinkle anywhere on his white suit, she noted. And his ears were remarkably small.

"Thank you, sir. I'll endeavor to—"

"Now why don't you join us in some cool refreshment? Reverend, if you'll show Mrs. Memory into the dining room?"

In fact, she was dismissed from the owner's sight. It was a perfunctory little ceremony, part of his week-long visit to show the flag of proprietorship and quicken the hearts of his retainers. She dwelled for an obligatory few moments over iced lemonade, confirmation of the legendary Flagler teetotaling, served with a doilied plateful of dry, sweet biscuits, and chatted with chief desk clerk Walters and Major Mackintosh, the music director of the hotel, whose interviews had preceded hers.

"Such a tragic figure," Walters said afterward as they made their way back across the hotel grounds. "A fine man like that."

Mrs. Memory said she was unaware of any tragedy surrounding Mr. Flagler. She knew only of the fortune he had amassed in the petroleum business and the reports of his sumptuous personal living arrangements.

"You noticed the name of his railroad car?"

"Why, yes—"

"But not the lady herself."

"Alicia? Who is that?"

"Mrs. Flagler, of course. Alice is her name, actually."

"What about her?"

"She's quite mad. He's had to move out on her. The woman is uncontrollable. He's living in a hotel in the city. People on staff there are friends of mine. The grisly details slip out—"

Alice, it seemed, had nursed the first Mrs. Flagler through her terminal illness and on her death married him, thirteen years ago, when she was thirty-five and the millionaire was fifty-three. He had lavished his riches on her, which she gladly accepted, Walters said, and all was well for a time. Then certain nervous inclinations surfaced in her, certain eccentric and emotional tendencies. Her speech took on exaggerated forms of grandeur as she became obsessed with her appearance and social position. Flagler, judging her a beauty, continued to dote upon her, even as her behavior worsened and she took to abusing him verbally. Temper tantrums grew into something worse until delusions set in, culminating in her insistence that Flagler had become unfaithful to her—there was not the slightest evidence to support the charge—and in his place she had taken the tsar as her imaginary lover and attempted to communicate with him regularly by ouija board. Flagler had obtained the best medical care available for her, but when her situation only deteriorated, he had reluctantly had her institutionalized at Dr. Choate's sanitarium in Westchester. For a time she seemed to rally, and on her release from confinement he had attended her dutifully. But she relapsed horribly, shutting herself into her rooms, issuing threats by turns suicidal and homicidal to the point where those closest to her husband feared for his safety as well as hers. He had had no choice but to leave the house and reside elsewhere. It was only a matter of time now until he would have to recommit her—for good, in all likelihood.

Yes, tragic was the word for it, Mrs. Memory agreed after hearing the avidly told tale. There was a moral somewhere in there, she supposed, having to do with the unpurchasability of happiness.

In the senior officers' dining room that evening the assistant manager remarked to her, "We all have the same staffing problem that you complained of to Mr. Flagler—in case you are unaware, madam."

"I was hardly complaining, Mr. Krause. I was merely observing—in response to Mr. Flagler's insistence on candor."

"His principal concern is with compliance, Mrs. Memory. Excuses are not appreciated. Our personnel difficulties here are well known to him— the man has, after all, built an entire railroad through the wilderness."

"But I was only—"

"I understand. You ought to be fully apprised, though. We are all, each and every one, on perpetual probation in Mr. Flagler's eyes."

"I believe that is the nature of employment, Mr. Krause. Thank you for your guidance in the matter."

At twenty minutes past four Mrs. Memory appeared in the women's cloak room off the lobby and, under the pretense of checking the towel arrangements, managed a hurried look into the mirror.

Her hand darted about her hair, pinning up wisps that had fallen, then adjusted the jet brooch that held in place the ends of her white lace collar. There. A touch more vividness would not hurt her complexion, she thought and pinched her cheeks and bit her lips. The five minutes it would take her to reach the Cocoanut Grove would help maintain the glow in her skin, considering that it was generally warmer and damper outdoors that inside.

At the edge of the grove in front of the hotel, she lingered for a moment or two, adjusting to the glare and letting the lilt of the hotel orchestra waft over her as she peered through the trunks of the palm trees. There he was, on the far right side, at a decorous distance from the center walk. Her heart offered sudden timpani to the music as her mind rushed back to those afternoons when she would fade into the folds of the parlor curtains and wait for the first glimpse of Russell, her Yale man, turning the corner in his springing gait and would count the unendurable moments before he would bound up to their doorway and bestow polished— and, as she knew, calculated—pleasantries on her mother. But what possible connection might remain between that agonizing schoolgirl crush and the appearance of this oddly appealing stranger? The long interval left her emotions a brittle mass of suspicion.

Monsieur Pinay, the maître d'hotel, raised his eyebrows when she asked for Mr. Loring's table. Her return squint told him to remember that it was she who took her meals in the first officers' dining room while he ate in the second officers' grill. He led her down the long aisle between the hundred tiny tables, her dark costume drawing no more than a few sidelong glances of curiosity. She was a calculated five minutes late.

"Ah," said Loring, bouncing to his feet at her approach, "I was beginning to think you were indisposed." He remained standing until the maître d' had seated her.

"They say lateness is a woman's prerogative, Mr. Loring."

"They say a lot of things about women, Mrs. Memory, at least half of which are true. The trick is to know which half."

"And do you, Mr. Loring?"

"On occasion. In general, though, I have found the fair sex to be exquisitely mystifying. It serves you better to keep us off guard."

This close to him, she could see that he was older than she had thought, with lines lightly etched in his broad forehead and at the corners of his playful eyes. Nor had the thin scar that began above his left eyebrow and disappeared into his dark hairline been visible to her before; it lent a slightly menacing and used quality to his looks without distracting from them. The face was rather too long for its width and the cheekbones too prominent to qualify for sculpturesque handsomeness, but it had character. A not quite aquiline bridge of the nose suggested an Indian ancestry, at once belied by the pretty gray-blueness of the eyes. "And suppose I had elected not to come for reasons other than of indisposition?"

"Then you would have so advised me in advance."

The man, she thought, was too pleased with himself by half. "With lemon, please," she told the hovering waiter. Loring took his tea with milk. "Tell me, Mr. Loring," she continued after the waiter had retired to fetch the pastry cart, "why would it have mattered if I had not come?"

He studied her directly for a moment before responding; her lack of coyness seemed to challenge his smooth tongue. "I was hoping to use the occasion to apologize properly and assure you that—"

"Your note was quite satisfactory on that score."

"Why, thank you, but notes are so impersonal. I wanted to let you know that you've so far seen only the more rambunctious side of my behavior. There are others, Mrs. Memory, I can assure you."

"I'm glad of it. But still, I cannot understand why my holding a good opinion of you should matter in the least." The fellow was behaving all too gallantly for his earnestness to ring true.

He was at a loss again for an instant as he gauged her resistance to being glibly disarmed. "Actually," he said, leaning several inches closer, "I was hoping that if you saw my better side, you might tell the chambermaid to bring me an extra towel or two."

She could not help but laugh. "Ah, I knew there had to be an ulterior purpose."

He smiled back. "You should do that more often, you know—laughing greatly becomes you, Mrs. Memory—if you'll forgive the impertinence."

"You're back to rambunctiousness," she said solemnly. "No, I shall not forgive you, Mr. Loring."

The arrival of the pastry cart provided a welcome respite. Her eye skipped over the fruit tarts and whipped-cream confections and settled upon a chocolate *gateau* flavored, according to the waiter, with raspberries and bananas—a sinful indulgence she would have devoured instantly if unattended. Loring chose several boring-looking cookies, appropriate to his slender physique. At the first succulent forkful, her mouth spread with pleasure. "There it is again," Loring said approvingly. "You must have no idea how a smile improves your face or you would do it more often."

"I do not calculate my smiles, Mr. Loring."

"Perhaps not. But you cannot plead innocence about your clothing. Must you wear things that drain all the color from your cheeks and that—that odd white hat? Surely the manager could be prevailed upon to permit you some other sort of uniform."

Plainly he had been paying her more attention from afar than she had supposed; she found it both pleasing and unsettling. "These unsightly clothes are not a uniform—they are my choice. I lost my husband several years ago."

"I see. So young a widow." He took a nibble at an oversized gingersnap and ruminated for a moment. "And how long is it since Mr. Memory passed away, if I may ask?"

"Whatever the duration, it is solely my business, I'm sure you'll agree—and restrain your disapproval."

"I was not disapproving, madam—I was regretting."

"It comes to the same thing, sir. If the queen of England adheres to the custom, so may I."

"And is she your model of suitable style?"

"She is the epitome of decorum, certainly."

"But I'd wager she has not deigned to laugh since 1859. And I know for a fact that she would heartily disapprove of what you did a second ago."

She looked up. "And what was that?"

"You licked your lips like a greedy child."

Lord, had she? The cake was just so—

"After you put your fork in your mouth, you felt a bit of frosting at the corner, and you reached for it with your tongue. The queen would reprimand you."

His keen attention was making her uncomfortable. "Well, I—"

"*This* is what the Queen would do." He pursed his lips and applied his napkin to them with dainty swipes.

She laughed. He was behaving altogether too disarmingly to warrant her studied aloofness. Such sporting came naturally to him; she decided to enjoy it for five additional minutes. What was it Mr. Loring did when he was not idling away his hours in the Florida tropics, she asked.

"I'm in investments." He said it without much relish.

"I see. And you find that absorbing?"

"Moderately. One does what one must."

He sounded almost mournful about it. She took him to mean that the acquiring of wealth was not as diverting as expending it. "Tell me if you will, Mr. Loring, what on earth possessed you and your friends to do such mayhem to the—those—sanitary devices?"

His eyes danced with interest. "I'm not sure I—"

"Those—personal—urns—"

"Urns?" His brow furrowed in puzzlement. "I still don't quite—"

She did not enjoy being toyed with. "Those—porcelain—objects that you and your friends purloined—"

"Ah, *that* again." He had the grace to look chagrined. The explanation was simple if not satisfactory. His crowd was to go hunting in the 'Glades the next morning, and since one of their number had never fired a gun and most of the others were rusty and all of them were in fine spirits in more ways than one—and there was a full moon out, besides—what more natural post-midnight pursuit than to take a bit of target practice down at the beach? And what more inviting targets than the hotel's splendidly painted pots? The practice did them a world of good, as it happened; they bagged a dozen rabbits and countless fowl of various species, not all of which he could identify for certain.

"I am pleased for you all," said Mrs. Memory. "There's just one other thing—if I may?"

"By all means."

"I must confess to a certain curiosity as to why you emptied a portion of your—beverage into the potted palm nearest you while playing cards the other day. It seems an unattractive habit."

"Not at all—in view of the parched condition of the poor thing. It was badly in need of attention, so I—"

"Nourished it with bourbon? How remarkably considerate of the hotel's property—in marked contrast to your—"

His teeth flashed with the impish smile of a naughty boy caught. "The truth is that I do not like to indulge in spirits while gambling. It destroys my concentration."

"But how thoroughly unsporting of you—not to mention deceitful—in view of your opponents' quite considerable—partaking."

"Ah, yes. I see your point. It requires a bit more elaboration of the truth." His avoidance of alcohol was deeply ingrained, he explained; he had seen its sorrowful effects on his own father, who had frequently lost control of himself when he drank. His acquaintances at the hotel did not share his qualms about liquor, so in the interest of compatability he saw no harm in his little deceit—and the gaming stakes were, after all, not very high. "It was a social engagement, not a contest in earnest."

She asked if he saw nothing odd in purchasing sociability by a form of pretense.

"I would call it cordiality, myself."

"Ah, I see." She sipped the last of her tea, then rose and extended her hand. "I've enjoyed this. And may I wish you a most pleasant stay?"

"You've made it more so."

"And if you're ever in genuine need of extra towels, Mr. Loring, it will not be necessary in the future to ask me to tea and bribe me with unspeakably delicious chocolate cake. Just leave a note for your chambermaid."

"I'll bear that in mind, Mrs. Memory." He stood aside as she left without looking back at him.

* * *

Stokes-Vecchio asked her to close the door behind her, an act that she instantly regretted: with the office window shut as well, the unventilated aroma of the pomade lubricating his scalp was inescapable. Why he doused himself so heavily with the stuff mystified her. If it was the better to groom his remaining thin thatch of hair, he ought to have wielded his comb with a lighter hand and not caused the streaks left by its teeth to reveal the widening encroachment of baldness. Perhaps the liberal application of stickum was intended to have a fertilizing effect on his fatigued follicles. Whatever the purpose, its result was infelicitous. She closed her nostrils by minutely opening her lips and sat staring at the general manager's hands, which he was busily assembling fingertip to fingertip, moving a few inches apart, then putting back together in indecisive spasms.

Finally he roused himself. "Mrs. Memory, I find this a very difficult subject to discuss."

"I'm sorry, but I don't—"

"No, of course. It's my place to take the—" He withdrew his hands from the desktop and folded his arms across his chest in a show of resolve. "I say, it has been brought to my attention that—that—" His resolve instantly curdled. "No, no—let me begin again," he said with a shake of his head that set the upturned ends of his waxed mustache wigwagging. "There are certain standards of conduct prescribed for members of the staff here that may strike you as—as perhaps excessively strict. But I can assure you, Mrs. Memory, there is a method to our little brand of madness."

"I have no doubt of that, sir."

"Splendid. That makes my task so much the easier." His fingertips embraced in front of his necktie, and he began to speak of her exemplary dedication to her duties before slipping over none too subtly to address the unenviable dilemma of a respectable woman in her profession.

Now she grasped his point. He had heard that she had taken tea with a guest, and he disapproved. "Allow me, sir, to spare you further concern. I understood that we are here to satisfy the guests. Not to have obliged the gentleman by joining him as he had requested—in a perfectly open and aboveboard fashion—"

"There is no question whatever of your deportment, I can assure—"

"—would have been rude in the extreme. The gentleman merely wished to apologize to the management for an instance of crude behavior."

"I quite understand, Mrs. Memory. It was not my intention to chastise you. It is just that you have a sterling reputation among . . . we all recognize that you have experienced a grievous loss—a truly grievous loss—and are entitled to the fullest courtesies and respect of a woman in your condition. But there are others who are less sensitive—and you are still a relatively young woman—who might quite unconsciously attract the attention of admiring males—who might all too eagerly prey upon your—"

"Thank you, sir, but I am entirely capable of defending my honor."

"No doubt. But that would require your full awareness of when it is imperiled—which gets me back to my original point. We frown on fraternization with the guests even for the good reason you gave for accommodating the gentleman—we do not want our staff people compromised—or in a position where they would find it awkward to—"

"I see."

"And not all the gentlemen here are what they seem." He could not forbid her, he went on, to exchange such pleasantries as might seem necessary in the fulfillment of her duties, but urged her to view with the utmost caution future advances made by any male guest.

He was addressing her as an underage child. "I am grateful for your solicitude, sir, but I surely did not consider the invitation you're questioning to be an 'advance' of any sort."

"My point precisely. You are vulnerable, Mrs. Memory—"

"All women are vulnerable, sir."

"Not equally, madam." He glanced at the ceiling, then suddenly adopted a far softer tone. "If I may, I wish to leave you with another thought. I can fully understand how a woman of—a woman like yourself—might from time to time welcome the conversation of—a—male companion. It is only human nature—and—therefore, naturally—you might seek such crumbs of comfort as are to be found among our guests—"

"Sir, you need not concern yourself with—"

His raised hand told her she was to hear him out. "Although you wisely cling to your wardrobe of mourning, I believe that you may still have need of the protection only a man can provide. And although we are relatively new acquaintances, it would please me greatly, madam, if you would look to me not only as your supervisor and taskmaster but also as a—protector and—and friend." Should she feel "at any time of day—or night—" a compulsion to open her heart and voice her concerns, he wished her to know that she might find chaste solace in him—"and a broad shoulder on which to place your—troubled—brow."

It would have been difficult to say which emotion moved her the more—giddiness or revulsion. The notion of placing her brow against his shoulder or any other section of his repellent being was so preposterous as to compel laughter, loud, barking and certain to produce his mortification, likely followed by her dismissal for insubordination. Instead she bowed her head for a moment in which to control her impulse, then brought it upright, hoping her eyes appeared to be just a tad misty. "Mr. Stokes-Vecchio, I hardly know—what to say—"

"Say nothing, then, my dear. I just wanted you to know that so long as you are in my employ, there is always a friendly corner for you to turn to—a lighted candle for your—dark hours—"

She could think only of the cylindrical Mrs. Stokes-Vecchio, up in St. Augustine, whom he elected to abandon for the hotel season, ostensibly the better to serve under the Flagler banner. "Your kindness—overwhelms me, sir."

"That was not my intention. But I should take it as a kindness in return if you did not refer to me as 'sir.' My given name is Anthony, and you should not hesitate to call me by it—in the privacy of this room—or wherever you might wish to seek counsel or share a confidence."

"I—" She was running out of permissible things to say to him. "Thank you—so much—Anthony." She rose, turned and hurried off, in dramatically swift sequence that she hoped he would accept as overwrought feeling.

No one was visible to her through the gate to the service yard. Even the kitchen noises were subdued at that hour on a Sunday morning. Clutching her basket and parasol together in one hand, she used the other to push open the gate and quickly slipped through.

Her eyes kept sweeping the grounds to be sure she was unseen as she took the path that circled the Cocoanut Grove. Her black outfit may have looked ridiculously unfashionable to the guests, but she did not care. If anyone questioned her presence, she was simply out for an early-morning stroll.

She inhaled deeply, relishing the cleanliness of the moist air, the fragrances of the hotel gardens and the perceptible tang of salt water. The next few hours were entirely her own, and she meant to luxuriate in their enjoyment. She moved past the croquet field, the tennis courts and the vegetable garden in a northeasterly direction out toward the golf course, carefully skirting the railroad siding, where the servants of the guests still slumbered in Sabbath respite. On any other morning the golf course would have presented a formidable obstacle, since many a guest liked to get there early and play a round before breakfast, but such sporting activities were discouraged on Sunday at the Royal Poinciana in deference to the Reverend Mr. Reynolds' sermon in the hotel chapel.

She admired the velvet of the putting greens with their little pennants aflutter in the breeze and the lusher growth beyond them. Farther out she could see the beige-white strip of beach sand and the ocean, its wavelets glimmering with sunbeams, composing an endless tapestry of mottled green and gray and blue. It was all so quiet she could hear bird calls usually drowned by man-made sounds as she passed beneath a sapodilla tree. The sand traps and water hazards required her to make little excursions around them. She used a small Japanese-style bridge spanning a pond as a vantage point to check behind her that no one had monitored her progress. Then she beelined for the ocean.

At the edge of the sand she sat to remove her shoes and stockings, rolling the latter over her garters into fatter and fatter doughnuts, which she tossed into her basket. Her bare toes dug into the delicious softness of the beach. The sun was not yet high enough to have heated the surface of the sand, and the cool moisture beneath provided a treat of pure sensuousness. Flexing her toes and ankles, she rose and hurried onward to the north.

With her parasol open now, she trotted to the water's edge, where the outgoing tide had compacted the sand, making it easier to walk along. Under the shade of the parasol she could afford to remove her hat, which she stuffed into the basket. Next came her hairpins, extracted a few at a time and dropped among her other garments. She gave her head a vigorous shake, letting her hair blow free in the wind.

Her destination was a huge palm tree, its trunk blackened and split by lightning, which she had heard Mr. Bedient, the groundskeeper, describe as indicating where Mr. Flagler's property ended and the Seminoles' began. The collar of her shirtwaist had come to feel oppressively like a noose the farther she went, so she put down her basket and parasol to unhook it. The air felt good rushing against her damp skin. She began to run, until the boundary-line palm came into view. Finding a spot where the sand was relatively free of shells, wood slivers and other sea detritus, she deposited her basket and pulled a sheet from it that she tried to spread open on the beach. The wind battled her hard for mastery over the cloth until she awkwardly managed to anchor the first two corners with her shoes; the basket and parasol secured the other two.

The ocean beckoned to her powerfully. She twisted the waistband of her skirt around. The lower buttons yielded easily, but the top one, usually fastened over her tightly laced corset, resisted. Impatiently, she took a deep breath, compacting her body and maneuvering the join apart, then folded the skirt carelessly and dropped it onto the sheet. Her petticoats were easier because they fit her uncorseted natural size. First the red silk with the black chantilly lace flounce; it fluttered to the white sheet against which it contrasted almost violently under the brilliance of the mid-morning sun. The second, a pale green satin with rose- and mauve-ribbon beading, looked more genteel lying against the red one: the hidden, clashing impulses of the widow Memory, bannered on her private beach.

Ready now, she ran to the water's edge, wearing only her combination. A one-piece, unconstricting garment mating a chemise with pantalettes, it was so much more sensible for bathing than those absurd woolen sailor suits women wore with their yards of ruffles and collars and sleeves and peplums and stockings and corsets. Corsets in the ocean! Such total nonsense. But then, the women who so outfitted themselves were not truly ocean bathers, she thought, but preening poseurs who ran to the water to get their toes wet and shrieked the first instant they were so much as spat at by a wave.

She lifted her arms above her head, delighting in the liberation of her body as the breeze caressed it, then dashed into the water, splashing and challenging herself to withstand the sudden shock of it. Hip-deep now, she waited for a moment for a wave to come rolling in on her, and when it was almost ready to break, she dove beneath it, drove forward, then relaxed in her own buoyancy and emerged well on the far side. Fully acclimated, she swung her arms and legs easily, glorying in the motion, the enveloping water, the look of her hair as it floated weightlessly beside her—this was the utter abandonment of restraint she waited all week to enjoy.

She swam parallel to the shoreline until betrayed by her hair, which refused to stay behind her ears and kept intruding on her line of sight. Again she had forgotten to bring a bit of ribbon to secure it. Unsure of her direction now, she slipped over and floated on her back for a while, letting the current take her. Slowly she became aware that her sense of time had abandoned her. She spread her arms and legs, letting the water flow around her body as her limbs passed through it resistlessly. Then she turned toward the shore and headed in to resume her narrow land-life, wrapped in the protective black shroud that concealed her inner luster. She swam mindlessly until her fingertips brushed against the sandy bottom, then stood up—only to fall down at once onto all fours.

A man was there on the beach, watching. He was seated on her white sheet, right beside her clothes.

"I'm coming out now," she called to him. "Please go away."

"I'd rather not," he called back.

The unmitigated gall! But what to do? She could not wait him out—her skin was beginning to wrinkle and she had to go on duty by noon. She felt trapped, put upon, disadvantaged. Rage began to rise in her invigorated system. For an instant she gauged herself nearly capable of pummeling him into submission. But reason prevailed: she would have to appeal to whatever, if any, gentlemanly instincts he had.

"I can't keep shouting," she shouted. "Come to the water's edge."

He got up and came toward her while she backed away, keeping only her head and neck out of the water. It was imperative that he conduct no further inspection of her state of undress. She squinted in to guess from his appearance what sort of person she was dealing with. He was wearing a navy blue jacket and white trousers; a red, white and blue band decorated his boater. Clearly he was not hired help.

"Will you let me by, sir? Surely you must see that I—"

"Oh, I have seen—quite enough—and I am awesomely offended."

The voice was suddenly familiar, but the distance and the pulsing heat waves prevented her from positively identifying his features. "May I ask what it is that offends you, sir?"

"The very idea that a"—he cleared his throat—"young woman should remove her garments in public and go into the ocean and—and disport herself like a mermaid is shocking—*and* reprehensible."

The lack of conviction in that upbraiding voice sealed his identity. And he must have known who she was; her black shirtwaist and skirt were right there next to him on the sheet. And her pretty, bright petticoats, besides.

"Mr. Loring, I would be grateful if you could restrain your outrage long enough to show a little civility and let me get dressed. We can discuss the moral issues afterward."

He took a coin from his pocket and began tossing it in the air and catching it. "I'd prefer to discuss them here and now, Mrs. Memory. I have plenty of time."

"I, sir, do not. I'm due at work by noon."

He dropped the coin into one pocket and pulled a watch from another. "In that event, you have precisely one hour and seven minutes and, let me see—twenty-five seconds—to make it. You therefore better get on with explaining yourself."

There was barely time to dress, walk all the way back to the hotel, bathe the sand away and dress again, properly corseted this time; she would surely be late, all because of this—this incorrigible playboy. Damnation.

"I have nothing to explain, Mr. Loring. I don't consider this a public place. No one comes here. I've never caught sight of another soul on the previous Sundays I've come out—"

"So! You're a habitual offender, are you?"

"You are not amusing, Mr. Loring. Now I must appeal to your honor—about which you protested to me so vigorously at our last encounter. Would you kindly move away a proper distance and turn your back so I may dress? My position at the hotel may be at stake."

"As you wish, madam. Harrison St. John"—he pronounced it Sin-Jin, in the British fashion—"Loring is, above all, a man of honor. I'll be thirty yards away, with studiously averted eyes. Just call out when you're ready."

Without waiting for him to complete his retreat, she ran ashore, hair dripping, soaked combination clinging to her skin. If Loring had not been there she would have taken a few minutes to sit on the sheet and dry off; now she would have to dress over a wet undergarment. Her only consolation was that it would keep her cool during the walk back.

With a near-frenzy she assembled herself: first the green petticoat, which she flung over her head and hooked, somehow; then the red one; next her shirtwaist—the upper and lower buttons she reached around for and fastened readily enough but the ones in the middle would have to wait till she was drier—the shirtwaist would not slide up over the wet combination. She yanked the skirt over her head, leaving the top button undone—no time to fuss with it. What to do with her feet? They were thickly crusted with sand. Usually she put on her shoes and stockings at the last moment just before turning off the beach for the hotel golf course. But what did etiquette dictate about the disclosure of naked feet to a strange man, especially this one? Instinct told her they should be covered, but to do so would sandlog her shoes and stockings and make for a singularly uncomfortable trek. Etiquette be damned. This was an emergency.

"Ready yet?" came the call from Loring, his voice barely audible above the surf.

"Just a minute!" She dumped the remaining contents of her basket onto the sheet and grabbed for the comb. There was no time to pull it all the way through to the tangled, sodden ends that had already drenched the back of her shirtwaist. She yanked it halfway, rolled the ends around her hand, and with savage thrusts of hairpins attached the mess to her head. Over it she gingerly lowered her hat, pinning it in place and taking care not to lance her scalp. Finally she yanked up the sheet, letting it blow in the wind for a moment to rid it of sand, stuffed it unfolded into the basket along with her shoes and opened her parasol—she did not intend to let him examine her. "All right," she called.

His long strides ate up two thirds of the distance between them as she moved reluctantly toward him. "Very rapid recovery," he said. "I thought it took women hours to get dressed."

"On occasion. This is not one." She moved past him, forcing him to match her determinedly rapid pace.

He reached around to lift her parasol away from her face with his finger and assessed her from hat to hem. "I must say, your exertions seem to agree with you. You look positively radiant, madam."

"Don't 'madam' me, Mr. Loring," she said, jerking the parasol back to a shielding angle. "Who told you about this place?"

"No one. I followed you."

"Impossible. I looked behind me repeatedly."

"So I noticed." He had awakened early, he explained, and taken a little walk around the grounds. He was looking at the guests' cars on the rail siding when he saw her go by on the far side of them. Curious, he pursued, but at a distance—"a considerable distance, I'll admit, since your backward glances disclosed your uneasiness."

"What stopped you from calling out to me?"

"If you knew I was there you would likely have changed your intriguing plans. I had no intention of depriving you of—"

She looked around the edge of her parasol to find him studying her movements. "I trust your curiosity has been fully satisfied."

"On the contrary. You become a greater enigma to me with every encounter."

"Then I should not confound you any longer. If we each pursue our appropriate activities here, the subject will not arise."

He let the coldness of her dismissal hang in the limpid air for a moment, then said, "I could report you to the manager, you know."

"My off-hour activity is none of their affair—or yours."

"That remains to be seen. As I understand it, Mr. Flagler is not partial to employees who practice indecent exposure—even in their off-hours."

She walked ahead, more briskly than ever, refusing to rise farther toward his bait. They marched on in silence for the next few minutes. Finally he broke in, "I must say, you were awfully good out there—for a woman. How did you learn to swim so well?"

Her downward glance strayed to his feet; he had not shed his shoes. In all likelihood he was extremely uncomfortable. Good. Let him pay at least a small price for his hijinks. Still, he was not such a bad chap, she had to admit, nearly as engaging as he was maddening. Her anger with him subsided. She had grown up beside the ocean, she told him, in New Haven. Her family's circumstances at the time did not include employment of a nanny, and so during the summer when school was out, she was often left in the charge of her brother, several years her senior. He would drag her along with him, warning her never to say a word to their parents or his friends about their recreational activities. "If it was cool, we played ball. When it was warm, we went to the beach. To win his respect I had to become a proficient swimmer."

He smiled as she finished. "Admirable. You're a most resourceful woman, Mrs. Memory."

"I've had little choice," she said testily. But his flattery pleased her, since it seemed to reflect a glimmer of understanding. "I can hardly expect anyone like yourself, however—someone with investments rather than a genuine working man—to grasp how the necessities of life often dictate the actions of common folk."

"You do me an injustice, madam—although perhaps I've brought it on myself by not being entirely forthcoming with you. When you asked me over tea about my occupation, I was vague in my response if you recall— and you tactfully did not pursue the matter. The truth, the real truth, is that I don't do much investing myself." In fact, he now said, he worked for the firm of Whitacre and Oldfield as an agent, and his job was to induce friends and acquaintances to make their investments through that office. And so naturally, the more friendships he cultivated, the greater would be his financial reward. Over the years he had discovered that the surest way to attract the friendship of others was to appear as much like them as possible, and so when his hotel friends drank, he drank, and when they gambled, so did he.

"One might say, then, that you are here under false pretenses."

"I deny that, madam. I am every bit as much a gentleman as the other guests—just not quite so well-heeled."

"But you are here to work, not play, if I understand you correctly."

"I don't find the two incompatible."

She felt an instant sympathy with that: they were both at the hotel to further their livelihoods. The difference between them, though, seemed profound: he dwelled in the world of the guests; she did not. What more was there to say? Relieved by their arrival at the edge of the golf course and the separation it would force, she thanked him for behaving, in the end, like a gentleman and started across the grass.

"Mrs. Memory," he called after her. She turned her head not quite halfway. "Your buttons," he said, and closed the space between them. "You seem to have forgotten them. Turn around."

She did as she was told, unthinkingly. As she felt the easy brush of his hands at the back of her shirtwaist, her mind flooded with the conflicting emotions of pleasure at his attentiveness, chagrin at her own forgetfulness and annoyance that he had touched her, without permission. The jumble of feelings reduced her to an incoherent mutter of thanks before striding off anew.

"Mrs. Memory." His call brought her up short again. This time, in her annoyance and confusion, she did not turn at all.

"Your shoes," he said. "You may want them on."

She turned back with a sheepish smile, but he was already moving away, circling around behind the golf course, hands dug in his pockets and looking as jaunty as a man can with two shoesful of sand.

TWO

She had just instructed one of the cleanup men to realign a white wicker sofa that had been placed a few inches out of position by the night crew when her attention was distracted by the appearance in the lobby rotunda of Arthur Timmons, artfully juggling a breakfast tray in each hand and a third on his head as he attended to his first room-service assignment of the morning.

The slender black boy, who had been employed in one minor capacity or another since the opening of the hotel, was a favorite of the staff and guests alike, but his insistence on cutting through a corner of the lobby to exhibit his acrobatic skills was intolerable to the head housekeeper. One misstep, and the largest carpet in the state of Florida would be hideously stained. She had spoken to the boy once, urging him to take a different route, but the message had apparently not registered. Perhaps his parents could administer a reprimand; his father, Oscar, was an assistant cook at the Poinciana, and his mother, Cleo, a laundress. But Arthur was a showman with an infectious smile and disarming good cheer, and showmen needed an audience. His breakfast room-service performance, tapping on guest doors with a light toe and spectacularly skating inside, to the delight of the hotel's clientele, was only ninety-nine percent affective; twice since the beginning of the season he had dropped one of his trays, once in the kitchen, the other time in a hallway off the dining room. Mrs. Memory was determined that it should not happen in an area under her supervision.

Her concern on the score proved all too well-founded. While she was meeting later that morning with Miss Sanderson and Miss Prentisse, her second and third in charge, to see what supplies needed reordering, word reached her that Arthur Timmons, triply laden, had lost his footing on his spectacular entry into room 418 and deposited the entire contents of all three breakfast trays on the middle of the sitting room floor. It was, plainly, his final performance as a waiter.

During luncheon at the senior officers' table the boy's fate was the chief subject of discussion. "I say we sack the little devil," Mr. Krause declared. "He's had his chance and dropped it—so to speak."

"This is not, after all, a charitable institution," added Mr. Burdette. "His ineptness has already cost the hotel a pretty penny."

"I wonder," said Mr. Stokes-Vecchio, "if we are not being a trifle unkind. He's just a boy, really—something of a pup about the place, as I understand it."

"Pups that make messes are not generally admitted to civilized quarters," said Krause. Most of the heads around the table nodded in agreement.

"You might, however, wish to consider the effect of the boy's dismissal on the morale of his parents," Mrs. Memory suggested. "I understand them to be dependable members of the staff."

"Perhaps the boy could drive one of the Afrimobiles," put in Mr. Bedient. "He's personable enough—and his chances for mischief would be slight."

A covered wicker chair with wheels attached to a bicycle at the rear and operated by the pedal-power of a black man, the Afrimobile was a contraption requiring the least skill of any job at the hotel. The pay was only what the drivers could coax in tips from their passengers, but since there was no other means of transportation in the immediate area due to Mr. Flagler's having outlawed horses from the premises for sanitary reasons, the drivers' opportunities for reward were plentiful. It was a better solution, Stokes-Vecchio ruled, than sacking the boy.

The wisdom of retaining the services of young Arthur Timmons was reinforced several days later when, during the absence of Mr. Stokes-Vecchio, who had gone to Jacksonville on banking business, a crisis erupted that threatened the entire operation of the hotel.

"I told Mr. Krause that wasn't the way to deal with it," Miss Prentisse declared, her voice piping even higher than usual. "You catch more flies with honey than you do with vinegar, I told him, but he wouldn't listen—not him. He's too all-fired high-and-mighty to listen to the likes of me. Oh, what *are* we going to do?" She twisted the lock of hair she had pulled from her coiffure around the middle and index finger of her right hand.

"And neither of you thought it proper to consult with me first?" Mrs. Memory asked rhetorically.

"There wasn't the time," the second assistant housekeeper replied, almost weepy now. "But I suppose I ought to have made some—"

"You suppose?"

"Mr. Krause was so insistent—" The poor woman was barely audible.

"The time to have done so was when he first brought up the subject."

"I—yes—well—but—"

It was pointless to pursue the question of protocol when a remedy was needed urgently. The story, as she pieced it together from Miss Prentisse's nearly incoherent outbursts, was that Mr. Burdette had happened to mention to Mr. Krause the previous week that the sum the hotel was paying out to guests so far this season for articles of clothing ruined by the laundry service was fifty-seven percent above the figure for the premiere season. Such a performance could not be tolerated, Mr. Krause asserted in his most forceful fashion to Miss Prentisse, whose responsibilities included supervision of the laundresses. Miss Prentisse duly passed the warning along to the black women who labored in the steamy basement chamber, but she did not make it sound like an imminent threat.

Then shortly before eleven o'clock on this morning, Mrs. Lancelot Hilliard, a guest from Boston, marched into Mr. Krause's office, bearing a favorite dress made of batiste with Irish crocheted lace insertions, and displayed the large black scorch mark that it carried on its return from the hotel laundry. The woman wished to be compensated for the garment. Krause dispensed the money on the spot and offered abject apologies, but the moment Mrs. Hilliard was gone, he summoned Miss Prentisse and demanded that she skin the hide off the laundress involved. Reluctantly, Miss Prentisse tried to comply, fully aware of the difficulty ironing a dress like that. Thick lace, she explained to Mrs. Memory, required a very hot iron whereas the delicate batiste needed a cool one, and even at a charge of two dollars, her girls could not take proper time ironing a dress of that delicacy without falling behind in their workload.

Afraid she would be fired, the guilty ironer declined to identify herself on Miss Prentisse's inquiry, and the rest of the laundry staff refused to give her away. Detecting only insolence instead of esprit de corps in this display of solidarity, Krause ordered Miss Prentisse to tell the black women that unless the guilty party stepped forward within the hour the collective payroll of the entire laundry staff would be docked by the amount paid to Mrs. Hilliard—and would continue to be docked in that fashion each time an article of clothing was damaged. Apprised of their Hobson's choice, the laundresses began a sitdown strike. Krause, growing hotter by the minute, retaliated by instructing Miss Prentisse to go back down to the laundry and tell the women that if they were not back on the job by two P.M. he'd sack the lot of them.

Nearly beside herself by now, Miss Prentisse returned to the laundry to relay the assistant manager's ultimatum, only to be greeted by a barricaded door. No one could get in or out. Desperation brought her running to the head housekeeper.

Mrs. Memory recognized that if the women persisted and Krause made good his threat, it would be necessary to hire thirty laundresses within a couple of days, as well as six or eight skilled ironers, of whom there could not be more than one or two in all of West Palm. And since there was only several days' supply in the linen closets and the guests' clothes had to be tended to in addition to the hotel's needs, the Royal Poinciana might have to suspend its operation, possibly for the season, if the impasse could not be resolved speedily.

It was at this point that Arthur Timmons proved his worth to the management. Summoned to the head housekeeper's office from the Afrimobile stand in front of the hotel, where he had been idling at the moment, the boy was instructed to go directly to the laundry and seek out his mother, telling her that Mrs. Memory would appear at the barricaded door in ten minutes' time and had respectfully requested an audience with the overwrought women. She could not risk the indignity of being denied admission to a portion of the building under her command.

As she neared the end of the corridor behind the vast kitchen complex, Mrs. Memory could feel the heat increase, causing prickles of perspiration to break out on her chest and back. Outside the double doors to the laundry she paused to gather her thoughts, reminding herself that just then she needed the laundresses far more than they needed her. She knocked on the door firmly.

There was a rustle inside, then a voice that asked, "Wha' chu want?"

"Just a few words with you."

She heard a heavy object, probably one of the oak ironing tables, being dragged across the floor inside. Then one of the doors opened a crack, and she could see an eye and sliver of black face behind it. The face withdrew, and the door opened just wide enough for her to pass through. As soon as she did, she felt the heat and humidity assault her like an explosion. Ranged behind the oak ironing table were the sullen faces of the laundresses, beads of sweat dotting their dark faces, streaking their cheeks and foreheads. Though the ceiling was high and the windows open, no air flowed through the room. To offset the unventilated heat, they wore the scantiest of dresses, little more than undergarments, really, their upper bodies barely covered for decency. Some of them had tied rags around their heads or necks to absorb perspiration, and two or three were fitfully waving straw fans that provided too little relief for the effort it took to work them. Three dozen pairs of eyes regarded her with hostility.

Why, she began, were the windows open now but not, as she had noticed on passing by one day, when they were normally working?

The question was unexpected and confusing. What had it to do with the problem at hand? The women looked at one another. Perhaps it was some sort of trick. "Wha' chu mean?" one of them asked.

By now the perspiration was coursing freely down Mrs. Memory's face, chest and back. She could even feel it on her legs. The steam from the washtubs and the irons had condensed on the cooler glass surface of the windows, which appeared to be sweating in sympathy with the inhabitants; the place was unfit for human habitation. She pointed to the windows and carefully repeated her question.

The woman who had opened the door for her, mopping her heavy round face and neck and unselfconsciously reaching all the way down into her garment to swab between her breasts, stepped forward to say that when they kept the windows open to let out some of the heat, flies and other insects often swarmed in. The women, preferring the heat to the bugs that sometimes left stains on newly cleaned clothes, therefore elected to open the laundry doors rather than the windows for what little ventilation it could provide. "Now why you askin'?"

"Because I think there's a better way to make you all a little more comfortable when you're working in here."

More murmurs, of skepticism rather than hostility now. Their leader asked Mrs. Memory what she had in mind.

"You leave that to me. Meanwhile, let's see if we can settle this other business." She said she knew that they worked hard and well, and she for one appreciated it. She said their work was important to the operation of the hotel and required skill and strength and perseverance. She said she understood how accidents sometimes happened, even to the best and most skilled workers, and that she herself did not think it was fair for them to be charged for the cost of any garments that were unintentionally ruined in the laundering. On the other hand, she said, anyone who repeatedly made mistakes could not expect to be rewarded by continuing employment. So she had a proposition to make to them: they would all go back to work now, and from this point on, anyone who caused damage during the washing or ironing had to come forward and admit the mistake promptly—no ifs, ands or buts. Anyone who made mistakes two times would be penalized—the ironers would be demoted to laundresses for a week, and a laundress who, say, twice ruined garments in the mangle would be suspended for a week. A third mistake would result in dismissal. If anyone who damaged a garment failed to confess, however, then all of their salaries collectively would be docked to pay for the amount the hotel had to reimburse the guest—or, if it was hotel property that was damaged, whatever it cost to replace it.

For a moment there was a look of bewilderment on their faces, possibly over the stunning reasonableness of the proposed arrangement, possibly because it was too complicated for quick comprehension. Slowly she went over the conditions a second time until heads began to bob in agreement. "And, as I said, I'll try to make things a little more pleasant for you in here."

"Wha' bout dat girl wha' burned de dress?"

"You all know who she is, so maybe you'll keep an eye on her and make sure she's more careful from now on. After this, any mistake she makes and doesn't admit to, you'll all pay for."

"Wha' bout Mistah Krause—an' all dat?"

"I'm responsible for the laundry, not Mr. Krause."

That brought smiles and stirrings, and even before Mrs. Memory was through the door, they had resumed working. On her way out she was tapped lightly on the shoulder by the large woman who had answered the door and served as ringleader. She identified herself as Cleo Timmons, Arthur's mother, and thanked Mrs. Memory for coming.

In the hallway, where the temperature was fifteen degrees cooler, she mopped her face and forehead with the back of her sleeve—an act of relief she had refrained from with difficulty in front of the women, most of whose waking existence was passed in that horrific hotbox. How could they tolerate it, she asked herself, daubing her handkerchief about her eyes, which were tearing from the perspiration that had seeped into them. Often she had passed their door unthinkingly and heard them chattering and sometimes laughing or even singing. It was, she decided, their brand of fortitude.

Back in her office she pulled her shirtwaist away from her clammy body and leaned forward to look hard at Miss Prentisse. "Do you consider the working conditions in the laundry to be satisfactory?"

Miss Prentisse, anxious for news on the outcome of Mrs. Memory's peacemaking mission, was confounded by the question. "Why—yes—of course. They have the most modern and efficient equipment made."

"I was thinking less of the equipment than the extreme heat."

"The heat?" Plainly the subject had not occurred to Miss Prentisse. "How can you have a laundry without heat?"

"I found it excessive."

"Well—because you're not used to it. Those women are. They like it like that."

"And who told you that?"

"Why, it's well known the colored love heat—that's the way it is where they came from. Where white folks get exhausted, niggers thrive in the heat. Up North, maybe you folks aren't—"

"Miss Prentisse, those women down there are human beings, just like you and me, and when it's hot, they are hot—just like you and me. I think they would be more productive and careful in their work if things were a little more pleasant for them." She was therefore instructing Miss Prentisse to see to it that three buckets of iced water were brought to the laundry each morning and again in the afternoon. Furthermore, would she kindly go to Mr. Jenkin's office and ask him to arrange at the first opportunity for screens to be made for the laundry windows so a breeze could flow through the room without bringing a plague of insects with it? Finally, she would appreciate it if Miss Prentisse inquired about the cost and availability of those new rotating electric fans, which might be installed in the laundry to relieve the oppressive heat; if it was too late for this season, perhaps they could be obtained in time for the next one. Mrs. Memory looked aside now in dismissal of her subordinate. "If I find you have not complied with my instructions, I will not take it at all kindly. Thank you."

Miss Prentisse rose with a look of bewilderment. "But—"

"Yes?"

"How have you resolved the—"

"Oh, yes. Everything will be fine. The women are back at work." She briefly explained the new arrangement and asked Miss Prentisse to be good enough to advise Mr. Krause of the resolution of the crisis.

"Me?" she trilled. "But—he'll be—"

"Thank you, Miss Prentisse."

The second assistant housekeeper, head bobbing as if palsied, dissolved through the door, to be replaced within minutes by the assistant hotel manager wearing a fiery glow. Without invitation Mr. Krause dropped heavily into the chair in front of Mrs. Memory's desk and glared at her as she put down her pen and made a neat pile from the papers scattered over the desktop. "Yes, Mr. Krause," she said, hoping her voice betrayed no emotion whatever, "is there something I can do for you?"

"*Do* for me?" He pushed his large head over the desktop toward her. "Haven't you already done quite enough?"

"I beg your pardon?"

His face darkened with emotion. "You have countermanded my instructions and undermined my authority by taking things into your own hands—"

The little black eyes in his wide shapeless face reminded her of the buttons on her shoes. "Are you referring to the former problem involving the laundresses?"

"What else *could* I be referring to, madam?"

"I'm sure I don't know."

"But you do know, do you not, that when Mr. Stokes-Vecchio leaves the premises, I am in command of the hotel?" He brought both of his fists up to the desktop and leaned over still farther toward her so that his face floated no more than two feet from hers.

"In nominal command, I should say."

"There is nothing nominal about it, madam. What I say is the law as far as this establishment goes. You have no right to take that law into your own hands—that is rank insubordination."

"And you, sir, if you will forgive my candor, were guilty of rank foolishness, unbecoming behavior for a commanding officer and in gross violation of the hotel's chain of command."

His eyes narrowed to pinpoints of fury. "Madam, you leave me no alternative but to report your behavior to the hotel manager."

Mrs. Memory tilted her head back to escape Krause's hot breath. "I think you will not, sir. And I think you had better reconsider the facts." The first fact, she told him, was that she was in charge of the laundry, not he, and the second fact was that Miss Prentisse was answerable to her, not to him. And if there was a problem connected with excessive laundry expenses arising from damaged clothing, he should have advised her of it. "Mr. Stokes-Vecchio comes to me about all housekeeping matters— that is my job—and you are hardly less obligated than he to do the same—wouldn't you agree?"

"The situation did not allow—"

"Furthermore, sir, it was apparent that you had not considered the possible consequences of your rash actions. What would have happened if the women had called your bluff? Where do you think we can find reliable replacements for them in a hurry?"

"They never would have continued to—"

"How could you be so certain? People treated badly are capable of reacting unpredictably." And what did he think might have happened to the hotel without a functioning laundry? And who was to say that, in their anger, the departing women might not have done serious damage to the equipment? Had any of those questions occurred to him? "I suspect not, sir—which is why I thought it best to take matters in hand before you succeeded in putting us all out of work."

The upper part of Krause's body slowly receded, coming to rest against the back of the chair, and the color began to drain from his face. "I—really—don't—"

"And if you ever again issue orders to my assistant or otherwise interfere with my supervisory duties, I will go at once to the general manager and make my position clear." She rose from her chair, hoping the desk would hide her shaking knees. "I am prepared, however, to overlook your conduct today and say nothing to Mr. Stokes-Vecchio—and if you are wise enough to learn from your mistakes, you will do the same. Now I would appreciate it if you will excuse me so that I may make my afternoon rounds."

She spotted him coming along the shore parallel to her only after she had turned and started swimming southward again. He was walking rapidly, his jacket a dark smudge at that distance, his tan trousers almost lost against the sand. She did not have to acknowledge that she had seen him just yet, but soon.

She went on swimming for another few minutes, knowing she was under his scrutiny.

"Hey, hello out there!" he called out to her, waving.

If she kept swimming in his direction, it would appear as if she were welcoming him, but to turn away and swim in any other direction would be taken as downright hostility. She treaded water for a minute, considering proper aquatic etiquette, then finally lifted her arm in something less than a hearty hail.

He took off his jacket, slung it over his shoulder and increased his pace. His boots were in his other hand, she could see now, and his trousers were rolled up well above his ankles; this time he would not stand on ceremony as a beach walker. As he neared the pile of clothes on her sheet, he dropped his boots, then slipped the jacket off his shoulder and folded it carefully before placing it down beside her things.

She turned away and began swimming northward a bit. When she looked back in again his shirttails were hanging out over the top of his pants and he was doing something with the front of his shirt. What was he up to? She could not pull her eyes away. He was fiddling with his cuffs and then with a single motion of both arms that startled her, he pulled the shirt off his body. Now what? As his hands began to move over the front of his trousers, the answer was all too apparent. He was shedding his clothes and coming to join her in the water. Good Lord!

She changed course suddenly, veering to the right and swimming away from him. Her arms flailed through the water, faster and faster, her legs in a churning counterpoint.

"Hey," she heard him call to her, "come back!" The words were faint above the surf.

"Stay away," she called back, making a megaphone of her hands. "I was here first . . ."

"I can't hear you," he yelled. "Come back."

She swam a few strokes more, then squinted and saw that he had in fact shed his trousers and waded into the water wearing only his drawers. Her view was obscured momentarily as a breaker of rare height reared up and began rolling in toward him. When the sea quieted, she looked again toward the spot where she had last seen him. There was nobody there. Her eyes scoured the shoreline but he was not to be seen. "Mr. Loring?" she called, at first suspecting him of coyness, then an alarmed "*Mr. Loring!*"

There was no response. She started to swim in, heart suddenly pounding. "Mr. Loring!" she shouted, struggling not to gulp water. "Where are you?" Dear Lord, what could she do for a drowning man? There was no one around to help her. And how, the thought flashed through her mind, could she ever explain the circumstances of her presence? Then she saw him rise out of the water, standing in it waist-deep. "Are you all right?" she shouted at him, arms slowing.

"Wave knocked me down. Not used to this. I'm fine now. Stay there— I'll come join you."

"No, you won't!" To make it sound more playful than offensive she turned and began swimming as strongly as she was capable of out toward the horizon. She had a good head start on him as it was, and even if he proved a vigorous swimmer, it would take real exertion for him to catch up.

After sprinting away from him for a time, she glanced back to check his progress. What she saw broke her forward motion and reduced her to hilarity. The poor man had advanced only a few dozen feet, doing a preposterous dog paddle. It would take him the rest of the morning to reach her even if she did not swim another stroke. He was clearly immersed in an alien element. That he had nevertheless risked himself and her ridicule, knowing how much more accomplished she was in the water than he, melted her initial upset at his coming. She started back toward him. She could neither leave him there, windmilling about absurdly, nor swim on at her own pleasure as if oblivious of him.

"I want to come out now," she called to him when she was within earshot.

"Come on," he shouted back. "I won't stop you."

Knowing that his eyes were on her all the while, she felt herself exaggerating her movements, making them as fluid and graceful as possible, as if to point up the difference between their abilities in the water. It was not so much that she was flaunting her skill, she told herself, as it was a compulsion to show him she possessed something that his money could not buy. She stopped when she had closed to perhaps a dozen feet of him and, remaining in the water so as not to allow him to see her body through her combination, said, "I want to let the sun dry me off. I'd appreciate it if you'd stay out here for a few more minutes."

"I'll stay out for as long as you'd like—I'm just getting the hang of this thing. I was hoping, actually, you might offer me a little instruction."

"Some other time, perhaps."

"Splendid. I consider that an ironclad pledge. Now you come ahead—I promise to avert my eyes if that's on your mind. Just call me when you're done sunning."

She circled around him somewhat, looking over her shoulder to see if he was as good as his word. He appeared to be absorbed in splashing away with joyous energy and little forward motion. She wondered whether he was truly so inept or was staging the demonstration to win her sympathy and future tutelage.

When her combination was dry enough to slip her shirtwaist over it she dressed quickly and easily. Finished except for her hair and hat and stockings and boots, she lifted her skirts and walked to the water's edge. "I'm ready, Mr. Loring," she called to him. "You can stop your—your—"

The ridiculous splashing ceased, and he turned toward her and shouted, "Sorry—what did you say?"

"I'm—ready to go back now. Thank you very much for—"

"Wait, I want to come with you."

Her impulse was to turn and hurry off, now that she had him at a momentary disadvantage for a change. But her feet stayed anchored in the sand as she watched the water around him leap and dance while he flailed toward her and rose up as soon as his feet touched bottom. For the first time she was aware that his upper chest was covered with dark hair. The sight told her more than she wanted to know about him, but her eyes would not turn away. With each foamy step he took, the level of water around him dropped until she could see that the entire upper half of his wiry form was similarly pelted. His drawers, fortunately, were of a heavy fabric that had none of the diaphanous quality of her combination. Aware suddenly that she must have appeared to be gaping at the spectacle of this unlikely sea god emerging from the not-very-deep, she turned and began walking mindlessly back toward the sheet.

"Mrs. Memory"—she heard Loring's voice directly behind and above her left ear, so close she thought she could feel his breath on her neck and cheek—"you're walking directly between me and the clothes I would like to put on if you don't mind."

"I—I'm so sorry, perhaps it would be wisest if I just—"

"On the other hand, I don't honestly relish jumping into my things in soaking wet drawers. Perhaps you can spare me a few moments to—"

Her eyes remained averted as she addressed this disembodied presence hovering within inches of her. "And do what in the meanwhile, Mr. Loring—gather driftwood?"

"Driftwood, cocoanuts, whatever you'd like—I won't be long. Would my drawers dry faster, do you think, on or off?"

She began to pivot around but checked herself midway. "Your— personal attire is not a fit subject for discourse with a lady, Mr. Loring. Furthermore, it is no concern of mine what degree of discomfort you must endure under these circumstances. You were not invited here, so I am hardly sympathetic with—"

"As you wish, madam."

Sensing him pad around her to the sheet, she wandered off a few yards, her eyes fixed on the ocean horizon. This simply could not continue. She would have to tell him that if he did not stop his outrageous behavior she would be forced to—to—what? Stop coming to the beach? Stay in her rooms Sunday morning when every nerve and muscle in her body were begging for release that only her sea bathing could decently accomplish? And what, really, was his crime? It could scarcely qualify as voyeurism. The beach, after all, did not belong to her. Nor was he unpleasant to talk with. And for all his cheeky manner, he was not really ungentlemanly. No, she thought, stooping to scoop up a shell and pretending to examine its convoluted structure, the only truly disturbing thing about his presence was the unsuitability of her bathing costume. It was as if she were wearing nothing at all. But that she could remedy—

"I say, Mrs. Memory?" she heard him call. "Do you have a mirror?"

She tossed the seashell into the bath of an oncoming wave, which bore it back to the deep, and glanced over at him before calculating his state of undress. Propriety had retaken command of him. The only indecorous note was his tie, its ends dangling below his collar in disarray. "No, I do not," she said, moving toward him. "Is there some problem?"

"The sad truth is I'm hopeless about doing up this thing without a mirror. I've tried three times now, and each time it comes out worse than before. Do you suppose you could—?"

As with his swimming, she was not certain whether he was shamming incompetence to arouse her interest or was otherwise so pleased with himself that he risked nothing in so appealing to her. She marched over a pair of sand hillocks and confronted him directly at one arm's length. "I can try."

"You'll have to come a little closer, I'm afraid."

She took a step forward and suddenly became so conscious of her nearness to him that it was almost suffocating. She could detect the rise and fall of his chest as he breathed, and when her eyes strayed to his face, carefully avoiding his look, she could see the minute ends of the hairs in his freshly shaved beard. "What is it you'd like me to do with it?"

"Tie it, if you don't mind."

"How, I mean—just an ordinary bow or is there some special way? I haven't had much practice at—"

"Just any old bow, thanks."

She picked up the silken ends with delicacy, trying not to touch the body that bulked so palpably just behind them, and guided by the wrinkles already in the fabric, bowed the loops as quickly as she could in a haphazard arrangement. "There," she said, taking a step backward, "will that do?"

He reached up to his neck, felt the tie with his right hand and said, "About as well as my swimming." Then with both hands he pulled her shoulders toward him and kissed her gently on the forehead. "But you can be my valet anytime you wish, madam." He smiled and went no further.

Her shock came and went in an instant, succeeded by a small responsive smile, but the place where his lips and mustache had brushed her still tingled. The breeze suddenly whipped over the beach, heightening the sensation already assaulting her and lifting a strand of her hair across her eyes. Loring brushed it away before releasing her from his light grip.

"Your eyes," he said, "what are they exactly?"

"They—don't seem to be exactly anything, I'm afraid."

"I don't know as I've ever seen such a color—that green-brown—it almost becomes gray but not quite. What do you call it?"

"I don't. No one's ever much noticed them."

"Because you spend too much of your time in the shade. In the sun all your color comes alive. Out here there's red in your hair and green in your eyes. Yet you persist in hiding all that and always wearing black. You make it almost impossible to see how lovely you really are."

It was too much—his kiss, his words, his acute awareness of her. She broke away while she still could, sensing a rush of fear from suddenly remembered wounds that had never properly healed, and of excitement that might render her susceptible to a fresh delusion. "My hair—I've got to pin it up."

"Why? It looks so much better this way—loose and free."

"I am neither, though, and it would not do at all for me to be seen in such a condition." She went to her knees on the sheet, upending the basket with a clatter, dragged the comb quickly through her hair and shoved pins into her coils with a recklessness born of discomfort from the steady gaze she knew he had fixed on her. Only after she jabbed the large pin through the crown of her straw hat, which provided her with a shield from his shameless stare, did she look up at him again. "Would you help me shake out the sheet, Mr. Loring?"

On the walk back their talk was light and impersonal, then lapsed entirely for a time until Loring cleared his throat and said, as if addressing the surf, "You have great strength, Mrs. Memory. Where does it come from?"

"I—didn't I explain satisfactorily last time? As a girl, I went regularly to the beach with—"

"Your swimming is the least of it. I mean your entire circumstances—with its dangers in more ways than one—and the bearing with which you seem to manage your position. There's nothing humble in all that. There's a defiance, really—"

The unexpectedness of this assessment, so different from the flattery he had applied earlier, again unbalanced her; he had that dangerous knack. "I hardly think of my conduct that way, I can assure you."

"No doubt. That's why it's so—beguiling."

"Mr. Loring, it can hardly be said that a professional housekeeper, of however exalted an establishment, indulges in defiant behavior. I do what I must to carry on—and try to do so with at least a modicum of dignity. Beyond that, I have no airs. And so I must ask you, please, to resist dispensing your undeserved and—and—inaccurate remarks, which serve no purpose whatever—for either of us."

"If that's your pleasure—"

The golf course was in view now. "It decidedly is."

"I'll not come anymore if you tell me not to."

"As you wish, Mr. Loring." Their worlds, she thought, remained unbridgeable, certainly under these conditions. It was all a muddle, this stirring he had provoked in her. Her farewell was little above a whisper.

She had not gone twenty steps from him when her senses returned: he was still holding the basket that he had carried for her on the walk back. Looking about to be sure nobody else was nearby, she ran back toward him, bracing her hat from the breeze with one hand. His face bore a slight smile at the sight of her swift approach. Her own remained expressionless as she reclaimed the basket and sat on the grass uncoyly to pull on her shoes.

Loring leaned over her as she worked the laces. "A word of advice, if I may, madam. When you're bereft of a certain unmentionable undergarment, you shouldn't run that way. The absence is pleasingly obvious to any uncouth onlooker."

There was *nothing* gentlemanly about him. If she had not been seated on the ground she might well have kicked Mr. Loring in both his shins.

Only four silly seams in the whole garment, and she had managed to sew one of them crooked. For shame, she scolded herself, picking up her scissors and beginning to snip at the offending threads. True, she was not sewing under ideal conditions, working late and without good lighting and in rather a hurry lest Miss Sanderson poke her nose into the sewing room to discover who was using one of the machines after hours. She felt almost furtive: how would she explain her need for a new black combination, especially one made without a drop seat in the back, to anyone wandering in on her just now?

At eight o'clock, the wayward seam restitched, she smuggled the peculiar garment upstairs to her room and began working on the buttonholes. Provided she persevered, she might finish half of them this evening. If only someone would invent a sewing machine that made buttonholes, the women of America would elect him President—if women could only vote. And why couldn't they? The degraded standing of her sex filled her with such fury whenever the subject came up in conversation or in her own thoughts that she dwelled on it as briefly as possible. There was no argument against it that did not violate all decency, yet the very notion of women voting, she had been told loud and often, was unwomanly. What, then, of women like herself, with a profession and real commercial responsibilities? What were they? Could no professional woman be a lady? Who made those rules? Who made *all* the rules? And why was she fashioning this fool garment if not to accommodate one of those tormentors of her gender? Mrs. Memory sighed at the state of things. She did not often yield to sighs; the world was the world, and there seemed little percentage, Loring's remark to her notwithstanding, in defying it. But she would not surrender to it, to all its punishing rules and false standards and cruel fates doled out seemingly at random to many who were least deserving of them. Perhaps the good and the wicked were meted their true desserts in the life everlasting; men, though, she suspected, arranged things to their liking in heaven and hell both.

She lifted the combination closer to her and began the second button-hole. It was a plain, shabby garment, with no lace or ribbons or ruffles to ornament it, but it would serve. She pulled a thread off the black spool and had just inserted the end into her mouth when a knock sounded at her door. She placed her sewing beneath a cushion, checked the fasten-ings of her dressing gown at throat and waist and went to answer the summons.

"It's Ruby Lee Eustis, ma'am. I'm a chambermaid."

"I know who you are," Mrs. Memory said, admitting her. The one who had run into Loring. "Is anything the matter?"

The girl performed some sort of twitch intended to pass for a curtsy and then slipped into the sitting room. "I got to ask you something," she asked, indicating the bunched blue cloth on her arm.

"Would you care to sit, Miss Eustis?"

The girl did not respond. She stood in the middle of the room, head swiveling. "All this b'longs to you?" she asked.

"In a manner of speaking. They take it away at the end of the season, I'm afraid."

"It's a reg'lar suite, just like fer the guests."

"More or less."

"They treat ya real good, don't they?"

Mrs. Memory nodded gravely and asked the girl to state her business.

She backed her way into a chair and perched at the edge of it, as if wary it would be snatched away from behind at any second. "It's about this here petticoat," she began, the silk taffeta rustling as she took it off her arm and spread it carefully over her knees. It was very beautiful, Mrs. Memory recognized, and must have been expensive when new, with its yards of ecru Valenciennes lace and rows of embroidered pink satin rosebuds. Ruby Lee had found it in the wastebasket in Mrs. Lockwood's room, No. 229—all stuffed in, as you could tell from the wrinkles in it, the girl hastily added. "I di'n't want to add it to the reg'lar trash so I just laid it in the basket, kind of." She supposed that Mrs. Lockwood had intended to throw it away because it was all torn up in back at the hem and the lace was ripped, too, she showed the housekeeper, but it was so pretty and she knew she could mend it—"I'm a real good mender, I am, ma'am"—and she could take it in around the waist to fit her, so she brought it to Miss Sanderson to ask if she could keep it. The assistant housekeeper had instructed her to take up the matter with Mrs. Memory.

Undoubtedly the garment had been tossed away; the girl would not make up such a story, and a theft would be too easily discovered. What was the harm? For a girl whose lingerie surely consisted of muslin and osnaburg, the silk and satin petticoat would be valued as a treasure and shown off to every female of her acquaintance.

"I'll tell you what, Miss Eustis. Keep the petticoat for one week and if Mrs. Lockwood makes no mention of it, then you may mend it, alter it or do whatever you care to with it. Would that suit you?"

Ruby Lee Eustis would go to her dreams that night in a rare, probably previously unknown, state of ecstasy. Gladdened, Mrs. Memory resumed her buttonhole making and considered whether she might not, after all, add a bit of white ribbon to her black combination.

The other officers had already begun to leave the dining table as Mr. Bedient continued his botany lesson largely for Mrs. Memory's benefit. On his chance remark that it was too bad the royal poinciana tree after which the hotel had been named did not bloom until mid-spring, well after the last guest had gone and the establishment was shuttered until the following November, the head housekeeper had asked the supervisor of grounds to describe the flowering process. The blossoms were red or bright orange or sometimes scarlet, perhaps four inches in diameter, he told her, and erupted in huge, brilliant sprays that caused the poinciana also to be known as the flame tree. The "royal" part of its name, Mr. Bedient went on, no doubt came from the flat, wide-spreading crown the tree developed, sometimes at a height of fifty feet in places of its origin, such as Madagascar; it had transplanted marvelously in the New World.

"How fascinating," Mrs. Memory said.

Others at the table were less taken with horticulture than she, and when Bedient began expatiating on the tropical garden he had planted at the southern edge of the hotel property, only the housekeeper and the general manager remained to listen. Perhaps, Mr. Bedient suggested, she would enjoy an escorted tour of his cultivated new specimens, some of which had probably never been seen by inhabitants of the American north. His plumbago and orange trumpet vine had begun to bloom just that week, and the African tulip trees were about to flower any day. If there was some late afternoon when he might accompany her on a tour of the garden, he was sure she would enjoy it.

She accepted the invitation, and their appointment was set for the following Tuesday at five outside the service-yard gate.

As the delighted grounds supervisor excused himself from the table and Mrs. Memory prepared to follow, she became aware of Mr. Stokes-Vecchio's mustache—in which he invested no little pride—quivering to her left. He busied himself wiping his lips with his napkin, carefully brushing his mustache upward at the end of each swipe to insure against its disarrangement. "I'm glad to see you'll be getting out a bit, Mrs. Memory," he said to her, alluding to the arrangement she had just concluded with Mr. Bedient. "A little excursion from time to time would do you a world of good—if you don't mind my saying so—Madeleine."

The familiarity implied in his using her given name in a public room put her on guard. "I—suppose you're right. The occasion does not often arise."

"I fully understand—which is why, if you'll permit me, I should like to propose one to you myself."

"How kind," she said, "but you needn't worry that I—"

"Ah, but I do. You are too valuable to this establishment for me to ignore your—recreational needs."

Hands in her lap, balled into fists, fingernails digging into her palms, she listened to him invite her to attend the Cakewalk as his guest the following Thursday evening. It was jolly good fun, he said, though rather frivolous; many of the guests considered the event a highlight of their stay. He was confident she would find it entertaining.

She had heard about the Cakewalks, of course, since coming to work at the hotel, but they were staged for the pleasure of the guests, and even senior staff members were not encouraged to attend. At any rate, she could not have come to one without an escort. They were held every week after dinner in the octagonal ballroom, where the little gold chairs were set out in rows to resemble a theater. As the hotel orchestra played a medley of lively popular tunes, black members of the hotel staff, garishly costumed for the occasion at the management's expense, struck attitudes, performed dances, often of their own devising, and generally strutted about in exaggerated fashion for the amusement of the onlookers. A panel of judges, chosen from among the hotel's most distinguished guests, selected the winning pair, who were awarded a modest cash emolument and the privilege of "taking the cake," an elaborate confection that represented the real prize of the evening.

Having accepted Mr. Bedient's thoughtful offer, how could she now spurn, even if more suspect, the invitation of her superior officer? But she was not anxious to encourage any lingering designs that the hotel manager might be harboring about the nature of their relationship. "Perhaps the guests might be offended," she ventured, "by the presence of a widow in their midst. My black wardrobe could easily violate the spirit of the festivities—"

"Balderdash, my dear. Your dignity and privacy are accepted by all who know you. The only question is whether the playfulness of the evening would violate your sensibilities."

He was not to be put off. "In that case," she said, "I accept." If not with pleasure.

The sky was a brilliant unbroken blue faintly edged along the southern horizon by little puffs of clouds. How far away was that on a day as clear as this—five miles or a hundred? The birdsong seemed to fill the air with a poignant intensity, carrying out onto the beach and challenging the crash of the surf. What kinds of birds were they, she wondered; too little time passed out-of-doors had denied her the keenness to distinguish among their calls. The green of the palm fronds levitating on the sea breeze signaled to her that the time for reverie had elapsed. Her new black combination, more sun-absorbent than her abandoned white one, had thoroughly dried, but her mood, while more meditative than at the start of her outing, had not improved from punishing the ocean.

She dressed herself leisurely, determined to enjoy the long, solitary walk back to the hotel. Almost fiercely she pointed her parasol over her head and moved at a steady gait, digging her heels into the moist sand more deeply than usual, deriving a perverse pleasure out of making the yielding surface conform to her will. Eyes focused on the beach immediately before her, she pounded along with almost martial purposefulness; wasn't it Caesar who was always driving his troops on forced marches across Gaul in pursuit of Vercingetorix? The memory of schoolgirl Latin exercises summoned up a happier time of life, when everything had seemed possible for her, even marriage to a Yale man from a gentried family, and transported her far from the pain that had dogged her all that morning.

Before she knew it, the edge of the golf course was in view. Damnation. She could have gone on for another hundred miles or to the clouds on the horizon, whichever was closer. But what was the—

"Hey!"

The shout flew out from a thicket in the corner of the golf course. No one, though, was visible. She slowed her pace, wondering whether to stop at once and put on her boots.

"Hello! Wait up!"

Still, no figure appeared.

Good sense sat her down on the spot, and as she opened her basket and withdrew her boots a man broke through the thicket and came striding rapidly toward her. He was dressed all in black except for his white shirt-front, an unlikely outfit for a Sunday morning in Palm Beach. His long-legged stride identified him to her well before his features were plain. He had on one of those new tuxedo coats without tails; his evening dress looked ludicrous against the sand under the noonday sun.

"Hello!" He panted, running up to her and, seemingly without a care who might see, throwing himself to the sand beside her. "I'm bushed."

He had gone to West Palm last night, he told her amid his panting, with a few of his hotel cronies. They got involved in a little card game, and before he knew it, it had become rather a large game and he was obliged to see it through to the end. By that time the last ferry back across Lake Worth had departed, and since there wasn't even so much as a rowboat available, they were marooned over there all night. To make matters worse, the first ferry on Sunday morning did not leave till half past ten. The moment it docked, he flagged down Arthur Timmons' Afrimobile, known to be the speediest of the lot, and had himself pedaled as far and as fast across the golf course as they dared travel. "I'm terribly, terribly sorry to have—"

"Yes, you missed a marvelous swim. The water was—practically effervescent—I can't remember its being so bracing and—and—a whole school of fish came by—you should have seen them—they were so bright and beautiful—pike or something, I think they were—though I'm not very good at underwater sighting—any more than I am with bird calls—I can't tell one from another, to be perfectly honest, even though I love to—"

"Madeleine!"

She had jabbered on without looking up at him, intent on not conceding in the least that he had been missed. His blunt, personal interruption destroyed her pose and threatened to rout her poise. She looked up and saw the distress lines contorting his brow. "I—can't recall ever having granted you the—the right to call me that."

"Forgive me, but you were rattling on and on, and I—"

"Some things may not be so readily forgiven as you seem to think, Mr. Loring." Her eyes fell away from his and focused on the laces she intently tightened.

"I—I'm sorry. You're quite right. I shouldn't have—but I'm glad I did, if you must know." His fingers were tracing a meander along the silk lapel of his jacket. "Besides, pike don't live in oceans."

A smile broke uncontrollably across her face. "Well, whatever they were, you missed them."

"I won't next week—I promise you."

"The world may end by next week. I should ration my promises if I were you, Mr. Loring." She rose and walked past his sprawled form. "I trust your night's labors were well rewarded."

Her feet practically flew across the golf course toward the hotel. For so long had she considered the absence of pain to be life's sweetest reward that she could not identify the sensation that came on her now in the heat of the day.

The music could be heard long before she and Stokes-Vecchio reached the ballroom. Major Mackintosh, second in command of the United States Marine Band before his retirement, was already flushed with exertion: this insistent four-quarter beat would exhaust the poor man by the time the evening was over.

Whatever it lacked in subtlety, the music served to enliven the crowd, which seemed more excited by the collective spectacle it was creating than by anticipation of the evening's entertainment. The men, in black cutaways or tuxedo coats, were the perfect monotonous backdrop for the dazzling display of finery, in every shade of the rainbow, by the women they escorted. Even on the few occasions she had dined at Sherry's and Delmonico's, Mrs. Memory had never seen so many extravagantly beautiful dresses at one time; several she recognized had been illustrated in Harper's Bazaar, which she read with regularity.

The jewelry bedecking all that silk and satin and lacework was still more fabulous. One woman wore an entire parure of emeralds and diamonds on her neck, ears and both wrists to complement her jade-green gown; matching rings had been made large enough to fit over her long white kid gloves. A woman nearby displayed a bib of glowing pearls that completely encrusted her décolletage from chin to the outermost protrusion of her bosom. The bearing of so much weight would have reduced a lesser spirit to stooping, but the pearly woman, with smiling fortitude, maintained her spine ruler-straight. The necklaces, brooches, pendants, bracelets, rings and tiaras, with their rubies, sapphires and topazes in modest complement to the profusion of diamonds, pearls and emeralds, winked and glittered in ten thousand facets with every slight turning of those elegant torsos beneath the blazing crystal chandeliers.

Mrs. Memory had worn her very best mourning costume for the evening—a silk faille *complet* with its jabot of white Valenciennes lace down the front and its passementerie braiding ornamented with dull jet on the skirt—but, confronted by such a panorama of matchless elegance, she felt irredeemably dowdy. Her sole piece of jewelry was the thin gold band on her finger. She was not there, though, to compete with the guests, she reminded herself, but only to witness the lavishness of their display.

The orchestra lustily rendered such current delights as "My Balalaika Beauty," "Dolly, Delight Me, Doodle-De-Doo," "Old Tray Ran Away with the Sleigh One Day" and a newly popular number that Major Mackintosh urged the crowd to join him in singing in his genial croak:

> *When Saucy Suzy skitters through the slough,*
> *There's only two or three things you can do.*
> *She'll hold your hand 'neath the pale moon above,*
> *And you can whisper softly to her sweet words of love.*
> *Her memory stays with you when you part,*
> *And there's no end of damage to your heart,*
> *But I love my Suzy girl and so would you*
> *When Saucy Suzie skitters through the slough.*

At the conclusion of this touching ballad, she glanced over at Stokes-Vecchio. He was caught up in the music, his hands, along with those of many in the audience, clapping gaily and only slightly behind the beat. He caught her glance and nodded his encouragement to her. "You should have a good time, my dear. Do try to enjoy yourself."

Following applause, a drumroll accompanied Major Mackintosh as he made his way from the orchestra enclosure at the side of the room to the platform that had been set up in the center of the dance floor. A signal from the leader brought the drumroll to an end with a crash of cymbals. "Beautiful ladies and charming gentlemen," the major began at a circus barker's shout, "I have the honor to present to you this evening an even dozen cake-contenders of rare virtuosity—six couples who will perform for you an amazing array of feats so splendid you will be sure to relate them to your grandchildren."

Stokes-Vecchio leaned over to her and whispered, "He says the same thing every week."

"Our first entrants of this gala evening," the major bellowed, "are Callie Williamson from the culinary auxiliary staff and Jonathan Ringo from our vehicular corps. A round of applause for encouragement, folks." That meant the female partner was a dishwasher and the male an Afrimobile driver, Stokes-Vecchio explained.

The major scurried off while the musicians struck up a twinkly number. Through one of the open French doors that led to the front lawn dashed a young black man pulling on the arm of his somewhat less mobile partner, a woman obviously twice his age. Up the lad leaped onto the platform while his companion took the more stately route up the stairs. His fireman-red shirt and black-and-white-striped pants melted together as he pinwheeled, somersaulted and flew about, limbs gyrating every which way. His partner was infinitely more subdued as she paraded about in a green-and-yellow-checked dress, peacocking her skirt, taking little steps from side to side and clapping vigorously in accompaniment to the young man's airborne antics. The art was all in the contrast between them.

A good round of applause and a second drumroll preceded Major Mackintosh's introduction of a woman "from our admirable fabric rejuvenation staff" and a man "from the Poinciana's remarkable department of haute cuisine"—which meant she was a laundress and he was an assistant chef—Cleo and Oscar Timmons.

Arthur's mother, in a bright green dress embroidered with flowers of many colors and a high headdress seemingly made of yard upon yard of scarlet fabric intricately wrapped and draped, looked an altogether different person from her workday appearance in the laundry. Her husband wore his chef's *toque blanche,* a white shirt with ruffles down the front and white trousers flared at the bottom like a seaman's. It was soon obvious that the couple, looking seven feet tall each in their extravagant headpieces, had rehearsed their performance carefully, for they moved together in smoothly coordinated steps, kicks and jumps. Belying her bulk, the woman was light on her feet and as graceful as her arrow of a husband. There was a certain disdain, which was not to say contempt, in their manner, as if they did not much care whether the audience appreciated the fluid harmony of their motions. Not once as they danced did they court their onlookers' endorsement with a smile or other ingratiating gesture. That their virtuosity was nonetheless recognized was manifest from the cheers and whistles mingled with the heavy applause. Indeed, Mrs. Memory was startled to hear the gentleman next to her tell the gentleman seated directly in front of him that he would wager that the second couple would take the cake and he was offering two-to-one against the field.

"How much?" asked the man in front.

"A hundred," said her neighbor.

"You're on."

Mrs. Memory leaned over to Stokes-Vecchio to ask, behind her hand, if this sort of wager was common. "All the time," he said. Many of them regarded the Cakewalk as more of a sporting event, rather like a horse race, than a cultural entertainment, which was how he preferred to view it. Indeed, some of the guests made the most outlandish bets. Why, he had even been told of a pair of this sporting ilk who took two pieces of toast slathered with jam from the dining room out to the veranda railing to see which of them a fly would land on first. Five hundred was said to have changed hands on the outcome of that contest. It was all so casual, she thought, so matter-of-fact, as if their money had no value at all to them. The more foolhardy the risking of it, the less jaded their existence; winning was beside the point.

None of the "cakists," as the major called them, who followed the Timmonses could, for all their gyrations, match them in flair and finesse, so the audience's reaction was muted when, after the final drumroll of the evening, the major announced that the couple had taken the cake and the fifty-dollar prize that went with it. But it had nonetheless been a lively occasion, as Mrs. Memory remarked when Stokes-Vecchio took her arm and guided her out of the ballroom.

"I'm delighted you found it so, my dear," he said.

Near the doorway, her practiced eye was attracted by a tiny gleam emanating from the soil at the base of one of the potted palms. She reached down and recovered a pearl earring pendant set in a cluster of diamonds, which had evidently been brushed loose from its wearer by the fronds of the dwarf tree as she passed too close to them. Mrs. Memory turned to show her find to Stokes-Vecchio, but he was absorbed in trying to steer them through the crowd and had not noticed her quick movement to recover the piece of jewelry.

Her hand closed over it for a moment, cloaking its glitter and luster and transmitting only the hardness and substantiality of the little treasure. Its owner must have been heavily laden indeed with gems not to have sensed its loss. The pearl and stones, Mrs. Memory thought, could be refashioned into a lovely ring for a woman of modest circumstances. Had anyone seen her bend and grab up the earring? There was no telling. It could not be risked. And it was not right.

When his attention had returned to her, she opened her palm to Stokes-Vecchio and displayed the earring pendant. No doubt inquiry about it would be made at the manager's office in the morning. He commended her alertness as she dropped the precious object into his hand. "Such things should be yours, my dear," he said. "Perhaps one day—"

"Happiness does not stem from vanity," she said with aphoristic righteousness. "There are inner glows in life to sustain those less materially blessed."

"Lord, yes." His eyes blinked as if bedazzled by her goodness. Perhaps she might wish to take a short stroll around the grounds, he ventured; it would prove a pleasant inducement to a healthful night's sleep.

"Not this evening, thank you," she said, one hand touching slightly above her heart as if to say that sensitive organ had already sustained quite enough adventure for one evening.

He was waiting for her at the edge of the golf course, and together they walked to her private beach opposite the old humbled palm tree.

Together they went into the ocean, he unselfconsciously in his drawers, she almost boldly now in her new black combination. They played in the waves, jumping them, diving under them, swimming through their crests. Hesitantly at first, she schooled him in how to use his arms to achieve a cleaner, more efficient stroke, to drive his legs for added thrust, to turn his head rhythmically for breath. He was an eager, grateful pupil, laughing at his own failings, then nicely getting the hang of it and encouraging her to accelerate his instruction. He improved so rapidly that she began to suspect anew that his previous floundering had been staged for her benefit. At a spot shallow enough for them to stand, she looked at him through narrowed eyes and asked him if it were so.

"Why, Mrs. Memory—what a foul canard."

"Answer me."

He answered her with a kiss, so long and deep and unexpected that she had to gasp for breath at the end. Out there, alone in the water, enveloped by nature and smiled down on by a glorious sun, it all seemed impossible to her, and altogether pleasing. The stunned sensation drained out of her as he took her in his arms with slow precision and brought her body against his. She responded with a surge of feeling she had not experienced for twenty years. The unfamiliar power of the passion that she thought had been buried in her heart frightened her. "Madeleine," he said to her, said her name three times more and fell silent. She said nothing back, fearing whatever words her lips might form would be too few or too many. He sensed the uncertainty in her response, and after searching her face for a long moment, gently released her from his embrace. Their play resumed, less innocent, more subdued, and wound up with a shoreward sprint in which she easily triumphed.

Before they parted at the golf course he asked if she would go to West Palm with him on Friday night. There was a restaurant he knew where they could have dinner, and no one from the hotel staff was likely to see them. She asked if any hotel guests patronized the place, afraid they might recognize her. "Have you anything to wear that's not black?" he asked by way of an answer. She did not. He pressed his lips in contemplation, then said, "That can be remedied easily enough."

The box arrived on the Thursday train. She found it waiting outside her door in mid-afternoon. It bore an iridescent evening dress of blue-and-green *mousseline de soie* and a little headdress of peacock feathers with a bit of veiling and was accompanied by a note that read: *"The wife of a friend has lent this. She is approximately your size but in no other way your match. It is, I'm told, the latest thing in Charleston. On the veranda at eight tomorrow. H."*

Taking care that she was not observed, she went to his room, tapped twice to see if he was in, then admitted herself with the passkey and placed the box on the chaise in his sitting room. Her note said, *"Your kindness is appreciated, but I cannot wear what belongs to others. Sunday, as usual, if you wish. M."*

It was back outside her door, awaiting her return after supper. *"It now belongs to you—on trial,"* said his note. *"The owner advises by wire it has never been worn. If it suits you, payment can be made at your convenience. If not, an admirer will stand the loss. Until tomorrow at eight."*

If not quite the style for evening wear at the Royal Poinciana, neither was it so flagrantly unchic as to call attention to its wearer. And it was, she recognized, a garment sufficiently attractive that it might do her in New York on those occasions she attended theater or dined out. Undoubtedly it would serve well to disguise her amid her present surroundings. And there were other steps she could take to transform herself from the shrouded matron who plied the corridors of the Royal Poinciana like a wraith.

Late Friday afternoon she directed a note to the first officers' dining room, saying that a slight indisposition would prevent her attending the evening meal. In fact, she attended to her masquerade—which was how she perceived the occasion—with assiduous care and growing apprehension that her normal good sense had abandoned her. Her hair she piled on her head in elaborate coils, bolstered by the fashionable pads they called "rats," and arranged in the latest French style as conveyed by *Bazaar*. Her eyes she outlined Egyptian-style, ever so faintly with an artist's brush, using the soot from matches she burned in a saucer—a theatrical trick she was taught by her New York landlady, refugee from a stage career. This woman in the looking glass was a stranger now even to her. And the dress, a trifle tight in places but a close enough fit, was a crowning triumph of deception to mask the widow Memory.

He was waiting for her on the veranda. In his cutaway with a white piqué vest he looked slim and dashing, the more so when contrasted with the elderly gentleman of portly physique and less than fastidious tailoring with whom he was chatting. The look on Loring's face when he saw her was more pleasing than any compliment he could have confected. "Oh, my dear!" broke from his lips in whispered astonishment. Then he quickly recovered his manners and said, "May I present Mr. Etherbridge of Chicago? And this, sir, is my friend—Mrs.—Mem—"

"Memphis," she said with a smile, applying a small squeeze to his proferred hand. It was the first thing that popped into her head. "*Je suis enchantée de vous connaître.* I yam so verree 'appee to meet you." She avoided Loring's doubly startled look.

"French is it?" Mr. Etherbridge asked.

"*Pas exactement.* I was born *canadienne,* but my late 'usband was *un americain,* so I 'ave become *une americaine* also."

"We'd better go," said Loring, taking her arm. "We don't want to miss the ferry."

He led her down the steps to the Afrimobile, where Arthur Timmons, having spurned all other customers, was patiently waiting. "Sorry," Loring said to her once they were on their way, "I could have ruined the game completely."

"Eet does not matter. I think we fooled 'im, *n'est-ce pas?*"

He smiled in appreciation. "I'd go easy on the oo-la-la, though—you never know when the Comte de Rochambeau might pop out from behind a palm. A lot of us down here aren't entirely what we seem."

The little ferry wharf was crowded with revelers, some of whose faces she recognized from the hotel crowd despite the dim light of the kerosene lanterns. He waited with her until most of the passengers had boarded before assisting her up the gangplank. It was best, he said, to avoid the hotel guests and social situations—if she would not mind remaining outside the cabin for the brief ride across the lake. She nodded, glad to have brought a cloak with her against the chill of the evening air.

At the wharf in West Palm he passed up the landaus waiting for the departing passengers and waved instead to a victoria so they would not have to share a carriage with another couple. Without her requesting it, he asked the driver to raise the hood to protect her from the rush of cool air. And when they were led to an out-of-the-way table set aside for them in the busy restaurant and he helped her into her seat she began to fear that the embrace they had shared in the ocean the prior Sunday had aroused unwarranted expectations in him.

He ordered them champagne, which was brought at once, and they toasted the evening ahead. The smooth effervescence pleased her and helped gentle the way further into this waking dream. The menu offered fewer choices than even the one in the officers' dining room at the hotel, and the preparation of the dishes appeared far simpler, too: no mention of sauces was made, either because there were none, she supposed, or the proprietors were not up to spelling them correctly. She settled on a bisque and roast chicken and scanned the restaurant while Loring was still making up his mind.

The diners were a varied lot. The hotel guests, easily distinguishable by their evening clothes, made up no more than a quarter of the clientele. An equal proportion of the men were without collars and ties, while plain business suits predominated in the intervening social spectrum. A few of the women had turned out in their best imitation of finery, but their little cotton muslins, most with the exaggeratedly full leg-o'-mutton sleeves that were in style only the year before, had a somewhat droopy, faded look. Other of the women, at once conspicuous to even the most casual eye, were the height of coarse fashion in brilliant, if slightly soiled, satins, cut so low as to leave only the smallest portion of their charms to the imagination. Their black-ringed eyes, carmined lips and cheeks and familiar way of touching the men they accompanied proclaimed their status as working girls.

"It may surprise you to know," said Loring, after placing their orders, "that this is the finest restaurant in West Palm Beach, though anyone with a couple of dollars in his pocket can come in for a dinner. And almost anyone does. Some local swells, too. The fellow in the gray jacket over there—"

"With the lady, shall we call her, in the yellow dress?"

"Yes, that one. He was in charge of laying the track on the railroad from here down to Miami. Supposed to have pocketed half a fortune on the way." He leaned closer. "The man on your right owns the local lumberyard and hardware—his fortune's assured, what with all the building going on around here. And the fellow over in the corner in the dark red jacket—that's Charlie Franklin—he already has his fortune. He owns the establishments where some of these lovely ladies, as you call them, live."

"I wouldn't have thought it was all that lucrative a business."

"Au contraire." When Flagler sent in his work gangs of railroad men, followed by the building crews for the hotel, West Palm had sprung up almost overnight, and there were lots of men hanging around with lots of money and no place to spend it on their days off. So bars had to be built and women brought in to accommodate the frontier laborers. "Old Charlie Franklin made so much money so fast that he hasn't figured out what to do with it yet. So he hangs around here, hoping he'll be picked up by the hotel crowd. He won't, of course, but he doesn't realize it."

"How do you know him—or shouldn't I ask?"

"We play an occasional game of poker here, after hours."

"Do you—approve of him?"

"You mean do I think putting lonely men together with desperate women who have no other means of income than selling their bodies is a decent and honorable form of enterprise? I don't think it's as despicable as you probably do. And he's no white slaver, at least." The naughty-boy grin reappeared for an instant.

She widened her eyes to study him as he attacked his soup. The candlelight that dilated her pupils, heightening the color of her irises, flatteringly softened her appearance as Loring glanced up and caught her watching him.

"All right. What's going on?" he asked.

"How do you mean?"

"I asked the widow Memory to have dinner with me, a woman who wears perpetual mourning, and instead of her I find that behind that veil I'm dining with one of the most confoundedly attractive women I have ever laid eyes on. Where did the widow Memory go?"

"Why, Mr. Loring, I'm beginning to think you have designs on me."

"Don't be coy. The least you can do is show a chap a bit of gratitude for his—"

"Extravagant compliments? Oh, but I am indebted to you, Mr. Loring—"

"Why won't you call me Harry?"

"I—I don't remember the subject's coming up before."

"It's up."

She sipped at her champagne and reflected. Then she asked, "Why does it matter what I call you?"

"It's a way of defining our friendship."

"I rather thought it defied definition—and that was its principal charm."

He shook his head and grinned. "The widow Memory is not easily smitten."

She leaned toward him confidingly. "Mr. Loring, the widow Memory has survived by thwarting the unwanted attentions of master flatterers and, I regret to say, far worse. She has no husband, no father, no lordly uncle, no great protector, so she has had to learn to protect herself." Her black wardrobe, she explained, was a prime element in her defensive posture. The world holds death in high respect but fears its contagion, so people of all sorts, she had discovered, shunned those who so openly draped themselves in its vestiges. Even the toughs in the New York streets that she was forced to frequent in the course of her professional duties steered clear at the sight of her mourning garb.

"And down here?"

Wherever she was, her clothes answered many unasked questions. In Florida, she had not altered her strategy. In black she became invisible. Rarely did anyone look beyond her garments to see who she was, to see *her.* "You, Mr. Loring, are one of the few who bothered."

"Then this is the real you, and the mourning Mrs. Memory is—an act?"

"If you will, though I wouldn't put it so sternly as that. The deception is not my choice but society's."

Over their main course, he touched lightly on his history—as a black-smith's boy growing up in central Pennsylvania, a footman at a men's club in Philadelphia, a mate in the boiler room on a riverboat out of Cincinnati, a clerk for a New Orleans importer-exporter, an apprentice cotton broker on Factor's Walk in Savannah, a junior partner in a Charleston brokerage house, and then the great world of New York finance, where his fortunes had undulated. She listened closely, wondering how much of it was true and what he had omitted. "And was there never a Mrs. Loring along the way?" she asked.

"Not quite. I'm rather the footloose sort, I'm afraid."

"And you see women as something between conveniences and encumbrances?"

"Now you're the one putting things sternly."

"I was simply asking."

"It sounded oddly like an accusation."

"Do I detect a sensitive side to your nature, Mr. Loring?"

"I am a mountain of sensitivity, madam," he said, draining the last of the champagne into their glasses.

Only when the waiter came to clear away their plates did she realize she had eaten her meal without ever tasting it. While they dwelled over coffee she was introduced to several of Loring's hotel friends who came by their table to propose a little card game. There was Tommy Somebody, who she had heard was connected in some august capacity with a New

York railroad, and Floyd Someone, who she had heard was involved in a silver mine—or was it copper?—out west, and soon good old Charlie Franklin, the whoremaster of West Palm, showed up with a large package of merchandise named Eloise on his arm. Through a light-headed haze Madame Memphis responded to them all with *"enchantée"* and as little else as she could get away with in her absurd *franglais* accent. Would she mind if he joined a game, Loring asked her quietly while the others hovered about a large round table nearby being cleared for the gaming. "You might find it a culturally enriching experience," he said; it was fascinating to watch the rich in their anxious quest to become still richer. Seeing his evident eagerness to join in and with no other likely source of entertainment in the vicinity, she acceded but noted her total ignorance of card games. Loring told her to pay attention and she would get the drift of play—poker was not a subtle game.

She positioned herself behind Loring's left shoulder. Eloise, the only other female in attendance, perched jauntily on Charlie's right knee on the opposite side of the table. The rest of the party was composed of the local lumberyard owner and a third hotel guest in evening clothes who, according to Loring's whispered information, was associated with the manufacture of a popular nostrum claimed to cure everything from apoplexy to warts; its principal ingredient was said to be laudanum.

While the chips were being distributed, Charlie asked Loring to perform a card trick or two for Eloise's pleasure. The request seemed to come as no surprise to Loring, who produced a pack of cards from his pocket and asked the doxy to shuffle and cut them a few times and return them. He then inserted the pack in his outer breast pocket and, without his looking but with much fumbling and grimacing, extracted all four aces from the deck one after the other. "That's cute," said Eloise. "How'd you do that?"

"Just lucky," said Loring with an affable wink to the rest of the table. Then he snagged a pencil and menu from a passing waiter and shoved them across the table to Eloise with the instruction to write down any four-digit number while he turned his back to her. Eloise giggled at the intellectual challenge and avidly complied. Turning back, Loring told her to add up the four numbers going across—"This is getting hard," she squealed, the tip of her tongue appearing at the corner of her painted mouth—and tell him the results. Then she was asked to subtract eighteen from the original number and take from the deck four cards, each of a different suit, corresponding to the numerals of the resulting total. Finally he told her to retain any one of the cards face down on the table and return the rest to him. "The one you've got left there," Loring said after a moment's calculation and with theatrical bravura, "is—if I'm not mistaken—and I rarely am—the—the four of hearts."

"Wrong," said Eloise and flipped over the eight of diamonds.

"Damn," said Harry. "The eights always throw me."

"Some trick," snorted the purveyor of wart killer.

Harry grinned innocently, reclaimed his cards and pocketed them before signaling Tommy the railroader to shuffle the fresh deck supplied by the house and begin the game. Tommy did so with practiced speed and snap, declared "seven-card stud," and began distributing the cards in a pattern that left Mrs. Memory thoroughly bewildered. The ensuing games did little to clear her confusion. Even the betting mystified her, though Loring hinted by sideways winks that often the winner had succeeded less by the cards he had assembled then by the certitude or feigned hesitancy with which he declared his wager.

The fortunes of the contestants waxed and waned, and she could not be sure, given the uncertain values of the different colored chips, who was doing best. Loring won his share of the games but often dropped out well before the end of some, bantering with the others who seemed rather more intent than he on the outcome. Indeed, his comportment intrigued her more than the baffling game itself. He appeared relaxed, whether winning or losing, arms spread away from his body, one thrown over the back of his chair, the other holding his cards in a tight pack that he occasionally spread open with his thumb for a quick glance, then flicked closed and held indifferently at arm's length. At times he slipped down in his chair, on the edge of his spine, looking behind droopy eyelids as if he were about to fall asleep. But then he would spring back to life, dispensing little jokes between hands. They were not very funny stories, but they did serve to keep the temper of play from turning mean-spirited, as did Loring's intermittent chatter about recent developments up north. The *Gianlorenzo Bernini* had just docked in New York, he reported to Tommy, and suggested that the Countess Contalfini was no doubt roaming the streets of the city, looking for him that very minute. And what did Floyd think the likelihood was that the newly open Serena Padre mine in Nevada had struck a mother lode? And the nostrum king was tickled by Loring's disclosure, gleaned from a report in The New York *Herald,* that the police had raided Mrs. Carver's intellectual meeting hall in the capital and the girls were threatening to reveal the names of their favorite conversationalists.

When it was Loring's turn to deal, the lumberyard owner urged him to demonstrate his dexterity to the rest. Loring obliged by picking up half the deck with his left hand, spreading it into a fan shape with his right one, then picking up the other half with his right hand and making it into the same shape with the use of only his right thumb and middle finger. "That's real cute," chirped Eloise. "Do it again." During the encore, as he was attempting to spread the right-hand fan, the cards flew from his grip and tumbled over the table.

"Out of practice," Loring explained with a shrug. As the bets were placed, he reached forward and flipped a white chip into the bottomless crevice bisecting Eloise's décolletage. "Dealer's tribute," he said with a wink. She retrieved it with a throaty laugh and presented it to Charlie for his opening bet.

By now the rest of the table had settled down to determined play. The hotel guests in particular sat upright and stony-faced as the pots grew in size. Tommy puffed harder on his mellow pipe. Floyd dropped out at the end of Loring's deal, tossing his cards in with disgust as Charlie shoveled in the pot. Mrs. Memory judged, from the size of stacked chips beside him, that Loring was running a distant second in the contest to the medicine man. He seemed now to slip down farther in his chair, his chin approaching the tabletop, but his posture and offhand manner belied his growing success. A pair of aces won him the final big pot just before the restaurant owner came by to advise that they would have to break it up if the hotel guests were to make the last ferry back.

They rode inside the cabin on the way back, out of the wind that was combing the lake more sharply now. Though weariness was coming over her as they huddled into a corner away from the other returning passengers, she said she had a few questions for him, if he did not mind, by way of clarifying his triumphant conduct at the card table.

"It was just a little fun," he said. "I hope you didn't mind."

"Not in the least," she said. "It was quite instructive."

"Perhaps we should leave it at that, then."

"If you'd prefer. But I was wondering—"

"Ah, the observant madonna of the gaming table."

She would not be deterred. "When you did the first trick," she said, "I had the feeling the four aces were in your pocket all along and you just put the shuffled deck in front of them—"

"Dastardly suggestion!"

"But then why did the trick with the numbers not turn out right?"

"Oh, it does—sometimes."

"I don't—"

"And sometimes the trick with the aces gets bollixed up."

"I—oh, my heavens! And that business with shuffling the cards and dropping them the second time?"

"The same."

"And—and who is the Countess Contalfini or whoever it was you told Mr.—Mr.—that Tommy person—was running around New York look- ing—"

"I haven't the faintest notion. It was the first name that came to me."

"Then why did Tommy laugh?"

"Not to show his ignorance."

She studied him through her lowered veil. "Mr. Loring, I do believe you are a very cagey fellow."

"I," he said, "am a sportsman."

"You," she said, "are a charming conniver."

"Madeleine, lower your voice or they'll chuck us both overboard."

"But if I could see through you when I don't understand the first thing about cards and I'm even a tiny bit tipsy from all that glorious champagne, how come they couldn't?"

"Because you, my dear," he said, drawing her cloak closer about her in a sheltering gesture, "were not intent on proving how much craftier you are than I."

At the dockside a small fleet of Afrimobiles waited for the passengers, but Loring asked the other drivers for the whereabouts of Arthur Tim- mons, whose services he had reserved, and was told the boy would be right along. As the other vehicles glided away with passengers from the ferry, she saw Loring's agitation increase. "That little scamp," he mut- tered, ready to make other arrangements as the lights on the dock started going off one by one.

"Mist' Loring! Mist' Loring!" the sudden call erupted from the dark- ness as Arthur came pedaling up at full speed, ripe with apologies and the widest grin he could manage at that hour. "Had me a little bit o' business, Mist' Loring. I'm real sorry."

"I don't pay you to do business on the side."

"No, suh—it won't happen no mo'."

Loring helped her into the little vehicle, which took off, the instant they were settled, on a somewhat circuitous route to the hotel—no doubt part of the prearrangement that had been made with the driver. The easy, swaying motion lulled her into closing her eyes for a moment or two. When she awoke hazily, the front entrance of the Royal Poinciana was hardly a hundred yards in front of them, its veranda lights dim and its hulking vastness darkened and silent in a way she had never seen it before.

As she lifted her head she realized that it had been resting on Loring's shoulder and that his arm was around her in a light but protective loop.

She sat up, took a deep breath of the moisture-laden night air and patted her hair to make sure her short slumber had not mussed it. With her revival he enclosed her free hand within his larger one and drew it, along with the rest of her, toward him, encircling her with his arms. Her envelopment was too swift and comforting to resist. Nor did she turn away his kiss, as intent and demanding as the one they had shared in the ocean but still longer and more satisfying. Wide-awake now, her body responded, and she felt his breath on her face, could hear the beating of his heart—or was it her own?—and wanted to look at him and touch him and deepen their embrace. But she could not, would not, not then, not yet, and he did not ask her to, for which she was grateful and clung to him till the last instant of the ride. All she said to him at the end, like a soft caress, was "Harry."

She heard quick footsteps approaching behind her in the dim hallway and turned around to spy the dark green uniform and starched white apron of one of her chambermaids. "Mrs. Memory—ya got to help!" the girl panted, hurrying to catch up. "Kin ya come with me, please?"

Retreating two steps, she was able to identify the pale, narrow face with its damp cheeks and red-rimmed eyes. The girl had plainly been crying. "What is it, Ruby Lee?"

"It's Mrs. Lockwood, ma'am—in two twenty-nine. The one with the petticoat I came to ya about. It's real important—kin ya come, please?"

Stifling a sigh, she accompanied the girl, who required three steps to her every two to keep pace down the long corridor and around a corner. At the door to 229 Mrs. Memory paused, squared her shoulders and nodded to the maid to knock.

"Who is it?" demanded an ill-tempered voice from inside.

"It's the chambermaid, ma'am. I got Mrs. Memory here."

"The door is open."

Ruby Lee turned the knob and pushed the door timidly, then stood with her back against it to let Mrs. Memory precede her into the room. Mrs. Lockwood was reclining on the white wicker chaise lounge, her back propped up against the pink and green upholstered cushions provided by the hotel and supplemented by a collection of her own white lace-trimmed and embroidered pillows. It was hard to tell where, precisely, the pillows ended and the well-upholstered form of Mrs. Lockwood, in a billowy white dressing gown, began. As Mrs. Memory got closer, she could see an oval tin of licorice pastilles on the table beside the grand lady and an open book face-down on her lap.

Mrs. Lockwood regarded her two visitors for a moment, then beckoned the senior one nearer. "So you are the housekeeper, are you? I've seen you flitting about but had no idea what exact function you performed. Come closer—I can hardly see you."

When the housekeeper closed to within a yard of her, Mrs. Lockwood held up her hand. "Now sit. You are entirely too tall for a servant."

"I am not a servant, madam. I am an employee of the hotel, as are all the members of the staff."

"Yes—well—whatever you are, sit down. I'll get a crick in my neck looking up at you."

Mrs. Memory withdrew a chair from the nearby table and sat. Ruby Lee remained standing in place. "Now how may I be of assistance?" asked the housekeeper.

Mrs. Lockwood popped a pastille into her mouth and then related how, in the three weeks she had been at the hotel, Ruby Lee had been making up her quarters with exemplary efficiency—"and she was quiet as a church mouse. In fact, that's rather how I thought of her." But lately, she could not fail to notice that the girl's undergarments were producing a great deal of frou-frou as she swished them about. Suspicious, Mrs. Lockwood had deliberately left some items on the floor this morning, and when the chambermaid bent to pick them up, Mrs. Lockwood looked up her skirts and recognized her own blue silk petticoat. "This—this hussy had stolen it!" Mrs. Lockwood's bulk shifted slightly upon her great white tuffet. "I would not have minded so much if the little tramp had only been forthright about confessing, but no! she kept insisting that it rightfully belonged to her—imagine!—and that she had not stolen it, but actually received *permission* to keep it—from whom I couldn't imagine—until she blurted out your name and said you could explain it all." The woman looked intently at Mrs. Memory. "Are you in on this, too? I think I heard your frou-frou as well when you walked in, or could I be mistaken? Perhaps you've developed a little enterprise on the side—"

"Mrs. Lockwood," said Mrs. Memory, in as soft a voice as she was capable of when confronted with blatant idiocy, "let me assure you that my undergarments, along with the rest of my wardrobe, are entirely my own. Neither I nor my girls engage in dishonest acts—and if any of them did and were detected, they would be instantly dismissed." She turned to Ruby Lee and asked her to wait outside the room, adding, "I'll call you, if necessary." When the girl had left, she turned back to Mrs. Lockwood. "May I ask you, madam, what you do while you are here with any items of apparel that you no longer find suitable to your use?"

"I beg your pardon?"

Mrs. Memory, displaying no impatience, carefully repeated the question.

"Every item of my apparel is suitable, my dear, or else I would not have brought it with me—or indeed purchased it in the first place."

"And suppose you discovered that an article of yours was unaccountably in disrepair—somehow torn or damaged by use?"

"Since my maid is not with me to do the mending, I would likely discard any such item. Hotel seamstresses are notoriously incompetent."

"And how would you go about discarding it?"

"How? I don't know—toss it aside, I suppose, or into the trash."

"And would that apply to an older petticoat that you discovered to be ripped in several places with a hem that was shredding—and that, in any event, you had probably begun to tire of?"

"I—why—oh." A thin light penetrated the woman's padded brain.

"Mrs. Lockwood, that is exactly what you did with the blue taffeta petticoat. Miss Eustis found it in your wastebasket, in badly wrinkled condition and damaged in the fashion I described. Her natural assumption was that it had been discarded. Even in disrepair, it is a beautiful garment, and Miss Eustis is a girl who has very few beautiful things in her life. Yet she was too embarrassed to tell you that she intended to salvage it after removing the basket to empty it—"

"But she might have asked me if there was some mistake."

"Perhaps you are right. Instead she came to me—and I chose not to insist that she return it, since the circumstances seemed to make your intentions toward the garment entirely clear. If I was in error, I am prepared to apologize, and the hotel will make restitution for the value of the petticoat. I saw nothing to be gained, however, by instructing the girl to humiliate herself by coming to you—"

Mrs. Lockwood held up her hand and emitted a vast sigh. "Yes, yes, of course—the pathetic pride of the working class." She inserted a fresh licorice beneath her tongue and waved the housekeeper away. "Next time she must ask or I will summon the authorities directly. Good day, miss."

The pathetic pride, thought Mrs. Memory, letting herself out, of the idle rich.

THREE

February, 1897

"*A*re you cold, dearest?" The elegant little man with short sandy hair and reddish mustache bustled about the large, angular, gray-haired woman installed in the rocker next to his, adjusting the shawl around her shoulders and tucking the multicolored afghan more securely about her knees.

"I'm fine, Royal darling," his wife assured him, patting him on the arm with a long-fingered hand covered with a little black half-glove that revealed the fingers but enclosed the palm.

Such devoted concern, in view of the late-morning temperature reading of eighty degrees on the Royal Poinciana veranda, would ordinarily have seemed absurd in even the fondest of husbands. But readers of Royal Postlethwaite's semiweekly column, "Society Scenes," in the *New-York Evening Examiner* had often been apprised that its author's wife, Virtue, suffered from extremely thin blood that was the result of aristocratic ancestry traceable back at least as far as Eleanor of Aquitaine. Postlethwaite's rival in the *Herald* sniped that Virtue stemmed from Ohio farm yeomanry nicely leavened by inbreeding with Kentucky mountaineering stock that had taken its inevitable toll on her physical constitution. Whatever the truth, the Postlethwaites, on their incessant social gad-flights, were always heavily weighted with shawls, lap robes and other heat-inducing garments.

Anthony Stokes-Vecchio's heart had turned palpitant upon the arrival of the wire from the Postlethwaites ten days earlier requesting accommodations for a fortnight's stay. Since the columnist was known to write about every place he visited, the general manager was anxious that his grand hotel, in only its third season of existence, should be favorably noticed by so prominent a scrivener from the New York press. It was

important, he stressed to every officer on his staff, that the Postlethwaites'
stay be perfect in every regard. Mr. Eristoff was commanded personally
to oversee every meal that the couple took, Mr. Bedient to harvest the
hotel gardens for bouquets of exotic blooms for every horizontal surface
in their suite and Mrs. Memory to be certain that their rooms were
spotless even if it required three cleanings a day.

They were sitting out now amid a cluster of guests and admirers,
regaling them with a fulsome report on the most gala ball in memory, held
in New York shortly before their departure for Florida. The columnist's
rather shrill, nasal voice carried up from the veranda and through the
open windows of the lobby, where Mrs. Memory dallied for a moment
or two. Eavesdropping on the conversation of guests, she felt, was hardly
more couth than pawing through the possessions in their drawers and
closets. This case, however, was slightly different. For the last twenty
years, almost since the day she had gone to live in New York, she had
been a regular reader of the *Examiner*'s social column. It was not that she
cared a fig for the doings of New York society—not in the least—but on
rare occasions she would note the mention of a certain family, citing its
whereabouts and activities, which held a special significance for her.
Royal Postlethwaite's column had become her sole means of maintaining
a link, however tenuous, to that gilded household, and the very sight of
him in the flesh quickened her hope that the name so precious to her
might be dropped and her enduring curiosity fed.

"There was *no* frivolity about it whatever," Postlethwaite piped. "Mrs.
Martin's motives were en*tirely* benevolent, let me assure you—which is
not generally the case with affairs of this sort. She did it to stimulate trade
in New York. For those of you rarely attending our city, I regret to say
that economic conditions there have been absolutely appalling of late. On
the other hand, one could not properly describe the function as a charity
ball in the normal sense—"

"She invited everyone only a month beforehand," Virtue Postlethwaite put in as her husband paused for breath, "which is practically the
last minute for a grand cotillion, so no one had time to order their
costumes from Paris as they normally would have. Everything had to be
done in New York. The dressmakers were *in*undated with work!"

"Not to mention the tailors, the shoemakers and the jewelers," the
columnist resumed even before it was apparent that his wife had subsided.
The booksellers and print shops were also enjoying a land-office business,
he explained, thanks to the rigid conditions the hostess had prescribed
for the event. Every attendant had to be authentically got up in keeping
with the theme of the ball—"A Night at Versailles"—in eighteenth-

century French costume. "Positively *no* mythological characters were allowed, and historical accuracy was essential to the spirit of the thing—no little Napoleons and Josephines were to be flying around the place, disturbing the peace of the Dauphin—of whom there could not have been fewer than four dozen re-creations, don'cha know? Originality is not easily come by under such circumstances. Elegance rather than cleverness was the desideratum of the evening." Mr. Belmont came in a suit of armor inlaid with gold, which, he confided to the *Examiner*'s social reporter, cost him a goodly ten thousand. Annie Morgan, J. P.'s daughter, on the other hand, came as a fetching but slightly anachronistic Pocahontas, in a leather dress replete with gold beads and fringes, moccasins and a great feathered war bonnet. *"Incroyable!"* Postlethwaite reported.

"And the decorations," Virtue Postlethwaite picked up the slack, "were no less." Following perhaps fifteen separate dinner parties held at various mansions about the city—all of which of course required the employment of countless extra servants and carriages, thereby further stimulating the economy—the entire vast guest list converged on the grand ballroom of the Waldorf-Astoria and spilled over into the dining and reception rooms adjoining it. Mrs. Martin had had the place done up in Gobelin tapestries and mirrors and scarlet and yellow draperies. "And the flowers, thousands upon thousands of them! My dears, it was sheer rococo! Orchids and clematis and three kinds of fragrant roses—the aromas were positively *pagan!*"

"Mrs. Martin herself told me in strictest confidence," Postlethwaite inserted, "that for her part alone in this remarkable occasion she spent three hundred sixty-nine thousand dollars—every last penny of it going to relieve the financial distress of the city. The woman is an angel. The little people of New York should fall on their knees and remember her in their prayers every night, if you ask me." He exhaled a sigh of reverence.

Mrs. Memory drifted away from the window and made her way, as if by reflexive command, to the Postlethwaite suite to assure herself of its tidiness. Nothing was too good for these camp-followers and chroniclers of the unconscionably extravagant. The Postlethwaites had been assigned rooms 211 and 212 with their lovely view of the lake, but not so high above it that the nobly descended Virtue would have difficulty ascending the stairs if she chose not to expose herself to the provincial riffraff one might encounter in the elevator.

Mrs. Memory assessed the Postlethwaites' sitting room. The afghan thrown over the arm of the sofa looked more strewn than folded, whereas the cashmere shawl draped over the end of the table appeared rather too premeditated in its arrangement. She refolded the afghan carefully and moved the shawl more toward the diagonal in asymmetric attitude that was better suited to please Virtue Postlethwaite's sense of contrived naturalness. Her eye roamed over to the pin-neat writing desk, on one side of which stood a little pile of books, each almost precisely the same height, width and thickness. Curiosity drove her to inspect their titles; what did New York's leading social arbiter read on vacation? The top three were *Mansfield Park,* the verse of Bayard Taylor, and *Florabunda of the Cotswolds.*

The first two volumes aroused no further interest in her. What more appropriate selections for him than the Austen novel and the pleasingly lyrical verse of the peregrinating Mr. Taylor, whom she had heard lecture once during her early years in New York? But the Cotswolds title was unfamiliar and odd. Was it travel literature or a romance? She opened the slim, elegantly printed book, which featured an engraving opposite the title page of a bonneted, buxom maiden languorously contemplating a cottage set at the edge of a meadow. A tale of bucolic sweetness, no doubt. As Mrs. Memory fished through the pages, her glance settled on ". . . *removing the garments from my body until I was unclothed as at the moment of my birth, my master proceeded to observe me minutely, noting, for my benefit, the various points that pleased him greatly . . .*" Rural innocence, indeed! She read on: ". . . *surprised to find, though the defloration had been accomplished with much outcry and no little pain on my part, that the elasticity of my outwardly small envelope could ensheath his distended engine fully. The animal side of my nature was uncaged and rose to meet his with the throbbing intensity that bespoke the appetite I had never known I possessed . . .*"

Why, that prurient, posturing old goat. The nerve of him to prance around passing judgment on the values of others while secretly degrading himself by taking pleasure in perfumed pornography. The man should be taught a lesson.

But the only one that came to her mind under the circumstances was to wrench the offensive page right out of its binding, leaving behind a telltale jagged edge to alert the book's owner that someone was on to his unsavory literary preference. In the unlikely event he wished to protest the act of retributive vandalism, let him—and then his hypocrisy would be revealed to the world.

With the balled-up page clenched in her hand, she unhurriedly let herself out the door and briefly relished the smile that crept across her face in the dim corridor. By the time she reached the service elevator, her mouth was reset in somber composure.

* * *

In a brown tweed Norfolk jacket with matching knickerbockers and argyle stockings that rose gaudily from the tops of his high-laced boots, he was almost unrecognizable when he turned to meet her at the edge of the golf course. "A new outfit, Mr. Loring?" she asked, drawing abreast of him.

"My tailor just sent it down from New York. What do you think?" He spun around full circle for her to admire and then dropped onto the grass to begin unlacing his boots.

"Very handsome, indeed." She sat beside him and started slipping off her shoes and stockings. "Only I was under the distinct impression you did not think very well of dudes."

"A dude is someone dressed to the nines when the occasion doesn't call for it. This outfit, however, will prove very useful down here. In fact, a few of the fellows have asked me to join them on a fishing expedition this afternoon and I thought—"

"What every well-outfitted angler should wear."

"Precisely."

"I think," she said with a laugh at his boundless insouciance, "that you may find something a little more rugged to be practical."

"What's practicality got to do with it? This is sport."

"Have you *been* fishing?"

"Once or twice," he said, pulling off one argyle stocking and attacking the other. "A painfully slow business—but a good way to learn about your companions' character."

"I should think your temperament would be better suited to lawn sports—croquet or tennis or even golf, although they all seem to take those terribly seriously."

"As it happens, I'm thoroughly accomplished in each of those—I excel at nearly all the dry-land sports." He stuffed his stockings into his boots, tied their laces together, slung them over his shoulder and helped tug her upright. "Good for business," he said with a smile and looped an arm around her waist as they walked. It felt to her as if it belonged without in any way becoming possessive in its hold.

A pregnant silence enveloped their progress, and her mind dwelled on the scene played out a few afternoons earlier when, on her way into the Lakeview Lounge to check the cleanliness of its immense stretch of windows, she had heard a burst of male laughter spilling out of the Writing Room, a place generally graced with a sepulchral silence. She retraced her steps in that direction and reached the Writing Room in time to hear the end of a traveling-salesman joke being narrated by a fellow in the midst of a dozen or fifteen guests clustered toward one side of the room; no writers were present at the little desks along the wall. As the storyteller concluded with a mildly salacious double entendre and was rewarded with a round of snorts and guffaws, one of the women bent her head, convulsed with laughter, and Mrs. Memory recognized the profile of the man whose arm was draped comfortably over her shoulders. She stared at him from the entranceway as long and as hard as she dared before hurrying past. Stomach churning, she asked herself what such behavior meant. A man did not physically attach himself to a woman in public unless he wanted to convey some sort of proprietorship over her to the world at large. Nor would a woman who valued her good name allow herself to become a leaning post unless she wished to announce that she enjoyed filling such a function.

"May I ask you a somewhat personal question?" she said, breaking their silence and slipping free of his hold as they splashed through the remnants of a wave that had wandered far up onto the beach.

"Anything."

"Provided you retain the privilege to be charmingly evasive in your reply."

"Of course. We mustn't disillusion each other."

A smile flickered over her face behind her parasol. "Why is it, Mr. Harrison Loring, when I myself have seen you escorting a very attractive woman guest around the hotel and there must be heaven-knows-how-many others who would be pleased to share your company, that you find it diverting to spend your Sunday mornings here on the beach with me? I am neither rich nor beautiful, and I am surely several years older than you. What do you want with me?"

He stopped walking and brushed her parasol aside to look at her. "Have you so little conception of what and who you are, Maddy?"

"I—I'm perfectly aware of what my—"

He lifted her chin so that she was forced to look at him. "You may not be beautiful in your own eyes, my dear woman, but when you smile your face takes on a glow that transcends mere physical beauty. The fact that you are not rich means you fully appreciate—as I do—the things money can buy since we both have had to earn them for ourselves. You have something beyond wealth that few, if any, of the decorative women here possess. You have a kind of grit, a determination and strength of purpose that I find wholly estimable. I simply admire the way you conduct yourself. And as for your being older than I, age is meaningless when two people care for each other. I care for you, Madeleine Memory." He released her chin. "Furthermore, you swim like a mermaid—and I'm ready for another lesson." And he started trotting off ahead of her, forcing her to hurry after him and close down her parasol lest a sea zephyr catch her and waft her up and out over the waves.

By the time they reached the stretch of sand she had adopted as her own, she was gasping for breath and perspiring. He shed his outer clothes speedily and folded them neatly while she proceeded more slowly. Disrobing in the presence of a man, any man, and especially *this* man, was an overt act of submission that did not come easily to her. She tried to busy herself without regard for his nearness, but as she emerged from her second petticoat, she glanced up to see him looking at her fixedly.

"Is something wrong?"

"Not in the least."

"Then why—"

"I like to see you take your clothes off, that's why. It gives me pleasure."

"I—wish—it makes me—uncomfortable to be—watched so intently. I'm not on exhibition."

"Of course. Making you uncomfortable is the furthest thing from my mind. I just thought you'd like to know how the sight of you pleases me."

"I do like it, actually—but I'm not used to—being observed. It makes me very aware of myself."

"Is that an ordeal for you? You should take pleasure in your gifts."

"I—it's just that—I'm so unaccustomed to—"

"Didn't your husband ever—survey you and tell you what you looked like—and how remarkable you are?"

She shook her head. "I can't remember—it was so long ago. I was little more than a girl then. In three more months, I'll be thirty-nine—almost old enough to be a grandmother. That's far too old for me to be dwelling on what I look like."

He circled his hands around both her wrists and kissed her gently on the forehead. "Well, Grandmother Memory, it so happens you are just five years and two months older than I, and if you don't want to think about what you look like, you can't stop me from doing it. But out of deference to your modesty, I'll be more subtle from now on." He released his hold on her and began to unbutton his shirt, keeping his head bent and eyes fixed on the sand.

Feeling now just a bit silly—she reached behind her to start undoing the buttons on her shirtwaist but was less punctilious than he about not viewing the other in the act of unpeeling: out of the corner of her eye she saw him pulling off his shirt and revealing his pelted chest. An uncontrollable impulse seized her. "Wait," she said, dropping her shirtwaist on the sheet and coming around in front of him. "May I—?"

"Whatever you'd like."

Shyness momentarily restrained her. No lady dared ask a gentleman what she was about to, and yet here she was, a more than willing presence in a place where no lady should find herself, reduced to deshabille and utterly vulnerable to his advances. Her impulse was overwhelming by now. "Russell—my husband—my late husband," she said, not quite venturing to look Loring in the eye, "didn't have any—and I was just wondering—I'm sure it must strike you as odd—but—I was wondering if—" She could feel her face flushing even in the heat of the sun.

"If it would please you."

She reached out, tentatively at first, her fingers slightly spread, and stroked the fleece on his chest, down with the grain and then up against it. It was soft, and springy, and it tickled the palm of her hand.

"Well?"

"It's quite—"

"Not excessively beastly, would you say?"

"Not—excessively. It's—"

"But not quite decorative—correct?"

"I—I'll—it's a matter of taste, I suppose."

"And it's not to yours?"

"I—wouldn't say that." Indeed, she would say nothing more.

Hand in hand, they ran to the water's edge, then past it, not stopping until they were waist-deep and she was shivering slightly from the shock of the cool water and the excitement of his company. They waited as a big breaker rolled in above them, then broke their handclasp and dove under it and swam out beyond the waves. She modulated her stroke so he could keep pace with her, but the usual ocean-buoyed elation was absent for her. The problem, of course, was Loring. She was entirely too aware of him; the ocean was a secondary presence now. Even when they were a distance apart, she was overly conscious of him, her eyes scanning the surface until she saw him there bobbing along happily in the water. And when she was close to him it was worse still. The water felt warmer near him, as if heated by a focused beam of the sun's rays. Her breath became shallower and faster, and it was difficult for her to stay underwater for more than a moment. Her legs and arms felt unmanageable, and there were times when she thought they would actually drag her down to the ocean bottom.

"I have to get out for a while," she called over to him and headed in to shore. Lying on the sheet for a while might calm her light-headedness.

She opened her parasol and pushed the handle deep into the sand. Its pool of shadow shielded her face while the rest of her body lay exposed to the sun. She closed her eyes, luxuriating in the golden heat, and tried to drain her mind. No storm clouds gloomed her Sunday sky. It was as if an angelic nimbus had settled on her portion of the shoreline, suffusing it with heavenly grace and nature's utmost glory. Why, then, did her yearning sensations not abate now but boil up still higher without the cooling quality of the sea to numb them? She was searching for an unguent to remedy her inflamed feelings when the heat crisping her legs was momentarily eclipsed. She opened her eyes to discover the source. Loring was standing over her.

"Are you unwell?"

She sat up. The symptoms suddenly pounded with increased vehemence as he knelt beside her and extended his hand to feel her forehead. His gentle touch released what scant restraint remained within her. No such powerful force had overflowed inside her in years and years—she could not recall the last instance—but the ache it stirred was demanding and unmistakable.

She reached for Loring's hand and pulled him down to sit beside her on the sheet. "I'm not ill—you needn't concern yourself. I'm fine—finer, thank you, than I've been in a very long while."

"A—um, female complaint?" He had the grace to look embarrassed.

"No. More of a human condition, I'd call it." She looked at him and smiled. "And if you weren't such a gentleman, you'd admit to the same—um, affliction."

He looked at her wide-eyed as droplets of ocean inched down his brow. "I don't really—"

"Do you mean to tell me, Mr. Loring," she said, picking up his hand and holding it between both her own, "that in all the times we've been alone together practically unclad on this beach you haven't once wanted to do this?" She brought his hand to her breast, eyes closing, lips parting in an instant pang of pleasure as his fingers spread and encircled her almost involuntarily. His hand brought a warmth through the still cool dampness of her combination. She shivered from the sensation.

"Mrs. Memory," he murmured, getting to his knees and circling her body with his unoccupied arm, "I swore to myself—on my honor as a gentleman—that I—"

"Lord, you are the most peculiar gentleman I have ever—"

"—that I would never touch you beyond a chaste kiss—"

"Your kiss is not chaste, sir."

"—until you made it abundantly clear to me that—"

"Is this clear enough?" She reached up to open the top buttons of her combination and drew his hand inside it.

"I—Maddy—I—was beginning to think you were made of stone," he whispered and brought his mouth over hers while his hand slowly began exploring the contours of her unveiled body. The fusion of feeling as his lips and swirling palm swept over her drove her back against the sheet, her body too pliant to support her any longer and her arms clasping his neck and bringing him down with her. Her breasts felt enlarged under his touch; all of her was swollen, moist, heightened.

They lingered there for a timeless spell, sharing the delicious joy of discovery as his presence pressed hard against her without further invitation. "I want to know all of you," he said, pushing at her undergarment.

The dampness prevented her from sliding it easily over her body; she had to sit up to remove it. "And you?" she asked. "No more of this one-sided ogling business."

Rolling on his back, he slipped down his drawers and flung them off into the sand, then reached over and drew her urgently against him, and they swam upward in constant, breathless motion, kissing, tasting, caressing, teasing and inciting, fiercely entwining in a spiral of tension that flew out of orbit from the energy of their pure abandon.

But when he attempted to bring their embrace to fulfillment, her hands flung up toward his chest. "No—I—we can't—I mustn't—" The words tumbled from her in a gasp.

He propped up an elbow and looked down at her in bewilderment. "Have you taken vows?"

She cringed. "I—it's not—"

"There'll be no pain, I promise."

"I—I'm not—"

"Practiced? It will come back to you in a moment."

"Please—don't force me—"

"Maddy, what is it? We were—"

"I wasn't expecting—I'm not—prepared—"

"You—seem very well prepared—"

"Not that way! My womb veil, Harry—I don't have it."

"Ahhh." He rubbed a hand over his eyes and pulled it through his hair. "That's easily remedied. I don't have to—finish there. I can—"

"No!" Her eyes and voice rose in unison. "That's what Russell did—and it happened anyway."

"Forget Russell. Maddy, your life has to go on—"

"No—not that way." She spun away from his hold. "Next time I'll be—ready."

"I want you now, Maddy."

"Please, Harry. Be a gentleman—"

He fell back, his engorged passion as evident as his frustration. "Maybe you *are* made of stone—"

His unhappiness sent a fresh surge of heat through her.

Resisting mightily, she reached out between his jackknifed knees and gripped him with both her hands, tentatively at first, then tightly, then moving and gliding in motions she had not practiced for so long they felt as strange as they were igniting. "The hell I am."

"I—take it back," he said, yielding to a spasm of pleasure. "You don't—need to—"

"I want to." She knelt over him, her fingers in quickening pursuit as he emitted small moans that broke his appreciative smile. "I want you to." She cupped and lavished him and held him as he shuddered, his warm wetness flowing through her hands. He drew her down against him as he ungently subsided. He lay motionless for a moment, then took her wholly in his arms and kissed her, lightly at first, and after with growing urgency that set her spiraling, higher and higher as his hands found the core of her feeling, and drew her onward and upward into a torrent of sensation. His hands and mouth moved fluidly over her, driving her aloft until she balanced precariously, excruciatingly at the pinnacle, engulfed in the imminence of release, moment upon shortening moment, pain and pleasure colliding, and finally, in an explosive instant, driving her over the edge into convulsive, shattering ecstasy. She was sixteen again, and a thousand sixteen, it made no difference. She was ageless and unending, fractured and whole, soiled and immaculate.

They clung together for a long, motionless while, his arms wrapped around her, their bodies pressed into a unit while she felt her heartbeat return to normal. "I believe," he said softly, "that beats ocean bathing."

She laughed and lay her head on his shoulder, her arm encircling his chest while he held her chin in his hand and bestowed little kisses on her forehead and cheeks and nose. When he suggested a last dip in the ocean, she went in almost against her will. Nothing should intrude on her reverie. There was no point in putting on her combination—he was acquainted now with her every contour. She floated on the waves, letting them foam and soothe every inch of her, while her hair massed lazily around her head, her eyes shut.

They dressed slowly and silently, only the glances they exchanged betraying their new intimacy. She fixed his tie without being asked.

On the walk back, their private thoughts filled the time and deepened their fondness. Midway, he stopped and turned and took her by the shoulders. "Maddy, what happened—about the child?"

"Child?"

"Forgive me, but I couldn't help noticing—what you said—and the marks on your stomach—"

His eyes would not release hers. "I—had a daughter—for a few days—" She forced her glance past and then away from his. "And then she was taken from me." She shrugged and looked out toward the ocean, squinting against its fierce glitter. "That's all."

"*All?* Maddy, I can't begin to—"

The stab of pain in her voice denied its message. He reached around and hugged her body to his. "I'm so—terribly sorry," he said. "You—and the child—deserved a kinder—"

"I don't believe in that, Harry. Life doesn't trade in kindnesses."

He nodded and gave the side of her face a touch. "I can see the depth of your loss. I shouldn't have brought it up."

"Perhaps not." She took his hand and swung it slowly between them as they resumed their walk. "I'm glad you know, though."

Seated around the general manager's desk were Mr. Krause, Mr. Burdette, and a Mr. Rutherford, who bore certain responsibilities for all of Henry Flagler's Florida hotels. They turned together to regard Mrs. Memory, who had come through the open door, plainly interrupting some sort of high-level conference. "I'm sorry," she said, backing away, "I was asked to be here at eleven-fifteen—"

"No, not at all," Stokes-Vecchio said, rising. The other men hastily joined him on their feet. "Come in, madam. Our meeting is over, I believe." He cast an inquiring glance at the others, who nodded. They removed their chairs from the vicinity of the manager's desk, placed them against the wall and drifted out with dispatch.

"Sit down, please, Mrs. Memory," the manager said affably, gesturing her toward the solitary chair remaining across from his desk. "There were several things I wanted to discuss."

She sat, hands folded on her lap.

"We had a most perplexing matter to settle at our meeting this morning," the manager began. The hotel had received written inquiries about accommodations for the final fortnight of the season from a Mr. Marcusohn of Cincinnati and from a Mr. Pradesh, secretary to His Majesty, the Maharajah of Chalmoograh. The former wished to reserve a suite for his wife and himself; the latter, a dozen rooms for the potentate and his entourage. "There was nothing said about elephants," Stokes-Vecchio added with a simper.

"How fascinating," Mrs. Memory said. "It would add an international flavor to the clientele. But is there space open? I hadn't thought the east wing was quite ready to receive—"

"The readiness of the wing was not the issue we had to resolve, Mrs. Memory. It was, as you so nicely put it, the flavor of our clientele."

"I see."

"We were of the unanimous opinion, after careful deliberation, that the result would not be suitable if, shall we say, too much spice were added to the broth."

"Meaning—what, precisely?"

"Meaning, in the instance of the royal applicant from India—and this would apply as well to our native Indians, so there is no xenophobia whatever involved in our policy—that their skin is of a detectably different pigment from our Nordic strain."

"And therefore undesirable?"

"Quite. No doubt a goodly number of our guests would be honored by the presence of such an exotic dignitary—especially one whose fortune probably exceeds that of any ten of our most affluent guests. But we are also certain that a perhaps equal, if less enlightened, portion of our clientele would make no distinction between this dusky ruler from the East and the lowliest of his subjects—to them, a nigger is a nigger, and they would not care to associate with such sorts. The very notion would be offensive. And since we are still in the building stage of our grand hotel—"

"And the Israelite family from Cincinnati—they would prove equally offensive, I gather?"

"By the same token."

"If you will forgive my impertinence, sir, I have—"

"Anthony."

"Anthony"—*damnation*—"I have encountered not a few of Mr. Marcusohn's faith among the guests at the New York hotels where I have served, and their presence seemed to cause no untoward incidents."

"Ah, but you are discussing commercial establishments in a city in which Mammon is king and moneychangers are legion, my dear. The Royal Poinciana is rather more of a private social club for Christian ladies and gentlemen."

"Perhaps this particular family is genteel?"

"We cannot submit each application to such a test in advance of the guests' arrival. So rather than confront them on a case-by-case basis, it made far more sense to us . . . ."

"I fully understand, sir—Anthony."

"—and although I personally have nothing whatever against the Hebrews, aside from their slaying of our Lord, it is a fact of life that once one of them is permitted to get a foothold, others are drawn immediately into their wake, and our fine establishment would soon be overrun with—"

"No doubt the decision must have proved painful to you and the other gentlemen."

"Do I detect a mildly disapproving tone in your remark?"

"It's not my place to pass judgment on such policies. My function is to serve whatever guests are present."

"Of course, my dear. I was merely making small talk." He fussed for a moment with the letter opener in front of him. "My—principal reason for asking you in was to ascertain—what I am hopeful of settling on in the next several weeks, before the staff disperses, is the composition of our officers for next season. But before making a final evaluation of the performance of my principal assistants and determining which of them to ask back, I thought I ought first to inquire which ones might wish to return. The other way is putting the cart before the horse, one might say."

"I see."

"It would be most awkward to extend the invitation—should I so decide—to those uninterested in coming back to this—glorious location—away from the wintry blasts of the north."

"I see. I—really had not—yet—begun to—"

"I quite understand. Perhaps, though, you might give the subject some attention in the next few days. I, meanwhile, will proceed with my evaluations." He cast aside the letter opener he was tightly gripping. "I trust you can understand, my dear, that I must separate objective from subjective considerations—"

"Of course."

He cleared his throat, made a furtive swipe at the right side of his mustache to tame an unruly hair or two and reached for the round glass paperweight with floral patterns imbedded in its base that normally sat upon a small stack of loose papers to his immediate left. He fondled the object for a time, then began again. The other matter he wished to put to her was strictly personal and unrelated to the previous one: in view of the affable evening they had passed together at the Cakewalk, would she perhaps enjoy taking dinner with him one night later in the week at a place he knew in West Palm? "It's nothing special, frankly—the food is mediocre at best and the clientele somewhat raffish, but I thought the change of scenery might be a welcome one for you."

Such a thoughtful, such a subtle solicitor for her favor. If she wished her job back next season, she had best consider the nature of their relationship along with other factors that might affect his deliberations.

"Thank you—Anthony. But I remain a widow—in mourning—and I'm not sure it's at all seemly for me to be seen cavorting at a—"

"I do not *cavort,* my dear Madeleine."

"I—stand corrected. But surely you can understand. It's not—"

He replaced the paperweight with a disheartened thud. "I don't wish to discomfort you. Perhaps you'll reflect on my invitation—along with the other matter?"

Your drift, Anthony Stokes-Vecchio, is all too apparent. "Of course."

"A sun-drenched paradise run with exquisite concern for the merest whim of every guest," Royal Postlethwaite had called the Royal Poinciana in his *Examiner* column, a copy of which Stokes-Vecchio had taken to posting on the staff bulletin board in the hall leading to his office. It was with precisely such encomia in mind that the general manager had instructed his senior people to attend assiduously to every aspect of the society journalist's stay.

Mrs. Memory was glancing at the latest posting of his column when an item in it jumped off the paper and set her pulse gyrating. Among the guests imminently due in Palm Beach at Mr. Flagler's palace-by-the-sea, wrote Postlethwaite, were the newlywed couple, Mr. and Mrs. Edwin Holcombe Caldwell of New York.

Lord in heaven! It could not be. But why not? What more natural place for a winter wedding trip? She had understood there would be a June wedding, according to the engagement announcement in the paper, yet no notice of the wedding itself had appeared before she had come south to take her position at the hotel. There must have been complications, she had supposed—perhaps second thoughts or health problems or a question of ultimate compatability between the two of them. The wedding notice had in all likelihood appeared in the society section only recently when the New York papers were inaccessible to her.

She headed to the front office and busied herself as unobtrusively as possible with the registry. Her eyes scanned the pages until she came to the weekly list of incoming guests—and there they were! Down for room 350, the bridal suite. Their arrival was slated for just two days hence; their stay was scheduled to last the final three weeks of the season.

Her heartbeat was irregular, she was certain, for all the ensuing forty-eight hours, and little else occupied her thoughts—not even the charms of Harry Loring—but the prospect of the Caldwells' presence. It all seemed an answered prayer, even if she were not able to exchange a single word with the former Miss Rachel van Ruysdale. The nearness of her, perhaps a protracted glimpse or two of her, would suffice.

At the scheduled arrival hour of their train, Mrs. Memory positioned herself in the lobby behind a particularly healthy pair of potted palms, the fronds of which she examined minutely while trying to calm herself and peer through to the throng of newcomers waiting their turns to check in. There they were—without a doubt. The couple was some twenty years younger than all the rest. She was slender and demure, dressed in white eyelet, her head bent slightly and her face all but hidden by her large, beribboned straw hat. He was stocky and dark-haired, in a light gray linen suit, and not at all hesitant to survey his surroundings with curiosity.

Mrs. Memory shifted her vantage point to another plant to get a better look at the young couple, but as she did, they moved up in line, turning their backs to her. Retreating from the rotunda, she forced herself to breathe more slowly. There was no hurry; there would be time and occasion—she could surely arrange it—to confront Rachel Caldwell. Why, though, did she feel as much dread of the event as yearning for it?

As Mrs. Memory was rearranging the curtains that the chambermaid had left artlessly gathered in the Postlethwaites' rooms, her attention was drawn out the window to a rowboat race about to begin on the lake.

Three boats, each containing a man and a woman, had lined up close to the shore where the starter, bearing a small American flag, was busy gesturing so that all the prows would be headed in approximately the same direction. Some fifty yards distant, a second gent positioned under a canvas canopy held aloft a larger flag plainly signifying the finish line. When all the rowers had maneuvered their boats to the starter's satisfaction, they proceeded to change places with their passengers; it was to be, Mrs. Memory saw with amusement, a race among the three women. She opened the window a bit further to follow the event better.

The women grasped the oars with conviction, their partners sat facing them in the rear seat with hands cupped over their mouths to cheer them on in coxswain fashion, and the starter swept the flag down in front of him with a great flourishing arc. The few spectators along the shoreline began to cheer on their favorites. The rower farthest from the shore, Mrs. Memory observed, seemed to be making almost no headway whatever, despite her determined bending and pulling. Her partner leaned forward as if to instruct her, but his guidance did not help.

Even after the middle boat had swept smartly to victory, the third boat continued on a zigzag course to nowhere, then abandoned its effort to reach the canopy and drifted aimlessly toward the shoreline, where its exhausted rower received a kiss of consolation from her passenger before she debarked and left him to row the craft to the finish line. When she pulled off her straw hat, dislodging a very dark ringlet that fell across her pale décolletage, which was more revealing than most sundresses permitted, Mrs. Memory recognized her as one of Loring's regular companions. Her rowing partner was dressed in a brown Norfolk jacket with knickerbocker trousers, she saw now, as he came trotting toward her along the lakeside lawn, his delivery completed. "How does it feel to lose for once, Harry?" someone called to him.

"I only lost the race," he called back, "but I won the girl."

Of course. And how many others had he squired and flattered and fondled and no doubt bedded over the weeks while he was meeting her Sunday mornings on the beach and intermittently taking her to a masquerade dinner? But then what had she expected? He was an active, healthy, attractive single gentleman, free to pursue what pleasures he wished; she had no hold on him. Yes, he had been attentive and kind to her and they had exchanged intimacies, but there was no pledge or even hint of exclusivity in his declarations to her; neither of them was, after all, a child, and each was free to practice whatever forms of self-indulgence their spirits dictated. That custom and opportunity encouraged his philandering and all but degraded her very thought of it to strumpetry—well, could he be blamed for that? It was understood that a red-blooded chap like Harrison St. John Loring was entitled to sport around with the ladies—and the more the merrier.

But it would not wash with her, not finally. Even if his behavior may have been excusable by society's prevailing rules, she could not condone it, giving herself over in such fashion to an unapologetic ladies' man adept, whenever pressed, at convincing her she was his favorite morsel, indeed a blue-ribbon special, and all the rest mere playthings. She let the curtain fall back in place and turned from the window with its expansive view. Why had she allowed herself to be used? Because, she answered herself savagely, right here, right now, he was all she had, and whatever portion of his true heart attended her did so with diverting skill and every semblance of sincerity. It could not be said that she derived nothing from the arrangement. What, then, was the crime of it? Simply that he practiced numberless such arrangements that he had not managed, or even tried, to keep from her awareness. It was not fair. And she did not, could not, know if he had invested his being in any other ladies to the same extent that she had begun to reserve hers for him. Not fair at all.

Back in her office, she dashed off a note to Stokes-Vecchio, accepting his open invitation to accompany him to dinner across the lake.

The manager proved as unctuously attentive as his scalp was excessively pomaded for the occasion. At the Cakewalk, they were in the midst of a crowd and the dancers provided adequate distraction; at the restaurant, though, she was at his mercy. To discourage any lingering seductive intent of his, she inquired doggedly after his wife in St. Augustine, his grown children—"Why, you'll no doubt be a grandfather any day now, Anthony," she remarked in a pointed pleasantry—and the details of his home life, including his favorite dishes and which species of tree grew in his front yard. By dessert she had lapsed into silence until a renewed conversational initiative of his, dealing with hotel business, required a series of monosyllabic replies.

Just as the fear seized her that she might fall into a stupefied sleep before he released her from captivity, she was bestirred by the approach of Loring in evening clothes, accompanied by the woman on whose shoulder she had seen him drape an arm in the Writing Room. As they neared her table she caught his eye with an uncharacteristically broad sweep of her arm. Loring paused to nod to her and the hotel manager, who promptly rose to shake the guest's hand. Loring responded by introducing his companion; the manager did the same. "Ah, yes," said Loring, "I believe Mrs. Memory and I have met—under nearly calamitous circumstances."

"Is that a fact?" Stokes-Vecchio asked, turning to her for elaboration.

"I—I'm afraid the occasion escapes me."

"Not me," Loring grinned. "In fact, I was quite bowled over by it." He turned to Stokes-Vecchio. "She kindly helped me off the floor after one of her young women upended me in her eagerness to discharge her duties. No lasting damage, though, I'm happy to say."

"Of course," she said in contrite acknowledgement. "The halls are dimly lit, so I'm afraid I didn't have the opportunity to—"

"Naturally." He looked back to the manager and added, "I can assure you, sir, that Mrs. Memory's department has tended to my needs admirably ever since."

Stokes-Vecchio beamed.

"You're too kind, Mr. Harrison," she said.

"Not at all," he said, his smile broadening, "only it's Mr. Loring—Harrison Loring."

"I'm so sorry—I thought it went the other way around. I'm not getting anything right this evening." Her smile outlasted his.

"Very nice chap," Stokes-Vecchio said after Loring and his friend had moved on. "Part of the sporty set at the hotel. Old Boston money, they say—a fortune from the China trade. His uncle, I think it was."

"And no doubt the slave trade before that."

"I shouldn't be surprised," said the manager, flicking at his mustache with the corner of his napkin and signaling the waiter to bring them coffee. "At any rate, it's a pleasure to have his sort around for the whole season."

"Hurry, ma'am!" The maid gestured to her, too upset for politeness. "I'll tell ya on the stairs."

They scurried through the halls and up a flight of narrow steps never used by the guests. "She's cryin' an' cryin'—all balled up in a heap and lyin' on the floor in the closet," the maid gasped over her shoulder. "Can't tell what's ailin' her—she ain't talkin'."

Emerging on the third floor, they moved down the main hallway to avoid alarming any guests who might see them. In front of room 350 the chambermaid stopped and knocked on the door. Mrs. Memory felt a rush of colliding emotions surge through her: pity, dismay, dread—even anger because of the abruptness of the circumstances. This was not how she had hoped it would happen, not a frontal assault on a sick young woman. It was supposed to have been a gradual unfolding, an opening up like a flower under the loving sun.

When there was no response to her knock the chambermaid hurried the passkey into the lock, quickly let herself and the housekeeper in and shut the door tight behind them. The sitting room was empty, but a series of muffled sounds escaped from the bedroom beyond. The maid nodded and signaled Mrs. Memory to follow her.

The bed had been slept in but there was no other sign of habitation. Through the closed closet door came intermittent sounds that were readily identifiable at close distance as those of a woman softly weeping. The maid rapped gently on the door. There was an audible intake of breath, then a small, low voice: "Go away—please, go away!"

Mrs. Memory steeled herself with professional correctness. "Madam," she began, trying to make her voice firm yet sympathetic, "I am the head housekeeper. My name is Mrs. Memory, and I cannot leave until you come out and assure us of your health."

The sobs had stopped while she was speaking; the distraught Mrs. Caldwell could not cry and listen at the same time. It was an encouraging sign. But the voice that broke the short silence was not. "I shall come out when I'm good and ready. This is my room, and I may do as

I wish in it. Now—please leave me.'' There was a decidedly forlorn tone to the defiant words, which were shortly followed by a renewal of sobbing.

"Madam,'' Mrs. Memory said with more urgency now, "are you ill?''

No answer. No letup in the crying.

"Perhaps it would be better if I came in, madam—''

"*No.*'' It was emitted with the subdued anguish of a wounded animal.

"Madam,'' Mrs. Memory said, "you *must* either come out or allow me in. The hotel cannot permit its guests to continue in obvious distress.''

Silence, then heaving breathing. "The door's open,'' said the voice, feebler than it had been.

Mrs. Memory gestured the maid to back away, then slowly clutched the doorknob and inched it toward her, allowing a faint patch of electric light from the bedroom to slant across the closet interior. On the floor, pressed against the side wall, sat a slender figure in a white garment, her long, strawberry blonde hair in disarray, knees drawn against her chest, arms clasped tightly around her ankles and hugging her legs to her body. She turned her head away from the light.

"May I leave the door open—or would you prefer me to close us in?''

"I don't care,'' the young woman said behind her knees in a voice just above a whisper. Her body gave a final small tremor and then seemed becalmed.

The housekeeper left the door ajar so she might see the being dearest to her of all the dwellers on the earth. Just at the moment, however, there was nothing very rewarding about the sight. She paused, standing against the wall opposite the folded young woman, before deciding that she could not communicate with her at that altitude and slid slowly down until she, too, was seated, facing the object of her profound concern. "Thank you,'' said Mrs. Memory, "for allowing me in.''

The young woman said nothing for a time, as much in embarrassment as unhappiness, the housekeeper surmised and thus kept her own silence. "Is it anything physical, madam?'' she finally inquired.

Rachel van Ruysdale Caldwell shook her head without lifting it.

"Well, that's something.''

The young woman ran a hand through a strand of her long, lovely hair and revealed the corner of one puffy eyelid. "You needn't worry,'' she said at last with a mighty effort to be civil. "I'll be fine in a moment.''

"Perhaps if Mr. Caldwell were—''

"No!'' It came out with a snap.

"Where *is* Mr. Caldwell—if I may ask? It's usual in these circumstances to notify the—''

"Out—he's out." She recognized the sharpness of her reply and modulated it. "At breakfast, I believe."

"I see. His appetite got the better of him, perhaps?"

"Yes."

"Perhaps he was unaware of your—"

"Yes!" she said with a rush. "His appetite got the better of him and he was unaware—" There was a moan and then a sudden burst of fresh tears. "That's—it—exactly—" She was crying now as if she could not stop.

Mrs. Memory reached a firm hand across to the young woman's shaking shoulder and stilled it. The rest of her quickly regained self-control. "Forgive my impertinence, madam, but I gather that you and your husband have perhaps suffered a lovers' quarrel. Such things are not unnatural among newlyweds. Many adjustments are required before—"

"*Quarrel,*" Mrs. Caldwell said with more scorn than anger, "is not the word for it."

"I see. Perhaps if you cared to share with me the—" She moved her hand more tightly around the young woman's shoulder and let the warmth of the gesture finish the sentence for her.

Still without looking at her, the girl asked, "Did you say you were *Mrs. Memory?*"

"Yes—dear."

"You have a husband?"

"Once."

"Then do I need—explain—to you—?"

"I'm not entirely certain that I—"

Rachel Caldwell's smeared face turned suddenly to her, revealing red-rimmed eyes and blonde lashes and brows that gave her a babylike look, as if her features had not completely formed as yet. "He *hurts* me, Mrs. Memory. Do you—understand?"

"I—"

"Perhaps now you'll let me be."

The full contents of her heart flowed out through Mrs. Memory's fingertips before releasing her hold on the younger woman's shoulder. Then she moved closer to her and asked in quiet sympathy, "And you dare not tell him?"

"He—I can't—it's my *duty.*" Her body shuddered in a brief convulsion from the effort of explaining.

The delicacy of the matter reminded Mrs. Memory that they had an audience. The housekeeper excused herself and leaned out the door to tell the maid to fetch a pitcher of iced water and a washcloth, leave it on the sitting-room table and go. "I can take care of this, thank you." She took a deep breath after the maid hurried off and let it out slowly, giving herself a little extra time to think. "Mrs. Caldwell," she began, "I think perhaps you ought to stretch your legs. You'll get all cramped sitting on the floor this way. Come, let me help you out of—"

"You're very kind, but you needn't—"

"Please allow me—to offer you a little comfort."

She led her past the bed out to the sitting room and instructed her to lie down on the wicker sofa, beside the table where the maid shortly brought the water pitcher, a cloth and towel and left them. Rachel Caldwell's skin, she saw, was very pale, paler even than her own; her eyes, very definitely green, more deeply set and far lovelier than hers.

Mrs. Memory wet the cloth and ran it gently over the young woman's face, all the while searching it intently, noting the shape and arrangement of its every feature and storing each away for future reference. The overall resemblance to her own was striking, and the telltale differences a stabbing reminder of the love that had created her. Rachel's face was heart-shaped, too, but slightly squarer than her own because the girl had inherited the heaviness of Russell's jaw at its juncture with the ears. Her right cheek had a dimple; Russell had had one in each cheek, she herself none. The girl's nose had that same insouciant tilt as her father's, but her mouth was formed identically like her mother's, with points rather than curves at the center of the upper lip and the lower one the fuller of the two. The teeth, too, were similar, the upper ones straight and even and very white, the lower set irregular and somewhat crowded so that one of the incisors jutted out of alignment. The girl was pleasingly narrow-waisted, her bones almost elegantly long and graceful. Her feet were the same length as her mother's but not as wide. The long, slender hands bore fingernails that exhibited the soft sheen of regular buffing; they looked to Madeleine Memory like small, pink shells. Her own were decidedly less shell-like and pampered.

The girl emitted an appreciative smile as the housekeeper withdrew the cooling cloth and wiped the moisture from her face. She wondered whether Mrs. Memory would mind terribly bringing her hairbrush to her from the dressing table in the bedroom so she might comb herself. "I always find it soothing," she explained, "and a little of that might help just now."

"Of course."

She went on the errand with a happiness that nearly overflowed into song. She found the silver and ivory brush, fit for a princess, and on returning was so reluctant to part with it that she drew over a chair for

Rachel to place her feet on and began, without asking consent, slowly, rhythmically to stroke her hair. The sheen and fragrance of it induced such exquisite pleasure in her that no words could be permitted to break the momentary spell. The brushing revealed that Rachel had the same distinctive widow's peak as her own. Mrs. Memory's only thought as she brushed away was that if she could, she would lift this moment of her life out of its sequence and conceal it in a box with a tight-fitting lid, to be uncovered only when in desperate need, and then she would repair to the most solitary spot she could find and examine its contents minutely, running her fingers over its satiny surface and deriving comfort from its feathery weight within her palm.

"You have a very comforting touch," said Rachel, half-turning her head toward her. "Nicer than my nanny's."

"But less expert, I'm sure."

"I wouldn't say so. Have you no children, Mrs. Memory?"

"I—did." Tears gathered just behind her eyes, threatening to cascade her into helplessness. She brushed on, lips sealed, heart in turmoil, savoring an intimate physicality she had never expected to know, and yet knowing it, was reluctant now to end. "May I ask you, Mrs. Caldwell, whether your mother never told you anything about marriage other than—that you must—do your duty?"

The girl's head gave a little bob. "The social things, mostly. Very little of a—personal nature. She's quite old, you see—sixty-two on her last birthday—and talk of such things greatly upsets her. She is a very formal sort of person."

"I see. And—your nanny—might she not have—?"

"Nanny is a maiden lady, and even older than Mother."

"Of course." She pained for the girl, for her innocence, angered at the ignorance and uncaring of Marianne van Ruysdale, so busy with her social obligations that she could not find the time or the courage to speak candidly with her cosseted daughter. "And Mr. Caldwell—may I ask you—is he—a man of the world?"

"In the way you mean, I can't say—although we have known each other almost all our lives. He would scarcely confide such things to me."

"No—of course." But here was surely the true source of the problem, and what counsel could she offer without appearing impertinent to a young woman who considered her a total stranger?

She continued brushing until Rachel turned around and reached for her arm. "Thank you, Mrs. Memory." The girl lifted the brush from the housekeeper's hand and set it beside her. "I think I shall be quite all right now." She raised her feet from the chair Mrs. Memory had placed in front of her and sat up. The puffiness of her eyelids had receded now, and the striking greenness of her eyes was fully apparent.

Mrs. Memory patted her shoulder twice, then withdrew her touch. "I wonder, though, if you'll permit me to offer a word of advice."

Rachel motioned her into the chair beside her.

She took the young woman's hand as a bond to strengthen her own nerve. "I would hazard the guess that Mr. Caldwell is not very experienced himself in these matters—and that he has heard improper things from some acquaintances of, shall we say, a coarse nature—about the prerogatives of manhood."

The girl's lips parted in apprehension. "I really—don't think—"

"Please—permit me this—much. Anyone as anguished as you were earlier—in there—is needy of a bit of guidance—even from—someone outside her circle. Have you any doubt, my dear, that Mr. Caldwell cares for you deeply?"

"I—that is not in question."

"When a man loves a woman—as I am sure Mr. Caldwell does you—his principal thought is to please her—not himself only. Love is a two-sided affair—it cannot be any other and qualify. With its commitment there comes a responsibility. His is, above all, to be considerate and tender and giving. Yours, by the same token, is to be honest and devoted and unafraid."

"But I cannot tell him—he would not understand. He would take it for—my repugnance—a childish fear—that I was not yet ready to assume my wifely role."

"He will not. Or if he does, you must have the courage to correct him. The marriage bed was meant to bring joy, not misery. Both partners must be kind—and patient. He needs to understand, and that will require your help. You were not born to endure brutalizing—no woman was."

She gave the girl's hand a squeeze and removed it from her hold. For a final time she studied the attentive face before her, marveling at its loveliness, comparing its formation to the bits and pieces that had been indelibly engraved in her memory. It was a face she would never forget. She would age it in her mind, adding a line here, a droop there, whitening the hair perhaps, creasing the cheek a bit, but it would remain with her now and always.

"You're remarkably kind, Mrs. Memory." Her long fingers reached out and encircled the housekeeper's wrist for a reciprocating instant. "I don't know how to thank you enough. I wonder if you would consider—accepting a small gratuity? I have no other way—" She loosened her grip and looked about the room for her purse.

"I do not accept gratuities, madam." The voice was soft, struggling not to betray injury at the suggestion. "Your appreciation and the happy resolution of your problem will be more than ample reward, I can assure you."

Rachel smiled. "Then please accept this instead," she said, darting her head forward and planting a small kiss on the startled housekeeper's cheek.

Love and rage collided inside her in almost equal proportion as she hurried down the hallway, desperate for a few moments of privacy. Heart pounding so hard that she thought she might faint, Mrs. Memory grasped the rear stairway handrail and let herself sink slowly down to the top step.

The pain she felt for Rachel Caldwell's situation, Mrs. Memory recognized, traced from precisely the same ignorance and inexperience she herself had suffered in bearing the child. Instead of guidance she had won her own mother's contempt. Was this emotional deprivation to go on for generations? Her mind flew back to the agony she had endured for the five months spent at Mrs. Pinckney's Home for Erring Women, the hideous, foul-smelling brownstone with bars on the window. Even now she smelled the whiskey-soaked rag clenched between her teeth during the endless, arduous labor and heard once again the alleged doctor's brusque assurance that the first labor was always the hardest—when he'd help her whelp again, the baby would pop out easy as pie. Worked alike for women as for bitches; the two were all the same to him.

She remembered the ache of inspecting her beautiful baby girl, the pink scalp barely feathered with the palest golden down. She had wanted to put the baby to her breast, but Mrs. Pinckney forbade it because, she said, such displays of affection would make the love-tie between mother and infant all the harder to break when the time for permanent separation arrived.

She remembered, too, stuffing her pillow and blanket under the comforter on her bed and hiding all afternoon long in the little unheated entryway under the high brownstone steps on the day she knew the baby was to be given away or sold or whatever it was the Pinckney woman did with the tiny new lives whose mothers could not sustain them. By the time she witnessed the arrival of the large, lacquered maroon carriage, with the initials "W. M. van R." embossed in gold on its door, she was shivering and feverish from her vigil. All she had seen of her baby daughter's new parents from her cramped lookout were their backs and the unmistakable signs of finery.

She remembered, finally, the tale she had made up and told month after month about the woman in the carriage marked "W. M. van R."

who had come into the shop where she worked and how she had given the grand lady the incorrect change and now wanted badly to make restitution. On her day off she would wander from bank to bank, throughout Manhattan, telling the story to any officer who would hear it, in the hope that the initials would mean something to him. After getting laughed at all over the city, she finally encountered a young clerk who took pity on her as she was about to leave and checked his files; the initials, he told her, were more than likely those of Walter Martin van Ruysdale, a well-off financier whose wife most certainly did not need her few coins of change. That was not the point, Madeleine Memory insisted and was duly rewarded with the van Ruysdales' address.

In whatever spare time she could manage, she would walk around and around the block bounded by Broadway, Fifth Avenue, Twenty-second and Twenty-third streets, hoping for a glimpse of a perambulator, propelled by a proper nanny, with a golden-haired baby girl inside. Once, on a warm Sunday in the fall when the baby was a few months old, she saw her sitting up in the pram, dressed in white lace with an embroidered pink blanket soft as a cloud covering her legs. She went back to her room then and wept, knowing she could never give the child what the van Ruysdales were able to without effort—and that the infant was certainly more likely to live a happy life with them than with her real mother. After that she never again looked for the child; to find her would only be to prolong her own heartbreak.

But she could not stop following the society column in the New York *Examiner.* Royal Postlethwaite's worshipful pen informed her whenever the van Ruysdales left for their summer home in Elberon or took their pretty little daughter on a tour of the chateaux of Provence or the churches of Tuscany or the English lake district. And she knew that Rachel van Ruysdale had been introduced to society at a decorous party given by her parents at their gracious home, No. 17 East Twenty-second Street. And at another party just a year ago, the van Ruysdales had announced her engagement to Edwin Caldwell, of the shipbuilding Caldwells, whose antecedents Postlethwaite avidly traced back to the Massachusetts Bay Colony.

So much for the civilizing effects of pedigree on the scions of gentry, Mrs. Memory thought, reflecting on Rachel's bridal ordeal, and drew herself to her feet. The second floor, she ordered herself, was awaiting her semiweekly inspection.

In order to continue seeing Harry Loring in public she had no choice but to perfect her disguise as the exotic Madame Memphis, a role that her

New York landlady and confidante, Agatha Agapé, relished helping her create through several shipments of items scavenged from her own wardrobe. The contrast between the unsmiling, unpainted, black-garbed Mrs. Memory, her hair pulled straight back from her face without a hint of wave or fringe or ringlet, and her alter ego became all the more striking with each passing week that she and Loring dined at the Silver Swan in West Palm. Greasepainted in alluring hues, hair piled in fashionably high rolls around her face, bedecked with multiple strands of bright beads that complemented her gaily colored dresses, a sector of shoulder and more than a hint of her womanly charms revealed to the tropical night air, Madame Memphis smiled extravagantly whenever she was not chewing and gestured liberally with her arms by way of establishing the outgoing nature of her character.

The sternest test of this elaborate deception came on the inevitable evening that Anthony Stokes-Vecchio, accompanied by the Reverend Mr. G. Edmonton Reynolds, spiritual advisor to Henry Flagler and Sunday morning sermonizer at the Royal Poinciana, passed by their dining table and paused to exchange pleasantries with the demonstratively Dionysian couple. "Here they come," Harry warned her not a moment too soon. "Into your oo-la-la." He bounded to his feet and made the introductions.

"*Ah monsieur,*" she said in ludicrous falsetto, opening wide her carmined lips and exhibiting two dozen teeth, "*je suis enchantée de vous connaître.* I yam so 'appee meeting you—yes?" She raised her gloved hand to an absurd height, wrist limp and hand dangling, in invitation to the manager to implant his lips upon the backs of her fingers. Charmed by her Gallic manner, Stokes-Vecchio bowed deeply and complied, affixing his moist mouth to her fortunately covered hand. He then presented to them the somber Mr. Reynolds, to whom Madame Memphis displayed only six teeth and no gloved fingers; Mrs. Memory had met him formally, if briefly, at the staff reception in Flagler's private railway car at the start of the season and had nodded to him in passing in the hotel corridors on several occasions since. For a divine, she sensed something rather too secular in his manner.

Mr. Reynolds scrutinized her with an attentiveness that suggested less bedazzlement. "If you were not French, madam, I would have bet—were I a betting man—that you and I have met before. I rarely forget a face or a name—it is a modest enough talent but of great use in my line of work."

"Ah, and what ees your work, *exactement,* eef you don't mind my asking, *Monsieur* Ray-nolds?"

"I'm a man of the cloth, madam."

Madame Memphis looked momentarily puzzled. "A holy man," Loring put in.

"Ah ha. In zat case I must confess, *monsieur*—I yam not *française*, as you say, but *une canadienne.*"

"Forgive me for thinking you were French. Then perhaps you and I—"

"*N'importe.* A natural error, monsieur."

But the revelation seemed only to heighten the clergyman's curiosity. If, as she claimed, she was originally from Quebec, had she later lived in Boston or perhaps Philadelphia? What was her maiden name, then? If she was not at the hotel, who were her hosts in Palm Beach? No, he did not know the Millers—and the Reverend Reynolds knew, or thought he did, most of the other property owners in the area. Perhaps the Millers were tenants? He would not relent, and his prey grew more anxious and less effusive with her interrogator's every question until at last Stokes-Vecchio summoned him away to their waiting table across the room.

"What do you think?" she asked, exhaling a deep breath as soon as they were by themselves again.

"I think your boss is in love with you in two languages," Loring said with a grin, "and that the minister may be on to you. The Lord has blessed him with supernatural powers to penetrate the deceptions of sinners."

"Harry, it's nothing to joke about. The man could do me in."

"Nonsense. You're merely having a good time—off the hotel premises. Is that against the rules?"

"I am not supposed to fraternize with guests at the hotel."

"But you're not *at* the hotel, dear Maddy. Are you supposed to be a prisoner there, never to wander off its grounds? Relax and enjoy yourself." He smiled and toasted her with their third glass of champagne, a beverage for which she was developing both a taste and a tolerance.

It was less the effects of alcohol than the apprehension of discovery that had vexed her on awakening the next morning and left her with a stomach too queasy for breakfast. As a result she was snappish and edgy to the point where she was nearly relieved by the appearance in her office, shortly before eleven, of G. Edmonton Reynolds, now adorned in clerical collar. "Yes, Mr. Reynolds," she said without a hint of recognition of their exchange the night before, "please sit down." She arranged the papers on her desktop with exaggerated efficiency as her visitor slid into the chair across from her. "How may I be of help, sir?"

"Oddly enough, that was precisely what I was going to ask you, Mrs. Memory."

"I—was unaware I was in any special need of help, Mr. Reynolds."

"I would not have thought so, either, madam, until I awoke this morning and remembered where I had met the ravishing Madame Memphis before."

She clasped her hands on the desk in front of her so they would betray none of the fear that was surging through her. "I beg your pardon, Mr. Reynolds? You seem to have me confused with someone—"

"Come, come, Mrs. Memory. This little game does not become you in the least. I believe I understand the reasons for it—though I cannot say that others here would be similarly understanding if apprised of your conduct."

"Sir, I beseech you to reconsider your remarks. I cannot conceive what delusion you are under, but I am a widow in mourning and do not indulge in any 'little game,' as you put it."

"Mrs. Memory, I do not—"

"Now, unless you have some specific business in mind, Mr. Reynolds, you must permit me to excuse myself. I have a great many duties to perform today." She rose from her desk and glanced from him to the door.

The minister remained seated, his eyes narrowed and forehead furrowed in a glower of disapproval. "It is my function, madam," he said slowly, "to attend to the spiritual well-being of this establishment—and that supervision extends to the staff members as well as to guests in need of moral guidance." He began to rise now as he brought increasing force to his words. "I cannot therefore urge you strongly enough to cease and desist this shameful practice of yours, Mrs. Memory, the disclosure of which I am sure would lead to the conclusion of your services in Mr. Flagler's employ." He turned to her sideways and added over his shoulder, "May I further suggest that you would derive a great deal of benefit from attending the service I conduct here each Sunday morning—you have never availed yourself of the opportunity for such moral instruction, unless I am mistaken. I shall look for you this coming sabbath. Good day to you, madam."

The prospect of losing Loring, both their evenings out together and Sundays at the beach, plunged her first into fury and then despair. She had not recognized, until the threat of its deprivation materialized, how much the time with him gladdened her and quickened the spirit with which she fulfilled her duties when they were apart. She confided the smallest possible measure of her sentiments in a clandestine meeting she had hastily arranged with Loring, by a note tucked under his door, for dusk at the edge of the golf course.

He took her hands in his and kissed her gently on the brow. "Ah, the spiritually healing powers of the reverend clergy," Loring said. "Where would we poor mortals be without them?"

"Harry, he *means* it. I could see it in those vile little eyes—"

"No doubt." He gave her fingers a reassuring squeeze. "Fortunately, we are dealing here with a singularly profane example of a healer who is badly in need of healing himself." Why, just the other night he had seen the Reverend Reynolds passing him unsteadily in the opposite direction in the hotel corridor that the guests affectionately referred to as Hypocrites' Row, connecting the grand ballroom, where the main social activities were conducted each evening, to the barroom, where women of social standing were disinclined to appear and where male guests repaired when eager for an interlude of stag companionship and a bit of liquid refreshment. The unmarried minister was plainly en route for a refueling when Loring spotted him. "It's my understanding that our pious friend has spirits other than the holy kind on his mind for a goodly portion of the day—and night," he told her. It would be no trick at all, through the inquiries of Arthur Timmons, "that little scamp whose services I pay dearly for," to obtain detailed information on the watering habits of G. Edmonton Reynolds.

"Oh, do," she said, kissing him fondly if briefly on the mouth and then hurrying away.

Accordingly, she greeted the return of Mr. Reynolds to her office on the following Tuesday morning with something close to pleasure. "Yes, please *do* come in, reverend," she said, restraining her mouth from forming a catlike smile. "You're always welcome here."

"I would not have thought you so eager to see me again, Mrs. Memory," said the minister, settling easily into the chair without being invited, "in view of our last conversation—and your failure to attend my service on Sunday."

"Alas, I was otherwise engaged on Sunday, sir. It is one of the few times all week that I'm free to attend to personal needs."

"I should think the health of your soul qualifies as a personal need, madam."

"The condition of my soul is best left to me, Mr. Reynolds, and just at the moment I do not find it in special need of your counsel. If I sense a change in the situation, I'll no doubt avail myself of your kind offer." She swept a hand over her desktop, scattering whatever motes of dust might have accumulated. "Now to what, may I ask, do I owe the pleasure of your visit?"

"It is not a pleasure, madam, believe me—it is a duty."

"Namely?"

"You still refuse to acknowledge this Jekyll and Hyde game you're playing, Mrs. Memory—or shall I call you Madame Memphis?"

"Any social arrangements I may or may not have made, sir, are no concern of yours or anyone else's so long as they do not hamper my duties or impinge upon the sensibilities of the hotel guests."

"Then you admit the masquerade?"

"I admit nothing, Mr. Reynolds. I have had my say."

"Such an attitude, I'm afraid, is likely to cost you your valued position here."

"I think you are mistaken."

"You are leaving me no choice, madam, but to share my discovery of the true identity of the flamboyant Madame Memphis with the manager. I cannot think he will be pleased."

"You must do as you think wisest—"

"Your attitude baffles me. I only wish that—"

"—but should you persist in assaulting my character in this fashion, Mr. Reynolds, I have no choice but to advise the manager of discoveries of my own"—she reached into the drawer in front of her and withdrew a folder—"regarding conduct I think he would find highly unattractive in a man of the cloth, especially one ministering to the clientele at an establishment such as this." She slid several sheets of paper out from the folder. "It is my understanding, sir, that on Friday last, for example, on no fewer than six separate occasions, commencing at eleven-thirty in the morning—the *morning,* sir—you were served a complimentary glass of bourbon and branch water by hotel personnel. I have here the precise times and places when you so indulged."

The minister's jaw froze, leaving his mouth open more than one full inch.

"On the following day, Mr. Reynolds, you partook of similar spirits on seven occasions—*seven,* sir. And while you apparently restrained yourself on the Lord's day, you compensated for your temperance by indulging amply again on Monday. My information is that—"

"This is scurrilous, madam." His arms were folded across his chest in defiance. "Many clergymen engage in a bit of social drinking. I see no harm in my—"

"I doubt if Mr. Stokes-Vecchio would so classify it."

"He and I share an occasional glass. It will hardly be news to—"

"I disagree. Moreover, I should strongly doubt that Mr. Flagler, whose disapproval of alcoholic drink is well known to the entire world, would be charitably disposed if advised of your—unfortunate tendency."

"Flagler—" The name flew out of his mouth with dread.

"I hope, sir, that we understand each other now—and that you will restrict your activities to the Lord's business and none other. Good day, Mr. Reynolds."

For the final Cakewalk of the season, Stokes-Vecchio explained over luncheon to the senior staff, only the previous winners would be permitted to participate for the grand prize of two hundred dollars, a hefty sum, he said, for black folk. The general manager proposed that each of them at the table join in a pool among themselves, at five dollars a head, to predict the winner of the event four days hence. "All the guests do it," he said, "so I thought it might be diverting if we did likewise. I wouldn't call it gambling, really—just a little sport among us to get into the spirit of the occasion."

Mrs. Memory was not greatly attracted to the idea, but since, like the rest of them, she was awaiting word from the manager as to whether she would be invited to return to the hotel for the following season, it did not seem a politic moment to play the killjoy. And when Stokes-Vecchio indicated that she, as the only woman present, would have the privilege of choosing first from among the list of six participating couples in the dance contest that he passed around the table, she graciously consented to choose the Timmons couple.

Her selection was greeted by a small chorus of groans.

"Have I done something remarkably foolish?" Mrs. Memory asked.

"On the contrary," said Stokes-Vecchio, adding that the Timmonses were the only entrants to have won more than once; the weekly winners were invited back, and the Timmons couple had triumphed on each of the three evenings they participated. "They are the odds-on favorite."

"I had no idea," Mrs. Memory said, all smiles. "Well, aren't I the lucky one?"

To sustain her luck and obviate the general manager's almost certain intentions, the head housekeeper asked Mr. Bedient if he would be agreeable to accompanying her to the grand finale Cakewalk. The invitation, extended casually as they were departing from the dining room, was so unexpected that the grounds manager blushed with pleasure and instantly accepted.

Mrs. Memory's schedule that same afternoon drew her to the veranda, where she was to determine which of the rocking-chair cushions would require reupholstering for the next season. The western veranda that overlooked Lake Worth was not popular during the late afternoon. The sun there burned with intensity, and most guests preferred the cooler shade of the eastern exposure. She greeted each unoccupied chair as an old friend, some of them rocking eerily at her approach as they were caught by a trick of the breeze.

Partway down the row on the other side of the front doors she stood up. All the bending and stooping had tired her, and her back was beginning to ache. As she relaxed for a moment, her eye was drawn to the line of Afrimobiles below the veranda steps. At the far end of the line Arthur Timmons was engaged in intent conversation with his principal customer and benefactor, Mr. Harrison St. John Loring, in a snow-white suit that looked as wilt-resistant as its wearer.

When the two of them broke off their exchange and Loring strolled off around the corner of the hotel to the remainder of his afternoon's amusement, Mrs. Memory watched with interest as Arthur ventured up the steps onto the veranda and smilingly approached the few guests lounging there. To each he presented a small white card and made a brief explanation, laughing easily when engaged in an extra moment's conversation. As he completed his canvass, Mrs. Memory summoned Arthur to her side with a short but unmistakable wave of her fingers and inquired into the nature of his unauthorized solicitation.

"It's de Cakewalk, ma'am," he said, mopping the sweat from his brow with a clean handkerchief, which his mother no doubt saw he was provided with each morning. All the guests were being invited to wager on the gala event, Arthur reported, and showed her one of the cards he was handing around. It was similar to the one she had seen over luncheon, listing the names of the entries, but this one disclosed, unlike the other, that the Timmonses had been multiple winners in the earlier competition. Bets of fifty, one hundred and two hundred dollars were permitted, said the card; those wishing to participate ought to retain the bottom portion of the serrated card, fill in their selection on the top portion and leave it at the front desk for Mr. Postlethwaite, who had graciously consented to serve as master of ceremonies for the event; a committee of volunteers among the guests would retain the wagers for safekeeping.

"And who assigned you to distribute these, Arthur?"

"Mist' Loring—he in charge o' de bets."

She nodded and pleasantly waved the boy off, but something about the entire arrangement smelled foul to her. Sunday at the beach, she asked Loring about it. "Just a little diversion to stir up interest," he explained. "This is not exactly the most stimulating playground in the western world, in case you hadn't noticed."

"And what have you to do with it?"

"I? I am helping the distinguished society columnist from New York, a man of scrupulous honesty and towering tedium, administer the event. The wagers are placed in a safe deposit box in the hotel's vault twice each day," he explained.

She told him it was all of no concern to her; she had picked the Timmonses in the senior staff pool and fully expected to win.

"You won't," he said.

"That's your opinion."

"As you say, madam."

"What do you mean?"

"Ask me no questions," he said, scrambling to his feet and spraying sand behind him as he raced for the water, "and I'll tell you no lies."

The ballroom looked, if anything, still more glittering than it had when she attended the earlier Cakewalk. Electric globes blazed everywhere, and the guests, shimmering in the reflected glow, pinwheeled in an excited hubbub resonating with louder voices and more raucous laughter than she had remembered from before. Champagne coolers on their little tripods stood interspersed between the rows of gilt chairs, and waiters and bellhops were everywhere underfoot, bringing magnum bottles and passing trays of glasses among the crowd. The steady clink of crystalware and the burble of nearly giddy conversation suggested more of a carnival mood, she thought, than an entertainment at the most socially prominent resort hotel in America.

Mr. Bedient, wearing evening dress that he had no doubt borrowed for the occasion, led her to a fourth-row seat and brought them a pair of champagne glasses that they sipped slowly as Major Mackintosh's orchestra filled the packed room with sound by turns lilting and syncopated but always festive. Two rows in front of her and a few chairs to the left, she spied the strawberry blonde head of Rachel Caldwell, clinging to the arm of her young husband. The pale blue she had on was a good color for her, Mrs. Memory thought, but it should have been a little deeper and bolder; with the girl's high coloring, she did not need to confine herself to childish pastels. Perhaps there would somehow be an opportunity to tell her so . . .

A long drumroll followed by a thrilling clash of cymbals subdued the crowd, and Major Mackintosh turned over the program to Royal Postlethwaite, wearing white tie and tails. In his mincing, parlous manner, the society journalist explained the rules of the contest and noted "the extreme pleasure that it instills within me to participate. Because it is no secret," he went on, "that the evening's competition has furnished an opportunity for sport among quite a number of the gentlemen present—

not to mention a few of our dear ladies as well—I will not dally a moment longer except to announce that in addition to the six previous winners there is to be a surprise couple among the performers who will go last but will unfortunately be ineligible for the grand prize."

The second couple to perform—a bellman and a scullery girl—left Mrs. Memory mesmerized. Young, slender and supple, they danced together sinuously, shoulders and hips moving in ways she had never seen executed on a stage. Had they been white, she supposed, such a performance would have shocked and possibly outraged the onlookers, but because they were "darkies," and therefore primitive, their motions were perceived as exotic rather than suggestive and thus all the more diverting. The lower orders were there, after all, to provide for the pleasure and well-being of white civilization at its apex.

As the audience sang merrily along with the orchestra between performances, she surveyed the room for Loring. Her search, undertaken with nonchalance lest it arouse Mr. Bedient's curiosity, was rewarded with a glimpse of him in the front row on the opposite side, arm intertwined with that of his companion, a pretty auburn-haired woman who was apparently a late-season find. When the music again broke into a drumroll, however, she noticed Loring separate himself from the woman and seemingly grow tense, leaning forward in his seat, eyes glued to the conductor and no expression at all on his usually animated face. At the announcement of "Cleo and Oscar Timmons," Loring sat up and watched with folded arms, as if vigilant over their expected virtuosity. The rest of the audience greeted their arrival with a burst of applause, signifying their status as the favored entry.

They were dressed as they had been on the night she had seen them take the cake, and their mien was unchanged. Grave and reserved, they looked over the heads of their audience as they moved together as effortlessly as before, in perfect synchronization with the music yet somehow appearing to float beyond it in their own space to a tune and tempo of their own creation. All at once, though, while executing a particularly intricate series of steps, Oscar stumbled over his own feet and fell sideways onto the platform in the middle of the floor. His sprawled legs interfered with his wife's nimble maneuvers before she could avoid them, and she, too, tripped, landing heavily on one knee. The audience emitted a collective gasp at the inexplicable mishap.

The dancers picked themselves up quickly and tried to resume their routine, but the spell was broken, and Cleo, in apparent pain, was having trouble sustaining the tempo. So strong was the competition that it was apparent the Timmonses could not triumph after their spill, and rather than disgrace themselves with a hobbled performance, they halted, bowed deeply and retired from the floor to the accompaniment of sympathetic applause.

Mrs. Memory's eyes shifted to Loring. He looked relaxed now, leaning back against his chair and chatting with his companion as he contributed to the hearty clapping. If the very thought were not so unseemly, she would have sworn she saw a faint smile flick across his face. But why? If he was fond of the Timmons boy, then why not back his parents to win the prize? Surely they could use the money. She remembered now, though, that he had predicted their defeat; exactly how had he known?

The final couple, consisting of one of Bedient's gardeners and an ironer in the laundry, courted the crowd shamelessly, waving and winking their way around the floor and drawing beamish approval from Mrs. Memory's companion of the evening. But they were not up to the standard of the others, and speculation rippled through the audience about the judges' choice. While the decision was being pondered, Postlethwaite called out the names of the last performers of the night, the ones ineligible for the cake—Miss Diana Davis of Merion, Pennsylvania, and Mr. Timothy Faraday of New York City and Lenox, Massachusetts. The announcement drew whoops and whistles and even some good-natured hissing from the crowd.

The couple ran in not through the French doors as the other dancers had done but through the main doors at the entrance to the grand room. Obviously guests of the hotel, they had blackened their faces with greasepaint, leaving a margin of white skin showing around the edges in case there was any doubt of their race. For maximum shock value, Miss Davis was dressed as a man, in oversized gray trousers and jacket with a straw boater, her hair tied against her scalp with a thick black net, while Mr. Faraday had on a billowy red-checkered dress with a large white apron over it and a red bandanna wrapped around his head. As he tromped across the dance floor he affixed a hand to his mammoth false bosom, which tended to separate and roam randomly about the upper part of his dress. The audience's amusement was boundless.

The couple struck a pose, and then Miss Davis, with an imperiously outstretched finger, gave Major Mackintosh the signal to begin. To the strains of the ever-popular "When Saucy Suzy Skitters Through the Slough," they paraded around the platform, kicking, stomping, leering, eyes rolling, arms fluttering, in a blatantly inept imitation of various elements of the evening's earlier performances. The audience roared its pleasure as the clowning grew still broader. Soon the couple was stomping on each other's feet, and their smiles gave way to kicks in their partner's shins as the whole performance degenerated into a pushing, shoving, hair-tugging Punch and Judy bout with the principals winding up prone and still on the floor.

It was a funny parody, and very cruel: rich whites mocking poor blacks whose presence on the long narrow strip of sand called Palm Beach was tolerated only because wealth had to be served. Mrs. Memory looked about her. Though a few of the guests sat grim-faced, and Mr. Bedient had the grace not to join in the laughter, most were caught up in the general hilarity. She could not read Loring's reaction—his face was turned over his shoulder to the couple behind—but Rachel Caldwell, she saw with a sinking heart, was apparently reduced to a paroxysm of glee, her shoulders shaking, a lacy handkerchief held delicately over her mouth to contain her display. Damnation! Had the child been brought up to have no compassion? Could she not perceive the vicious nature of the burlesque? If only she might spend a week with the girl she could teach her—what? The hard ways of the world that she had been mercifully spared? Yes, that and a hundred other things—all that her honest-to-God mother had been denied the chance to imbue in her. But Rachel Caldwell was an adult now, living her own life, the course of which had been set long ago. In her high distress Madeleine Memory could only rise in her place, amid the disgraceful din, and march out of the room, her backside to the crowd. Mr. Bedient scurried in her wake.

The next night at the Silver Swan she demanded that Loring explain his involvement. "I still do not understand. Because the Timmonses were easily the best cakewalkers, you bet *against* them? What was the sense of that?"

"For a smart woman," he said, "you are terribly thick-skulled. It was not a bet, my dear—it was a business transaction. The whole thing was arranged." He glanced around to make sure his voice had not attracted any listeners. "Arthur and I concocted it with Oscar. What we weren't certain of was whether his mother would go along. She's a mighty proud woman—especially of her dancing."

"You mean their fall was no accident?"

"Precisely."

"But that's—dishonest. You knew they were going to lose."

"Not entirely. Arthur said his mother was against it right up till the end." But Cleo Timmons, he explained, wanted to open a laundry service of her own in West Palm Beach, and unless they could get their hands on a sizable piece of cash somehow, it would take them years to put enough aside to buy the necessary equipment.

"But how did their losing the prize money help them?"

"Oh, Lordy. You have a remarkably undevious brain, my dear." Instead of the casual betting that surrounded the weekly Cakewalk contests, Harry had decided to organize the heavy wagering over the season's finale. The first step was to inveigle Postlethwaite into serving as chairman of the process; his celebrity lent cachet and propriety to the betting. And by volunteering to form a committee to handle the accumulated pool of cash, he had relieved Postlethwaite of the messy details. Because of the Timmonses' sterling record, it was no trick at all to lure the majority of guests into betting on them; that was why the card listing the entrants had noted their three victories in the earlier contests. Of the 187 bets placed, 124 had been on the Timmonses; only sixteen bettors had chosen the victorious second couple. "And they were paid off at the healthy odds of five-to-one."

"And how was that decided?"

"By the committee."

"Which consisted of—?"

"Your obedient servant."

"And no one else?"

"It didn't seem necessary."

"And Postlethwaite—didn't he ask for an accounting?"

"I offered. He said, 'Mr. Loring, I would not *presume* . . .' "

The total wagered had come to $18,640. Of that, fifty-three hundred dollars went to pay off the winning bettors, two hundred dollars to the winning dancers, and ten dollars to print up entry cards, "leaving a profit of thirteen thousand one hundred thirty dollars." He gave a hundred to Arthur and divided the balance equally between himself and the Timmonses. "Cleo plans to open her place in the fall," he concluded, "and a good time was had by all." He produced a thick cigar from his tuxedo coat and rolled it between his fingers. "Would you care for some more champagne, Madame Memphis?"

"Yes, Mr. Stokes-Vecchio—just a moment, please." Mrs. Memory reached out to hook the garland of ivy over the nail protruding from the molding atop the French doors and carefully dismounted from the step-ladder.

The manager was waiting for her against the side wall of the ballroom near the orchestra enclosure. "I had no idea you took part in the actual decorating yourself, madam," he said. "I was under the impression there was staff adequate for the task, so you would not have to go climbing—"

"They seemed not to be getting it quite right," she replied, smoothing a few wayward wisps of her hair back into place, "so to save my voice I thought it easier to do it myself."

He shook his head with evident admiration for her industry as the two of them surveyed the brigade of gray-clad maintenance men bustling about the vast room, carting ladders and boxes, hanging floral decorations and Japanese lanterns, and otherwise transforming the scene into one properly festive for that evening's Washington's Birthday Ball, which marked the unofficial end of the Royal Poinciana season. A few guests were scheduled to linger until the end of the month, but preparations for closing down the facilities until the following November would begin the next morning. A small problem had arisen in connection with the ball, the general manager confided to his head housekeeper. Two special friends of Mr. Flagler wanted very much to attend the festivities that evening, but because there was not a single empty room in the entire hotel, he wondered if Mrs. Memory would mind, for this one night only, sharing her suite with her assistants, thus freeing the two rooms they occupied for Mr. Flagler's friends. He could move two cots into her sitting room so she would be inconvenienced as little as possible.

"I am afraid not, sir." She had other plans for the evening that could hardly be disclosed to him.

"I beg your pardon?" His eyebrows drew together in a severe fret.

"I would like to accommodate you, but that will not be possible. Perhaps one of the other senior people could—"

"I am asking *you*—Madeleine—because I felt I could—that you would be more understanding of my predicament than—than—Well, I am shocked, to be frank."

"Then you are being unfair to me. The terms of my employment for this season were clearly that I would be given an apartment of my own for the duration." She happened to be a very light sleeper, she went on, and would find it most difficult to get her needed rest with others intruding on her privacy, and the next several days were to be filled with extraordinary activity that demanded the maximum use of her energies, so she did not choose to jeopardize her health merely because—

"It is not a matter of 'merely.' If it were so small a matter I would not have troubled you in the first place. As to your terms of employment for this season, that is not in question. It is next season, frankly, that has been on my mind. I saw this request—I don't mind telling you now—as a test of your loyalty and goodwill. Therefore, I'm dismayed by your reaction. I consider this request the equivalent of a royal command from Mr. Flagler."

"I hold Mr. Flagler in the highest regard, sir, as I do you—although

I do not quite view either of you as royalty"—she smiled briefly—"but you have made a bargain with me and I do not find it honorable for you now to seek to break it, especially for *this* evening above all others."

"My honor? You question my honor when I simply ask that—"

"Furthermore, I find it distressing that you would ask the sole female member of your senior staff to discomfort herself rather than making the request of the gentlemen. Mr. Burdette, Mr. Bedient and Mr. Krause all occupy facilities comparable to mine. I think it hardly fair, sir, that your first impulse is to—"

"I have your point, madam."

"And with regard to your testing my loyalty as a prerequisite for my further employment here—"

"I will be discussing that with each of you starting tomorrow."

"—if my performance to date has not persuaded you of my value, then the sacrifice of my comfort for this evening is unlikely to alter your judgment of me—nor should it."

He brushed at his mustache with a knuckle of his index finger. "I had not thought you would take the matter so—let's forget the entire subject, shall we?"

"If you don't mind."

He expected her at his office with the rest of the senior staff at twelve-thirty that evening, he reminded her, at which time he would lead them all in a procession into the ballroom for introduction to the guests as part of the farewell ceremonies of the season. If she wished to join him in his office fifteen minutes early, he would be pleased to share some sherry privately with her to mark the season's successful completion.

"Perhaps," Mrs. Memory said, and turned to oversee the rest of the decorations.

"Piece of cake," Loring reported with a large grin as she closed and locked the door behind him, removed the champagne bottle cradled in his arm and set it on the table next to the wicker sofa in her sitting room. He reached into his bulging cutaway pockets and produced two champagne glasses. "I simply"—he opened his coat and stuck his hand into his breast pocket—"unfurled my little American flag"—he brought out the small party favor—"waved it in front of me like mad and sang 'Columbia the Gem of the Ocean' to it all the way upstairs. Sometimes I even staggered a bit for effect but didn't draw so much as a second look."

This was the fifth visit he had made to her suite, and each had required considerable guile so that no observer could guess his mission. The risk of their being detected, of course, was entirely on her but he was thoroughly sensitive to it, and she was in no doubt after his first visit that the rewards were in keeping with the danger of the gamble. "Stagger over here," she said, sinking onto the sofa, "and tell me all about it."

"Let me shed this monkey suit first," he said, unpeeling his coat, which he tossed onto a chair, and kicking off his shoes, which he propelled over the matting back toward the door. "Much better," he murmured as he joined her on the sofa, pulled her gently onto his lap and closed his mouth hungrily over hers.

She arched her body and fit it snugly under his light touch, which grew increasingly firm and exploratory until he suddenly hesitated and wandered off the mark. "Something wrong?"

"I'm stuck on your ruffles," he growled. "How do you undo this damned thing?"

She laughed and opened her dressing gown for him, then shuddered with delight as his hands engaged her bare flesh. The delight dwindled a moment later when she felt herself lifted from his lap and deposited farther down the sofa.

"You're ruining the crease in my trousers," he said, standing and unbuttoning his waistcoat. "Won't do at all." He slipped out of his garments until he was left only in his drawers. "Better," he said, then snapped his fingers. "I forgot about the champagne, dolt that I am." He went to the table and began attacking the wire securing the cork. "How can I seduce you without champagne?"

"How can you seduce me unless I resist?"

"You leave that to me," he said, prying his thumbs beneath the lip of the bottle and driving the cork across the room with a satisfying report. The bubbly foamed over the side for an instant until he neatly trapped the flow in one of the glasses. "What shall we toast?"

"The Royal Poinciana, of course. If not for the hotel we'd never have met. Or perhaps we should toast Henry Flagler—without him, there would be no hotel."

"Not to mention the rest of Florida," he said, presenting her a glass. "To Flagler—a man with a driving dream."

"To Flagler—my teetotaling patron saint."

They sipped and intertwined their drinking arms and sipped some more, and then she pressed closer, eliminating the gap between them, and placed her mouth on his. "You're doing a grand job of seduction," she said, lifting away his glass and placing it with hers on the table. "Follow me." She pulled him behind her by the hand, dropping it only to push open her bedroom door, and let her dressing gown fall to the floor in a lazy heap. With a sweep of her arm, she drew back the spread and covers, propped herself on the edge of the bed and regarded this Harry Loring, this rampant male animal, this superb companion and exquisitely accomplished lover, who was so kind and patient with her, who hovered over her now, contemplating her womanliness and marveling at the directness of her appeal. "Don't be bashful, sonny," she said.

With a little growl he dropped his drawers and sprang onto the bed beside her, pulling her down and gentling her over and saying, "I tell you, Maddy darling, this beats the beach every time."

She laughed until he silenced her with lips and hands and limbs and all of him. She caught the faintest whiff of clean bay rum before abandoning herself totally to his suffusing power, and then her own ignited response took sudden command of their thrashing embrace.

A *most* satisfactory ending to the season, she mused afterward, pleasingly sated, lying on her side with her breasts pressed against his motionless body, his arm around her neck and a leg thrown over hers. He looked—she opened an eye and glanced at his face in the dim light seeping in from the sitting room—utterly contented. Was she enough for him? Had he pleased himself half as much as he had her? Or did he prefer more tender, nubile female flesh? Did he inventory the charms of all the beauties he bedded, rate their quotient for passion, their outcries of ecstasy?

"Harry?"

"Mmmm."

"How many women have you—been with this season?"

"Been with?"

"Yes—including me."

"What on earth are you talking about?"

"You know perfectly well what I'm talking about. How many women have you *had* here this season?"

Now his eyes were wide open. He turned to look at her. "What the devil's got into you, Maddy?"

"That is not an answer."

"That is not a question worth answering—or one that a lady puts to a gentleman."

"I don't see why not. You're a socially active gentleman—who's no doubt proud of his—attainments and—and conquests—"

He gripped her by both shoulders. "Maddy, did you or did you not have a good time in this bed a little while ago?"

"Wasn't that apparent? In fact, that's why I'm asking—whether you give—all your companions so good a time of it."

"I don't see why that should be any concern of yours so long as you—"

"Actually, I was wondering whether you are lying there contented or just itching to go downstairs and get back to the party."

"No, I most decidedly do *not* want to go downstairs." He sat up and fixed her with a stern look. "Maddy, I'm here because this is where I want to be. Do you want me to go—is that it? Just tell me what the matter is."

He was right, of course. Her words and feelings were unbecoming, were beneath her dignity. "I—don't know. It's just—that I've seen you with so many women here—"

He flopped back onto his pillow and gathered his thoughts. "Look," he said, curling an arm around her body and tugging it close to his, "I don't give a damn about anybody else you may have seen me with—or not seen me with. They're all part of the game I play, can't you understand? Just forget about them, will you, please?" His mouth was beside her forehead, and she felt his breath as he spoke. "This is where I want to be—by your side, whenever I can be. What I was thinking about before, when you rudely interrupted my reverie, was where you and I will go from here—what'll happen to us—when I can see you up north. Do you understand? There aren't any others—they're only decorative bodies so far as I'm concerned."

How she wanted to believe that. She lay quietly, reflecting, her head on his shoulder, listening to the soft sounds of his breathing, his even exhalations slightly stirring a few hairs on her scalp. She felt enveloped by his nearness, his solidity, the earnestness of his protestation, that faint scent of his bay rum. But did that cosmetic aroma cover something foul beneath it, the same way his silver tongue and easy charm might so readily be deceiving her? Could their tropical idyll survive the harsh test of a colder clime? The distractions of the city were innumerable, and fragile things crumbled easily there. No doubt he was saying what he knew would please her, but honesty was required now, at season's end. If their time here together had been simply a joyful accommodation for them both, she would relish it as such, and without a moment's regret, and harbor no hopes or expectations of permanence for something that had been built on sand. There was only one way to determine his sincerity: he had to be told the truth about her, all of it, and now.

"Harry?"

"I was beginning to think you'd died."

"Harry, there are things I haven't—wanted to tell you—things about my past I wasn't ready to reveal—to you or anyone."

Their eyes were inches apart. "Maddy, you needn't. I know as much as I need to." He caressed her face, brushing a strand of hair back from her forehead.

"Not as much as I need you to, though," she said.

"Your qualities are far too apparent for you to—"

"Hush. Hear me first."

Her future was set even before she was born, she began, when her mother, Catherine Reynard, a transplanted French-Canadian mill worker from Woonsocket, Rhode Island, met Hiram Memory, a bank clerk at the New Haven Trust Company, while she was vacationing at Savin Rock. For the mill girl a man who occupied such a responsible position and wore a clean collar to work every day was a real catch, and she married him as soon as possible. But Hiram Memory was no world-beater and did not advance as quickly as Catherine had hoped. Money was scarce, especially after their home was blessed with children, first a son, then six years later a daughter. As soon as Madeleine was old enough to help by wielding a needle, Catherine Memory opened a small shop selling ladies' hats and notions on State Street in New Haven.

Business was slow at first, but when Catherine, on a buying trip for supplies in New York, hit upon the idea of millinery inspired by Parisian styles and insistently called her creations "chapeaux," the store began to prosper. After a couple of years she had enough money to open a place around the corner on Chapel Street, the best business address in the city. She called the shop "Madame Catherine's" and thickly laid on her crude Acadian accent whenever a customer was within earshot.

It would not do, of course, for the daughter of "Madame Catherine," whose shop was now patronized by New Haven's most refined women, to attend school with working-class children, so little Madeleine was sent to Miss Wilson's Female Seminary, where the daughters of New Haven quality were taught, besides grammar and mathematics, etiquette, speech, posture and all manner of feminine graces that every gently born lady-to-be was expected to have mastered. Catherine had plans for Madeleine. After being "finished" by Miss Wilson's, she was to be sent to a school in Paris that Catherine had heard all about, where her daughter would learn style and color and fashion, and when Madeleine returned to New Haven with all her accumulated knowledge, Madame Catherine's shop would become the finest millinery establishment in the state, if not the nation. Accomplishment and wealth would naturally follow, promoting for Madeleine a brilliant marriage into a family of means and position.

First, however, Madeleine would have to know the French language perfectly, displaying a proper Parisian accent, which would instantly authenticate her mastery of *la mode française.* A suitable tutor of French had to be engaged; mere classroom instruction at Miss Wilson's would not suffice. An advertisement placed in the *Register* drew to their doorstep a fine young Yale student named Russell Giles Corwin, the son of a small-town minister from upstate New York and a French mother who saw to it that her son spent his summer vacations in her native Normandy. Russell's blond good looks and wholesome pedigree added to Catherine's conviction that here was the ideal candidate to instruct her daughter.

Three evenings a week after dinner, starting early in October, Russell sat with Madeleine in the Memorys' front parlor, conversing with her, reading with her, enchanting her, as Catherine flitted in and out in order to refine her own accent and to make certain that the young tutor and his pupil were engaged in things strictly Gallic. The trouble began in the spring, when Russell suggested that he and Madeleine meet in the after-noons instead of evenings to familiarize themselves with the outdoors as seen through French eyes. A knowledge of the vocabulary of the natural world would prove enormously useful to Madeleine, the young man solemnly assured her mother, inasmuch as smart Parisians often walked in the Bois de Boulogne and took holidays in Brittany. That it would enhance her daughter's opportunities was all Catherine needed to be told, and she gave the youngsters permission to take walks after classes for each of them had ended. The two of them explored the streets of New Haven, and in time they took to wandering farther afield up to the reservoir north of the city or to Hamilton Park on the west or the waterfront on the south, but most of all they enjoyed the spectacular vista from East Rock, the promontory overlooking the city and all the places they had navigated on foot and the wide world beyond.

It was on East Rock, in a secluded niche, that they made love for the first time. Madeleine, frightened but curious, was avid for the experience, passionately enamoured of the Yale student, her teacher and sophis-ticated companion, as only a sixteen-year-old in love for the first time could be. Young Russell swore that so long as he did not spend himself within her, nothing could happen—that was what everybody did in France. It was all part of her cultural training, so to speak.

And nothing did happen, that first time. But after the fifth, or perhaps the twenty-fifth time—for by then Russell was teaching Madeleine with relentless enthusiasm nearly every afternoon—the girl knew something was wrong. Russell left for France at the end of June, and by the middle of July it was apparent that some wasting malady was afflicting her. She was seized by lassitude, and a peculiar discomfort every morning caused her to reject her breakfast, sometimes before rather than after it was consumed. Her breasts were so sore she had to be careful easing them into her corset, and worst of all, her monthly did not arrive. By August, when she had to loosen her corset laces for the first time, she understood that Russell had not entirely mastered the nuance of French civilization that discouraged impregnation. She had been irreparably "caught." And there was no one for her to confide in. She dared not tell her mother; her father had been reduced to spineless impotence as the weekly income from Madame Catherine's shop had long since surpassed his salary by several times, and her brother had gone west years earlier after a fight with their parents.

When Russell returned to Yale in September, Madeleine tearfully related her situation, only to be told that he had become betrothed over the summer to a very special young woman, the daughter of a former French nobleman from a fine Huguenot family, and although he was very fond of Madeleine he was not about to break his vow and thereby throw away his future on—he would not say an ordinary girl from an ordinary family—her. And, by the way, he said, he could no longer tutor her since a betrothed man should not be seen in the company of another woman, but he would offer her what money he could. Under the circumstances, however, it would not amount to very much.

"Little bastard," Harry muttered.

"Shhh," she said. "It was very long ago—and he was not little."

She would, at any rate, not accept his money if she could not have the rest of him, and a man that dishonorable no longer commanded her starry-eyed love. She had no alternative but to tell her mother. Catherine Memory's instinctive response was to demand the name of the villain who had wronged her daughter, but Madeleine, knowing full well her complicity while now despising her own trusting nature, refused to disclose his identity. Her mother guessed it, of course, but Madeleine's lips were sealed, forever until now, on the subject. Betrayal of all Catherine's hopes for the girl and her own resulting rise in the social world were the least of the charges mother lodged against daughter; it was the first time Madeleine had heard the word "slut" uttered in their home. As her last maternal act, her mother arranged, instead of her final year at Miss Wilson's, for her to stay at Mrs. Pinckney's Home for Erring Women in New York. For her to have remained in the Memory house would have brought endless shame to the family and infamy to Madame Catherine's shop, inevitably causing a sharp decline in trade. After the baby's birth, the door to her parents' home would be barred to her, her mother said, washing her hands of a child who had proved so utterly ungrateful for the opportunities lavished on her, so disrespectful of the values taught her in an upright Christian household. Madeleine Memory was on her own now, for good. And so, after the baby had been turned over to the van Ruysdales, the infant's mother, who had not even reached her eighteenth birthday, was forced to make her way alone in the great Sodom of New York City.

He kissed her brow. "What did you do?"

"Whatever I've had to in order to survive—but nothing dishonorable, I assure you." She forced a smile. "I just wanted you to know who I was—that my 'husband' never existed—that my mourning clothes are a complete and utter sham—"

He held her tight for a long, silent moment. "I don't care who or what you were or, within limits, what you've had to do. And if you thought I'd think the less of you because of what you've had—"

"I felt only that you ought to know—whatever the consequences."

"Ah, Maddy. You are too, too good. But some things need not be said or ever revealed—what good can they do? You make me ask myself how much of the truth I need to confess now to you."

"You have no obligation to me."

"No less than you had to me, yet you told me."

"I can't believe you're harboring things that I haven't—"

"Do you think you're the only one with dark secrets? We all carry them around with us. Surely you've gathered that the life I lead is not an entirely ethical one by conventional standards."

"You don't hurt people, do you?"

"Only in their pocketbooks—and only people who can afford the injury." He separated from her and propped himself up on an elbow. "The Wall Street firm I told you I'm connected with—that I seek clients for—is as mythical as your late, lamented husband. My business, Maddy, is card playing, which I am spectacularly good at—"

"Is there a living in that?"

"A precarious one, but it can provide certain amenities."

"But how? Where does one go to—"

"You're not hearing me, Maddy. I am a *professional* gambler."

The news numbed her. "But I thought such people—"

"Lived on Mississippi riverboats and wore big diamond rings? Not at all. Sometimes we look—in fact, the best of us always look just like the people we play with. We're members of the same clubs, eat the same foods, drink the same wines, patronize the same tailors—in short, we blend in with our prey so we don't arouse their suspicions. Sometimes we lose to them at cards, and for the very same reason. The only difference is that when we lose, we lose small, and when we win, we win very big. We live by our wits, our dexterity and our powers of observation, which must be kept very sharp, my dear, every minute of the time so that we can turn any situation that might arise to our advantage. And at the Royal Poinciana, opportunities abound."

A thousand questions rushed into her head, but before she could begin to sort them out, they both reacted to a sharp rapping on the door to her suite. "Oh, Lord, what time is it?" she said, lunging for a closer look at the clock on her bedstand. "Twelve-fifteen! I'm going to be late—"

The rapping on the door persisted. She threw on her dressing gown and hurried out through the sitting room, calling out to whoever was intruding on her to wait a moment. Barefoot and breathless, clutching her thin garment closely about her, she inched open the door. It was Stokes-Vecchio, in full evening regalia.

"I—yes—is there something the matter?"

"Madeleine—forgive me—I thought you'd be dressed and ready."

"I'm afraid—I must have dozed off."

"I was thinking I might escort you downstairs to my office—"

Lord in heaven. "Thank you—Anthony—but that's really not necessary." She kept the door open only the merest sliver.

"It would be my pleasure. I could wait while you got ready—"

"Really, no—thank you. It's not—appropriate—your being up here—with me—"

"Actually, there was something I wanted to say to you—before the others—in private—"

"Surely it can wait until tomorrow."

"I had hoped—I'll take only a moment of your time—if you'll just fetch something proper to wear—"

How could she leave him out there, begging admittance, when she badly wanted him to offer her a return engagement for the next season? Damnation, how she disliked the smarmy man. "I—if you'll come in and wait just inside until I can get on something—"

"Of course."

As she turned and began to retreat to her bedroom for slippers and a less filmy garment, she spotted the champagne bottle and glasses behind her on the sitting room table and Harry's clothing littering the vicinity. There was no choice but to wheel around and confront Stokes-Vecchio before he took a step farther. As she pivoted, she nearly tripped over one of Harry's discarded shoes; the other, she saw, rested on its side midway between her and the hotel manager, who in the dimly lighted entranceway remained transfixed by the sight of her and had not yet let his gaze wander to the indicting piece of male footwear. She scurried toward him, stopping directly over the shoe and covering it with the skirt of her dressing gown.

"Madeleine," said Stokes-Vecchio, taking her advance toward him as a delayed sign of affection, "you're quite—radiant in that—garment."

"Anthony—you have me at a disadvantage. What is it you wish to say."

"Must I say it here in the hallway, my dear?"

"I'd rather—if you don't mind—"

"Can't we speak in your sitting room for a moment?"

He was practically pleading with her, like a schoolboy. Cruelty, though, was her only defense. "I think not. It would make me most uncomfortable."

He drew a handkerchief from his pocket and mopped the oozing front edge of his scalp. "Madeleine, you are—an exceptionally principled woman—and I respect that—in you—a great deal. But really, I can not see why I must be made to—"

"Because I insist." She suddenly reached for both his hands to show a softening in attitude but kept them locked at waist height to form a barrier rather than a bond between them. "Now please speak your piece, Anthony, or I'll be hopelessly late for the ceremonies downstairs."

Well, he began, he wanted her to know—her, especially, to know—how proud he was of the way the hotel looked at all times. Why, just the other night he had been unable to sleep so he came downstairs to clear up some paperwork that had accumulated on his desk, and he was delighted to see that the rotunda appeared as lovely at three-thirty in the morning as it did at three-thirty in the afternoon.

Was that the urgent message he had come to deliver? The man was a hopeless ninny, but he had to be humored, and right out the door. "It's terribly nice of you to come all the way up here to tell me that, Anthony, but really it's all part of my duty. Now if perhaps you can let me proceed with my dressing, we can—"

"No, no, Madeleine—it's more than routine. Your notion of dividing the housemen into two crews for morning and evening work—it's been an inspired arrangement. I hadn't realized till then just how well it's worked out." He withdrew one of his hands to smooth back the quivering right side of his mustache.

"Thank you, Anthony, but I think you are too generous in your—"

"No, not in the least. You are superb at what you do, Madeleine—you are superb in almost every way—"

"Anthony—really—you must not—"

"You must rejoin us next season. I shall be quite lost without you."

"That's most kind of you. I'm just not entirely—"

"At a handsome increase in your salary, of course. I've not worked out a budget yet with Mr. Flagler, but I was thinking of an additional five hundred for the season—if that would suit you, I mean."

"I—well, that's most generous, of course. But I think I ought—"

"A thousand, then. I think I'll be able to work that out. You must say yes, Madeleine."

"I—well—if you'll promise to leave the next instant and let me attend to my appearance for the ceremony—"

"Yes, of course!"

She beamed at him with full magnitude. "Then yes—thank you so very much. I'm proud to be part of this fine establishment." She gave his hand a fond squeeze and then cast it free. "Now forgive me, Anthony, but you must scat—absolutely at once."

He retrieved her hand for another moment and kissed her fingers in gratitude before departing, nearly at a bound.

Whether more exhilarated over having averted disaster or being handsomely rewarded for her season's labors, she could not say as she lifted the hem of her dressing gown and danced back into the bedroom to tell Harry the news. She found him bunched in the bottom of her closet, sound asleep.

FOUR

New York, 1897

Patricia Dane, blinking her wide blue eyes rapidly as she focused on a chocolate-sauced cream puff, finally reached for it. In a trice the first bite had made its way decorously down her throat, adding to the maintenance of the Rubenesque form that even three or four daily trots up to her third-floor flat could not diminish. She was a sweet young thing, Mrs. Memory thought, if excessively given to quoting, as she had been for the past five minutes, from that morning's sermon by the estimable Reverend Hill at St. Stephen's Episcopal. Mrs. Dane had confided to her, shortly after moving in, that for the first two decades of her life she had wanted to be a missionary, bringing enlightenment to the heathen in a distant desert land, but "darling Robert" had swept her off her dainty size three-and-a-halves at the age of twenty-one and compelled her to follow the more sensible dictate of her ardently beating heart. Now the only heathen she tried regularly to convert was her Sunday-afternoon hostess, who withstood the spiritual onslaught with smiles.

"Darling Robert" Dane—Mrs. Memory could think of him in no other way—was as spare as his wife was plump. Mrs. Memory felt uneasy for days after referring to them as "the Sprats" in front of Miss Agapé, who had hooted throatily for a full minute over her first-floor tenant's brief lapse of Christian kindness. In truth, the Danes were a trifle self-righteous. Mr. Dane read the editorials in three newspapers as he rode the streetcar downtown to work every morning and two when he returned at night, so that he was certain, if invited, to offer a carefully balanced opinion on almost every conceivable subject. Bankers, Mrs. Dane told Mrs. Memory, needed to have a great deal of knowledge in many fields, and if her husband was to rise to vice president of the Corn Exchange Bank, which he was currently serving in the capacity of secretary and assistant loan officer at the Chambers Street branch, he had to prepare himself.

It had been difficult at first for Mrs. Memory to unpuzzle what it was exactly that her other co-tenant, Benjamin Sprague, did for a living. A tall, slender, balding man who dressed in black suits always pressed with geometric precision, he had moved into the second-floor flat just two days after she had taken possession of the one on the first, and it was only natural that they were soon exchanging hallway pleasantries. On the second occasion that they went to dinner and the theater together, Mr. Sprague allowed that he was a "professional comforter—in a way" and then promptly changed the subject. It was months later that he confided, almost apologetically, that he was the manager of the Fourteenth Street branch of the Oldfield Funeral Home. Most people, he explained to her, unconsciously feared that his daily consorting with the fact of human mortality was somehow contagious and therefore were likely as not to shun him. He earnestly hoped, Mr. Sprague added, that he had demonstrated to her the absurdity of that misapprehension. Mrs. Memory could not deny it, having accompanied him to nearly every theater and lobster palace in New York and found him a perfectly agreeable, gentlemanly escort and a serious student of the stage. He liked nothing better than dissecting the evening's performance during the intermissions and on their rides home together. That he expected no favors other than her company in exchange for his generosity made him an even more attractive companion in Mrs. Memory's eyes, because if truth be told, there was always the slight aroma of something medicinal about Mr. Sprague that made the prospect of physical engagement with him repugnant to her.

Agatha Agapé, as far as her first-floor tenant was concerned, was a jewel of a landlady. Her gaiety more than compensated for the decided stiffness of the Danes and Mr. Sprague (in whom she feared the characteristic was indeed occupational). As a young and not-so-young actress, Miss Agapé had been *every*where and done *every*thing, she told Mrs. Memory, shaking her hennaed head for emphasis. One of her keen admirers—of whom, she implied none too subtly, there had been scores—had given her this house as a testament of his high esteem. Others had similarly bestowed trinkets of value, several of which she generally wore in jangling conjunction when attending Mrs. Memory's teas. She was glad, she said, that a lady like Mrs. Memory had rented the first-floor flat, thereby lending to the house a certain elevated tone that her own raffish demeanor denied it. She would have kept the first floor for herself instead of the ground-floor apartment, but it was far more convenient for her friends not to have to climb the steep front steps in order to visit her. Elderly gentlemen—she winked—had enough problems with their hearts without encountering additional physical obstacles to the demands of romance.

Mrs. Memory looked around inquiringly. Well, yes, Mrs. Dane yielded, her hand darting, she would have another; she had been wondering what the cherry-dotted confection on the left might taste like. The Reverend Mr. Hill had exhorted his flock that morning to feed the hungry, and Mrs. Memory was performing her Christian duty by providing this delicious little repast. Now if only—she slid the cookie bite to the pocket of her cheek—Mrs. Memory and the others present would join her and Mr. Dane to hear their divinely inspired minister Sunday next, their shriven souls would surely rejoice.

"Thank you, dear," said Mrs. Memory, beginning to move the dishes to a tray for return to the kitchen, "we're always grateful for your concern. But there are private ways as well to make peace with the Lord."

"But those," replied Mrs. Dane, swallowing, "are not sanctified."

"The Lord may be less inclined than you think to draw that distinction. But I shall be glad to join you this Wednesday in your work at the orphanage—that seems an exemplary project for St. Stephen's sponsorship."

Mrs. Dane beamed over the recruitment and surrendered her cup and saucer. "Heaven will thank you, Mrs. Memory."

"Perhaps we should await the usefulness of my efforts before expecting too much in the way of approval."

"Say," said Mr. Sprague, leaping to his feet to reach for the kitchen door as Mrs. Memory, laden with the tea tray, approached it, "if any of the musicians among us would oblige, I'd enjoy hearing a song or two."

"I thought you'd never ask," Miss Agapé said in her best mock basso profundo. "I've been practicing all morning."

Mrs. Memory, promptly reemerging from the kitchen, pleaded that she had not sat down at the piano since having left for Florida and that her accompaniment would as a result be even weaker than usual. "But I'll do my best." The little spinet had been an impulsive purchase, acquired secondhand at an attractively modest price, and seemed a decent enough use of the "accomplishment" that her mother had been so proud of in that long-ago time when she still acknowledged the existence of a daughter.

Miss Agapé, prepared as always to perform, spread her music out on the rack. Ah, yes—Mrs. Memory by now knew the song to have been the highlight of Miss Agapé's role in *Banks of the Thames*, in which she had portrayed a winsome fishmonger who managed to ensnare the Earl of Edgmere after many slippery complications. Mrs. Memory played the introductory bars as the actress quieted the swinging pendants around her neck and the bangles on her wrist, then began in her slightly hoarse alto:

> Me father never met me,
> 'e never cared to stay,
> And when I asked me mother why
> This is what she'd say:
> Your daddy's got no moss on 'im 'cause 'e's a rollin' stone . . .

After the first few verses, Miss Agapé, skirts flying as she twirled to the beat, asked everyone to join in the chorus, and they all complied, the Danes no less lustily than the rest despite the rakish overtones of the ditty. At the end the songstress curtsied prettily to the applause led by Mr. Sprague, whose appreciation of the merriment, Mrs. Memory had concluded, stemmed from immersion in its precise opposite all week long. He turned to Mrs. Dane next and urged her to take the stage.

She at once turned a becoming rosy hue and said she had not brought any music with her, but if her hostess didn't mind her rummaging through the piano bench she was sure something suitable would surface. Mrs. Memory moved aside to let the younger woman poke through her songbooks. "I think we might manage this one, don't you?" Mrs. Dane proposed. Mrs. Memory scanned the accompaniment and nodded with restrained enthusiasm. "In Thee, Fond Love, My Spirit Resideth" was slow, silly and sentimental, but to scorn it would hurt her guest's feelings. Mrs. Dane sang it to the ruffled lampshade on the corner table in her sweet high soprano, too embarrassed to direct it to the person for whom it was meant. He was nonetheless moved, and his applause, genteel but unremitting as a fiduciary trust, lasted longer than anyone else's.

Would the hoarseness she had detected in Miss Agapé's throat, Mrs. Memory wondered aloud, be soothed by a little sherry? It would, indeed. Mr. Sprague was likewise agreeable. The Danes, she knew, would not indulge in alcoholic beverages but refrained from judgmental comment on the morally debilitating practice. Including a glass for herself as she poured, Mrs. Memory remarked that the sherry would surely have a therapeutic effect on the flow of her fingers across the keyboard. And her playing did, in fact, seem to improve during Mrs. Dane's rendition of "The Light from the Distant Shore," which contrasted nicely with Miss Agapé's finale, "Bibulous Bacchus" from Cymbals and Myths, with its special bass effects demanding a certain virtuosity from the accompanist.

She confirmed, as they filed out, that she would join Mrs. Dane on her visit that Wednesday to the orphanage on Fulton Street and would be delighted as always to accompany Mr. Sprague to dinner and a new musical play on Saturday night; Miss Agapé she would meet and engage, without appointment, in numerous conversations throughout the week.

Yes, these neighbors were all very pleasant and comforting, but as she wound a towel around a teacup while washing up after her guests had gone, she asked herself if this was all there was to be for her. Would the rest of her life be given over to periods of well-paid work with interludes of joyless diversion? Would there ever be anyone with whom to share her days and nights as the juices of her youth ebbed now without prospect of her achieving serenity? Which was not, she reminded herself, to complain about her lot—she had, by any standard, attained a level of comfort denied to most in this life, and she did not believe in any other. It was just that—that she had glimpsed something much more in the company of Harry Loring, and having known it, she regretted now its sudden withdrawal. She had not heard from him since her return to the city. He was the sort of man who truly meant what he said at the moment he said it, but his attention span was brief and memory shallow. Not a man to have put her faith in—was there any?—and, of course, she had not.

The afternoon before her first visit to the orphanage she went to the library and hunted among the children's books for a promising title. She settled on *How the Little Elephant Found Wisdom,* which she read over that evening by way of preparation; it seemed just the proper mixture of adventure and instruction. Now, though, surrounded by a dozen lifeless little faces, she wondered if she had badly miscalculated.

"Once upon a time there was a little elephant who lived in the jungle, and, sad to say, he was not very bright as elephants go." She looked up hopefully to gauge her listeners' immediate response. None was apparent. "Does everyone know what an elephant is?" she asked.

No one said anything.

"Well, does *any*one know?"

Silence.

"Well, perhaps it would make things clearer if I explained." She leaned down a bit and showed them the small picture on the title page, the only illustration in the book. "An elephant is a very large animal—one can't quite tell that from this picture, I'm afraid—and is not native to America. It is much larger than a horse—oh, two or three times larger, I should say—with a very thick skin and a nose shaped rather like an arm—a very large arm, indeed, if you can imagine such a thing—and it is highly flexible—that is, very bendy, one might say—so that the elephant can not only smell with it but also lift things—large things—as large as a log, for example—"

The children's faces remained blank. Could they not understand English? Or were her words too difficult for them? Or had no one before ever tried to explain such exotic subjects to them? One little boy finally said, "What's a jungle?"

"Does anyone know?" Mrs. Memory asked the rest of them.

No one did.

"A jungle is—well, sort of an overgrown park—if you can just imagine what Central Park would look like if—" Oh, Lord, were they ever taken up there from this dingy place for a frolic among those grassy banks and wooded ways? "Well, suppose the park had very high grass, as high as your tummies—and many, many more trees, so many and so thickly together that they nearly blotted out the sun—and vines that hung down everywhere and made it hard to walk through—and hundreds and thousands of animals, big and tiny, some of them savage and poisonous—"

The boy who had asked the question began to cry, evidently from fright at the horrific scene she had painted for them. "Anyway, jungles are far away from New York," she said quickly and returned to her text. Before she could continue, however, the room was suffused with a sudden organic stench. *Tsssuuh.* It was difficult for her not to acknowledge in front of them the assault on her nostrils. The little fellow there on the left pulling at the crotch of his baggy trousers was evidently the perpetrator. Surely the child was old enough—he had to be three or four—to know how to control his bodily functions. Couldn't the orphanage people manage to instill a little discipline in their institution? She gestured to the child to come to her. The odor grew with every step he took. "What's your name?" she asked softly.

The little boy shook his head.

"Donny," shouted one of the older children, a girl with brassy, carrot-colored curls. "He don't say nothin', ever."

"Donny, would you go out into the hall, please, and ask Miss—" Her head swiveled toward the carrot-top.

"Eversham," the girl shouted, a self-satisfied smile bisecting her round face and revealing two central incisors with ragged edges just beginning to protrude through her upper gums.

"Ask Miss Eversham to—to—" She turned away from him again, her eyes blinking rapidly, as much from the frustration of instructing the mute to speak as from the smell of him. "Could you," she addressed the orange-haired girl, "take Donny to Miss Eversham and tell her—?"

"He needs changin'. He allus needs changin'," the girl said, wearily climbing to her feet. She was a heavy child, Mrs. Memory noted sadly, so overweight that the faded, dun-colored dress she wore, with a waist-line big enough to fit her girth, hung down nearly to her ankles. "Come on, Donny." She clamped a hand around his wrist, jerking him along behind her as she tramped to the door and closed it quietly behind her.

They would wait, Mrs. Memory announced, for the missing children to return. Meanwhile, she wanted to know all their names and ages. That information imparted, silence ensued. How was she supposed to get through the next two hours? Could her elephant story hold any meaning or magic for them? What value could her visit possibly have for these tiny creatures whose lives had been stunted and fates determined before they were even born? Their patched, threadbare clothes, donated by charitable Manhattan Episcopalians, appeared at best a month or two shy of the rag bag. Above their garments, each grave little face wore a halo of gray around the edges, only the depth of which varied. Had no one in this place ever heard that soap and water should be used to the boundary of the skin, down the neck and beyond? The poor things would surely develop ringworm from their own filth. Was there any hope for these misbegotten, abandoned children? Occasionally, Mrs. Dane had told her, one of them would be adopted, but it must have taken a potential parent with far-seeing vision indeed to detect the spiritual beauty shining under-neath these pinched, ashen faces.

The doorknob turned. The round-faced girl had come back with her charge in tow, his wet gray trousers exchanged for brown ones rolled several times at the bottom. Her name was Letitia, she told Mrs. Memory, and she was six and a half, older than everyone else. Next year she would go to school; all the rest of them were still babies who had to stay home.

Her contentious remark, as it was designed to, provoked the others into a cacaphony of responsive insults, including a sampling of the foulest words in the language. The boy seated to Letitia's left actually punched her in the arm. Donny cavalierly punched him in return and began gnawing on his knee. In short order, the room had turned into a minature melee, and Mrs. Memory was beside herself. Calling on them sweetly to stop misbehaving produced no result whatever; she could barely hear herself above the din. Almost desperately she stamped her foot and clapped her hands together as hard as she could in a single percussive outburst that startled the children into frozen attention.

"Listen," she said in a tone like the one reserved for the most delin-quent chambermaid under her command, "I did not come here to watch you behave like little animals. We are all here to have a good time—*do you understand?* Now either you will learn to control yourselves or I shall not come back—*ever again.*"

The instant the words were out of her mouth, enunciated with the exaggerated clarity she had adopted from her first moment among them, she regretted their harshness. Life had doled them enough cruelty without her contributing more at first provocation. Even if the children did not take to her readily nor she to them, they would have to learn to endure each other for their mutual benefit.

"How would you all like to sing a song about the moon?" she asked them brightly, putting the storybook about the elephant to one side for the moment. "Now you all know what the moon is, don't you?"

"The bright light in the sky at night," said the punching instigator.

"Good! All right, then, I'll sing it first, and then you follow along whenever you think you know the words."

The inhibition she would have felt delivering a solo a cappella in a roomful of adults remained submerged; this was combat, and she had no other weapon at her disposal for winning them over. In a quavery alto she began,

> *Glowing, growing, up above,*
> *The Moon looks down on us with love . . .*

The boy who asked her what a jungle was began crying again, whether at the quality of her rendition or perhaps the bad dreams it reminded him of, Mrs. Memory had no idea. Her voice grew more uncertain as she groped for the lyrics, which suddenly escaped her and Letitia announced that it was a dumb song and snatched the storybook about the elephant from the tabletop for her private inspection. This behavior proved contagious, for soon some of the children were singing along with her more or less, some were singing counter to her in mocking tunes of their own devising and some were tumbling across the floor without reference to the music. It was bedlam once more.

"Perhaps," she said to Patricia Dane on the streetcar ride home, "I would have done better with a piano. I think they'd have been more attentive."

"You mustn't blame yourself. They're naturally unruly children."

"Is it that—or because they've not been properly attended to?"

"There's only so much that can be done for them, I'm afraid."

"I still think a piano would help. Would the church consider making such a contribution?"

"I'm afraid it would strike them as somewhat frivolous. The children are there for sustenence, not recreation."

"I myself would not dismiss the uses of recreation, Patricia dear. It seems to suit you and Robert and the rest of us well enough on Sunday afternoons—don't you think?"

Mrs. Dane was not good at coping with that sort of moral dilemma. "That's—quite a different thing, wouldn't you say?"

Mrs. Memory would not. Instead she pressed Mrs. Dane to ask around at St. Stephen's whether a well-worn spinet might be contributed to the orphanage by a generous parishioner. "Only," Mrs. Dane dickered in the Lord's behalf, "if you promise to come every Wednesday that you're not otherwise occupied—"

Mrs. Memory promised.

"And to church on Sundays?"

"We shall see," said Mrs. Memory, a past master by now at repulsing those who required that she apply for salvation on bended knee. The Lord, she was certain, was less presumptuous.

Scouring the "wants" for a promising summer position, she put down the *Herald* and picked up the less-engaging but more respectable *Tribune*. Time was growing short for her to find a satisfactory summer situation to supplement her income from the Royal Poinciana. Perhaps a nice private placement with a family summering at the Jersey shore or one of the New England resorts would be preferable to working at an establishment. That would be a change for her, at any rate. But a hotel or an inn was likely to prove less emotionally entangling. A lodge in the Adirondacks or a hotel in the Finger Lake district would suit her best, perhaps.

She squinted down the columns of tiny type and, finding nothing suitable, was about to drop the paper onto the floor with the rest when a small notice at the bottom of the page caught her eye. "Housekeeper wanted. Excellent credentials only. Apply Mrs. Caldwell, 898 Fifth Avenue, Tues.-Fri., 3–6 P.M."

Rachel. Why would she need a housekeeper so soon after returning from her wedding trip? Surely one had been engaged beforehand. Perhaps her mother-in-law had made the selection for her, and the housekeeper didn't suit the younger Mrs. Caldwell.

The girl had been on her mind lately with damnable frequency, no doubt as a consequence of her weekly attendance at the Fulton Street orphanage. The more she saw of those small unfortunates, the greater her rejoicing that her own flesh and blood had been favored by fate. Was it so unnatural that she would wonder about the particulars of the home Rachel Caldwell lived in? It was bound to contain a swarm of servants, superb furnishings, intricate woodwork and other architectural flourishes—it would all be such a pleasure to see, as if in a living story-book: the daughter she had never known until now, installed amid surroundings beyond her own wildest dreams.

She couldn't. She would not dare. Would she? The very idea, though, was as intriguing as it was preposterous—and not a little frightening: barging in up there under false pretenses just to satisfy her curiosity. But if Madame Memphis had served her purpose in Palm Beach, surely she could manage a disguise that would in no way summon to Rachel Caldwell's mind the kindly housekeeper of the Royal Poinciana. The girl had probably wiped their previous meeting right out of her mind, anyway. Still she could take no chances. The disguise would have to be expert.

How, though? The bold, boisterous Madame Memphis would not do, of course, but her accent, properly muted, might be suitable and further help deflect Rachel's memory. The imposter would have to radiate competence, like her authentic professional self, but her appearance and manner had to be somewhat different. She brooded in her parlor, trying to hit on the perfect persona, then glanced out the window and spotted two nuns passing by with their starched white headdresses flapping in the wind that coursed down Eleventh Street. Ahhh. She could pretend to be a former—what did they call them?, women apprenticing to take holy vows? A postulant. She would be a postulant who had changed her mind. Yes, that would do nicely. And she was from Montreal, where she had kept house for—for the convent of the Little Sisters of—of the Holy Family. It was a quite sizable convent—two hundred or so in residence—so she was well versed in the needs of housekeeping for a large residence. After leaving the convent she had been with a family in Buffalo, people of considerable means, occupying one of the city's more splendid residences. And now she wished to locate with a fine family in New York. She would reveal all this in a voice slightly above a whisper, with just a soupçon of an accent. Some makeup would be needed, perhaps a little blue-gray under the eyes to age her. And perhaps a birthmark on her cheek, though nothing too disfiguring—hadn't Agatha Agapé once told her that a single prominent feature like that tended to distract from all the rest? And spectacles—definitely spectacles. She could buy them at the notions store on Eighth Avenue, and if she wore them low on her nose, she would not actually have to look *through* them. And she would rent an old dress and hat, clean and suitably unstylish, from the place on Hudson Street; an ex-postulant could look somber and even a bit shabby but never soiled.

* * *

The spectacle of upper Fifth Avenue unrolled before her eyes two days later as the hack made its way northward through the thinning traffic: palazzi, chateaux, villas, fortresses, all set down next to one another with little or no greensward in between, most running right out to the edge of the walkway in a hodgepodge. Each of them shrieked at the top of its voice that its owner possessed or was the beneficiary of a fortune. Her heart pounded in syncopation with the horse's hooves. Would Rachel's house be crenellated or columned, Gothic or Georgian? Did the girl crave such aesthetic excess? Well, perhaps she had had no choice. The lures of luxury were irresistible, especially if heaped on the young couple as a wedding gift.

No. 877 . . . 885 . . . 892 and there it was—898 Fifth Avenue. The house, built of white limestone with a gray slate mansard roof and arched windows on the first two stories, was rather smaller than most on the avenue but undeniably still a mansion. The place had a pleasing simplicity about it, and the little stone balustrade leading to the front door gave off an inviting air.

She paid the driver, unthinkingly adding a tip far too large for someone of her unfashionable, impecunious appearance. When he tried to return part of it to her she thanked him but declined, pleased that her incognito was working well. But a rush of uncertainty assaulted her as she mounted the front steps. She hesitated on the brink for a long moment, studying the enormous brass door-knocker and unconsciously fingering the silver crucifix that hung from the chain around her neck—the crowning touch and sole ornament of her drab costume. What if Rachel saw through it all? Well, what of it? Where was the immorality in what she was doing? Was it a crime to wish to observe the surroundings of the offspring of one's womb? With her cracked kid glove she lifted the knocker and let it fall. The deed was done.

The door was opened almost at once by a spritely maid whose light gray uniform much resembled the caller's dress. Shown into the great hall that proclaimed itself the height of fashion with its brass fireplace hood and dangling lamps, inlaid little tables, Oriental carpets and hanging draperies embroidered in Arabic calligraphy and flamboyant cartouches, the would-be keeper of the house was stricken by its massive overindulgence. It was, she had to remind herself, the latest thing; even Royal Postlethwaite, that peerless arbiter of fashion, had advocated in a recent column the inclusion of such a "Turkish corner" in the au courant home. The house, she decided, must belong to the senior Caldwells, who had assigned a wing to Rachel and her husband till they could find a place of their own.

She seated herself on a velvet settee with an extremely high back at the perfect angle to afford no comfort whatever. Two other women were there already, awaiting their turn to be interviewed. They eyed her furtively at first, then relaxed their scrutiny, secure that the shabby newcomer would offer them little competition.

The maid returned shortly with another applicant in tow, looking somewhat the worse for the ordeal, showed her out and ushered the first of the waiting pair into the drawing room at the end of the hall. Her interview lasted so briefly that Mrs. Memory wondered if the poor woman had suffered an attack of incontinence under the tension of the encounter. The next interview ran rather longer.

The effrontery of her ruse grew in her mind as the pendulum in the great hall clock beat against the quiet of the house, broken only by an occasional murmur escaping from the drawing room. What really was she doing here? While she was at it would she perhaps like to rummage through Rachel's closets and drawers, examining all her belongings in detail? Defiantly she raised her chin. She was merely applying for a job; no harm in that. And if the pay and the terms and the conditions and the people were adequate, why—why she might even consider taking it!

After she had taken mental inventory of every object within sight and speculated on its country of origin and price of purchase, she was at last shown into the drawing room. In contrast to the dimness of the hall, the large chamber, with the late-afternoon sun streaming through its west-facing windows, dazzled her eyes. She had to blink several times to allow them to adjust, adding somewhat to the humble appearance she projected. Rachel, she saw now, was seated at the far end of the room on an enormous, heavily carved armchair with an embroidered satin seat that looked very like a throne. A short distance away an elderly woman was perched on its twin, the seat so high for her short legs that only her toes reached the floor.

"Mrs. Caldwell?" She dropped a curtsy to the space between the two women in her uncertainty as to which of them she should be addressing.

"I am Mrs. Caldwell," Rachel spoke regally, pulling herself up farther in her chair. "Please come down this way so that I may speak with you." Her notion of protocol—or was it just bad manners?—excluded the need of identifying her older companion.

She moved past exquisitely carved Belter, with its curved cabriole legs, past velvet and brocade and silk, past depending yards of tassels and fringes and pom-poms on every shade and hanging, over bare parquet and ferocious tiger skins, fangs and glazed eyes intact, until she was within six feet of the two women. She curtsyed again.

"You may sit over there," Rachel directed with a sweep of her hand toward a low armless chair upholstered in a velvet stripe.

"Thank you, madame."

"And now would you kindly remove your hat so that we may have a better view of you?"

Damn. "As you wish, madame."

"And would you be good enough to speak up? My mother-in-law is slightly hard of hearing."

Double damn. "As you wish, madame."

"Now then—is that a French accent I detect?"

"Yes, madame—but I can assure you that my English is perfectly—"

"No need to explain. Being bilingual is hardly an impediment to a position here, Miss—?"

"De la Tour. Marie de la Tour, madame." There seemed to be not the merest glint of recognition in Rachel's look.

Invited to state her experience and credentials for the housekeeping position, she recited these slowly and clearly, gaining conviction with each new fabricated detail. She presented herself as a plain, even homely, woman with a sure sense of discipline and spiritual wholesomeness. Her want of beauty meant that few suitors would pursue her and intrude on the performance of her duties. The absence of family and friends nearby would likewise bind her more firmly to the household. And her obviously pressing need of self-support still further assured loyalty and perseverance. She could supply them, moreover, with several excellent references, Miss de la Tour concluded, reaching into her drawstring purse with confidence born of knowing she was herself the author of the commendations.

"That will not be necessary at this time," said Rachel. "The applicants who seem to us most promising will be asked to return next week. We will take references at that time."

"Very good, madame."

"You're wearing spectacles—how severely is your vision impaired, if I may ask, Miss de la Tour?"

She looked up at Rachel over the tops of the rims. "They are merely corrective, madame. With the years my sight has lessened fractionally. It is not unnatural. I can assure you it would in no way interfere with—"

"What does she say?" the elder Mrs. Caldwell asked her daughter-in-law. The first words she had uttered during the interview, they had a harsh, imperious edge to them.

"She says she sees quite well enough," Rachel told her.

"Does she always wear that large cross around her neck like that?"

The question, as Rachel's expression showed she knew, was wanting in tact, but it was too late to rephrase the offensive words. "Do you?" she asked the applicant as softly as the accoustics permitted.

"It is the symbol of my faith, madame. I am a regular worshipper, if that is the purpose of the question." She shifted her look from one Mrs. Caldwell to the other. "I had not thought the cross to be unseemly in appearance. If there is some restriction, however, against any display of the sort, I'd be quite happy to—"

"Does she say she's Catholic?" rasped the elder Mrs. Caldwell, a hand cupped behind her ear.

The applicant's eyes engaged Rachel Caldwell's. The young woman blinked several times in obvious embarrassment, but again she yielded to the indelicate thrust. "Are you, Miss de la Tour?"

"Is that pertinent, madame? The advertisement made no mention of—"

"No—of course. We're simply trying to—"

"At least she's not Irish, too," came the croak, "or is she?"

Embarrassment was giving way now to annoyance as Rachel turned to her mother-in-law. "Miss de la Tour is French Canadian, mother, and I should appreciate it if I were allowed to conduct the—"

"This is a Christian home, Miss—Whatever-Your-Name-Is—and someday soon there will be little ones, and we don't want them brought up with a lot of Latin mumbo-jumbo and endless fairytales about the saints."

"Mother!" broke from Rachel's mouth. She turned quickly back to the interviewee. "Miss de la Tour, would you please go to the far end of the room so I may speak in private—"

She retreated hastily, conscious with every step of the sharp whispers being exchanged behind her. The girl had some spunk, after all, thank the Lord.

On either side of the pair of windows facing out onto Fifth Avenue she encountered a set of life-size portraits of Rachel and her husband, dressed as they must have been on their wedding day. How unfortunate for the young woman, to be confronted for the rest of her life by an idealized vision of herself at the height of her bloom. A portrait should never be painted, she thought, until the subject's face had achieved a certain degree of character. That took some living. Forty years of age was the minimal span. The faces on the wall before her were too un-formed, too empty to express any meaning beyond the good fortune of their station.

"Miss de la Tour?"

The two Mrs. Caldwells had apparently resolved their wrangling over who would be mistress of the house. The applicant returned, but seeing that Rachel was standing now and her mother-in-law had abandoned her chair and positioned herself beside a window gazing out sternly, did not resume her seat.

"Your credentials are impeccable, miss," said Rachel, her voice tremulous with suppressed rage, "but I greatly fear you would not be happy employed in this household."

"If it is my faith, madame, I would swear an oath not to proselytize. It is many years now since I was in orders—"

"I am afraid that would make no real—"

"I believe faith to be an entirely private matter."

"I do not question your sincerity, miss, but it simply would not—"

"If madam would only take a moment to examine my references, I think that my character and conduct would be amply—"

"I'm sure you come highly recommended, but I cannot—cannot—"

"Cannot what, madame?"

"I—I need not justify myself to you, miss." Rachel turned aside.

"Certainly not, madame. I meant no impertinence. I just wish to understand what is the nature of the objection."

"I'm sorry, Miss de la Tour. Thank you for coming."

"I am very fine with children, madame. I think you would find—"

"Good day, miss."

She stood before her daughter in silence now, unable to retreat, unwilling to accept the girl's abject surrender to intolerance. Her eyes met Rachel's for a moment, then fell to the floor. "I—I—only wish—"

"You will not do, miss. Now you must really and truly leave."

"I—I—am badly in need of work, madame."

Rachel's bosom rose in a heavy, silent sigh. She blinked and fought to regain command of her emotions. "Are you hungry, Miss de la Tour?" she asked, her tone far softer.

"I—try not to—give in to—" Her shoulders slumped. "I am, madame. There are so many expenses in a strange city, and I was not prepared for—"

"Yes. Well, Katherine will show you to the kitchen, and cook will fix you something."

"Thank you, madame—"

"And now, good day, miss."

"—but I could not permit myself to break bread in a home that is ruled by such unjust and unmerciful standards. I should rather starve, madame. You are not worthy of my services. Good day to you."

Mrs. Memory, who had not prayed in years, addressed the Deity directly now as she hurried away down the avenue in search of a hack. Do not, dear Lord, she implored, allow this lovely child to succumb further to the petty and brutish values of her new relations as the price for accepting their wealth. And then she allowed herself to wonder, for the first time, if the manifold blessings visited upon the girl might not have come at the cost of her soul. "Cabbie!"

Without asking her, Mrs. Memory knew how Agatha Agapé had just happened to be at the front door to let Harry Loring in when he arrived to call for her. The landlady had been watching for him through her front window with the curtains drawn back and the lights out, and when the carriage clatter stopped before the house she peeked out to confirm the identity of the arriving passenger. As he climbed the stoop to the front door, she had scooted up the inside steps in time to receive him just at the moment his hand reached for the bellpull. The incorrigibly romantic old woman was no less aroused by Harry's appearance than the object of his attention was herself.

Perhaps if he had chosen a less showy means of inviting her out for the evening than the three dozen roses—by way of partial compensation for the unavoidable hiatus in their friendship, his card said—the actress would not have been so intrigued. But the gesture recalled her own glory days, and she pined to associate, even fleetingly, with a young sport again. If, furthermore, Mrs. Memory had been home instead of at the orphanage with Mrs. Dane when the flowers came, Miss Agapé would have remained in ignorance of Harry's existence. Once having discovered it, however, she was not satisfied by Mrs. Memory's perfunctory explanation that he was "just somebody" she had met in Florida. His extravagance suggested a greater intimacy, meriting Miss Agapé's closer inspection. Behind his back now, as Madeleine Memory opened her door to readmit Harry Loring into her life, her landlady stood nodding emphatically in approval of this devilishly attractive physical specimen.

No embrace followed the closing of the door. She kept a clearly understood distance between them. Harry, if he was surprised, gave no hint of disappointment. "Very pleasant," he said, scanning her parlor, then took possession of her sofa without an invitation and spread his arms expansively across its back. "How have you been?" he asked, the sweep of his eyes taking her in from hemline to coiffure.

That damned, calm self-assurance, the assumption that he could do no wrong that she had thought so stimulating and attractive in Palm Beach she now found infuriating. How dare he treat her as an object of convenience, to be ignored for two entire months until someone or something reminded him of her existence—and then to materialize in her parlor without a hint of contrition and only a shower of rose petals having paved his way. Could he believe he was so alluring to her that nothing had changed between them?

"Just fine," she said with a mechanical smile, taking the chair opposite the sofa. They exchanged chatter no weightier than a feather, Harry forfeiting the chance that every lull provided to explain himself, until he looked at his watch and announced they had better leave. He had arranged with Charles, the manager at Del's, for them to arrive for dinner at nine; the carriage was waiting. He hoped she would not mind, he said, as he helped her with her wrap, that he had already worked out the menu. And afterward there was to be a little surprise entertainment that he thought would amuse her. Harry Loring was back, in his customary style. The scoundrel.

She sat in the corner of the carriage, as far away from him as possible, and still he made no effort to narrow the gap—a tacit acquiescence to her pique? "Maddy," he said at last, breaking the uncivil silence between them, "there were reasons—"

"Of course."

"A number of things happened all at the same—"

"They're of no interest to me, I can assure you." Then why had she accepted his invitation for the evening? She had struggled with the question a dozen times since his roses had arrived. There may indeed have been reasons for his long silence, but none could excuse his behavior. If there was to be any relationship between them, it would have to begin over. She would give him that much chance and no more.

"Maddy, you should at least hear what I—"

"The subject is closed."

His lips tightened and eyes strayed from hers. "As you wish, madam."

It was her first visit to Delmonico's new location on Fifth Avenue, opened only a few weeks earlier. She was enchanted by the elegance of the small, baroque palace with its little balcony punctuated by electric globes that threw down a softening glow on the wrought-iron-covered doors. As they swung open, Charles the manager greeted Harry so promptly that he appeared to have been awaiting their arrival. He led the two of them across the main dining room through a set of French doors to a small private room off to the side. Harry guided her firmly by the elbow as they followed the manager, waving with his free hand at diners who hailed him, but not stopping to chat or introduce his companion.

"I've never seen you in that color before," he said after the manager had seated them. "Violet is most becoming to you."

"Thank you." Reflexively her hand went up to touch the string of amethyst beads at her neck. "You look well yourself—I trust your health has not been impaired?" That at least would have explained his disappearance; even so, he could have sent word to her . . .

"Maddy, my health had nothing to do with—"

"I'm so pleased." She reached at once for the little card on the table in front of her. "Now what clever thing have you planned for us?" Her eyes ran down the menu to the bottom of the list: *Gateau Chocolat Madeleine.* How beguiling of him to have remembered her weakness for pastry. But she steeled herself against playing into his hands by softening her manner.

Magically a waiter appeared to open their champagne, and then another with their oysters. She had never seen so many. Cool and sweet, they effortlessly disappeared down her throat. "The last of the season," Harry said. "Charles told me that after tomorrow there won't be an oyster left in the city."

Their carefully circumscribed talk dwelt on the food, the city's latest curiosities, plays they had seen, inconsequential stories each had heard, as the waiters replaced platters and refilled their glasses. The beef was tender enough to cut with her fork edge, the asparagus properly piquant, the mushrooms huge yet succulent. And the chocolate cake, layered with crushed raspberries and laced with *framboise,* tasted as sinfully exquisite as the slice she had had with him at their hotel tea. Probably she had never had a better meal in her entire life. Its cost, she reflected, could undoubtedly have paid half the price of a used spinet for the orphanage.

The carriage was waiting when they emerged. Harry had conspired a deluxe evening from beginning to end. Without instructions the driver turned them around and trotted the carriage up Fifth, then left before the park, stopping at a massive structure on the corner of Seventh. It was not her part of the city. Her eyes inquiringly surveyed the building. "The Navarro Flats," Harry said. "We're going to see a friend of mine."

The elevator rose slowly to the ninth floor and let them out into a small hallway with two doors, both open. Leading her through the one into the salon where guests in evening clothes were consuming champagne in tall, fluted goblets, he brought her at once to a bald, portly fellow who was dispensing pleasantries in all directions. "Eric Bemis, the best producer in New York—this is Madeleine Memory, the loveliest lady in town."

"Why not the entire nation?" he asked with a grin and took her hand in greeting. "That's Harry for you—always understating the case."

"It befits his modesty," she said with a smile.

Both men laughed agreeably, and Bemis wished the couple an enjoyable evening before excusing himself. "The show must go on, you know."

The crowd had already begun drifting across the hall to the other room, where a dozen rows of chairs had been set up to form a miniature theater. By the time she and Harry took seats at the extreme left of the front row, Bemis was standing at the front of the room, looking every inch the impresario beside a grand piano framed by a high-arched window. He waited for the clatter to die down. "Ladies and gents," he began, "it's my custom to skip the rigamarole on these happy occasions. Let me simply introduce the incomparable stars of my forthcoming production, *Belle of the Balsam Woodlands,* who will perform several of its musical numbers for you this evening. Without further ado, please welcome Cicely Fanshawe and Anthony Porter!"

Goodness! There they were in the flesh, not three arm-lengths in front of her—the stellar musical performers of the New York stage. She and Mr. Sprague had seen them just before her departure for Florida in *Gertrude's Golden Gladiator,* a delightful confection that had run for a good eight months. How inspired of Harry to bring her here. Why had he not mentioned in Palm Beach, when she spoke of her fondness for the theater, that Eric Bemis was a friend of his? What else had he omitted? A very great deal, no doubt.

The songs, accompanied on the piano by Bemis himself, were gay, the singers radiantly persuasive, trilling to each other as if truly in love— which, according to Miss Agapé, who heard it from a friend who had a friend who knew Porter, they most definitely were not. But they were masters of illusion, conveying the intensity of young love by locking onto each other's eyes, touching hands ever so lightly and blending voices in fine harmony. The well-heeled audience appeared spellbound.

At the close of the performance Bemis came around the piano to thank his guests for attending—"and imbibing," he added slyly—and noted that his office was in the Old Knickerbocker theater on Fourteenth Street west of Sixth Avenue, in case anyone had forgotten. He expected that he would be seeing many of his listeners there in the near future.

"Eric has a problem," Harry explained as they settled back into the carriage. The producer lived on a constant merry-go-round, staging plays, a high proportion of them successful, and gambling away his profits in card games. Presently deep in debt, he had included some of his gambling associates among the guests invited to the recital in order to convince them to buy shares in his next venture; it was their best hope of getting repaid.

"Then strictly speaking, he is your prey rather than your friend?"

"The two are not incompatible, my dear."

"I see," she said, aligning her beads. "And will you back him in this new play?"

"I might. The earlier creditors among his backers get paid first." He was closer to her now. "What do you think I ought to do?"

"I'd say it really isn't much of a gamble. Fanshawe and Porter perform beautifully together—" She let the words hang for a moment, at once regretting their unintended application to themselves. "The new play should be a rage." She slid away from him.

"If it's such a sure thing, perhaps you'd like to take a piece of it yourself?"

"I think not. Widows and orphans are ill-advised to risk their meager lucre on the stage." She looked out the window. They seemed to be retracing their route down Fifth Avenue. "Not more food?"

"No, my dear," he smiled and patted her ambiguously on the wrist. "Canfield's Saratoga Club." It was located right next to Del's.

She had heard of the place, of course, but never dreamed of visiting it. Its clientele was reputed to consist of the wealthiest people in New York—nearly everyone she had ever read about in Postlethwaite's column had been there at one time or another.

Harry took her arm, more firmly now than before, and guided her on a tour of the downstairs rooms furnished with the finest of carpets, sofas, tapestries and paintings, all corroborative of the reports that Richard Canfield was a peerless connoisseur as well as a panderer to the vices of the socially elite.

"You come often?" she asked Harry.

"A couple of times a week—mostly to see who's in town. Occasionally I avail myself of the gaming facilities."

The scarcity of women on the premises aroused her curiosity. Were they unwelcome, she wondered. Not in the least, he reassured her; women could attend but neither observe nor participate in the gambling. "Most of the regular fellows prefer to come alone because they don't want to be distracted." He suggested they head upstairs, where she might be more comfortable among the other women in the reception area.

The second floor was still more sumptuous than the first—the carpets thicker, cushions softer, paintings larger and by more renowned artists. She recognized a Landseer on the wall that had been reproduced as an engraving in *Harper's Weekly* several years earlier when Canfield had bought it at auction. Her glance was distracted by a group of men moving purposefully through a door into the room behind them. "That's where the low-stakes card games are played," Harry murmured. "When the pots are big enough and we don't want anybody looking over our shoulders, we repair to a strictly private room on the fourth floor." Unfortunately, she was barred from viewing the action.

"And why exactly is that?"

"Chivalry, madam. The fair sex must be shielded from unpleasant sights and potentially explosive displays of temperament, as happens on rare occasion." On the third floor, he explained, were rooms devoted to faro and roulette, games that did not attract him, he said, because they offered so little opportunity for him to apply his talents; luck played too heavy a part in them for any real money to be made.

"And you don't believe in luck?"

"Believing in it is different from relying on it. Only nincompoops rely on luck."

"Hear, hear," called out a dark-haired, thickset man of medium height and perfect tailoring who had come up behind them and overheard Harry's last pronouncement.

Harry wheeled around. "Richard!" he said with a smile. "You must forgive the heresy."

"My heresy is your creed."

"Touché. Mrs. Memory, may I present the honorable Richard Canfield, proprietor of all this splendor."

He turned a broad smile on her. "Welcome to Canfield's, madam." He did not faintly resemble "the wickedest man in New York," as she had seen him referred to in the papers; he struck her more as a kindly, clean-shaven uncle than the devil incarnate.

"You have a lovely establishment, Mr. Canfield—handsome beyond its praises."

"We aim to please, madam," the proprietor said with a slight dip of his shoulders meant as a rudimentary bow.

"The decor and appointments are as greatly appealing to our so-called gentler sex, I should say, as to your male patrons."

"That was surely the intention. Women grace our little home away from home with their presence."

"Their presence, though, I gather from Mr. Loring, would be awkward at your tables."

"Unfortunately, Mrs. Memory, a certain profane character sometimes accompanies the play. I fear the ladies would be offended by it—"

"Or the players uncomfortably inhibited?"

"Just so."

"How sad. I should think some of your female guests might find the contests highly diverting."

Canfield's professional smile thinned. "Perhaps. But—as I say—the ungenteel aspects—in view of women's more fragile sensibilities—"

"Some women—if I might venture the opinion, sir—have more rugged constitutions than men are generally inclined to credit them with. I should hazard the guess, Mr. Canfield, that there might even be some women who would relish participating firsthand in your stimulating activities."

Canfield flicked a look at Harry, then turned back to his companion. "Mrs. Memory, do you believe a true lady would ever indulge in such a pastime?"

"If a true gentleman taught her how."

"But then they would no longer be true gentlemen, madam—in my humble view." Canfield bowed, more deeply this time, and took his leave.

"Maddy!" Harry growled.

"I was merely making conversation."

"You were practically making a speech. Suffragists are not among his clientele."

"Nor are they ever likely to be." She lifted her chin.

"Nevertheless, it's a model establishment of its kind," said Harry, "honest as the day is long—aside from the fact that, strictly speaking, the place operates outside the law." It was far easier for the operator of a gambling house to be honest than to try to cheat, Canfield had told him; gamblers took money from each other, after all, not from the house. Canfield's secret was that he was not greedy, settling for a profit of little more than five percent on the gross receipts—quite enough to fill the owner's pockets and maintain the civilized atmosphere of the establishment. "Why, I'd like to own it myself."

She took his arm as they reached the head of the staircase. "Is that your ultimate ambition in life, Mr. Loring—to operate an illegal casino?"

"Of the best sort only. Not quite so airless as this one, though. It's too dark in here. You can't find the windows. In my place you could breathe—"

An outcry on the staircase a floor above them interrupted him. "You run a crooked wheel," someone was heard shouting. "I don't owe you a thing—I want my money back!"

"Just a moment," Harry told her and bounded halfway up the landing to see what the disturbance was about. She followed him up at a slower pace. Midway, she saw a cluster of five men, including Canfield, surrounding a singularly agitated customer. "His name's Rudge," Harry whispered to her over his shoulder; the man was a poor gambler and a worse loser. He had borrowed from the house that night to cover his losses and proceeded to lose some more; in his fury he had grabbed back his IOU from one of Canfield's aides and torn it up, claiming the roulette game had been rigged against him.

Rudge pushed through the circle of Canfield's men, waved his fist at them. "I'm going straight to the authorities! I'll tell the world what kind of sty you're running here—and you'll be out of business by morning!"

As the man charged down the steps Harry intercepted him with open arms. "Excuse me, sir," he said loud enough to be heard by Canfield and his crew above them, "I couldn't help noticing the disturbance and wondered if I might be of some assistance. Burbank is my name—Assistant Chief Inspector Burbank."

Forehead moist, eyes watery, jaw trembling, Rudge stopped to catch his breath and mop his face with the handkerchief Harry offered him from his own pocket. The gesture seemed to recall him to his senses. "Inspector?" he said, the meaning of Harry's words dawning on him. "What sort of inspector?"

"The usual sort," said Harry, declining the return of his kerchief. "In here we prefer not to wear our badges."

"*We?* You're all in on it?"

"I'm not sure what you're referring to, sir. Mr. Canfield is a gentleman running a gentlemen's establishment. All gentlemen are welcome here."

"I—how can you—" The short-necked, roseate Mr. Rudge was reduced to speechless rage before shoving past Harry and half-stumbling downstairs in his futility. When he was out of sight a chorus of laughter and applause cascaded down from the third-floor landing. Harry replied with a single crisp salute, then waved farewell and guided his companion down to their carriage.

He was quiet on the ride back downtown, letting her decide how the evening would conclude. But she had made that decision before it began, and no amount of his disarming conduct, no expenditure of cash or charm or derring-do, would shake her resolution. If he cared for her truly, he would understand.

As they neared her house she asked him to come in for a nightcap; that would be very pleasant, he allowed, squeezing her hand before opening the carriage door to help her out. He had a discreet word with the driver, to whom he handed some bills, and as Harry came back to walk her up the steps, she saw the carriage pull away from the curb and continue down Eleventh Street.

She poured them sherries and came to sit beside him on the sofa. Their knees were almost touching as she slowly turned the stem of the little glass between her fingers. "It's been a wonderful evening," she began, "and I'm sure it must have cost an enormous amount—"

"Not worth your thinking twice about."

"And I did have a glorious time—"

"The effect I was hoping to achieve."

"But I have to tell you"—she stopped to take a breath—"that if you think you're going to climb into bed with me in five minutes, you had better think again."

His head shot backward. "Maddy, I don't understand—"

"I think you understand perfectly."

"Some unexpected things happened—and there were a lot of loose ends I had to tie up before I felt I could—well, it took me some time to—"

"And it never occurred to you to wonder what I might be thinking or doing all that while? If there had only been so much as a postcard from you to say you were aware I existed. Would that have been too much to ask?"

"A postcard! You mean a very great deal more to me than—"

"But how was I to know? I can't read your mind. I felt—deserted—abandoned. Do you think I'm the sort of woman who"—her hands groped the air for the proper euphemism—"dispenses her favors lightly?"

"Hardly. But I—"

"No one who truly cared would just disappear the way you did, without a word. What had I done? I went back over all the time we'd spent together, and I hadn't a clue."

"Maddy, it had nothing whatever to do with you. It was simply—"

"Insensitivity and selfishness."

Reprimand had turned to rebuke, and equanimity deserted him. "Look, Maddy, when all is said and done, I don't owe you any—"

"I emphatically disagree—but I don't wish to debate the matter. I'm pleased you asked me to join you this evening, and I had a splendid time of it, but I'm not going to thank you in bed—not when you hurt my feelings so. You've been thoughtless and presumptuous and—and utterly impossible, that's all." She turned away from him and tried to control her shaking long enough to take a sip of her sherry. "Now get out of here before I change my mind."

By the time she looked around again, he had let himself out the door.

Mrs. Memory held the needle closer to the window and tried to thread it again. No good. She bit the end off the wisp of thread and attempted it a third time. Finally. Was her hand less steady or were her eyes going bad? A thing like that used to be no trouble at all for her, and now . . . Perhaps eyeglasses for use just around the flat were in order.

She picked up the petticoat. The chore itself was nearly as disagreeable as her apparent inability to accomplish it any longer with ease. Of all the pointless, irksome tasks women had to perform, sewing protective strips of cloth to the bottoms of their petticoats was the most tedious.

The clink of the bronze mail slot and the thud of the morning post hitting the hall floor outside her door readily drew her from her sewing. Not that she was specifically expecting to hear from anyone that day, but she had written to Miss Sanderson a while back and a response might arrive any time now.

Picking up the letters that lay scattered on the carpet, she noted that, as usual, most of them were for Mr. Sprague with a few items for the Danes; perhaps every second day something came for her. She made two neat piles of them on the hall table as a courtesy to her neighbors. The last item in the collection was a postcard depicting the golden thrust of *le tour Eiffel,* set against an impossibly blue Parisian sky with a mass of greenery at its base. She had seen pictures of the tower in the papers when it was opened seven or eight years earlier. Peculiar thing, thrillingly but unnecessarily tall.

She flipped the card over and found it addressed to her. Instinct told her at once who had sent it and drove her scurrying through her open door so she could read the message in private: M., it said, *here is the postcard you wanted. Touring la belle France on business. Will be here till approx. mid-July. Be well. H.*

The damnable man! When she had not heard from him for two weeks after the evening they had spent together she concluded that ultimately he cared only for her physical favors. What *other* inference could she possibly have drawn? Now this.

She picked up her petticoat again and took two stitches, but the postcard had so upset her that she could not go on. If he was no longer interested in her, why had he bothered sending the card? If it had been intended only as a farewell gesture, a sort of wave from a distant shore, why the allusion to his midsummer return? Unless he had sent it as an insolent act to pay back her rebuff, a way of saying that even if she dearly wanted him now, she would be unable to see him for months. The wait would be even longer than he knew, for two days earlier she had concluded arrangements to serve, for an attractive wage, as assistant manager/housekeeper at a resort lodge of heavily upholstered rusticity in the Adirondacks, a two-hour carriage ride west of Saratoga Springs; the position would keep her out of the city until September.

Her head was growing muddled from the turbulence the postcard had stirred up. She had to talk about it with someone or she would scream from frustration. Who better than Agatha? A similar situation must have arisen in her life, perhaps repeatedly.

Shown in by Rose Maude, Agatha's former dresser who had continued in her employ after the close of her stage career, she found the retired actress seated at her dressing table, back to the door, carefully massaging her right cheek. "Take the big seat, Maddy," she called cheerfully over her shoulder. "I'll turn around in just a minute."

Like a grateful patient anticipating expert release from distress, she did as she was told, feeling enveloped in the yards of velvet that covered the enormous wing chair, a prop, no doubt, from one of Agatha's stage triumphs.

"There." A final swish of a feathery powder puff, and the ex–leading lady spun around on her revolving stool to face her visitor. "What do you think?"

The right side of Agatha's face had taken on a distinctly Oriental cast with a yellow-brown tint to the skin, a circle of red cheek and an eye upswept at the outer corner. The left side of her face, devoid of makeup, looked eerily lifeless by comparison. The effect, heightened by the actress's incongruously red hair, was both bizarre and a little sinister. "Mr. Pangborn is coming for a visit this evening," she explained, "and he remembers me best as Oo-Ling in *Pigtail Paradise*. I was just making sure I hadn't forgotten how to do the makeup, but it seemed wasteful to do my whole face."

"Agatha, I'm sure he'll love you, however you look."

"Illusion is all, my girl—why take the chance?" She got up and moved briskly to the chaise longue, her dressing gown trailing gracefully over its side as she composed herself on it. "Now to what do I owe the pleasure of your unexpected visit? Let me guess—it's about a man, isn't it? That devilishly good-looking one who sent the flowers, I'd say. Oh, I do love the look of a man with a scar. It gives him a rather piratical air, don't you think—so roguish."

That thread of tissue that ran vertically along his upper forehead and disappeared beneath his scalp line she had never considered a disfigurement; rather, it added interest to his otherwise too even features. Its origin, now that Agatha called her attention to it, he had never disclosed.

"He's presenting you with a problem and you want my advice?"

She nodded but did not know where to begin. Delicacy was not Agatha's strong suit, and restraint was Madeleine Memory's habit.

"Out with it, my dear girl. It won't be anything I haven't heard before."

It came out with a rush. Not every last detail, but enough for the older woman to understand it all.

"And after your dinner at Del's," Agatha said, with her severely plucked brows raised, "and the musicale at Eric's—oh, the poor man must be in a terrible pickle—he would never have sold off parts of his productions in the old days—and after the visit to Canfield's and the carriage and all that effort on his part, you sent the man packing without—his reward?"

"I will *not* be taken for granted, he badly hurt my feelings—"

"And he arranged that glorious evening to apologize to you."

"He didn't seem apologetic—"

"Did you give him a chance to apologize—or were you standing on your high horse, the way you sound now to me?"

"I—well—I wasn't interested in stories. The fact of his behavior was undeniable—"

"So was the fact of his apology. The man set up the most elaborate seduction I've heard of since Vinnie de Montvert bought a yacht to cruise to Long Beach Island with me back in seventy-seven. Forgive me, dear girl, but I think you missed the boat. Some men don't apologize well. Their coming around is the best they can arrange."

"Perhaps. But can't I have my dignity, Agatha?"

"He wanted your *acceptance,* Maddy—not your damn dignity. He knows all about that." She shook her head. "What's happened since?"

"Just this." She handed Agatha the postcard from Paris.

The actress scanned it, then snapped her fingers as if instructing Rose Maude. "Maddy, darling, reach into the right drawer of my dressing table, like a good girl. There's a box of cigarettes and some matches in there. And fetch that little dish on the tabletop. A cigarette helps concentrate the mind." Agatha set the postcard on her lap as she lit the cigarette, then studied the writing while she inhaled. "What does he mean by 'the postcard you wanted'?"

"I think I told him it was the least he could have done when he was avoiding me for whatever reason. All I meant was—"

"Well, now you have it—but not him." She let a plume of smoke gather above her head. "I must say, though, that the tone does border on the arrogant." The oriental and occidental eyes both regarded her fixedly. "Does he know you'll be away when he's due back?"

"No."

"Ah. Well, then, I think I have it. When you were a child, what did you do when you wanted to mock someone—but not too severely?"

"I stuck my tongue out, I suppose."

"In my neighborhood we inserted our thumbs in our ears and waggled our fingers. If we felt *very* naughty, we put a thumb to our nose and did likewise. I think that's what your Harry is doing to you. It's a schoolboy gesture. He's thumbing his nose at you, telling you that you can't see him even if you wanted to—so *there*. But he's thinking about you, all right. Yes, indeed. It's a little like the time when I toured in *Fedora*, and Baron von Einhaupt decided to—" She cut herself short. "But we needn't go into *that* now." She stubbed out her cigarette. "I would place a very large wager that you will see this Harry again."

Mrs. Memory was uncertain whether to be cheered or chagrined by the prediction. "And what of it?"

"I have no wish to pry, my girl, but answer one question for me if it's not too personal. When you were—intimate—with this gentleman, were you—pleasantly occupied?"

Mrs. Memory gave a single nod.

"Then I have a short piece of advice for you, dear child, that you will ignore at your everlasting peril. Grasp every opportunity for pleasure in this life with both hands and hold it tight. The world is too hard and our time in it altogether too short to spend it standing on principle." She drew herself upright. "This principle business becomes very tiring."

WHITE PLUME INN

South Corinth, New York

20 July 1897

Dear Agatha,

Greetings from the wilds of this bracing country!

I have never worked amid such surroundings before. It is a finicky crowd, pretending to rough it but truly wanting all the comforts of Murray Hill and Beacon Hill. They are on horseback half the day and in canoes the other half, or so it seems—all very athletic and redolent of leather, pine and perspiration. At night everyone appreciates the great crackling fire in the main room, finding it all the more hypnotic in proportion to the port and brandy that both sexes consume in amazing quantities.

The cuisine is tasty but gamy, bear steak and porcupine pie being local delicacies with which I had been previously (and not unhappily) unacquainted. The decor runs heavily to knotty pine and antlers—I cannot believe there is a buck left alive in all the Adirondacks since every room and corridor here is outfitted with one or more sets of horns. The air is marvelously refreshing, dry and clear by day, chilled and wild but fragrant after dark, with far fewer insects than I was prepared to tolerate.

The only trouble is that my time is never my own. It is a round-the-clock sort of job, seven days a week, and I must fight for time off now and then to read and do a bit of mending. Alas, it is too far to go anywhere else when I manage to wangle free—my carriage should have to turn right around by the time I reached what is laughably referred to as "civilization" up here. Aside from feeling thus imprisoned, all is well and I trust the same with you. I remain,

> Yours fondly,
> Maddy

> 131 West Eleventh St.
> New York City
> 30 July 1897

Maddy dear—

Thanks for remembering this old trooper. Yrs. of the 20th most welcome.

Curiously your letter and the enclosure arrived almost together. I am sending it on immediately, knowing as I do who the writer is. I hope you don't mind my reading it, but it *is* a postcard, after all. Since you conferred with me about the previous card, I've taken the liberty of addressing some thought to this one.

She removed the card, its front picturing Anne Hathaway's Cottage, and flipped it over. Its message, in the flowing hand she recognized at once, read: *Delayed return. Am in England with a friend. Here till end of August. H.*

How odd. No fond wishes, no promise of reunion. And why the cryptic reference to "a friend"? She turned back for counsel to Agatha, who wrote:

Even if, as I first thought, there is some nose-thumbing going on here, I believe the amount has diminished. I am not certain I like the anonymous friend he refers to. If female, then in writing about her, he is no gentleman, in which case you must forget him completely. But that is not at all the impression you gave me, so we must assume H. to be a gentleman still and everything is on the up-and-up.

I think the card actually brings good tidings to you, Maddy, if you care to read them so. Of course, I may be wrong in this, as I was with Fabian Carruthers—remind me to tell you about *him* when you get back. He was one of my real disappointments.

Things here are much the same, the heat beastly. I do the park and visit the Rockaway beach now and then but mostly fan myself and wait for blessed autumn. Your arrangement sounds far preferable. Enjoy it.

Best love,
A. A.

The hotel canopy, she saw, had been done over. In her time at the Buckingham it had been green with gold lettering. The new maroon one with white writing would not clash so gratingly with the blue carpeting in the lobby, which remained just as she remembered it. The gilded statue of the Duke of Buckingham was still waving his plumed hat under the Buckingham coat of arms. The heavy mahogany woodwork continued to gleam waxily. The draperies with their thick velvet folds and rows of silk fringe retained their wispy patina of dust no matter how often they got brushed. And the navy-blue walls and carpeting exuded the same funereal refinement as ever. Rejoicing inwardly that the lobby's appearance was no longer her responsibility, Madeleine Memory judged that the whole effect would have been less suffocating if done in lighter shades.

Miss Armbruster would meet her in the Villiers Dining Room, her note had said. The captain who showed her to the table was a new man and did not know her, but the dining-room manager and the wine steward both smiled and bowed in her direction. It was gratifying, she thought, to be recognized at one of the finest hotels in New York, even if not as a distinguished guest.

Her hostess rose to greet her, kissing her on both cheeks. Miss Armbruster looked splendid, Mrs. Memory told her; the complexion that she remembered as sallow was now prettily flushed, and her gray-streaked hair, formerly worn in a plain bun, was now almost stylishly ringleted. "It's because I have a secret," the head housekeeper of the Buckingham Hotel told her former chief assistant, "and no one must know." She was to be married the following spring; Mrs. Memory recognized the prospective groom's name as that of the hotel's longtime house physician. The bride was to acquire three stepchildren in the bargain.

"How splendid for you," Mrs. Memory said quite sincerely, for Miss Armbruster had a tendency to mother everyone around her, from the chambermaids to her chief subordinate. Still, it would be a sizable household for her to manage.

"Yes. And Gideon—Dr. Maxwell—has said he will not tolerate the idea of my working under any roof but his, so I'm afraid the Buckingham will have to do without my services after the first of next April."

Between the broth and the lamb stew Miss Armbruster proceeded to elaborate on her reasons for asking Mrs. Memory to the luncheon. "My present assistant—no doubt you'll remember Miss Attles—has the approximate disposition of a gallon of vinegar. She does her job well enough but she's very hard to swallow. None of the girls likes working for her. Frankly I should hate for her to take over for me—the job pays nicely, by the way—so I was hoping, Madeleine, that I could persuade you to fill the vacancy when I leave."

Before Mrs. Memory could react, Miss Armbruster hurried to meet all her possible objections. "I presume you must be committed to go back to Florida this winter, but you would not have to take over for me until at least several weeks after your return. It would not conflict with your schedule at all. And you know the hotel inside out and almost everyone in it—they're mostly nice, reliable, very professional people. And I know Mr. Chambers would be delighted to have you back—he still asks about you, you know."

To become head housekeeper at the Buckingham had once been the pinnacle of her ambitions. The salary would certainly be satisfactory, and the conditions could not be improved upon. Minerva Armbruster was a truly splendid soul to have remembered her in this fashion—and she told her so while wiping a corner of her eye with a monogrammed napkin.

But returning to work full-time was hardly an appealing prospect, not so long as she was able to cover her expenses nicely and put a little something by while working no more than half the year and in places more comfortable than New York, with its often severe winters and oppressive summers. And in the more temperate seasons she was able now to live like a lady, in pleasant surroundings, with the leisure to follow her random pursuits, or none at all, as her mood dictated. She had been thinking lately that perhaps she might devote herself more seriously to the piano.

"You've a strange expression on your face," the older woman said, "as if I've brought you a very mixed blessing. There is no reason you need to give me an answer now. This is October sixth—take the next few months to think about it. You can let me know any time before mid-February—though, I daresay, the sooner, the better. I would like to have something positive to tell Mr. Chambers when I go in to see him. The shock of my leaving would be greatly mitigated if I could tell him that you would be taking over for me."

It was highly reassuring to know that the top position was waiting for her at the Buckingham should any complications affect her situation at the Royal Poinciana this winter. She smiled back her agreement not to decide until required to. "Meanwhile," she added, "I do hope you and Dr. Maxwell will come visit me sometime—he must be told what a jewel he's going to be getting."

Mr. Sprague, though unaware of her prior exposure to the production, had chosen *Belle of the Balsam Woodlands* with her in mind. True, the critics had been dour in greeting its opening the previous week, but the fact that she had heard some of the music during the recital at Eric Bemis' made discovering where the songs fit into the story all the more appealing for her.

What pleased her most of all was her capacity to separate this performance emotionally from the one she had attended in the spring the last time she saw Harry Loring—and to enjoy it without bitterness; it was as if the evening marked the opening of a new chapter in her life.

On the sidewalk after the final curtain call Mr. Sprague took her arm and headed them down the block toward Benedetto's Ice Cream Parlor, where they had made it a habit to indulge in a post-performance phosphate. They were still caught up in the exiting crowd when she thought she heard a male voice behind her shout her name. She glanced back but saw no one she recognized. Whoever it was had probably called "Matty!" She hurried to match Mr. Sprague's quickening pace; he did not like being stuck in throngs.

"Mrs. Memory!" This time the voice was close by. As she turned, a hand reached out for her shoulder and stopped her. Even in the mid-block darkness she saw that it was Harry Loring, breathing hard from running to catch up to her. "Didn't you—hear me call you?"

Emotions fused and dissipated in a numbing instant. "Excuse me, sir. You must have me confused with another woman."

"Maddy!"

"I don't know you." She turned her head away and shook her shoulder, freeing it from his grip. As his hand fell away her feet unfroze and drove her in pursuit of Mr. Sprague, who had become separated from her by the flow of the crowd in the few seconds she had been delayed.

"Who was that?" Mr. Sprague asked, regaining her arm.

"Don't give it another thought—I certainly won't."

Alone in her parlor, gathering her senses after Mr. Sprague had bid her his usual chaste adieu at her door, she told herself that what she had done was right. He had not written a line to her after the postcard from England, had communicated with her in no way whatever. She was better off with no Harry Loring in her life, forever wondering about him and his whereabouts and what feelings, if any, he might still have toward her.

She sat at the piano and derived almost perverse pleasure from softly picking out the notes to the title song of *Belle of the Balsam Woodlands*.

Agatha, having elaborately recounted how she had received the rope of very large pearls that descended to her waist, wanted to go on to the provenance of the intricately carved jade bracelet on her wrist. But with more than customary tact she decided that the story would likely offend Mrs. Dane, who, in order not to hear it, was saying something that Mrs. Memory was not listening to.

"Excuse me? Do have another one of these apple tarts, they're very good," Mrs. Memory urged, all but angling the contents of the tray onto Mrs. Dane's lap.

"Thank you," said the well-padded guest, removing one of the tarts to her plate. "I asked whether you were up to playing this afternoon. I brought music with me this time—if that was all right."

"And why not?" She reached out for Mrs. Dane's copies of "Quite Lonely the Sunset" and "Sands Through the Hourglass Are Tumbling." Thank the Lord for Agatha's saucy selections or they'd all wind up a mass of congealed treacle.

The loneliness of the sunset as the grains of sand tumbled through the hourglass caused Mrs. Dane's voice to become thinner and thinner until, at the end, it was just a tiny whisper—a most dramatic effect that prompted Agatha, smiling through teary eyes, to call "Brava!" three times and announce that she herself would be unable to perform unless fortified by a drop or two of sherry. It was promptly provided. She swallowed the contents of the glass in a single recuperative gulp and handed Mrs. Memory a sheet of dog-eared music that she told them all had first been performed by Amelia Llewellyn at Niblo's Garden more than forty years before. "I had the privilege of singing it in Baltimore in sixty-five—it was just a month after I had narrowly missed being cast in *Our American Cousin* and thus being in Ford's Theater the night Mr. Lincoln was killed—but I can't remember now whether this came from *Delaware Dahlia* or *Mermaid's Lament*. We were also doing *Guinivere's Other Love* that season, but of course that wasn't a musical."

No sooner had Mrs. Memory sounded the final chord on the piano than the front door bell rang. No one, it seemed from their collective looks, expected any guests, certainly not on a Sunday afternoon at tea-time. Mr. Dane went to see who it might be, leaving open the door to Mrs. Memory's flat. They could hear murmurs in the hallway, and then

Mr. Dane reappeared with someone immediately behind him. "Mrs. Memory," he said with a quizzical look, "this gentleman asked for you. I thought rather than—"

Only one image sprang to Mrs. Memory's mind, and the instant after it had done so, Mr. Dane stepped aside and the figment came to life on her threshold.

"Sorry to be late," he said with a thin smile at her across the room and a half-bow to her guests. "Deucedly difficult to find a cab—half the city must be out for a ride on such a golden day."

The unalloyed brass of the man. To waltz in this way, brimming with cheerfulness in front of all her friends, when she had made her feelings toward him unmistakably clear on the street the night before, was unforgivable. Mr. Sprague had even witnessed the—or had he been too far in front of her to hear their exchange or recall Harry's features?

She had to say something. The others were looking at her for their cue. "Why, Mr. Loring—I'm—so glad you could make it—after all. Won't you come in?" She got off the piano bench to take his hat, dropping it on the end table and narrowly missing the plate of leftover pastries. "We're having a little musicale—you must have heard us—"

"Indeed. I delayed ringing until the number was done."

"How very considerate."

"I was most assuredly impressed."

She made hasty introductions. Mr. Sprague gave no sign of remembering the latecomer from the previous night. It had been dark, after all, and the street was packed. Agatha, though, had no trouble whatever recognizing the new arrival and observed his effect on their hostess. She hurried over to the table where the sherry decanter sat—it was too late for tea now, but a guest had to be offered something—and presented a glass of it to Loring, who was by then talking animatedly to the Danes and Mr. Sprague. Leaving Mrs. Memory to compose herself, she squeezed onto the sofa next to Mr. Dane to face Loring, head cocked and eyes wide open, as if to miss no detail of the man.

"Miss Agatha Agapé," Loring announced at the extended sight of her and snapped his fingers. "The name was familiar, but I've just now placed it. There was an Agatha Agapé on the stage when I first came to New York—but that was so long ago she would have to be—you're far too young. Are you related to her—a daughter, perhaps?"

The sly dog. He knew perfectly well from the dinner-table stories she had told him of her ex-thespian landlady who she was. "Maddy"— the tone was imperious—"bring that sherry decanter over here at once. Your charming Mr. Loring has suggested I'm young enough to be my own daughter. We're going to get on famously—I can tell already."

Mrs. Memory delivered the decanter and used the opportunity to collect the cake plates and teacups and escape through the kitchen door. Behind her she heard the burst of laughter as Harry told a little joke. She nearly dumped the china en masse into the sink but reached instead for a tea towel that she lashed against the nearest cupboard. Why hadn't she thrown him out the door? Her damned dignity again—and the fear of humiliating herself in front of her neighbors? And now here he was, drinking her sherry and appearing to be thoroughly amiable and amusing when she knew his performance was just that. Her anger built as she emerged from the kitchen in time to receive the Danes' thanks for "a lovely afternoon, your very best tea ever." Mr. Sprague, too, soon deserted her—a dinner appointment waited for him up in Chelsea. Agatha, though, appeared prepared to remain for the rest of the evening. She had stretched out along the sofa, the hem of her dress turned back a trifle to reveal several layers of bright petticoats and just a bit of pink-silk-stockinged ankle above her little black slippers. She regaled Harry with her harrowing theatrical adventures, concluding with the time in Kansas City when the set caught fire on opening night and the cast was forced to escape into the audience, which thought it was part of the performance and applauded appreciatively.

"And on that stirring note, children," said Agatha, "I think I'll take my leave." She swung her feet to the floor.

"Must you?"

"Yes, my darling. I've lots to do before Alfred arrives." She bid an extravagant farewell to Harry, adding the earnest hope they would meet again before long. At the door, to which her hostess accompanied her, she whispered, "Do remember what Vinnie de Montvert said to me, Maddy." She pecked the younger woman on the cheek. "Every now and then Vinnie would be extremely wise. *Adieu, amour.*"

She closed the door behind Agatha, lingered in the foyer, struggling for self-control, then turned back slowly to face him. "Maddy, I'm sorry," he began before she had crossed into the parlor, "but there was no other—"

"You are not welcome here, I would like you to leave—"

"I came to explain—and to apologize."

"The time for that expired some while ago."

"You must give me a civil hearing, Maddy." He was standing in the middle of the room, palms opened toward her.

"I must do nothing of the kind. Please leave, Harry." She should not have uttered his name.

"I will not leave until you give me the courtesy of hearing me out."

"You're being brutish, you know. I've made my feelings abundantly plain to you."

Momentarily speechless, he looked as abject as she had ever seen him. "All I ask then," he said quietly, "is that I be allowed to state my feelings equally plainly."

Refusing to meet his eyes, she waved him into a chair and perched herself on the edge of the sofa, acutely wary of his gift for blandishment and charm. He reseated himself slowly, adjusting his posture to the chair's plush contours, crossing his legs and then recrossing them the other way until he had taken possession of his assigned place with the same fixity of purpose that he had once displayed in taking hold of her heart. His words, however, were noticeably more measured and their delivery far less buoyant than customary.

There was a young man some years ago, he began, who fell in love with the daughter of a wealthy candy maker, the Licorice King, as the tycoon styled himself. Eventually the young man declared his entirely honorable intentions to the young woman's father, who withheld his approval, telling the suitor that he would receive an answer in a few weeks. Meantime the young people continued to see each other, becoming more attached than ever. Then the Licorice King summoned the young man to his study and advised him of the facts he had recently learned. It had seemed proper, he said, to call on the Pinkerton organization to look into the background of his prospective son-in-law. The investigators found that he had none to boast about; that he was the ne'er-do-well son of a humble blacksmith from some small town in northeastern Pennsylvania; that despite his fine tailoring and well-spoken manner he had no real education and few prospects beyond what he might garner with his infamous knack for excelling at the card table. With that, the father ordered the young man to leave his house forthwith and never to see his daughter again. She was hurried off to Europe by her mother and a year later was married to a Swedish baron.

Harry paused dramatically. "I was that young man, Maddy. The girl's father made me feel as if I had no right to hold my head up anywhere, much less in what he referred to as 'polite society,' in which he said I should not be permitted to prowl. The bastard couldn't speak a single sentence without using 'ain't' and 'he don't,' but I didn't have the nerve to say back to him that neither was he good enough for his precious daughter." He drew a deep breath. "But I had a friend I traveled with in those days, and several months later we encountered this sterling character while we were sailing from New York to Cherbourg. I laid low while my friend engaged him in an amicable game of poker that lasted most of the voyage—and by the end had relieved him of five thousand dollars, which he generously shared with me."

He uncrossed his legs and leaned forward, resting his elbows on his thighs. "Try to see what that experience did to me, Maddy. Those proper girls, the daughters of merchant wizards and financial kingpins and the whole social set—they were not for me. I couldn't stand up under their fathers' scrutiny. And if I couldn't have those girls, well then, by George, I'd have the other sort. So I did—lots of them. And, to be truthful, I still do. Actresses, secretaries, salesgirls, women of the demimonde. They're fun—some are even quite intelligent—and they rarely make demands. A good time is all they want—and all they get from me. I like that easy life, the life without strings—and responsibilities. I'd grown conditioned to thinking of myself first and last—and everyone else be damned." He sat straight up. "But then you came along and upset all that."

She was different from him and from all his women, he explained. "I didn't know what to make of you at first." She was better educated than many of the rich men's daughters he had known. She held the most responsible position of any woman he had ever met, had ever heard of, even. There was no question that she was a woman of quality, a lady, and yet—she had gone to bed with him, without any trace of coyness, as openly and hungrily as he had with her. And she intimidated him and even frightened him a little because of her forthrightness and self-possession. She could be haughty as a duchess one minute and provocatively earthy and natural the next. In a sense, she was much too good for him, and yet she had given birth to an illegitimate child in her youth—a most unfortunate happenstance that was surely beneath her present dignity. The pieces of her simply did not fit together in his mind.

When he returned from Florida he had been confused and uncertain how to deal with her. She meant too much to him to try to impose his itinerant, improvised way of life on her. At the same time he felt incapable of reforming and trying to pursue some other, more conventional livelihood. The dilemma she presented him with was profoundly distracting, and his card playing suffered from this preoccupation. In fact, he became caught up in a losing streak that left him so financially pressed that he was, for the time being, unable to entertain or care for her in a manner he considered suitable to her quality—and he could not face up to confessing his straitened condition to her for fear she would dismiss him as shiftless and improvident. "A successful gambler is one thing; a loser is a hopeless addict," he said with a weak grin.

The longer he delayed seeing her, the more tangled his emotions became. He told himself that he did not need her, that she would only encumber him, but he knew he nevertheless wanted her badly. Yet she was entitled to someone better than him, a stable and reliable character who had a solid income and wanted supper on the table every night at seven. True, she seemed attracted to him, but if their relationship was to deepen into a permanent attachment he knew he had to bring to it traits that would wear well. What really could he offer her, though? Only a life of highs and lows, rich one week, poor the next, an existence spent trooping around the country and the globe in quest of prey. How could he do that to her? Weeks passed while he debated it all with himself. When he began winning again he decided he would make it up to her by arranging an extravagant evening together and confessing his misery to her. But she was resistant to his every effort to unburden himself that night and in the end practically threw him out the door.

No one since the Licorice King had done that to Harry Loring. He was both infuriated and doubly fascinated by her and went off to Europe to lick his wounds and, as was his practice, to play his way around the summer-resort circuit. Perhaps she would mellow toward him by the time he returned. While on the continent, though, he received word that the man who meant most to him in the world lay mortally sick, and he went to England to tend him. "For you to understand where I've been the past three months, I have to ask your indulgence a bit longer," he said, slumping back in his chair. "It has everything to do with who and what I am."

The ordeal of revelation was taking its toll on him. It was the first time, she sensed, that he was baring his soul to her. To anybody. "I'm listening," she said, her tone markedly less severe now.

His mother, he told her, was his father's second wife. His first had been the only child of a prosperous farmer in Sullivan County, New York. Harry's father had worked on the place for several years and married the girl, assuming that when the old man died his daughter would inherit the farm. A couple of nephews got it instead, and his father became so furious that, his plans turned to dust, he left with only the clothes on his back.

How he wound up in Hawley, Pennsylvania, Harry never knew, nor what became of the farmer's daughter. His father might, in fact, have been a bigamist, or his parents might never have formally married—it made no difference to him. All that mattered was his own existence, which was far from pleasant in his youth. He was the oldest of six children, and his father, by then an extremely bitter man, never smiled and spoke little except to issue orders and reprimands. When they were not heeded at once he would reach out and give the offender a swipe with the back of his large hand. "That's how I got this," Harry said, running his finger along the thin scar on his forehead. He was nine or ten at the time and had been helping his father in the smithy, operating the bellows probably—the details were unclear to him now—when his father lashed out at him for some small failing and sent him head first into the fire. Pulled out almost immediately, he still lost most of his hair. Luckily his burns were superficial, and if his head had not landed on a burning ember, he would probably have escaped unhurt.

As the oldest child he was expected to devote himself to the family, especially since his mother, having given birth to six children in eight years, was an exhausted, chronically sick woman. But he hated his surly, brutish father and was alternately sorry for and contemptuous of his whining, bedridden mother, and in desperation ran away on half a dozen occasions, to be greeted on his grim return by his father's razor strop. He was determined not to stay in Hawley a day longer than necessary, and after laying his eyes on the first gentleman ever to set foot in the smithy—he had come by on a superb roan that had tossed a shoe—Harry knew what station in life he intended to occupy.

Soon after his thirteenth birthday he ran away for good. Gifted at spelling and arithmetic and able to write a finer hand than any other boy in his schoolhouse, he filched five dollars from his father's britches and set out with these meager resources to become a gentleman. He slept in fields and haylofts, working his way down the Delaware Valley, earning whatever he could by doing chores and mostly settling for a meal or two in payment. Philadelphia was his goal. He had never been there, but from what he had heard about it he knew he could lose himself in the great city and never have to go back to Hawley.

He worked first in a livery stable, mucking out stalls, watering and brushing the broken-down animals and sleeping in the tack room. When the stench—his own included—grew too much for him he became a delivery boy and then a clerk in a dry-goods store, using his employee's discount to buy himself the first decent clothes he had ever owned. With the little knowledge of bookkeeping he had picked up at the store he was able to land a clerking job with a shipping concern and proved adroit with papers and numbers. The mustache he had grown for his new position was a thin, wispy thing, but he kept it because it made him look older than his sixteen years.

So far he had done rather well for himself, he thought, but even at that tender age he knew there was a certain tone missing from his life if he was ever to attain the status of a true gentleman. Accordingly, he began to scour the newspaper want ads, and when he discovered that the position of assistant to the secretary of the Susquehanna Club was open, he eagerly applied. The musty atmosphere of the place entranced him the moment he entered: the dark paneling, the creaking leather upholstery, the soft-voiced members, gentlemen all, lounging in oversized chairs with their long cigars, delving through the newspapers and discreetly drinking themselves pie-eyed. Polite and well-spoken, humble yet confident, and using "sir" at the end of every sentence, Harry convinced the manager that he was twenty-two years old and able to perform all the tasks required of an assistant club secretary. His handwriting, samples of which he had brought with him, was not only elegant but, more important, also unblotted. Meals and a tiny basement bedroom came with the salary.

If he spent more time among the club members than most assistant secretaries had in the past, his overseers did not object, since it meant the rough edges were being the more quickly sanded away. Among those who witnessed his metamorphosis at the Susquehanna Club was an Englishman named Neville Maskelyne, a friend of one of the clubmen who had obtained guest membership privileges for him during his extended visit to Philadelphia. Perhaps because he, too, was an outsider and more acutely attuned to his surroundings than the Susquehanna's regular membership, Maskelyne soon noticed the alert lad who was so busy absorbing every aspect of club life. Eventually he struck up a conversation with young Harry Loring, found him an engaging fellow and invited him to dine one evening at a small restaurant not popular with the club crowd. On that occasion he managed to elicit from the youngster his true age, his past and his principal desire in life.

Something about Harry's tale touched the older man, who at once began to correct the boy's table manners and to offer him advice on haberdashery. Unmarried and without close family of any kind, Maskelyne must have relished the notion of becoming a surrogate father to a young man in whom he sensed great potential and a fervent willingness to adapt himself to a caring counsel. Harry proved so dedicated a pupil that he was soon receiving guidance in all his nonprofessional activities as well; he was told what books to read and cultural sites to visit and matters of social and political moment to familiarize himself with if he hoped to consort with gentlemen. Maskelyne even shared with him the flotsam of two misspent years at Cambridge, entering into quasi-Socratic dialogues that taught Harry to think about loftier matters than his immediate somatic and emotional needs. Under Maskelyne's tutelage as well, Harry lost his virginity in a visit to the most respectable brothel in the city where the girls had to meet stringent standards of health and decorum. Detailed advice in that particular realm, Neville said, would be saved

until Harry was a bit older; it was enough for the present that he understood the nature of the performance expected of him.

After more than a year of such instruction, the Englishman's guest
membership at the Susquehanna finally exhausted the club's collective
patience, and Maskelyne told Harry it was time to quit his secretarial job;
he was about to be taught, if he wished, the rudiments of the profession
that his mentor pursued—one that, once perfected, could sustain him in
style for the rest of his life. It was a talent that would grant him welcome
into the company of the most elevated ranks of society as a gentleman
and a sportsman. Maskelyne himself had become a virtuoso at practicing
it with many members of the British aristocracy, not excluding the titled
nobility—and on two occasions with the Prince of Wales himself.

Neville proposed that Harry work with him in the capacity of secretary/
factotum. He would accompany him everywhere and acquaint himself
with a wide variety of surrounds, from baronial drawing rooms to ocean-
going yachts, furthering his education at every stop. Harry, who would
have leaped at anything Neville suggested, including emptying the Atlantic Ocean with a spoon, readily agreed. They moved into a suite of rooms
Maskelyne found not far from Rittenhouse Square, and a woman was
engaged to do their cleaning and prepare their meals.

Every morning at nine Harry would meet with Neville to be instructed
for three hours in the theory and practical elements of card sharping; how
to read paper, dealing seconds or bottoms, the use and practicality of
holdouts, stacking the deck, double-duking, substituting coolers and how
to shoot up the pot. Strictly for nostalgia, Maskelyne also demonstrated
several mechanical devices that he had used in his youth for secreting
cards up his sleeve and producing them at timely moments—the "kepplinger," he called his favorite spring-action accessory—but had eventually abandoned as too risky. Then Harry would be left alone to practice
what manipulative exercises were called for. At one o'clock dinner was
served, followed by a half-hour for recreation. For the rest of the afternoon Harry practiced again, this time in front of the mirror to insure that
all his moves were smooth and undetectable. Neville would drift in and
out of the room, observing, encouraging, correcting when something
went wrong. In the evenings Harry often joined his mentor in places
where Maskelyne could demonstrate his mastery of the arts he had been
teaching his pupil. After several months the time had come for Harry to
obtain some practical experience and for Maskelyne to find fresh pas-
tures. They entrained for Boston, and on the ride the younger man was
presented with a distinctive new middle name—after St. John's Wood,
where Neville had grown up off Abbey Road.

They took a room at a small hotel, and Harry waited while Maskelyne went to the Sussex Club to see an old acquaintance. The next morning they moved out of the hotel and into the Sussex, where guest memberships had been arranged for them. Through the club, they gradually met other Bostonians, and thanks to Neville's British accent, unfailing good humor, perfect tailoring and indubitable sincerity they began to be invited into some of the finest homes of the city, where extra men for the dinner table were always in demand. It was a small step from the dinner table to the gaming table—one that Maskelyne was adept at taking.

Harry, presented as Neville's orphaned, half-American nephew, was equally welcome, and no one questioned his disinclination to have remained at Oxford longer than the single term he professed to. He had been badly tutored as a boy, he would explain, and now, by way of compensating, he and his uncle were traveling, absorbing what America had to offer. For the moment there was Boston and its delightful outskirts to explore while he was investigating some possible investments in the area with the proceeds of his parents' estates.

Eventually they invaded Newport for the season and then moved on to New York. "Neville wanted me to perfect my English accent before we went to California because the British were greatly welcome out there at the time. That's changed, of course, but we were a novelty in those days and enormously popular. It was an extremely profitable stay for us."

In time Neville's health grew less robust and he elected to return to his homeland, dividing the year between his club in London and a cottage in Dorset. Harry's prospects were far brighter as a gentleman-sportsman (that is to say, honorably unemployed) in America, where the species was rare, than in England, where it abounded, and so pupil and beloved tutor came to a painful parting of the ways. Harry would send him a small but steady portion of his winnings as an expression of his gratitude, and Neville, appreciative because he was no longer flush, welcomed him for a few weeks' visit each summer. But the older man's last years were for the most part lonely and brightened only by news of his protégé's progress. When Harry came to see him the past summer Maskelyne's strength had so deteriorated that it was plain the end was not far off. Harry was at his bedside in early September when death came, and he had to stay on to clear up the estate, which, though not large, was complex and encumbered by debt. After its settlement nothing was left, really, except Neville's extensive library and several rusting antiques of his trade, including his cherished "kepplinger," all willed to Harry.

"I got back to the city only ten days ago," he concluded, "and have been putting my own affairs in order. I had every intention of writing to you within the next several days, explaining some of this and asking forgiveness—I swear it, Maddy. Then I saw you last night and got your terrible cold shoulder." He stood up wearily. "It was more than I could bear. I decided there was nothing for me to lose by coming here today and risking your renewed anger—crawling to you if I had to—to have my say. Fortunately you were entertaining, and I—"

"And you are not fond of crawling—or as good at it as double-talking your way through doorways."

"Maddy, for God's sake, don't be heartless!"

She patted the seat next to hers on the sofa and beckoned to him. "My heart is convalescing," she said, taking the fingertips of both his hands as he joined her and holding them lightly in her own for a long moment of reflection. Then she pulled on his fingers, wrapping his arms around her, and brought her lips to his. It was a kiss calculated to soothe, not excite. They broke apart slowly, her head resting on his shoulder, his arm still tightly encircling her waist in silent communion.

Over dinner at a small, dimly lit chophouse, she was cordial but subdued, and he was uncharacteristically somber, uncertain to what extent she had been won over by his disclosures. What little she said revealed none of the struggle inside herself to gauge his true intentions toward her.

"What's to become of us?" she asked finally over coffee.

The question caught him unprepared. "Whatever you'd like," he said.

That was too much for her to accept. The most she might hope for was that the death of his friend had sundered Harry's strongest tie to his old way of life. The thought of him domesticated seemed a denial of his nature. It would all take time to sort out.

She fumbled with the key in her lock, and Harry had to open the door for her. He tossed the key on her table, slid the bolt home and turned to face her in the shadowy illumination from the street lamp down the block. "Or was I being too presumptuous just now? I'll leave if you'd prefer."

"I have a way," she said, pressing the full length of her body against his, "of letting my guests know when their company is not entirely welcome."

On the last Wednesday that she attended the children at the Fulton Street Orphanage before leaving for Florida, she was pleased to discover that a new Chickering spinet had been installed there the previous week. When she asked the identity of the donor, Mrs. Memory was told that the gift was anonymous, but Miss Eversham directed her attention to the small brass plate mounted on one side. It bore the inscription, "In Memoriam, Neville Maskelyne, 1832–1897." No one at the orphanage knew who he was.

FIVE

She felt herself more vulnerable in her second year at the hotel even though her position there, on the face of it, had been much strengthened by her performance the previous season.

Most unsettling to her was the behavior of her chief assistant. Almost from the start, Bettina Sanderson had poorly hidden her resentment that, despite her undeniable competence, she had been passed over for the top job after her superior had resigned at the close of the hotel's premiere season. Mrs. Memory's credentials for the head housekeeper's position were beside the point; all that mattered to Miss Sanderson was that a newcomer from the north had been imposed on her by Mr. Stokes-Vecchio without explanation—or, in her view, justification. Mrs. Memory had quickly detected that the lanky spinster had the obsessive efficiency of a martinet and the approximate disposition of a cobra. These charmless traits notwithstanding, a formal, if fragile, cordiality prevailed between them during Mrs. Memory's first season at the hotel.

Now, though, Miss Sanderson was behaving toward her with poorly veiled hostility. At staff meetings under Mr. Stokes-Vecchio's direction, the chief assistant housekeeper lost no opportunity to remind her superior that certain essential supplies were rapidly dwindling—a matter that could have been readily disposed of in private between themselves. And then there was the occasion when Mrs. Memory recommended to the manager that two additional maids be hired due to an increase in the hotel's guest capacity, and Stokes-Vecchio unaccountably turned to the chief assistant housekeeper for her opinion. "I do believe," said Miss Sanderson, "that we can manage as is." Not eager to add to his payroll, the manager asked the housekeeper to delay the matter until the need was inescapable.

"That may leave us with improperly trained personnel in mid-season," Mrs. Memory said.

"I know some girls in Tallahassee we can likely get in a pinch," said Miss Sanderson, ingratiating herself with the manager.

Her transparent zeal to undermine Mrs. Memory's position was further evidenced by her appearance at the head housekeeper's door one midnight early in the season to inquire sweetly if all was well within. The gentleman in the suite below Mrs. Memory's, it seemed, had phoned the front desk to complain of a creaking ceiling—a problem referred to the housekeeper's office, where Miss Sanderson had been on night duty. Through gritted teeth, Mrs. Memory quietly rejected her assistant's offer to help search for loose floorboards in the bedroom; Harry, meanwhile, was forced to retreat on tiptoe to the bathroom as Miss Sanderson's eyes scanned the sitting room for clues of any indiscretion. Miss Sanderson's own unimpeachable chastity was, of course, known to all by virtue of the singleminded devotion she displayed toward her chronically ailing mother, who lived in a bungalow in West Palm.

The incident served, besides further alerting her to her assistant's viperous nature, to underscore the uneasy nature of her renewed relationship with Harry Loring. It was both better and worse.

They still frolicked Sunday mornings on the beach, though she was doubly vigilant now against prying eyes. And thanks to the replacement of the Reverend Mr. Reynolds by a less wrathful spiritual advisor at the hotel, she was able to resume her weekly dinners out with Harry in her guise as the exuberant Madame Memphis. In joyful addition, Harry joined her in her suite for a second evening each week, taking pains to avoid detection both coming and going.

This heightened pleasure, however, made it all the more difficult for her to insulate herself against his flagrant tomcatting about the hotel and its environs. To say so to him directly was beneath her dignity; to deny the anguish it bred was beyond her capacity.

A source of particular distress was Harry's frequent appearance in the company of Miss Angela Prettyman, a willowy, darkening blonde who happened to be—or claimed to be, according to Mr. Walters, who specialized in such intelligence—the niece of the Viscount of Bennisford. It was said the Miss Prettyman devoted herself to the game of golf and the hope of restoring her branch of the family to its ancestral wealth by a successful marriage. And where better to pursue that end than at the Royal Poinciana? Still, Mrs. Memory told herself that she would be incapable of performing her duties at the customary level if she were to grow alarmed about every skirt that Harry attended. This one, though, was attached to a particularly fetching form that he seemed to be pursuing assiduously rather than playing the field as was his habit.

Over a luncheon at the senior officers' table, Mrs. Memory learned from a cryptic exchange between Mr. Stokes-Vecchio and Mr. Burdette that Angela Prettyman's purse was as shallow as her aristocratic claims were suspect. For the second week in a row, the hotel's financial officer told the manager, "our British lady visitor is in arrears"—an affront to his gray-clad soul. The delinquent guest had told him, Mr. Burdette went on with tight-lipped omission of her name, that the bank draft from her London solicitor must have been delayed in the mails and that she was profoundly embarrassed. "What shall I tell her, Anthony?"

"Don't trouble yourself further, Parker," Stokes-Vecchio said. "If her unfortunate predicament isn't cleared up by next week I'll have a little talk with her myself. These things happen."

As it happened, one of her green-clad chambermaids beckoned Mrs. Memory into a linen closet as she marched by one morning the following week and confessed to a gross intrusion on the privacy of a certain guest. The girl related how a few minutes earlier she had knocked on the door of a suite normally occupied by a single lady, and hearing no sound from inside and seeing no sign on the door to warn her off, she assumed that the guest had gone off to her morning activities. But on attempting to make up the room she found the bed occupied by the guest and a bearded gentleman.

By guarded inquiry Mrs. Memory learned that the suite in question belonged to Angela Prettyman; golf, evidently, was not the only game she played with avidity. More to the point, she learned the following day through a chance remark she heard Mr. Burdette pass to one of the bookkeeping clerks that "the delinquency in that British account" had been cleared up. Had Miss Prettyman's bearded friend perhaps advanced her a discreet and timely sum in anticipation of her overdue draft from London? Or, more plausibly, was it payment for tawdry services rendered? Either way, there was both more and less to her than met the eye. On the beach with Harry that Sunday, she told him her concern.

"I must say that your taste in young women has improved this season over last," she remarked as they lay sunning themselves after a long swim.

"I beg your pardon, madam?" said Harry, his face shielded from the sun by a straw hat.

"Your Miss Prettyman has turned quite a few heads."

"Ah, Angela." He gave a yawn. "A most presentable lass."

"They say she exudes British charm."

"Some."

"To which you are no doubt immune?"

"She's available and fun—more fun than most of the women I meet down here, which is not saying a great deal. The woman also happens to be loaded. Her grandfather left her a bundle—and I mean to persuade her to part with some of it."

"How, pray tell?"

"Rich ladies give me things sometimes."

"In return for . . .?"

He slowly lifted the hat off his face and cranked his neck upward toward her. "Maddy, you're worth ten Angela Prettymans. Now stop this."

She relented for a moment while he seemed to doze back off. "Harry?"

"What?"

"She's an eighteen-carat liar."

"Who?"

"You know who. She's no more loaded than you are. In fact, I'd say you're both playing the same game."

"You're daft."

"And you're blind."

He jackknifed his upper body to her level. "What *are* you talking about, Maddy?"

Having finally commanded his full attention, she would not satisfy it for fear of being charged with petty jealousy. "Professional ethics prevents my saying any more." She rose and, her eyes studiously averted, began to gather her things for the walk back to the hotel.

"A very special party" was what Stokes-Vecchio had called it, adding no more than that it was to be held in the hotel's Rose Suite.

In accepting his invitation, which she took to be a kind of command performance, Mrs. Memory was both intrigued and wary. Whatever the occasion, it would have to be a quiet affair. For one thing, the Rose Suite accommodated only a dozen for dinner. For another, a married man who did not want his reputation sullied as a philanderer did not appear in social circles accompanied by another woman—and Anthony Stokes-Vecchio worshipped propriety. If he retained designs on his head housekeeper despite her continually discouraging them, the manager would have chosen a more clandestine rendezvous than the most ornate and intimate private dining room in his own hotel.

On the afternoon of the affair Mrs. Memory had gone to the Rose Suite to oversee its cleaning and the placement of the piano and huge bouquets of pink and white roses in accordance with instructions that had been left. But by whom, she did not know, and the Special Events book kept by Mr. Krause offered no clue; it merely said "Reserved" beside the Rose Suite for that date. Even Mr. Walters, for whom such information was addictive catnip, seemed in the dark when probed on the subject.

Whatever it was about, she decided now, looking at her mirrored reflection, she would endure the occasion in good spirits; on evenings when Harry was under the same roof with her but decidedly not under the same sheets, any distraction would do. Yes, her old black taffeta still served. And the little necklace of jet was in perfect keeping; just a touch of understated decoration.

The manager, done up in a racy white piqué double-breasted waistcoat under his swallowtail jacket, was waiting anxiously for her in the lobby. "Lovely, my dear," he breathed, emitting his usual *eau de pomade* and propelling her, taffeta swishing, toward the Rose Suite at a purposeful gait.

"Anthony, you have me consumed by curiosity. I think it would appropriate, now that we're practically on the threshold, if you'd tell me—"

"It will all become clear momentarily." The hand on her elbow guided her along with assurance. At the entrance to the suite Stokes-Vecchio paused and brought his mouth close to her ear. "I know I can count on your good sense in this situation, Madeleine, but please remember not to bring up any subject that would seem to be even the slightest bit indiscreet."

"I can't think what you—"

He brought his index finger to his lips. "And disregard any cheap gossip that you may have heard—it has no place in these rooms this evening." With ceremonial aplomb he reached for the large brass doorknob shaped like a rose in bloom and turned it slowly.

As she stepped through the door and saw who her host and hostess were, she understood—everything. Beside the slender, white-haired man with the full mustache and peculiarly small ears stood a little freckled woman, dressed in lush blue lace and five strands of the most exquisite pearls she had ever laid eyes on.

"Miss Kenan," said Stokes-Vecchio, "may I present Mrs. Russell Memory, our highly esteemed head housekeeper here at the hotel?"

Every now and then in Royal Postlethwaite's column, she had seen mention of Mr. and Mrs. Henry Flagler's social activities, but in recent months the references had become more veiled. The column would allude to him only as "Mr. Florida" and did not shrink from disclosing that his wife had been unfortunately confined once more to Dr. Choate's famous "rest establishment." Although Mrs. Flagler was thus removed from public view, her husband, to judge by Postlethwaite's cryptic reports, felt no such need. With relish that suggested he did not plan a return visit soon to the Royal Poinciana or any of Flagler's other resorts, the columnist reported that "Mr. Florida" could occasionally be glimpsed in the company of a small, sweet North Carolina woman of "milk-white skin." Lest anyone think the worst, Postlethwaite went on to note that Mr. Florida was a devoted music lover and "Miss Milkskin" possessed a lovely voice: art for art's sake, don'cha know?

This, then, had to be Miss Milkskin in the flesh. The hand that reached out to hers, encased in a white glacé kid glove that extended nearly to her freckled shoulder, was tiny. Mrs. Memory found herself having to suppress the most absurd urge to squeeze the little fingers until they fell off. She was, however, surprised to find that they responded to her touch with a sure, firm grip. Clearly the woman possessed a strength not apparent from her unremarkable, even plain, surface.

"And Mr. Flagler, I believe you and Mrs. Memory met last season," Stokes-Vecchio said, bobbing between them.

"Indeed," said the great man. "I'm delighted you've rejoined us, madam. Anthony speaks of you only in superlatives."

"Employment under such ideal circumstances is a pleasure, sir."

The manager steered her nimbly through the other introductions. There, all sipping champagne, were Mr. and Mrs. Eugene Ashley, Flagler's cousins, in whose beach house Miss Kenan was staying for the season; Mr. and Mrs. Pembroke Jones, friends of both Miss Kenan and Mr. Flagler; the Duke and Duchess de Fragonetta of Iberia and Mr. and Mrs. Weems-Alford of Toronto. How better to limit the gossip than to include only their close friends and relatives, foreigners and employees of the hotel? Yes, discretion was all. Of them, Mrs. Memory had heard only about Mrs. Jones, who, according to the society column, was the owner of "Sherwood," a Newport "cottage" in which she notoriously served mint juleps to a select group of young female friends every summer day before luncheon. It was at Sherwood, Postlethwaite reported, that Flagler had first encountered Miss Kenan, then seamstress and companion to the Jones family. She had stitched her way into his heart as she beguilingly sewed a button on his coat one summer afternoon several years before.

As they made their rounds before being seated, Stokes-Vecchio displayed a dazzling gift of innocuous small talk, remarking at length upon the weather, the decor, the condition of the golf course and the pleasing mood of the holiday season. It was not for nothing, Mrs. Memory reflected, that he had advanced to the pinnacle of the hospitality industry. With relief she was finally borne into the dining room on the arm of the Duke de Fragonetta, who, unaghast at being seated beside so common a commoner (and yet the most attractive woman at the table), pushed her chair in as gently as he would likely have Queen Victoria's. Her glance fell at once on the glittery display of sterling, crystal and bone china; five forks resided on the left of her setting—an unthinkable number until her eye wandered to the silver-bordered parchment menu resting at each place. It read:

Consommé Royal

Croustades Dieppoise

Filet de Boeuf Renaissance

Timbale de Suprêmes de Volailles

Salmis de Faisans et Perdrix

Dinde à la Perigueux

Foie gras à la Française

Salade de Laitue

Pointes d'Asperges Veloutée

Glace Maltaise

Gateaux

Dessert

Chef Dzugashvili had outdone himself.

The duke inquired politely into the nature of Mrs. Memory's duties and expressed due admiration for her manner of discharging the high responsibility she bore for the comfort of the guests—"of whom I am a most contented one," he added. "The service here is exemplary, under the circumstances—the remoteness of our location, I mean to say, and the limited supply of workers."

"I quite understand—and thank you sincerely." She in turn inquired into the location of his duchy. He was doubly titled, the duke explained, since his ancestral lands spanned the border between Spain and Portugal and had been in the family since late Roman times, well before the Iberian peninsula had been divided into two monarchies. Thus his was the only family in both nations to bear the noble designation "of Iberia." Mr. Weems-Alford, to her left, was less forthcoming. When he was not attending to his interests in Saskatchewan wheat, he disclosed, he represented a riding southwest of Toronto in the Canadian Parliament—"a weary sort of diversion, really, but one has one's duty."

As the white-gloved waiters moved soundlessly and deftly, changing plates and wine glasses with each course, seemingly without supervision, Mrs. Memory suspected that there had to be a peephole somewhere in the paneling between the kitchen and suite's dining room through which Monsieur Rempli, the *sous-*chef, was monitoring the scene.

Over the beef course Flagler asked the Duke de Fragonetta if he had had recent word from home on the Cuban situation. Everyone in Spain was eager to have done with the Cuban mess, said the duke, and there was wide support for the liberal measures taken by the cabinet. The decree granting the Cubans autonomy was due in Havana momentarily, and peace would be a reality, the Iberian predicted, within a month.

Mr. Ashley ventured that he had rather a different opinion, judging from reports that the Spanish army's honor had been offended by President McKinley's message to the Congress earlier in December.

"Not in the least," said the duke. "I can assure you all that Spain seeks only the friendliest relations with America and is not eager to fix a quarrel with her."

"A wise policy—under the geographical circumstances," suggested Flagler.

"And it is our hemisphere, after all," put in Mr. Jones.

"Really, dear," said his wife, "I think Mr. Weems-Alford might take offense at quite so sweeping a claim. We do share the continent with a few neighbors."

Mr. Jones was nonplussed. "Quite so. I meant only in the sense of its being our sphere of influence."

Mr. Weems-Alford nodded appreciatively. "Spheres of influence," he said, "belong to those with the might to impose them—and in that, I am forced to concur, you have no equal among us."

That led to an extended discussion among the men on the continuing importance of naval armaments, and Mr. Ashley commented on the maiden voyage in Baltimore harbor that week of a new kind of craft called a submarine that had survived four hours under twenty feet of water "and cruised about as prettily as you could want at that depth. I should think the views were on the dismal side, though."

"What a preposterous invention," said Mrs. Jones. "Of what conceivable use is it?"

"Military surveillance," explained her husband. "We measure progress nowadays by our enhanced capacity to inflict destruction."

Everyone nodded at the poignancy of the remark, and the discussion, still on the subject of subterranean travel, turned to the news from New York that the forces of Tammany, in deference to the streetcar and elevated-line owners whom they regularly plundered, had quashed plans to build a whole new network of rapid transit tunnels underground.

"The submarine sounds preferable," said Mrs. Jones gaily. "They could run whole armadas of them up and down the rivers."

"As a resident of New York," Mrs. Memory ventured, "I think I should find descent into the earth in order to get somewhere to be rather like passing into the underworld. And the city has more than enough infernal aspects to it already."

Stokes-Vecchio's eyebrows gave a cautioning wag, but her little bon mot drew an approving nod from Flagler himself. Nevertheless, he put in, the underground system would soon have its day, given the steadily growing value of New York real estate and the city's swelling population. In connection with these new masses and the problems they had brought in the form of oppressive tenement life, Mrs. Ashley remarked on a recent article in the *Herald* that traced poverty to poor dietary habits. A grown man could be fed nicely on fifteen cents a day, the paper said, but many of the laboring class were bringing on their own impoverishment by squandering their pay on bananas, French rolls, butter and eggs, canned asparagus and fancier meats like round steak and pork chops.

"What are they supposed to eat?" asked Mrs. Jones.

"The article said that peas, beans, rice and peanuts are most nutritious, as are cheap stewing meats, and they ought to buy plain bread and fresh vegetables in season. Sounds sensible."

"Sounds unpalatable," said Mrs. Jones.

But Mrs. Ashley was determined to make her point. The article, she went on, described as typical a hardworking Irish truckman's family in which the fat wife was said to lie about the house swilling beer from morning till evening and sending her children to do the marketing; the results were predictably wasteful. "Such ignorance surely deepens their plight."

"But one wonders," said Mrs. Memory, "if they are ignorant because they are poor or poor because they are ignorant."

"Does it matter?" asked Mrs. Jones.

"Perhaps to them," replied Mrs. Memory, and sank the table into momentary silence. She avoided Stokes-Vecchio's chastening glance.

"No doubt they go hand in hand," said Mrs. Weems-Alford.

"Our poor remain impoverished because they are lazy," said the Duchess de Fragonetta. "Ignorance is the least of their sins. A little learning, and I daresay they would become more slothful still."

Miss Kenan had offered not a word during the cross-table portion of the dinner talk, having confined herself to pleasantries with her immediate partners at the opposite end of the table from Mrs. Memory. Her principal contribution to the evening, it appeared, lay just ahead, for as soon as coffee had been taken, Mr. Flagler cleared his throat, looked across the table with a benign smile and asked, "Mary Lily, will you honor us?"

"I'd be delighted." She smiled back and rose, signaling the conclusion of the massive meal.

Miss Kenan's full name reverberated in Mrs. Memory's mind. Mary Lily Kenan. M. L. K. Ah, yes—Miss Milkskin, indeed. Postlethwaite's subtlety was infinite.

The guests seated themselves in the salon during the pianist's rendition of a Chopin étude. Miss Kenan, as if in a ballet, tiptoed up to the piano with tiny, mincing steps and sheltered herself against its curve. She smiled demurely to the guests and with a nod to the pianist offered them as her opening effort "Pale Moonlight Streams O'er the Green Meadows (Illuminating the Sheaves)." She had a small, thin, pretty soprano, true to the notes but short on character. What it lacked in richness and control it sought to compensate for with vibrato. Still, it was not unpleasant to listen to, and if Mrs. Memory chose to concentrate her attention on the accompaniment, the low lushness of the cello underscoring the flights of piano and violin, rather than the singer, who would be the wiser?

After four more songs Miss Kenan sweetly remarked that though the climate was not conducive to such thoughts, Christmas was but three days off and so she would conclude her little program with "Waltzing Under the Mistletoe." Wearing a bright smile throughout, she blushed faintly in Flagler's direction upon reaching the line, "We share sentiment very merrily, / As I kiss you and you kiss me." More Christmas carols followed with everyone joining in, and the duke and duchess even obliged with a song they said had been a tradition for centuries among the peasants on their *estancia*—"Let Us Loudly Rejoice, For the Babe Is Born," rendered with a great deal of clapping and stamping of feet. Whereupon Henry Flagler was unable to contain a yawn that announced the evening's revels were ended. Mrs. Memory felt her elbow firmly gripped by Stokes-Vecchio as the guests bade their grateful farewells to the host and hostess.

"I think a breath of fresh air would do us both good," the manager said as they reached the hallway.

As promised, it had been a very special party. It would have been rude to turn down her superior under the circumstances. "As you like."

He directed her through the lobby to the veranda and down the steps to the lawn below. "Let's walk for a while," he said. "A little exercise is good for the digestion." The very model of a gastrointestinal Don Juan. He led them south, away from the other evening strollers, in the direction of Mr. Bedient's gardens. When they reached a stretch of lawn surrounded by shrubbery he put his hands on her shoulders, compelling her to stop and face him. "Madeleine," he whispered hoarsely, "you must know by now how I feel about you. You're so—very refined—and attractive—and efficient—the best housekeeper I've ever worked with—anywhere. I've never—met anyone like you—"

Lord, she should have known: more than appreciation was expected in return for elevating her into the company of swells. "Anthony—I—"

"I cannot be less than honest, my dear—whatever your response."

Her brain was scrambled by the heady evening and the soft warmth of the night. Yet somehow he seemed easier to deal with outdoors, where the faint breeze dispersed the smell of his hair tonic; for the moment, they were simply a man and a woman, not overseer and subordinate. "Anthony, you're a very—vital and—stimulating—person. I have not known anyone—quite like you, either." She slipped out of his pinioning hands. "But you're a married man, Anthony. Your very gracious wife was kind enough to allow me to share Thanksgiving with you again last month. I cannot put her—thoughtfulness—out of my mind. I would feel—most unhappy about any—"

"Ah, Madeleine." His right hand touched her chin. "Your reluctance so becomes you. But I must confess to you the truth of the situation. For the past, oh, I should say ten years now, Gertrude and I have been married in name only. We share the same roof for some months at a time, but that is all." Marriage to a woman sadly incapable of understanding her spouse was an empty shell, he contended. "The fruit has long since withered, you see." He would do nothing consciously to hurt Gertrude, of course, but it was only narrow-minded, benighted people who nowadays viewed the bonds of matrimony as imprisoning chains under conditions such as his. There was Mr. Flagler's own situation for them to behold as a guiding example. His life with his wife, despite his best efforts to accommodate her, had become a living hell, and now that she was so ill as to require permanent confinement, Mr. Flagler had been reborn and rejuvenated by the affectionate regard of Miss Kenan. Surely if a great and respected man like him could overlook the unreasonable strictures of a hidebound society, then why could not a somewhat less elevated but thoroughly respectable professional like himself be similarly allowed to . . .

"Anthony—I do understand. But you make it—so difficult for me. Russell Memory has filled my heart for so long now that I doubt it's possible to make room for another. I gave him my vows as he gave me his. They were not chains that bound us but our deep and abiding feelings. I do not think—in good conscience—that—"

"Your vows were required till death did you part—not forever, Madeleine. I cannot believe that your departed husband would have wished, especially in view of your tender age at the time of his death, that you devote the rest of your years to lighting votive candles in his memory. Most certainly you should carry him with you always—and your tender feelings for him—but life must go on for you. It is unfair to yourself to—" He lifted her chin a fraction. "We are fond of each other—we work well together—I cannot see why—"

The man was nothing if not persistent.

"But it is our very compatability that I fear will be fatally compromised. Don't you see, Anthony, how difficult it would be to work together efficiently if we were constantly distracted—absorbed with each other— always aware? I could not—I have not the ability to cut myself into parts—to divide myself into the vocational and the personal—" Was that enough? No, she must make it absolutely clear, now that his look hinted she was achieving her desired effect. "I cannot work well when my thoughts and emotions are otherwise engaged. I must have serenity to function at my professional best—and no less will do for the Royal Poinciana. I cannot believe you would not feel the same." She placed a hand over his. "Anthony, women have a sixth sense in these matters. Perhaps later—after the season is over—we might discuss it again—" Better a carrot than a stick.

His hand trailed down from her chin to her elbow, which he cupped in his palm and gave a little squeeze. "What a wonder you are, Madeleine." The promise of renewed consideration of his suit would sustain him; the poor man wanted only cause to hope. "You're right, of course— and I'm grateful to you, my dear, for reminding me of my duty. The splendor of the evening led me astray, I'm afraid." He took her arm, and they retraced their path toward the hotel. A narrow escape.

Stokes-Vecchio was in a less genial and pliant humor—indeed, he was detectably agitated—when she was summoned to his office the following week and confronted with more people than she had ever seen occupying the room at the same time. Present besides the manager were Miss Sanderson, three of the hotel's six Pinkertons and four young women with bags at their feet whom Mrs. Memory recognized, after a moment, as chambermaids—Maureen, Beatrice, Florence and—who was the last girl?

They had been hired barely six weeks ago; she could not remember every single one of them.

"Sit down, Mrs. Memory," Stokes-Vecchio directed, the edge of fury in his voice badly concealed. "Shall I tell you what transpired while you and I slept peacefully last night—that is, were in our beds—supposing all was well on the premises?"

The story was brief but distasteful to the manager, whose mouth curled downward as he narrated it. Beginning at around eleven the previous evening the desk clerk kept getting calls from guests annoyed by a great deal of noise and hilarity emanating from Suite 367. Repeated efforts by the deskman to ring up the room went unanswered, so Mr. Chance, the Pinkerton on duty—Stokes-Vecchio nodded toward the one on the right—was dispatched to make a personal call and scotch the disturbance. His sturdy knocks could not be heard above the uproar inside. At this point, in view of the dimensions of the din, Mr. Greenhouse, the Pinkerton seated in the middle, was also sent for, and the pair attempted to use their passkey to gain entrance. This attempt, too, was unavailing, for some sort of foreign substance had been inserted in the keyhole, preventing the key from engaging the lock mechanism. At which impasse Mr. Martin was awakened—Stokes-Vecchio turned to indicate the largest member of the Pinkerton contingent, who could not have been less than six-foot-four or weighed much under three hundred pounds—and his mammoth shoulder was employed to push in the door.

Inside they encountered a thoroughly disreputable sight: amid a clutter of liquor bottles, eight male guests in various stages of undress were cavorting all over the suite with the four chambermaids seated there in front of her; the young women had been clad in nothing at all.

"I had my corset 'n' stockings on," Beatrice demurred.

"That will do, young woman," snapped Stokes-Vecchio. He turned back to Mrs. Memory and said that since they had broken a cardinal rule of the hotel by fraternizing with guests *and* in this disgraceful fashion, he was about to dismiss them at once unless the head housekeeper or her chief assistant had any reasonable ground for objecting.

What was there to say in their defense? She supposed that all four of the girls were less depraved than eager to earn some extra money and not too particular about how they did it. But their disobedience of the rules was undeniable—even, the thought occurred to her, as was her own, but she at least did not carry on at the top of her lungs—and they would have to go. "All I can say, sir, is that they are good workers, and I'll be very sorry to lose them."

"But in view of their conduct, you are reconciled to their loss?"

"Sadly, though."

"Yes, of course." The manager turned to Miss Sanderson. "Is there anything mitigating that you can—"

"I say good riddance to bad rubbish," replied the chief assistant housekeeper. "I had opposed the hiring of those two from the first." She pointed to the pair huddled miserably in the middle. "But Mrs. Memory is a more charitable soul than I."

"But you concurred in the hiring of the other two, did you not?" asked Stokes-Vecchio.

"Without much enthusiasm, if my memory is not playing—"

"Thank you, Miss Sanderson." The manager directed the Pinkertons to take the girls to Mr. Burdette's office to pick up the pay due them and then directly to West Palm for shipment on the next train north.

"May I ask each of you please to give me your keys to the rooms and the linen-supply closets?" Mrs. Memory said, rising.

"Ah, yes," said the manager. "Good of you to remember."

"I've already collected them," said Miss Sanderson. "The short one says she lost her passkey."

Stokes-Vecchio's eyes narrowed, sensing a conspiracy; a misplaced or withheld passkey was an invitation to trouble. "I don't believe that."

"I ain't got it," the girl protested. "I had it last night—it was pinned to my dress so's I wouldn't lose it—but it was gone this mornin'. Wunna yer high 'n' mighty guests musta lifted it off me." She looked calmly and defiantly at Mrs. Memory.

"Very well," said the manager, voice lowered several notches as he turned to the outsized Pinkerton. "Mr. Martin, please escort this young woman to the housekeeper's office and wait outside while she removes her clothing and shows every article she possesses to Mrs. Memory. Nobody walks out of this hotel carrying our property with them." He paused for a moment to see if the threat produced any result. When it did not, he nodded.

"I won't!" cried the girl.

"You'd better," said the manager.

"Shit," said the girl.

Mrs. Memory led the way down the hall to her office. The girl disrobed sullenly, handing one article at a time to the housekeeper, who turned each one inside out, squeezing the fabric to see if the missing key had been pinned to a concealed fold. When she was down to her undergarments the girl turned and asked, "You wanna look at these things, too?"

A key could easily be concealed in a chemise. "Everything," said Mrs. Memory wearily.

The girl shrugged and continued undressing without apparent shame. Mrs. Memory, though, cringed inwardly for the girl's humiliation and withheld the reprimand she would otherwise have administered. Examination of her most intimate garments revealed that the girl possessed only a rudimentary conception of personal hygiene—and no passkey. The housekeeper told her to get dressed and turned to examine the contents of her bag.

It was not a carpetbag or valise like the other girls'. This poor misguided child had tied her belongings into a large square of sacking knotted at the corners. In it were a few pathetic items—a frayed and badly patched petticoat, a once-white muslin dress now grayed with dirt and yellowed with age, a few shreds of underwear, a toothbrush worn to a stubble. At the bottom of the sack was a collection of stained rags.

As the girl pulled her petticoat over her head, she explained, "My monthlies. I use 'em 'n' rinse 'em out."

"Take them out and open them up."

The girl, looking wounded now, complied. There were no keys among them. "All right. Finish up quickly—" Without a further word she left the girl.

Mr. Martin marched her down the corridor to join the others and pack her off to the train as Mrs. Memory looked on unhappily. Midway to the main service entrance, the girl exploded into profanity under the Pinkerton's ungentle goading. "Sure, you throw us out like rubbish," she said, "an' what about the fuckin' mucky-muck dudes what got us in there for a good time? Them dirty pricks get off scot-free—"

The Pinkerton raised his great mitt of a hand and swatted the girl.

Mrs. Memory had to resist the impulse to rush to the girl's aid; however abusive, she had a point. The housekeeper brought it up to Stokes-Vecchio after reporting that the passkey had not turned up. "It is not the sort of behavior that can be condoned among our guests," she said quietly to the manager. "I think a reprimand is in order on a man-to-man basis—if I may say so."

The manager nodded. "A ticklish matter, though. The guests have certain prerogatives that are difficult to ignore, sad to say."

"But I did not understand that they purchased the right to abuse the employees in such fashion."

"Excuse me, ma'am," said Pinkerton Greenhouse, "but the girls were there under their own free will—no one shanghaied 'em."

"But they were young and very vulnerable," the housekeeper argued.

"Be that as it may, Mrs. Memory, they are working girls, out in the world," said the manager, "and there are certain risks that cannot be foreclosed. I don't think it is our place to lecture the guests, who are here, after all, to enjoy themselves. Some of those involved are among our most devoted patrons." He turned to Greenhouse for confirmation.

The detective consulted his fistful of notes and read off the names of the males he had recognized and recorded in case further investigation was required.

Harry Loring was fifth on the list.

It was peculiar, she thought, how greatly her mental state had heightened her physical need almost to the point of pain. Her yearning for him this evening was so intense that her body nearly ached in anticipation. Scolding him first would certainly not fuel a worthy consummation. As it was, he was taking so long to begin undressing that she felt compelled to help him remove studs and unbutton buttons, hands moving over his body almost ravenously.

"You're quite a shameless hussy," he whispered, exploiting the truth of the charge by attaching one of her hands firmly to him with a squeeze and beginning his own slow ministrations through the folds of her dressing gown. "Don't be in such a rush. We have the rest of the evening."

Frustration from his teasing deliberateness constricted her throat. She could feel herself all but growling with impatience until, finally, Harry lifted her in his arms and carried her to her bed as if delivering an urgently overdue cargo. Familiarity need not breed contempt, she thought—not in bed. It can enhance satisfaction as well. No need to send subtle signals to register what is pleasing and what is pointless time-wasting. The familiar taste of him, the feel of him, the touch of him, all the collective passions of the past were resummoned and compounded in a surge of expectation and more appreciated for its knownness. His doing *this* sparked a pulsing trace of every other time it was done, the echoes gathering and reverberating inside her, and his *that* became infinitely sweeter because it differed from *this* yet added exquisitely to the wholeness of the act. Such a lovely and loving other on her, astride her, within her. All of her raced to the edge of exultation, then broke into a million ecstatic filaments.

Afterward, as he sprawled beside her, his left elbow denting her pillow while he drew lazy figure eights around her breasts with his right forefinger, she addressed the matter of his moral deficiencies. "How," she asked quite simply, "could you do such a thing with those poor girls?"

His hand stopped meandering and settled on her midriff. "Know about that little episode, do you?"

"A thing or two. It's only caused me constant problems for the past three days—shuffling room assignments, pushing all the girls because we're so shorthanded, desperately trying to find replacements just as we're on the verge of peak season. Not to mention the squalor of the thing."

His hand wandered away from her. "I'm frightfully sorry for your inconvenience—and for the girls getting the heave-ho. It was just supposed to be a little lark for an hour or two. But some of the others started putting away too much of the sauce, and things got out of hand."

"I should say."

"I tried to calm them all down, but that just made for a more fearful ruckus than ever. I had no idea it would wind up causing you trouble."

"But why were you there in the first place?"

"Maddy, I swear to you I never even touched a single one of the girls. I couldn't. They were too young and too poor and too—altogether sad. It was all—quite appalling."

"Then why were you there?"

He shook his head. "One goes along—for the ride. It's—rather like a business investment. So much easier taking money off pals you frolic with than total strangers."

"And the devil take the hindmost."

"In a manner of speaking."

"Some business," she said, rolling onto her side so that only her back confronted him.

The matter grew more troubling to her several days later when Stokes-Vecchio assembled the senior staff in his office immediately after breakfast and advised them of a new crisis. A Mr. Luther Stallings of Baltimore, the guest in Room 310, had concealed among his garments certain financial instruments, the face value of which was collectible by the bearer upon presentation to any bank or other party willing to cash them. And now they were gone. Mr. Stallings had of course known of the availability of safe deposit boxes in the hotel office but, as was common, preferred not to use one. The hotel therefore bore no liability for the disappearance of Mr. Stallings' bonds—the lines on Mr. Burdette's face suddenly relaxed—but they all had to be apprised of the sudden presence of a thief at the hotel. That the perpetrator of the crime, furthermore, was sophisticated in financial matters seemed apparent since the modest amount of cash that Mr. Stallings kept in the same place as the bonds had not been touched. This led to the deduction by the Pinkertons, the manager went on, that the culprit was almost surely not a chambermaid or any of the help. Which, by the process of elimination, meant it was likely one of the guests. Further, the detectives suspected, the crime may well have been linked to the recent sordid incident in Room 367 during which one of the chambermaids involved claimed that her passkey had been stolen from her.

"I don't quite see how that follows," said Mr. Krause. "There must be sixty or seventy passkeys on the premises. Any of them could have been used. Or Mr. Stallings might have left his door open by mistake."

"Mr. Stallings made quite a point, he says, of locking up each time he left his room—which would be understandable. As to the passkeys, how a guest might obtain one without being detected—other than in the circumstances of the—the orgy of the other evening—is unclear." The manager said he was not jumping to any conclusions, but suspicion did point to one of the so-called gentlemen involved with the chambermaids. Some of them had the finest possible backgrounds; of the others, less was known. But it was impossible to question them selectively or to risk a search of their rooms, with or without their knowledge, unless the hotel was prepared to offend them grievously. "Now this may have been an aberration—a one-time incident, perhaps undertaken for the sheer adventure of it," Stokes-Vecchio speculated, "or we may have a shrewd and very dangerous character on our hands with easy entry into every room in the hotel." Management's choices were to alert the guests to the peril, impossible without dampening the carefree mood of the season; to change all the room locks, far too expensive and time-consuming a measure; or to become exceedingly vigilant until they could be sure the perpetrator no longer stalked the corridors.

Over dinner in West Palm the next night, Madame Memphis asked her weekly companion if he was acquainted with a Mr. Luther Stallings.

"Yes. He's a perfect dunce," said Harry.

The judgment sounded consistent, she said, with behavior that had resulted in his being relieved of seven thousand dollars in securities. Had Harry heard about the incident? He looked neither surprised nor saddened by her disclosure. His equanimity deepened her suspicions, which had been aroused first of all by his presence at the seraglio in Room 367, second by his familiarity with financial documents of every sort and third by his recently expressed concern that things were slow for him in the gaming department this season—it was a more conservative crowd, and most of the men in it found poker playing beneath their dignity. Other sources of revenue, he had confided to her at the beach only the previous Sunday, would have to be considered.

"It doesn't seem to come as unhappy news to you," she said.

"Why should it? Luther is an extremely wealthy boob who never earned a dollar in his life, honestly or dishonestly. He lives off the fortune accumulated by his grandfather."

"You mean that makes him a quite suitable robbery victim?"

"As victims go. And at that, his grandfather came by his money by foisting on the public something called Buffalo Lithium Water—a cure-all certified by the most eminent of quack physicians—by the tens of thousands of gallons."

"You seem to know a lot about Mr. Stallings."

"What I know is that the money taken from him would otherwise almost certainly have gone to buy himself another stud for his racing stable—a sorry pack of nags they are, too—or gorge himself every night for a year at Delmonico's—which he practically does, anyway—or for a trip to Monte Carlo, where he specializes in losing whatever's in his pockets at the baccarat tables. The man is a useless parasite, Maddy."

"In short, the perfect prey for you."

His eyes became slits. "Now, just a minute. What are you saying?"

"You're the one doing all the saying about the man."

"You asked."

"But the vehemence of your response . . . it sounds a bit like a carefully considered justification for separating the unworthy clod from his riches—or, say, any portion thereof left lying around his room."

The eye slits became pinpoints. "Maddy, do you think *I* took the man's bonds?"

"Lord, I hope not!"

"You do, don't you?"

"Well—the remote possibility has crossed my mind. And nothing you've said has done much to chase the horrid thought."

He crossed his arms over his chest. "So—you think I'm no better than a common thief—is that it?"

"Oh, no—not common at all. Most uncommon. And highly selective."

"I don't see the joke."

"Nor I. But your remarks bore a self-incriminating tone."

"Nonsense. You asked me what I thought of the man, and I told you. Does that make me a thief?"

"It suggests a certain frame of mind on the subject. Stealing is stealing—the shortcomings of the victim are beside the point."

"Perhaps. My lack of any great sympathy for this particular victim was all I was confiding to you, though. Really, I don't understand your great concern over the matter."

"The hotel's reputation is involved."

"What of it? What's the hotel to you?"

"It provides me my livelihood—or a considerable portion of it."

"And you provide it with all your professional skills in return. It is an inanimate object, put up for profit by an industrial magnate who won his wealth as a prime accomplice in a thoroughly ruthless enterprise. He seems to me hardly more admirable than Luther Stallings, except that he worked for his money."

"You sound like a wild-eyed social revolutionary."

"And you sound like a slavish retainer for the Flagler family."

"I resent that—greatly. You're trying to twist the whole thing around and make me into—"

"A more thoughtful, intelligent person, capable of questioning the fatuous pretense she sees enacted in front of her every day. I want you to think about yourself, Maddy, instead of the people who pay you to serve them. You've been working too long for the comfort of others. Start thinking of yourself—and seeing where your opportunities truly lie."

"And where is that—in playing Maid Marian to your Robin Hood?"

He reached for the champagne bottle and refilled her glass. "I can think of worse fates."

The door to Room 273 was wide open, signaling the couple's imminent arrival. Through it Mrs. Memory saw that their black steamer trunk and two large red-brown valises had already been brought up. Other smaller cases, along with a hatbox or two and perhaps a small bag with the necessities for the train trip, would follow as soon as they had completed checking in.

There was no need, she had decided, to wait until afternoon to take inventory in the linen-supply closets. She might as well make her count in the one down this corridor right now, and if the Caldwells happened to pass by on the way to their room, it would be a happy coincidence. She smiled to herself at the justification; in fact, she had been planning her deployment for days, ever since a check of the reservations registry confirmed her guess that the young couple would return this season to the site of their wedding holiday. Had Rachel changed any since spring? Was she more self-possessed now or had she been drawn ever more deeply into the Caldwell web? Had her husband curbed his brutal ways in bed or had she somehow narcotized herself to his carnal tyranny? Actually, she realized, he did not matter at all to her, except as a fit consort; in her eyes he was a grayish presence, a cloud trailing after the sun, a blurred shadow cast by his wife's luminosity.

Twenty-seven, twenty-eight, twenty-nine—her ears picked up at the sounds of footsteps down the hall and a soft murmur of voices. She darted to the doorway for a peek. No bellman, no Caldwells. Just two women guests on their way out. What could be keeping them? Thirty, thirty-one, thirty-two—thirty-two extra pillows. Blankets next. She counted them by twos. Fourteen, sixteen, eight—there they were! She could make out the bellman's lilting tones, the vivacity in his voice as he told them there were two new lawn tennis courts available to the guests this season and the bicycle paths had been widened and lengthened for their pleasure. Her head poked out of the closet doorway for an instant, only to be quickly withdrawn in shocked disbelief; Rachel was obviously and unmistakably with child.

The high, wide waistline of the dress, the burst of gathers under the bosom, the disappearance of her willowy, girlish form—all were signs that left Madeleine quite breathless with elation at the prospect. But at once an opposite feeling set in. Was the girl, barely beyond childhood herself, so soon to lose her youth to the responsibilities of motherhood? Was it fair to have had so little time to be carefree? The availability of servants would no doubt ease the burden; still, it meant a new stage of her life. The birth was not imminent—she did not look large enough for that yet, nor would it have been wise to travel to a place so distant from expert medical care shortly before the baby was due. But soon, in three or four months perhaps, her little girl would give birth to a baby of her own.

She went back to the shelves with the blankets and clung to one of them numbly. In the spring she would become a grandmother! Her eyes brimmed. Would she ever see the infant? Ever share in the joy of its upbringing? Would it not have been better to remain in ignorance of Rachel and her life and family than to know of them and be tantalized by what she knew yet be forced to stay forever at a stranger's distance? No. Better this way, with all its bitter frustration, she told herself, than a lifetime of wondering.

Her need for contact, however brief, with Rachel Caldwell became urgent with the discovery of her pregnancy and seemed to become more pressing by the day. If not at the hotel, it was unlikely she would cross paths with her soon again. How should it be done, then? She could think of no plausible subterfuge. So on the fifth day of the Caldwells' stay, she simply timed her morning schedule so that she would ascend the main staircase when Rachel made her regular descent for breakfast while her husband was out golfing.

She saw her coming up above and restrained her footfalls in accordance, moving far more slowly than usual. Hold tight to the railing, darling, she yearned to call upward; a fall could be catastrophic. Does your doctor thoroughly approve of this form of moderate exercise? We have elevators here that a woman in your delicate condition would be wiser to rely on. Careful now. Three steps, two steps, one step, there! The girl looked tired even this early in the day. The rosy glow was gone from her skin. She appeared sallow, almost petulant with the corners of her mouth turned downward like that. The child must be having a difficult time of it.

"Mrs. Caldwell?" Great big smile, many teeth showing.

Rachel paused and looked pained, as if distracted from meditation. "Yes?"

"I thought I recognized you. I'm Madeleine Memory—we met last year—in your room." Her right hand was extended, ready to be shaken.

Rachel looked directly at her and inhaled. "I don't recall our meeting. Please forgive me."

"You were indisposed at the time."

"Was I?"

Could she possibly have forgotten? Perhaps she had exiled the unpleasant cause of their meeting and everything connected with it to the farthest recesses of her mind. Even so, it was unthinkable that she could not remember a kindness done her only a year before—or, worse, that she was unwilling to acknowledge it. "At any rate," Mrs. Memory persisted, "I'm delighted you've come back to us for a second visit."

"Thank you," Rachel said, and began to turn away.

"I can see by your present happy condition that everything has worked out well for you."

Rachel aimed an annoyed look over her shoulder. *"Everything?"*

"I—had reference to your domestic happiness. I'm so very glad for you, madam."

"I fear your concern for me is misplaced, Miss—"

"Memory. It's Missus."

"Yes—well, thank you." And on she proceeded at a steady, deliberate pace, as unaffected as if she had been detained by a moth.

In her mingled hurt and fury, the grandmother-to-be gripped the bannister as tightly as she could. Was this the girl's true attitude toward those whom she regarded as her social inferiors? Or had exhaustion perhaps drained her of all considerations beyond her own state of health? But even in her desperate eagerness to excuse the young woman, she could not dismiss the growing evidence that the daughter she had surrendered had been raised to regard herself as the center of the universe and all the rest of mankind as her handmaidens. She retreated to her office, angrier at herself for having harbored unreasonable expectations than at Rachel for disappointing them.

*   *   *

Miss Sanderson, agitated and perplexed, said she thought it best to review the matter first with Mrs. Memory before taking it up with Mr. Krause.

Gladys, one of the two telegraph operators at the hotel, had confided in the chief assistant housekeeper that she was earning a little something extra for doing favors for a female guest. The woman had come to Gladys in tears and begged for help. An attractive blonde, she had fallen in love with a married male guest vacationing alone and was quite convinced she was now carrying his baby. The man had promised to divorce his wife and marry her as soon as possible, but she had no way of knowing whether he was telling her the truth. So she had convinced Gladys to let her see a copy of the wires the gentleman was in the habit of sending out each day so that she might better calculate his sincerity toward her. Gladys knew it was improper, but the woman was so distraught and her situation so pitiable that the telegraph operator, full of commiseration as she was, thought no harm could come of it. Moreover, the young woman was British and could hardly return to her own country in such disgrace—and besides, she gave Gladys ten dollars every time she passed on his wires to her. As a result the operator was making as much as thirty or forty dollars extra each week, setting the sum aside for her future as Miss Sanderson had often urged her to do with her wages, which until then had left her little margin for savings. What was odd was that the wires from the gentleman in question were never actually directed to his wife, as the British woman had hoped—only to his stockbroker. Gladys wondered if she should continue to help the troubled woman.

Mrs. Memory smelled a rat. "It's thoroughly reprehensible, of course," said the housekeeper. "I'd urge her to desist at once and never to do such a thing again under any circumstances."

"I've already done that, of course. But more is required, I'm afraid."

"Why is that?"

"Because the hotel cannot afford to employ a telegraph operator of such deficient character."

"Perhaps it would be kinder to let Gladys know the strength of your conviction—in as pointed a way as you wish."

"But I have no authority over her whatever. She's free to disregard my warning—so how shall we ever be sure if she's reformed or not?"

"Then you have a duty to instill the fear of God in her."

"I know what my duty is—and you should as well."

"Indeed—except that Gladys came to you in good faith, seeking your counsel. To turn her in without giving her a second chance strikes me, frankly, as something of a betrayal of her confidence in you."

"She's the one who's done the betraying, if you ask me."

"But you would be compounding it. You know what they say about two wrongs not making a—"

"Now you're turning me into the one with the low character—and I quite resent your attitude, Mrs. Memory."

"All that I'm trying to suggest, Miss Sanderson, is that it's beneath you to do in this simple, good-natured woman."

"The woman's done herself in. As to what's beneath me or not, I'm the best judge, thank you kindly. Discipline must be instilled."

"Beheading the woman, though, is a rather dire means of moral improvement. I myself will not be a party to it—in the event you were seeking to enlist my collaboration."

"I fear that you and I do not share the same values."

"As you say, Miss Sanderson."

The instant her fingertips brushed bottom, she got to her feet and raced up the sand to the sheet, beating him by just seconds. Under her tutelage he had become a far better swimmer, his greater physical strength almost a match for her superior technique. "The winner—and still champion," she panted.

"But not for long," he said, chest heaving as he dropped to his knees beside her.

"I'm safe so long as you refuse to take your lessons seriously."

"It's more fun watching you instruct me so earnestly. If I take it too seriously the fun goes out of it."

"It *is* serious—if you care about swimming—"

"I care about you." He pulled her toward him and kissed her on the tip of her nose.

After twisting the ends of her soaking hair to squeeze the water out, she arranged her body to conform more comfortably to his. It seemed the place and the moment to broach the story of Gladys and Miss Sanderson. She omitted only the nationality of the woman who bribed Gladys. He listened with abstracted interest while scooping handfuls of sand and heaping them onto a steadily growing mound encasing his knee. At the end he said, "What a disgraceful business. Sanderson's right—the woman should be sacked."

"She confessed. She's entitled to another chance."

"Being a telegraph operator is a public trust."

Something in his tone told her Harry did not mean a word he said. His sincerity was too plainly manifest, therefore false. "And what of the guest who put her up to it?"

"Also reprehensible."

"If Gladys is let go, shouldn't the guest also be asked to leave the premises? After all, she was the one who conspired to—"

"Without a doubt. Off with her head."

"Even though she's your good friend?"

"Who?"

"Miss Prettyman."

"Angela? I scarcely see her. Don't tell me she's the one?"

"I don't have to tell you something you already know. I say the two of you are in cahoots in this little business, whatever it is exactly."

"Now where on earth did you dredge up that absurd notion?"

"From Arthur Timmons. He says you and she are together quite often."

Harry stopped playing with the sand. "He wouldn't say that."

"I bribed him. Why should you be the exclusive purchaser of his services?"

"That little black beggar! Wait till I get hold of him—"

"Then you admit it?"

"I admit I need money—and so does Angela—you were quite right about her."

"And I admit I was lying about Arthur. I was just guessing about you two."

His look said he did not enjoy being outfoxed. But he conceded the defeat manfully. Yes, he had worked out the telegraph scheme with Angela Prettyman. She had fed the operator the sad story of her pregnancy by a New Yorker named Ottaway and was then clever enough to convince Gladys that Ottaway's financial wires—the man was a big and obviously knowledgeable plunger in the current manipulations of the Sugar Trust certificates that were fluctuating wildly due in part to the Cuban crisis—were some kind of secret code affecting his matrimonial status. Actually, Ottaway was not even married. He was such a heavy and successful player in the Sugar Trust situation that it was minimally risky for Harry to take the information Angela brought him and wire his own broker to follow Ottaway's lead. So far, he had made twelve thousand dollars, which, of course, he had to split with Angela. "Quite a lucrative subterfuge," he concluded. "Best of all, nobody got hurt. Even if Gladys gets the sack, she'll wind up ahead of the game."

"And how did Miss Prettyman unearth this profit-making news in the first place?" she asked.

"Ottaway told her himself."

"Just like that—out of the goodness of his heart?"

"It took some questioning and quite a bit of coaxing, as I understand it—Angela's very good at that. She indicated that she was in certain difficulties and asked if Ottaway would be able to lend her a little something until she heard from her solicitor in London. Instead he put up money in her name as part of his transactions and told her all the profits would be hers."

"In exchange for?"

"A gentleman doesn't inquire into such matters."

"Especially if he knows the answer anyway."

"Don't be catty, madam. You have your profession, Miss Prettyman has hers—all comparisons are invidious." When Angela pressed Ottaway for additional financial advice so that she might continue to accumulate profits, he declined. "So she came to me and we cooked up our little scheme with Gladys."

"And why did she come to you—of all people?"

"We're friends. Good friends."

She traced a finger down the musculature of his upper arm. "Harry, have you been sleeping with her?" Her tone reeked of nonchalance.

His eyes engaged hers for an instant and then went past. "Why do you ask?"

"Because the answer is so very obvious."

"All the more reason, then, not to ask. Whatever my answer, it's not likely to improve your disposition."

"Is there something wrong with my disposition?"

"I didn't say that. I just mean that I try not to dwell on things that are likely to stir you up—that might intrude on us when they need not. I don't consider that the least bit beastly of me."

"For God's sake, Harry! I know what Angela Prettyman is—and so do you. And I do not understand why you need to be on such—intimate terms with her sort. It speaks poorly for you, if you'll forgive my saying so—and it demeans me—"

"If that's what you think, then you haven's *begun* to understand me yet—or how it is I survive. My involvement with her is not a comment on you—not in the least." He viewed Angela Prettyman, he said, as a congenial business opportunity. She was likable enough and usually in a position to uncover information that was potentially useful for his pocketbook.

"A horizontal position, I daresay."

"Sometimes. The woman has to earn her living somehow. She's bright enough to keep her eyes and ears open and is generous about sharing her news with me."

"And why is that, pray tell?"

"Because—dammit, Maddy—I give her a good time—something she doesn't often get. Does that satisfy you?"

"The question, I believe, is whether it satisfies *you*. Apparently that requires a sizable segment of the female half of the English-speaking peoples."

He shoved over the mound of sand he had accumulated. "Christ," he said softly. "Maddy, I never made you any promises. We're not married, and I've never pretended to be a saint."

"But the very notion of fidelity seems hateful to you—as if you'd find it unmanning."

"You make it sound as if you're a one-man woman while I gad about like some perpetually aroused satyr pursuing my pleasure. No one I've been with since meeting you has meant a fraction of what you do to me." He was holding her by the shoulders now.

"That's very prettily put," she said, blinking back tears that the sun caught at the corners of her eyes, "and I'd dearly like to believe every word, but you've an odd way of demonstrating your—"

"I adore you, Maddy."

"Then why must you sleep with this—this harlot of a gold digger—and flaunt the fact all over the hotel. I wouldn't call that very considerate or respectful of—of someone you—claim to adore."

He shook his head. "I haven't flaunted anything—I haven't even conceded it. You extracted it from me—"

"What's the difference? It doesn't alter the truth of it."

He relaxed his hold on her. "I knew one day we'd have this very argument—which was why I was so hesitant to see you again in New York after last season." He glided his finger along her brows and down her nose in a little T shape. "Dear, dear Maddy—I'm not insensitive to your feelings, believe me—but I can't remake myself for you."

"Can't—or won't?"

"Does it matter which?"

"Yes—to me."

"Is that what you want me to do—become something different from what I am? I give you everything I'm capable of—"

"Which amounts to friendship that costs you nothing in restraint—and me everything. Does that seem a fair bargain to you?"

"You're under no restraint from me—I've asked nothing of you I haven't offered in return."

"Perhaps that's very generous of you, but if you're being dead earnest about how you feel for me, you should want me to be a one-man woman—yours."

"What I want and what I have a right to ask aren't the same. You're free to do what you think best with your life."

"Thank you very much. But the difference between us is that I don't consider a deeply felt attachment to someone of my choice to be a form of bondage. The freedom comes in being able to choose—it needn't end when the choice is made—unless what follows proves hateful." She shook her head and looked out to sea. "For such a worldly man, you're remarkably unaware that women thrive on emotional security, not free love."

His eyes narrowed. "I took you for a different sort of woman—hoped you were strong enough to be your own self, not a man's reflected image."

Her top teeth dug into her lower lip. "And I took you for a different sort of man—one strong enough to share himself fully and become larger for it." She placed a hand on his still damp chest and guided it to rest on his heart for a moment before removing it. "We both seem to have miscalculated rather badly."

The conversation did not improve with the lengthening evening. Like the man himself, there was a juiceless quality to his words. Little sustained his interest beyond the hotel's occupancy rate, the durability of wicker (or lack thereof), plumbing in its countless permutations, and the latest thing in electrical devices. Finally he hit on a subject of mutual concern: herself. Why did she choose to live in New York, he wondered, in view of its notoriously deficient graces? Didn't all the clatter and dirt daunt her? Wasn't it hard to make acquaintances without ulterior motives? That a woman could conduct her own life sensibly in the midst of an enormous city thronged with strangers and dangers amazed him. He could understand the life of a man in the city, he said—he had visited New York on five occasions and observed the infectious energy of the place—but he shuddered to think of a woman alone there, buffeted by the crowds, riding public conveyances, traversing the teeming thoroughfares, prey to the most unwholesome elements and unprotected by a male presence.

"One gets quite used to it," she said with a plucky little smile that she was not sure he could see in the faint glow cast by the pathside lanterns. "Indeed, after a while one even begins to enjoy the challenge."

"I cannot believe you mean that," he said, his voice husky with emotion. "I shudder for your safety. I—care—so—oh, Madeleine—" He stopped abruptly. The arm that had been locked to her elbow snaked about her waist and pulled her tightly against him while his other hand found the back of her head and held it in place as he lurched toward her, his nose bumping hers en route, and clamped his mouth more or less against hers. His lips and tongue began working.

What his attack lacked in finesse it made up for in suddenness, leaving her only a reflexive instant to respond. To receive him would only encourage further advances; to keep her mouth closed would be a humiliating rejection of her professional superior. It was only a kiss, after all—a business investment, as it were. Her lips and teeth parted.

It was over quickly. With a shudder, the manager pulled away, leaving her with a mouthful of sawdust. "I'm—so terribly sorry, my dear." He reached in his pocket for a handkerchief to pat his moistening brow. "I didn't mean for that to happen. The thought of you alone—was too much for me to bear." His eyes swam toward hers, lids heavy. His breathing was becoming more audible.

Dispassion would no longer suffice to mute him. This pathetic pining would only worsen unless she acted unequivocally. But how—without embittering him? If there was an ounce of theatricality within her soul, now was the moment to dredge it forth.

"Anthony—I have not been entirely fair to you."

"Say no more, Madeleine—"

"No, I must. I gave you leave to think that I—that we—that there was even the possibility that—there might eventually be a certain—intimacy between us. That was unfair—and deceitful—because, you see—I have not told you the whole truth." Could she produce tears and keep them flowing? "Oh, Anthony—I have been so frightened and miserable." *Believe it!* There. More bereft still. That's it. Now blink and the tears will spill over beautifully. Fine. More. "It's not that I've lied to you—" More feeling, please.

"What are you trying to say to me?"

"I—I've been so terribly agonized"—a few dabs of her kerchief. "I feel so guilty and ashamed for having misled you, Anthony. The truth is— that—I am engaged to be married!"

The manager's parched lips parted in shock.

"Yes, it's true—I am to be married after Easter." A wan little smile would be appropriate. Not too much now. Just right. It evoked an identical curl of Stokes-Vecchio's mouth, along with a large measure of confusion. Her mind churned and improvised under threat of execution for failure. The tale hurried from her lips almost before she could weigh it for plausibility. She had turned an ankle in stepping off a streetcar last spring, she began, and darling Evan—her fiancé—was kind enough to help her to curbside and walk her home. He was a most correct gentle-man—a detective, as it turned out, on the New York City police force, who had been cited for extraordinary bravery several times. Yes, she thought, that was precisely the right occupation; it lent a certain touch of menace to him, useful in case the manager were to harbor any vengeful instincts.

But Evan, she hurried on, did not earn a great deal of money, and his dear departed wife had left him with two small children whose health was frail and needs were large. So they had agreed to delay their betrothal so that she could return to Florida for this season; her salary for the three months of work would meet many of their impending expenses. But since Mr. Flagler did not approve of married women on his hotel staffs she had hoped to keep her imminent marriage secret in order not to preclude the possibility of her future employment at the Royal Poinciana—"should my work continue to prove satisfactory." Another tear trickled down her cheek and off it into the night.

"Madeleine, I am—stunned—no, astounded—by your revelation—and forthrightness." His hand reattached itself to her elbow and launched their resumed walk to the hotel. "I understand fully now why you have been so reluctant to—accept my—overtures. How could you do other-wise?" The kerchief in his free hand swabbed the rim of his scalp. "And you were right, for your own sake, to keep your secret. Mr. Flagler will never condone the notion of a married woman living here apart from her husband—he is too great a believer in the institution of marriage to permit it."

"I understand." Under the cloak of darkness between the lamps that lighted the path, no further tears were required. "But after your impulsive gesture back there on the path, I cannot—I must not—continue to deceive you—even if it may mean the severing of my connection with the hotel—which I greatly love."

"Believe me, you have nothing to fear from me—dear Madeleine. I shall keep your secret close to my heart. I cannot help myself—from remaining your devoted admirer—and protector—"

"Anthony, I cannot tell you how greatly moved I am by your—charita-ble instincts and—and your many kindnesses. Evan and I will always be grateful."

"No, I am the grateful one, Madeleine—for your honesty and courage and—the pleasure of your professional company." . . .

Agatha Agapé would surely have stood and cheered her performance. But it had been, she noted as she later slumped onto her bed, very hard work indeed.

*   *   *

Sweet and gentle, David Bedient had asked her with utmost diffidence on their way out of the dining room to meet with him in the gardens late that afternoon. She could not tell from the gravity of his expression whether he was worried more by uncertainty over her response or by the nature of the subject prompting the request. Whatever the trouble, she assumed it pertained to him and said of course she would join him.

Her stomach began to ache, however, almost from the moment she heard Mr. Bedient's first words. A chambermaid had been watching as an apparently intoxicated guest in evening clothes was permitted entry into Mrs. Memory's suite late one night the previous week. The maid happened to be passing after she had left a room where she had gone to change the sheets on the bed of a very young guest with a weak bladder. There was no mistaking it, either: room 555 had been assigned to the head housekeeper partly because the number was hard for the chambermaids to forget in case she had to be summoned. The maid had even walked by the room right afterward just to see if she had made an error.

Next morning, mindful of the hotel rules that had resulted in the dismissal of four of her fraternizing workmates several weeks earlier, the maid dutifully reported what she had seen to Miss Sanderson. Mr. Bedient was unsure as to what precise use the chief assistant housekeeper planned to put the information, but from the readiness and abhorrence with which she had related to him the news of Mrs. Memory's evident transgression, the housekeeper had best be on guard. Since, in the event of a confrontation over the issue, it would come down to the chambermaid's word against Mrs. Memory's, Mr. Bedient speculated that Miss Sanderson was perhaps hoping instead that the slander would reach Mr. Stokes-Vecchio's ear via a third party—like himself—and do its damage indirectly but no less insidiously.

"It's none of my business," Mr. Bedient said, absentmindedly picking up a terra-cotta pot from the bench in the potting shed, where they had gone for privacy, and ladling rich, dark soil into it with a trowel, "but if I were you and I wanted to retain my position here I would find some means of stopping her. The woman is no friend of yours."

Mrs. Memory reached for the hand that held the trowel and gave it a squeeze. "Thank you for the advice—and for being so circumspect. I wish I could say more, but I have no desire to burden you with my—personal life." She poked a finger into the soil in the pot, as if testing it for dampness. "I used to think I had no friends at all in this place, but I see that I was wrong. Your friendship means a great deal to me, Mr. Bedient—more than I can say." She glanced off toward a table full of incubating Chinese hibiscus awaiting transplanting. "For the rest of my life, whenever I come upon a lovely blossom, I'll be reminded of you."

Her brain worked furiously on the walk back to the hotel. Sanderson could not be permitted to spread her venom. If Stokes-Vecchio heard that she had entertained a man, any man, in her suite, he would know she had lied to him about being engaged. And since her visitor was a hotel guest, her malfeasance was surely grounds for instant dismissal. And then Sanderson would have what she wanted.

Perhaps her viperous assistant was only biding her time about going directly to the manager, knowing as she must have that the head housekeeper was the apple of his eye. Their occasional dinners together in public and his courtly behavior toward her could not have eluded the web of gossip that enmeshed the staff. If Sanderson herself had come forward too zealously, her designs on the head job would have no doubt been transparent and perhaps inspired the manager's sympathy for the target of her disclosure. Even with the chambermaid in tow, Sanderson may have been hesitant to confront Stokes-Vecchio with an indictment of the housekeeper, who was older and wiser than the girl and whose word was infinitely more reliable. If the maid knew what was good for her, she would restrain her tongue, and at season's end, the whole thing would blow over. But Sanderson might not hold back much longer if her scandalmongering proved fruitless. The woman had to be dealt with before she went to the manager. But how? Should she seek her out—and say what? All that a confrontation could achieve would be Sanderson's undying enmity for Mr. Bedient as well, and the threat she posed would intensify. No, there had to be another way.

Over breakfast the next morning, her mind full of the plan she had settled on during a sleepless night, Mrs. Memory was jolted by the news that Mrs. Edwin Caldwell had taken a nasty tumble on the ballroom dance floor the previous evening and there was fear for its effects on her pregnancy. A specialist was due in on the first train from Jacksonville to check her condition.

Madeleine Memory's personal concerns were gone in an instant. All she could think of was the health of the girl and the safety of the baby. Why oh why had her dolt of a husband been waltzing her around the dance floor in that delicate state, she thought as she bolted from the dining table and headed for the Caldwells' suite. The grief and annoyance that had grown in her from the last two encounters with her daughter were forgotten. Rachel's failings, could be explained away by social conditioning and terrible in-laws. What was needed was a mother's presence.

Mrs. Memory could hear whispered altercation escaping from the sitting room even before she reached the open doorway. Edwin Caldwell and the house doctor were deeply divided over the course Rachel's treatment ought to take. "But she's spotting, sir," the doctor was saying, "and no risks at all should be taken with her condition." He prescribed confinement to bed for at least a week. For his part, Edwin was convinced it was best for him to return his wife to New York as quickly as possible and to the care of her European-trained physician, a man of the highest scientific credentials. The train ride itself would imperil Mrs. Caldwell, the doctor insisted; he was certain his colleague en route from Jacksonville would concur. He would abide by the judgment of no Florida doctor, Edwin replied; whatever specialized knowledge the Jacksonville man laid claim to, young Mr. Caldwell went on to suggest, was likely derived from the birthing of cows and horses.

Mrs. Memory's knock interrupted. Edwin Caldwell glanced over at her with an expression of puzzled hostility as she stepped uninvited through the doorway. "What is it, Miss?"

"I am the head housekeeper. I was saddened by the news of Mrs. Caldwell's mishap and—thought perhaps I might be of some assistance."

"Yes, thank you. If you'll come back in an hour, Mrs. Caldwell should be awake. I'll want you to pack up her things for our trip back north."

"Yes, sir," she said, but remained in place, casting a look at the disapproving face of the house physician.

"That will be all, thank you, miss."

"Yes, sir—but I just wonder if—if it is wise under the circumstances—to subject Mrs. Caldwell to the rigors of a train ride."

"Are you a doctor, too?" Edwin snapped at her.

"No, sir, but I am a woman—and aware of the possible effects of the jolts and bounces that the train inflicts—not to mention the other uncomfortable aspects of train travel that are unavoidable and might—"

"Your expertise has not been invited, miss. Now if you will kindly—"

"Forgive me, sir, but it is not a matter of my expertise but of yours. Perhaps it would be wisest to defer to the medical opinion of Dr. Lyons, who I cannot believe would approve such a course."

Edwin hunched his shoulders. "My wife's health is *my* responsibility. If you will have someone else in here by ten to help with the packing, miss, I would be grateful. And you may close the door after you on the way out."

But the Caldwells did not leave that day or the day after, either, Edwin having tempered his impulsive judgment. Mrs. Memory lingered in uneasy vigil close by the Caldwells' second-floor suite, constantly inquiring of the maids about the patient's condition. So far as any of them knew, there had been no further complications. But she could not take their word as authoritative any more than she could inquire directly of Rachel's attending physicians.

On the third day she decided to risk Edwin's anger by appearing at the door to their suite, her arm draped with clean linen, prepared to make up the rooms herself and thereby determine firsthand how Rachel was. Edwin, still in his dressing robe, answered her knock. "She's resting now. Come back in an hour or two, if you don't mind."

But she had other duties to attend to then and could not appear to be excessively concerned with this particular guest. "I'll be very quiet, sir, I assure you."

"I'd *rather* you do as I ask, miss."

"Edwin?" Rachel's voice drifted out from the sitting room. "Is anything the matter?"

"It's only the housekeeper, darling. Go back to sleep." His annoyance with Mrs. Memory was nearly palpable as he began to close the door on her.

"It's all right, Edwin—I'm just catnapping."

Grudgingly, he reopened the door. "Be as quiet as possible."

Mrs. Memory made her way through the sitting room, hardly daring to turn her head for a glimpse of the coppery gold of Rachel's hair as she lay stretched on the chaise longue near the window. The girl appeared to be lifeless. A massive expenditure of willpower drove her by without pausing and on into the bedroom, which she proceeded to make up swiftly. The bathroom, with its heavy ring around the tub and minute dark flecks and curds from shaving soap filling the sink, presented a more difficult problem: to clean them would require noisy gushes of water. As she was weighing what to do, Edwin came into the bedroom. "I must change," he whispered harshly.

Mrs. Memory tiptoed from the bedroom, leaving the door closed and the bath uncleaned. Immediately her eyes sought the face and form of her slumbering daughter. Edwin had not forbidden her to tidy up the sitting room, so she circled warily about the chaise, studying the averted features from a distance. The floor on either side of the chaise was littered with objects that Rachel had been using to keep herself occupied. Mrs. Memory inched closer and knelt to pick up the strewn articles one by one. The petit point the girl had been working on was uninteresting, she decided after a moment's inspection, turning it over and placing it on the table near the chair, and the poor darling had botched the stitches on the wrong side rather badly. A book she had been reading was left open and face down to save her place—*The Decoration of Houses.* Ahhh. Perhaps Mrs. Wharton's guidance would provide some enlightened notions of decor—badly needed, from what she remembered of her painful visit in disguise to the Caldwells' home the previous spring. Finally, some combs and Rachel's ivory-and-silver-handled hairbrush. Mrs. Memory cradled the brush in her hand, gazing at its owner's face and remembering with what joy she had wielded it a year earlier to relieve the newlywed girl's distress. Just as she was about to place it on the table Rachel's eyes fluttered open.

The sight of the housekeeper with her hairbrush in hand drew a little smile of recognition from the girl, who blinked a few times as if to separate reality from her dreams. "Oh, hello again," she said and then seemed to fade off.

The glimmer of acknowledgment brought a rush of satisfaction to Mrs. Memory. Did Rachel really remember her or was the greeting directed at her as the embodiment of all housekeepers in the universe? Her gaze dwelled on the girl's long-fingered hands and then returned lovingly to her face. She gave a little start as the green eyes opened again and looked directly into hers.

"How—how are you feeling now, madam?"

"I'm quite fine, actually." She began to yawn but remembered her manners and covered her mouth. "I really am. I'm so fine I'm tired of all this resting." With that she began to swing her legs over the side of the chaise.

Mrs. Memory hastily dropped the hairbrush on the table and lunged to help the girl. "Really, madam—is it wise for you to be up? I had understood it was best for you to remain—"

"Oh, pish-tush. I'm fed up with all this lying about. I'm not so fragile that—" She paused and her eyes widened. "Oh," she said as she rose, "Oh, my oh my."

"What is it, madam?"

"The baby. I can feel it kicking this very minute." A great wide smile lighted her pretty face. "It must be doing well, too."

"I'm so—very glad for you—madam—"

Rachel reached a hand out and touched her mother's wrist. "Thank you. You're very kind, miss—no, it's missus, isn't it? You are the very same housekeeper from last year, aren't you—the one who was so—"

"Yes, madam—Mrs. Memory."

"Of course." She took two stiff-legged steps toward the table and picked up the hairbrush. "I hadn't thought you were still at the hotel—

not having seen you at all this season." She moved with heavy steps to the window and slowly began to brush her hair.

"We met briefly on the main stairway during the first week of your stay, but you seemed not to—"

"We did? I don't recall. Perhaps I was unwell that morning. You should have reminded me, Mrs. Memory—I hope I'm not in the habit of being impolite."

"I actually—it's not important. Only your health is."

"Now wait," Rachel said, brushing her long burnished hair with more vigor. "I do remember meeting someone one morning who asked if—who seemed to—was that you? Oh, my goodness. I took you for one of the guests—one I feared was rather too familiar with my—well—please, do forgive me. If you had identified yourself as the housekeeper I should never have—"

Edwin exploded out of the bedroom and cast an accusatory look at Mrs. Memory. "I did not want her awakened!" he declared.

"Edwin, Mrs. Memory didn't wake me. It's time that I—"

"And she is not to stand about engaging in conversation with strangers. Miss, I would like you to leave our room this instant and have one of the other maids finish up inside. You've done quite enough—"

"Edwin, Mrs. Memory is not a maid. And she did not—"

"I—did not mean to—"

"Whoever she is, she's a busybody and I won't have her—"

"Edwin!"

When she came by the room later that afternoon, hoping that perhaps Edwin was out and she might have a final word with Rachel, Mrs. Memory found the Caldwells' suite unoccupied and a maid making it up for incoming guests. The couple had left, the maid told her, on the afternoon train. The brute, Mrs. Memory thought.

"Oh," said the maid, "this was left for you."

It was a small package beribboned and bearing the name of the smart gift shop in the ground-floor arcade. She took it to her office and opened the box in private. Inside was a tortoise-shell comb, its edge and handle cunningly chased with silver in a graceful floral pattern. It was the loveliest comb she had ever seen. With it was a note written in a flowing, overly rounded hand with idiosyncratic punctuation:

Dear Mrs. Memory—

Please accept this small token of my affection—both as a form of apology for unintended slights and gratitude for the several kindnesses you have shown me during our stays here—I am feeling so well that we have decided

rather hastily to return north, else I would have given you this in person—
my fondest good wishes to you.

Rachel Caldwell

Her fingers slowly encircled the comb until they encased it in a fierce
grip that she wanted to sustain forever.

Feeling so blessed by Rachel's gift, Mrs. Memory found it especially
difficult to act uncharitably that evening after dinner to safeguard her own
interests. But Miss Sanderson had left her no choice.

It grieved her, she told Mr. Stokes-Vecchio in his office, to report that
her chief assistant, apparently moved by ambition to replace her next
season, was stooping to the vilest means to blacken her superior's reputation.

"What is it that she's saying?"

"I'd rather not elaborate. Suffice it to say that it has to do with my
moral standards."

"But they're impeccable. What could anyone possibly say to—"

"Nevertheless, she's attempting it." Mrs. Memory sighed and dropped
her voice. "You know, things happen to some women as they become
older—they undergo certain changes. Perhaps she's entered that stage of
her life."

"I'll speak to her at once."

"I implore you to do no such thing. It will only compound matters."

"Then—what?"

"I wish you to dismiss her—at once. With her full season's pay, of
course. She has an ailing mother, and I would not like to—"

"I see. But Madeleine, there are two full weeks left to the season
and the cleanup period afterward. She's a good worker—highly competent—"

"Miss Prentisse and I can handle the added work, I'm sure. Nothing
will be neglected."

The manager sat back and attacked his mustache with little pokes and
prods. "I understand your upset—fully—but I think your solution is a
little extreme."

"Her continued presence here is an affront to me, Anthony."

"Suppose we say you're free to select a new chief assistant for next
season, but Sanderson can finish out this one. It would be so much more
orderly—and without your having to overtax your strength—"

"I want her gone. The woman is treacherous. I ask you for her dismissal with pay—and a letter of reference as consolation, which is more than she deserves."

"You're putting yourself ahead of the hotel, Madeleine. We have fifteen hundred guests to attend to. We should not be left shorthanded at peak season if it's humanly possible—"

"Either she goes or I shall."

He shook his head. "Now you're being rash and—forgive me—vindictive. It's out of character for you."

"I have a full-time position awaiting me at one of the leading hotels in New York—all I need do is wire them that I accept the offer. My preference is to remain here, Anthony—with you—now and in coming years. It's a less taxing and more pleasant arrangement all around. But if you cannot see your way clear to accommodate me in this matter of principle, you leave me no choice."

He drummed the desktop with his fingertips and grimaced. "Very well."

Ugly business. She left his office with pounding heart. Why, of all the men in the thousand miles between New York and Palm Beach, had she become enamored of Harry Loring? The bounder had vitiated her brain and chipped away at her conscience from the moment he had begun to impinge on her heart. And now her infatuation forced her to this base expediency. She did not much care for him at the moment—and even less for herself. Would Mr. Bedient understand?

Among the hotel's senior staff, hastily convened in the manager's office for a pre-dinner emergency briefing, she supposed herself the only one able to unpuzzle the sensational events unfolding on this the final night of the season. To be sure, the crime had been imaginatively conceived and daringly executed but was not so subtle as to leave her in doubt about the likely identity of the culprit.

According to her reconstruction, the first step in the plan had to have been the theft of the maintenance man's gray uniform. That could have taken place almost any time during the season, but she guessed the plot had not been hatched until the beginning of February at the earliest. The workman's outfit had probably lain inconspicuously in a drawer in a certain hotel bedroom until about six on the evening of the Washington's Birthday Ball. With all the fuss lavished on the final social event of the season, few people would have paid much attention to an apparent member of the maintenance staff, in a nondescript gray uniform and a mechanic's cap worn low enough to shadow his face and carrying a few tools, who had placed an "Out of Order" sign on the door to one of the gentlemen's bathrooms off the second-floor hallway in the north wing. Plumbing breakdowns were not extraordinary events, and for the men who were not well heeled enough to afford a room with private bath, the inconvenience of walking another hundred feet to the nearest facility was not so great that anyone would have complained. The whole interval to repair the supposed disorder had certainly not consumed more than a quarter of an hour.

At some time during that interval, the occupants of the rooms nearest the bathroom began smelling the smoke. Everyone in the vicinity was swiftly alerted to the danger by a passing bellman who ran down the hallway, knocked on every door shouting "Fire!" at the top of his lungs and directed the room occupants to the stairway and then down into the lobby. In reminding the guests of the highly flammable character of all-wooden structures, the bellman had been most insistent on the need for haste, witnesses later recalled. A few guests remembered having seen a maintenance man in the hallway as they hurried through it toward the stairs.

Only moments after the final escapees arrived in the lobby, they were advised that the flames were already out and the peril past, so those in the rear of the procession simply turned around and trooped back upstairs to their rooms. The smoke smell still lingered but was already dissipating, and everyone resumed dressing for that evening's gala event. No one gave the minor disturbance a further thought until Mrs. Westerley's piercing screams echoed through the wing.

It was less than an hour later when Stokes-Vecchio summoned the senior staff to his deskside to consider what measures to take in response to the situation. The problem was Mrs. Westerley's jewels. On returning to her suite after the fire scare, she had continued her preparations for the evening's glittering social affair. It was only later, after she had completed her wardrobe and gone to the dressing table to open her jewel case, that she discovered the gems were missing. She did not remember unlocking her door when she returned after the fire alarm, she told the Pinkertons—indeed, in their haste to escape the danger, many of the guests had neglected to lock up behind them before they fled. All the wily thief had to do then was step through any open door he happened on and help himself to whatever conveniently placed jewelry the guests had removed from the hotel safe that afternoon and brought back to their rooms in preparation for the ball.

The fire, Stokes-Vecchio told his senior staff, had obviously been set to abet the robbery, which was just as obviously committed in the few moments following the guests' hasty departure from the wing. By the time the manager and the detectives reached the scene, the thief's trail had grown cold. In the men's bathroom where the alleged repair work was being done, they discovered a large pile of wet, burnt rags and some old soggy newspapers in the tub—once he had got the blaze going long enough to generate smoke detectable beyond the door, the thief must have merely turned on the water tap to douse it—and a hammer and wrench, the props of his pretended trade, lying on the floor. That was all. Missing from Mrs. Westerley's suite were a diamond necklace and tiara, a stomacher and several bracelets including one that featured fabulous emeralds unearthed in Brazil a century earlier, the largest of them weighing twenty carats.

The Pinkerton house detectives were doing all they could for the moment, Stokes-Vecchio told them. The compound of barracks where the maintenance men, laundry workers, bellmen and chambermaids stayed was being thoroughly searched. The guests' rooms, unfortunately, could not be similarly gone over without alarming their occupants and massively insulting them. But the manager would have dearly loved to undertake a room search because the jewel theft, like the one earlier in the season of Mr. Stallings' financial securities, displayed too much sophistication to have been perpetrated by just any petty crook; no one on the hotel staff seemed capable of such wiles. In Stokes-Vecchio's office right now the Pinkertons were questioning the bellman who had spotted the fire and alerted the guests in order to see if he had any additional information. Since he had accompanied the last of the guests down the stairs, the bellman himself was exempted from suspicion, except that he might have been an accomplice to the crime. Stokes-Vecchio was not sanguine about achieving a swift solution. The thief was a clever fellow who appeared to have planned every move carefully.

Only when Mr. Krause asked the identity of the bellman and the manager said it was the Timmons boy, Arthur, did Mrs. Memory begin to develop deep and immediate suspicions.

"What was he doing in the vicinity in the first place?" the assistant manager asked.

"Passing by, he says, on his way to deliver a drink to a guest on the third floor."

"That's a peculiar route for him to have used."

"The boy says he was taking a shortcut. Niggers, alas, are not known for their mastery of geometry." The guest to whom he had been delivering the drink had, at any rate, confirmed the boy's story.

"And who was the guest?" Krause wondered.

The manager consulted a paper in front of him on which he had scribbled notes on the crime. "One of our regulars—Mr. Loring."

The Washington's Day Ball, of course, would go on as scheduled that evening. There was no point in spoiling the fun for the rest of the guests, Stokes-Vecchio ruled, although he supposed the news of the theft was spreading all over the hotel even then, but there was nothing that could be done to stop it. The manager's only real recourse was to implore his senior associates to stay alert and report any suspicious behavior to him or the Pinkertons. At the end, he reminded them that they were to reconvene in his office at twelve-fifteen A.M. for their annual presentation to the ball guests.

As they filed out, Mrs. Memory was agitated by the thought that any man who would not scruple at relieving a wealthy if wastrel guest like Luther Stallings of his valuable bonds, or who was capable of conspiring to intercept another guest's communications with his broker, might not be above snatching exquisite jewelry of a third guest. A most uncommon thief, but a thief nonetheless. This chain of thought led her to reflect that there was no point in her possessing the passkeys if she could not use them whenever the occasion warranted—and now, she decided, was such an occasion.

She hurried first to Angela Prettyman's suite and found it empty. Most of the guests were by then in the dining room, where they would be enjoying for at least another hour their last festive meal of the season. Even the Englishwoman's kindest friends, Mrs. Memory noted with distaste, would not have described her as "tidy." Dresses, petticoats, stockings and shoes lay over any and all horizontal surfaces. Her dressing table was strewn with white powder, smears of red cream and bits of false hair in various lengths and conditions. If the jewels were stashed in the midst of such a mess, it would take a whole team of investigators a far longer time than she had available to uncover them. She sampled the hem of a petticoat, the bottom of a golf bag and the lining of a parasol on the chance that some of the gems had been hastily sewn into them. Nothing. A look into the middle drawer of the bedroom chest yielded only more chaos.

Abandoning the effort, she opened the door slowly to be sure nobody was in the hall—there was no guarantee that all of the guests had in fact gone downstairs—and finding the way clear, hurried up to the third floor, where with racing pulse and cold dread now enveloping her she slipped into Harry Loring's room. It appeared as spotless as if the chambermaid had just left it. Not a ripple disturbed the surface of the bedspread; not a cushion bore a wrinkle imprinted by human use. An uncommonly orderly man, Harry.

If Harry had taken the jewels—was there a streak of madness in him she had failed to detect?—where might he have hidden them? Not sewn into his clothing—that was a woman's trick. Probably he could not even thread a needle. Then where? The jewelry would have to make quite a large sparkly pile. He would probably wrap it in a shirt and drape other things around it. Like soiled linen? She darted back to the bathroom, but the wicker hamper had been emptied. Of course—he was departing in the morning and would not have left his soiled clothes where they could so easily be forgotten. His luggage, then.

She opened the closet and found two small valises, a portmanteau and a large steamer trunk bearing his initials and a patchwork of labels left over from frequent transatlantic crossings. Only the trunk was locked. The loot had to be in there. But how to get at it? She would simply have to break open the lock. With what? The writing desk in every room held a brass paperweight and a letter opener; they would have to do. She ran to get them. The paperweight proved an effective enough hammer to loosen the lock and allow her to wedge the letter opener under the hinged flap. With a strength born of urgency and mounting certainty that her guess was right, she yanked with all her might, snapping the opener right out of its leather holder but prying free the hinged section. He would know, of course, that someone had broken in and was on his trail—but what of it? It would throw a deserved fright into the scoundrel.

Temples pounding now, she opened the top drawer of the trunk. Leather cases, neatly arranged, with his small items of jewelry and valuables; stacks of handkerchiefs and white linen, carefully folded; rows of stockings, sorted by color. No lumps formed by diamonds or emeralds. The second drawer held more linens; the third, shirts and collars, edges carefully aligned, smelling slightly of soap and starch. Nothing suspicious.

Only when she reached the fifth and deepest drawer and encountered a jumble of soiled clothes did her search intensify. She poked through it with care. Shirts, stockings, drawers, handkerchiefs. And—what was that? Something gray or filthy white, uncharacteristic of his usual sartorial perfection. She tugged it out. A gray shirt, of precisely the kind worn by the hotel maintenance men. Good Christ! She probed through the drawer wildly now, tossing the contents from side to side in frantic quest of the other parts of the outfit. And there they were—the gray trousers and soft cotton hat with a peak to hide his face. All purloined for him, no doubt, by Arthur Timmons, who at almost any time could have slipped easily into the laundry room, where his mother had formerly worked and the women all knew him, and made off with the uniform. The plumber's tools left behind in the bathroom the boy had probably snatched from the maintenance shed and smuggled to Harry. The fool, the goddamned fool! To take such a chance, however shrewdly calculated. And to corrupt the boy that way, no matter how amply he rewarded him. And yet—the daring and ingenuity of the scheme could not be denied. What cold nerve he had. As to Arthur, no doubt Harry would say the boy was insulated from the crime by his shepherding the guests away from the fire while the theft was being committed, and for his troubles would earn more than he could in ten years of menial labor. And the victim was, after all, one of the idle rich, almost surely unredeemed by her own or any of her family's contributions to society.

As she draped the incriminating garments over one arm and carefully covered them with her shawl, Mrs. Memory felt a sudden chill and began to tremble. Was it brought on by the sense of complicity, she asked herself, hurrying to the door, or the rage that gripped her and overcame her readiness to excuse the act? She inched open the door to make certain the coast was clear and darted out into the corridor unobserved. Her feet were moving but with what destination in mind she no longer knew. Her first impulse had been to race up to her room and instantly reduce the maintenance man's uniform to a pile of gray rags, unidentifiable and easily disposed of among a dozen different hiding places. But why? He had betrayed her. Fancy clothes, smooth words, good looks—none of them changed the basic fact of the matter: he was a crook, however glibly he rationalized it, and she had played into his hands, surrendered him her heart, served as his confidante and accomplice, however unwittingly, out of some pathetic emotional weakness within herself. The man was a menace, a marauder—she saw it all too clearly at last—and could not be left free to prey on victims whose privileged condition he invoked to justify his wickedness.

At the top of the stairway she headed down, not up. She would go directly to Stokes-Vecchio's office, drop the gray uniform onto his desk and—and Harry Loring's vile little game would be up. Why had it taken this long, why was so blatant a transgression of the rules of society required to bring her to her senses? Why had she let pure carnal satisfaction blur her growing knowledge of what he was when he was not caressing her? Yes, the time had come, his betrayal of her trust richly deserved its reward in kind.

How would she explain the discovery, though? She—she had decided to take it on herself to—to search the rooms of the six men who had been involved in the orgy with the chambermaids early in the season because—

because she had always suspected a link between their presence there, the missing passkey and the theft of Luther Stallings' bonds. Yes, that was plausible enough to divert any suspicion of her involvement with Loring that might be awakened if she had singled out his room for inspection. And where had she found the uniform? In Loring's trunk; no need, though, to mention her having pried it open. And why had she taken it on herself to make the search? Because—because she knew that Stokes-Vecchio had hesitated to order a massive invasion of the guests' privacy but it galled her to think of the criminal getting away with such a—a disgraceful act, one that threatened the reputation and—and the future economic well-being of the hotel to which she was so devoted. Yes . . .

But as she reached Stokes-Vecchio's office, her towering resolve was shrivelled by the sight of Harry Loring, at his polished best in formal attire, being guided to a seat beside the manager's desk by Pinkerton detective Greenhouse. She halted next to the open door, just out of sight of the room's occupants, and chose to listen to the proceedings before marching in with her indicting find.

"Really, gentlemen, I understand your concern," Harry was saying as he settled into the chair, "but I do not appreciate being hauled away from the dinner table on the final night of my stay."

"I'm afraid it cannot be helped, Mr. Loring," said Stokes-Vecchio.

"Surely this could have waited until after coffee had been served. I told your detectives earlier all I know about the unfortunate incident."

"That remains to be seen, Mr. Loring."

"I don't follow. You can't mean to say that I am under suspicion in any way for—"

"Everyone in the hotel is under suspicion, sir."

"That's preposterous. Your clientele have no need of reducing themselves to jewel thievery. We are all people of considerable means."

"Appearances are sometimes deceiving, Mr. Loring. Now if you'll just cooperate with detective Greenhouse, we won't have to detain you for more than a few moments—"

"But I resent the very implication of my being brought in here like some back-alley yegg. What possible connection is there between me and this—appalling crime?"

"It's the nigger boy, for one thing," said Greenhouse.

"Arthur? What of him? I thought he was something of a hero—the way he sounded the fire alarm—and so forth. I was proud of him when I heard the full story."

"Yes, but his actions paved the way for the thief to do his dirty work," said the manager.

"As it happened, yes," said Harry, "but how can you blame the boy for that?"

"It could've been set up that way," said the Pinkerton.

"You mean—that Arthur was part of the robbery?"

"Possibly," said the manager.

"Ridiculous! I know the boy—"

"So we understand. It's one reason we've asked you here. It seems peculiar to Mr. Greenhouse that Arthur should have been passing by just at the right time to serve the thief's purposes."

"But as I understand it, the boy saw the smoke coming from the bathroom and simply did what any alert, intelligent person should have done under the circumstances."

"Or so we are apparently supposed to believe."

"Really, Mr. Stokes-Vecchio—I'm afraid your people are grasping at straws—to try to vilify the boy for his meritorious acts—"

"You sound rather defensive about the boy, Mr. Loring. Almost excessively so, if you don't mind my saying."

"Yes, well, I'm quite fond of him. I've gotten to know him over the past several seasons—I used to request his services when he was an Afrimobile driver and I was delighted to find him promoted to bellman this season. I always ask for him to serve me when the chance arises—in fact, I had specifically asked for him to bring up the drink I ordered this evening while I was dressing for dinner."

"Exactly so," said Stokes-Vecchio.

"Meaning what, if I may ask? Is there something suspicious in anyone's ordering a drink in his room? I should imagine dozens, perhaps hundreds, of your guests do likewise."

"But Mr. Greenhouse has learned that you, sir, are not in the habit of indulging in a pre-dinner drink in your room."

"I—well—true enough, but I simply felt like one—to get into the festive mood for the ball. Look here, you're seizing on the most obscure circumstantial evidence, and, frankly, I resent all this—"

"Your room," the Pinkerton interrupted, "is right next to the stairs leading down to the wing where the robbery happened."

"So what? So are a lot of other people's rooms. Are they being questioned, too?"

"None of them, though, Mr. Loring, was party to the unfortunate immoral episode earlier in the season involving the chambermaids—"

"My God—not that again! It was all just a dreadful lark, and I deeply regret its happening, but you can't hang a man for—"

"One of the girls' passkeys was never recovered—and Mr. Stallings' bonds were taken not long afterward—"

"Yes—and what of it? How is there the remotest connection? There must be dozens or hundreds of passkeys floating about the hotel—why worry about the bunch of us?"

"The nature of the crime, Mr. Loring, suggested a knowledgability that would not exclude guests from being among the possible perpetrators."

"Now see here. I know Mr. Stallings, and it is just as possible that he tucked the securities into his swimsuit and lost 'em in the ocean! Why muddy the reputation of guests whose worst crime is an occasional excess of high spirits?"

"Mr. Loring, perhaps we can abbreviate this unpleasantness if you'll simply grant us permission to examine your suite for—"

"What!"

"Including the luggage," put in the detective.

"I will allow no such thing—unless you can assure me that every other room in the hotel will be similarly intruded upon."

"Not every guest falls into the same category."

"Mr. Stokes-Vecchio, I greatly protest your continued—"

"We're just trying to do our jobs properly, Mr. Loring. I beg your cooperation."

"You have absolutely no right, sir—no right at all—to—to—"

"Then you object to our searching your room and possessions?"

"I do, indeed—unless, as I say—you plan to do likewise with—"

"It's unfortunate that you take this position, Mr. Loring," said the manager. "If you had not objected, we should have taken that as conclusive testimony that you have nothing to hide. Under the circumstances, you leave me no choice but to have Mr. Greenhouse instruct Detective Martin to go directly to your room now while you remain here with us. I'm truly sorry to offend you in this fashion, but—"

"This is infamous!"

He looked drained and on the edge of panic as she broke in on the scene. Perspiration was plainly visible along the upper edge of the suspect's forehead as she skimmed a look past him to the manager. "Excuse me for intruding," Mrs. Memory said softly, removing her shawl and revealing the gray uniform folded over her arm, "but I came across these items a few moments ago."

Harry was sitting bolt upright now, his hands clutched to the arms of his chair like talons.

Stokes-Vecchio looked up wide-eyed as the head housekeeper deposited the garments in front of him on the desk. "Splendid, Mrs. Memory. And where did you find these?"

"They were in"—Lord protect her!—"the main linen closet on the second floor, sir. I was making a routine check and—found them folded and rumpled in a corner—as if hastily discarded—"

"Is that closet normally locked, Mrs. Memory?"

"Certainly."

"But could it not be opened by any of the chambermaids' keys?"

"No, sir. Only the senior girls have access to the main supply closets."

"And the dismissed maid—the one who claimed her key had been taken from her during the—the unfortunate episode in which Mr. Loring and the other—gentlemen—participated—"

"No, sir. She had only the room passkey."

"I see. Then it is possible that one of your own girls might have participated in some fashion in this—"

"I suppose it's possible, sir, but I would find it most unlikely. I know each of these women to be of high personal character."

"Of course." The manager looked over at the detective. "Nevertheless, you ought at least to speak with them individually."

"Right away," said Greenhouse and headed out the door.

Stokes-Vecchio turned to the guest, who shot his cuffs full-length and now wore a triumphant look of indignation. "Mr. Loring, I most humbly ask your forgiveness. I felt I had no choice but to—"

Harry was on his feet and sporting a thin smile. "If you will kindly reduce my charges to half the normal tariff for next season," he said, "I shall consider it ample apology." He shot his cuffs a second time and breezed out the manager's door with the merest nod of recognition to the housekeeper, who had, for reasons she could not have satisfactorily explained at that moment or any other, just saved the rogue's bacon.

Early in the blustery March afternoon of her second day back in New York, a package arrived for her without a return address. She tore it open and found a box containing a magnificent diamond bracelet centered by a giant purple amethyst. A little souvenir of their recent stay in the tropics, read the card in Harry's swirling hand.

That evening he explained it all, filling in the gaps. Even if the hotel detective had come to his room, it was unlikely that they would have discovered the jewels in the false bottom of his portmanteau, that useful object which his mentor, Neville Maskelyne, had willed him. But the uniform he had worn to commit the act was another matter entirely. Time had not allowed him to strip off the incriminating items and ditch them elsewhere on the premises. His gratitude to her was boundless; she was surely entitled to a reward for all the trouble she had gone to.

"Thank you," she said, "but I cannot possibly accept such a thing."

"Nonsense. You're far more deserving than its previous owner."

"The law is not hospitable to that theory of rightful possession."

"I care more about justice than the law. What really matters is not where the bracelet came from but how it was given to you."

"And how was that?"

"With love."

"Love," she said, "is not usually associated with contraband."

"That's what makes it a special gift. Anyway, I say it's not your conscience that objects to it—it's fear of incrimination."

"The thought did cross my mind."

"That's why I had it reset with an amethyst in place of the emerald."

"You call that love?"

"I call it practicality—no one will ever recognize it now."

She dropped her head onto his shoulder. "Harry, why have you worked so hard to corrupt me?"

"What a thoroughly ungrateful thing to say."

"I'm entirely serious."

"Also quite obtuse. I am not corrupting you, dear Madeleine. The truth is that we're birds of a feather, and I'm trying to get you to face the fact. Proper society has scorned us both, and each of us in our own way is paying it back for the insult. Only I'm more forthright about it."

"I hadn't realized."

"Exactly. I've managed to recreate myself in the image of my betters in order to prey upon them all the more readily—and I do not shy from admitting it to myself. Indeed, it sustains me in my profession. Your revenge is to serve them faithfully while secretly holding them all in contempt. But you cannot concede the resentment, however justified. Accept that in yourself by accepting the bracelet."

"Harry, that is—without a doubt—the most perverted bit of—"

"I am saving your soul, madam."

"You are a certified loon. I should have let them put you away."

"But you see—you did nothing of the kind. We're naturally and spiritually allies." He slipped the bracelet onto her wrist. "Now wear this with pride."

She broke into exasperated laughter. "I don't know whether to crown you or hug you."

"Hugging is regarded as the more affectionate."

So she hugged him, and they passed the rest of the evening devising other ways to express their mutual esteem. After he had left in the morning, she put the bracelet inside a spare biscuit tin that she stored on a high kitchen shelf and tried to forget it.

SIX

*D*uring her third and final season as head housekeeper of the Royal Poinciana, Madeleine Memory grew increasingly concerned over the suitability of a more permanent form of alliance with her lover. A domesticated rake, she told herself, was doubtless a contradiction in terms, but no other sort would serve if their relationship were ever to attain true dignity. Yet she feared, borrowing a tenet from Harry Loring's odd philosophy, that the longer their affair lasted and the more conventional it became, the more certain the excitement ignited by its scandalous nature was to drain out of it. The pressing question to be settled between them was which view—the morally upright or the lazily tolerant—would prevail; who, in short, would yield to whom? Or, assuming that neither conquest nor submission was acceptable to the other party, would they be able to split their differences?

Their lives had in fact become too intimately intertwined in New York for them to be happy under the restraints that governed them on their return to Palm Beach. They had shared so much since the close of the hotel's last season—dinners at glittering places and cozy holes-in-the-wall, theater and concerts and museums, excursions by carriage and boat and train, their hopes and dreads, jokes and reminiscences, propensities and frailties—that their forced separation at close hand was an all but unbearable prospect for her. It had been so very pleasant to wake up with him beside her in New York or in the bedrooms of his friends in Newport or Saratoga, now that her salary at the hotel had allowed her to stop working summers. He was with her several times weekly, on no special schedule—she understood fully by now that he did not function on other than a spontaneous basis—and when the demands of his purse required his occasional extended absences, she neither questioned nor caviled. The authenticity of his feelings for her (if not their depth), as demonstrated in a hundred different ways, large and small, satisfied her. Among certain of his friends and in the eyes of one of hers—namely, Agatha Agapé—they were an established couple.

The subject of marriage, though, was not raised except to ask how could it but inhibit their happiness together. "I don't see that it would make anything better" was all he said. For her, at any rate, a precondition for matrimony was his constancy, a subject not readily broached with him out of fear he would take it for dependency and disappear. He never spoke of his love for her, only in terms of adoration, which lent a slightly holy (if unsanctified) glow to their flame. Love, he implied at every opportunity, was for sentimentalists—too fragile, too vaporous, too altogether insubstantial to describe what fused them. Love was fickle and flighty, love was silly and he had no time or taste for silliness. He liked simplicity: she was his woman, and he was her man—most of the time. Any involvement of his with other women, he was at pains now to explain, was entirely vocational. Better yet, he sought to keep any such sallies from her attention while she largely controlled the impulse to inquire into matters that could only exacerbate her longings for him when they were apart.

It was therefore doubly hard on her to resume the character of the widowed and celibate Mrs. Memory after they had been cohabiting with regularity the rest of the year. The impediments to their lovemaking in the environs of the hotel were formidable. Having been discovered trysting in her suite by a chambermaid near the end of the previous season, she could no longer risk that arrangement. Harry's room was even more perilous. And Sunday-morning frolics at the beach were too far apart and too prone now to discovery, in view of the resort's rapid growth in popularity.

So they both welcomed the news that Charlie Franklin, that enterprising seigneur of the local demimonde, with whom Harry still played cards on occasion, had sensed the growing need for a suitable place of assignation away from the hotel among certain of its clientele. Charlie was now the owner of Miss Emily's Corset Shop on Magnolia Street in West Palm and two ample rooming houses around the corner on Yucca Avenue, conveniently connected to the shop by a trellised corridor hardly noticeable from the street. Bedrooms, attractively furnished and spotlessly maintained, to hear Charlie tell it, could be rented in the houses on Yucca either by the day or, more economically, by the week, month or season. Miss Emily, a most efficient former employee of Charlie's too far along in years to practice her arts profitably, presided over the enterprise with high discretion. A visit to the corset shop was an ideal alibi for women meeting their illicit lovers; what husband could object to such an errand, which could plausibly take hours at a time? The male half of his patronage, as Charlie explained his new undertaking, simply entered the rented premises directly from Yucca, with nobody the wiser.

On learning the details of the arrangement, Mrs. Memory was not overly enthusiastic. "But it's so obvious," she said, "and so—so—"

"I believe 'tawdry' is the word you're looking for."

"The very one."

"Charlie insists the sheets are clean and the better rooms reserved solely for the contract customers."

"But how would one know? Charlie, when all is said and done, is still a cheap panderer—"

"Disreputable but not cheap."

"—and will surely try to realize the maximum return on his investment. The very thought of hopping into a bed that's used all the time by others for that sort of—of—"

"You don't seem to mind sharing hotel rooms with me."

"That's different, somehow. One uses hotels for a variety of reasons, some even legitimate. Their function is not so singular and so—so—"

"Tawdry."

"Yes."

Then, too, there was her concern about Miss Emily and the potent use that might be made of the knowledge she possessed of her patrons' identity. "Now you're just being absurd," Harry reasoned. "It's her business—she's got to be discreet or Charlie'll cut her gizzard out."

"Maybe. But I still don't like it."

"I know, but there's nothing better—and I need you—and may I assume the need is mutual?"

"You may."

"Then think of it as a home away from home. You're home to me, Maddy, wherever we are."

Such rhapsodic sentiments from him were rare, and so she relented . . .

"Can you bear the place?" he asked her after they had left the room for the first time and were headed for the ferry landing.

"Actually, I think the commonness of it is rather stimulating."

"I noticed."

"The walls are on the thin side, though, and the quality of the bedding is deplorable. Do have a word with Charlie."

How very like her, he thought—that strict but offhand propriety, that precise yet funny way of putting a thing, that directness, that coiled strength, that intelligence that seemed to light her features from within, that mysterious marrow of soul that beautified her smile, rationed her tears and lent such unencumbered joy to her lovemaking with him. She may not have been the most gorgeous creature on earth or the most sensuous and supple partner he had ever encountered beneath the bed-covers, but nowhere on earth now did he hope to find a more desirable or satisfactory woman than his Maddy. Having won her, though, was no assurance of his keeping her, he knew, when there was so much about the life he led that still offended her. He would do anything to please her, short of pawning his manhood. He would speak firmly to Charlie about the walls—a corner room would be required—and demand linens fit for a queen, for she was no less to him in the secret realm they shared.

"Oh, Mr. Loring—there you are! I've been looking all over the hotel for you."

The young woman hiked up her skirts to ease her course toward him with quick little running steps, causing a single ebony lock that had somehow escaped her elaborate coiffure to bounce adorably next to the creamy gold of her neck. Could she possibly be unaware, Harry wondered, that her motion also disclosed her rose-stockinged ankles and several ruffled petticoats trimmed with lace? The girl needed to be taken aside and taught a thing or two about proper feminine deportment.

He had been doing his best to repulse the advances of Victoria Tor-rance, but she was not easily deflected. She had first thrown herself at him, quite literally, a week earlier on Children's Game Night, the hotel's regular Tuesday-evening entertainment, during a fast-paced round of musical chairs. He had fallen into one of the last seats available just as the music ended, and she, a fraction of a second later, slid herself right onto his lap. Courtesies at once took over, and he was soon caught up in her disarming chatter. Miss Torrance was too obviously pretty for her own good; only time would soften the sharply contrasting tones and planes of her youthful beauty. She could not have been much more than eighteen, though all she would say when Harry asked her age directly was that it was a woman's prerogative not to reveal it—"but I'm old enough," she added. He thought not.

In the ensuing week, nevertheless, Miss Torrance made a point of coming into daily contact with him somehow or other, whether at the seaside or the tennis courts, on the golf course or in any card room he happened to be occupying, where she would turn up with a less pretty friend or two for a game of hearts. Without excessive effort she also managed to get herself included in whatever evening activity his set engaged in.

Tracking him in this fashion was not difficult, for year after year the hotel's guests broke down into groups readily determined by age, marital status and social distinction. It was the unmarried set under thirty, with a few exceptions allowed for those older single men who were particularly attractive or spirited—the sub-category into which Harry Loring fell— who tended to enjoy the Royal Poinciana most. The group was linked less by age, actually, than the inclination of its members to pleasure-seeking ways, with couples and combinations forming and dissolving throughout the season in patterns heavily affected by the rose and mauve of the sky at sunset, the wafting fragrance of the frangipani and the whim of an eyelash fluttered one time too many. They tended to favor a certain sector of the lobby for post-meal gatherings to plan their activities and determine who would accompany whom. It was there that Victoria Torrance approached Harry each morning to gaze up into his eyes and ask if perhaps he would have time that day to improve her tennis game or help her overcome her errant golf swing.

The girl was so flagrant an exhibitionist with regard to her claims on his time and attention that her behavior could not for long escape Maddy's notice. Harry's sensitivity to her feelings was by now so acute, at any rate, that he knew it was impossible for him to cavort, however innocently, as he had in the past under the hothouse conditions prevailing at the hotel without causing her distress. So he confided in her wholly. Miss Torrance, he conceded, would have aroused his interest a few years earlier. A blend of artless, vulnerable child, transparently eager for his companionship, and calculating, self-centered woman, intolerant of any frailities except her own, she was at the very least diverting. He was uncertain what this ravishing woman-child needed more—to be taken over his knee or into his bed. She was far too old for the former and, alas (he told Maddy with a wink), too young for the latter. The only sure way to avoid temptation—not to mention the scalding reprimand of the head housekeeper—was for him to keep out of the girl's sight, an economic impossibility: he could not afford to cut himself off from a prime source of income in the form of the attractive young people with whom she was so adept at surrounding herself.

To complicate matters, Harry had learned that her grandfather had died recently and that her widowed father had inherited sole proprietorship of the Connecticut Cotton Company, the world's fifth largest spinner of thread. Attractive as his daughter was, her father was the worthier prey. If he could be cultivated through her, she had to be dealt with. A tricky but promising game.

"Why should it bother me in the least?" asked Madame Memphis in response to his disclosures, leaning back in the restaurant chair and batting her heavily made-up eyes in mockery of the girl's demonstrative wiles. "Merely because the child is less than half my age—and her skin is soft and smooth and without a wrinkle? How could I be envious of your dallying with such a gorgeous young creature who's picked you to educate her into the mysteries of adulthood?" She emitted a little cadenza of false laughter. "Beez-nees ees beez-nees, *n'est-ce pas*, Monsieur Loring?"

In light of his vow to her not to employ his light fingers in larceny or his lithe limbs in fornication with any other woman—she had made clear to him she viewed the hotel season in its entirety as a test of his fidelity—Maddy was untroubled by the flirtations of Victoria Torrance, until, that is, Harry let himself be trapped into accompanying the little vixen on a ride out to the Everglades after dark with a party of other gay youngsters. "Don't you love the tropics at night?" Victoria had asked. "It's so soft and dank and slightly menacing. Florida reminds me of—I don't know what—India or Cathay or some place exquisitely exotic. It smells so different from dreary old Waterbury." Harry resisted the lures of the wild, especially after dark. There were crocs and gators out there, he said, and quicksand and twenty kinds of snakes, not to mention spiders and scorpions and millions of mosquitoes the size of coconuts just lying in wait for them. "Why, Mr. Loring," the siren sang back to him, "I never thought you of all people would be a scaredy-cat about a few baby insects."

His masculinity challenged, Harry found himself at the end of the long jolting carriage ride in the vicinity of Wilson's Pond and Black Bottom Creek, where a three-quarter moon illuminated the way in places, but the deep shadows of the tangled trees and shrubbery obscured it completely in others. Victoria hung back from the rest of their party and, her hand creeping into his, announced, "I don't want to see the pond. I'd rather wander around here on our own—with all the smells and strange noises and wild things. I want to feel the way it must have been just outside the Garden of Eden when the world began." Then she grabbed his hand more firmly and tugged him after her as she plunged into the wildwood.

With his free hand he batted at things that swarmed around his face and ears, yielding to his better judgment. Suddenly the girl was out of his grasp, tumbling earthward and emitting a small squeal of pain. Her foot had become snagged on a wayward tree root, and her twisted ankle left her temporarily immobile, she said. It was not a good place to be marooned, especially with a seductive enchantress. He had no choice but to scoop her up from the moist ground, encountering the silk organza of Victoria's skirt and the several layers of her lace-swagged petticoats, and to carry her to a safe spot to recover, while trying to gather his strength to carry her over the nearly invisible terrain. It was slow going, and when she said her ankle was no longer throbbing he asked her to try to stand on it. "All right," she said, "but first give me something to ease the pain."

"Like what?" he asked.

"Like this," she said, reaching around his neck, pulling his head down and fastening her lips to his.

In the heat of the moment he reacted instinctively as he would have to the kiss of a more experienced woman, and she, an apt pupil, perceiving at once what might be expected of her, returned what she was receiving with the avidity of a hungry child offered a luscious chocolate.

"I'm glad it was you who showed me—about kissing," she said afterward as she hobbled back to the carriage, seeming to gain strength with each step. "My instinct was right about you, after all. I'll always remember this, Mr. Loring."

Harry, of course, respectfully suggested that she forget about the incident at her earliest convenience, and he faithfully reported the proceedings, with amusing embellishments, to Maddy, whose equanimity, he could see, wavered only slightly before the fullness of his revelations. Still, they made her uneasy, and she confessed her yearning to see more of him after dark and something other than the inside of a rural restaurant and a squalid rooming house. "Right you are," he said. "I think it's time for Madame Memphis to join me as a guest in the hotel dining room."

At first the risk seemed too great to her, but in view of the improvements to her disguise that Agatha Agapé had equipped her with—a subtle shift in the set of her shoulders, a drawerful of theatrical makeup with elaborate instructions for the use of every vial and bottle, a wig of human hair far darker than Maddy's own natural shade—she let herself be persuaded. All went well until Victoria Torrance sailed by their table on her father's arm, and in no time she had intruded on their privacy by extracting from Harry an invitation to join them in an after-dinner drink. Tall, ruddy and going to suet, Caleb Torrance proved by no means charmless, and a spirited conversation developed. The girl, with light touches on Harry's arm, was so transparent in her coquetry that Maddy seemed to him more amused than annoyed by her. Here, truly, was no rival claimant for Harry's heart. Indeed, she found Victoria so curious about her origins and attentive to the conduct of an assured older woman that Madame Memphis did not protest when the girl's father took Harry off to the bar for a cigar. In their absence Miss Torrance wasted no time in confiding the secrets of her young life to her captive listener.

"You see," she said, nibbling at the last of a dismaying number of petit fours she had consumed since gaining a seat at their table, "I *had* to go away to the Phoebe Blackwood Seminary—to be finished. There was simply no place to carry on with my studies in Waterbury." And growing up without a mother was such a dreadful handicap for a girl; why, she had never even made a proper debut. Her Aunt Thelma, her mother's sister, had tried to be kind, she supposed, but they never got along, not even at Christmas dinner. "Auntie hates me because I look just like my poor mama who stole her beloved Caleb away from her and she had to settle instead for boring old Uncle Harold and his churchful of adoring parishoners. She never forgave my mother, so she takes it out on me. I think she smells funny because she's decided that taking baths is unwholesome in God's eyes. She washes herself beneath her underclothes. I'll bet you anything Uncle Harold has never seen her in the altogether. Did you ever *hear* of such a thing?"

She had not. Nor had she ever heard any woman, of any age, reveal intimate family relationships or discuss personal hygiene with such sang-froid. Her father should have demanded his money back from the Phoebe Blackwood Seminary; the girl was decidedly unfinished.

"Your father must have loved your mother very much never to have remarried," said Madame Memphis. "They say every girl needs a mother."

"I don't. I have Daddy. And why should he remarry? He can have a new doxy every month if he likes—and he usually does."

Her words were shocking. A proper young woman was not supposed to know of such things, and surely not to acknowledge them, much less discuss them with a stranger. Perhaps the girl seemed so unbridled because she had rarely had the chance to talk with a woman of the world. "Indeed," Madame Memphis replied, concluding that the effusive Miss Torrance would benefit more from a cautioning older female than a male mentor of Harry's libidinous inclinations.

Victoria's designs on Harry, it turned out, were matched by her father's on the exotic Madame Memphis. "He asked my permission to request the pleasure of your company some evening soon," Harry told her after the Torrances had gone on their way. "And I would be far better off, he advised, escorting his daughter. I believe he sees me as a suitable candidate for her hand."

"And why not? The nubile child is probably the prize catch in all of Waterbury. You've reached the age, Monsieur Loring, when you ought perhaps to think about settling down with a buxom wife and her father's hefty fortune."

"It's the fortune I'm applying for, not the wife. And with your delightful cooperation, I think he can be parted from some small part of it."

"Cooperation?"

"Yes. Go out with Caleb and show him a good time—and sing my praises to him in the process. I think we can soften him up with a two-pronged attack."

"Harry, don't be an imbecile! I will not be an active party to any underhanded scheming of yours. And I most assuredly will not make myself available to that—that lecherous man. No doubt he thinks anyone of French extraction is nimble in the amorous arts."

"No doubt. But you'll know how to deal with him. He's a highly respectable industrialist whom Madame Memphis should be honored to have escort her. He can call for you at the rooming house."

"*Our* rooming house? No, I couldn't. He might assume—"

"So what? Just makes you a more delectable French pastry."

"Harry!"

"Maddy, he's one fat pigeon. With your help I can land him."

"And the girl?"

"Merely an avenue to her daddy's heart—I swear it."

She sighed. "What is it you have in mind exactly?"

The opening that season of a gambling casino in Palm Beach just a short walk north of the Royal Poinciana, everyone agreed, was an inspired stroke by Henry Flagler. The great tycoon was said to have no part in the ownership of the new enterprise but had blessed its creation and arranged for it to be operated by a thoroughly knowledgeable professional. The hotel's male guests—females, by Flagler's genteel edict, were not permitted access to the casino—needed more stimulating entertainment in the evenings than the tame musical and cultural programs regularly presented on the premises. Besides, nearly every other first-class resort community in the world, from Cannes and Deauville to Newport and Saratoga, boasted a casino.

What was good for Henry Flagler's hotel business, however, was not necessarily good for Harrison St. John Loring's pocketbook. The easy availability of organized games of chance in an attractive setting, Harry discovered at once, was cutting into his potential victims' interest in a nice little friendly game of high-stakes poker. Indeed, the resulting drop in his income was the chief reason for his interest in cultivating Caleb and

Victoria Torrance. He was nonetheless determined to turn the existence of the casino to his advantage.

Everything about the place, he related to Maddy, was discreetly understated, starting with its exterior, which resembled a cluster of gray-shingled barns that gave no hint of the strictly illegal activity inside. By assuming the guise of a private club (admission by membership card only, a mere formality in the case of the hotel's guests), the casino took on an aura of exclusivity that appealed to the Royal Poinciana's socially prominent clientele while placing it beyond the reach of the law. The only identifying insignia on the outside of the place were the initials "B. C." in Old English lettering incised into the frosted glass panel in the formidable front door. Could there be a less provocative name for a casino catering to *la crème de la crème* than, simply, the Beach Club? Most people, though, called it Bradley's after its somewhat mysterious impresario, Colonel Edward Reilly Bradley, who as a young buck, according to the story going the rounds, had served as an Indian scout with the army and played a vital role in the capture of the warrior chieftain Geronimo. Not a figure to trifle with, they said.

The light in the doorway of Bradley's establishment, Harry noticed on his first visit, was tactfully dim so that entering customers, many of whom held high financial responsibilities in their home communities, might avoid easy detection by passersby. Inside, the club greatly resembled the Royal Poinciana, with its white walls and green carpeting, rattan and wicker furnishings and ubiquitous jardinières thick with tropical foliage. In the foyer, one nodded to but avoided encounter with a squad of guards in dinner jackets that did not quite conform to their stocky shapes. Intruders on either side of the law risked a rude welcome.

Next to the blank on the membership application asking his occupation, Harry wrote "Investor" and for references listed the names of several acquaintances at the hotel and those of his banker and broker in New York. Then he joined Caleb Torrance and two other gentlemen from the hotel for dinner in the club restaurant. In place of a menu the waiter recited the available selections; no mention was made of prices on the implied understanding that if one had to ask, one had no business being there. The food proved superb, incomparably better than anything in West Palm and one full notch above the hotel's fine cuisine.

They tarried at table long enough for cigars and port, since neither drinking nor smoking was permitted beyond the dining area—a curiously unclubby stricture, by Harry's reckoning. Perhaps it had to do with the wealth and social standing of the potential clientele; anything less than the most proper and fastidious setting might have discouraged their attendance. And the high stakes of the gaming required a decided sobriety in the security arrangements: in addition to guards tactfully scattered throughout, Bradley was said to have stationed a sharpshooting rifleman at a strategic shielded post to repulse any ill-advised holdup men. It was as much an armed stronghold as a sportsmen's gathering place.

The gambling itself was confined to the club's "ballroom," an approximate replica in miniature of the Royal Poinciana's octagonal grand ballroom, and a second-floor room, reachable only by elevator, for card games. The two-story ballroom was divided into quarters, one each allotted to the roulette, faro, hazard and *chemin de fer* tables. A sign just inside the door instructed guests to refrain from loud talk and laughter. Overhanging the room was a balcony with a high lattice-work railing, behind the diamond-shaped spaces of which, Harry supposed, more guards (Bradley's rifleman likely among them) monitored the players and housemen below.

In place of the murmuring undertow customary in gambling palaces was a hushed void in which the only sounds were an occasional cough, the low call of dealers telling the customers when to bet, the tiny rattle of jumping roulette balls and the click of the croupiers' sticks working the chips back and forth. To further deaden the feeling of the place, in Harry's view, there was no rustle of silk or fragrance of perfume in the air. For him, the one ingredient essential to the elixir of Palm Beach was the presence of women, highly positioned and brightly costumed, passions awakened by the heat of the day and the evening breeze, all ripe for flattery, bedazzling and possibly embezzling. Without them, it was a sterile outpost.

He would have preferred to wander upstairs to the card tables to allow his special gifts full rein. But he was not after a killing, certainly not on his first visit to such a policed establishment. If he was spotted as a sharp, he might well be invited never to return. Instead, he drifted over to the roulette tables, resolved to play for a modest gain by pursuing the systematic approach that his late mentor had taught him but that he rarely used.

The Maskelyne system for beating the roulette wheel was based on the theory of mathematical probability. The gambler, betting only on which one third of the board would hold the winning number, put down two bets, thereby covering two thirds of the winning possibilities. With a two-to-one payoff, the bettor could thereby make steady but unspectacular gains. But since there was still a sizable chance for losing in any given round, the system required the bettor to raise his wager to slightly more than double the amount put down on his previous losing bet—and to keep it up, raising his stake in that proportion no matter how many consecutive defeats might be suffered. If the bettor's nerve held, sooner or later the numbers would fall his way and his losses would be covered, with something left over for profit. Then he started all over again with a small initial bet.

By the time he quit that first night—and before his winnings had attracted much attention—Harry was $1,150 ahead, enough to cover a week's expenses at the hotel. He gave a fifty-dollar chip to the croupier with thanks and went to collect his winnings. At the cashier's window, though, he was told that payoffs of more than a thousand dollars were made in the office just off the ballroom floor; Mr. Bradley himself liked to do the honors in such cases, if Mr. Loring did not mind. Mr. Loring did not. In fact, he rather wanted to make the acquaintance of the proprietor who was so wreathed in legend. Besides his repute as an Indian-fighter, Colonel Bradley was said to have been, at various times, a cowboy, a miner, a steelworker, a racetrack tout, a horse-breeder, a Chicago realtor who made and lost a fortune, and a casino operator in places as far flung as New Mexico and Long Branch, New Jersey.

Bradley was standing at his desk when Harry was ushered in—a man slightly taller and a good deal stockier than himself, with a rigid posture suggesting a severe dignity. His eyes, blue agates so transparently pale that the irises seemed almost to disappear when the room light struck them at certain angles, gestured his new customer into the oversized wicker chair opposite him and coolly took his measure. "I think it's good manners to congratulate our big winners, Mr. Loring."

"Good business, too," Harry said with a grin.

"I hope so," Bradley answered soberly.

From the touch of gray in his hair and the crow's-feet at the corners of his eyes, the man was perhaps six or seven years his senior, Harry calculated, but there was a definite weathered character to his look, as if he had survived some very tight squeezes in his wanderings. "I'm highly impressed with what you've done here, Colonel—it's different from any other gaming establishment I've ever been to, and that includes most of the better casinos around the country and abroad. I notice, though, that you're a stickler about keeping the wicked weed and the demon rum in their places."

"The Flagler influence," Bradley replied. "We're trying to maintain the Beach Club as a haven for gentlemen of the highest order. Alcohol and spittoons seem inappropriate." He glanced over Harry's membership application, which had been brought to his desk for approval. "Well, we're pleased to have you with us, Mr. Loring." He scrawled his initials on the form and slid a club card across the desktop to Harry. "What kind of investing do you do—if you don't mind my asking?"

"Oh, a little of this and a little of that. Anything that strikes my fancy. Just at the moment I'm in with some people pursuing the African ivory trade. Risky business, of course, but it can be highly rewarding. We've got a few shares still open, Colonel, if you happen to be interested."

"Thanks, but I leave the gambling to others." He reached into his pocket and withdrew a thick wad of bills. "By the way, Mr. Loring, you needn't bother with that 'Colonel' business—I'm plain Mr. Bradley."

"I'd understood there was an illustrious army career somewhere in your background—injuns and such."

"There's some truth to that, but the 'Colonel' part is strictly window dressing. I raise a few thoroughbreds in Kentucky, so they made me one of their tinhorn colonels. Not that I'm ungrateful to my Kentucky friends but I'm leery of people who pass themselves off as something they're not—starting with myself." He unclasped his bills, counted out Harry's winnings and pushed them across the desk. "I hope you'll give us a chance to win some of this back, Mr. Loring."

"That shouldn't be too hard. I usually do better at roulette as a spectator than a player."

"Either way, you're welcome here." He rose and extended his hand. "But I wouldn't stick with that system of yours too long," he added. "I've seen it drive men to ruin."

The two next met ten days later on a Thursday afternoon at the hotel golf course. Bradley, playing with a foursome that was just behind his, greeted Harry after he had driven off the fourteenth tee. The latter took the liberty of asking the casino owner how his business was faring. "You've got pretty heavy expenses there, I'd guess," he added. "I hope you're luring enough customers."

Circumspect in his response, Bradley nevertheless indicated that all was not going quite as well as he had hoped and wondered, in that connection, whether he might have a word with him in the clubhouse at the end of play.

Over rum coolers, Bradley said, "Since you were kind enough to ask, we're not getting enough people in the door to cover expenses, which, as you noted, are large. I thought that given your apparent familiarity with establishments similar to ours elsewhere, you might have an idea or two to help us out. Needless to say, I'd appreciate your keeping this exchange confidential."

Harry nodded, expressed thanks for the flattery implied by the inquiry and asked whether anything could be done to reduce costs.

"Not without altering the character of the place. I intend to run a first-class club here, Mr. Loring, or no club at all. That's what Mr. Flagler asked me to do, and that's what we've arranged."

"So you have," Harry said with a sympathetic sigh. "Perhaps Mr. Flagler would consider subsidizing you for a season or two while the clientele builds up."

"My understanding is that Mr. Flagler doesn't operate that way."

Suddenly recalling Maddy's spirited exchange two years earlier with Richard Canfield at his club in New York, he savored it for a moment before broaching the inspiration. Then he said, "Actually, I do have a thought that you might want to entertain. I ask only that you hear me out before rejecting it."

"Fair enough."

Most of the Royal Poinciana's guests, Harry began, were married, and the wives by and large resented it, he had heard, when their husbands went off to the Beach Club to gamble without them. And because not a few of the wives grew testy imagining what went on at Bradley's den of iniquity, their husbands gave in to them rather than quarrel. "So they stay away in droves—and you lose their business." He was of course familiar, Harry went on, with certain traditions of the casino world, among the most widely subscribed to being the belief that women around a gambling table were bad luck—and were thus barred from most establishments for that reason as well as for propriety's sake. "But suppose you stood that superstition on its ear, Mr. Bradley? After all, this is a rather special resort—and remote from the nation's more populous regions. You've got to make do with what potential customers there are in the immediate vicinity—and I would suggest to you that there might be a great many of them among the women here. I cannot conceive that your business would suffer one iota if, instead of barring the female of the species from the premises, you greeted them with open arms. Then they'd see the quality of the establishment and be far less inclined to object to their husbands' coming. And they themselves would almost certainly enjoy the gaming and come frequently as well."

Bradley sat motionless for a time, musing on the idea. "Leaving the question of propriety aside, I'm afraid it would entirely change the character of the club."

"I don't see why you couldn't insist that the ladies abide by the same rules as the men."

"The ladies," said Bradley, "are different sorts of creatures."

"Yes, and *vive la différence*—but in view of the nature of the crowd that the hotel attracts, I doubt you'd have a bunch of banshees on your hands."

"Perhaps not. It just goes against everything I've ever—"

"Yes, and that may be precisely why the time is ripe for risking it. Why don't you consider running an experiment? Why not proclaim a 'Sweethearts' Night' or some such thing and invite the ladies into the club? The Bull's Head in Saratoga used to run Women's Nights there every Monday when business was normally very slow, and the pace picked up beautifully. I believe you'd have the same result here."

Bradley was plainly intrigued. "I doubt Mr. Flagler would approve of the idea, though. He specifically told me he didn't want women in the club. He has a very exalted notion of womanhood."

"Oh, hang Flagler! Listen, Mr. Bradley, you're fighting for your financial life here. What have you got to lose? You simply *must* fire all your ammunition. Flagler's a businessman—he'll understand what you're up against."

A tentative smile played across Bradley's fixed features. "Thank you, Loring. You've given me food for thought—food for thought, indeed."

On an overcast Sunday morning inhospitable to ocean bathing, Mrs. Memory and her lover passed up their usual frolic on the beach and repaired instead, by separate routes of arrival, to their rented room on Yucca Avenue in West Palm, where they passed several hours in languorous dalliance. At its conclusion, the couple returned together across Lake Worth, she in the guise of her flamboyant alter ego, whose wardrobe she divided now between her West Palm and hotel accommodations.

As they headed back from the ferry dock along the shaded path that wound through the hotel grounds, they recognized the white-haired old gentleman with the abundant mustache and his female companion, a small, freckled woman looking young enough to be his daughter, approaching in the opposite direction. They slowed to pay respectful greeting. "*Bonjour,* Mademoiselle Kenan," said Madame Memphis, executing an elaborate curtsey. "A *play-zhur* to see you, Monsieur Flagler." Whatever inhibitions Maddy had retained in the display of her incognito were swept away in that impulsive moment; who better to flaunt it at than the absolute potentate of Palm Beach and his petite consort? Harry marveled at her daring.

Though he did not by nature welcome such familiarity, Flagler nodded cordially to the other couple, who introduced themselves, and was so pleased at the spontaneous warmth of their greeting that he paused to make their acquaintance. Harry had always said to Maddy how he wanted to meet the multimillionaire and probe for the secret source of his seemingly infinite aptitude for making money. Given the opportunity, he did not fail to make the most of it. While the women chatted about the unkindness of the sun for having deserted them on the sabbath, he sang the praises of the Royal Poinciana and told its builder how greatly he had enjoyed his three seasons in attendance, each more so than the preceding one. "And apparently I'm far from alone—I hear there are plans afoot, sir, to increase the size of the hotel at the end of the season."

"I appreciate your kind words, Mr. Loring—and your patronage as well. That's the final test, isn't it?" The expression on the old man's face was unchanging despite the pride evident in his voice. The architects had nearly completed their designs for the expansion, he acknowledged. "We're going to add another couple of hundred rooms and of course enlarge the dining facilities as well. I can't tell you how many people we've had to turn away simply because there was no room at the inn." The breathy gusts that erupted from the back of his throat just then might have been either laughter or the effects of chronic catarrh—it was impossible to tell which; his mouth did not turn upward and his teeth and upper lip remained hidden beneath the mustache that projected forward like a small shelf under his nose. To be safe, Harry smiled at the remark and hazarded the guess that the resort would soon become so popular that additional hotels were likely to flourish there in time.

Their pleasantries were interrupted by the raucous approach of a horseless carriage, chugging and sputtering toward them and filling the entire width of the path. As it bore down on them, emitting a series of small explosive bursts, Harry shepherded the pedestrians onto the lawn, leaving the way clear for the jangling vehicle to proceed on its course to the lakeside. "Ahoy, friend Flagler!" called out the driver over the noise of the machine, raising his white yachting cap with one hand while trying to maintain control of the steering mechanism with the other.

"Commodore Kane," Flagler replied without raising his voice, and touched the brim of his elegant panama. The halfhearted gesture and the softness of his greeting betrayed a lack of enthusiasm. "Commodore, indeed," he confided to Harry. "The man owns a bunch of beat-up old barges that run down the Delaware from Trenton to Philadelphia. If an ocean wave rose up and swatted him in the bow, he'd be the first man overboard." More catarrhal gusts. "Man's a hopeless landlubber. I tried to buy his property here a few years back, but he wouldn't sell then—and the stubborn coot won't sell now. Can't say I blame him, though—everything we're doing here only makes his place more valuable—but that dreadful gadget of his is something else again. He keeps it here all the time now—infernal combustion, I call it." Another genial wheeze. "Roars like the fires of hell and smells twice as bad, if you ask me."

"But they say they're the coming thing," Harry countered. "Very twentieth century and all that."

"I'm rather attracted still to the nineteenth," said the mogul. "It hasn't done too badly by us."

"I should think, though, you'd be pleased by the arrival of these contraptions, what with their being powered by petroleum—in which, I'm told, you take some interest."

"Oh, I do indeed, sir, and any new use for the stuff suits me fine. But new machines take time to develop—to get the goblins out of them. I don't think they should let 'em out of the barn till they can run with the herd, so to speak. Now with enough time and tinkering, these buggies might well prove useful for carrying goods to market or helping farmers till their fields—I have no doubt of that. But they shouldn't be used just to cart every blamed fool from place to place when there are other perfectly satisfactory and unobjectionable means of transportation. And these mechanical horrors most certainly do not belong on this beautiful island. Our bicycles and Afrimobiles are clean and quiet and get you around with dignity and all the speed a sensible man needs." He tipped his hat and turned abruptly toward Miss Kenan. "We'd better let these youngsters go on their way," he said. "A pleasure, Mr. Loring—and you, madam. We're particularly delighted to have French visitors with us at the hotel."

"Alas, monsieur, I cannot afford your 'ospitality—I stay across ze lake."

"Ahh. The misfortune is ours, my dear."

"*Charmant*," said Madame Memphis as they moved off.

"If only," said Harry, "the man played poker."

On the second evening that he escorted Madame Memphis to dinner at the Silver Swan in West Palm, Caleb Torrance spotted Harry Loring across the room from them in the company of several card-playing cronies whom he had not deserted despite the opening of Bradley's Beach Club. To the great pleasure of Torrance's companion, the thread manufacturer invited Harry to join them for dessert and proceeded, in remarkably unsubtle fashion, to solicit his attentions to the charming Victoria, who was back at the hotel, he said, "in the company of some little pantywaist I wouldn't use to mop the floor with. The child needs a man of the world to direct her life—I won't be around forever."

Over a new bottle of a full-bodied '78 Bordeaux, the two men began to discuss the merits and drawbacks of bachelorhood, to Madame Memphis's amused indulgence. "The trouble is," Harry said expansively, "I like my good times too well. I crave the theater and fine food and traveling in style and having my clothes made by the best tailors in New York and London. It's true my investments have done well for me, and I can afford to spend the whole season down here, but it all comes to a pretty penny. Why give all that up to the snares of domesticity?"

"I don't see why you can't have it both ways, my boy. Living in Connecticut may be a far cry from that New York high life of yours, but I manage to run a business and a home and still have a good time of it."

"Yes, but without a wife."

"I just haven't found the right woman," Torrance said, then with a look at Madame Memphis added, "yet."

"Maybe you don't really want to," Harry ventured. "Or maybe I'm a slave to the license of a fellow who's never been hitched. When a man takes a wife, he can't go on living like a gypsy. He's got to move out of his club and acquire a proper home with a full clutch of servants, and a carriage and horses, and go through the whole social rigamarole that respectable married folks do. I'm not sure someone like me could get accustomed to that sort of thing."

Torrance drained his wine and, finding no waiter nearby, reached for the bottle himself. "For the right woman," he said, refilling their glasses, "a man makes sacrifices."

"No doubt," said Harry, his eyes fixed on Torrance, "no doubt."

" 'Course a fella like you, now, can afford to be choosy. If it was me, I'd hold out for a gal from people of means who'd expect to do their share in setting up a fine household for their daughter. Certainly any fella who wound up with my Vicky would be entitled to that sort of generosity— not to mention the bequest her grandfather left her that I watch over like a hawk. And then there's the balance of her mother's estate that she'll come into on her twenty-fifth birthday. Oh, my little girl's going to be a distinct asset in somebody's ledger—which is why I've got to be danged sure whoever gets her has the right reasons."

"Caleb, with or without all that, your little girl would be the brightest star in any man's firmament. It's just that . . ." Harry groped momentarily before deciding which way to lead his prey.

Torrance's eyes narrowed. "Just what?"

"I was brought up by old-fashioned, hardworking folks in a little Pennsylvania town you've never heard of, and my father raised me to—"

"I didn't catch what it was your father did for a living."

"Some folks said he was the best judge of horseflesh in the whole East. He bought and sold 'em, bred 'em, trained 'em, raced 'em. Called our place Meadowberry Farm—and did right well with it. What I remember most about him, though, was his preaching to me that I had to be my own man. Oh, he helped me along, made sure I got some schooling, but anything beyond that he wanted me to earn by myself—that was life's principal satisfaction, he used to say. And that's stuck with me ever since."

"That's all well and good, but some of us have to suffer with inheriting the thing—and I don't see any shame in that—not so long as you—"

"That's not my point, Caleb. I'm saying that if I ever married a gal who came from money, that's all fine and dandy, but what's hers is hers, the way I look at it—I could never consent to sponge off any woman. And I sure as shootin' wouldn't take on the responsibility of a wife and the little ones that are sure to follow and all the rest of it until I felt thoroughly secure about my own finances. That's why I keep looking for promising investments—and like to wander around so much, talking to people. You never know what's going to turn up. Why, I was talking with Henry Flagler just the other day, for example, about the horseless carriage. He's convinced, like I am—though not everyone else agrees—that they're the invention of the future."

"He thinks that? They tell me it's still a pretty primitive gadget."

"Sure—and that's why now's the time to get into it." As a matter of fact, Harry said, working on his wine as he warmed to his task, only a few weeks before he'd left New York he heard about an old fellow up in Dutchess County who had developed a very special kind of horseless carriage—he'd been tinkering with the thing for years and had finally got it to the stage where it was ready for manufacture and he was willing to let a small number of investors come in with him to start up a factory. "So I hopped the train to Poughkeepsie and then it was another couple of hours by carriage out to the place. He was in the middle of nowhere, all right, but by golly, the oldtimer had really come up with something out there in the wilderness."

Torrance's eyes began to widen with each sentence of Harry's account. "What was it, man?"

"The damnedest-looking thing you ever saw." The carriage part was conventional enough, but the wheels were like great big India-rubber doughnuts. And you could hardly see the spokes at all. In the middle of each wheel, the savvy old mechanic had imbedded a row of metal prongs—looked as if he'd hammered a hundred dinner forks into the hub. "Now, I thought to myself, this geezer has to be the craziest loon in the country. But those things had a purpose."

Harry paused to let out some more line. "What?" asked Torrance, grabbing it.

"He claimed those prongs gave his carriage the ability to run over ice and snow, sand and mud—anything that covered the ground—and when it was bare, the prongs retracted right up inside the wheel frame so the carriage could go like blazes over stone or brick or earth." The oldtimer took him for a ride over his frozen pond, and then up and down a mound of sand in his barnyard, and then, since it had rained during his visit, there was a big mess of mud near his stables that the vehicle cut through like a hot knife slicing butter. The thing even rode roughshod across neighboring cornfields where the stalks had been cut down but not yet turned under. "It's a real miracle worker. And best of all was its engine. Purred right along like a kitten without all the racket that you hear all these other contraptions make."

Torrance was in a near-trance now.

"He intends to call the finished machine The Zephyr because he thinks it feels like you're riding the wind in it. He wasn't far wrong, either."

Torrance shook his head. "Isn't that something?"

When he got back to the city, said Harry, readying for the kill, he spoke to his friend who'd put him onto the deal and said he wanted in. There were to be five partners sharing equally in the factory, with the old-timer to receive a quarter of the profits and a small royalty on every unit sold. "I put up five thousand in earnest money with the promise of another fifteen by February first if my friend wires me the go-ahead. The factory should start up in June or thereabouts. Within a couple or three years, the money should be pouring in—unless I was dreaming up there."

Torrance studied the dregs of his wine glass. "And you say all the shares are taken in this little venture?"

"I've no idea, Caleb. I gather that's what the February first date is all about. But that's only a little ways off. I can be patient."

Torrance cleared his throat while Madame Memphis poured herself some more wine, the better to anesthetize herself to Harry's scalping operation. "But if somebody else wanted to get in right now," his subject inquired, "is it too late?"

"Beats me."

"Could you find out?"

"Sure. The only thing is, Caleb—and I have to be honest with you— this friend of mine always plays his cards pretty close to his chest and rarely deals with strangers, especially ones who aren't used to taking a plunge now and then. He doesn't want recriminations if his ventures come a-cropper—which means he'll only take in people with a little money to burn."

"Well, it wouldn't bankrupt me to try my luck at something a little more exciting than thread."

"That's the right attitude—only I wouldn't like to see you riled up if the answer still turns out to be no to a stranger."

"Hell, you and I aren't strangers anymore, Harry. We might even get to be kissing kin somewhere along the line. You could vouch for me. Tell him we've got a bank account as long as your arm—"

"Well, I could give it a try."

Torrance snapped his fingers. "Listen, even if your man says no, maybe you could buy in for me in your name. I'd give you a bank draft and we'd shake on it."

"I suppose that's possible—assuming the deal's not already set. But I'm still uneasy about your going into it strictly on my say-so."

"Your judgment's good enough for me, son—yours and Henry Flagler's." He gave a hoot of a laugh and raised his wine glass to the venture. "Say, why not wire your pal tonight?" Torrance added, licking the wine from his lips and clapping Harry on the shoulder. "The telegraph desk's open till twelve—and you know what they say: strike while the iron's hot."

The transaction was consummated the next forenoon, while the iron was nearly molten. To celebrate, Torrance had Harry join him and Victoria for luncheon on the terrace. Under the circumstances, Harry could hardly rebuff Miss Torrance's further invitation to play a round of golf later in the day when the sun was subsiding.

"Now just try to remember what I've been telling you," he said as she reached toward the caddy for her club on the seventh tee.

"You must think I'm a terrible cretin, Mr. Loring." She placed the ball on the tee with a graceful kneel, then took two steps back and raised the club for a practice swing. Down it swished with youthful force. "Bam!" she said, "right on the green."

"Bam, yourself. You won't hit it ten yards if you keep turning the club in your hands that way."

"Right, right—Vicky's a bad girl."

He stepped toward her to help adjust the position of her hands on the club just as she decided to take another practice swing to correct the problem. His outstretched right arm and the arc of her furiously wielded driver intersected on the upward journey of her swing. The crack of hard wood against bone was audible to all three sets of ears in the immediate vicinity. Instantly he felt the white-hot intensity of pain that shot through the right side of his body from fingertips to knees.

The head housekeeper was on hand when he awakened in his hotel room and groaned at the sight of his heavily bandaged arm. "Divine retribution," she said.

"Whoever heard of a one-armed professional cardplayer?" he said, ignoring her unkindness.

"Perhaps the time has come," Mrs. Memory suggested, "to consider a different profession."

"No," he said, gazing out the window, "I think that fate has just furnished me the greatest challenge of my career. Now if you would kindly have a bellman bring me up a whiskey and soda, madam, I'd be much obliged."

On the evening that Bradley's Beach Club threw open its doors to women for a one-night trial, Harry arrived with Madame Memphis on his good arm to assess the goings-on. The early signs were not encouraging to anyone who took his gambling seriously.

Society people who were normally possessed of the most impeccable decorum made a mad rush to get through the casino door for fear they would be excluded if they arrived too late. The line in front of the cashier's booth grew so long that a makeshift one had to be set up to accommodate the demand. And the gambling itself was something to behold. The women, probably because so few of them had ever enjoyed the opportunity to play at a casino, were making the most outlandish bets, staking large sums on absurd combinations, devising implausible reasons for "lucky" numbers that behaved in no such fashion, backing faro cards without the slightest reference to which ones had already been dealt. Rarely in the annals of games of chance had there been such profligate spending for so few rewards.

Amid the tumult, Harry refrained from play, preferring instead to observe and call to Madame Memphis's attention the finer points of the establishment. "It's like an armed camp," she said. "I should think that would detract from the sporting aspect of it."

"I would rate Mr. Bradley more of a businessman than a sportsman."

The proprietor himself, looking slightly bewildered by the antics of the overflow crowd and more than a little harassed by the problems of trying to control it, nevertheless managed to shake Harry's left hand as he slid past them midway into the evening and murmur, through a conspiratorial half-smile, "Welcome to the Club Pandemonium—and I owe it all to you, Loring. How can I ever repay you?"

"Things'll settle down—you'll see."

In the end, as it always does, the lure of profit superseded the strictures of taste, and Bradley, his eye on the club's bulging coffers at evening's end, declared the experiment a success and promptly abolished the casino's former ban on women; only Wednesdays were henceforth to be preserved as stag night.

* * *

Self-conscious about the heavy cast encircling his right arm and the large sling supporting it, unable to enjoy any of the hotel's sports activities, and badly bored, Harry fell into a foul humor aggravated by the deepening depletion of his resources. His sole daytime diversions were walking and working jigsaw puzzles with Victoria Torrance, whose compassion for Harry's condition—for causing which she acknowledged only minimal complicity—was boundless. Caleb Torrance, too, would join in the therapy, marching Harry off to long lunches and longer tales of bringing up a motherless daughter. He could not stand to see his beautiful little girl in tears and so had yielded to her every whim. "We've got a dollhouse in the attic, I tell you, Loring, that's big enough for a family of Hottentots to live in comfortably. Her dresses take up three large closets, and her petticoat collection looks like an explosion in a lace factory. There's no doubt about it—the girl needs a strong man to rule her."

Torranced to his gills, Harry welcomed Maddy's suggestion that they pay a return visit to the Beach Club, now that women were welcome, so that he might try to replenish his wallet by some means other than poker. She promised not to distract him in this pursuit. "I'll just watch," she said, "and count the guards."

They steered clear of the roulette table; he found the game tiresome. Hazard and "chemmy" he considered equally unchallenging, and so his interest settled on the faro tables. He had once been tutored in all the variants of the game, and memories of those priceless lessons flooded his mind as they drew close to one table and followed the proceedings.

The play was on the lethargic side; for all its popularity, faro was not a dramatic game. He explained its rudiments to Madame Memphis in a whisper. The six players seated around the outer edge of the table placed their bets between each turn, which consisted of two cards. Suits did not count; one wagered only on the number or the picture on the face of the card to be drawn from the dealer's box on that turn. More adventurous bettors would "string" their wager by placing chips between any of the thirteen card faces imprinted in replica on the cloth-covered playing table, in effect doubling their chance to win—or lose—in any given turn. Whoever had correctly bet on the first card to emerge from the dealing box on that turn was the winner; whoever had bet on the second and final card dealt lost to the house. If a bettor neither won nor lost, his bet remained on the table, where he could leave it on the same card or cards he had played the last turn or shift it as his instincts directed. To the dealer's right, the house's case-keeper operated the cue box, an abacuslike little wooden contraption with thirteen wires corresponding to each of the four-card groupings in the deck. Each wire held four small balls, and as each card was played, the case-keeper tolled it off by moving one of the balls from left to right on the appropriate wire so that even the most casual bettor could tell at a glance what cards remained to be played and could bet accordingly.

After watching while two decks were played through, Harry took his place at the table and joined in with nonchalance, betting modestly. By the end of the third deck of play, his acute powers of observation began to reward him. "Something's up," he murmured over his shoulder to Madame Memphis, who remained utterly in the dark but followed with keener attention now. During a normal run through any given deck in a faro game, Harry would explain to her later, two consecutive cards of the same face value would come up in any single turn perhaps once and no more than twice. This phenomenon, known as "a split," worked solely to the advantage of the house, which took in half the chips wagered on the twice-appearing card and paid off nothing. This provision of the rules gave the house a slight advantage—of approximately three percent, Maskelyne had once informed Harry—in the course of playing out the deck. But as the game unfolded under the hand of this Beach Club dealer, a leathery-faced operative whom the case-keeper called Sam at one point in the play, Harry noticed that splits were occurring with greater frequency—never fewer than three per deck and in several cases four or five of them. Sam, Harry told his companion as they retreated to the café for a brandy, was a cheat.

But how had he managed it? The possibilities were limited, Harry mused aloud. Since each deck was played through numerous times and thoroughly shuffled between each runthrough, stacking it ahead of time was not the answer. No, Sam had to be doing it before their eyes. There was therefore only one plausible explanation. The other players were lax in their attentiveness as Sam separated the cards after each turn into two piles, as the rules dictated—winners to his right, losers to his left. But instead of piling them neatly on top of one another, he did so with apparent indifference, and every now and then, Harry thought he had detected, Sam placed a card slightly to one side, protruding from the others in the pile. Seizing the opportunity to straighten these apparently careless heaps, Sam must have nimbly stripped the the two cards he intended to match up in a split in the next runthrough of the deck and placed them at the bottom of the pile or, more nimbly still, in an identical position higher in the stack. It took a certain sensitivity of the fingertips and a good deal of practice to do so unnoticed; Harry himself had mastered the technique in a week under Maskelyne's tutelage, but he was rusty now, of course, and could not have performed the feat. Sam then must have merely taken the two stacks, once the deck was played out, and given them what was known among connoisseurs of the craft as "the faro dealer's shuffle"—two cuts and a mix that perfectly alternated the cards from each half of the deck—so that when the cards were reinserted in the dealing box, the splits were nicely in place.

They went back to the faro table. Five splits turned up in the next game, convincing Harry he was right. Sam was relying on the inattentiveness of the wealthy bettors at his table. And of the extra profits his quick fingers collected for the house, he must have been pocketing a portion and turning it in later as if part of the chips he had received as gratuities from winning players. If these gifts to him were somewhat higher than the house average, so were the house's winnings from his table, and no suspicion fell on him.

Before leaving the club they returned to the café, where Harry ordered them another brandy apiece—not to drink but as a pretext for him to remark admiringly to the barman on the merits of the faro dealer named Sam. In response, he extracted the intelligence that Sam came from Chicago, training ground of the best faromen in the country; that Sam, like all the housemen, lived in the clubhouse under the dormitorylike arrangements Bradley imposed on his well-paid help, and that Sam's last name was Suggs.

"I have a little project in mind for our Mr. Suggs," said Harry on their way back to the hotel.

"Must you?"

"The exchequer's low—and so is Mr. Suggs."

"Harry, I don't like that place. It's very cold—and very menacing. I think it's dangerous to trifle with the dealer or any of them. For all you know, everyone in there is crooked, including Bradley."

He tightened his fingers over hers. "Maddy, this is my world. I know my way around in it. I don't ask you to like it, but don't expect me to abandon it. It's what I do best with my life—and being one-armed for the moment requires my taking a few calculated risks. Worry not."

Next day he mailed off a note to the Beach Club that read:

My dear Suggs,

I observed your conduct at the faro table last evening with great interest. You can discuss the reasons for your regrettable breaches of trust with me at the Lakeside Inn in West Palm at 2 P.M. on Thursday or, not finding you there at that hour, I shall bring up the topic with Mr. Bradley. The choice is yours.

Most sincerely,
H. St. J. Loring

"Don't lie to me!" she exploded the moment they were inside the door of the rented room on Yucca. "I can stand anything but that!"

"Don't scream, Maddy," he said, looking forlorn. "They can hear you all over the place."

"And they could hear the bedsprings going yesterday, too, when you were in here with—with—whoever it was you were fouling the sheets with. Harry, how *could* you do such a thing—and *here*, of all places?"

"You're jumping to conclusions—"

"What? Are you actually *denying* it?"

"I—am," he lied. What choice did he have? To confess would have been worse. The ironic part of it, he remembered, running his hand over the end rail of the brass bedstead, was that even as he had been administering—yes, that was the very word for it—*administering* coitus to the wan, supine form of Amanda Larrabee in this same spot twenty-four hours earlier, his thoughts were all of Maddy and how differently she answered to his touch. He loved to watch as the prim "widow" Memory gradually abandoned her self-control and emitted soft groans of cascading passion. Was it perversity that gave him such pleasure from her primal responses and the loss of the dignity she so studiously maintained out of bed? Her whole essence suffused that chamber of their pleasures; her dresses, the vivid ones she wore as part of her French Canadian disguise, were hanging in the armoire there, just a few feet from the bed, in silent censure of his hovering over another woman. But it had been a passionless exercise for him; by no stretch of the imagination could he be said to have been making love to Amanda Larrabee. She was merely someone he had serviced in the old days.

Amanda and her androgynous husband George had opened their home to him and Maskelyne; there were polite dinners and lucrative card games afterward while Amanda wandered up to her rooms and dreamed of lusty young Harry Loring and the thrashing of their locked loins. Even when Maskelyne returned to England, Harry continued to visit at the Larrabees' until one night he found a desperate note from her in his coat after he left, explaining the unfulfilled nature of her marriage and all but begging him to satisfy her when George was away on Wall Street. It proved a highly profitable arrangement for him, requiring only one afternoon a week—a nice complement to the money he took off George, sometimes in the evening of the very same day that he had lain with his wife. She asked nothing of him in return but minimal tenderness and reliability in scheduling. It lasted until he went to Europe one summer and lapsed by more or less mutual assent.

Now, fifteen years later, the Larrabees had shown up for the last month of the season at the Royal Poinciana. Old George, apparently less potent than ever, greeted him like a long lost son, and Amanda, by a note no less desperate than the one with which she had initiated their former intimacy, proposed its resumption. In view of his broken arm and greatly reduced income, Harry accepted, apologizing to her for a certain delicacy in their proceedings imposed by his injury. The room on Yucca seemed a safer place for their transactions than the hotel.

They were in the midst of the act the day before when he was distracted by the sound of pebbles pelting against the bedroom window. It had to be Arthur Timmons demanding his attention. The bellboy, who worked the evening shift at the hotel and as Harry's boy Friday the rest of the time, was stationed in the alleyway as a lookout in case Amanda's husband should suddenly turn possessive about her.

Harry slipped out of bed to answer the summons, hid behind the draperies while opening the window wider and heard Arthur hiss up at him, "It's Miz Mem'ry—she comin' in!"

He hastily instructed Amanda to remain where and how she was and to explain, if it came to it, that the room had been rented to her and a friend and that the intruder had better skedaddle or there would be trouble. He, meanwhile, grabbed his drawers and ran to the men's bathroom down the hall. Its window backed against the open rear door of the corset shop through which he could hear, unmistakably, Maddy's voice asking, and then demanding, the key to their room. What she was doing there—it was very definitely not her afternoon off—he could not imagine. Miss Emily, thank heavens, refused the request, claiming at first that the room was being cleaned and then, as Maddy grew more insistent, that it was being used. He hung by the window, listening to the exchange, and sent prayers of gratitude aloft when Maddy at last gave up and stormed off. After a decent interval, he and Amanda fled the premises, separately . . .

"It's pointless to deny it," Maddy resumed the onslaught that he had known would ensue. But to have avoided their rendezvous this afternoon would have been a confession of guilt—and he could not hope that she would understand and forgive his business with Amanda. She had not actually caught him in the act; possibly he could manage to talk his way out of it. "I saw your Arthur hanging around here before I went into the shop," she went on, "but he disappeared fast. And where Arthur is, you are."

"Oh, that," he said. "I asked him to take one of my suits over to his mother's place to be cleaned—she does a much better job of it than they do at the hotel."

"Harry—you're only making it worse!"

"No, it's true—I swear."

"You do, do you? Then I'm marching right over to Cleo Timmons' place this instant and ask her."

"You—just—do that."

"I most definitely shall." But she hesitated, the firmness of his denial, if not of his manner, giving her second thoughts.

"At any rate, just because they wouldn't let you in, why do you assume it was me in here?" Counterattack was his best weapon now. "It seems perfectly obvious that they were renting the room out to some other party, you caught them at it and they were naturally embarrassed. Why implicate me in their wrongdoing?"

"Harry, I *saw* you here!"

"Where?"

"At the ferry slip. I waited in the ticket office—in the women's room—for an hour. I *had* to know—"

"I see. And was there a woman with me?"

"No. But there were women coming and going. It could have been any of them. You're too slick just to go marching around with them in broad daylight—especially since she's probably someone from the hotel."

He began shaking his head sadly. "Yes, I was in West Palm. So what? I have certain—business arrangements I make from time to time—and some small clothing items I need—"

She glared at him across the bed, drumming the top of the nightstand with her fingertips. "Harry," she fumed, but softly now, "you are *lying* to me."

"Why is it," he asked, "that you're always ready to think the worst of me? Suppose I acted the same way toward you? How do I know that *you* didn't want the key to come up here with Caleb Torrance and do what-ever—"

"*What?* How *dare* you—even suggest that—" Her hand knotted into a fist. "I came over here on an errand for the hotel," she said, delivering each word with great deliberation. "We needed extra lace for the sheets in the two bridal suites that were just added. Miss Prentisse was off and Miss Duval was otherwise occupied so I had to do it. The corset shop just happens to have the best lace in West Palm—and so long as I was here I thought I'd take one of my Madame Memphis dresses over to Cleo's for a cleaning."

"That's *your* story."

"God *damn* you!" she shouted, reached for the pitcher of water on the nightstand and hurled it across at him with all her furious might. He leaned forward to avoid the flying missile, lost his balance, twisted and fell, bashing his left elbow on the hard railing at the corner of the bed and a second time when it landed on the floor just before the rest of him. Within the hour, both of his arms were in slings and Harry Loring was the saddest-looking man in southern Florida.

It was impossible, of course, for him to remain unobtrusive in the Beach Club crowd, rigged up as he was now in all those bandages. But the setup had already been worked out down to the last detail, and if he called it off, that would be the end of it.

Maddy would have to come with him to put down his chips—there was no alternative. He feared for her part in it far more than for his own. It was enough that she had agreed to help him collaterally with the Torrance scheme; this one with Suggs was turning her into an active accomplice. Whether out of pity for him or remorse for having wounded him on top of his other injury, he did not know, but she was at least willing to come to the casino with him. This was no small triumph, he told himself, because she must have supposed that the whole sordid business served only to confirm him in his conniving ways. Perhaps she had succumbed to his insistence that his entrapment of Suggs was designed as a benefit to Bradley and therefore a manifestation of his own newly respectable character. Or perhaps she had agreed to help her armless lover in the belief that it was at least remotely possible that she had been unjust in accusing him of infidelity. Her other reasons, he suspected, were love, admiration of his courage and the pledge she had extracted from him to turn away after the season's close from these risky exploits that she declared could lead only to his eventual ruination.

And so Madame Memphis made her third appearance at Bradley's club, this time in charge of placing the chips as her incapacitated companion directed. Suggs had told him he would finish off the old deck a little after ten-thirty, then switch to the prepared one. After that, it would all be up to Harry to carry it off in convincing style.

He watched Suggs working the cards. No need for concern, the dealer silently assured him, eyes glittering; the thing would work like a charm.

Yes, Harry could see what Suggs was doing with the splits—and he had to give him credit; Maskelyne in his prime could not have performed better.

Still, he felt his insides churning over the riskiness of the arrangement and the hostility of the place, full of probing eyes and hidden weapons. Suppose Suggs was setting him up—and was about to claim that Harry had tried to bribe him into cheating? Or suppose his memory failed him as play progressed and he forgot the arranged sequence of the cards? Or suppose the case-keeper, who was practically at Sugg's elbow, caught on? So many things could go wrong in a room packed with housemen alert for any sign of irregularity. It was a tight spot to work in.

He had been varying his play since arriving in the club an hour earlier. Whatever he won, he would do his best to lose back to the house within the next two or three turns. It was essential for him to project the image of a random player, as if any success that he might come upon were not due to excessive calculation. As he played, he instructed Maddy to switch from five-dollar chips to fifty-dollar ones, so that by the time Suggs tore open the arranged deck, Harry was wagering as much as five hundred dollars a turn.

Slowly, almost laconically directing his chips onto the playing table, he built up his stack as Suggs dealt through the deck. There had been only one minor mix-up from the shuffles the dealer had given the fixed cards at the outset. Harry had Maddy string many of his bets to appear cautious, bet low when the splits were due in order to minimize his losses, "coppered" on the house's card for variety's sake, made sure to lose every third or fourth turn and all the while he appeared to be studying the cue box to see what cards had not yet been played, as any marginally attentive better would. By the end of the deck Maddy had gathered in $9,650 worth of chips for him. Half of it theoretically belonged to Suggs.

"Thanks, Sam," he said coolly to the dealer and had his consort hand him two fifty-dollar chips, as any sporting gentleman would have done. At the cashier's window they were told, as before, that Colonel Bradley himself would cash in their chips.

They accepted the brandies the proprietor offered, and Harry smiled his thanks. The man disclosed not an inkling of resentment at the thought of surrendering nearly ten thousand dollars of his money. There was nothing small-minded in his attitude or about the operation he ran. Ingratiating himself to Edward Bradley, colonel or not, might someday yield benefits well in excess of the winnings he had just rooked him out of, Harry told himself as they chatted amiably, and he steeled his resolve to advance his own interest by sacrificing another man's. But Sam

Suggs was a cheat—and cheats who got caught richly deserved their fate.

"I never fail to be impressed, Mr. Bradley, whenever we come by here. This is a first-class operation." It was not yet up to the standards of Canfield's or the House with the Bronze Door in New York, of course, in terms of sheer elegance. And Etienne's in New Orleans had a special style of its own, due to its distinctive croupiers, the mulattos who were among the most exquisite women in the world. And Dockswell Hall on San Francisco's Embarcadero, he added, offered a greater variety of games and players than any ten other houses put together. But the Beach Club, with its outward simplicity and subdued atmosphere, reminded one of an orderly, gracious yet unpretentious home, he said. "We're treated as your guests here rather than mere paying customers—and that makes all the difference."

Bradley heard him out with an expressionless face that nevertheless carefully scrutinized the flatterer. "Well," he said at the end, "that's quite a compliment from a man as well traveled as you seem to be, Mr. Loring."

"I hope, then, Mr. Bradley, that you're not overly saddened by an unpleasant piece of news I have to deliver." He asked Madame Memphis to deposit his chips in a heap on a corner of the desk. "You're nurturing a viper here within your walls, and I feel that these"—he nodded toward the chips—"should in all good faith be returned to you."

Quietly he narrated the entire story of Suggs and his deft hands and the scheme they had worked out that would have netted them each nearly five thousand dollars for the evening's play. "Quite frankly, Mr. Bradley, now that it's over and I've proved the point I'd set out to, I was tempted to walk away with your money—I've never before had the opportunity to recoup the losses I've sustained in any house of chance. But I'd rather have your friendship than your money." He nudged the chips toward Bradley with both his slings. "Whatever disposition you make of Suggs, I can assure you, sir, that this unhappy little incident will remain in strictest confidence between us. Madame Memphis is a paragon of discretion. I have no doubt, moreover, that discovering this unpleasantness is far more troubling to you than it is to us."

A glazed look had settled over Bradley's blue eyes while he gauged the magnitude of the scandal and tried to measure the character of the smooth-talking stranger who professed such charitable instincts. "I'm shocked," he said, not looking or sounding it, "and very grateful to you, Loring." He had tried to assemble a decent staff of employees, he explained defensively, relying on the best recommendations he could find and then providing those he had selected with enough incentives to keep them honest. "Petty thievery can beggar anyone in my business—and cheating the clientele is even more unforgivable. I'm sure you understand that I have no need to take advantage of the guests in my establishment—the odds are sufficiently in my favor to begin with. But I suppose there's always going to be one bad apple in the bunch." He stood and came around to the side of his desk by way of demonstrating his concern. "I'll deal with Suggs in an appropriate manner, of course. And along with my thanks," he said, looping an arm around Harry's shoulder, "I want you to accept the proceeds of these chips."

"Mr. Bradley, I really don't—"

"I will not hear of a refusal. It's a small price for the favor you've done me. The reputation of this place must remain spotless." He reached into his pocket, counted out the money and raised his hand to still Harry's protest as he placed the bills in his pocket. "I'm a man of few friends, Mr. Loring—it's an occupational hazard, I'm afraid—but in the future, I'll be very pleased to number you among them."

Among the tasks Arthur Timmons performed, now that Harry's armless plight required him to hire away the boy from the hotel and employ him day and night as his personal attendant, was reading aloud, ostensibly for his employer's benefit.

They had attempted *Pendennis* together, Arthur at first turning the pages for Harry to read aloud and explain, then Harry asking Arthur to recite to him. This exercise, which became a nightly ritual, was painful for them both, yet Harry persisted in it, tirelessly correcting Arthur's halting, often ludicrous approximation of Thackeray's elegant prose. Arthur complained that he did not see the point of all the reading, but Harry told him it was important that he try to improve himself. That Harry's patience outlasted the boy's was due largely to his appreciation of Arthur's devoted attendance to his needs, which were now nearly total. Arthur not only fed him, dressed him, scratched him, brushed his teeth for him and turned the pages of books and newspapers for him but even assisted him in performing the most primal of human acts. That Arthur did so without complaint or letting his good nature slacken—his jibes and jokes saved their forced intimacy from degrading either of them—was the surest testament of his gratitude for Harry's tutelage in the ways of the white world, polite and otherwise.

Arthur's devotion notwithstanding, he was unable to meet all of Harry's elemental needs. Only Maddy could collaborate with him on the one most pressing at the moment. But how could it be satisfied without awkwardness destroying its entire beauty?

Well, yes, she could help him with his clothes and in maneuvering onto and about the bed, but he could hardly pleasure her in their usual ways. He would have to lie there, largely impassive, while she did the moving for the both of them. It was not impossible, just demeaning and not a little absurd. But there were parts of him that still operated acceptably, if Maddy proved willing to assist in the maneuvers.

She was tender in the removal of his garments, her care growing the nearer she approached his drawers. But her extreme delicacy ended when she saw how ready he was for her. "It would appear," she commented clinically, "that all your energy has abandoned your other parts and gone to lodge—*there.*"

"Be still, woman," he scolded, "and sit down here next to me."

She perched on the edge of the bed, and they kissed, she somewhat gently at first and then, sensing that restraint was unnecessary, with intensity. As he felt her hand move from his shoulder to close around his swollen pride, he broke away from their embrace. "No," he said, stifling a gasp, "not that way. I've been giving this project a great deal of thought. You are to take off your clothes and do exactly as I instruct."

She stood up, slightly bewildered, and began to comply under his close scrutiny. The frustration of being unable to reach out and touch the ripe softness she progressively revealed elicited a pitiable groan from him.

"Are you all right?" she asked, bending over him. Her breasts, visible practically in their entirety through the gauze of her linen chemise, swayed in front of his eyes.

"I'm—just fine." He inhaled deeply. "This is a form of torture entirely new to me. On the exquisite side, though."

"Are you sure you can manage this? There are other ways we can—"

"If you do precisely what I ask."

"Whatever you want."

"First, help me lie down," he directed. He kept his eyes on her breasts as she eased his head onto the pillow. It was extraordinary, he thought with the enhanced power of concentration awakened by his reduced mobility, how the laws of physics caused the shape of her breasts to change as her body bent and shifted.

"Now what?" she asked, lying down beside him.

"Kiss me," he ordered.

She did as she was told, tongue and lips sending unspoken messages to him—of apology, forgiveness, desire and plain, simple human need.

He eased her away from him. "All right," he said softly, "enough of that. Help me move to the center of the bed—please."

She took him by the shoulders and slid his body, with its arms pressed tightly to his chest, toward the middle of the bed. "Far enough." There followed detailed instructions on the placement of the pillow and the position and location of her body—on her knees and above him. She wound up with her face close to his, within kissing distance. "No," he shook his head, "that's not what I'm after. Move past me—farther—farther—stop. Now, lower." His tongue flicked out and reached her right nipple, hardening it instantly. "Lower," he murmured, and she crouched to oblige, her breast against his face as his mouth moved over her flesh. He could feel her body trembling, hear her breathing, ragged and irregular, pneumatic sighs and little groans escaping from the back of her throat. "Other one," he whispered. All his carnal knowledge was devoted now to what subtlety of lips and tongue might please her most.

"Now higher," he ordered. She lifted up and pulled away from him completely. "No, no, no—over this way." He jerked his head back to show her what he meant. She obeyed; he rewarded her with a line of kisses down her body, between her breasts and on past her naval, stopping at the base of her abdomen. "Now I need some help."

She sat upright and looked at him mistily. "What—what?"

"Help me up."

"Up? Now?"

"Please just do as I say."

She clasped him under his shoulders and slowly helped lift him, her puzzlement growing with the expenditure of effort. She watched closely as he got to his feet and then dropped to his knees beside the bed. "What do I do?" she asked, looking totally bewildered.

"Come toward me."

She crawled to the edge of the bed and knelt there, waiting.

"Now lie down on the bed with your feet on the floor."

"Why?"

"No questions—just do it."

"This is the most ridiculous thing I've—" She flopped around on the bed, adjusting herself to his satisfaction, then sat up on her elbows to look at him questioningly. "Now what?"

"Put your head back and spread your divine legs."

"*Whaaat?*" She almost shrieked with the realization of what he intended. "I will *not.*"

"Do it, Maddy."

"That's—it is—thoroughly—indecent. I'm not—" Her knees remained locked.

"Oh, yes you are. And you won't be sorry."

He regarded her steadily, willing her to relax, to enjoy, to sip at the sensation he was about to offer her. Slowly, the rigidity began to leave her body, and her knees parted slightly.

"More, Maddy."

Her knees parted still farther.

"It won't hurt, I promise. Bear with me, angel." He murmured more soothing words, cursing inwardly that he was unable to gentle her with his hands, to smooth her thighs, to effect a transition between the sensation of nothing but air around her and the full shock of intrusion she would experience in another instant. It could not be helped. He leaned toward her, exhaling gently, warming her with his breath, and then reached for her the only way he could.

At his touch, a tremor coursed through her body and she inhaled with a violent gasp of a sort he had never heard her utter. "Cover your mouth with a pillow, sweetheart," he urged. "We're not alone here."

She did as he directed, and he renewed his attention to the most delicate and sensitive part of her, slowly, lovingly heightening her pleasure as her thighs pressed against his ears. Even through the pillow, her muffled sounds of ecstasy reached him. Her timidity receded, and she was caught up in her quest for sensation, heels pressing against the floor, her body slightly elevated now, unable to pull away from him even if she had wanted. The pressure of her thighs relented as she seemed to forget him completely. Higher and higher she rose, farther from the edge of the bed, forcing him to go upward with her, carried along by the angle of her body as she reacted to the caresses of his lips and tongue.

Her breathing became shallower and more rapid, then he could hear it no more. Had she fainted? He opened his eyes to see if he could get a glimpse of her when suddenly, with a great heaving inhalation, she gave a convulsive shudder followed by a piercing cry only partially insulated by the pillow. Tremor after tremor raced through her, her hand opening and closing pointlessly at the edge of the mattress, and then it was abruptly withdrawn as she jerked upright onto her elbows. He was about to pull away from her, but her legs closed once again, holding him to her like a vise. He had not known she was capable of such strength. One final spasm and then her body sagged; her legs fell away, freeing him at last. He looked up at her as she pushed the pillow away from her exhaustedly. "Oh, my God" was all she said, her eyes still closed.

"Was it so bad?" he whispered.

She shook her head slowly, eyes still shut. "Not bad." Her breath was short and uneven. She took a moment to compose herself. "Unbelievable, actually." Her eyes opened and regarded him with mock sternness. "Why didn't you ever—"

"You weren't ready for it—and I needed to have two broken arms before I was."

The taste of her was still in his mouth. He leaned over, his balance precarious, parted her lips with his tongue, and, sharing the final intimacy with the woman who had become so much a part of him, filled her mouth with the taste of herself. He half-feared she would recoil, but instead she came alive again, pressing her lower body against his, feeling for him as if in desperation. "I want you in me," she whispered fiercely, "*now.*"

Her words, her actions ignited an intensity he had not thought he could generate under such conditions. His need was no less urgent than hers. She got to her knees, helped him onto the bed and straddled him. "Lower," he said. "Get off your knees. Lie on me. Put your weight on your hands."

She more than acquiesced. He felt himself surrounded, engulfed, overwhelmed by her femaleness, her otherness, their oneness. It took but four thrusts, each shorter than the one preceding it, and his world, as hers had moments earlier, surged and detonated in bursts of uncontainable bliss.

He opened his eyes to find her smiling down at him. "I never saw you—like that—before," she told him. "I'm always so involved with myself—"

"Have you missed much?"

"Oh, I've missed a great deal, Mr. Loring."

He was not in much of a celebratory mood toward the season's close, preferring in general to remain sulkily in his rooms rather than to mingle as an unsightly intrusion among the exquisitely garbed guests at their evening revels. But he could hardly have refused the Torrances' invitation to join them and Madame Memphis at their table for the after-dinner dance on the final night of their stay at the hotel. Victoria absolutely insisted upon his presence, bandaged or not; besides, his being there was essential to delivering the coup de grace to Caleb Torrance—no easy feat in his condition.

As the strains of "The Cherry Tree Waltz," a composition of Major Mackintosh's own devising, swirled slowly downward from the bandstand like dying pink petals from the song's blossoming namesake, a radiant Victoria Torrance closed her eyes in a semi-swoon and gently touched the fingers that protruded from his right-arm sling. "I so hate for us to be leaving tomorrow. I wish it would go on forever—don't you?"

"It's been a grand time," he agreed, "not counting broken bones." His eyes wandered off to the dance floor, where her father was steering heavily about with the plucky Madame Memphis in tow. What a marvel she was of social grace under duress. The woman must have loved him inordinately to endure this pretense of cordiality for his benefit. His feeling for her at that moment turned every other emotional involvement he had known into the rank shallows of sentiment.

"Will you miss me?"

A harder volley to dodge. "Without you here, Miss Torrance, I would have been desolated."

"Does that mean you'll come to see us in Waterbury?" she asked, lifting his wine glass to his lips for him to sip at like a wounded bird.

What in the hell had Arthur done with the wire he had carefully arranged to be sent from New York for delivery to his room during the dance? If the boy could not be relied on he would not be suitable for the plan Harry was devising for his future employment. "I'll do my very best on that score, Miss Torrance."

She tilted her head in a pert little moue. "But you're not promising—and I can't and won't accept anything less from you."

"Your kindness is much appreciated. But I hate to make promises that my prior obligations may prevent me from keeping—business trips, social engagements, lady friends more mature if less exquisite than you, dear Victoria."

"Mist' Loring, Mist' Loring!" the bellman paged, the moment the music ceased. "Wire for Mist' Loring!"

Thank the Lord. Arthur's timing was only a minute or two off. "A wire," said Harry, "at this time of night? Why on earth—boy!" He swiveled his head to the bellman by way of identifying himself. "Are you sure it's for me?"

"Yassuh, Mist' Loring."

He asked Victoria to fish into his jacket pocket for a coin to give the bellman and then had her tear open the wire for him. His face bent forward over the table, its expression souring as he read the message:

OUR ZEPHYR HAS FLOWN THIS EARTHLY COIL. SAMPSON SUCCUMBED TUESDAY EVENING TO THROMBOSIS. EVERYTHING IN MUDDLE AS NO APPRENTICE TO CARRY ON. DEBTS NOT PREVIOUSLY DISCLOSED APPEAR TO IMPERIL SOLVENCY OF VENTURE. OPENING OF FACTORY INDEFINITELY POSTPONED. WILL ADVISE FURTHER DEVELOPMENTS IF ANY. SORRY TO BEAR ILL-TIDINGS. MCPHERSON

"Oh, no," he said softly, his color drained as he finished.

"What is it, Harry? You look as if the roof just fell on you."

"Not quite." He shook his head and then indicated she was free to read the wire.

"Oh, my," she said, taking it in at a glance, "that sounds dreadful. What does it mean?"

"Perhaps your father had better explain."

"Some business thing you two have cooked up?"

"I wouldn't put it quite that way."

"But Daddy doesn't know anything except the thread business. I don't understand why he'd decide out of the blue to—"

"You two aren't looking very festive," boomed Caleb Torrance as he led Madame Memphis back to their places at the table. He was flushed from his exertions on the dance floor and weaving from an evening of accumulated alcohol.

"Daddy, look at this!" Victoria said, and pushed the wire across the tabletop before Harry could say a word.

"My glasses are in the room. You know I can't read a blessed—"

"I'll read it to you," his daughter said, alarm in her voice.

As she did, Maddy's brows wrinkled with sudden comprehension and Torrance's bleary eyes narrowed, not quite catching the gravity of the news.

"I—I'm terribly—I just don't see how it could all—" Harry groped for words of fitting commiseration.

Torrance blinked several times, as if to clear his brain. "What's all this mean in terms of our investment?"

"I—I'm afraid I don't know anything more about it than you do. It sounds like it's going to take a while to sort this thing out. But if anybody can salvage a difficult mess like this, it's McPherson."

"And if not?"

"Then we're in the soup, I guess."

Torrance sat there stunned for a time, slowly digesting the totality of the setback he had suffered. "Good Christ," he said softly, "that's the fastest twenty thousand I ever lost."

"Twenty thousand!" Victoria shrilled, clamping a hand over her mouth an instant after the number escaped from her pretty lips.

"I—I don't know what to say, Caleb—except that I tried to warn you these things don't always—"

"Daddy, how could you—?"

"Please, sweetie—don't mix into something you don't know—"

"I know what I'm hearing. It sounds as if you let Mr. Loring talk you into some very silly investment scheme that suddenly—"

"It was *not* silly, darling—it was a highly inventive—very practical—new kind of horseless carriage—with—with—"

"With what?" Victoria demanded.

"Very large wheels that—that allowed it to—uh—go over all kinds of terrain in—in every sort of weather and—and—"

"Daddy—did you ever see this remarkable creature?"

Torrance's expression had turned forlorn. "Not actually. But Harry here did, and he felt that—it was really quite—"

"I didn't know that Mr. Loring was an engineer."

"Vicky, I really don't think you should get into—"

"And I really don't think you should let any smooth-talking gentleman talk you into investing in something you've never—"

"Nobody talked me into anything, Vicky. In fact, Mr. Loring did his level best to discourage me from—"

"I'll bet."

"Vicky, you owe Mr. Loring an apology. He's behaved in a perfectly—"

"Caleb, I think Miss Torrance's upset is very natural. She's lived a highly protected and, by your own concession, somewhat indulged life without encountering much adversity. She needn't apologize for trying to share the hurt of a father she dearly loves."

"Daddy, can't you hear the man?" Victoria's eyes began to blaze. "He's trying to twist it all and make me into a—"

"I think Miss Torrance is getting overwrought," said Harry, not dignifying her with a direct look. "Perhaps you and I should take a walk."

"Oh, no, you don't!" She turned her growing fury on him. "You think you can talk your way out of anything, Mr. Harrison Loring."

He now ignored her entirely and addressed Torrance. "Frankly, Caleb, I think Victoria's little temper tantrum is directed at me for entirely other reasons than this unfortunate news from New York—reasons that a gentleman ought not to impute to a young lady of proper breeding—"

Torrance wore a blank look. "I don't follow you, Loring."

"I believe Victoria feels that I'm not, let us say, entirely appreciative of her charms, so she's understandably seized on this—"

"What!"

"—bad news out of peeve that I haven't totally succumbed to her fetching—"

"That's a damned lie!"

"Vicky—"

"—ways, and you know what they say, Caleb, about hell having no fury like a—well—like a—"

"Ohhh, you snake!" Victoria cried, and lashed her hand wildly toward Harry's defenseless face. He ducked too late, into, rather than away from, the blow.

"Vicky!" Torrance shouted as the whole ballroom looked on.

A thin trickle of blood appeared on Harry's cheek where Victoria's fingernail had caught his flesh. They all sat there staring at it in grim silence, aware that the situation was by now irreparable. "I think," Victoria finally said, rising with majesty, "we'd better go home now, Daddy."

The moment they were out of sight, Maddy drew a handkerchief from her purse and applied it lightly to Harry's cheek to absorb the bleeding. "You know," he said to her with an appreciative nod, "I think Torrance might have been good for fifty if I'd played it right."

"I wanted to have you to the club for dinner, Mr. Loring, but I assumed that—"

"Call me Harry."

"Harry—but I assumed that's awkward for you without assistance, so I thought we might just chat instead."

"Suits me."

Bradley folded his hands on the desktop. "Harry, you're a fellow who interests me. Ever since your suggestion to let the ladies in here and then your cottoning on to the scheme of our former Mr. Suggs, you've been on my mind. So I began asking some questions about you—and getting the oddest answers."

Harry shifted in his chair as Bradley elaborated. He had checked with Harry's acquaintances, the people with whom he came to the Beach Club, and had made discreet inquiries at the hotel. He had even had a New York friend look into Harry's city address, the Thalia Club, where his man went for a visit to learn what he could of the Loring family tree.

"You're a very puzzling man, Mr. Harrison St. John Loring—if that's really your name." Bradley's tone turned icily brittle. "No one seems to know very much about you. You were apparently born at about the age of twenty to a mother and an unnamed father who had three or four occupations all at the same time but in different parts of the country. The only story all of my informants agreed on was that you were somehow related to an Englishman who was, for lack of a better term, a bon vivant. Nobody was familiar with any of your so-called investments but everyone knew that you spend a good deal of your time playing cards, particularly poker, and that you appeared to have Lady Luck riding on your shoulder whenever you played. Peculiarly, though, no one seemed to question your good fortune—and still less to resent it. The words 'professional gambler' never crossed anyone's lips to describe you, but even so, I've been able to come to no other conclusion."

What was there to gain now by obfuscation? Harry smiled. "Your informants sound like a conscientious lot."

"And I've drawn the proper inference?"

"I'm afraid you have me dead to rights, Mr. Bradley."

"Excellent," said the club owner, his tone warming now though his look remained austere. "If there's one thing I don't like, it's a liar. So I'd prefer to believe that the story you told me at our first meeting about your financial affairs was an essential expedient to cloak the true nature of your professional activities around here."

"You might put it that way."

Bradley folded his hands behind his head and leaned back. "Fine, fine—and so long as we're being honest with each other, I should confess that I've checked up a bit on the background of your lady friend as well. Now with her I've had less luck. Nobody over in West Palm seems to know much about Madame Memphis. Even her comings and goings are hard to determine. She seems to disappear into thin air with regularity. So I've come to the conclusion that she, too, is not quite what she seems—and serves more or less as a collaborator with you in some of your activities."

Harry remained silent.

"You deny it?"

"We are fond of each other. I will say nothing to compromise her."

"Ah, good for you, Loring. You're a gentleman of the old school." Bradley suddenly unclasped his hands and snapped forward in his chair. "Be that as it may, the fact remains that you're also one damned tricky operator—and the lady is probably no lady—no offense, but I am entitled to pass my own judgments."

"You may not cast aspersions toward her in my presence," Harry said, climbing to his feet.

Bradley waved him back down. "Hold your horses, Loring. I apologize. Nevertheless, it's plain to me that you are not the sort of person who ought to be left loose around Palm Beach, preying upon our distinguished guests. You're certainly not good for my business—and even less so for the hotel's. I therefore came to a decision recently to pass along all my information about you to Mr. Flagler and Mr. Stokes-Vecchio, who would, I'm sure, bar you from the premises in the future. Together, we can run you and the lady both out of town for good, is what I'm saying."

"I have no doubt."

"Can you think of any good reason why that shouldn't be done?"

"I'm sure one would occur to me, Mr. Bradley, given half the chance."

Bradley got to his feet and poised his fingertips against the desktop. "You're quite a wiseacre, Loring. I don't see anything in the least amusing about all of this."

"You have me at a disadvantage, Mr. Bradley. I'm just trying to be civil. What's the point in—"

"Civil? You speak of civil when you skulk around here like a slick smart aleck, figuring you can pull the wool over everybody's eyes?"

"I never *skulk,* Mr. Bradley."

The casino owner stuck his hands into his pockets and turned to look out the window for a time. "No, you don't, do you? In fact, Loring, there's something rather appealing to me about your brass—almost as if you're ruled by some twisted sense of honor."

"Thank you."

"The truth is," said Bradley, pivoting back toward him, "that the longer I thought about you, the more convinced I've become that instead of ridding Palm Beach of such a dangerous pest, I'd be wiser to try to use your peculiar charms to my advantage. What would you say, Harry, to coming to work for me next season as my right-hand man—assuming, of course, your right hand is working by then?"

Harry's lips parted in silent amazement.

His duties, Bradley explained, a touch of warmth now in his forbidding eyes, would be few but vital. The club would bear the cost for his season's stay at the Royal Poinciana, and Bradley did not particularly care what activities Harry pursued during the day—the ones he had enjoyed in the past were perfectly agreeable to the casino owner—but his evenings were to be spent exclusively at the Beach Club, keeping his eyes and ears open. He would be expected to maintain a watch over the tables, to make sure both the players and housemen remained honest and that the membership was treated politely but abided by all the house rules. No one other than Bradley would know he was in the club owner's employ—he was to remain, one might say, a secret weapon. He would gamble along with the other guests, but the money he used would be Bradley's, and all his winnings, should there be any, would be turned over to the house at the end of every evening. Whatever suggestions Harry could make to improve any area of the club's operation would, of course, be greatly welcomed. His salary would be a guaranteed ten thousand against three percent of the club's profits at the end of the season, so that the more customers Harry could induce to play, the higher his ultimate take.

"I don't keep books—for obvious reasons," Bradley concluded, "so you'd have no proof that anything you wound up with in excess of the guarantee was your fair share. But I can assure you that if play continues next season at a level anything like what we've enjoyed since admitting women to the tables, you wouldn't be sorry to have associated yourself with me."

Harry offered an appreciative nod. "I'm mighty pleased that you think well enough of me to make such a generous offer. But I'd like to think about it all overnight—"

"Understandably."

"And might we say five percent of the profits?"

"Out of the question, I'm afraid."

"You mean it's take it or leave it?"

"I do."

Harry tilted his head to study the ceiling. "Well, then there is just one other thing that frankly would make your proposal more attractive to me."

"Namely?"

"My friend Madame Memphis is possessed of, shall we say, great social acumen—she is a most vivacious, intelligent and persuasive person. She is also a very good organizer, and I feel certain that, in her own way, she could manage to escort a sizable group of unattached women here every evening, in addition to others generally attracted by her high spirits. In my estimate, her efforts would greatly swell the club's receipts. If you would undertake to pay her hotel bill as well as mine, you would not regret it."

"That's not impossible—if she can do what you say."

"She can do almost anything, Mr. Bradley, once she sets her mind to it."

"Harry," she said, "the whole thing's perfectly absurd."

"Not in the least. And you could finally become a lady of leisure all year round."

"Leisure? Why, I'd have to be playacting the entire time—keeping up the accent every waking minute, always worrying I might slip."

"Nonsense. Madame Memphis would naturally take breakfast in her room and not appear in public until just before lunch—she needs her sleep. And only part of her afternoons would have to be devoted to cultivating business."

"I think the person you want for this performance is Agatha Agapé, not me."

"Agatha, bless her, is not quite my style. Furthermore, Mr. Loring, devil that he is, could arrange to have his room connect directly to Madame Memphis'."

Her flinty tone faded, and her eyes softened. "Could you really?"

"Why not? For fifty dollars, Mr. Walters can do anything—and for another twenty-five he can manage to forget that he ever knew about it in the first place. And what do you suppose you'd be doing in the mornings instead of exercising your adorable accent?"

"What?"

He moved his head closer to hers on the pillow until their noses touched. "A little of this," he said, tracing the outline of her lips with his tongue, "and a little of that."

"Mmmmm. But my chambermaids—"

"They won't be *your* chambermaids anymore. You'd be a guest at the finest resort hotel in America while escaping New York's nastiest weather. And the maids would get generous gratuities not to come to our rooms until lunchtime. And if you put that stuff on your hair that Agatha uses to make it turn red and paint yourself up just a bit more, no one on the staff will ever recognize you. Meanwhile, you're having a high old time of it, free of charge."

She was silent for several moments. "Plus," she finally said, "a quarter of your salary and half your share of the profits."

He bit her nose. "A third."

"Fifty-fifty or forget it."

"Damn. Everybody outbargains a man without arms."

When Harry Loring went north at the end of the season a week later, his arms had not yet quite mended. He therefore took Arthur Timmons with him as his manservant, promising to sustain him in New York at least until the hotel's following season. On the train, he began instructing the boy in the theory and practice of card playing, poker in particular. It gave him pleasure to do so and brought back most agreeable memories.

SEVEN

(O)n arising the third morning out on their westbound voyage home, Mrs. Memory heard her traveling companion groan through the open door linking their compartments. "It's suicidal to stay out there," Harry said weakly, appearing at her bedside after his usual pre-breakfast tour of the deck but looking more frazzled than refreshed by the exercise. In fact, she detected a slight chartreuse tint to his usually ruddy cheeks.

"I thought you were the seasoned seagoer," she chided.

"Sane people don't cross after late September," he said, flopping onto her narrow bed and emitting a smaller but more pitiable groan than the prior one. "Never again."

"Mind over matter," she said, and vaulted his prostrate form. On attaining the vertical, though, she had a keener appreciation of his condition. The ship seemed to leap to the top of a wave, linger there in shuddering immobility for a long moment and then plunge into the trough below with a sudden, appalling effect on the hollow of her stomach. It was as if the good German iron and dense Black Forest oak of which the *Fürst Bismarck* was constructed had been replaced by balsa wood. And between heaves and pitches the ship swayed from side to side with an irresolution that was decidedly non-Teutonic.

But she was determined not to succumb to mal de mer. Dressing swiftly to escape the confines of her cabin and depositing a kiss of commiseration on Harry's dampish brow, she made her way through the undulating hallways and out into the open, spume-filled air. It was merely a matter of mental discipline, she told herself. Her head would stay firmly in place, with stiff-necked perseverance, while the rest of her shifted and scrambled to accommodate the ship's motion. She could *think* her way through to internal equilibrium. The trick was not to dwell on the physical present;

instead, she resolved to cast back over their dreamlike six weeks in Europe—her first trip abroad—and decide which had been its most glorious single day. Perhaps the one in London when they had spent the morning at the British Museum, where Harry dwelled transfixed over the coins of antiquity; the afternoon in Spitalfields, where she lost herself amid bolts of old silk in a little shop of impenetrable dustiness; teatime at the Ritz, where the pastries left them too gorged for supper; twilight in Kew, where they kissed on a broadwalk all at once empty except for themselves; and the evening at Drury Lane for a rousing performance of *The Pirates of Penzance* and then a roundabout cab ride home through Mayfair. Or was it the still more exhausting day in Paris when Harry trailed dutifully after her through the Louvre, kept manful pace with her up and down every narrow street on the Ile St. Louis, dozed off for the better part of the Molière at the Comedie Française yet managed to perform at full amorous capacity on returning to their balconied room overlooking the Tuilleries? Surely it was not the day they had nearly missed the train at Montreux because she had become transfixed by the exquisite craft of the bobbin lacemakers while Harry overslept. Or the two evenings they drifted among the gaming tables at Monte Carlo— though she had to admit how much more elegant *"Faites vos jeux, mesdames et messieurs"* sounded then the "Place your bets, ladies and gents" they had heard all summer at Newport and Saratoga. It was just that whenever Harry came within sight or sound of gambling paraphernalia they were no longer on vacation; the man was a consummate (and incorrigible) professional.

It had all been hideously expensive, she thought, but worth every centime and ha'penny. If she and Harry had been more like ordinary people, it would have seemed like a perfect honeymoon. As it was, the magical interlude was as close as she was ever likely to come to a wedding trip with—let alone marriage to—Harry Loring. A formalized bond, as he continued to claim, would end the specialness of their relationship, and she did not, would not, could not, press the issue. Just as beautiful crystal if squeezed too hard was prone to shatter, so might the jewel of their enduring affection. All she could do was live with it and for it, savoring it with every fiber of her being for as long as she was able. Ahead of her loomed a whole season in Palm Beach to be spent for the first time as a guest instead of an employee of the ranking hostelry in North America, and all she had to do for the exchange was to become a character of her own invention. The prospect both excited and terrified her.

Braving the choppy sea had left her unaccountably hungry. Her stomach was more likely to remain stable, she decided, if it obtained some ballast. But the thought of attending their dining-room table without Harry's jaunty company was not appealing. Their ten companions at table were a dreary lot: a German couple who spoke no English and little *Deutsch* but ate with a wolfish heartiness; the three McIlhenney sisters from Charleston, who had followed the pilgrimage trail of Gothic cathedrals all the way to Santiago de Compostela and spent their mealtimes correcting one another over minor details of every relic encountered en route; a Mr. and Mrs. Dewey of New Jersey, whose special interest in their grand tour had been the udder capacity of Lowland cows, he being the owner of the third largest dairy herd in his state; and a stocky, balding gentleman of about Maddy's height named Newell Forbes, a sedate Bostonian in the paper business of some sort, who was traveling alone and did not volunteer the nature of his visit abroad. To this array she had presented herself as the widow Memory and Harry as her mother's second cousin—they comported themselves in non-adoring ways at the table, fond of each other but no more, and if the rest thought the worse of them, so be it.

Only the Germans, the gauntest of the gaunt McIlhenney sisters—in unaccustomed and no doubt prayerful silence—and the proper Mr. Forbes were sufficiently undaunted by the ship's bobbing motion to appear for breakfast. The Boston man seemed oddly buoyant under the circumstances, as if thriving on the adverse conditions. He had become used to such rough voyaging in his youth, he said, when the family business required his regular shuttling on cargo ships between Boston harbor and Portland, Maine. "Decidedly choppy going," he said, dispatching his eggs and sausage with neat mouthfuls. "Eating's the best antidote."

Maddy, nevertheless, contented herself with a single poached egg and a lonely triangle of toast with a half-cup of tea. Afterward she returned to her cabin to check on Harry's health. He had tactfully withdrawn to his own bed next door and was snoring away in peace, so she read for a bit, then returned upstairs to the mostly empty public area, and electing to avoid the wind-lashed deck until the sea subsided, wandered into the music room, a symphony of polished brass and mahogany. Not even a steward was present. Well, why not entertain herself for a few moments at the grand piano—if she had not forgotten how?

Her fingers seemed to fly of their volition through "Full Moon, the Fireflies and You," filling the room with a lilting echo. Without a mistake she sailed equally well through "Your Face Is Engraved 'pon My Heart," but then she tried a new arrangement for "Desert Sands," a particular favorite of Agatha Agapé's, and ran into heavier going. "Try it with an F sharp," a voice said behind her. "I believe it's a D major chord."

Her head swiveled to meet the attentive gaze of the unprepossessing Mr. Forbes, whose fierce dark eyebrows contrasted starkly with the grayness of what little hair remained to him. "Oh," she said with a quick smile, "I didn't think I had an audience—certainly not a knowledgeable one."

"Forgive me, madam—I was passing by and recognized your—I don't mean to intrude."

"You're not—it's just that I'm not very good and tend to confine my performing to small private groups of tolerant friends."

"Actually you play quite nicely. Your touch is confident—I should think a singer would find you a splendid accompanist."

She nodded. "Accompaniment is about the limit of my ambition."

"But if you enjoy playing at that level or simply to amuse yourself, what's the harm?"

"None, I suppose. I'm just reluctant to inflict my limitations on—"

"You shouldn't be so self-conscious—though, if you'll forgive my saying so, your modesty becomes you, madam."

She smiled demurely; the man was not charmless. "You play, I take it?"

"A bit."

She yielded the piano stool to him readily, though he assumed it with reluctance, then proceeded to perform half a Beethoven sonata. Maddy marveled that his square, blunt fingers could address the keys with such adroitness. "And so forth," he said, cutting short his own performance.

"Oh, don't stop," she said. "You're marvelous."

"Passable," he said, rising. "It's rather a consuming hobby with me. I keep thinking the Boston Symphony will summon me on short notice one night and I'd better be prepared." His smile revealed a beautiful set of teeth and an unexpected dimple in his right cheek.

Others, attracted by Forbes' playing, drifted into the music salon, and Maddy, unwilling to give a recital of mindless popular melodies, declined to resume the piano stool he tried to surrender to her. Instead, she thanked the Bostonian for his encouragement and headed off for a circuit of the deck now that the sea seemed to have calmed somewhat. Forbes did not press his attentions on her, for which she was appreciative; Harry had warned her that all sorts of predators and poseurs made the transatlantic crossing in search of prey.

Supposing that Harry had by then recovered, she searched the ship for him and nearly gave up. Could he have possibly staggered to the railing and been blown over? She had heard of such things. But he was not the sort; no man who lived dangerously would let nature grab him off so casually. A second tour of the public rooms yielded the sight of him in a corner of the petit salon, surrounded by half a dozen eager card players. Having abstained from his beloved poker for two whole months, couldn't he have waited at least until they were back in New York before resuming his trade?

She brought up the subject while they were dressing for dinner. Her view was that their vacation had not yet ended; his was that he was entitled to pass part of their shipboard time as he chose and that, at any rate, it was necessary to recoup some part of the money they had lavished on their European jaunt. It was not an argument she could win, and pursuing it would only turn him petulant and more stubborn. So far as she was concerned, their holiday had ended. He was back in business as usual.

But she could be as independent as he, and when he excused himself at ten o'clock for a late-evening session at cards she remained in the grand salon, listening to the ship's orchestra play waltz music. While the strings swept her off into a brown study Newell Forbes happened by, paused to be sociable and inquire into the health of her absent companion and on learning he was otherwise occupied asked if he might join her for a few moments. She was glad for his easy, understated company; the moments became hours. The more they talked, the plainer it became to her that he was no bounder but a man of means and refinement. And there was ample intelligence behind his large brown eyes.

His business was the manufacture of pulp paper for newspapers and periodicals, and if it was not the most amusing of enterprises he did his best to make it sound an engaging pursuit. As a young man he had hardened himself working in the family's logging camp during his summer vacations, taking pains to hide his relationship to the proprietors. He had once even ridden the logs down the Androscoggin River to the sawmill, but "my rather rough-hewn mates had begun by then to suspect me for the Harvard man I was at the time—and by virtue of the fact I was the only one of us carrying a somewhat soggy copy of Thoreau's tract on the Maine Woods." Such a testing apprenticeship aside, he had about decided to enter the ministry instead of serving Mammon when his older brother died in a carriage accident. "I lost my faith at about the same time—no coincidence, I suppose—and was therefore susceptible when the family pressed me to join the business. I've not regretted it—paper's an honest product, and it never talks back. And what with the proliferation of the automatic typesetting machines, the printing industry has been having a great boom of it, so we're kept busy enough." There was none of the self-made go-getter's bravado in his recitation and no apology, either, for the privileged position he had inherited. If providence had doled him more modest circumstances, she thought, his character would not have differed.

By the next afternoon, with Harry again engaged in fleecing a fresh flock at cards, she welcomed Forbes's companionship. He was a man as wide-ranging in his tastes and interests as Harry was not. In the arts he acknowledged a decided leaning toward the avant-garde: the new French composer Debussy pleased him as well as Bach and Mozart; the painters Cezanne and Lautrec as well as the Dutch masters; Chekhov and the young Irish playwright Shaw he preferred to Sheridan and French farce; the poetry of Byron, Browning and Whitman to Tennyson and Longfellow; among the novelists, Stendhal, Thackeray and lately Mr. Hardy to Fielding and Austen, with only Hawthorne and Mark Twain among the Americans. "Not Mr. James?" she asked.

"I find Mr. James somewhat epicene—if I may say so."

Not knowing what the word meant, she nodded and began to suspect that she was beyond her intellectual depth. A Harvard Brahmin, she consoled herself with an inward smile. Yet he did not wear it on his sleeve, and he was droll—and becoming better-looking by the hour. Even his politics were surprising. A conventional-enough protectionist Republican, he nevertheless confessed to being moderately sympathetic with the compassionate policies of W. J. Bryan—"if only he weren't quite so windy about it all."

On their fourth or fifth, or possibly eighth, circuit around the prow of the ship, while the wind continued to assault them, he ventured to probe delicately into the nature of her own situation, about which she had said almost nothing. Even then she yielded the least possible. Her late husband had left her enough to live on comfortably, she said in not quite those words; to acquire a few of life's luxuries and busy herself, she had entered employment in the hotel field, directing the housekeeping operations of several large establishments. She gave no names, and he did not pursue them. "Admirable" was all he said of her self-elected choice to work. It was only over tea that he gingerly asked after her traveling companion. "A most attractive and amusing chap," said Forbes. "You're luckier in your relatives than I."

"Cousin Harry can be delightful company," she conceded, "but he's something of a wastrel, I'm afraid. Never did settle down to a proper career. He finds me dreadfully stodgy."

"He miscalculates—by a serious margin, I should say."

She sipped her tea and kept silent. The time had unavoidably arrived to press Mr. Forbes regarding his own domestic arrangements. It was hard to conceive that so engaging and accomplished a gentleman was altogether free of the ties that bind.

"I am in the midst of obtaining a divorce," he answered her without shilly-shallying. "My visit abroad was by way of putting time and space between me and Mrs. Forbes."

A hundred questions came to her mind about the details of his sundered marriage, but none fit to raise. Divorce in his social world was scandal enough not to need elaboration. But who had been the more offending party? His ingratiating manner all at once suggested to her that Newell Forbes might be as accomplished a womanizer in his disarmingly formal fashion as he was a pianist. But his conduct toward her for the remaining three days of the voyage gave no hint that his intentions extended beyond the transient pleasures of a shipboard friendship.

Early on the morning of the bleak day they were to land in Hoboken, Maddy took a final brisk walk around the deck. Heavily wrapped to ward off the damp, she paused to study the low Long Island shoreline twinkling in the haze and to reflect on what lay ahead for her. He materialized beside her, rather as he had in the music room, uninvited but hardly unwelcome. "You've made it a marvelous crossing for me—if you'll forgive my forwardness," he said in a voice as softly mellow as the shrouded dawn. "Would you be offended if I asked your address? My business takes me to the city from time to time."

To refuse so civil a request would be to confess the true nature of her relationship to Harry, which she feared was transparent enough to a man of Newell Forbes's sophistication. "I'm often out of town," she said with a smile.

"Perhaps I can schedule my visits to overcome that," he said. Then he led her to the leeward side of the ship, next to the railing, where a lifeboat shielded them from all but the most inquisitive passersby, and said, "Unless the prospect appalls you, Madeleine Memory, you haven't seen the last of me." He wrapped her in his arms and kissed her with a warmth, gentleness and expertise that took her by surprise. In its breathtaking aftermath she considered for the first time the propriety of entertaining the affections of more than one man at a time. The prospect did not distress her altogether. Absorbed as she was when they parted, she took no notice of the observer on the far side of the deckhouse who had been watching them all the while and then disappeared among the ventilators and deck piping.

Over luncheon during the final hour of the voyage she virtually ignored Forbes and dwelled, guiltily perhaps, on the charms of Harry Loring. His mood was made all the more chipper with the announcement that the winner of the ship's pool for the person who had come closest to guessing the exact time the ship would pass the Statue of Liberty was none other than himself. The prize came to $2,360.

Maddy skewered him with slitted eyes. "How clever of you."

"It's only half mine," he whispered. "Half goes to Hans."

"And who is Hans?"

"Our esteemed first engineer," he hissed, then signaled the captain to bring champagne for the entire table.

"For crissakes, Otis—it's lift, turn, walk—three simple steps." Harry's voice, while below a shout, revealed his exasperation with the new croupier. The man could handle the wheel and the stick with adequate finesse, but unless he could master this little emergency drill he would not survive the preopening training week.

Even as he worked the staff, Harry marveled to himself at Bradley's foresight. If the owner of the Beach Club had not thought of everything, he had come damned close. Things that even a seasoned gambler like Harry himself would not have guessed at. All the gambling equipment, for example, had been made to Bradley's design so that in the event of a raid the tabletops could be lifted off easily and what remained resembled nothing more incriminating than ordinary dark oak dining tables. Beneath the cashier's enclosure in the ballroom a trapdoor leading to the cellar had been concealed. And the cellar was planned to the last detail; its walls of smooth-faced stone that was dry to the touch were unbroken by windows or any other form of outside access, making it impregnable except through the overhead trapdoor. A series of small ventilation ducts provided air in the event the premises had to be pressed into service as a human hideout. The whole exercise of removing every trace of the equipment ordinarily in use in the casino room—tabletops off and hustled down the cellar steps, felt cloths removed and rolled up, cashier's bills, chips, cards, wheels and every other gambling device concealed in the basement enclosure—was not to consume more than five minutes. It would take at least that long for any invading party of lawmen to get by the doorman and Big Tip on watch in the club vestibule. They would not rush the place as if it were occupied by desperados—this was Palm Beach, not Dodge City.

Harry struck his hands together three times, the signal to begin the concealment operation. This time Otis got it right and earned a wink from Harry. Considering their rewards and working conditions, the men ought to be expert at every phase of their craft, including evasion of the law. The pay was twenty-five dollars a day plus gratuities to the men who worked the floor, plus a ten percent bonus to all at season's end. First-class food and lodgings in the club dormitory were on the house. Only the somewhat monastic nature of the work, Harry noted while helping Bradley recruit the staff, discouraged enlistees. They had to leave their women at home, live in barracks-like conditions and avoid fraternizing with the clientele. Still, half the staff had returned from the premiere season.

No corner of the club escaped Harry's ministrations during the week they prepared for the arrival of the early-season crowd. He was determined to show the proprietor that he was well worth his salary—only the chef, famed for his delicate lobster dishes, was paid more, but then only Harry was permitted to live off the premises at the hotel so that the customers would take him for one of their own.

The rules of the house were drilled into them eight hours a day. No one resident in Florida was permitted to play—a dubious gesture to the anti-gambling laws of the state. No one under twenty-four was admitted. Any patron who felt he had been cheated or dealt with unfairly was to have his money returned promptly and without argument and his membership card withdrawn on the way out the door. He rehearsed their technique with the card dealers, taught the roulette men how to spin the wheel with an added flourish the way they did it at Monte Carlo and warned them all how to spot a sharp and counteract his play. Even the dining room attracted his touch. He urged the maître d' to have the waiters fold the napkins into rosettes like the ones provided at Le Faisan d'Or in Paris, and when the linen proved too limp to hold the desired shape he instructed the laundresses to add more starch. Above all, he preached discretion and clamlike conduct in every circumstance; the Beach Club was to be second to none in good manners among the casinos of the world.

Even as he warmed to his task Harry brightened at Maddy's improved attitude, which had cooled to him at the end of their trip. Their protracted tour had been rewarding in all ways but financial, so he had had no choice but to get back in harness while on the return voyage: too many pigeons not to join in the shoot. Surely she had no need to be possessive toward him. And if he had thereby encouraged her to wander a bit, what was the harm? Their current arrangement at the hotel was ideal; it put them in proximity and into bed on a regular, indeed deluxe basis, but gave them each ample rein.

From the first week of the season Madame Memphis proved a great favorite among the female guests, with her friendliness and contagious gaiety. Invitations to her informal little musicales, held on a more or less weekly basis, were eagerly sought, but there was no exclusivity at all about them. Everyone was welcome to participate in the singing, dancing and skits that were performed in one of the spare hotel card rooms for all who chose to attend. These fetes of hers provided the women with entertainment away from the hot and sandy seaside while their men were off golfing, fishing or hunting. And if the vivacious French Canadian was perhaps a bit too partial to gambling at Bradley's in the evenings rather than engaging in the hotel's tepid after-dinner amusements, her habit attracted to the gaming tables many a society matron who would otherwise have felt too conspicuous on the club's premises. After all, they would tell one another, echoing Madame Memphis' exuberance, one is only not-so-young once, *n'est-ce pas?* Why not enjoy themselves in this heady clime, where rigid social strictures could be temporarily loosened. Under Maddy's incognito sponsorship, the club's coffers were plainly benefiting from heavy play by the distaff clientele.

Harry's own value to Bradley was likewise manifested early in the season when Big Tip, who doubled as club secretary and chief bouncer, appeared at the proprietor's office late one afternoon while Harry was conferring with him. A rather distraught woman was asking to see the owner, Tip reported. Rarely did a visitor come to the front door without an accompanying club member, and it was well known that Bradley did not conduct business until after the club opened at seven. She was not a large women, Tip added, and appeared to be an unlikely carrier of a concealed weapon. Bradley agreed to see her.

Her name, she said, was Myra Gordon, and her husband, Lawrence, was a new club member. Bradley nodded, recalling the name from the application he had signed a few nights before. Harry murmured into his ear that the aforesaid Mr. Gordon had been a small but steady loser over the past several evenings. "And what is it we can do for you?" the proprietor asked, suspecting he knew the answer.

Her husband had lied on his application, she said miserably. There was indeed a wealthy family by the name of Gordon in Binghamton, New York, who owned the biggest harness factory in the state, but her husband was only a distant relative. The two of them were at the Royal Poinciana on their honeymoon and her husband had taken all the money that had been given to them as wedding gifts and gambled it away. She broke down at the end of her brief recital, and Bradley had to look away in his discomfort. "How much was involved?" he asked when her tears had subsided to sniffling.

"Five," she said, gulping painfully, "—thousand—dollars."

"And you'd like it back, I take it."

"I'd—like—we'd—a chance for a fresh start—"

Bradley drummed his desktop with heavy fingertips. "What do you think, Mr. Loring? This woman has a heavy burden on her heart. It couldn't have been easy for her to come here."

Indeed, her grief was too persuasive by half; it took a confidence man to spot a confidence woman of equal virtuosity. "I'm highly sympathetic to her plight, Mr. Bradley. But I think if her money is returned to her the lesson this good woman should otherwise have learned will be lost on her. If her husband is an imprudent fellow—or possibly a fool—she'd best find out at the start of their life together."

Bradley nodded as the woman's tears resumed. "Mr. Loring has the right idea," he said, rising, "but I have a softer heart, especially where the gentler sex is concerned." He went to the wall vault and counted out the money. "I suggest you tell Mr. Gordon that the only lucky thing he had going for him this week was you." He patted her wrist as her face lighted with gratitude.

The selfsame Mr. Gordon reappeared at the club the following night. Big Tip ushered him at once into Bradley's chamber, where he heard the tale of Mrs. Gordon's plea in his behalf. "Mrs. Gordon and I have been married twenty-two years," the man said with more amusement than rancor, "and I can assure you that if I could not sustain the modest losses I've suffered at your establishment—and enjoyed the process immensely—I would not have come. I'm afraid, Colonel Bradley, that somebody has taken you for a ride—and it wasn't me."

"Harry," said Bradley when his chief assistant responded to his summons, "you're in charge of the Beach Club court of appeals from this moment on. It's my head that's going soft, not my heart."

Harry saluted, about-faced and returned to patrolling the tables.

The costumes were not exactly original, but Agatha had been a princess to send them down from New York on such short notice. Maddy blew her a mental kiss and adjusted the red wig, pinning it more firmly to her hair. What with the rush to unpack her European things, have them cleaned and repack for Palm Beach she had forgotten all about the New Year's Eve masked ball the Royal Poinciana had apprised its guests of in writing as a festive way to greet the twentieth century. And Bradley hadn't yielded until a week beforehand to Harry's suggestion that he close the club on The Big Night rather than compete with the hotel's extravaganza, so his outfit, too, had to be sent at the last minute.

She walked through the doorway joining her room to his. Harry was installed before the cheval glass, altering the position of the tricorn on his head in order to settle on its least ludicrous angle. When he turned around to face her, she burst out laughing. "Let's have a little respect, please, for the founding fathers."

"I don't know which is worse—the mustache or the wig. One of them has got to go."

"Well," he said gravely, "we certainly can't have a wigless first president."

"Then I guess it's the mustache. I just can't picture George Washington wearing one."

"In the first place," he said, "you're a victim of historical inaccuracy. I know for a fact that Washington wore one all the time, but Martha made him shave it off every time he got his portrait painted. He'd grow it back in between pictures." He twisted both ends of the hairy appurtenance for emphasis. "In the second place, I am not going as George but Jim Washington, twin brother of the president, who always—"

"I know—had a mustache in his portraits but shaved it off in between." His antic mood was infectious. "Harry, you're daft."

He put his finger to her smiling lips. "So long as you're going to ruin the occasion by being a stickler for accuracy," he said, "I don't think you look a whole lot like Queen Elizabeth. From my glancing familiarity with English history, you are entirely too pretty for your role, my dear."

She kissed him lightly on the lips. "Well," she said, "all your friends will be amused by your dressing as a historical figure so like yourself—neither of you ever told a lie."

But her little jest evoked a frown from him that broke their giddiness. "I'm afraid all my friends couldn't care less—and they're down to a handful, at any rate."

It was true, she knew. His planned dual role as the perennial jaunty hotel guest by day and Bradley's hawkeyed assistant by night did not play at all well. By the second week of the season Harry had to confess to his acquaintances among the clientele that financial reversals during the intervening year had necessitated his becoming an aide-de-camp at the Beach Club in order to defray his costs for the season. The old crowd grew cautious toward him and he was invited to join few poker games now that it was thought that the petty sums he might win or lose were meaningful to him. "Welcome to the real working world," she said, taking both his hands and applying fond squeezes.

"That's easy for you to say—now that you're the life of the party."

The irony had not been lost on her. For the most pragmatic of reasons the withdrawn, impassive head housekeeper had become the effervescent center of attraction, while the glib, fun-loving reveler of seasons past had become a sober, calculating sort, on professional retainer and ostracized by his former chums. This reversal of their roles took its toll on both of them. Denied natural outlets for his self-expression, Harry had become subject to spells of moodiness. For Maddy, playing the role of her constantly sparkling alter ego was more than a little exhausting at times; she marveled at her lover's old prowess for sustaining frivolity.

Even in greeting the new century they had to be on the job. Madame Memphis presided in the Royal Poinciana ballroom over a large table of masqueraders who comprised the inner circle of her friends, women who thrived on her reflected gaiety. And since there were too few men in the party, Harry had to perform as multiple consort. In attendance were Annie Sheppard, sent south each winter by a doting father so she could escape the rigors of Massachusetts winters, who came as a lightly armored Joan of Arc; the elfin, affectionate Joanne Cole, whose husband was generally out in the 'Glades collecting gator hides and insect bites but showed up for this occasion as a low-slung Robin Hood to his wife's perky Maid Marian; Maxine and Constance, ebullient widows, who came respectively as Diana, goddess of the hunt, and Demeter, goddess of the harvest; and Sylvia, who might as well have been widowed since her husband drank himself into oblivion late every afternoon. Sylvia, no doubt thinking to arouse her husband's appetite on this once-in-a-century occasion, came dressed as a gauzy Salomé—to no avail; her spouse, still in the golfing knickerbockers he had donned for a late round on the links, was early into the champagne and spent much of the evening snoring on the tabletop.

Spirits were elevated among the rest of the masked revelers, who took delight in guessing the true identity of the others at the gala. None of the women at the table was permitted to feel left out as the genial Jim Washington, mythical brother of the father of the country, asked each of them to dance at least once and escorted them to the heaping buffet tables that edged the room. *"Tu es très angelique,"* Maddy whispered to Harry during one of their brief interludes together, and gave his knee a most un-Elizabethan squeeze beneath the tablecloth. *"Naturellement,"* he said with a reciprocating movement. "And now I shall hold forth on my memories of that terrible New Year's at Valley Forge." But the arrival of the latest bucket of champagne spared the table that recital.

Mingled with the dancing, drinking, feasting and general forced merriment was the costume judging. Prizes were to be awarded for the best men's, best women's and best couples' outfits; every entrant in the competition was required to parade briefly by the judges, preferably with a gesture appropriate to his or her costume. Madame Memphis limited herself to what she hoped was a suitably regal curtsey, but her friend Sylvia, who had had more than a little champagne, was less restrained. As Salomé, she naturally elected to offer the judges her version of the Dance of the Seven Veils, but during the difficult maneuver of wafting one of the veils over her head while simultaneously rotating her shoulders, she unfortunately managed to snare a judge's hand in the chiffon. The hand, still more unfortunately, was wrapped around a lighted cigar at the time, and for several tense moments it appeared that Sylvia might soon be out of the competition for lack of any costume at all. Quick reflexes among the other judges and two handy bottles of champagne prevailed, and Sylvia emerged unscathed except that her number of veils had been reduced by four and a half.

The promenade of contestants ended shortly before Major Mackintosh announced that only sixty seconds remained until the arrival of the new century and that everyone should find his loved one for a very special midnight kiss. Maddy looked around, but Harry was nowhere in view. Damn him! Last time she saw him, wig askew and tricorn canting to the left, he was with Maxine, in her diaphanous huntress costume, who said something about their going out for a breath of air and a glimpse of the gibbous moon. How could he be *so* insensitive? Didn't he know by now she was a sentimentalist about a few very special things? What did it matter if he had kissed her at the top of the Eiffel Tower or in the middle of London Bridge or when her number came up in roulette at Monte Carlo if he wasn't with her now to see in the new century?

She sat smiling benignly but inwardly fuming while the bandmaster counted down the seconds. She was smiling when the lights went out at midnight, and she was still smiling thirty seconds later when they came on again. And by the time Harry and Maxine arrived back at the table shortly thereafter, swearing they had seen a shooting star at what must have been the precise moment the new century was born, her fixed smile felt as if it had been formed of concrete. "Happy nineteen hundred, sweetie," Harry burbled, sliding into the chair beside hers and kissing her fondly if briefly on the mouth.

"Same to you, dearie," she said softly, her left hand rising to his shoulder. With her right, she reached for the neck of the champagne bottle on the table in front of her and proceeded to dump its contents over Harry's wigged head and down his face and neck.

"What the hell—" he gasped, then muted his astonishment at once and emitted a series of gay honks that passed for laughter among those who did not know him. "Aren't you the little madcap, though?" he hissed at her through gritted teeth.

"The party's just beginning," she said, shaking the last drops from the bottle over his nose. " 'Appee New Year, *mon amour!*"

Their tablemates, much taken with the hilarious spectacle of the doused patriot, followed suit, showering one another with the bubbly and then turning their aim on friends at neighboring tables. Soon the whole room was awash in squirting champagne.

Amid the uproar Harry grabbed Maddy's arm and yanked her from the table across the foaming ballroom and through the French doors to the lawn beyond. "What the hell's the matter with you?" he demanded, tugging his soaked collar away from his neck.

"And what the hell's the matter with *you?*" she shot back, her smile turned to savage anger. "At the Big Moment you're outside baying at the moon with Maxine Esterhazy in her goddamned nightie—"

"Oh, for crissakes, Maddy!"

"Nothing's sacred to you, is it, Harry?"

He sighed hugely. "Look, I had no idea how close it was to midnight when we went outside. Neither of us knew what time it was until we saw the lights go out in the ballroom. So I gave her a little kiss for good luck—was that so terrible?"

"She wasn't the one you should have been kissing."

"I was only with her in the first place because she's your pathetic friend. She probably hasn't been kissed since she left the cradle."

"There's a proper time and place for everything."

"Then I should have made a commotion over that little performance you and the exquisitely mannered Mr. Forbes gave on deck the morning the boat docked. That was no small peck, my darling, so long as we're—"

The fire went out of her fury. "How do you know about that?"

"How, indeed? I came up on deck looking for you because I wanted to be at your side when we first sighted land—*that* seemed a special occasion to me—not unlike tonight. I found you, all right, just before the two of you scooted behind the lifeboat and—"

"Nobody scooted anywhere. He led me—"

"I didn't hear you cry out in protest."

"It was—just—a farewell kiss—"

"It looked more intimate than that to me."

"He was nice to me—a thorough gentleman—while you were off playing your damned poker day and night!"

"Fine—that's how I took it—a little shipboard entertainment for you while I was busy at my trade. That's why I didn't make a fuss. And neither should you when I'm away with your dog-faced pal at the witching hour by some perfectly innocent miscalculation."

She looked out across the lake, calming herself. "Well, maybe we both have something to apologize for."

He moved behind her and looped his arms over her breasts, drawing her against his still sopping costume. "Does it matter what time we kiss to celebrate? Do you think the new century is offended?"

"I—that isn't—exactly—"

"I want so much for this to be our century—and bring us every good thing imaginable. I want us to—"

"Like what?"

He turned her around and enfolded her in his arms. "Like good health to begin with," he said, kissing her forehead, "and great happiness," kissing her eyelids, "and excellent luck—can't forget the bitch goddess, can we?" He kissed the tip of her nose. "And making lots and lots of money—the twentieth century is the ideal time," and he kissed her on the mouth, slowly and deeply while he pulled her tight against him and let his body express the remaining sentiments he could not put into words.

"Harry," she said after they had at last disconnected, "why do we have to make a lot of money? Greed breeds ruination."

"Prosperity isn't greed."

"Aren't we prosperous enough?"

"I wouldn't call hand-to-mouth living the last word in happiness."

"Then go to work at an honest occupation, like other people."

"I want a club of my own, Maddy—of *our* own—someday soon—and in New York. I'm learning a lot about the business from Bradley—things I never realized before. I think that between us we could do very well at it. Does that seem so crazy?"

"It would take a fortune, Harry, to do the thing right. You couldn't get away with anything tinhorn in New York. Where's that kind of money going to come from?"

"Oh, I've got a few ideas stirring."

"Oh, lord."

By the time they returned to their table, the names of the individual male and female prizewinners had been announced, and Major Mackintosh was going through the runners-up in the best-costumed couples category. Maddy listened with half an ear until she was suddenly brought up short by the trumpeted names of the second-place recipients—"Mr. and Mrs. Russell Corwin of New York and Paris." The words stabbed at her, causing a pain that swiftly occupied her whole body. Harry saw her shaken look and asked what the matter was. A headache, she said; it would pass momentarily.

She could not take her eyes off the platform as the couple, costumed as Louis XVI and Marie Antoinette, lumbered across it to claim their prize. All she could tell for certain at a distance was that the once slender young man who had been the first love of her life—who had loved her back and then wronged her irreparably—had thickened quite a bit. She squared her shoulders and looked away. It was a large hotel. If they had not run into each other yet, chances were fair that they would not—and, at any rate, her role-playing precluded any possibility of his recognizing her after so many, many years.

She had managed to exile Russell Corwin from her thoughts over the next several days, but in the end was defeated in this effort by her friend Joanne's childlike fondness for finding a congruence of interests where none existed. The sweet little woman had met Mrs. Corwin at the hairdresser's and thought it would be amusing to bring together the two French speakers of her acquaintance at a little party on Thursday afternoon, along with the rest of her—and Madame Memphis'—crowd.

Maddy could not readily refuse the imploring invitation. Besides, she was consumed by curiousity. What confluence of qualities had lured away from her the adored Yale boy of her youth, who had tutored her in French and then so many more things and in the end abandoned her to her desperate situation? Madame Memphis would go to Joanne's little social hour but keep her distance and drench her anxiety in sherry.

Thérèse Corwin, it turned out, had a waistline seven or eight inches larger than her own. But the extra poundage, Maddy thought, trying to be fair, could very well have been a recent acquisition. Her face was attractive if not obviously pretty; as a younger woman she must have seemed all the more so—though not, Maddy decided, prettier than she herself had been twenty-five years before. The Frenchwoman's winning qualities plainly resided in some area other than the decorative. Her brain, perhaps. Madame Memphis would explore the possibility.

Where did the Corwins live in Paris, she asked, alluding to her own visit there only a few months prior. The answer was returned with gravity—on Avenue Montaigne, off the Champs—as if to ask was a breach of etiquette, and no question followed about her visit to Paris. Since the Corwins lived both there and in New York, Madame Memphis pursued, which city did the couple find more suitable and stimulating? Mrs. Corwin pondered that meringue for a time, then replied firmly that each city had its virtues and she was glad frankly that she did not have to choose between them. Ah-ha. Well, then, how was Mrs. Corwin finding Palm Beach on her first visit, especially in comparison to European resorts? Warmer, she said, and more soothing—and the food, she added, brightening, was far better than she would have expected in a, shall we say, frontier environment. Having delivered herself of these daring judgments, she fell silent and assiduously addressed her teacup.

The woman was pleasant enough, in her way, and not mentally defective, Maddy concluded, but she lacked verve and curiousity. She did not or could not make the connections between subjects that opened up a conversation and took it along new paths. She was either terminally phlegmatic or considered herself far above the social rank of these *arrivistes*. Either way, sad to say, she wanted wit. Could it be perhaps that the not-so-poor thing was merely shy? Not possible; anyone who traveled between Paris and New York as the Corwins did would have overcome that phobia years ago.

And yet Russell Corwin has chosen her for his wife. Maddy looked harder at the woman as others in the group tried to lure her into their chatter. There could be but one explanation, and it was right there in front of her, in the hundreds of tiny stitched tucks in her white batiste shirtwaist and the lavish satin-stitch embroidery on her Irish linen skirt. Those little items had to come from a fine Parisian couturier—possibly Mr. Worth himself. Russell had chosen Thérèse because she came of wealth while the Memorys were of New Haven's petit-bourgeois stock; there was nothing more to it. Given that he was the son of a minister of distinguished ancestry but impecunious condition, she could almost forgive him his choice. She sat back and sipped her sherry with something close to serenity. He had made his bed with satin sheets, so to speak, and now had to slither in it. She followed the conversation around her with desultory interest and yearned for the hour to be over.

Before she could manage her escape, the door opened and Russell Corwin walked in to pick up his wife for their late-afternoon bicycle ride. A *frisson* of dread swept her into the corner, out of his view. No doubt they would beat a speedy exit. She could not bear a face-to-face confrontation. Why, though? She was the injured party, she bore the scars—why should *she* cringe?

Madame Memphis swirled forward and drew the latecomer's eye. His wife, all civilities and no substance, insisted that he meet the ladies and most especially the delightful French Canadian. He gave her a brief continental bow and at once began to speak with her in French, professing a keen interest in her Canadian accent, which, he noted for the benefit of the other women present, so resembled an American one. Few native North Americans were able to master the French "r" with the authentic catarrhal roll that he himself had been fortunate enough to learn in his youth on family visits to Paris. "It takes practice," he said brightly, to which Madame Memphis responded with her customary cadenza of confected laughter. Afraid of giving herself away, she told him of growing up in a little village about fifty miles from Quèbec—far enough, she hoped, to account for any discrepancy he might detect between her speech and that of a genuine *Quèbecoise*—and leaving Canada at the age of fifteen when she married the late Monsieur Memphis. All the while her eyes pranced over him, wary of meeting his look for fear her own would turn into a scorch.

The years had not been kind to him. His pale blue eyes, once so large and luminous, had receded into the thickened folds of his lids, while the broad jaw and bold chin she had once thought worthy of a bust by Houdin or Bernini were enveloped by mounds of skin on the verge of becoming certifiable jowls. His complexion was ruddier now, almost unhealthily so, and his posture had begun to sag. Too many seasons of self-indulgence had left their irreparable mark. It was just as well, she decided, noting his curiously dainty hands, the fingers swelling fleshily, that he had not chosen her. The thought of those pudgy fingers running over her body, holding her, caressing her, was repulsive. Yet she jabbered on, perversely enjoying the falseness of the encounter.

His curiosity at last satisfied, he thanked her for the pleasure of their conversation, rose to collect his abundant wife and left. Her ruse had scored its ultimate triumph.

Two days later on her way to the veranda, where she usually met her friends after lunch, he came up behind her and softly spoke her real name. Her head swiveled around and saw the pained intensity in his look. She stood frozen for an instant, struggling to regain her composure. "Ah, Monsieur Corwin—so very nice to see you again. And how is Madame—"

"None of this is necessary for my benefit, Maddy."

"Monsieur?"

"Did you think I wouldn't recognize the girl I loved when I was at college? We've aged, Maddy, but I'd know you anywhere."

The role-playing was pointless. "How very touching," she said.

He studied the hardness of her eyes. "Would you join me for a short walk—we can find a shady place to sit—"

"I don't see the point."

"I think we owe each other a little conversation."

"I owe you precisely nothing, Russell."

"I don't think it would hurt you to be civil to me for a few minutes. You were quite good at it the other day, despite the appalling accent."

"I had no choice then—but I do now. You of all people have no right to talk to me of being civil."

"If you don't want me to ruin your little game—whatever it is—I urge you to come along and not make a scene here."

Reluctantly, powerlessly, furiously, she followed him, keeping silent as they sat on a small stone bench at the edge of the Cocoanut Grove. Even then she would say nothing.

"What is it you're doing here, Maddy? Your French isn't even good enough to pass for—"

"You're not my tutor anymore—don't lecture me another instant, Russell, or I'll pay the delightful Mrs. Corwin a visit and fill in some pages that I assume are missing from—"

"That would be a mistake."

"You made it, not me."

"The mistake was collaborative—and being the girl, you ought to have known what precautions—"

She put her hands over her ears and cast so fierce a look at him that he broke off. "The accent you find so deplorable," she said after a moment, "is a part of my professional role here." She was at the hotel as a sort of entertainer, she said quietly—and someone who could befriend unattached ladies and ignored wives and help to amuse them during their stay. Their acquaintance with the outgoing and slightly naughty Madame Memphis added a touch of intrigue to their otherwise stultified routine. She had been forced to earn her living for the past twenty-five years, and this was the best job she had ever had. She hoped, she added pointedly, that he would not compound his great unkindness to her in the past by making it impossible for her to continue in her present employment.

Corwin shook his head. "That you're reduced to pretending, Maddy—to acting a role so at odds with your—"

"You're quite wrong—I am not reduced in the least. I spend the entire season at the finest hotel in America. I enjoy what I'm doing and am really quite fond of my ladies. I earn my own keep—and how I do so is no business of yours, Mr. Russell Corwin."

"I—whatever you say. I was only—"

"You needn't."

He sat in silence, then asked blandly, "What became of the child, Maddy?"

"Why should it matter to you in the least?"

"Because—I've carried this guilt with me—all these years—"

"I trust the burden hasn't been too great an inconvenience."

"Maddy, I don't expect your forgiveness—I don't deserve it. I ask only that you understand my circumstances for what they were. I was a boy, with very little wherewithal and—"

"And an eye ever on the main chance—whereas I was weaned in the lap of luxury." She stood. "Russell, I think this conversation has gone on quite long enough for—"

"The child, Maddy?"

"It was a girl, Russell. She was taken from me when she was only a few days old—I thought it best. As to the rest, I can't help you."

"Can't—or won't?"

"Your solicitude is too late, Russell—by twenty-five years." She gathered up her parasol. "My friends are waiting for me on the veranda."

The note from Newell Forbes that Agatha had forwarded to her was, as she might have anticipated, a model of propriety. His business would bring him to New York at the beginning of April, at which time he hoped she might allow him to renew their acquaintance. Her reply, written on the personal stationery she had brought with her rather than on the hotel's, was properly thankful and regretful. "My social obligations at this time, I am required to advise you in candor," she concluded, "would make the course you suggest, while otherwise agreeable, both awkward and impracticable. May I nevertheless add the wish that our paths shall cross again someday?"

For a moment she pondered how to sign it, then wrote, "Kindest regards," and sealed the envelope after rereading the note.

That sensitive chore accomplished, she snatched up a package of henna and went into the bathroom to attend to a far more irksome one. The coloring had to be done then because this was one of the few times that Harry's special duties would keep him occupied all day at the Beach Club and he could be spared the sight of her looking like Medusa. The henna business was ticklish as well as time-consuming, boring and possibly dangerous, and it made her arms ache from being held up for so long.

She had rubbed the sticky paste into the left half of her hair, checking the results in both the mirror in front of her and the one on the dressing stand she had pulled up behind her when a noise in the bedroom made her start. "Who's there?" she called out angrily as a bit of the dye stuff trickled down her forehead and channeled periously close to her eye.

"It's the chambermaid, ma'am. I come to give you this here—"

Thinking only of the need to finish up the job as quickly as possible, forgetting for the moment where she was and who she was supposed to be, she charged out of the bathroom, glanced at the familiar young woman and let loose her annoyance. "Ruby Lee, haven't you girls been told a hundred times that you aren't ever to enter a guest's room without knocking first? What's the matter with you? Have you lost the few brains God gave you?"

As the girl's face froze with astonishment at the apparition before her, Maddy caught herself short. Oh, damnation! Damn it all to hell! She could have cut her tongue out with a knife. Her unkindness to the poor child was the least of it. Cross to begin with from the hateful henna, forced to present herself in little more than a camisole, half her head oozing stuff that constantly threatened to run into her eyes and blind her, she had allowed her wits to abandon her and in one careless moment blew away the disguise she had worked so hard to create.

Ruby Lee's homely face ran through its limited repertoire of expressions and settled into one of complete incredulity. "Is that you—reg'lar Mrs. Memory—from last year an' all before that? But Jeannie tol' me you was French. She said—"

"Why didn't you knock?" Maddy asked frostily.

"I *did* knock, ma'am—I really did. You was prob'ly in the bath—and when I didn't hear no answer I came in with my passkey. I brung ya some fruit, ma'am—it's Thursday, fruit day. Jeannie would've come herself only she got cramps real bad so I done it for her—" She cut herself short, eyes blinking at her former supreme supervisor and uncertain what to do or say next.

"I'd like you to come back here in exactly one hour, Ruby Lee—we'll have a little talk then."

"Yes, ma'am."

"Meanwhile I strongly suggest you say nothing to anyone about this meeting. Do I have your word on that?"

"Oh, yes, ma'am," the maid said and left on the run.

Maddy's mind raced, too. She simply could not afford to be found out. Stokes-Vecchio would be furious. A former employee staying at the hotel as a guest was unthinkable: it shattered all the niceties of class distinction between the payers and the paid. The finest, most socially desirable people in the country would be scandalized by the notion of mingling unaware with a poor widow who had to earn her own living. Worse still, questions would be asked if her ruse was exposed—very embarrassing questions. The simple fact of her resorting to a disguise smacked of some nefarious purpose. And who, furthermore, was paying her bill? It would not even take the Pinkertons to solve the nature of her primary function, what with her attendance at the Beach Club every night and the way she induced her lady friends to gamble along with her. The evidence would point directly to Colonel Bradley, and since Harry had persuaded him to hire her, the uncovering of the whole dubious arrangement might very well threaten the club owner's relationship with Flagler and cause him to take his revenge against the offending couple. No, she could not let that happen, she thought, applying the gooey stuff to the other half of her scalp.

A tense Ruby Lee reappeared seven minutes early. She would not sit down—standing was easier. It sure was nice of Mrs. Memory to be, um—so concerned about her when she must have so many other things on her mind, what with being a regular guest at the hotel now and—

Maddy raised a hand to stop the girl's nervous gibbering. This was a very important matter, she began, and one that would require Ruby Lee's utmost cooperation. She stared hard at the girl, who nodded at once. The fact was—Maddy looked around the room as if checking for unseen listeners—she was staying at the hotel at Mr. Flagler's request.

At the mention of the revered name, Ruby Lee's eyes grew large.

It seemed that last year, Maddy went on, certain complaints about the service and the facilities at the hotel reached Mr. Flagler's ears. When he spoke of these matters to Mr. Stokes-Vecchio, the manager denied them, but the hotel owner was determined to get to the bottom of it all. Last spring, therefore, after the season had ended, he asked his head housekeeper whether she would be willing to return the next season as his special investigator. Only she knew the hotel and all its workings as well as Stokes-Vecchio, and some areas of its operations she knew even better. But it was plain to both Mr. Flagler and herself that she could not be an effective observer if she came to the hotel as "regular Mrs. Memory," as Ruby Lee had so nicely put it, so she would have to assume a disguise. Did the girl follow all of that so far? She nodded. "And so," Maddy whispered, looking around again as if an eavesdropper might be hidden behind the curtains or under the bed, "here I am as Madame Memphis, with everything changed—my hair, my clothes, my speech—so that no one, especially Mr. Stokes-Vecchio, will recognize me. Now Ruby Lee, do you understand why you must not breathe a word of this to anyone?"

"Oh, yes, ma'am." The conspiratorial tone of the former housekeeper's disclosure left the girl thrilled but unsettled.

"Very well then, Ruby Lee—I'm counting on you. Both our jobs, you see, depend on your keeping my secret."

"I swear, ma'am."

But Maddy grew uneasy the next day. The threat of punishment or even dismissal might not be enough to seal the girl's lips. An irresistable impulse might seize her at the wrong time, and the secret would get spilled. A positive reward might be a more effective inducement to silence. But what sort?

The answer came to her as she watched Arthur Timmons through the door connecting her suite to Harry's as the young man arranged his employer's wardrobe and removed several of his suits to take to his mother's laundry in West Palm, where he stayed with his parents during the hotel season. Arthur had proven a highly useful if expensive retainer for Harry since he had brought him back to New York with him the previous winter. Might she not be the beneficiary of similar help? But could she afford the luxury? That would depend on how she and Harry came out financially with Bradley when the season was over. At least the possibility was there, and she would have to use it on the girl even if in the end she were forced to rescind the lure.

Devoid of makeup and adopting the authoritative mien of the head housekeeper the girl remembered, Maddy resummoned her to her room before dinner that night. "Have you mentioned our secret to anyone?" The girl swore she had not. "And I have your solemn promise you will not break your word?" The girl swore she would not. "Well, I have been giving our arrangement very careful consideration, Ruby Lee, and if you keep your sacred word to me, I have something in mind that I think may please you." There were many chores she had to do every day at her own home, she told the girl, sewing and mending among them—skills Ruby Lee had once told her she was good at. And she had an active social life with all that it entailed: elaborate hairdressing, evening clothes that needed attention, fine lingerie that required special laundering, guests who had to be served when she entertained. All these things consumed a great deal of her time and energy, and she was reaching the point in her life when she had to think about conserving her strength. So she had been thinking of hiring a personal maid, someone who wasn't afraid to work hard when it was necessary. Of course the person she hired would have to live in New York, as she did, away from her family and friends— but New York was an exciting place, so much to see and do. The person she hired would have her room and board paid for and receive a modest wage in addition. "I'm wondering, Ruby Lee, if you might like to be that person?"

Numb disbelief gave way to delight that filled the girl's eyes to overflowing.

"I take it the idea might suit you?"

"Oh, yes—yes, ma'am—it would suit me fine—I swear."

"We could do it on a trial basis—for three months, say—and if either of us didn't like the arrangement I'd pay your fare back to—where is it you live?"

"Palatka, ma'am—Palatka, Florida. It's up—"

"Yes—well, I'd pay your way back there if things didn't work out, and that would be that. Do you understand?"

"Oh, yes, Mrs. Memory."

"No—don't use my name, please. You must absolutely swear not to say a word about me to anyone. If I even hear the name 'Mrs. Memory' around this hotel, our arrangement will be canceled at once."

Ruby Lee crossed her heart and bit her lip. It would be very sad, Maddy thought, to have to disappoint her.

"We'll use birthdays," Harry heard the chesty young man address the pretty blonde on his right. "I'm September eighteenth," he said, removing two chips from the roll nestled in his left palm and placing them down on the number with his right hand, "and you're November fifteenth." He gave her two more chips to cover that number.

"But will your memory be as good in November," she asked with a small laugh, "as it is in February? You didn't remember my birthday until eleven fifty-nine P.M. last year."

"You're distracting me, sweetheart." He surveyed the table. "Now let's do the kids. Let's see—Billy's birthday is April twenty-ninth—"

"Twenty-*eighth*. Our anniversary's the twenty-nineth—of January."

"I always get those mixed up."

"Some romantic you are," she said, delivering him a tiny punch on the upper arm.

"And Amanda's," he said, ignoring the love tap, "is—is—was it the ninth or tenth?"

"Eddie! It was just three months ago."

"But I can't remember if it was before midnight or after. All I remember is the waiting. She certainly took her sweet time."

"It was three minutes after midnight—and it wasn't the poor thing's fault." She took the chips and placed them on the ten.

"Two more," he said.

"Save them, Eddie—you *could* lose."

"We'll buy some more. The birthday method requires you to put down all the chips in your hand."

"Who says?"

"I just made it up." He turned to the older woman on his left and inquired which day of the month she was born on. More pleased than offended by his bluffness, she obliged.

They were an attractive couple, Harry thought, and it was amusing to watch them bet. Surely they had no experience whatever around a roulette table—although he had to concede their system made about as much sense as any other. He watched as the young woman grabbed a fistful of her husband's sleeve and clutched it fiercely, her eyes never leaving the wheel, as the little ball clicked furiously around its course. When it dropped into number ten she bent her knees slightly and took a little jump. Any bolder display of joy, she knew, violated the starchy spirit of the Beach Club.

"You're a genius, hon'," she said, darting a small peck to his cheek as the croupier pushed a pile of chips in their direction. "Let's cash these in and call it a night."

"Not yet, dear—I'm feeling very lucky. You can go inside if you'd like, but I'm staying right here."

Harry had seen the pattern hundreds of times, although occasionally it was the wife who became addicted. He moved on, making his usual round of the tables, trading quips with the players he knew, keeping an eye fixed on the croupiers and dealers, glancing into the cashier's enclosure, walking slowly through the hallway and vestibule to make certain the doorman and Big Tip were encountering no problems. He even visited the men's room to ensure its cleanliness and to check if any overindulgers had chosen the floor in there for taking a short rest, as they tended to do from time to time. The restaurant, too, underwent the scrutiny of the proprietor's chief assistant; no one could accuse Harry Loring of shirking on the job. He seemed a man perpetually in quest of something.

Once in the café he treated himself to a little rest. He had not realized until the season began how much time the job would require him to be on his feet. He gestured to Ned, the bartender, who quickly presented him with a tall glass of iced Apollinaris water. He sipped it slowly, estimating the size of the crowd and the night's likely take, then wondering what part of the club Maddy was working just now and marveling at her durable patience. She had borne her assignment in far more than a perfunctory manner. The woman could probably command an army if asked.

Halfway through his refreshment, Harry saw Ned jerk his head toward a nearby table. It was the young wife he had seen with her husband at the roulette table an hour before. She sat with only a tall, half-filled glass of brownish liquid for company. A rum cooler, no doubt—it was the stylish drink in Palm Beach at the moment. But he did not care for the spectacle she presented: no lady was supposed to be seen in public consuming hard liquor, particularly when she was by herself. He picked up his glass and glided over to her table. "Forgive me, madam," he said pleasantly, "but didn't I see you earlier doing very well indeed at the roulette table?"

The young woman looked up at him slowly and somewhat bleary-eyed. "Very well indeed," she echoed him in an almost mocking tone. "My husband's still there—no doubt breaking the bank."

"And you can't bear the spectacle?"

"Haven't the stomach for it."

"Roulette?"

"Gambling. I hate it."

He smiled down at her. "Those are bitter words to a man whose business is watching people take their chances with Lady Luck."

She eyed him warily. "You're in the gambling business?"

"In a manner of speaking. I manage the Beach Club for Mr. Bradley."

"Ah," she said. "You must be amused by the—the nightly spectacle of—mass asininity." Her head shot upright. "That's hard to say—'mass asininity.' " She smiled to herself.

"Exactly what is it you don't like about gambling?"

She studied her drink reflectively, declining to meet his look. "Oh, what it does to people—it changes them—they become—what?—*maddened* by it. It's a kind of sickness, isn't it?" She cast him a sideways glance. "I guess you can't admit to that, though—being professionally involved—if you can call that a profession—"

She was skirting with abrasiveness as she sipped her drink. He watched her for a moment. "Do you find rum coolers refreshing, madam? Some people claim they're lethal—and not entirely suitable to a lady's constitution—"

"Oh, hang suitability! Hang all conventions. I'll do what I please so long as certain people insist on doing what they please—even though other people think it's—very stupid and—wrong."

"If you insist, madam."

"I do insist—so there you are." She lifted the glass and polished off the remainder of her drink.

Harry had nothing left to say to her. She was an adult, and he could compel her neither to rejoin her husband at the gaming tables nor to stop consuming rum coolers so long as she behaved herself. But he could, and did, have a word with Ned to tell him to go very light on the rum if the

young woman continued ordering. On his way out of the café he spotted
Maddy and asked her to leave her friends for a few minutes to talk to an
overindulging young wife.

The sudden sight of her daughter—miserably alone and drinking for
solace—caused Maddy to stagger for an instant in the café doorway. She
had not been aware of the Caldwells' arrival. Rachel looked sad and
vulnerable. Her maternal instinct surging, Maddy forced herself to regain
composure. She was needed. As the head housekeeper she would have
had qualms about approaching a strange young woman in such circumstances, but as Madame Memphis she was undaunted. Besides, she had
not seen the girl in a very long while, and there was no telling when, if
ever, the opportunity might come again.

"Bon soir, ma petite amie. You are, perhaps, *un peu fatiguée* with the
games of chance, yes? I, too, am tired and would welcome some company.
Permit me to introduce myself—I am Madeleine Memphis. May I—?"

" 'Course. Be my guest, madam. I'm Rachel"—she gave a small smile
and gulped for breath—"Caldwell. Very nice to—et cetera."

"You are unaccompanied?"

"It's Mrs. Caldwell. Mister's in there—" she indicated the casino with
a jerk of her head—"having the time of his silly life."

Rachel's speech was more than a trifle slurred. How many coolers had
she consumed? It would not take many to souse a non-imbiber. "I 'ave
not seen you 'ere before. You will be staying at the hotel long?"

"If Eddie hasn't lost everything we have before the night's over. The
bank gave him two whole weeks off—the Corn Exchange is not very
generous in its vacation policy."

The girl had to be tipsy or else she would not have so casually confided
her husband's occupation and employer to a perfect stranger. "Ah, *quelle
coincidence!* That is the name of my bank as well—on Fourteenth Street.
You are from New York, then?"

Rachel nodded and volunteered that her husband worked in the bank's
Broad Street office.

"Aha! That is the most important one, *n'est-ce pas?* Your Eddie must
be a very able man indeed to be working there. And he cannot be very
old if you are still a very young woman."

"I'm older than I look, madam—and I have two whole children—a son
and a daughter."

A daughter? The baby must have been born while Maddy was in
Europe. She had seen no mention of it in Postlethwaite's column. Two
children so close together. And she was not a robust woman. Apparently
she had not learned to tame Eddie's animal instinct. Madame Memphis

made a mock-stern face. "And no doubt they are ten or fifteen years old—and that evil-looking potion you're drinking is straight out of the fountain of youth." She asked the waiter for soda water for herself and deliberately neglected to offer Rachel a refill.

The younger woman had the grace to smile. "My son is not yet two, and the little girl came only three months ago."

"You are not afraid to leave such a young one?"

"A little. But she has a wonder of a nanny, and her grandmother is there to keep an eye on everything."

Which grandmother—the ancient one or the deaf one? *"Quelle chance.* You young people today are so—very modern and free. When I was your age we wouldn't have—ah, but we were living in caves back then—"

Rachel started to laugh. "You tease me, madame. You're scarcely old enough to be my mother."

Maddy swallowed hard. Her every impulse was to reach out and gather up the girl and rock her gently till her discomfort passed. "If I had a daughter, Madame Caldwell, I would be delighted if she were as lovely and charming as you."

Rachel rose. "Thank you for the compliment—especially since I'm not exactly myself at the moment. I really must excuse myself. I have to"—she gestured vaguely—"excuse myself. You understand, I'm sure."

"I hope I'm not breaking up the party." A male voice. Maddy looked over her shoulder. Russell. Good God in Heaven: a family tableau. "I had hoped to spend a moment with two of the most attractive ladies in the place."

The man had no right, none at all. Did he know, by some preternatural instinct? The irony of the moment blurred her brain. She performed the introductions with a heart beating so violently she feared it was visible to the two of them. But Rachel departed quickly, easing some of Maddy's explosive tension. "Well," she said calmly, "I'm surprised to see you here, Russell. I would have thought Yale men were above engaging in mindless games of chance."

"Nevertheless, they beat the *tableaux vivants* at the hotel this evening. Thérèse and I gamble with ten dollars apiece, and when that's gone, so will we be." He smiled cordially, but when she failed to respond in like fashion he leaned closer. "But I didn't follow you in here, Maddy, to discuss my gaming habits."

"Is that so? I can't imagine, then, what we have—" She pushed her chair away from the table, ready to stand and leave. "Don't let me detain you, Russell."

"Maddy, wait."

"There's really nothing more we have to say to each other."

"But there is—more than you could know. Thérèse and I are childless."
He quickly narrated how over the years they had tried various regimens
and exercises, had avoided certain foods and gorged on others till they
gagged, how Thérèse had visited the best physicians in Europe and America and undergone painful surgical procedures, but his wife would never
produce the child they both so wanted. "Now can you understand,
Maddy—how that child—yours and mine—matters to me? She's all
there'll ever be of me—that I'll leave behind. All I want to know is that
she's well and lacks for nothing."

She drew a fortifying breath. "And suppose you weren't childless? The
girl wouldn't matter to you in the least—any more than she did when she
was born. You're a supremely selfish man, Russell."

He folded his plump fingers together in front of him on the table.
"You're repaying my cruelty with your own now, Maddy, when all I want
is to make up to her—and to you—what you were deprived of a long time
ago."

"Life doesn't work that way—you're too late, Russell. And don't tell
me I don't understand your plight—I have no other children, either. But
that young woman we—created—will be twenty-five years old in a few
months, and she doesn't belong to me or to you. Whoever she is, wherever she is, I'm sure she's doing very nicely without either of us. And as
for me, I have no need of your assistance in any shape, manner or
form—and if I did, I would sooner die than accept anything from you."
She stood now. "I suggest for your own piece of mind that you forget
about the girl and me both—as you were able to so readily at the time
you were badly needed."

He slowly got to his feet to confront her. "I accept your claims about
yourself and understand your feelings toward me. But as to the girl, I
know you're lying to me. I used to watch you lie to your mother about
where we had gone, and your eyes used to make the same nervous little
darts from one of her eyes to the other—just the way you did a moment
ago." He bent across the table. "Maddy, where *is* our daughter?"

She made a determined effort to keep her eyes fastened to his, willing
them not to waver. "I'm sorry—it's as I told you. She was taken from me
just after she was born and I have no idea—"

"Bye-bye." Rachel walked by their table on her way from the ladies'
room, giving them a little wave as she went. Then she turned. "Very nice
meeting you both," she called back, and headed for the doorway.

Maddy felt the edges of her vision going black. The well of emotion
inside her was so near the bursting point that she had to wonder how

much longer she could hold back the urge to cry out the truth at this moment that coincidence or fate had put the three of them under the same roof for the only time in their lives. She bit her tongue, hoping to pin it in place as Russell's eyes scoured her face.

"I don't believe you, Maddy," he said. "Not that I blame you. But I want you to know that our meeting under these conditions has been emotionally jarring for me. Please believe that my intentions are altogether benign—and if you or the girl ever needs anything at all at any time in the future—"

"I'll remember," she said more gently than she intended. "And now I must excuse myself."

In the ballroom casino Harry's head spun around as the shout cut through the hushed chamber. "*Yow-wow-wow-wheee!*" He began to stride rapidly in the direction of the roulette table from which the sound had come. As soon as he reached the table Harry saw that the noisemaker was the young husband with the birthday betting system. A quick conference with the croupier, made difficult by the exultant whoops of victory, revealed that the fellow had placed five bets of $125 each on five numbers and one of them had come through. Against odds of thirty-five to one, he had just enriched himself of $4,275. The winner was crowing as if he had won the legendary pot of gold.

Harry pushed through the throng and reached his side. "Would you mind accompanying me, sir? We have a tradition here—Mr. Bradley prefers to pay off big winners personally."

"All right, all *right,*" he shouted. "Meet me in the bar, everyone," he called to the others at his table. "The drinks are on me."

Harry tucked his hand under the fellow's elbow and began guiding him out of the ballroom toward Bradley's office. "May I suggest, sir," he said, "that you enjoy your victory at a little lower volume?"

"Sure, sure. Inside in ten minutes, everyone—on me!"

"I think you'll find, sir," Harry persisted, "that such generosity is out of place here. All the Beach Club members are more than able to purchase their own beverages."

"Hey!" The fellow stopped in his tracks, just inside the ballroom doorway, and shook his arm out of Harry's grasp. "Are you trying to tell *me* how to behave, mister?"

"Sir, I'm merely trying to suggest it would be better—"

"You're not *suggesting*—you're telling me—" His hands balled into fists.

Harry signaled one of the housemen by the door to join him. Right behind came the young man's wife, pushing her way through the crowd that was collecting around them. "Eddie, please," she begged in a low voice, "don't carry on."

"Look, Rachel, we hit it big"—he shook his pocketful of chips—"and this flunky of Bradley's is trying to tell me what to do."

"Eddie, *please*—let's just go." She began tugging on his arm.

"I *won't* go," he cried, shaking her off. "I want my money," he demanded, pushing his face close to Harry's.

"You'll get your money in the morning—it'll be delivered to you at the hotel."

"What's wrong with now?"

"Mr. Bradley is not fond of guests who—"

"I don't give a damn what Mr. Bradley is fond of—I came here to—"

"*Eddie!*"

The young man's angry fist was interrupted in mid-arc by the bulky houseman, who in tandem with a second lifted the offensive fellow off the ground and propelled him out into the vestibule, with his wife miserably trailing. "I'll take your membership card now, sir," Harry said as his aides unlocked Eddie's right arm.

"Here, take your damned card—I won't be back! Just see that my money's there in the morning—or I'll have the authorities on your neck."

Maddy materialized at Harry's side as the din receded. He did not see the unhappiness in her face as he inspected the surrendered card. "Edwin Holcombe Caldwell, New York," he read aloud. "Know anything about them?"

"A little," Maddy said mostly to herself.

"Anything I should—?"

"Some other time."

Maddy groaned softly along with Sylvia, Constance, Annie and Elspeth, a latecomer to the hotel, as the little ball clicked past twenty-seven and followed the arc of the wheel with what seemed like agonizing deliberation until it dropped into fifteen. The truth was that after more than two solid months of every-night-but-Sunday visits to the Beach Club, she understood the urge to gamble no better than she had before she began. Thank heavens she used none of her own money during her evenings at Bradley's; she had worked too hard to throw it away so fecklessly. For her companions, of course, it was throwaway money, sheer time-killing caprice, except for Joanne, who had a tendency to bet and lose more than she could afford; Madame Memphis tried gently to break her of the habit. It was the gamblers who struggled to earn their daily keep whom she truly pitied—but none of their sort was ever seen in the environs of Bradley's.

As she led her friends through the hallway to the café, where the grandfather clock chimed eleven fifteen, Maddy idly noted the absence of the guard in formal wear who was usually posted in the corner. He had gone to the gents', no doubt. She gave the matter no further thought as Sylvia asked her whether bombazine could be worn in April. Madame Memphis was of the opinion that any material could be worn whenever its wearer decreed. Elspeth, overhearing, pronounced bombazine suited only to fall and winter wear; any other time it would be lamentably unstylish.

This weighty talk continued over drinks in the café as Maddy listened with half an ear to her ladies appraising the relative stylistic merits of barathea, bengaline and bouclé. This gave way to a yet more deeply felt exchange on the advantages and drawbacks of merino, *merveilleaux* and *mousseline de soie*. These women, Maddy thought, attention wandering, were not quite as empty-headed as they often sounded; they simply lacked adversity in their lives. And they were considerably more pleasant and amusing, she had to admit, than the chambermaids and hotel officials with whom she had consorted in seasons past. Their being exceedingly rich no doubt improved their dispositions; they could afford to be kind and gracious to one another. Having arrived at so lofty a level of social standing and material comfort, they could not conceive that anyone was their superior. Perhaps the wealthy and privileged were, among themselves at least, the ultimate democrats.

To numb herself slightly from the mindless chatter about her, she ordered a second cooler but carefully instructed the waiter on the proportions of rum, lemon juice and soda water she preferred. Across the room she spotted Harry in conversation with one of the hotel guests, an older gentleman named Lucien Dougherty, who had arrived the previous week in his private railway car and turned out to be a longtime acquaintance of Harry's. "A great good pal of Neville's," he had explained on introducing the substantial citizen to her. Harry was offended afterward when she asked him which Neville. His beloved mentor, Maskelyne, he said, which stirred momentary suspicions in her that he waved away. Dougherty had made his fortune in the import-export business, but just what it was he imported and exported Harry didn't know for certain. At any rate, the oldtimer seemed a hearty sort, if rather a diamond in the rough.

She watched Harry break away from Dougherty and speak briefly to the guard at the café entrance; in a moment, the two of them exited together, leaving the room without its usual protection against distasteful incidents. Peculiar. She nevertheless took Harry's departure as a signal to lead her band back into the casino for the evening's final round of wagering. Rising, she felt slightly muzzy-headed, but not to the extent that while passing back through the vestibule and hallway, she failed to notice the absence of the doorman and Big Tip. The place was virtually unguarded. It was more than peculiar, she sensed; something was happening—yet the place seemed to be operating as normal.

Her suspicions were intensified when on entering the ballroom she saw that none of the housemen other than the game operators was on hand and Harry was now nowhere to be seen. Yet the gambling continued. Fifteen minutes later, though, the casino operations halted and all eyes in the room were turned on a procession of waiters, each bearing a lighted silver candelabra from the restaurant, followed by the maître d', the bartenders and the white-clad kitchen staff. At the head of the line in evening clothes was a large, attractive young blond man with a magnificent set of waxed handlebar mustaches—apparently a newcomer to the club staff. Immediately in their wake came the remaining club members on the premises who had been ushered into the ballroom by a second stranger, a tall fellow with long blond hair and a flowing reddish mustache. As the casino became a hubbub of surprise and wonderment the second usher called out to quiet the assemblage and said that Mr. Loring would be along in a moment to make a special announcement of interest to all.

Maddy's brain flooded with apprehension that drove off the fuzziness from her drinking. A moment later she looked on with horror as Harry stumbled through the ballroom entranceway, one eye swollen and almost closed and a reddish streak of what appeared to be drying blood running down his chin from the corner of his mouth. Behind him, having administered a stiff shove that propelled Harry over the threshold, was a third stranger, still larger than the other two, this one brandishing a large silver revolver. The sight of it signaled the other strangers to pull out guns of their own and level them at the panicked crowd. "Shut up and listen, all of you—and nobody'll get hurt," the second intruder called out above the noise. Harry held up his hands, too, urging them all to stay calm, and staggered over to the cashier's enclosure to gather himself together.

The crowd hushed, and Maddy had to apply all her self-restraint not to rush over to Harry. But aside from looking wobbly and beat up, he appeared to have sustained no life-threatening injury. He pulled himself upright and addressed the room in a loud if halting voice. "Ladies and gentlemen—I beg all of you to listen. All our lives are at stake—and most especially Mr. Bradley's. These—people—have him in his office—along with all the guards—who were lured there one by one and disarmed and bound and gagged and are now being held there along with him."

An undertow of outrage flowed through the room. He held up his hand. "These—gentlemen—have assured me that they mean none of us any harm. All they're interested in are objects of monetary value. It's essential, though, that you do just as they say. I have no doubt that they are desperate or else they would never have attempted such a vicious—"

The gunman on Harry's left raised his weapon and pointed it just below Harry's ear. A woman across the room shrieked.

Harry gave a little nod of understanding and continued, his voice hoarse now. "Yes—well—your cooperation with these—people—is therefore urgently recommended. They've told me that at the first sign of trouble they'll fire a shot—and when their confederate in Mr. Bradley's office hears it he will shoot Mr. Bradley. And then all of us may be subject to their violence."

"You heard the man," the gunman next to Harry said in a voice low and mellifluous, as if he were a singer or an actor used to projecting his words to a full auditorium. Then he turned back to Harry. "Please tell two of your casino men to roll back the carpet and open the trapdoor."

Looking dazed, Harry shook his head and turned up his palms in assumed ignorance.

"The trapdoor, Mr. Loring." The command was louder and more menacing now.

"I don't know anything about a trapdoor. Where did you—"

The man clipped Harry on the side of the head with the handle of his revolver and sent him to his knees, then prone on the floor.

"Oh, you filthy—" Maddy cried out before she could stop herself.

The gunman looked around and spotted her. "I want no more of that." He waved his gun in a sweep across the packed room. "If you'll all behave like the ladies and gentlemen you're supposed to be, everything will be all right." He bent down to Harry, who was sitting up now and shaking his head to clear the pain. "Now, then, Mr. Loring, will you do as I ask or will I have to—?"

Harry weakly summoned one of the croupiers and a faro dealer out of the crowd. "Do as they say," he told them.

As the club members watched in amazement the two housemen set their shoulders against the cashier's enclosure and shoved it, chips and coins rattling in the drawers, a dozen feet from its original position. From where she stood Maddy could see that a U-shaped cut had been made into the carpeting. The men rolled the flap of carpet back, revealing a trapdoor with a brass handle set into the flooring. With an upward snap of his head the ringleader signaled the croupier to pull up the handle. The door lifted smoothly. The hole underneath looked very black to Maddy.

The basement, the gunman in charge told the onlookers, had been designed for rapid storage of the gambling equipment in case the law authorities arrived unexpectedly. "But tonight it will be the gamblers who are to occupy the facilities." The guests were to file by while one of his accomplices relieved them of their purses, billfolds, jewelry and any other valuables, the men's studs and cuff links very definitely included. "Although that will leave you gentlemen in a slightly disreputable-looking condition," he added jauntily, "I'm sure the ladies will forgive you on this special occasion." After they had been lightened of their valuables the guests would be escorted down the steps into the basement, "which, let me reassure you, is more than ample to accommodate all of you in comfort and without any fear of suffocation—isn't that right, Mr. Loring?"

Harry's lips tightened as he gave a grudging nod.

"You will be detained there no longer than absolutely necessary," the gunman concluded, "and let me save you any thoughts of trying to make an escape. The room has no other means of entrance or exit than this stairway you're about to go down—and it will be firmly locked after you."

He then signaled one of the other gunmen to lead the candelabra-bearing waiters down the steps to light up the basement. They were followed in swift order by the kitchen staff, the casino men and the remainder of the help—none of whom, Maddy noted with curiosity, was asked to surrender his valuables. Only the rich were to be victimized. As thieves went, she supposed, these were not entirely unconscionable. She could hear murmurs and movements coming from below the stairs as the staff obediently settled into its prison. And why should they risk their necks for the clientele's sake? The thieves seemed to have thought of everything.

"And now, ladies and gentlemen, it's your turn," the armed leader announced. "To expedite matters I suggest you ladies begin helping one another remove your pinned and clasped items, and you gentlemen take off your accessories. Ernie will escort you safely down the steps after you've deposited your things on the floor here in front of me. Each man's coat and trouser pockets will be searched as he comes by, and we're keeping a close eye on the women to make sure none of you attempts to hide anything in your clothing or on a private part of your person. Anyone we find withholding valuables from us will be dealt with. We'll begin with the people on my left and work our way around. The better you cooperate, the faster we can end this."

As the club members started forward for their shearing, Harry struggled to his feet. "Just a minute." The gunmen eyed him. "Can we at least be allowed to keep a list of what you take? The authorities will have to know, anyway—what harm can it do you?"

Their young leader looked puzzled, and then a smile lit his face. Even his accomplices began to laugh at the outlandish suggestion. "You want us to let you help the—police?" The gunman spat the last word and began to laugh to himself for a moment.

"Why not?" Harry said. "It can't harm you any, and it might help these people somehow—with their insurance or some other—"

The gunman shrugged. "Suit yourself, Mr. Loring—but it won't do you any good. Where these things are going they'll never be traced."

"Madame Memphis," Harry called out. "Is she here?" His voice was weak, barely louder now than a hoarse whisper.

She brushed by a couple standing in front of her and hurried to Harry's side. "Are you all right, darling?" she whispered, feeling the gunman's cold eye on her and catching the dim sheen of his revolver barrel reflecting the chandelier light.

He nodded. "Inside the cashier's cage—top drawer—there's paper and pencil. Get it."

She ran and did as he asked, then brought the things to him as the gunmen moved uneasily about.

"You keep the list—I'm too weak and dizzy," Harry told her in a tight whisper. "Just the major things."

"How will I know?"

"Use your common sense."

She nodded and knelt on the floor, scribbling furiously as the first couple moved forward and placed their valuables on a bedsheet that one of the thieves had spread beside the cashier's cage. "*Onyx and gold studs & c.l.,*" she wrote after taking the couple's name, "*blk. leath. purse, 3-strnd pearl neck. w/ruby rng.*" But they were already on the way down the stairs, the wife moaning and her husband supporting her, by the time Maddy was done; she could not keep up. For the second couple she listed only, "*sml. plat. & diam. neck., gld & slv brclt, lg. diam.-emrld rng.*"

The little pile grew steadily larger, Maddy's fingers flying as Bradley's lightened patrons slowly, steadily descended and the ballroom crowd thinned. Sylvia's opal and gold pendant on a dainty filligreed gold chain was among the later objects added to the glittering heap, soon joined by Elspeth's little emerald and diamond necklace, its stones arranged checkerboard style, that matched the hem and bertha of her green and white evening dress. The women fluttered their fingers at Maddy in greeting as they trotted by. Near the end came Lucien Dougherty, who asked the gunmen if he couldn't hold onto the gold watch fob that had been a keepsake in his family for six generations. "Drop it, old man," he was told.

Finally it was Maddy's turn. Her amethyst and rose-quartz beads were, no doubt, the least costly item among the booty, but she hated losing them. She thought of appealing to the thieves on the ground that she was not truly a guest but a club employee. Now, though, was no time to risk a confrontation with these costumed thugs, who were becoming increasingly impatient to be gone. She slipped the beads over her head and got up off the floor, prepared to go down into the cellar.

"Your ring, madam," the second gunman said.

She had completely forgotten the small gold band she had worn on her finger for over twenty years, the symbol of the widowhood she had falsely professed for all of her adult life. Almost gladly she wrenched it off her finger and dropped it on the pile. Perhaps its loss signaled a more truthful and satisfying existence that lay ahead for her. She turned her back on the thieves and headed into the depths.

As promised, the cellar proved to be no dungeon. With candlelight and fresh air wafting in through ducts in the walls it was surprisingly habitable. And instead of a sullen mood enveloping the crowd, something approaching gaiety had taken hold, fueled by a distinct gallows humor, as if they had decided to make the best of the misadventure. At any rate, they could do little else—and besides, their lost possessions were likely insured or readily replaceable.

A footstep on the stairs turned Maddy's gaze upward. Harry was coming down, slowly and painfully. "Excuse me," he called in a weak voice, "may I have your attention?" Even in the dim light, she could see that the skin around his now closed eye was growing discolored. "Our captors have asked me to tell you," he said, indicating the gunman posted at the top of the stairway, his head protruding into the ballroom, "that once they have made good their escape they will telephone the hotel and advise them of our presence here. They have given me their word on this, and I want very much to believe them. Since they at no time resorted to violence—except on me—I think we can safely—"

He was interrupted by the arrival behind him on the stairway of the club's dozen guards, followed finally by Bradley himself, all of them bound and gagged but none seeming injured in any way. That they had failed—utterly—to provide the patrons the security for which the club had gained repute excited no resentment just then among the basement dwellers, who circled around them to commiserate. A moment later the trapdoor closed over them with a muted crash, sealing them all in their mass crypt. A woman toward the back of the cellar began to whimper as the ceiling creaked with what sounded like a very heavy object being dragged across the floor above to weight the trap door closed. Another woman began to moan, crying that she could not tolerate the sensation of being closed in. A third sank to her knees in prayer and then collapsed.

As soon as Bradley was freed he called everyone to attention, speaking with difficulty because of the dryness of his mouth and throat. A sip of brandy from a silver flask that one patron had been allowed by the robbers to retain for medicinal use quickly restored the club owner's voice. He climbed to the second step on the stairway to make himself more easily heard and thanked them all for their calmness and cooperation, "without which I am quite certain I'd have lost my life. I am appalled and humiliated that such a thing could have happened in our establishment in view of the elaborate precautions we take. I don't know how these men infiltrated the premises or obtained their obvious knowledge of our operations, but I can assure you that we won't rest until we find out." He reserved a final word for "the valiant efforts of my devoted assistant, Mr. Loring, who tried to intercede in my behalf at considerable bodily risk to himself. I want to thank him publicly for what he did."

A volley of applause, amplified by the chamber's echoing walls, was offered in tribute to Harry, who sat recuperating in the corner under Maddy's tender care. He smiled wanly and gave a nod of acknowledgment. Big Tip and several of the other beefier housemen then made a mighty effort to pry open the trapdoor, but it would not budge. Discussion followed about the wisdom of extinguishing some of the candelabra in order to preserve the oxygen in the room, but Bradley reassured them that the basement had been planned to provide a flow of air for such a contingency. Still, it was thought prudent, since there was more light than was strictly needed, to douse half the candles. In their shared indignity the crowd behaved with exemplary good cheer; spirited conversation developed, new friendships were made, even a few songs were sung to sustain flagging spirits.

As Harry's strength returned, Maddy asked for details of his heroism in Bradley's behalf. He waved off the question but she persisted. He happened to have been in the hallway when he saw two of the robbers walk into the owner's office, he explained in a rasp. Not recognizing the intruders and very definitely not having seen their weapons, he decided to follow them in—"just in case they meant trouble. I figured that Bradley must know something about fighting and it was two against two, so we'd have a decent chance." But the robbers had agile fists, several of which found Harry's eye and mouth, and lost no time thereafter in brandishing their weapons, forcing Bradley to open the wall safe and then tying him up.

Maddy stroked his forehead. "But how did they get all the guards to come to his office," she wondered, "and surrender like lambs?"

"I'm afraid they used me for that job." He was ordered to go to each armed houseman, explain the gravity of the danger to Bradley if any rescue was attempted and bring him to the office doorway, which was opened just enough for him to see the owner trussed up with a gun held to his head. The guard then surrendered his weapon to the second gunman present, who removed its cartridges and quickly bound and gagged him. Then Harry was dispatched to fetch the next guard. "All very methodical, I must admit," he said.

"You sound like you almost admire them."

"In an odd way, I do. They appeared out of nowhere and knew every detail of the place." He shook his head. "Damned mystifying."

It was two hours before their rescuers arrived, led by Stokes-Vecchio, the hotel doctor, a nurse and the entire Royal Poinciana Pinkerton contingent. A round of drinks was served on the house while the victims were divided into four groups, three of patrons and one of the club's employees, for questioning by the detectives. Bradley and Harry comprised their own separate division and were questioned more exhaustively than the rest.

The mystery of how the thieves had entered the premises was solved almost at once as one of the Pinkertons, using a lantern to explore the grounds surrounding the club on that moonless night, discovered a ladder abandoned beneath the window in the men's lavatory. The club's outside guard had been overcome in the darkness and the ladder placed against the building to reach the lavatory window, which by design had been installed too high to reach from the ground level and was normally locked from the inside during the club's operating hours. Somebody on the staff might have unlatched it for the thieves, or possibly someone had carelessly forgotten to lock it—though the janitor assigned the job swore he had done so as usual.

As it turned out, the inventory of stolen items that Maddy had composed with such frenzied effort was not needed. In their interviews the detectives were able to assemble a much more complete one. Harry relieved her of her shorter version, thanking her for the effort as he pocketed it and saying that at least it was a fine souvenir of the occasion they might be able to look at someday and laugh over. Just now, though, he said as he touched his darkening eye socket with a grimace, it was all too painful.

The robbery, valued well up into the millions of dollars although no precise figure was given out, was the consuming topic of interest for the final week of the Palm Beach season. Neither the Pinkertons nor the police, summoned on the pretext that the Beach Club was merely a private social establishment rather than a deluxe den of iniquity, unearthed any clues to the thieves' identity. Every train that passed through West Palm for the next week in either direction was thoroughly searched and its passengers interrogated, and every ship that docked at a port on Florida's east coast was similarly combed—all to no avail. Descriptions of the culprits were of little use since the authorities theorized that wigs and false mustaches had been worn by the gunmen. Police were forced to conclude that the escaping bandits may have gone west into the 'Glades, where they remained in hiding, and although three separate posses were sent out, led by native Indian guides, nothing turned up.

Bradley brooded over the crime, so massive a blow to his pride and his pocketbook, and shuttered his place for the brief remainder of the season. He and Harry pondered who had unlatched the lavatory window, concentrating on the kitchen staff and speculating that somebody delivering supplies had slipped in through the service entrance and done the mischief. But the kitchen crew vowed that it had been as vigilant as ever against such a trespass. More troubling still, how had the robbers known about the trapdoor? Perhaps a member of the original construction crew had told someone about it, Harry suggested. Bradley, however, felt a more plausible source was a current or former club employee, but he was at a loss to know how even to begin narrowing the possibilites. He settled instead for ordering iron bars installed on the inside of every window in the club and tastefully hidden behind the curtains. But the gesture, he conceded, was rather like shutting the corral gate after the horses had bolted.

The derring-do of the jewel thieves appeared at first to have cost Harry Loring dearly. Up until the robbery, Bradley told him, the season had been highly successful for the club, thanks in no small measure to his assistant's conscientious labors. But the thieves, in clearing out all the cash in the house and forcing him to make good on certain uninsurable items and close down operations for the last, and usually most lucrative, week of the season, had wiped out his profits. All the casino owner could pay Harry was the remaining half of the ten thousand dollars they had agreed on for his base salary. Bradley looked glum handing him a bank-draft for that amount.

Harry retained his sunny exterior. "I suppose we're the biggest gamblers of all," he said with a smile, "hoping to come out ahead in this line of business."

Bradley was appreciative of this plucky attitude. "And I hope you'll give some thought to rejoining me next season," he said. "I think the odds are against disaster striking twice."

"We shall see," Harry said, taking his hand firmly, "what we shall see."

On their train ride north Maddy shared her lover's good spirits. "Even though it was not half as remunerative as I'd hoped," she said, "I can think of worse ways to have spent the winter." Her sole regret was having promised Ruby Lee a job as her maid, which might now prove a drain on her resources but could not—both in justice and her own self-interest—be avoided. She leaned over and kissed Harry for having included her in his arrangement with Bradley.

Toward the end of the trip, as she was settling down in their compartment after breakfast to resume reading the book she had brought along for the ride, Harry reached into his pocket, withdrew a string of amethyst and pink-quartz beads and tossed them onto Maddy's lap.

"Harry!"

"I thought they might have a high sentimental value to you, so I persuaded Lucien to remove them from the—collectibles."

"Dougherty—that old man?"

"One of the finest retired jewel thieves in North America."

"*Harry!*"

"His private car is attached to the end of this train. He's a very estimable gent, but I thought it best not to let him wander too far out of my sight—considering the value of what he's got stashed about in various hidden compartments of his luggage."

Her look changed from wide-eyed disbelief to cauterizing anger. "How could you take such an insane chance?"

He shrugged. "I'd call it more calculating than insane." The opportunity was there from the beginning: lots of swag, no police, the isolated location of the club. All they really had to figure out was how to get into the place, neutralize the armed housemen and get the stuff out of Florida—"which we are in the process of doing."

"*You* left the men's room window unlocked?"

"Would the twin brother of the father of our country tell a lie? I confess."

"But your eye—your mouth—the way that man hit you with his gun in the casino?"

"Occupational hazards, my dear. We thought it best to establish my allegiance to the dear colonel beyond a shadow of a bloody doubt." He touched the still-tender area about his eye. "Emerson overdid it a bit in Bradley's office, I must admit."

"Emerson? You know those—people?"

"Since they were pups. Emerson and his brother are Dougherty's grandsons. The other two lads are their cousins—one of them a failed thespian, which is why he served as their spokesman. Their fathers—Lucien's sons—are in another area of the business—specializing, shall we say, in the disposition of valuables not obtained through strictly legal channels. Generations of craftsmen collaborated in our little enterprise."

"All under your—your insidious direction."

He patted her thigh. "Very nicely put." It had all been worked out to the last detail, Harry noted not immodestly. He occupied the gents' room a few moments before eleven o'clock to make sure no patron was on hand when the Dougherty boys clambered up the ladder. Then he stationed himself outside of Bradley's office to certify that the proprietor was there and so that he could conveniently attempt to come to the proprietor's rescue shortly after they invaded his office. The rest of it she knew.

"But—a thousand things could have gone wrong. You could have been killed—"

"Faint heart ne'er won fair fortune—and I daresay the rewards will be ample." After expenses, which were considerable—the rental of the railway car, all those evening clothes and disguises, the boys' miscellaneous travel costs—he estimated his share of the take at between two hundred thousand and a quarter of a million dollars, "being conservative, as I am by nature."

"So that's what you wanted my list of the stolen articles for—to be sure that—"

"Precisely. It was a last-minute inspiration—about the only thing that hadn't been planned—which is why the boys were amused when I proposed it in front of everyone. And since I was the mastermind, they figured it was best not to argue, under those awkward circumstances."

She shook her head, as much in wonderment as disapproval. "And how did the—the boys—escape?"

"Separately, over several days—wearing work clothes. And of course they're all dark-haired and clean-shaven so their appearance didn't match the police descriptions. They hid out at various rooming houses in West Palm where they'd checked in the week before on different days. Naturally they carried none of the loot on them."

"Naturally." She fingered her returned beads. "And why didn't you rob the club's staff while you were at it?"

"They're working men—you can't think I'm a heartless wretch."

"You didn't seem to have so much heart where Bradley was concerned. He trusted you, Harry—"

"He still does, I believe. I consider that the highest tribute of my illustrious career. He even wants me back." He stroked his adam's apple contemplatively. "I think that would border on the unethical, though."

"You have the ethics of a snake."

"I resent that deeply. My victims, per usual, can well afford their losses, the colonel included."

Maddy sighed and sat back, watching the landscape flash by. "And what are you going to do with all the money, if I may ask?"

"I could use a few new suits. And your wardrobe is beginning to look the tiniest bit shabby, if you don't mind my saying—"

"Harry, I will *not* be implicated in—"

"And then there's our club. I've already thought up the name—the Palm Beach—just the right touch of elegance with a hint of the exotic tropics. We'll bank the money in a joint account—"

"Harry, I'm not going—"

"We'll be equal partners—and the operation will be entirely legitimate—except for its illegality, of course. I figure this gives us half of what we need to do it up right. In another year or two we'll have—"

She shut her eyes. "I don't think my heart can hold out that long."

EIGHT

1901 Season

$\mathcal{H}$arry stretched his legs out in front of him and sat back farther. The Waldorf-Astoria certainly knew how to furnish a suite—and Flagler's was no doubt the grandest in the hotel. The chair was so comfortable that he might easily have drifted off, except for the obvious gravity of the business they had summoned him there to discuss. But the great financier's cigar smoke, wreathing him invisibly on the far side of the sitting room, and his attorney's singsong voice added to the drowsiness that the overstuffed furnishings seemed designed to promote. Why couldn't this wisp of a man, whose tongue constituted four-fifths of his entirety, just get to the point?

"You come very highly recommended to Mr. Flagler by Colonel Bradley," Lionel Teasdale, Esquire, of the firm of Addison & Teasdale, had begun his remarks that November morning, "although your particular professional specialty is not one of which we are normally in need." But a certain project now presented itself, the gnomelike Mr. Teasdale went on, that "because of its extremely delicate nature requires a somewhat unorthodox approach. And to accomplish it, our representative—and we hope it will be you, Mr. Loring—must have a thorough appreciation of Mr. Flagler's Florida operations."

"I'm a keen admirer of Mr. Flagler's achievements," Harry said with a respectful nod toward the pillar of smoke twenty feet distant, "both in Florida and generally."

"I wonder if you know, though, Mr. Loring, how dubiously his efforts down there in the wilderness were viewed within reigning financial circles." His Florida East Coast Railway was termed the height of folly ten years earlier, Teasdale related, "and candidly, it's still not a moneymaker and may not be for years to come. But Mr. Flagler has patience to match

his vision—and, shall we say, pockets deep enough to sustain the cost."
While it was true there was not yet enough traffic to keep the rail line busy,
the seasonal tourist trade at the Flagler hotels was turning a profit and
the Model Land Company was bringing in enough settlers and farmers
to justify Flagler's faith. It was important to Flagler's way of thinking that
his Florida enterprise eventually pay its way, but adding to his own wealth
was not the principal incentive for the undertaking. "Mr. Flagler has
provided a livelihood for thousands down there—he is creating something quite splendid out of nothing." His own employees were well paid
and tended to, new settlers were given land without cost for their schools
and churches and municipal buildings, and the fate of the citrus growers
was foremost in Flagler's anxiety-tossed sleep. During the horrific frosts
of '95 and '97, the mogul went to great expense to help the growers stave
off ruin, giving them free seed and fertilizer and crating materials, spreading around cash gifts, propping up their banks, even ordering his trains
to stop repeatedly on their runs up the coast and blow their whistles six
times by way of warning that a frost was on the way and that the smudge
pots ought to be set out promptly. "Some cynical observers attributed
Mr. Flagler's generosity in those crises to crass self-interest," Teasdale
went on, recrossing his neat little legs, "but then there are always some
who fail to understand that Christian charity and good business practices
are often the coziest of bedfellows."

Now for all his extraordinary labors in behalf of the good folk of
Florida, Henry Flagler sought neither gratitude nor acclaim, his attorney
explained. "He is a most modest and retiring gentleman, to whom personal publicity is anathema." Repeatedly he had rejected proposals that
hotels, towns, even rivers, be named for him, and it was regularly necessary to put the kibosh on efforts to erect statues in his honor. "He has
asked nothing in return from Florida except the opportunity to proceed
unimpeded in his good works—nothing, that is, until now. And what he
asks is not only for himself but for others who do or may find themselves
in a personal dilemma as unfortunate as his own."

Money alone, however, could not achieve Mr. Flagler's most earnest
wish, although its availability, if adroitly applied, might be useful. What
was most essential, now that the financier had transferred his legal residence from New York to Florida, was a gifted confidential agent to carry
his cause at the coming session of the state legislature—"a man of special
talents, someone able to say one thing and mean another—a man of
enormous discretion in matters where the law is concerned, who can keep
his own counsel—and who is virtually unknown in the state and unin-
volved in the regular Flagler operations." When the subject was raised

tactfully with Bradley, that authority on sporting subjects was of the opinion that the ideal agent for Mr. Flagler's purpose was a superior poker player, a man with cool nerve and keen intelligence—"and he unhesitatingly named you, Mr. Loring, as the best recruit he could imagine."

The specific nature of his assignment was spelled out far more swiftly than its elaborate prelude, as if Harry had to be convinced of the righteousness of Flagler's cause before he would consider doing his bidding. But if he was to be an evangelist in the old man's behalf, perhaps Teasdale was correct in his approach. The rewards for the undertaking, though, were of far more interest to Harry than its justification; as a man of the world, he could fully understand Flagler's needs where matters of the heart were concerned. Harry's pay would be generous, the lawyer said toward the end, and he would be provided with one of Mr. Flagler's seaside cottages in Palm Beach from January till however long it was necessary for him "to achieve our purpose in Tallahassee." He would be free, of course, to bring any companions he wished with him to enjoy the comforts of the climate and the amenities, a cook and maid would be at his disposal, and all expenses he incurred when his duties took him to the state capital would of course be borne by Flagler. "And should this arrangement prove to be mutually beneficial," Teasdale concluded, "perhaps a more permanent one can be worked out."

Maddy was apprehensive about it all when Harry explained the offer afterward. "I cannot go on playing Madame Memphis one day longer," she said. "Whatever purpose she served is done with."

"Then you'll just be your charming, adorable self, my dear."

"But I don't travel in the same social circle as those people—"

"Perhaps it's about time you began to."

"Impossible. They'll know I worked at the hotel—that I'm pretending to something I'm not—and look down their long noses at me."

"That Mrs. Memory is dead and gone. The real one has beauty and exuberance she's no longer hiding in drab black clothes and a dour manner. I doubt if they'll even remember your previous incarnation—and if they do, so what? We're beginning to be people of means—and our patron owns the place. Besides, you can be a woman of total leisure the whole winter."

Put that way, the prospect was harder for her to resist. "But I'll be bored silly."

"Then cultivate the friendship of the rich and decorative. I've always found that a stimulating vocation. Besides, they may come in handy for us someday." And he gave her a necklace of kisses that ended their discussion and immediately preceded an hour of carnal delight.

*   *   *

Not even a glimmer of recognition sparked in Mary Lily Kenan's blue eyes when they were introduced at tea shortly after Maddy's arrival in Palm Beach by Norma Trask, who occupied the cottage just south of the one she and Harry were sharing. Indeed, Miss Kenan professed high pleasure on meeting Mrs. Memory and called her "a splendid new face among our younger set."

Nor, two evenings later, when she and Harry attended a dinner party at the oversized cottage Flagler and his beloved consort shared, did the tycoon give any sign of knowing that Maddy had formerly been in his employ. Nor did Flagler's niece, Elizabeth Ashley, and her husband, Eugene, seem to recall that they had sat at the same table with her several years before during a little pre-Christmas party that Stokes-Vecchio had taken her to at the Royal Poinciana. Not sure at first whether to be relieved or offended by this collective lapse of memory, Maddy chose simply to enjoy herself as the meal wore on and not to think of her presence among them as any form of social climbing.

They were a lively enough lot and did nothing, other than mentioning a hundred names unknown to her, to make her feel unwelcome. Flagler was at his courtly best, Miss Kenan a small, buxom bundle of charm and the Ashleys as acerbic and engaging as Maddy dimly recalled their having been on the earlier occasion. Also in attendance were the Lowerys of Philadelphia, Shirley being a willowy woman of perhaps fifty whose athletic pursuits turned her undaintily tan, and her husband Lewis, who spent only the first month of the season with her at their cottage before returning north to his insurance business; Vivienne and Alfred Gorman, Long Island people whose talk ran heavily to horses; Miss Kenan's brother, Will, who was serving as an engineer at The Breakers, the new hotel Flagler was putting up on the site of the old Palm Beach Inn directly across the island from the Royal Poinciana, and Will's wife, who spoke little; and Norma Trask, a New York widow and confidante to Elizabeth Ashley, who entertained various of her relatives at her cottage throughout the season. To these formally attired gentlemen and tastefully adorned, impeccably coiffed ladies, Mrs. Memory represented herself much as she generally did when traveling in Harry's company—as a widow whose late husband, a success in the shipping business in New Haven, had left her moderately comfortable. Yet here there was no pretense—for the circumstances of their cohabiting did not allow it—that Harry was her cousin and their friendship of the innocent sort. No opprobrium attached to this tacit admission since the nature of Flagler's relationship with Miss Kenan was equally illicit by conventional standards; if anything, it was all the more scandalous by reason of the wide gap in the lovers' ages.

Still, Maddy did not feel entirely at ease and could not disabuse herself of the sense that even with her Madame Memphis guise at last shed she was a poseur in such company. And she could not take her eyes off the astonishing strand of graduated Oriental pearls that adorned Mary Lily's throat. The largest one was the size of a robin's egg. And the strand was held by a diamond clasp that could not have been less than twelve carats. The woman had been lavishly rewarded for her favors by her multimillionaire admirer. And what was the harm in that? Only that the transaction seemed so blatant and the object of his affections therefore suspect for the sincerity of her feelings in return.

After dinner, Mary Lily drew Maddy aside, almost as if sensing her disapproval, and applied the full voltage of her charm to the newcomer to her Palm Beach circle. "I want us to be friends, my dear," she said, patting Maddy on the wrist, "especially now that Mr. Loring tells me you're quite accomplished on the piano. I desperately need some help in that department since none of the other girls plays and I'm no good at accompanying myself."

"I do play a little, Miss Kenan, but I'm afraid Mr. Loring has a somewhat exalted notion of my—"

"Oh, do call me Mary Lily—and I'll call you Madeleine, if I may, and you'll see how much better friends we can be." The smaller woman's hand clasped about hers.

"Thank you, Mary Lily. I'd be—"

"Calling friends by their Christian names fosters a closer spirit, I do believe."

"I—suppose so. Some people I know are simply more comfortable with formality—"

"As to the piano, Madeleine, I shouldn't concern myself—"

"You might call me Maddy—so long as we're to be—"

"Maddy?"

"Yes—if you'd like—"

"Somehow I've never been overly fond of diminutives. They seem to lack—I don't know—character, I suppose."

"That's—interesting. I can't say I've ever considered the matter at length. Perhaps you're right. Madeleine will do nicely, if it pleases you, Mary Lily."

"You're the one who must be pleased, my dear. But Madeleine is a quite lovely name—so there you are." A fonder pat on the wrist. "As to your piano playing, I'm sure you'll do splendidly. Our needs are quite modest, I assure you."

"I'm afraid, though, that I don't do any of the fine composers at all—they're quite beyond my patience to master. It's just the popular songs I'm familiar with—"

"Frankly," Mary Lily said, leaning closer to Maddy, "the Gormans give us all the Beethoven and Chopin we can manage—and, bless them, a fine thing they make of it. All I'm after, my dear, is someone to play the music I like to sing—songs that swell the heart or bring a tear—the sort that Henry so enjoys." She touched her pearls in unconscious tribute to their bestower.

"Well, then—perhaps I'm up to that modest—"

"But we must rehearse, you and I—we shouldn't make a botch of it, no matter the size of our audience. Do come to tea tomorrow—cook makes the most divine plum tarts—tiny ones—and we can begin to—"

"Thank you, Mary Lily, but I'm afraid Norma and I are to go golfing—"

"Pish-tush—bring her along. I know for a fact Norma prefers to play first thing in the day but probably thinks you're a late riser."

Was it a suggestion or a command? Either way, Flagler's bejeweled little songbird, beneath her bright feathers, seemed a disarmingly manipulative creature. "Well, perhaps I can try to arrange it with—"

"Do."

Norma Trask, as it happened, was glad to oblige. They played nine holes while the grass was still dewy and breakfasted afterward on the porch to Norma's cottage. Maddy liked everything about the woman—her easy grace in addressing the ball, her patience with a novice's play, the way she looked in windblown yellow linen, how she spoke without patronizing a newcomer of suspect social credentials. Best of all was her directness. "I can tell," Norma said, lightly buttering her toast, "you weren't entirely enjoying yourself last night."

"Wasn't I?"

"I'd say not—and it's natural, of course—so many new people to meet and assess. It all takes a bit of getting used to."

"Perhaps so."

"But I'll go further and risk saying that you don't find Mary Lily much to your liking."

"I—shouldn't say—she seems very pleasant, actually."

"But basically you don't approve of her and Henry as a suitable couple. You find it—"

"It's not my place to—"

"—all a little unseemly—their great difference in age, to begin with—and then there was the necklace. I noticed your noticing it."

"Oh, my. I didn't mean to—it's just that I've never seen anything quite so—so—"

"Appallingly lovely?"

"Yes—exactly."

"And when you get right down to it, you suspect Mary Lily of being rather a gold-digger—of a highly polished sort, to be sure."

"I should say—that somewhat overstates it."

"But the sentiment is there, nonetheless—I know it, Maddy, because we've all felt it at one time or another." She deftly veneered the toast with marmalade and did away with it between sips of coffee. "You can rest assured, though, that Mary Lily herself is no less sensitive to the appearance of the match—or shall we say mismatch? The notion of being taken for a kept woman is most unattractive to her—she lets her hair down with some of us when she's into her second mint julep—and the matter is of continuous concern to her family. They're very proper people—in the dreadful way that smalltown North Carolina folks of social pretension are bound to be—which is why her brother Will is around so much. He's more than a Flagler functionary—he's Mary Lily's ambassador plenipotentiary to Sir Henry's court, looking out for her interests in quite the way that my dear Elizabeth of Ashley looks out for her kindly uncle. For all his zillions, he's old now and highly susceptible to the wiles of charming Southerners." A final swallow of coffee. "And so you see, all this is out in the open between the parties—which is a far healthier way to deal with it."

So much instantaneous intimacy regarding the affairs of the high and mighty was more than Maddy had bargained for, but it was not without its fascination and, as Harry had suggested before their arrival, perhaps of future professional use to them. "Yes," she said, "I can see that."

As to the lovers' considerable age difference, Norma went on, it would be a mistake for Maddy to assume that Henry had one foot in the grave. "He still has great charm—at selected intervals, I grant you—and the life force has by no means abandoned him. Possibly that's the heart of the problem."

"Problem?"

"Well—the unseemliness of the—what shall I say?—carnal aspect of their friendship. He *is* nearly old enough to be her grandfather. One would think there would have been a certain abating of the fires of passion in him by now. No doubt Mary Lily arouses the embers—"

"I rather assumed—if you'll forgive my frankness—that was an essential part of her function—or should I say the attraction she exerts upon him?"

"Mmmm. And that's where I run into trouble. You see, I don't deny that Henry's wealth and power are part of his allure for her—just as her liveliness and refinement and good breeding—by smalltown North Carolina standards—are catnip to him. That's all a fair exchange as I see it. It's the carnal thing that I—you know, I have this unpleasant vision of a great old stallion rearing on its wobbly hind legs and mounting the fairest filly in the paddock—and I—well, it's repulsive to me, frankly, much as I'm fond of the two of them. What sort of beauty can there be in the physicality of such a—coupling? It is obscene—an ancient cock of the walk alighting on—"

"But if she invites it?"

"Equally obscene."

"Possibly the notion—the act—is less repulsive to Mary Lily than to you."

"Possibly—but I'm not at all sure. I suspect she closes her eyes—throughout—and sets her mind on the material rewards for her degradation."

"The necklace?"

"And all the other trinkets."

"They do make it seem rather more like a transaction than a—"

"That part doesn't trouble me. Why shouldn't she be lavishly rewarded for—allowing him—I mean to say that so long as the adultery is forced by circumstances and Henry's intentions to her are thoroughly honorable if conditions ever allow—but of course that's why your Harry has been enlisted in the cause—"

"The cause?"

"Their marriage. Surely you don't suppose Mary Lily will tolerate this limbo of illicit companionship forever?"

"I was unaware she had any choice, the divorce laws being what—"

"Didn't Harry explain it all to you?"

"Only that he's looking out in general for Mr. Flagler's interests at the legislative session."

"Mmmm, he does play his cards close to his chest. Perhaps he didn't want to concern you with the grubby details."

"I—will confess—that from time to time he withholds certain specifics—about his business arrangements—if he feels I will not altogether approve."

"How very gallant of him. But surely you've grasped that Henry is a prisoner of his marriage to an institutionalized woman—which makes the poor man as pitiable as Alice is in her madness. And if his wealth can buy him his freedom—and legalized happiness with Mary Lily—why not?

Which is where Harry comes in—assuming the Florida legislators will prove more pliable than—"

"I see." The assignment was less attractive than Harry had painted it for her. Perhaps he had not gone into the point of it for fear it would renew the discussions between them of his own studied avoidance of wedlock. Or perhaps he simply had some darker design on Flagler's fortune.

"Meanwhile, she has the necklace for solace—I'm told it's worth at least a million—though Mary Lily herself, of course, would never say as much. She has taste, you see—discounting the basic distastefulness of the relationship itself—if you grasp the distinction I'm drawing—"

"I'm afraid I don't. You seem to be fond of—"

"Well, but I am—I do like the girl—her brass—and her strength to endure the gossip and the looks—I mean she and Henry are not a proper couple—it cannot be denied. They're never asked out in New York by the reigning social set—so they hide out here, in a place of Henry's own devising, with friends who understand their situation."

"But?"

"But none of that mitigates my feeling that a man of his age carrying on with a—well, an old maid was what she was—and no doubt virginal before Henry swept her up—it's all more than a tad tawdry." Norma placed her napkin on the table and rose. "I suppose, though, that's what makes it so exciting for us. Excessive good taste wearies one so." She glanced out at the ocean before Maddy could untangle that nexus of warring judgments. "Mmmm, looks calm—how about a swim? I hear tell you're more at home in the waves than on the links."

Throughout January and February their life was one long, langorous idyll, warmed by the relentless sun and cooled by the ocean spray. Maddy had little to do but play, read, make marvelous love, and acquaint herself with the habits of her social betters. These proved to be hardly more ennobling in the area of amorous decorum than those of humanity's dregs. There was the annual arrival, for example, of Shirley Lowery's lover, who checked into the Royal Poinciana each winter two days after Shirley's husband returned to Philadelphia. The substitution of the one for the other at the regular social functions of the cottage circle was accomplished without comment, other than Norma Trask's remark to Maddy that Shirley's extramarital friend was a close business associate of Lewis Lowery, who may well have known of the liaison. The case of Vivienne and Alfred Gorman was still more egregious. Although they dined and entertained together, their mutual interests did not extend beyond music and horses—and certainly not into the boudoir. They maintained separate bedrooms and love lives, but all with supreme civility. As to Norma herself, she made no secret of it that she had long ago soured on men and that her emotions were vested heavily in her niece, lately graduated from Barnard and committed to the suffragist movement. "She is a most passionate child," Norma commented in showing Maddy the girl's photograph. "You can see it in the eyes and lips."

While Maddy's education advanced in the sybaritic arts, Harry's progressed in the political sphere. For a time he did no more than read the Florida newspapers intensively—a dozen a day—to familiarize himself with current topics of concern and the varying regional interests of the state. But the real training for his forthcoming foray up in Tallahassee began with the arrival of Flagler's Florida counselor-at-law, Judge George Raney, who, as it happened, also served as a prominent member of the state legislature. For a full week he and Harry talked politics from morning till midnight; Harry had not been the beneficiary of such enlightening tutelage since Neville Maskelyne taught him how to master the mysteries of playing cards. The two pursuits struck him as having much in common.

Florida was in the throes of vast social reforms, as was much of the rest of the country. Indeed, its governor, William Jennings, was a cousin of the great populist, Bryan, with whom he shared many of the same policies and a compassion for the plight of the unpropertied. "The man's a hopeless nincompoop, of course," Judge Raney explained, but the issues he identified himself with—cheap money, regulation of freebooting industry and the railroads, the graduated income tax, more education and electoral power for the masses—had an undeniable appeal in the new century of the common man. "But turning them into law is another matter entirely. If we humor him a little, he and his ilk will go away before long—none of that sort has the stomach for the dirty work."

Although Raney exercised considerable sway among his legislative cohorts it was essential that he not be identified openly as Flagler's man. "When you get right down to it, Henry's a rich old Yankee," the judge confided, "and a carpetbagger's a carpetbagger, however much good he's done for the state." It was necessary, therefore, that Harry carry most of the load in persuading the Florida lawmakers to pass the bill on which the great entrepreneur had set his heart. They went over every name in both houses until Harry knew them all by heart, along with their skills, ambitions, interests and pet venalities.

"Like Gaul," said Raney, "they are divided into three parts—and all of them, don't forget, are Democrats." The Republicans, of whom Henry

Flagler was a devoted pillar, had been but a flickering presence since the Reconstruction had ended twenty-five years earlier. "Many of them are corrupt—or, better yet for our purposes, corruptible when the right occasion arises. And this is one."

One of the factions was made up of "the railroad people," those in the pockets of the big vested interests like Flagler and the other railway men and industrialists. These would form the nucleus of the majority Harry had to forge, Raney instructed, "but it's a fatal error to take them for granted. Their allegiance must be courted and renewed—like an old lover's." Their opposite number was the reform camp, which tended to see Flagler as a predator and would be pushing hard for tighter regulations by the state railroad commission. The reformers had lately succeeded in pressuring the commission to drop the passenger rate from five cents a mile to four, with comparable slashes for freight, but there were all kinds of exceptions and side deals, with the lowered prices more honored in the breach than in the practice. "We're going to have to lay low with this crowd and say we want to be cooperative—then claim the moral high ground for Flagler in the divorce bill. Henry may even have to give a bit in the regulatory area to get his way." The final legislative faction was the entrenched Democratic ring, open to challenge from both sides but still very much in charge in the county courthouses from Miami to the panhandle. "Them we have to buy outright—they see straight through any trade-offs to what's uppermost in our heads. The only man in Florida they hate worse than Flagler is the governor."

When they were done reviewing the rogues' gallery of politicos, the judge offered Harry a few guiding principles of superior underhanded conduct, and in language he could not mistake. "First," he said, "don't put your chips down too early in the game or you'll scare away the players. Second, don't show your hand before you have to—but let 'em know you're dealing from strength. Third, if you're going to bluff—making promises you can't or won't deliver—don't get caught." To grease the wheels, Flagler was making a sizable war chest available to the pair of them to spread around as they saw fit—"but remember, not one cent before the votes are in. This is strictly cash on delivery."

"How much cash are we talking about?" Harry asked.

"A hundred thousand—plus the generous gift Flagler is going to bestow on the state agricultural college about ten minutes after you hit Tallahassee."

"Where am I going to put a hundred thousand dollars?"

"In my saddlebags," Raney said with a wink. "The old man knows me better than he does you."

"And how do I get my hands on it when the time comes?"

"Just send your nigger boy runnin' my way," said the judge, indicating Arthur Timmons, who was arriving on the porch with a fresh round of bourbon and soda for the lawyer and iced lemondade for Harry.

The night before Harry left for Tallahassee the Ashleys hosted a dinner party intended to buoy him with good wishes and deepen his resolve to bring back the prize—"the consummation of our dreams," as Flagler put it in a brief toast at the outset of the meal.

Eventually, in view of Harry's pending mission, the table talk turned to politics. The focus fell on Elizabeth Ashley's observation that Mark Twain had recently contended that the success of the suffragist movement would be highly therapeutic for the body politic because, as he put it, "Women never will tolerate corruption."

"Which, of course, is precisely why they'll never be given the opportunity," said Alfred Gorman. "Politics is a man's game, and men play it dirty. The ladies will ruin all our fun."

"And not a moment too soon," said Elizabeth.

"Ah, a cryptosuffragist in our midst."

"What of it? I can't for the life of me understand why men so scorn the suffragists' efforts."

"Because they are unwomanly."

"Then don't resist us so hard."

"Who is this 'us' of yours, Liz?" Vivienne Gorman asked. "Most of the women I know could hardly care less. They'd vote exactly as their husbands do—if only to avoid domestic civil war—so the outcome would be no different."

"Some women do care, though," Maddy spoke up, "and might well vote as they themselves choose—thereby affecting the outcome."

"Exactly," said Flagler, "and that's what we're afraid of. A chap with an appeal to emotion but very bad policies—like Bryan—might sway the ladies and pull down the republic."

"Then we women would suffer the consequences of our folly."

"Better to spare us in the first place," said Alfred.

Flagler invited Mary Lily to enter the fray. "If I may be pardoned a homily," she said, "I subscribe to the theory that the hand that rocks the cradle rules the world."

"Hear, hear," said Shirley Lowery.

"And what of women who have no cradles to rock?" Maddy asked.

The table fell still for a moment. "I meant it metaphorically, my dear,"

Mary Lily answered, not eager for combat. "Women influence their men in many ways."

"Not a few of them devious," said Eugene Ashley.

"To the extent that may be true," said Norma Trask, "it is your doing."

"Because we are oppressive?"

"There is some evidence along those lines."

"Because you prefer it that way."

"That," said Maddy, coming to Norma's aid, "is absurd."

Eugene swung his head toward her. "Dependency is women's role, or the Lord would have constructed you differently."

"I would characterize that as a patently brutish theology," Maddy shot back, feeling a flush heat her cheeks as her inhibition drained away.

"Are you calling us indecent?" Alfred fired from the other flank.

"Just mulish," she answered more tartly than she had intended.

"Speaking of mules," said Will, trying to restore lightness to the party, "I've made a careful study of the subject and I find a decided affinity between active participation in the suffragist movement and a lack of comeliness."

"Meaning what?" Maddy snapped.

"Good-looking women have better things on their mind."

"That's not mulish—that's swinish."

"Maddy!" Harry said.

"What?"

"Will was just having fun—"

"Actually, old boy, I meant it literally. These female marchers and hollerers are quite the most unlovely creatures I've laid eyes upon."

"That's idiotic!"

"Maddy!"

The table had fallen still as ardor was laced with venon. Maddy felt all their eyes flicker over her and then turn aside. She studied the residue of her peach melba.

"May I suggest we adjourn," said Mary Lily, "for a little music?"

The proposal was greeted with acclaim.

"I'm afraid I'm not much in the mood," Maddy told Mary Lily as they moved toward the conservatory.

"Nonsense, my dear—we must soldier on."

She felt blue the next day, both because of Harry's departure and the shrillness of her conduct the night before. None of the other women was in touch with her all morning; had she become an overnight pariah? The mistake was in forgetting herself and thinking for the moment that sex was a firmer bond than class. Without Harry about to bridge the gap she feared that her indiscretion would leave her isolated in enemy territory.

For a time she contemplated sending Ruby Lee over to Flagler's cottage with a note to Mary Lily, excusing herself from their standing teatime date at the piano attended by any of the other women who were so disposed. Better, she finally decided, to brave a frosty reception than to hide and thus promote her own ostracism. And Mary Lily had the inspiration to fortify them all for the occasion by substituting mint juleps, as was her intermittent custom, for tea. By the second round any lingering resent-ment Mary Lily may have been harboring toward Maddy for having insulted her brother at table the previous night was dissipated, and the women were toasting her independence of spirit—"if not," as Elizabeth put it, "the subtlety of your scorn. But Will had it coming."

"Will's a man's man, I'm afraid," said Mary Lily more protectively than apologetically. And soon they were off on a musical bender, giving rather more raucous voice to Maddy's playing than usual. Fed by a long swallow of her third julep, she took their antic mood as a cue to teach the others a favorite song of the Floradora Girls—"Darling Rosebud, Twine 'Round My Window"—but with a few slightly suggestive variants to the lyrics that Agatha had gaily offered to her that autumn. It was at this precise moment that Henry Flagler walked in on them.

Maddy played on at a somewhat thumping gait as the others' voices mysteriously trailed off behind her. Finally aware that she was performing solo, she turned around to see her companions all but shrinking into the corners of the room and Flagler advancing on her with a most peculiar expression on his face. Was he fit to be tied or just uncertain whether to reprimand them or laugh out loud? For an instant she was certain he was about to ask her to leave the premises for the corrupting influence she was having on his prim little darling. Instead he flashed a quick smile and asked, "Do you know any others like that?"

Maddy cleared her throat and fought to cleanse her brain, hoping she did not reek of bourbon. "Well—I—a friend of mine—who used to be on the stage—from time to time instructs me in—these slightly—I hope you're not offended—that I—" She gestured toward the other women, who were by then clustered near the door, saying their goodbyes to Mary Lily.

"Nonsense, Madeleine. You're a spirited woman—and you've made my little queenie a merrier girl than in past seasons. The weeks can drag on for her down here, I'm afraid. Your companionship has been a god-send to her."

"Well—I—"

"The Royal Poinciana's loss is our personal gain, I should say." His smile was positively beatific.

"You—you're aware that I was—"

"Of course, my dear. Your charms were far too evident that dinner Stokes-Vecchio brought you to for me to have forgotten."

"I thought—perhaps—"

"I had to let him go, you know. Anthony was not up to the job—though it took me several seasons to find it out."

"I hadn't heard. I thought it best not to appear at the hotel—"

"Quite."

"I assumed you didn't remember—Mary Lily's never indicated—"

"Of course not. She thought it might make you uncomfortable."

"I—you're all—too kind."

"Not in the least. Now let's hear one more chorus of that naughty number." And he reached into his breast pocket for an unlighted cigar, which he waved in approximate rhythm to Maddy's subdued rendition.

His first morning in the state capital Harry devoted to a carriage ride through the Tallahassee hills with their rich red soil so hospitable to growing cotton, and the parklike city with its great trees and elegant gardens full of wisteria and camelias and Cherokee roses. Men of evident means bred fine horses and fancy cattle in the neatly fenced fields that he surveyed in the outlying sectors. The lulling sense of overripe repose he drew from the local landscape was in marked contrast to the bustle surrounding the capital, with its gaudy patchwork of cheap hotels, taverns, rooming houses, surveyors' offices and lawyers' shingles swinging from every street corner. It may have been a sleepy little Southern city most of the year, but for the couple of months the Florida legislature was in session there was excitement in the streets and a purposeful gathering in every lobby and barroom.

He lunched on succulent Spanish mackerel fresh from the Gulf and used the occasion to win the favor of State Senator Owen from Lake City, site of Florida Agricultural College. "You've got a fine institution there, Senator—they say there's none better in the whole South when it comes to teaching agronomy." But it had come to Mr. Flagler's attention, Harry added, working at his molars with an after-dinner toothpick in a manner identical to the senator's, that it was deficient in one vital regard.

" 'Sthat so? I hadn't heard."

"A gymnasium to fill the students' physical needs would be the crowning touch. 'Sound minds in sound bodies' is part of Mr. Flagler's creed.''

Senator Owen peered at him through squinting eyes. Harry was uncertain whether the man was being cautious or was merely in need of glasses. "Gymnasiums are pretty fancy trimmings for poor folk," the senator said. "It's easy for Mr. Flagler to say—"

"But you agree that having one would be a real asset to the college?"

"I don't dwell long on pipedreams, Mr. Loring."

"But you don't oppose the idea—if it didn't burden the taxpayers?"

"Why, no—why should I?"

"And construction of a gymnasium would mean dozens of jobs in your neck of the woods—and a lot of money would have to be spread around for materials and supplies."

"Why, sure."

"And it would be good news for your district?"

The senator's eyes widened as he nodded.

"Then Mr. Flagler wanted me to ask you if you'd be willing to make the announcement to your constituents—and all the good people of Florida—of this bank draft for ten thousand dollars solely for the construction of a gymnasium for the college lads."

The senator's eyes were fully open by now. "Why, that's right generous of Mr. Flagler. It would be my great pleasure—"

"And the bearer of good tidings doesn't hurt himself too badly with the voters, eh, Senator?" Harry administered a small slap on the man's broad back.

Owen lifted the remnants of his third bourbon and water and toasted his new benefactor. "Not too badly, Mr. Loring." He swallowed thickly. "And if I can ever be of service to Mr. Flagler—in an upstanding way, of course—you just let me know." And he carefully inserted the bank draft in his billfold.

"I'll keep that in mind, Senator."

On his second evening in Tallahassee Harry had dinner with Napoleon Bonaparte Broward, whom Judge Raney had cited as the biggest fish in the legislative pond. A large man with a fierce mustache, he sized Harry up with care as the latter chatted easily about recent commercial developments in Jacksonville, Broward's home district. Throughout the meal Harry was careful to order no beverage more potent than ice water.

"I'm a newcomer to politics, Mr. Broward," said Harry as their pecan pie and coffee came, "so maybe I'm wrong to mention it, but a lot of people tell me you're the logical choice to be the next governor."

"Do they, now, Mr. Loring?" Broward's words and manner were affable enough, but the honey stopped short of his eyes, which assessed Harry with skepticism.

"They do, indeed—which is why I'm appreciative of making your acquaintance early on, sir. A novice like me has got a lot to learn."

"And you figure I'm your best tutor in the legislature?"

"Am I wrong?"

"Hard to say—but you could do worse." He reached into his pocket for two cigars and offered one across the table. "But if all this is a serenade to soften me up on the railroad commission, you're wasting your breath, Loring. I'm dedicated to protecting the interests of the growers along our coast, and Flagler's railway is costing them."

"Did I say anything about railways, Mr. Broward?"

"Not yet—but it's getting late, and I've got some other people to meet before the evening's over."

"Of course." Harry bit off the end of his cigar and ducked his head to light it in the candle flame that separated them. "Well, since you've brought it up, all I'd say on that score is that Mr. Flagler knows you're a businessman yourself—and recognize what it means to operate at a loss—which is what the East Coast Railway has been doing since he built it. And if the commission keeps cutting its rates—"

"I hope you're not going to tell me, Loring, that Flagler's lost a bundle on his Florida operations and he's continuing solely out of the goodness of his heart."

"You're the last man in town I'd try to fool, Mr. Broward. All I'm saying is that Flagler's efforts have been good for the people of Florida— but if his railway runs deep into the red he's going to have to curtail his investment in the state."

"I don't believe that—he's in too deep."

"But he doesn't have to keep on subsidizing rail transportation for its residents. There's simply not enough passenger traffic once the tourist season's over or enough cargo coming out of the state to justify indefinite losses."

"I've got my people to protect. The rail rates are too stiff for the little growers—and they can't afford to sustain losses the way Flagler can. These people have to eat."

"Are you telling me, Mr. Broward, that the growers would be better off without rail service—and you'd like to go back to the days of coastal schooners and mule trains to carry Florida's produce?"

"I'm not saying that. I'm saying Flagler can't have it all—"

"Then I respectfully suggest we agree to disagree on this subject and

get to the one that's on my mind and Mr. Flagler's—and yours as well."
It was his understanding, said Harry, that Broward was an ardent backer
of a bill to prohibit the manufacture of intoxicating liquors throughout
Florida and to outlaw the sale of same except through dispensaries licensed and operated by the state.

Broward raised a hand. "If Flagler's worried the law's going to hurt his
hotels, tell him not to—"

"Not in the least, Mr. Broward. He assumes they'll be exempted because the state wants to encourage tourist traffic. What I want to say is
that Mr. Flagler is no less devoted a foe of the demon drink than you
are—and he heartily approves of what you're doing—and if there's anything at all he—or I—can do to help you put this bill across we're at your
disposal."

Broward sat back and puffed warily on his cigar for a moment. "Well,
that's a different story."

"And believe me, Mr. Broward, I know the evil firsthand. My own
father fell victim to its insidious effects. I rarely indulge in spirits more
lethal than an ice-cream soda." Harry leaned toward him. "By the way,
I'd be grateful for the name of a good soda fountain in the area."

A thin smile at last lighted Broward's face. "I'm afraid, Loring, that
Tallahassee is a little weak in that department. They specialize here in sea
bass, rotgut and whores—and I can't do anything about the first and last
of those. But I'll gladly take your help on the liquor bill, and next time
you're in Jacksonville, I'll buy you the best soda in America."

"A deal," said Harry, taking the man's large hand and then reaching
for the check.

On his third afternoon in Tallahassee Harry was fortunate enough to
obtain a half-hour appointment with Governor Jennings. There seemed
little of the wild-eyed visionary in the man's look and speech, but Harry
had long since discovered that appearances could be deceiving, especially
among poker players—and any governor worth his salt had to know how
to play the game.

The first twenty minutes of their session were devoted to speculation
about the approaching statewide referendum over the proposal to move
the capital to a more centrally located city. The governor could see the
advantages, in theory at least, but practically speaking, those in favor of
the move were in total disarray, each favoring his own hometown as a
more suitable site. "And then there's the expense of the thing—however
uninspiring our public buildings may be, there's a considerable invest-

ment in them all together." He cast a glance at the clock on his desktop and added, "Why, is there some place that Mr. Flagler would like to recommend to us?"

"Not in the least, sir. As a brand-new resident of the state, he wouldn't presume for a moment to—"

"No, certainly. I was simply wondering why you—"

"Actually, Mr. Flagler wanted me to pay you his respects and let you know how greatly he admires the humanitarian program you've set out."

"Really? I would have thought my views were a bit heavy on the progressive side to please a man of his leanings."

"His leanings, Governor, are toward good sense and decency. Mr. Flagler may be a businessman first and foremost, but his record for generosity and fairness toward his employees and customers is well established. I'm sure I needn't remind you, either, of his prompt actions during the frosts of ninety-five and ninety-seven—"

"All Florida was grateful to him, Mr. Loring—even as we recognized that he was protecting his own considerable investment in the process."

"Is there something reprehensible in that, sir?"

"Not at all—unless investment turns into exploitation. My job is to prevent that from happening."

"And Mr. Flagler will be your foremost supporter in that goal." As to the governor's hopes for the legislative session, Harry added, Flagler stood wholeheartedly behind the proposed primary election bill—"the more democracy, the better, sir"—and the plan to provide free textbooks to Florida's schoolchildren; education was the only way to rescue the impoverished from a life of destitution. "Mr. Flagler's gift of a gymnasium for the agricultural college is a gesture in that direction." And the pure food and drug bill was one leaf borrowed from the book of reforms proposed nationally by the governor's famous cousin that all public-spirited citizens could agree upon. "And so, unless you object, sir, Mr. Flagler has asked me to work in behalf of your program throughout the legislative session."

"That's extremely generous of Mr. Flagler. And since they tell me it's a free country, Mr. Loring, I'd be the last one to discourage your activities in the capital." The governor idly polished a spot on the corner of his immense desk-top. "But I trust neither of you expects to exact any specific benefit for your participation. I'm not in the habit of—"

"Only one very small one, sir—and it's of a highly personal sort, yet one that common sense and decency are likely to commend to you." Quickly Harry explained the bill he had been sent to shepherd through the legislature—amending the matrimonial statutes to permit either party in a Florida marriage to obtain a divorce if the other were declared hopelessly insane and had to be institutionalized permanently—and the tragic circumstances of the Flaglers' union that underlay the effort. "Of course, it's not Mr. Flagler alone who would benefit from such a measure but anyone unfortunate enough to be similarly afflicted."

"I see," said the governor.

"The man has done many kindnesses for a great many Floridians since first coming to the state—and has asked nothing, sir, in return except the opportunity to spread his wealth for the common good. The favor he now asks is—"

"I understand fully, Mr. Loring." The governor rose to signal the end of their interview. "Let's see if the legislature passes your bill. Then—and only then—I'll be glad to consider all its ramifications and whether I can sign it in good conscience."

"Fair enough, sir. Meanwhile, I'm at your disposal if I can—"

"Good day, Mr. Loring—and I hope you enjoy your stay with us."

Maddy clutched the little calling card that Ruby Lee brought in to her bedroom face down on the silver plate that Mary Lily Kenan had presented to her the week before as a token of affection. A visitor at this hour? It was barely a quarter past nine. And who in Palm Beach would need to be announced in so formal a manner? Certainly not any of the girls, who usually marched right into the foyer and called out a greeting.

Apprehensively she turned the card over. In copperplate script it read simply, "Newell Forbes." What on earth—? A sigh. Was the man incapable of understanding plain English? She had contrived to be away from New York on all the dates he had proposed to visit her in the city, and shortly before she left for Florida she had written him to say that while she appreciated his continuing interest in her she had a commitment elsewhere, so there was no point, really, in protracting their occasional correspondence. Yet here he was. Why? And how had he found her?

Well, she was dressed and had done up her hair, and it would be rude to refuse to see him, at least briefly. She wished she had put on a prettier dress than her old blue muslin, but for an impromptu and not very welcome meeting it would have to do. "Why, Newell," she said, joining him on the screened porch, "I can't say that I expected—"

"Ever to see me again?" He took both her hands in his and gave them an affectionate squeeze.

In a cream-colored suit and matching Panama hat he looked more dapper than she had remembered him. "I shouldn't put it that way," she said, managing a decent smile.

"Please accept my apologies for barging in on you like this. Circumstances beyond my control conspired to—well, you must know it's not my way to—" He was flustered for the moment, then hastily explained himself. It seemed that he had recently negotiated a contract with a shipping company that offered him highly advantageous rates for deliveries below Charleston, so he had decided to take a trip to the southern coastal states to see if he might persuade some newspaper publishers to buy their newsprint from him. As it happened, friends of his from Boston who heard he was coming to Savannah and Jacksonville insisted that he continue on to Palm Beach to spend a week or two with them—did she remember meeting the Millers at Henry Flagler's cottage the week before? "Well, they were quite taken with you, Maddy, and your piano playing for Miss Kenan—and since you were apparently down here by yourself, they thought they might arrange an introduction for me. When they mentioned your name to me last night I said—well, I was so pleased that providence seemed to have arranged what all my overtures have failed to do that I thought I'd march right over here first thing this morning and surprise you."

"So you have." Her smile faded.

"You look less than delighted."

"I—it's just that—well, it's not true."

"What's not?"

"What the Millers told you. I'm not here alone. I'm with—my friend."

"But—you were unescorted at the Flagler cottage."

"My friend is in Tallahassee conducting some business for Mr. Flagler."

"Oh." Forbes's shoulders sagged. "I feel quite foolish."

"Why should you? You had no way—"

"Oh, but I did. Your letters made it clear enough. But I thought—I hoped—your feelings might have altered toward your friend and so you came down here to—"

"I'm afraid not, Newell. It's as I wrote you."

"I see. I hadn't thought, though, that your relationship was so—" He turned his face from hers and sank heavily into a wicker chair.

"I trust you're properly scandalized."

"Saddened, I should say." He twirled his hat in his hand for a moment. "It's that dashing young fellow from the boat, I presume?"

She nodded and stood over him, placing a hand on his shoulder. "I'm afraid I deceived you about cousin Harry. Forgive me, Newell, but there didn't seem to be much choice on shipboard—given the usual proprieties." She moved away and took a chair near his. "It's different down here. Perhaps it's the languid climate that lends itself to the relaxing of northern conventions—or that the leader of Palm Beach society is himself involved in—well, I'm sure you're aware of the nature of his—"

"I'm told there are mitigating circumstances in his case."

"There are always mitigating circumstances, Newell."

He sat silently for a time until she felt obliged to offer him coffee as commiseration. He shook his head with a wan smile of thanks, then suddenly asked, "But what of your reputation, Maddy? Is it of no—?"

She smiled sweetly. "You're too kind. But the truth is I have no reputation to speak of. I'm not a part of any respectable society you can name. I go my own way—and have for a long time now."

"I see." He stood. "And you're entirely happy with—your present situation?"

"Is anyone on earth entirely happy, Newell? One makes accommodations."

He nodded, took her hand briefly and left, clutching his straw hat so severely that she wondered, looking after him, whether it would ever recover its shape.

He had sent his card, along with Judge Raney's letter of introduction and a short note of his own, conveying his desire to make the acquaintance of the woman who had been described to him, he said, as "the best political brain in the state of Florida." Indeed, it was widely conceded that Evangeline Jeanguenin Summers could have served superbly as president of the United States if only she had been born a man. As it was, she had maneuvered her pallid husband into the decisive position in the Florida Senate before he had the ill luck to succumb to a tubercular hemorrhage. The widow Summers continued to hold court at Bramblewood, her plantation just outside Tallahassee, where the parties she gave when the legislature was in session were said to be the site of ninety-eight percent of the decisions that governed the state.

Her reply was prompt. Any friend of Judge Raney, she wrote, was always welcome at Bramblewood, and in view of Mr. Loring's association with the state's most eminent industrialist, perhaps he would join her there for a private dinner three nights hence. Harry sent Arthur off to deliver his acceptance note tied to a single red rose as close to perfection as Tallahassee offered.

To his considerable surprise the best political brain in Florida came wrapped in a package of superior form. She was somewhere in the fifth decade of her life, Harry gauged, but whether nearer the beginning or the end of it he could not be certain. Her hair, while streaked with white, featured several shades ranging from blonde to light brown so that the overall impression it created was of a golden aureole crowning her face. She was actually quite petite, he noted as they went in to dinner together, but her carriage, whether seated or standing, was so erect that it gave her a decided regal bearing and made those taller and less precisely vertical then herself seem almost shambling.

Eva Summers had the Southern gentlewoman's gift for uttering a great many words that, on analysis, amounted to very little yet radiated graciousness. Her low-pitched voice required her listener to bring his head close to hers as she riveted him with brown eyes so pale they could have passed for amber. When he complimented her on the beauty of the house and the elegance of its furnishings, she deftly narrated how her grandfather Jeanguenin, of Swiss-French stock, had left the exhausted soil of his South Carolina holdings some seventy years earlier and come to the Florida panhandle, where despite occasional forays by the Indians the cheap, rich earth made the cotton grower's life into a paradise. After the first crop bloomed so bountifully he had gone back home to Beaufort to fetch his betrothed, who brought with her an ample dowry of slaves to make the fields prosper, cuttings from her family's formal gardens and many of the furnishings, by Charleston's finest craftsmen, that still graced the manor house. Its veranda her grandmother Jeanguenin always referred to as "the piazza," the way folks did in Charleston, the widow Summers recalled in a moment of reverie. "Grandmama was a very old-fashioned lady, I'm afraid."

"And you aren't?" Harry asked, watching as she poured the coffee expertly from a rococo-patterned silver pot into tiny cups with an exquisite green and gold border.

"Oh, my gracious, no. My grandmother and mother were sweet Southern blossoms—very fragile in their way—who never let a political thought enter their pretty little heads. I suspect they'd be perfectly astounded to hear whatall I know about—and probably very disapproving."

Enchanted by his surroundings, the fragrance of the soft, moist air and the iridescent gossamer that his hostess spun about him, Harry invited her to recount the origins of her immersion in politics. "Boredom," she said wickedly. Her father used to bring home his colleagues from the senate, and having no brothers or sisters to play with and hating the piano and all other forms of music that girls of quality were supposed to embrace, little Evangeline would hide behind the draperies and listen to the blunt talk about politics, about the brokered deals, the seamy trade-offs, the arm-twisting and, when necessary, the clubbing down of uncompliant adversaries. "It was most ungenteel, of course, and I was shocked at first, but I came to grasp that was the way of the world even though I was spared it by the good fortune of my birth. Naturally I could hardly wait to grow up so I could apply those secret lessons I'd learned." She smiled at him over the rim of her coffee cup. "It's quite an unattractive tale, you see. The rest of it, I suspect, Judge Raney told you."

"But he neglected to mention, along with her other attributes, the loveliness of the widow Summers."

She laughed lightly. "Now I *know* you've come courting my political favors, Mr. Loring—not just to socialize on a balmy evening."

"Are the two incompatible, Mrs. Summers?"

"I should say not."

He sipped contemplatively at his coffee for a moment, then mentioned to her the heated discussion on women's suffrage that had been held his last night in Palm Beach and asked whether she favored it or subscribed to Mary Lily Kenan's position.

"I should put it slightly differently, Mr. Loring—if it won't disturb your sensibilities. I'd say it's the head that shares the pillow, rather than the hand that rocks the cradle, that rules the world. But then I see no reason why that head can't have the ballot as well."

"And hold office, too, I suppose?"

"And why not? Or do you think women are such emotional creatures, Mr. Loring, that they can't be hardheaded—and as ruthless as any man?"

"As manipulative, at any rate—possibly more so."

She conceded the distinction with a broad smile and proceeded to hold forth on what she condemned as "the nitwit policies" of Governor Jennings, whom she scorned as the enemy of everything she valued. "Once you start putting fool ideas into poor folks' heads—about cheap money and book learning and a laboring man's so-called rights to a job—you're two steps away from anarchy. I'm all for decency and kindness, Mr. Loring—and I do believe that charity is next to godliness—but these Jenningses and Bryans will be our ruination. They are bad for Florida— and for people like your employer."

Her reference to Flagler summoned him back to business. As she walked him out to the veranda to take the air for a few minutes before the insects took command of the night, he told her that he particularly wanted her counsel on a matter affecting both politics and the needs of the heart. Mr. Flagler, for all his success, had suffered great matrimonial unhappiness, Harry explained, for reasons entirely unrelated to his husbandly virtues; his first wife's illness and his second wife's madness had reduced his domestic life to a living hell—"and now, having come on a good Southern woman to share his life with him, he finds himself trapped by—"

"Tell me about Miss Kenan. They say she's something of a vixen."

"Suppose I just say she would make a formidable politician."

"Ahh—a woman after my own heart."

"Very much so—though she lacks your intellect, if I may say so."

"You must not be indiscreet, Mr. Loring."

"I must be honest, Mrs. Summers."

"Not *too* honest—or you may find yourself unemployed."

He grinned. "Actually, if I'm to remain in Mr. Flagler's keep for long I could greatly use your guidance." His appeal was somewhere between the plaintive and the seductive as he outlined the bill about to be introduced into the legislature for Flagler's benefit.

She listened sympathetically and pondered the matter a moment when he was done. "And what's to become of the unfortunate second Mrs. Flagler if this—convenient arrangement—is authorized?"

"She'll be very well provided for, I can assure you."

"It's sad, of course—"

"Of course." His eyes met hers. "But might you help—with a tactful word here and there to the right people—or am I too presumptuous to ask?"

"I'm used to this sort of thing, Mr. Loring. But I must choose my battles with care. This is not one I can embrace with all my heart—in view of all the other—"

"I fully understand."

"But I'll tell you what. I give a nice little party at the beginning of each legislative term—very informal—and everyone who's anyone is asked in. It's so much more suitable a meeting place for them than those dreadful hotels and boardinghouses they stay in. I don't generally ask men representing—what shall we say?—special interests, but I've been known to make exceptions, and then you'd be free to speak up in your own behalf—if that would be all right?" She placed a finger lightly on his wrist. "Beyond that, I can't—"

"It would be more than all right, madam—it would be superb of you." He gave her hand a grateful clasp. "If there's any way I can repay your kindness you need just say it, Mrs. Summers."

She returned his clasp. "Let me give the matter careful thought, Mr. Loring."

"Now that you've fleeced me, gentlemen," said Harry, leaning back in his chair and swinging his feet up on the table in front of him, "let's see if we can do some business together."

They were a singularly grubby crew of pirates, he thought—these dedicated foes of the liquor-control bill. But then he had hardly expected a bunch of Sunday School teachers to show up at his hotel suite for an evening of bourbon, cigars and poker. The two members of the Florida House of Representatives were doubtless the most bedraggled pair currently to occupy that esteemed chamber; the short one sported three-days' growth of beard and appeared to have borrowed his shirt from a stouter brother, to judge by the way its collar rippled out from under the taut edge of his cravat. The other gentleman of the legislature, older and taller, seemed to have shaved selectively, as with a tweezers, and had on a shirt so gray with grime that he must have worn it daily since arriving in the capital two weeks before—and slept in it besides. The three representatives of the liquor industry were better heeled and barbered, but from the savage manner they partook of Harry's hospitality—Arthur kept plying them with food, drink and tobacco throughout the marathon poker game, with nary a nod of thanks to the strapping lad or his master—they had apparently just broken a long spell of abstinence from all three.

"The thing of it is, Loring," said the shorter lawmaker, "these bluenose bastards have their heads so far up the governor's ass they can practically see daylight."

"Not to mention," put in the infinitely more civil leader of the liquor lobbyists, "that they are all fucking hypocrites."

Harry let them go on for a while, trying to convince him of the righteousness of their spiritual cause. Primarily, they argued, the temperance people were swept up by misguided morality; the private vices of humanity could never be legislated out of existence, and the harder government tried to do so the more certain it was to fail. "The thing can't be enforced," the dirty-shirted legislator insisted, "and one helluva lot of bucks'll be wasted in the effort." In the second place, the bill was undemocratic in the extreme. "People who want to drink, should," said the pithiest of the lobbying trio, "and them that don't, no one's forcin'." Last, and probably most telling politically, the real motive behind the proposed antibooze measure wasn't the improved health and morals of the public but the political spoils that would accrue. "It's just another way to tie us up and tie us down," croaked the taller legislator, a farmer from Ocala. "Who do you think'll get the special licenses to sell alcohol and make big money off it? The governor's pals, that's who. This whole scheme's nothin' but a fat payoff for all of 'em out there butterin' up Jennings' pecker."

Harry listened to them while sipping his tall glass of bourbon through clenched teeth. "My friends," he said when they were done, "I'm beginning to see the light. And I do believe I can be of some financial assistance, in view of the justice of your cause. But you've got to understand the delicacy of Mr. Flagler's position. He can't afford to be identified publicly with either side in this fight—be bad for his business. On the other hand I know he's with you in his heart, believing as he does in a minimum of government interference, whether it's with what people want to drink or how to run a railroad—if you get my drift. People ought to be free to do as they choose in this great land of ours." He was prepared to make a cash contribution to the liquor men's lobbying efforts as well as a sizable donation to the legislators' reelection campaigns. But there were two conditions. "First, mum's the word. You fellows noise this around, and next thing you know there'll be a line outside my door of glad-handers eager to relieve my boss of his hard-earned lucre."

"Shut my mouth," said the Ocala man, placing a hand over his heart, "and hope to die. What's the rest of the deal?"

Harry took a final swig of his drink, by now sufficiently watered to dilute its impact on his system, and said, "Do I have to give experienced gents like you lessons in politics? All I know about the subject is that one hand washes the other." He was glad to lend financial support to the cause dearest to their hearts and even plump for it on his social rounds—so long as they would side with him on a harmless little bill that meant the world to Henry Flagler.

Five minutes later the transaction was agreed on in all particulars. To seal it, Arthur served them a final round of drinks. But in doing so, he reached around the Ocala man just as the latter lifted his arm in a sleepy stretch and sent the full glass splashing over his foul shirt and trousers, creating a puddle on the uncarpeted floor. "You dumb nigger son of a bitch," he exploded at Arthur, who backed quickly away.

"Arthur's usually very sure-handed," Harry said. Actually, he thought, the accident improved the aroma in the gentleman's vicinity.

But the accident victim would not let it go. "Don't stand there gaping, you black bastard—dry me off!" He stood in place, his night's alcoholic intake fueling his anger. "Better yet, get over here and lick up this mess on the floor!"

Arthur's wide eyes blinked rapidly and looked over at Harry.

"You heard me—lick it up, boy—all of it." By now there was pure malevolence in his eye.

The foul-smelling room was still for a moment. Their evening's business was suddenly forgotten and might be wasted entirely if the situation got out of hand. Lord, he thought, give me strength to stomach lowlifes like these and use them for a worthy—or at least justifiable—purpose. He had dealt with his share of unsavory characters, and Heaven knew all too well that he was no angel himself, but this crew was surpassingly vile. If he could prevail over them only by outstripping them with duplicity of his own, well, then, he would have to do it. He hated himself for it, though, at that moment and swore he would desist from such degrading work the instant his finances permitted.

"Young Mr. Timmons here is in my personal employ," Harry said, "and is not in the habit of licking up floors." He stood and gave the offended party a hearty slap on the shoulder. "So I'd take it as a great favor if you'd accept one of my own shirts to replace that lovely one of yours—the size shouldn't be too far off." And he gestured to Arthur to go off in quest of same.

The Ocala man's rage subsided. "A thousand, you said—right?"

"Plus the shirt," Harry said with a grin that brought laughter all around. "Payable the day the vote is in."

"It's a pleasure to meet you, Senator Williams." Harry surveyed his visitor while they both sat back and sipped their lemonades for a moment of mutual inspection. A tall man with gray, thinning hair and a well-pressed suit of snow-white linen, he was easily the best assembled Florida legislator Harry had yet encountered. The half-smile he wore expressed a confidence that made Harry measure his words.

"The pleasure's all mine," said the senator. "It's always worth knowing the representative of a man as powerful and devoted to the interests of the state as Mr. Flagler."

They sparred for a few minutes, touching on the virtues of the primary election bill, Tallahassee's lodging provisions and lemonade, before Harry got to the point. "You've told several of the friends I've made here that you're unalterably opposed to the bill I'm working for in Mr. Flagler's behalf. I thought perhaps if we discussed it a bit you might find your opinion modified."

"I doubt that very much, Mr. Loring."

"Frankly, sir, I don't quite understand your vehemence in the matter. My friends say you're trying to rally opposition to the bill."

"Without much luck, either, so far. You're doing your work well, Mr. Loring."

"Only because of the humanitarian purpose behind it."

"I think not. I think it's because you're buying their votes, Mr. Loring, with promises to contribute to—"

"People are always ready to spread unpleasant rumors about men in Mr. Flagler's position."

"Let's not play games, Mr. Loring. I don't know what they call this sort of thing where you come from, but I call it bribery—and frankly I find it despicable. On top of which I find the bill you're pushing morally reprehensible. Laws aren't supposed to be made to suit the personal needs of rich old men."

On the face of it, Williams was exactly right, Harry knew and did not much appreciate being characterized as an unscrupulous potentate's slavish retainer. But the judgment, coming as he knew it did from a man of less than exemplary conduct in his own dealings, smacked of self-righteousness. And while Flagler's needs were unquestionably entwined with his personal pleasure and convenience, Harry never doubted the essential humaneness of the statutory act he had been sent to promote. Why should any devoted spouse be sentenced by law and custom to perpetual imprisonment in the form of wedlock to a certifiably mad mate? No one blamed Flagler for his wife's misfortune; why should it then be imposed on him in equal portion? The devices to which Harry was forced to stoop to gain Flagler's purpose were appallingly far beneath his dignity—thank the Lord that Maddy was not present to witness them—but he clung to the morally justifiable purpose of his mission and persuaded himself at trying moments like this that the money he was earning for such admittedly unsavory labors would one day soon help purchase happiness for him and his lady fair.

"Tell me, Senator," he said, bracing himself once again for his vexing assignment, "how's the dry-goods business back in Pensacola? Or is it hardware—I've forgotten."

The man's face hardened at the apparent diversionary tactic. "It's both—but what of it?"

"I'm just curious as to how it's going."

"Well enough."

"I should say so—judging from your appearance and manner. I'm told you're among the most successful store owners in your city."

"Well—I do well enough, I suppose. But what—"

"I'll tell you a funny thing. Mr. Flagler was saying to me the other week how he thought it might be a good thing for him to get into the retail trade around the state—businesses closely linked to the growth he's doing so much to promote. He actually mentioned Pensacola as a promising place for him to invest in—and you could hardly find a more useful and promising sort of business than dry goods and hardware—to judge by the success you've had, Mr. Williams."

"Just a minute, now—"

"But I'm wondering—just wondering, you understand—whether there would be enough business to go around if Mr. Flagler should open a place exactly like yours right across the street from you—or down the block—"

"You can't threaten me like that, Loring, because I—"

"—especially if his store charged a penny or two less on most of the items he stocked—which might be a sensible policy if he wanted to attract the patronage of the good citizens of Pensacola."

The senator's face began to redden and his manner grew heated. "You can't just waltz into this town and start throwing your weight—"

"I'm not throwing anything around, Senator—least of all malarkey. I'm merely speculating on the economic realities of the retail business. Free enterprise. It's something you might want to keep in mind, though, the next time you go out of your way to piss on Mr. Flagler's interests. He's not fond of people who do that to him, Mr. Williams—and he has his ways of getting even." He took a swallow of lemonade and reached into his pocket for the best Tampa cigar money could buy. "Meanwhile, I hope you'll accept this smoke with my compliments, sir."

Tedious as the days had become without Harry, she did not welcome the reappearance of Newell Forbes in Palm Beach. Word of his surprise return to the Millers' cottage reached her the day before the note from him, asking for a few minutes of her time. He was a fine, likable gentleman, but his persistence under the circumstances, however flattering to her, was beneath his dignity and a trial for her civility.

He looked weary and still more distressed than he had when she sent him from her door ten days earlier. "Newell, is anything the matter?" she asked, meeting him on the porch.

"I think you'd better sit down, Madeleine. What I have to say won't please you very much—and it surely gives me no happiness to—"

"What on earth are you—"

"I only came back because—because I had to—because I care so for you and—and I—"

"Newell, you scarcely know me. We're little more than strangers who met on a ship and became friends."

"Maddy, I can't tolerate the thought of your being hurt."

"You're talking in riddles. Come in the house and collect yourself."

He spoke at a less staccato pace but in a voice still plainly agitated as he narrated his travels since leaving Palm Beach. He had gone to Miami and then swung over to the west coast, making the acquaintance of publishers and printers as he went and stopping finally at Tallahassee for a few days. While there, he was taken to dinner at the best restaurant in town by the owner of the weekly *Observer*, a most agreeable fellow with roots in Boston. At the corner table, not far from their own, Forbes caught a glimpse of a familiar face in the company of one of the loveliest women he had seen in some time. Their heads were close together, and their laughter and general behavior left little doubt to any onlooker that they were on intimate terms. He asked the publisher if he knew the identity of the beauty and was told she was a local widow who owned a sizable plantation and involved herself extensively in the political affairs of the state, particularly when the legislature was in session. "Mrs. Summers is the queen of Tallahassee, the power behind the throne," said the publisher, "no matter who occupies the governor's chair." And her escort? "Some slick flunky for Henry Flagler—he's been hanging around the legislature, pushing a private bill to solve his boss's matrimonial dilemma." The fellow was said to be using bribes, threats and duplicity to put pressure on the lawmakers. So gifted was this operator that he had managed to entice the Summers woman to do his bidding—and provide his bedding as well. They had been seen together often since he had arrived in the capital, and he was known to have spent more than a few nights under her roof. Though normally a woman of propriety she had remarked to a number of acquaintances how charmed she was by the outlander and how his connection with Flagler might prove highly useful to her.

"I don't have to tell you, Madeleine, how disturbed I was by what I heard," said Forbes, his eyes fixed on hers throughout his recitation. "You told me you were quite happy with your Harry and I was prepared to accept your word—indeed, you left me no choice." He had spent the next day wandering the streets of Tallahassee, he said, oblivious to the buzz of politics in the humid air and tortured by indecision over what to do. "Should I come back here and tell you what I knew—and risk looking like an overgrown tattletale with a transparent motive? Or ought I just go on home and leave you to your Harry and whatever would befall you in your ignorance?" He mopped his face with his handkerchief and fought off the obvious strain that the effort was costing him. "Even as I got on the train south I was hesitant," he went on, "and since reaching Palm Beach I've been debating with myself over what to do." He gave his head a shake. "But I realized that—whatever it costs me in your regard—I can't let you be deceived by a man who doesn't deserve your affection, much less your trust." He stood and turned from her. "Now I've had my say."

She was not sure whether to respond to Newell with gratitude or chagrin for the unwelcome news he had brought. There could be, she felt, no questioning the sincerity of his feelings for her—or the advantage that he no doubt hoped his last-minute discovery might bring him. Still, there was something unattractive about it. Yet, how could she blame him? Or herself . . . ? Harry's carryings-on were egregious even by his own past standards of dissembling and manipulation. But always in the past there had been sustaining excuses—that his victims deserved being taken and could surely afford it, that greed and arrogance deserved their comeuppance, that even at his lowest he occupied higher moral ground than his prey. Now, though, in doing Flagler's work, and from the sound of Newell's terrible tales, he had forgotten altogether the protocols of minimal propriety. This was not her Harry, she told herself, however ardently he might insist that whatever he had done was for their combined sakes . . .

As for his womanizing, she was less angry than saddened. How very like Harry to find agreeable female companionship when he was not around her. He was a past master at rationalizing his dalliances seven ways from Sunday. How useful to his ends to acquaint himself with a woman who knew how to pull the proper political strings, he would tell her. And of course there were the awful state of the hotel accommodations available to him and the dreadful food in that benighted town—how much more pleasant and conducive to his work to adopt the Summers plantation as his headquarters, especially since the widow lady's cook turned out a superior syllabub and tipsy pudding, not to mention how much cooler her bedroom was than any chamber at a hotel. Emotion played a distant second fiddle to expediency in the line of duty—she had heard it all before. But Newell, creature of convention that he was, could not conceive of any response from her besides rage. Yet the truth of it was, simply, that when Harry's masculine needs grew rampant, they demanded an outlet, and so long as he and she were not ordained man and wife, she could not charge him with a breach.

To recognize all that, though, was not to forgive it, or to be unaffected by it. Harry's infidelity was now public; he was, it seemed, rubbing her nose in his soiled linens whether he meant to or not, and she could not deny the fraying effect on the tissue of her emotions. Her Harry was behaving badly, by even the most charitable measure. Was she not at least entitled, then, to stray from the straight and narrow? Were her own needs any less forgivable than his—particularly when an agreeable attendant, so long a supplicant, stood ready, as it were, to service them?

"Thank you, Newell," she said. "I expect this can't have been easy for you."

"It's not me I'm concerned about."

"I'll survive," she said, putting on a chipper tone. "Now what about you? I know the Millers are closing up tomorrow and taking the afternoon train—and none of the hotels is still open."

"I thought I'd join the Millers on the ride north."

"Must you?"

"I don't see that I have much choice."

"Why not stay here?" she said, without even a pretense of coquetry. "There's a spare room."

He sat back, more in surprise than triumph. "Thank you, Maddy, but I hadn't any such—"

"There's no piano here, sad to say, but you might enjoy the ocean bathing for a few days—and perhaps some other forms of entertainment will occur to us."

He gave a grim little smile. "No doubt we could say I was your long lost cousin Newell."

"If you wish to be cruel, I won't detain you."

"Maddy, I didn't mean to—sound bitter—"

"Then say no more."

"And Harry?"

"Harry's not due back for at least a week, according to his last wire."

"So you'll have your revenge—and then I'll be dismissed from your life again."

His sensitivity and intelligence were borne home to her anew with a sudden surge of fondness. Newell Forbes did not go in for consolation prizes. "I don't know," she said, taking his hand and entwining it with hers, "I just don't know."

Harry stood in front of the mirror, his comb in one hand, a little nail scissors in the other. Slowly he drew the comb through his mustache, seeing if he could spot the six or eight tiny hairs that were out of alignment and gave a slightly asymetrical appearance to his face. He knew he should not have trusted the hotel barber but the only other tonsorial shop in Tallahassee looked so disreputable that he would not have been surprised to have his pocket picked while he was under the hot towel.

A bellboy bearing a sealed envelope interrupted. *"H—I suggest you get over to the Senate this morning,"* the note read, *"Events are proceeding faster than you or I could have imagined. E."*

How did that woman always know things ahead of him? She had predicted relatively clear sailing in the Senate, but if unexpected opposition arose it would signal a tooth-and-nail fight in the House. What secrets did she know about each legislator that allowed her to gauge the outcome with such confidence? What favors had she granted that she could call in at will to affect the course of government in a sovereign state, even if a still primitive one? Her mind was plainly as supple as her body; the former had withheld from him what the latter did not.

He bolted a cup of coffee thick with chicory and hurried to the capitol. The gallery was almost empty when he arrived, and only a handful of senators were in their places, reading the papers or gnawing on chicken parts or aiming at—and generally missing—the spittoons spread about the floor. Bootblacks wandered the aisles, forlornly looking for customers, and purveyors of iced water stood off to the side, awaiting the signal to refill the pitchers on each senator's desk. A sultry lassitude pervaded the chamber as the speaker droned on, oblivious to his audience's indifference to his remarks. The man might as well have been orating in Swahili. He was against revising the convict-release system so that the state rather than certain licensed crew bosses might profit from the hard labor of its felons. The next fellow to the podium wanted the state to assume the costs of maintaining the roads throughout his impoverished county—a request that drew raucous laughter from his colleagues. A third senator proclaimed the virtues of St. Augustine to become the new state capital and noted its historical claim on the honor; playful hoots of derision followed.

And then Mr. M. L. Buxton of Orange County mounted to the lectern, and Harry felt his pulse begin to race. He had deliberately kept at arm's length from Buxton, leaving the honors to Judge Raney; it would have been unseemly if Henry Flagler's representative had been seen consorting openly with the legislator who had been chosen to work the great man's will. The floor was about half-filled as Buxton began to speak in his strong, resonant voice. Without fanfare he read out the text of Senate bill No. 87, which was intended to amend the Florida statutory code governing matrimonial relations by making incurable insanity a ground for divorce of husband and wife if either resided within the state limits. "Simple humanity cries out for this modification," the senator declared, saying he hoped Florida would lead the rest of the nation out of the dark ages of divorce law, which in many states, like New York, recognized violation of the Seventh Commandment as the only ground for ending wedlock.

Neither applause nor groans greeted the proposal. But Harry noted with satisfaction that Senator Williams of Pensacola rose to second the motion and assert that he had, on careful reflection, reversed his initial opposition to the measure. Harry braced, though, for an onslaught from certain senators who had been unapproachable or whom Eva Summers had urged him to avoid.

No one, however, came forward to speak against the bill. It was as if they were not listening. Perhaps unknown foes would be laying in wait when the bill went to committee behind closed doors later in the week.

A new speaker was carrying on now about the state tax code. Harry rose and slipped out of the gallery. All his work to this point had been ground tilling; the harvest was close at hand—unless the locusts suddenly descended.

What the others must have thought of her, sharing a cottage with two men in sequence, she could only imagine. For appearance's sake she had told them that Newell was a close friend of hers and Harry's who had been lately divorced and was taking a leisurely business tour of the South. Even to Norma Trask she would not confide the truth—there was no need of explanations or forgiveness in that emancipated social set. And Norma's own carryings-on with her niece was sufficiently deviant to seal her lips against disapproval of Newell's presence. Indeed, they were all living in glass houses—or a fishbowl, to put it more aptly, but the perils of stone throwing at those close quarters were identical.

She had known that Newell would not take the first step. His presence under her roof had compromised her enough already, he said, and so he held back, kissing her gently and sweetly, truly more like a cousin than a lover while the cook and Ruby Lee were asleep in their rooms off the kitchen. But since their living arrangement implied an intimacy they both desired, what point, she asked him, was there in withholding consummation?

When he took her at last, the affable, balding and very proper Bostonian proved an adroit, surprisingly masterful lover. He seemed to know where she was most sensitive and how to draw out her responses, but he would not travel straight toward the mark, preferring to circle about until she was brought almost to a frenzy of frustrated desire. He was gentle yet adamant, directing her with his hands or deflecting hers when they pleasured him to excess. She could hear herself gasping in his urgent but never oppressive embrace, feel her own shudders and his in return. When he pulled himself away from her once to vary their deployment, she opened her eyes and saw him smiling; she had forgotten to turn off the bedside lamp. The sight of him, beyond the feel of him, intrusively awakened an image of Harry, damn him, hovering in the shadowy corner, assaying their performance, condemning her wanton behavior. It didn't even matter that he, after all, was the far more culpable party. No, she was cuckolding him and, worse, relishing it—and in that savoring she knew sin, by her own lights if not his . . .

For several moments, she grew self-conscious, lapsing into passivity, an object for Newell's delving, until she *forced* herself to rout Harry's specter from her conscience. This new lover ministered to her patiently, as if he perfectly understood the conflict affecting her, inhibiting her, and finally won back her undivided attention.

How, she wondered afterward, depleted in the darkness, had a monogamous gentleman of his pedigree achieved such virtuosity in the amorous arts? The man obviously had dimensions she could not have guessed.

Ten to one. Harry looked at his notepad. Only one name left on the House list. Judge Raney was to meet him for lunch in the hotel dining room at one thirty, their only public meeting during the entire legislative session. But the moment was ripe for him to make known his allegiance to the Flagler bill. A knock announced his final caller.

Harry opened the door, expecting to see Senator Naery of Madison County, come to collect his campaign contribution in return for services faithfully rendered; the Senate had passed the divorce law overwhelmingly. But instead Harry encountered Representative Lockwood, a legislator of poor-white stock whom Raney had told him to avoid like the plague; the man was a swamp of resentments against the Flagler interests and all monied power in general. "James Joseph Lockwood, Mr. Loring," he said, not apologizing for his intrusion. "My friends call me Jimmy Joe."

"Oh, sure—I know who you are, Mr. Lockwood," Harry said, taking his hand but not asking him to sit.

"And I know who you are, too, Mr. Loring."

"Well—I guess it's about time we got acquainted. What can I do for you, Jimmy Joe? I've got some folks coming by here in just—"

"I'm from Wakulla County—from Crawfordsville, a little town you never heard of, 'bout twenty-six, twenty-seven miles from here."

"I've never had the pleasure, I'm sorry to—"

"One thing the folks I represent feel strong about, Mr. Loring, is honesty and decency. They're good folks down in Wakulla."

"I have no doubt of that, Mr. Lockwood."

"Well, now, Mr. Loring, I been hearin' all manner of things about you and your so-called 'campaign contributions' "—his bluff manner turned suddenly truculent, and his eyes became hot needles of retribution—"and I want to tell you that you and your kind make me sick, mister. You ain't doin' nothin' but bribin' the decent men of Florida—corruptin' 'em with your oily city ways—"

"I guess I can't call you Jimmy Joe anymore, then."

Facetiousness was lost on the fellow. "I know Clem Nevers was just in here for his loot," he ran on, " 'cause I seen him walk out of this room myself not five minutes ago with his hands in his pockets lookin' like a fox just out of the chicken coop and whistlin' up a storm."

Was this doughty backwoodsman really aroused at Harry's tactics—or just offended by not having been included in the payoff list? A thousand dollars could go a long way in Wakulla county. "Well, Brother Lockwood, Senator Nevers may have been by here, and then again maybe he wasn't."

"No maybes about it, mister. Now I'll tell you what I'm aimin' to do soon as I leave here. I'm gonna see Malcolm Battle from the Jacksonville *Metropolis*—that's the biggest paper we got in the state—and I know he's sure gonna be interested in what I got to tell him."

Of all the scum he had had to treat with so far on his mission to the political sinks of Tallahassee, this character was coming closest to unhinging Harry's self-control. Perhaps he had just run out of patience . . . or had finally arrived at the point of detesting himself for the tactics he had had to adopt in wrestling with the oily body politic of Florida. Still, this was no moment to draw back. This swamp snake was baring his fangs and had to be dispatched, or else all the unappetizing work he had put in till then might be revealed for what it was—*and* the battle lost . . . "I see," said Harry. "Then would you mind telling me, please, since you've got your mind made up about me, why you stopped by here first?"

"I . . . thought maybe you'd deny it flat out—"

"I don't have to deny scurrilous charges by you or anybody else."

"In that case—"

"And you can go see Mr. Battle and tell him anything you'd like. But I'll bet you dollars to doughnuts the *Metropolis* won't print a word of what you say to him."

"I figure if he does a little scoutin' around he'll find out quick—"

"Have you got any idea who the owners of the *Metropolis* are?"

Lockwood's face fell. "Flagler?"

"He's one."

"Well, he don't own 'em all."

"More than you'd guess."

"Well, I'm gonna find me one that he don't an' I'm gonna tell 'em—"

"And do you have any idea what I'll tell the gentlemen of the press if they happen to ask me about your charges? I'll tell 'em that Jimmy Joe Lockwood, that upstanding pillar of Wakulla County, came by here looking for a pay-off for his vote—and that I was thoroughly offended by his request and sent him packing—which is what I believe and what I'm doing right now, mister." Harry walked to the door and opened it wide. "See you in Crawfordsville someday—and I'll keep an eye out over my shoulder."

* * *

Norma's complaint that she had been neglecting her friends was true, Maddy supposed, but it really wasn't fair. None of them had extended visitors like Newell, who was so—well—"endearing" was the very word for him. He had never been to Florida before, and the wonders of the place were endlessly appealing to him; even a banana tree was a splendid sight to someone who had not beheld one. And he loved swimming in the Florida ocean—it was so calm and turquoise and altogether different, he said, from the gray-green surf that pounded itself into a froth against the Maine coast he knew so well.

At his suggestion they had taken up the southern European custom of napping during the hottest part of the day, and now, as their shadows crept across the beach, they could linger as they liked on the sand or in the water. It had been a dreamy time, perhaps the loveliest and most serene ten days of her life. Where they would lead she could not tell and would not dwell on. If it was an interlude, then it had been a tonic for the two of them; if it was a prelude, her heart would determine it in good time—and Newell had been wise enough not to press her to name which she thought it was.

She could see him swimming lazily out just beyond the breakers. With Harry due back at the end of the week she would have a few days to be by herself and reflect on it all; meanwhile, the cook was making them leg of lamb with mustard and rosemary for dinner, and she could look forward to a lovely evening—and lovelier night—with Newell before he took the morning train. She closed her eyes and fell back against the sheet she had spread on the sand: another few moments of sun soaking, and she would join Newell in the ocean.

A shadow eclipsed the sun on her face. She opened her eyes and blinked them several times to be sure they weren't deceiving her. "Harry?"

"My dear."

"But—your wire said—"

"The House passed the bill two-to-one—and the governor signed it last night—mission accomplished. So I thought I'd surprise you—apparently more than I had intended."

She climbed to her feet, mind spinning as she struggled to stave off the panic. "I'm so glad, Harry," she said, planting a congratulatory kiss on his mouth but sensing the coldness of his lips.

"Who is he, Maddy?"

"Who's who?"

"The man whose clothes are in my house, who's evidently been eating at my table—I see Camilla has two settings out for dinner—and who very likely has been sleeping in my bed, goddamn it!"

"What are we playing, Harry—'The Three Bears'?"

"You tell me, Maddy."

"Never in your bed, *mon cher*—only in the guest room." She could see Newell heading up the sand toward them, hoisting a nonchalant wave of his arm. "We'll discuss this another time, if you don't mind. Now be polite to our guest."

Harry studied the somewhat bulky figure advancing on them. "Forbes—for crissakes!"

She would not cry, or beg, or implore the earth to swallow her up. She would brazen it out and maintain her dignity: that's what a lady did; a lady was dignified. Even one found by her lover consorting with another. The morality of her predicament, she consoled herself in the instant, would require a philosopher to sort out. All she was certain of was that Harry had given her ample cause for her conduct. Just then the most she could manage was to adhere to the amenities and try to prevent a horrid scene.

The lamb, though peony-pink, had no taste at all for her, and the celebratory champagne Harry had brought with him from Tallahassee failed to jolly any of them. Newell carried off his part, playing the houseguest stuck for a place to stay till Maddy had rescued him. Harry remained icily well mannered on the outside, spinning tales of Florida politics at its grimiest to fill what would otherwise have been unmercifully long gaps in the dinner conversation, but inside, Maddy knew, he was boiling. A short but thoroughly uncomfortable evening was passed on the front porch—there were moments when she half-expected their bristling silences to turn into a barroom brawl—and then they all retired early.

She and Harry spent the night with their backs to each other, hardly sleeping. In the depths of the darkness she thought she could hear Newell breathing across the hall. Was he as restless as she and Harry were, simmering in their mutual anger, lying rigid and afraid to move lest they touch each other?

Next morning Newell declined Harry's offer of assistance to the ferry. His bags were light, he said, ever the thoughtful guest. After a stiff handshake with Harry and an even stiffer one for Maddy, along with his thanks for her hospitality, Newell walked down the path toward the ferry landing. He had not had a single moment alone with her since Harry's return. She would write to him at the first opportunity, Maddy told herself, fighting to display no undue emotion as she watched him recede from her life now with far more regret than when she had turned him away a month earlier.

She and Harry did not speak to each other until nightfall. He appeared in formal wear, though only the two of them were to dine, and poured himself a tall gin and quinine water. "Just don't tell me you weren't sleeping with him," he said, stirring the drink with his middle finger.

"Just don't tell me you weren't sleeping with the Summers woman," Maddy shot back. "And I'd appreciate your fixing me one of those."

"Fix it yourself." He sat stonily across from her in the big chair.

"All right—if that's the way you want it."

"How else should I want it? I've been cuckolded in my own cottage—"

"It's not your cottage."

"When I'm in it it's my cottage—dammit!"

"As it happens, you weren't in it—at the time."

"Stop being cute with me, Maddy. Everyone must have known what's been going on in here. You've made me a laughingstock—"

"And what have you made me?"

"You can't compare the two situations. I'm a man with responsibilities—"

"And what am I—just your kept woman?"

"You know damned well that's not how I—"

"I know nothing of the sort—except that you refuse to make me an honest woman and manufacture a dozen excuses when the truth is you just want to keep tomcatting around whenever it's convenient. And I damned well resent it—and if you can't tolerate my acting just as you do for a change, then you're jolly well free to live your life without me, Harry Loring."

"Well, I just might—"

"And you needn't bother to have me declared insane if you want a divorce. Just go. Better yet, I will—on the morning train—if that's how you prefer it."

But that night they made love, more passionately than they had in several years. And when they left Florida that season, they went together.

On June 3, 1901, thirty-eight days after the new bill was signed into law, Henry Morrison Flagler sued for divorce from Ida Alice Shourds Flagler on the grounds of incurable insanity. The divorce, following the testimony of many experts and acquaintances who traveled to Florida at Flagler's expense, was granted on August 13. Eleven days later, the multimillionaire was married to Mary Lily Kenan at Liberty Hall, the bride's modest ancestral home in Kenansville, North Carolina. According to

Royal Postlethwaite, the New-York *Examiner*'s society columnist, the bride wore a long-sleeved dress of white chiffon over white satin, appliquéd with lace as was her veil, which was further adorned with orange blossoms, "the perfect emblem of their union." The groom wore a dark Prince Albert coat with light trousers—"and a smile," added the columnist, with a thrust from which his disapproval of the spring-winter union could be readily inferred, "as wide as his wallet."

"Why weren't we in the wedding party?" Harry asked, tossing the newspaper account of it aside.

"Why should we have been?" Maddy adjusted her new floral hat in the mirror as they prepared for a Sunday stroll down to Washington Square. "We're not exactly on intimate terms with the happy couple."

"Without me there would have been no wedding."

"Possibly. Or possibly someone else would have oiled the waters."

Harry came up behind her and wrapped his arms around her still slender waist. "I didn't *oil*, my pet—I arranged."

"Whatever you did, angel, you were paid for. And casual business associates are not often included in wedding parties, especially those gathered in remote Southern hamlets."

The imagined social slight was nevertheless still in the back of Harry's brain when he was invited several months later to Flagler's estate in Mamaroneck by his officious little attorney, Lionel Teasdale, to discuss a new assignment requiring, as the lawyer put it in his letter of invitation, "your deft hand." Harry had other plans in mind, but his prior engagement for Flagler had been remunerative enough for the time it required to justify his entertaining an encore. But the price for his services rose whenever he thought about the idea. He really did not care for wearing another man's yoke, *whatever* the reward, especially if it involved dirty work that Flagler's regular retainers apparently would not sully their hands undertaking.

And dirty work was precisely what Teasdale had in mind. Flagler, the old goat, had been named the correspondent in a divorce action filed earlier that year in Syracuse. Happily wed now, he had decided, on advice of counsel, to try to settle the matter quietly for a certain cash consideration rather than risk a court appearance, particularly since the Flagler name was now being muddied in Florida for what many felt was the unseemly haste with which he had discarded his second wife under the divorce law that his wealth and influence had purchased.

"I don't think I'm your man," Harry told Teasdale in Flagler's study after listening to the particulars. "But I have a proposition of my own I'd like to put to Mr. Flagler—if I might have the opportunity."

"He's a bit indisposed this morning, I'm afraid. And frankly, Mr.

Loring, Mr. Flagler isn't very receptive to propositions these days, or he'd spend his whole time fending off—"

"I think he might be interested in this one."

"Well, I'd be glad to convey the particulars but I wouldn't get my hopes up if I were you."

He had been planning and saving for years, Harry explained, to open a club of his own in New York, a place with a charming atmosphere and fine cuisine where ladies and gentlemen could come to be entertained as well as to engage in games of chance. He intended to call it the Palm Beach Club, a name that he felt would appeal to a clientele of taste and means. He himself was widely experienced in the casino world and felt thoroughly confident that with the assistance of his friend, Mrs. Memory, he could run a first-class and quite profitable establishment. But the Palm Beach Club needed to be done right, and that would take an additional investment about equal to the amount he had already assembled; he hoped Mr. Flagler, given his role as the veritable creator of Palm Beach, would be the one to make that investment, either as a silent partner or in the form of a loan.

"But aren't there already a couple of dozen gambling parlors in New York of the sort you describe?" the attorney asked.

"I'm not talking about a 'gambling parlor,' Mr. Teasdale—I have in mind an establishment quite up to the quality of Bradley's place in Palm Beach, but a bit jollier."

"I see," said Teasdale, oozing skepticism. "But whatever you call it, it will still feature gambling, and gambling is illegal, Mr. Loring, and I can hardly imagine that Mr. Flagler would want to get involved in—"

"He's done it with Bradley in Florida."

"Because he had a vested interest through his hotels, and Florida isn't—"

"It's just as illegal in Florida as it is in New York, which didn't stop him from cooperating with Bradley. And if he were my partner in New York that would certainly qualify as a vested interest."

Teasdale shook his head. "I'm afraid I couldn't in good conscience urge Mr. Flagler to risk his direct involvement in any such—"

"It needn't be direct. A loan would do just as well."

"Mr. Flagler is not in the lending business."

"Oh, but I'm sure that from time to time he's been willing to help out in a good cause."

"Even if he were, what sort of collateral could you possibly put up, Mr. Loring? You could hardly expect him to—"

"The business itself—I'd give him a note against the whole thing.

If for any reason we fell into arrears, he could simply foreclose on us."

"I doubt that a chattel mortgage would meet—"

"You doubt everything, Mr. Teasdale. You get paid to doubt."

The lawyer crossed his legs uneasily. "Really, Mr. Loring, you're missing the main point. Don't you see that even in the unlikely event Mr. Flagler agreed to your proposition, he'd be besieged by every other Harry, Tom and Dick who came down the pike? Word of these things gets around."

"It needn't. I'm a most discreet fellow—or he'd never have brought me in for the Tallahassee project."

"That was a different sort of thing."

"But the same question is involved—namely, can I keep my mouth shut? I have so far—and have every intention of continuing to do so." Harry touched the lobe of his right ear. "Might I add, Mr. Teasdale, without your mistaking my point, that if Mr. Flagler were to join with me in this venture my lips would be glued still tighter."

Teasdale's narrowed eyes began to perceive Harry in a fresh light. "And if Mr. Flagler were not to join you?"

"I'd be saddened."

"And vengeful, perhaps?"

"Oh, nothing so crude as that. But conceivably a bit less discreet."

"You mean you'd blab about the way the divorce law was passed."

"Did I say that, Mr. Teasdale?"

"I'm trying to get your meaning, Loring."

"I'm trying to strike a legitimate business deal."

"It sounds to me as if you're trying to coerce us into one."

"That's a most unattractive way of putting it. I'm a gambler by profession, Mr. Teasdale—I make do with whatever chips are at my disposal. Sometimes that requires a creative approach."

"I think I know blackmail when I hear it."

Harry smiled. "Come, come. A man would have to be a little mad to try to blackmail someone of Mr. Flagler's eminence. And no doubt he has his ways of dealing with such threats—ugly ways, too, I'd guess."

"I wouldn't know. But I'm told, Mr. Loring, that blackmailers have been known to wind up floating in the North River."

"I resent your use of that term. I've simply made a proposal."

"And a threat."

"Nothing of the sort."

The lawyer gave a small grunt. "And if Mr. Flagler were to tumble for your scheme, what would prevent you from coming back here in six months and asking for more money?"

"My honor as a gentleman, Mr. Teasdale."

"I see. And you assume comparable honor on our end, I take it—rather than certain ruthless expedients that might be—"

"Ah, yes. Well, perhaps I should add, then, that I have recently deposited with my attorney a lengthy letter, along with instructions for it to be copied out and sent to every newspaper in New York—in the event of my death from any other than natural causes."

"I see. And shall I guess the contents of your letter?"

"My lips are sealed, Mr. Teasdale—as always."

The little lawyer drummed his fingertips on his kneecap for a reflective moment. "And how much did you say you needed?"

"I didn't. But a quarter of a million will do nicely—to be lent, shall we say, at three percent, with interest alone to be charged for the first two years and the principal to be repaid over the ten years following."

"He'll never agree to it."

"Ask him." Harry stood. "And I'd appreciate your drawing up the legal instrument at your earliest convenience."

NINE

Spring, 1902

"Harry, you're not paying attention." She brushed at the hand that was massaging her calf muscle and slid her body out from under his pinioning leg, letting his head sink into the soft cushion.

"I am, too. You have a most remarkable limb, my dear—long and firm yet very shapely—"

"You were *not* thinking about my leg—or the rest of me—even before, while we were—proceeding."

"Actually, I've been thinking about wicker all day. I'm just not sure you're right. There's something—I don't know—insubstantial—about it that may give an impression of—"

"Harry, you're becoming obsessive."

He could not deny it. But if their lovemaking had turned somewhat perfunctory, the exhilaration of all their non-horizontal hours together more than compensated. The four-story brownstone Maddy had found on Thirty-fifth Street in Murray Hill was just right in size, layout and location to house the Palm Beach Club, though the exterior grillwork needed repairs and the interior, of course, would require considerable alteration. Harry negotiated a two-year lease, the shortest commitment the owners would agree to, and scheduled the club opening for the first of May. As a result, that winter was the first that the pair of them did not spend in Florida since they had met, but there was simply too much to do to indulge themselves in that fashion, particularly since neither of them was on anyone's payroll.

Their days were full of decisions and the hundred details that flowed from each, and their nights—and embraces—distracted by second thoughts and small squabbles over every aspect of how their plans should be executed. From the first, however, they were agreed upon the basic idea for the club. It had to be different, or it would not succeed. The very use of the Palm Beach name would at once set it apart from the other such establishments in the city: their place would be both elegant and exotic, stylish but not flashy, selective yet not exclusive to the point of limiting the clientele to the socially prominent and the filthy rich. "Anyone who can pay the freight and doesn't chew with his mouth open is okay with me," Harry ruled.

"I'm afraid, though," Maddy cautioned, "that the hoity-toity aren't going to relish the notion of rubbing shoulders with hoi polloi."

"It's time they did—this is the twentieth century, my dear. Besides, we can't rely on one social set or another. We need to cast a wider net."

Apprehensive as she remained, Maddy was persuaded by Harry's conception of a "one-stop club." The most luxurious gambling palaces in town offered comfort and atmosphere but no cuisine; one dined at Del's before proceeding to Canfield's next door, or at the Waldorf before entering the House with the Bronze Door. The Palm Beach Club—or the P.B.C., as Harry had taken to calling it—would offer superb food. But at Johnson's and Kelly's, among other clubs, a decent meal was available along with the gaming. The P.B.C. would provide entertainment as well so that customers could stay all evening and, relieved of the fuss of hailing cabs or worrying about inclement weather, would gladly part with more of their money for the convenience of the thing. "Nothing too elaborate," Harry said—"a singer or two, possibly a quartet, perhaps a few dancing girls and some sort of tasteful novelty act—a midget briefly reciting Shakespeare, say, or a trained seal riding a very short bicycle."

Maddy laughed at his exuberance. "I like everything but the dancing girls—they might make it a touch too déclassé, don't you think?"

"Déclassé may be just the ticket to draw a crowd."

"I can see a lot of gentlemen of unwholesome tendencies sitting around examining pretty dancing ankles and doing very little gambling."

"The ankles will be on display only briefly—and just one show to a customer. Furthermore, we ought to change the bill every couple of weeks so our regulars won't get bored."

Maddy shrugged. "As long as you don't insist on calling it 'The Palm Beach Follies.' "

"That's not bad," he said, and ran an appraising hand up her right leg from ankle to knee. "Say, would you—"

"No, I will not dance for your customers, Harry—or sing, play piano or juggle coconuts."

"Coconuts! Why didn't I think of that? Just the authentic Palm Beach touch. We could hollow out a hundred halves and use them for finger bowls. Or spittoons, possibly—"

Maddy took command of the basic decor, given Harry's limited knowledge in that area. The color scheme, she felt, ought faithfully to resemble the Royal Poinciana's light verdant tones but in a slightly subdued fashion more suited to New York's cosmopolitan air and temperate climate. "Remember our evening at Canfield's club—how dark and airless you felt the place was? He's got all that dreary walnut paneling, those somber Oriental rugs and maroon wallpaper and those horrid dark green brocade draperies. We want a gay, light atmosphere." Sage green carpeting, perhaps, and the paneling painted a soft cream; the walls a cheery but unaggressive yellow. And the furnishings, she suggested, ought to be comparably recreational. "Why should we go charging around Europe hunting up fancy oak chairs that old French kings used to seduce little girls on? We could use the same cushioned wicker that the hotel and Bradley's—"

"Can you really seduce someone on a chair?"

"—do. Paint it white, use pretty patterned cushions—it would save a great deal of money—though of course we'd have to keep the paint handy to make sure everything looked—"

"I'll bet Eric Bemis would be delighted to help us with the entertainment," he ran on, recalling his theatrical producer friend. "He knows hundreds of performers, and every act on the continent, not to mention England and—"

"Harry!"

It was in the middle of that night, while they spent their passions and immediately thereafter, that Harry duly noted his reservations about Maddy's proposal for the wicker. "I'm just not sure it's the right thing," he said. "It's not New York. It's too provincial."

She gathered the sheets around her. "I thought you wanted your club to be different."

"Yes, but not ludicrous."

"Wicker is not ludicrous, it's refreshing. It will say 'Palm Beach' to the customers the moment they come through the door."

"Hmm. And potted palms all over the place?"

"Dozens," she said.

"Hundreds," he said, rolling over on her in a giddy embrace, "and we'll water 'em with bourbon and soda."

Enlisting a staff of prime quality was their next concern once the decorating work was set in motion. The proprietors themselves were of course to be the principal overseers; their division of labor called for Harry to manage the gambling part of the business and all customer relations while Maddy had charge over the food (excluding alcoholic beverages, which she insisted he take under his wing) and maintenance of the premises. The entertainment they would decide on together.

To bring an authentic Palm Beach flavor to the staff, Harry took the train south and spent a week at the Royal Poinciana, trying to woo head chef Ivan Dzugashvili into the club's employment. Since the P.B.C. was not slated to open until a good six weeks after the hotel season ended, there would be no conflict, Harry said—till the following December, at which time chef Ivan could choose which place he preferred. "You hire me," said the chef, "you go broke from cost of me." Besides, he had a job with the White Star steamship lines when he wasn't at the Royal Poinciana. But his younger brother Josef was available and almost as good as Ivan. "First month I come help—and teach him Ivan's best tricks, okie-dokie?"

Before the night was over, Harry and Ivan worked out the basic P.B.C. menu, featuring one French, one Italian and one Southern dish each night in addition to the obligatory fare. And before his stay was over, Harry had snared two other Royal Poinciana regulars. Mr. Walters, the hotel's thoroughly knowledgeable—not to mention indefatigibly nosy— front deskman was perfect to perform a similar function at the club, greeting guests, seating them according to their social and professional rank, screening out undesirables. He would have to learn the New York crowd, to be sure, but his instincts had been well tested and his general hauteur would lend just the right note to a club hoping to attract customers from a broad social spectrum. The dining service itself would be under Raoul Pinay, the hotel's maître d', who told Harry he could not promise that he would stay on at the club during the Royal Poinciana's next season. "Theez people, they are like my family, n'est-ce pas?"

"I'll make it worth your while," said Harry.

"In zat case, maybe I get a new family," said Monsieur Pinay.

To man his gaming tables Harry enticed the renowned Joe Fisher, impresario of Wheeler's Grotto in Saratoga Springs, to come to the city for three months and help him hire and train the crew. Fisher's place in Saratoga operated as a kind of training school for dealers and croupiers. "He takes boys straight off the farm," Harry explained to Maddy, "and turns them into aces. Almost everybody in New York uses some of his boys—they're honest and dependable, and with us he can start from scratch."

"Wouldn't you rather have older, more experienced men?"

"No, they're tired and looking for easy money, which makes them susceptible to being bought off. I want 'em young, fresh and innocent. Also cheap. Anyway, I think Joe'll stay on for our first month of operation to make sure our recruits are panning out. After that—well, I'm not exactly a novice in this department."

"Harry, you wouldn't dream of—you wouldn't possibly—"

He shot his cuffs in annoyance. "The P.B.C. will be above reproach in every aspect of its operation. Even the drinks will be only very slightly watered—a measure I regard to be for the benefit of our customers' health." In that connection, he reported, he had just enlisted Ned, the expert bartender at Bradley's, to join the club staff. And he had decided that his private man Friday, Arthur Timmons, who was by then a strapping youth of twenty-one, would serve as a security man and chief bouncer at the P.B.C.—"and in time I'm going to try him as the first colored dealer in town. He's ready to move into the profession—the boy comes back from his days off with a small bundle. I've taught him well." And finally, Harry persuaded Eric Bemis to part with "Pinkie" Dawson, one of his assistant producers and himself a former trouper on the musical stage, for two days a week to coordinate the P.B.C.'s entertainment program; the rest of the time, Harry himself would keep an eye on the performers.

"An eye and what else?" Maddy asked the night after the first shapely showgirls arrived to audition.

"This is business, angel," he said.

"With you, it's always business."

"Are we back to that?"

"We've never left *that*."

To attract a large turnout for the opening, they had engraved announcements printed and sent to a carefully assembled list of two thousand names. Mr. Walters, while still in the employment of the Royal Poinciana, surreptitiously copied down from the registration ledger the addresses of hotel guests, past and present, from the New York area and mailed them up to Harry. Eric Bemis, grateful to Harry for past favors and always eager to arrange social settings where he might prime future investors, provided a long list of names and addresses from the theatrical world and its backers. Lucien Dougherty, Harry's erstwhile partner in the plundering of Bradley's, was glad to provide him with access to the Tammany crowd through his brother-in-law, Pete O'Rourke, one of the Wigwam's leading sachems. And Harry and Maddy themselves added a considerable number of names from among those casual acquaintances and unsuspecting marks they had encountered over the years at Saratoga, Newport and other stops on their professional rounds. Harry did not even object when Maddy offered Newell Forbes' name. "Why not?" he said. "I'm not allergic to Boston money. So long as the man doesn't come with it.

After due deliberation they included on the announcement cards two items of information intended to broaden the club's appeal. The first was that women were "decidedly welcome" to enjoy all the facilities of the P.B.C.—in marked contrast, it was implied, with Canfield's and other of the loftier casinos where the fair sex was not invited to attend the gaming tables. The second item noted that "informal wear" would be permitted on Monday and Tuesday evenings—which, not incidentally, were the two slowest nights of the week at gambling establishments of the better sort— by way of saying that the P.B.C. clientele would not be limited to the stuffiest stratum of New York society. To address the expensively engraved announcements, a chore for which Harry's ornate handwriting was ideally suited, the two of them devoted an hour every evening before retiring. The task so numbed their hands and wrists that their sexual prelude was reduced to a minimum on those nights they had enough energy left to attempt lovemaking.

Late one morning three weeks before the opening, Harry was paid a call by the captain of the Murray Hill police precinct. "A pleasure to meet you," Harry said, leading him through the maze of ladders and sawhorses as workmen hurried to finish the renovations. "I think you'll find that the Palm Beach Club will be a welcome addition to the neighborhood."

"Some of your neighbors don't share that sentiment," the captain said. "I thought we might go over your plan of operations."

"Delighted," said Harry and brought the visitor, who curiously enough was not in uniform at the time, to the club's little second-floor office, where Maddy was sifting through bills and trying to master the rudiments of bookkeeping. After pleasantries were exchanged Harry directed a curled brow at his partner that said unsavory business was at hand and she was to excuse herself from the premises. She did not need a second hint to beat a speedy departure.

"I understand you plan to allow gambling games on the premises," said the captain as soon as they were alone.

"Now where did you hear a thing like that?"

"You're hiring—word's around town."

"Is it? Well, you know how rumors spread."

"I take it, Mr. Loring, that you don't want your club to be raided or men from our force to pay frequent calls that would—"

"How much, captain?"

The gentleman of the law sat back and stroked the side of his neck contemplatively. "I'm glad you know the ropes, sir. Sometimes these arrangements turn into a tug o'war, which doesn't do anybody any good."

"I think you'll find us as cooperative as possible. The public's welfare must be protected."

"Exactly."

There was an "initiation fee" of three hundred dollars, the captain explained, which went to cover the costs of checking into the reliability of club owners, their past business operations and whether they could be depended on to run an honest illegal enterprise. If the P.B.C. met this test, then the "Gambling Commission," as the captain called it, would set a monthly fee for the club's safe operation—that is, without intrusion by the police so long as the place was run discreetly. The "commission," as Harry had made it his business to discover, consisted of a prominent city councilman, two state senators of high seniority and a Tammany Hall stalwart; the take was divided, in proportions held a deep secret, between the ad hoc commission and the police, from the highest level to the cop on the beat, so there was little or no possibility of a chink in the protective armor the club proprietor was purchasing. "It's a good investment, Mr. Loring—for everybody's benefit."

"I've no doubt of it," said Harry. "And I hope you and the missus will come by sometime as guests of the club."

"I'm afraid," said the captain, taking the small wad of bills Harry pulled from the cash box, "that would be against our rules. But thank you, anyway."

A week later the lawman returned with the news that the club was sanctioned to open and its "licensing" fee for the first year of operation would be a thousand dollars, payable in small bills on the first business day of each month. "Promptly," the captain added. And at an appropriate time, the "commission" would request a modest percentage of the club's profits.

"What's modest?" asked Harry.

"You'll see."

"And how do you know what our profits are?"

"Instinct, Mr. Loring. Our people are very experienced."

For the first week, Mr. Walters had to turn people away at the door. He managed it, though, with such tact and apologetic good humor, cordially suggesting that the rejected book reservations for the following week, that the Palm Beach Club operated at full capacity, and then some, for its first month in business.

On opening night, her heart racing for much of the evening, Maddy hovered near the door to watch the faces and listen to the voices of arriving customers. Their jaws literally dropped and eyes rounded with surprise as they swept through the vestibule and took in the striking decor of the club. The immediate response was overwhelmingly favorable except for that of two imperious matrons, obviously one full level below the upper crust, who felt the yellow and cream walls did not flatter the delicate peach tones of their painstakingly embellished complexions.

The place had indeed turned out splendidly, Maddy told herself as she drifted through the rooms, greeting those she knew with a residue of her best Madame Memphis exuberance and casting an eagle eye on the housekeeping details. The pale green-and-yellow floral linen print she had found for the wicker-chair cushions lent a graceful note of gaiety, while the lacy white undercurtains behind the silk faille of the draperies, which were only a shade or two lighter than the sage carpeting, hinted at blossom-scented breezes about to waft through the tall windows. Particularly pleasing to her was the effect created by the dozen chandeliers she had rescued for a pittance from the strange little shop in Brooklyn that had advertised them in the *Herald* as part of a going-out-of-business sale. It had cost more to electrify than to buy them, but the price, she decided, seeing their faceted tear drops wink and glitter above the excited crowd, had been worth every penny.

The guests were a thoroughly mixed bag, as she and Harry had hoped. Among those she met or brushed shoulders with the opening week were the Duke and Duchess of Devon, he being twenty-third in line to the British throne; Carlo Amalfitano, the best known tenor on three continents, whose platinum larynx barely cleared the top of Maddy's decolletage; Townsend Peale, president of the Bangor & Aroostook Railway, and two of his chief lieutenants; Wenceslaus Bartolescu, illegitimate son of the reigning king of Rumania; Bobby "The Gentle Brute" O'Hara, the current middleweight boxing champion, whose muscles bulged thrillingly beyond the confines of his evening wear; the four beautiful Hanford sisters, heiresses to a baking-soda fortune, whose identically dressed heads featured golden coils interwoven with aquamarines that vibrated with the same extraordinary shade as their fabled eyes; Florian Ziegfeld, the young producer who joined Eric Bemis at the large table he took for the occasion; Francis "Fisty" Boland, Tammany's No. 2 man, who joined the Dougherty crowd at the gaming tables upstairs soon after arriving, and perhaps most important of all, those journalistic arbiters of the city's high life, Royal and Virtue Postlethwaite, the latter swathed in cashmere shawls. *"Ecco Palm Beach assalutamente verismo!"* she was heard to trill before her husband wisked her off to the dining room, cashmere fringes trailing over the polished floor.

There were, of course, a few small near-disasters attributable to opening-week jitters. Like the brief kitchen fire on the second night that, though rapidly quenched, leaked a pall of acrid vapors throughout the first floor for an hour or two. Dining-room service was too slow and a bit sloppy until Monsieur Pinay directed admonishing hisses toward the dilatory waiters each time they came off the floor. Lucille Bingham, the charming chanteuse known as "The Indiana Thrush" who headed the entertainment card, sang with sweet refinement, but her prim manner and church-choir selections left the crowd impatient for more spirited fare. Upstairs, too, there were some problems. At the faro table, play ended abruptly on the third night when the dealer came up one card short at the end of the game. Harry promptly refunded all the players' bets and soon established that the problem was nothing more sinister than a defective deck. But the young dealer had to be fired, as an example to the rest, for his failure to count the newly opened deck before putting it into play. More unsettling still was the intoxicated guest with the oversized diamond stickpin who regurgitated all over the roulette table an hour before closing on the fifth night. Heroic efforts to fumigate the green baize cloth failed, and a new one was in place when the club opened the next night.

Generally, though, it had gone well. The food was every bit as good as anything Maddy had ever had at Del's or Sherry's. The mood upstairs was effervescent, with ripples of laughter occasionally arising from the tables as Harry moved easily among the players and wisecracked to relieve the tension in between the high-stakes games. Most satisfying of all was Postlethwaite's column in the *Examiner* the day after the opening. In glowing terms he commented on the lighthearted mood of the new club and "the spectacularly eclectic crowd drawn from the raffish and the *raffiné* alike, with exclamation points of nobility and notoriety thrown in for good measure." Chef Dzugashvili came in for plaudits, especially his chicken Kiev—"no doubt a family legacy"—and the entertainers, aside from "a certain tendency toward the saccharine by Miss Bingham," were likewise commended, with gushing kudos for the six dancing-singing girls whom the columnist dubbed "the Bouquet of Sweetheart Roses, every one of them dewy-faced and sparkle-eyed, inviting the arrival of a swarm of honeybees." The item concluded: "Messrs. Canfield, Kelly and Johnson, take note: here is competition worthy of your esteemed pleasure palaces. We predict a fabulous future for the P.B.C.—all they're missing is a cakewalk!"

On the third Wednesday the Palm Beach Club was open, Maddy invited her Eleventh Street neighbors—Robert and Patricia Dane, Benjamin Sprague and their mutual landlady, Agatha Agapé—to share a table as her guests. It was a small way, she felt, to repay them for years of kindness.

The non-tippling Danes limited themselves to dinner, since Patricia was expecting their second child and fatigued easily. Their growing family and Mrs. Dane's swelling abdomen had dictated their imminent move from the third-floor flat to a larger place uptown. Her lusty appetite had not diminished, Maddy noted, as Patricia helped herself to a goodly sector of the baked Alaska after polishing the last spot of gravy from her dinner platter. Mr. Sprague, these days more redolent of Wildwood hair oil than ghastly human preservatives, excused himself to visit the casino upstairs, where Harry gave him a guided tour and counseled him on the mysteries of faro, at which the undertaker proved adept. That left Maddy and Agatha to watch the entertainers together. The dancing girls Agatha pronounced spirited and decorative but slightly out of step and tune; the knife thrower, thrilling but monotonous despite his accompanying recitation of Poe's "The Raven"; and the sterling-tonsiled Miss Bingham, Kokomo's gift to the muses, the old trouper found to be "best suited to christenings and wakes—if you'll forgive me, dear. You must do something to lift the caliber of your talent—or don't bother with it."

Two afternoons later the Indiana Thrush came down with laryngitis. The administering of heavy quantities of honey-laced tea followed by brandy and lemon juice did not avail, and it was plain that Miss Bingham would not be able to perform that evening. A hurried call went out to Pinkie Dawson in Eric Bemis' office to locate a substitute singer. The only available candidate was an operatic soprano who knew not a word of English and was described by Pinkie as "tending toward the unsightly—but some pipes." Harry thought not.

With four hours remaining before the first of the club's two nightly shows was due to begin, Maddy had a thought. "Now don't laugh," she said to Harry in naming her choice for the emergency performer. "I think it will be all right—at least for one night."

Harry shrugged. "If she'll do it. Otherwise, you and I'll have to do a few arias from *Tosca*—and my Italian's rusty."

When Maddy put the proposition to her, Agatha looked blank, then flattered, then frightened. "Me? You can't be serious, child."

"Why not? When you put your mind to it you can charm the birds out of the trees. I'm sure the club crowd would love you."

"Maddy, sweet, when I retired in Eighty-five I vowed never to get back onstage. I don't have the energy anymore. I'd be an embarrassment."

"It's just for this one evening. You've done it in my parlor on Sundays for ten years now, and still sound in fine voice to me."

"Then you have a tin ear. There's an enormous difference, my dear girl, between doing something for indulgent friends and doing it for paying customers. In the case of your living room my audience gets value precisely equal to what it pays."

"I won't have you saying that. You're a star, Agatha, and always will be."

Agatha sighed and took Maddy's hand. "Darling, in the theater we have a tradition that says always leave the customers wanting more. And that's the way I left—before they stoned me off the stage." She considered the matter a moment longer. "Besides, nobody wants to hear my silly old songs."

Maddy saw her opening. "Agatha, they'll love them. Everyone's got a vein of nostalgia in them. We'll explain the circumstances of your one-night unretirement—they'll understand—and cheer your courage. And it's a small house—they don't even pay for the show, exactly. It comes with the dinner, so nobody could claim—"

"Four hours' notice is just impossible, Maddy, even if I—"

"Why? Just do your favorites. You know them inside out."

"But your accompanist won't know them, or how I—"

"*I'll* play the piano for you."

"Lord," said the old trouper, "you must be desperate."

Maddy laughed. "So the truth is out at last."

"Child, I didn't mean—"

"You've wounded me to the quick." Maddy tugged her to her feet. "And the only way to make amends is to say yes."

"Well," said Agatha, "I couldn't be worse than that Bingham person."

"That's the spirit!"

"But what'll I wear?"

"Anything. Something simple, preferably."

"I don't own anything simple. And what's left is shabby and faded—just like the wearer."

"Stop that nonsense." She took Agatha by the arm. "We're taking a cab right over to Hudson Street and renting you whatever your heart desires."

Agatha threw back her head. "In that case—"

Maddy proved twice as nervous as Agatha. But Harry's introduction of their act was so gracious and mitigating that the audience would have had to be cruel to greet them with less than high tolerance. In fact, from Agatha's first line—"Me father never met me" from her triumphal role in *The Banks of the Thames*—the crowd was wildly enthusiastic as the aged performer sang her heart out and gyrated to the beat, her last jeweled pendant swaying in counterpoint. Maddy embraced her at the end to a roomful of huzzahs. And with the help of two drams of cognac, Agatha's voice held out for the second performance as well; the late crowd was equally responsive. In the corner, Harry wiped his brow in relief.

Deluded by the ovation, Maddy prevailed on Harry to let Agatha perform her old repertoire once a week—on Monday, which was a slow night anyway. There was novelty value in featuring her, Maddy argued, "and besides, the sweet thing can use the money."

But when Monday night came it was not the same. The professional pianist who accompanied her had not mastered the sheet music and was not accustomed to Agatha's slight divergences from the text; they repeatedly fell out of synchronization. And there could be no pretense now that the performance had been arranged hastily under dire conditions. The songs sounded hopelessly outdated, and their singer still more so. The crowd clapped politely, but by Agatha's last number she could hardly be heard over the table talk.

"A little more rehearsing," Maddy soothed her afterward, "and you'll be just fine." Agatha, exhausted but not defeated, concurred. During the following week she devoted herself passionately to improving the act.

But the next Monday was worse still. After her second number people got up and drifted away, some upstairs to the gambling tables but more out the front door. Harry cast a baleful look across the room at Maddy and gave two quick shakes of his head.

She was overcome with grief and guilt as she made her way to the dressing room after Agatha came off. She had lured the woman from happy retirement, her memories of the glory days intact, and now she would have to humiliate her. It was an unconscionable thing. Probably her heart would break when her dear young friend applied the hook that dragged her from the limelight for the last time . . .

"Don't say a word, darling."

"Agatha—I—"

"It's all right."

"It's the audience—they just don't understand what you're trying to do. It's a cheap crowd—insensitive and—"

"Maddy, don't try to soften the blow. I've had my share of disasters."

"You're not being fair to yourself."

Agatha patted the chair next to her dressing-table stool. "Come over here and sit down."

Maddy sank into it, suffocating from gloom. "I don't want you to think that it's got—"

"I think you're a sweet wonderful girl," Agatha said, picking up Maddy's hand and nestling it between hers, "and none of this is your fault. The truth is I let my heart rule my head—like an old fool. It won't happen again, I assure you."

"I feel I never should have—"

"Hush your fuss, child. Now, I know you want this place to succeed, and if there's anything at all I can do to help—short of performing—just say the word."

Maddy closed her eyes, and before she reopened them in tear-filled gratitude, an idea flashed into her mind. "Actually, now that I think about it, there is something of value you could do for us."

"And what is that?"

"I don't think this Pinkie Dawson fellow has got quite the right sense of what the club needs in the way of entertainment. I wonder if you'd become our—what could we call it?—our artistic advisor and help us select the right performers." She glanced at the pendant around Agatha's neck and the last remaining baubles adorning her wrists. "We couldn't pay you what you're worth, but it would be something. I'm sure Harry wouldn't mind, and we surely can use the—"

"Harry might or might not, but Pinkie surely would. It's a sweet thought but there's really no need to—"

There was an interrupting knock on the door by Arthur Timmons delivering a box of a dozen yellow roses with an accompanying card that read, "To Miss Agapé, the brightest star in the firmament, from a long-time admirer." Their loveliness and bouquet brightened the woman's lined face that no pigments or ointments could make young again.

When Maddy saw him next, in the vestibule on his way up to monitor the casino take, Harry gave her a wink and a moving kiss on the cheek. The shameless charmer.

Business slowed down during the Palm Beach Club's second month—the dining room was operating at about two-thirds capacity and the casino take was off proportionately—but that was to be expected. Time was needed to build a steady clientele. And over the summer things normally slackened at every club in the city as the wealthy encamped for out-of-town resorts. It was in the middle of August, during their quietest week yet, that Maddy decided to alter her routine and pour herself into another activity beside the club. Harry did not much like it.

She had customarily arrived at the club around ten in the morning and worked until noon or so on the accounts. There were bills to pay and the previous night's receipts to check over, the dining-room and bar checks to be squared with the actual cash handed to her by maître d' Pinay and then added to the gambling profits Harry left in the office safe. Arthur Timmons would then accompany her for protection to the bank on Thirty-fourth Street, where she made the daily deposit. Their balance there was declining, to be sure, but at the approximate rate Harry had foreseen; if the club was breaking even by year's end he would be well pleased, he had told her. On her return to the club she superintended the cleanup crew, telling them to pay closer attention to the sink in the women's dressing room or the kitchen floor, making sure the laundry had added enough starch to the table linens and that the waiters were folding the napkins properly, arranging for the hem on one of the gambling-room curtains to be restitched where a careless customer had stepped on it, reviewing the next day's menu with the chef. The details were endless, but she applied herself to them in her usual meticulous manner; she was doing all she could to make Harry's dream come true.

This need not extend, though, she now concluded, to devoting all her evenings as well as her days to the club, appearing there each night to oversee its routine function. Harry, of course, had to be there nightly, closely watching the casino operation; that was where their profits were, or would be in time. But her end of the operation was in the hands of capable professionals, and coming by one or two nights a week was sufficient to check up on them and to spot any problems. Besides, she wanted—and felt she was entitled to—some time of her own. She had spent the last twenty-five years earning her living, and she was getting tired. Even when she was trotting around the resort circuit with Harry she had considered herself at work—always required to be pleasant and sociable, always on guard, always answerable to his needs, his priorities, his whims. Her life was never her own. The time was at hand to change that.

Thanks to her insistence that they save their money instead of frittering it away on the high life as Harry had been accustomed to doing, they had enough now between them to buy a small house and carry the mortgage. She was weary of living in the cramped first-floor flat in Agatha's building; it afforded her no real privacy, and what with Harry's constant comings and goings and their being away much of the year, it was not a real home to her. When she broached the idea, Harry had objected at first, arguing that it was imprudent to tie up their capital in such a fashion and thereby possibly imperil the future solvency of the club. "You're the one who's being a spendthrift now."

She was resolved, though, that if he would not give her his name, he would damned well provide her—and them, if he could bear being tethered—with a fit dwelling and the semblance of a normal social life. But she could not put it to him quite so bluntly. Instead she prevailed upon Dr. Maxwell, husband of her friend and erstwhile supervisor, the former Minerva Armbruster, to convince Harry that New York real estate was a very sound and liquid investment. And when Maddy put on paper the numbers showing him that even with the taxes, mortgage payment and maintenance expenses the total outlay would not greatly exceed the sum of what each of them was paying for the separate lodgings they maintained to keep up the facade of propriety, Harry relented.

It was a sweet little house, Maddy thought, as she turned the corner from Park Avenue the second Sunday after the transaction had been completed. No one was stirring on the street except for a churchgoer or two hurrying to the ten o'clock service. True, she conceded, looking at the house from a distance, its brownstone exterior left something to be desired in the way of aesthetic appeal, but since every other house in its row bore a similar facade, there was a certain complementary propriety to it that she had instinctively liked. Their house, furthermore, was distinguished from its immediate neighbors by the giant wisteria vine—it was more like a tree, really, with that thick trunk—that climbed up the front between the window and the doorway all the way to the third floor. In May, when it flowered, the front rooms would be suffused with its perfume. Window boxes would be pretty, she imagined as she glanced up, with red and white geraniums and trailing ivy. But since the wisteria bloomed purple, perhaps only white geraniums were in order. She surveyed the site for another moment, pleased with the little rectangle of garden just below the stoop. And there was the bigger garden behind the house, too. It was close to perfect—and it was all hers as well. Harry had insisted that the house be in her name alone, and for no more convincing reason than that she was the one who had badly wanted it and was therefore entitled to its rightful ownership. She suspected him of less altruistic motives, but if this was the only way he would agree to the purchase, she chose not to cavil. Perhaps the club was truly all he ever wanted to own in life.

She let herself in through the oak-paneled front door. At once her eye fell to the encaustic tile floor in the vestibule, with its pattern of chevrons and diamonds in black, buff and terra-cotta that yielded immediate delight. The inner door, its beveled-glass window outlined with golden oak dentils, seemed to beckon her warmly within. She loved coming here on a Sunday morning when everything was still and no workmen were clambering about and she could picture the place as it would be when they moved in a month from now.

It riled her that Harry had absented himself almost entirely from the adventure of putting it all together. He would enjoy living there, no doubt, once it was finished, he had told her the other night before they went to bed, but he could not involve himself in the petty details of colors and patterns and furniture styles and run the club as well. Since the house was her idea she should have the joy—and headaches—of its assemblage. "Some partnership," she said to him.

Her piano would fit excellently into the alcove *there*, she thought, pacing through the house now like a wily cat appraising its territory, and yes, the mint wallpaper with the scrollwork would serve beautifully here in the parlor. Images of poetic perfection flickered through her head as she moved into the library. The bow window that overlooked the garden was the ideal place for a little conservatory. She would have a tinsmith in to make a tray that would fit snugly within the curve of the windows, and she would fill it with pebbles and set dozens of pots of plants on top. With the sun streaming through the windows the effect would be charming and especially welcome in winter.

On the way up the main stairway to the second floor she paused to run her hand over the top of the newel post, which was carved, she noted now with tactile satisfaction, in the shape of a pineapple, symbol of hospitality. The small gem of craftsmanship augured well she thought. There would be intimate dinner parties sometime in the not so distant future, with Harry pouring fine wine and narrating some mildly embellished misadventure or other . . . crackling logs in the fireplace . . . song and laughter and introspective talk between them . . . prosperity and serenity. A smile crept over her face. The workmen had finished the master bedroom. It was a symphony in shades of rose set against a pink background, evoking memories of an English garden she had seen when they were abroad. Would it be too dainty and feminine for him? Well, he had had his chance and left it all to her; it would give her pleasure enough for both of them—but damn! the man grew more remote and enigmatic with the passage of time. Was their love now to be measured only in profits and possessions?

Harry had breakfasted by the time she returned to her flat and was sitting wrapped in his dressing gown and wreathed in cigar smoke, with a pile of Sunday papers at his feet. "Don't tell me," he said, "let me guess—a sudden yearning to communicate with the Divinity. I just hope you put in a prayer for the club and your obedient servant."

"Oh, Harry—it's so absolutely splendid, just *right*. You'll love it—wait and see."

"Are we talking of holy matters or domestic tranquility?"

She kissed his forehead. "It's so dignified, darling, it makes me proud— yes, house proud, I admit it."

"The deadliest of vices among the smug and bigoted—"

"I think we should wrap ourselves in the same sort of dignity as the house."

"How's that?"

"Marry me, Harry."

His eyelids lowered and stayed there.

It was all perfectly clear to her, though, and came pouring forth. "For the first time in our lives we're property owners—"

"*You're* a property owner."

"—we've put down roots—we're substantial citizens about to establish our very own place in the world—a little safe chunk of the universe that's entirely ours. We ought to celebrate that by—"

"Surrendering to convention."

"Convention has nothing to do with it. I mean taking joy in our—our togetherness—announcing to the world that the two of us are united, that we're a—a wholeness, a oneness—instead of two separate people."

"I call that surrendering."

"To whom?"

"To a world that doesn't give a tinker's damn about us and whether we're linked in holy bloody matrimony—a world that has to put everything in neat little piles of good and evil and dictates to me who and what is moral. I don't want to be shoved into this pile or that one, Maddy. I want to be what I am."

"Not what *we* are?"

"*We* are already—can't you see that? Can't you see that it's our very rejection of all the polite hypocritical rules that makes us special—and what we share very rare?"

"What I can see is that we've done everything your way for years. And now I'm ready for you to come and meet me halfway because you've made your point and I've granted it. Is that so hard for you? Why must you be so damned stubbornly selfish?"

"Selfish? The house is in your name—the club bank account and the lease are in your name—what more can I give you by way of assurance of my affection? What woman has more security?"

"I'm not talking about security, damn it. I want to be able to shout to the world that Harrison St. John Loring loved me enough to make me his wife. I want respectability and acceptance—some modest esteem among real, decent people. I want to be able to take my place in the society you scorn so. I don't want to live in the shadows the rest of my life."

"You're living a delusion," he said, opening the last of the papers on his lap. "Society has sentenced you to exile, Maddy—for life—and me as well. The difference between us is that I've never accepted its right to tell me how to live."

She was a pretty little blonde, this new one, Harry thought, with a sure flair for comedy, the way she kept an absolutely straight face as if unaware that her garter was gradually sliding down her leg during the routine, attracting all eyes to its descent until finally she spied the offending object and, feigning enormous surprise, kicked it off and out into the audience at the end of the dance. It was a cute trick and closed the entertainment with a bang. He wondered idly whether it had been the girl's own idea or Pinkie's. Perhaps he ought to find out; it was always a boost to morale to let the newcomers know that management appreciated their efforts.

The post-dinner odors were offensive to his nostrils as he made his way backstage through the kitchen. His knock on the dressing-room door was answered by the tall redhead, wearing a green dressing gown, the opening of which revealed her long muscular leg. "Oh, Mr. Loring! I told them you'd be by."

"What made you so sure, Celeste?"

She looked him up and down. "Because you don't miss a trick, Mr. Loring—and Mona's little number was sure to catch your eye."

"Yes—well, I just wanted to tell all the girls—may I come in for a minute or is this a—"

"Whatever you say, Mr. Loring—you're the boss." She turned her swan's neck and called out over her shoulder. "Man coming in—*the* man." Muffled shrieks and giggles were heard within. "Just a second, Mr. Loring, some of the girls are—"

"I'm Harry."

Her plucked brows arched. "Swell. It'll be just a minute, Harry—I know you wouldn't want to embarrass any of the girls."

"Surely not."

The room reeked of femininity: perfume, greasepaint, perspiration and a subtle other scent he could not quite isolate filled the air. The girls sat in various stages of undress and makeup removal, the long table in front of them a jumble of jars, bottles, tubes, bowls and brushes. Their five faces were upturned toward his in anticipation as Celeste ushered him in. "Excuse me, girls—I didn't mean to—" He stood there motionless for a moment like a small boy at a candy store, bedazzled by the tempting merchandise.

"You didn't come to bring us bad news, did you, Harry?" Celeste asked.

"Oh, no—not in the least," he said, squaring his shoulders and adopting a businesslike stance. "Quite the contrary, in fact. I just wanted you all to know how well I thought it went tonight." His eyes sought out the new girl. "And you, young lady, were especially fetching."

"Yeah," said the little blonde, "well, thanks," and turned her head back to the mirror to continue wiping away her paint.

"That's Mona Geiger," said Celeste. "Mona, say a proper hello to the boss."

"Hello, Mr. Boss." She flicked him a look and went on attending to her pretty face.

"Mona's very talented," said Celeste, "but a little short on manners."

"And she's a show stealer, too," one of the others piped up.

"I wouldn't look at it that way," said Harry. "A trick like that helps the whole act." He took a step in Mona's direction. "Whose idea was it, Miss Geiger?"

"Mine," she said, looking up at him now. "I showed Pinkie I could do it, and he put it in the act. I can do it with a petticoat, too, but Pinkie said this is a high-class joint—place, I mean—and it wouldn't be right."

"Pinkie has a point."

"No, he don't," said the girl who had complained about Mona's exhibitionism. "That's what's wrong with him." Giggles abounded.

"Well," said Harry, feeling warm around his starched collar, "keep up the good work, girls. The Palm Beach Club appreciates your—etcetera."

Too bad, he thought, climbing the stairs to the casino rooms, that Madeleine Memory had put a damper on his taste for dalliance. But he could no longer regard a woman's ungrammatical speech and crude manner with indifference. Nor were a pretty face and shapely body the only measures of pulchritude. To excite his interest now, a woman needed brains and style as well—and dignity; that was Maddy's ultimate allure. Tarts were a dime a dozen, and the time when he had gorged on them was long past. Still, it was unsettling to have so lovely an array of young female flesh right there, at his fingertips, so to speak. Ah, youth . . .

He moved around the tables, watching the play, greeting familiar customers with a quip, checking on the dealers and croupiers. Joe Fisher's boys were working out well, and they responded to the tips the winners gave them with an enthusiasm that was genuine.

As he edged around the baccarat to the faro tables he noted a small crowd in front of one of them and wondered who was drawing so much attention. Was someone making a killing at his expense or losing his shirt to the house? Either way he had better find out. He slipped in closer and stood on tiptoe. There, trying his luck against the cards, was none other than Richard Canfield, proprietor of New York's best-known gambling club. Why had no one told him Canfield was on the premises? Mr. Walters had probably sent Arthur to find him, but the lad had no doubt steered clear of the dancing girls' dressing room.

Harry watched with unsmiling satisfaction as the pile of chips in front of Canfield dwindled and was finally exhausted. And yet he slipped the dealer a folded bill of appreciation. The man had style.

"Good evening, Richard. Sorry it wasn't your night."

"Harry, old boy. So nice to see you—and your charming place here."

"Busman's holiday?"

"Not at all. I'd call it keeping an eye out on the competition."

"I doubt that we really qualify—not yet."

"Any dollar spent here is one less available for spending at my place—don't sell yourself short, Harry. I certainly don't."

Canfield was too gracious by half. "Any advice for me, Richard—or complaints about the place?"

"Not at all. Everything seems in order at your tables. And your notion of providing entertainment is interesting—even if it doesn't suit my own tastes. I just worry that it will put too much strain on your exchequer. I'd hate to see you go bust, Harry."

"Would you?"

Canfield paused at the head of the stairs. "Harry, that's not a question a gentleman should ask—or have to answer."

Harry smiled, his point nevertheless made. "I stand corrected."

"But I do want you to know that if things don't work out for you—if you discover, as I very much fear, that when the novelty value of your place here wears thin and the customers stop coming—I can use a man of your talents. I'm not getting any younger, and I'd very much like to be able to ease up a bit, if there was someone else I could—"

"Your concern is greatly appreciated, Richard—and the very same applies to you. I find there just aren't enough hours in the day, and if things turn sour for you ever—well, you have my drift."

"Thank *you*, Harry."

As the last of the night's crowd filtered out through the vestibule, he had begun to turn into the barroom to check with Ned and Raoul on the evening's receipts when he felt a light hand reach out and pluck at his jacket cuff. "Mr. Loring—I just wanted to—"

"Mona. I thought—don't you girls all leave right after—"

"I wanted to apologize to you." Her dressing-room haughtiness had been replaced by a tender smile and warm green eyes.

"For what? I shouldn't have come in like that—a bull in a china shop and so forth. It probably didn't help you with the other girls for me to single you out like that. But I did want to—"

"Oh, I understand, Mr. Loring, and I want you to know I appreciate it. But my behavior was not very nice."

"Then we're even, all right?"

She reached her hand up tentatively and brushed her fingertips the length of his mustache and back. "I want you to know I think you're a very attractive man—all the girls do."

"Well, thank you—I guess we're even on that score, too." He felt his face grown warm where her finger traced down his cheek and outlined the bottom of his chin. "I imagine all you girls have plenty of—young escorts who are—eager to—"

"Younger men are boring, Mr. Loring—and clumsy."

"Well," he said, "then you'll have to teach them, won't you?"

"I'd rather be taught than do the teaching."

"That's—well—I'll keep that in mind, Mona."

"Do," she said. "Good night, Mr. Loring."

"Harry."

"Good night—Harry."

The letter from a Mr. Andrew Payson of the law firm of Jameson, Finley & Purcell, 26 Broadway, was short and cryptic. It read:

Dear Mrs. Memory:

I write in behalf of my client, Mr. Russell Corwin, who is currently resident in Paris.

He has asked me to discuss with you a matter of deep concern to him. I am, accordingly, hopeful that you will be willing to come to this office, at any day and hour of your convenience, so that I may disclose the nature of Mr. Corwin's instructions to me. If it would facilitate matters, I should be glad to have a cab call for you at your residence and return you there at the completion of our interview.

With all due regard, I am

Yours very faithfully,
Mr. Andrew Payson

She reread the letter twice. What could possibly be on Russell's mind except the identity of the child he abandoned? By withholding the knowledge from him she was plainly punishing him as no other means could have achieved even if she had set her mind to it. And just as plainly, whatever guilt had gnawed at him over the years was now ripe and devouring his conscience. Well it ought to.

She cast the letter aside for a moment and went to water her plants. Then, lest temptation lure her to the attorney's office to learn the severity of Russell's agony, she crumpled his note and dropped it into the refuse. Ruby Lee would dispose of it within the hour.

Harry groaned in response to the knock on his third-floor office door. He had hoped to get another five minutes of rest for his aching feet before having to resume his rounds downstairs. No wonder Canfield was looking for an understudy. "Come in," he called in resignation.

It was the assistant cashier, a young fellow whose performance as a deskman at the Thalia Club, Harry's former residence, had reminded him of his own youthful efforts at the Susquehanna Club. "I have a gentleman outside, Mr. Loring, whose last bank draft failed to pass muster—and he insists that we honor a new one."

"Which gentleman would that be?"

"The demonstrative Mr. Caldwell."

Just my luck, Harry thought. The name of Edwin Holcombe Caldwell had been imprinted on his memory from the night that the fellow carried on like a wild Indian at Bradley's, and Harry had had to lift his membership card and lead him to the door. When he showed up for the first time at the P.B.C. in mid-September, Harry kept his distance from the unpleasant young chap—business was business, and no doubt he would not patronize the place if he recognized Harry and learned he was the proprietor. But he watched Caldwell from the edge of the room, and since luck was not with him, there were no victory whoops. He continued to play when his cash ran out; Harry himself had approved honoring his bank draft after having a word with Mr. Walters, who well remembered Caldwell and his attractive young wife from their stays at the Royal Poinciana and believed that there was considerable family wealth behind him. When the bank draft for a thousand dollars came back marked "Insufficient Funds," a polite note was dispatched to his residence asking him to meet his obligation as soon as possible; meanwhile, his name went on the club cashier's list of the verboten.

"Show him in," Harry said, tugging himself upright.

The young man looked not in the least chastened as he strode through the doorway and took Harry's hand. If he recognized the owner of the Palm Beach Club, he gave no sign of it. "This is all terribly silly," he said. "I trust we can get it straightened away, Mr. Loring."

"Nothing would make me happier, Mr. Caldwell. I gather you've been experiencing some no doubt temporary difficulties."

"Not at all. It was simply an improper transfer of funds. The damned bank couldn't keep track when I moved some assets from one account to another. A royal nuisance. Bunch of idiots, if you ask me." He wore a bleary look, and his tongue sounded thick from drink.

"I think perhaps if you had been kind enough to advise us to that effect when we informed you that—"

Caldwell nodded prompt assent. "Meant to—absolutely meant to. Slipped my mind. You go ahead and redeposit the old check."

Superiority and combativeness oozed from him. Even the way he occupied the chair Harry had invited him to take, dangling an arm over its back, crossing one leg over the other at a sharp right angle, was a declarative statement of the divine right of the wellborn. The very tilt of his head, elevated slightly so that he looked down his nose at him, was annoying to Harry. Others he had dealt with in young Caldwell's predicament had had the grace to apologize. This one's etiquette did not seem to extend beyond the varieties of arrogance.

"I'll certainly do that, Mr. Caldwell."

"And I take it you've no objection, then, to honoring the draft I've presented just now? I've dropped a bit here tonight, but I feel my luck turning."

"How much did you have in mind?"

"Fifteen hundred."

"The house rule, Mr. Caldwell, is that we do not extend credit to any customer in arrears. I'm sure you can appreciate that this business would not remain very businesslike if we—"

"But I *said* there was no problem—it was a mix-up at the bank. Are you doubting my veracity, Mr. Loring?"

Harry struggled to restrain the contempt he felt toward this overgrown squirt. "That's not the point, Mr. Caldwell. It's a matter of rules and honor. Gentlemen are expected to meet their gambling debts within twenty-four hours—or they ought not to participate."

Caldwell uncrossed his leg and leaned forward. "And I thought honor among *gentlemen*," he said, "dictated that those who are losing be permitted to rewin their money. You seem to want me in here only when I'm losing."

"I reject that Mr. Caldwell."

"I'm not surprised." He sat back. "Tell you what. Let me have the fifteen hundred in chips, and the first twenty-five hundred I win will be repaid to your cashier on the spot. Could anything be fairer than that?"

"And if you lose?"

"Then I lose. You have my checks—just deposit them."

Harry shrugged. Such impudence deserved its comeuppance—and business, after all, was business. "How you elect to spend your money is not my concern," he said, leaning over his desk, "but whatever the outcome of your wagering this evening, Mr. Caldwell, the club cannot extend this courtesy to you another time." He glanced over at the young cashier. "Issue the chips to our guest, please."

Eddie Caldwell ran his stake up to four thousand within the hour, but neglected to fulfill his promise to substitute the larger portion of that sum for the two bank drafts he had given the club. His luck then soured again, and he wound up the night having to borrow cab fare home from Mr. Walters.

Two days later, both bank drafts were returned to the club, and the name of Edwin Holcombe Caldwell was entered upon the list of those who were permanently persona non grata at the Palm Beach Club.

The precinct captain reached into the humidor on Harry's desk, removed three cigars, stuck two inside his coat pocket and lighted the third, sucking the smoke into his mouth and smiling contentedly. "That's how you can tell the success of a club, Mr. Loring—by the quality of the cigars the owner gives out."

"I wouldn't be so sure of that, Captain. A good cigar is the cheapest form of self-promotion."

"You're not pleading poverty, are you?"

"Neither poverty nor prosperity—we're coming along."

"Yes. Well, that's why I've come by. In the judgment of the Gambling

Commission, the Palm Beach Club is doing a whole lot better than they had imagined possible. You're to be commended, Mr. Loring."

"I don't know where the esteemed commissioners get their information. Maybe they know something I don't."

"I wouldn't be surprised. But the fact of the matter, sir, is that the commission has decided to increase your monthly fee so that it's more in line with your receipts. From now on, if you value a trouble-free operation, they'll be expecting a monthly payment of fifteen hundred—"

"For crissakes! How the hell am I supposed to—"

"—plus ten percent of your profits."

"What profits? I'm still fighting to get the place out of the red!"

"Yes, that's what they all usually say—so let's call it five percent of your gross, then, shall we?"

"That's—outrageous. It's out and out robbery. I've seen greed in my time, but this beats all." Harry stood, fuming in his impotence.

The captain shrugged. "I know how you feel, but I'm just the messenger. No point in taking it out on me."

"They're nothing but a bunch of shakedown artists."

"Possibly. But I think you have your competitors to thank for this little piece of news—or so I've heard."

"What do you mean?"

"I mean they don't like your taking their business away, so they've complained to the commission—to squeeze you a little. It's the price of success, Mr. Loring."

"I'm running a decent place, why should they—?"

"Come, come, Mr. Loring, you weren't born yesterday. I'll be glad to register your objections with the commission, but it won't do any good. Your choice is to pay up or close down—or we'll do it for you."

He was habitually tired. He did not have to say so; she could tell from his posture, once so erect but often slumped now, whether he was seated or standing. He was looking older, too, she realized, sitting there in the parlor waiting for him but not acknowledging it to herself. The gray had fanned out from his temples and covered much of his head, and his mustache was more silver than dark. Even the hair on his chest had begun to turn a while back, although—she had to admit to herself—she really hadn't had a good look at it for quite some time. That fact, too, she supposed might be another sign of his advancing age. A man past forty could not be expected to have enough energy to run a complex business and meet and joke with a wide variety of people till all hours of the night and still make love as frequently as he once did. Yet she missed it. Nothing so rejuvenated her like feeling his arms around her, hearing his breath grow agitated, sensing the surge of his passion . . . She had lost her place in William Dean Howells' new book.

The clock had just finished chiming half past two when Harry came in and threw himself down on the sofa without even delivering her a perfunctory kiss on the brow. "Slow night?" she asked.

"Rotten weather never helps."

"Don't people gamble when it rains?"

"Harder to find a cab—you know that." He wished she would take off her glasses. They detracted from what remnants of her youth he could still find among the encroaching lines that gave her face added character but had begun to make her look matronly, even a bit grandmotherly. And perhaps she ought to go back to using henna on her hair; it was a touch garish, to be sure, but more flattering to her, he thought, than the drab, gray-streaked mass that she had now. But how could he tell her without being insulting? She was entitled to age without pretense.

"How were receipts?"

"About the same."

"Upstairs, too?"

"Upstairs, too."

He had been like that lately—unresponsive, even testy, as if put upon, and short of patience with her, with everything, it seemed. Was it the demands the club made on him—or the ones she did not? Every little thing having to do with her and the house now seemed an imposition to him. Was he dissipating? How else to account rationally for the hours he had begun to keep? He made the usual facile excuses, of course, but with less and less conviction. But did she really expect him to resist exercising his *droit du seigneur* when she let him out of her sight for most of every evening? If she had to police him constantly, though, what meaning could fidelity have for her? For him it had never meant more than involuntary servitude.

"I—gather you decided to wait out the rain," she said.

"What do you mean?"

"I mean—I guess you didn't want to get soaked walking home."

"That—and there's always a dozen things to do after closing—personal problems with the help, customers who insist on hanging around till I throw 'em out—the receipts to check on—"

"Why do you have to bother with the receipts? I do it in the morning. You've got enough to do without—"

"Because I *care*, Maddy—because it's my place, and it's not going as well as I want. Don't you understand?"

"I understand that wrecking yourself doesn't help any."

Her questions had begun to annoy him. She wanted a strict accounting of everything now, it seemed—the club's finances, all his activities, how he felt and what he thought. If she was so concerned about how things were going she could damned well come over to the club in the evening and see for herself instead of staying home reading. She was turning into a recluse, consumed by the house, and starting to sound and act as well as look like an old woman. She would stand there in the parlor trying a dozen different shades on the lamps as if they were hats, whispering things to herself about the comparative virtues of ruffled silk or lace tiers, as if the choice of one or another was an act of vast significance. Or she would ply him with endless illustrations of fences and ask him which style he would prefer in their garden, or whether they should replace the crumbling flagstone with brick on the little path that circled the flower bed. All he knew, or cared, about gardens was that the flowers that grew in them should be red, mostly. He hated to admit it, but his Maddy, the woman who had magically transformed herself from the role of widowed housekeeper to radiant lover a few short years ago, seemed to be reverting to drabness—and becoming stodgy, cranky and habit-ridden in the process. She had even taken to serving him the same menu week in, week out on those nights he stayed home for supper with her—chicken Mondays, lamb Wednesdays, beefsteak Fridays; it saved the cook from bother, she told him, if it was all the same to him. But he did not want to live under such a smothering regimen. Hell, he was still a relatively young man and had not lost his attractiveness, even if he was getting a bit gray at the temples and his mustache had taken on a silvery sheen. The assessing glances and advances by the showgirls at the club continued unabating, and no week passed when he did not turn aside an invitation from the wife or companion of a customer, who apparently was drawn to him. There was more to life than Maddy was letting him experience, or was willing to share with him now; she was abdicating as his charmed and charming consort to become a captive of domesticity. If that was what she wanted, all right, but he would not be roped into it. Not yet, anyway.

"You know, there's no need to wait up for me this way," he said.

"I'm not, actually. I'm reading."

"You've got most of the afternoon and the whole night after supper to do your reading without staying up well past midnight. It's getting on to three o'clock."

She glanced over at the clock on the mantel. "So it is. I wasn't sure you noticed."

"Maddy, you're turning into my truant officer."

"Am I? And here I thought you might like the idea of my wanting to have a glimpse of you now and then under our own roof."

"Let's not exaggerate the situation, shall we?"

"You're right," she said, closing her book. "I guess it speaks for itself."

Rachel paused on the threshold of Maddy's tiny office and beamed at the sight of its occupant. "Lord, you really *are* Mrs. Memory. I couldn't believe it when Mr. Walters said you were the very same person who—"

Maddy rose in delighted surprise and grasped both the girl's hands with her own. "Mrs. Caldwell—I do believe! What an unexpected pleasure, my dear."

"How did you—I mean, isn't this—" Rachel stopped herself. "This is such an entirely different direction for you—I would not have assumed your connection with this sort of—establishment." The word came out sounding just short of disreputable, but there was also warmth behind the implied disapproval.

"Life takes us on odd turns, I'm afraid." She noticed that once Rachel's smile had faded, she looked drained and uneasy. There were circles under her eyes that Maddy had not seen before, and her cheekbones pressed against her flesh, adding to the impression that she had suffered a marked loss of weight. "But how are you, young lady? Frankly, you look—not entirely yourself. Sit down, please."

"I'm afraid I'm intruding. Perhaps some other time would be—"

Maddy pushed the club bills to one side. "These can wait."

"You're too kind—still. I probably never should have come—"

She could not imagine why the girl had sought her out, but she was grateful for it, whatever the reason. "Let me judge that."

"This sort of thing must come up all the time here—but with me it's all very—harrowing and unpleasant." Her voice began to break.

Maddy reached over and placed a comforting hand over Rachel's. "What is it, child?"

"This—it's very hard for me to talk about." Her eyes filled up.

It was Eddie, of course; it was always Eddie. He was gambling to excess and losing heavily. And it was not just at the Palm Beach Club; it was five or six other places as well where he owed considerable sums. "He gets into trouble at one place and then moves on—it's like an illness, Mrs. Memory. He can't stop himself. He's gambling all the time, or thinking about it—planning strategies, dreaming up combinations of numbers. It's all he ever talks about anymore—how to win our money back and more. I've tried to stop him, of course, but he won't listen. I'm at my wits' end—I don't know what to do. He hates his job at the bank, he takes no interest at all in our children and he's not very fond of me, either. I'm afraid. We had to sell our house and take a smaller one—"

"I was under the impression that you lived with your in-laws."

"Oh, that was some time back. Eddie's mother is rather—imperious. We took a place of our own a few years ago. But it was too grand to maintain, what with Eddie's losses, and I'm afraid we'll have to mortgage the new one if Eddie is to pay off what he owes. Even then, I'm not sure there'll be enough."

He was twenty-five hundred dollars in debt to the Palm Beach Club, she said, and Mr. Loring had turned the matter over to collection people who were not very nice. They came to her front door every few days while Eddie was working at the bank and demanded payment; lately they had threatened to go to his employers and tell them about it if he didn't meet his obligation.

"I see," said Maddy. Harry had never mentioned the matter to her, but then why should he have singled out Eddie Caldwell's debt to the club from the others that he kept in his head? She felt that their records ought to list bad debtors, but Harry was always fearful of a raid someday and wanted no incriminating evidence to show up on paper. "And you think that I might help somehow?"

"I'd heard this place—your establishment—was co-owned by a woman, and so I thought that perhaps—well, that a woman might be a bit more understanding of—" She lowered her head. "And then I was given your name and thought—well, I supposed it couldn't be you—who had been so very understanding—"

Maddy sat back, appalled by what she had heard and furious at the pampered, utterly irresponsible young man who needed a good thrashing, which his wife was hardly capable of administering. "But surely your family are people of means. Couldn't you borrow the required sum from them and arrange to repay it over time? I'm sure they—"

Rachel's eyes glassed over. "I have no family." Her parents had moved out of the city to the van Ruysdales' ancestral place at Kinderkamack on the Hudson, where they had died within the past few years.

Maddy had seen no obituary notice in the papers; no doubt their living so far out of the city was the reason. "Forgive me for prying, but was no provision made for you by way of a legacy?"

Rachel's bosom heaved as she struggled for composure. "The man I always thought of as my father died three years ago and left everything to—to the woman I supposed was my mother, except for a thousand-dollar bequest to me. That's gone now, of course, to help pay Eddie's debts." And when Mrs. van Ruysdale died two years later there was a little family history included in her will.

Maddy's temples pounded; a scalding light was suddenly playing on the innermost secret of her life.

"My mother"—Rachel laced the word with scorn—"said that she could not in good conscience leave her estate to me since I was not a true van Ruysdale, not a blood member of her family but a child adopted in infancy from a destitute woman who had abandoned me." The wealthy but childless couple had taken in the unfortunate child and given her the best that money could buy all the time she was growing up. They had seen to it that she was wed to a man from a respectable and very comfortable family, and now that their little foundling had produced two children of Caldwell blood, it would be up to them to provide for the well-being of Rachel and her family. That's what she was told. "She left her money to my van Ruysdale and Blessington cousins. I haven't a pittance."

Everything inside her cried out to the girl. She ached to rush to her and hold her in her arms, to soothe her humiliation, to weep for her material degradation—and to reveal to her the sole remaining secret that life had conspired to keep from the young woman. Could the news other than comfort her? But this was not the moment, and these not the circumstances, for the traumatic revelation. Maddy fought for breath. "And the Caldwells? Mightn't you speak to them?"

"They're very angry with us—and with me especially. They've never forgiven me for our moving out of their grand house, as if we were not entitled to our privacy. And then came the news of my lack of proper breeding—it was as if I had conspired to keep the information from them. They've partially forgiven me that because they're fond of the children, but they believe it's the effect of my bad blood that's causing their darling Eddie to gamble. A stronger, more refined woman, they're convinced, would have curbed him long ago. They'll give us no further help at all."

No wonder the girl was desperate, forced to confide in a relative stranger. "Oh, my dear," Maddy said, coming around behind Rachel's chair and placing her hands on her shoulders. How she yearned to brush the child's hair as she had done that bittersweet day they had met in the bridal suite at the Royal Poinciana. "And what is it I can do to help with your troubles?"

"I—I'm not sure. Perhaps you could ask Mr. Loring to be a little patient and call off his bloodhounds. The moment we have some money I'll see to it the club is paid back—I *swear* to it."

Maddy nodded. "But I fear that's attacking the effect rather than the cause of your unhappiness."

"I'm not sure I understand."

"Your Eddie must be brought to his senses."

"But I've tried everything—"

"Perhaps if—may I speak my mind, Rachel?" There was no longer any point in formality. The girl was her flesh and blood and closer to her at this instant than any time since she had given her life.

"Of course."

"Men are usually nearer in spirit to their more animal instincts than women are. I assume Eddie is no different in that regard from the rest. There are times when a woman must take advantage of nature—since we are so often its victims—if you have my meaning?"

Rachel's shoulders slumped beneath Maddy's hands. "I'm afraid that sort of thing wouldn't work very well for me, Mrs. Memory. Eddie seems not very interested in me—in that particular regard. All his—appetite— seems to go into the roulette wheel, and nothing can distract him."

"Then perhaps a more dire step is necessary."

"I'm not much good at—what could I—"

"You could tell Eddie that unless he reforms you'll have no choice but to leave him."

The harshness of the proposal was greeted by momentary silence. Then Rachel's head swung around toward Maddy. "But—where would I go? What would I do? How could I pay for the food to put in my children's mouths?"

"And won't you have to ask those very same questions if you stay with Eddie until he's gone through every cent you have and put your family hopelessly in debt? I'm suggesting you instill the fear of God in him right now, before it's too late."

Tears were rolling down the girl's gaunt cheeks. "My head tells me that you're right, Mrs. Memory—but in my heart, I don't know." She reached a hand back and placed it on Maddy's wrist. "You're a stronger woman than I'm capable of being."

"I'm not so sure. If I'm strong, Rachel, it's because life has been hard on me at times. I've learned—I've had to learn—to rely on myself, and I'm trying to pass along that lesson. You must take care of yourself, my dear, because no one, not family nor friends nor, goodness knows, society itself will do it for you." She reached into her sleeve for her handkerchief and began wiping away Rachel's tears. "Promise me you'll think about what I've said?"

By way of an answer Rachel stood up and threw her arms around Maddy's neck with a hug so fierce that she feared for an instant that it had been pulled out of joint. But of course it did not hurt in the least. How could it?

* * *

With the utmost reluctance she broached the topic to Harry that same evening. It could not be done, though, without her revealing a part of her that she had calculatedly chosen not to share with him. Until that moment he knew no more, or less, about her child than Rachel's father did.

"Lord, how awful for you," he said after hearing of her daughter's quandry. Yet he was not sensitive to the painful irony of its effect on Maddy and how it drew her suddenly closer to the girl. He promised to have the club's collection agency stop badgering Rachel, but he would not forgive her dishonorable husband his debt.

"I'm not asking you for that," she said. Or for much else these days, she added silently.

The second letter from Counselor-at-Law Payson of 26 Broadway arrived two weeks after the first. She left it unopened in her desk drawer for several days before deciding not to throw it away still sealed. It read:

> Having no reply from you to my earlier note in behalf of Mr. Russell Corwin, I am obliged to suspect that you may be uneasy over the prospect of an interview in a setting as formal, and possibly unnerving, as a legal office.
>
> If it would ease your anxiety in any fashion whatever, I should be pleased to call upon you at home at any hour of any day of your designation to discuss the pressing matter Mr. Corwin has asked me to raise with you.
>
> May I add, at risk of offending your sensibilities, which I assume to be delicate in any matter pertaining to my client, that it would be greatly to your financial advantage to entertain the proposition I have been instructed to present. Please do, madam, allow me the courtesy of an audience.

Courtesy, indeed! The man was paid to press his case. And the harder he pressed, the more surely Russell was discomfited by his past sins and hankering to expiate himself. But she had endured too much for too long to respond generously to his grossly tardy attentions. Silence was all the retribution she needed—or cared to inflict.

As she had done with the earlier one, Maddy balled the lawyer's artfully penned note and dropped it in the refuse, along with the other discarded business of the day.

* * *

"Mr. Forbes, ma'am," Ruby Lee announced. He was right on her heels, giving Maddy no chance whatever to have the maid make excuses for her.

"Newell! How did you—why didn't you—?"

"I've come from the club. They said you weren't on the premises in the evenings, so I assumed—" He stood on the far side of the parlor, waiting for an invitation to come closer. "I hope I'm not intruding, Madeleine, but it's only half-past eight and I thought rather than—"

"Risk a cool response to a proper approach you'd barge in and trust me to forgive it?"

She had not seen him since the weekend they had spent together at the hotel in Providence—an interlude she somehow felt she owed him, although it had made her feel painfully deceitful—while Harry was down in Palm Beach seeking to hire staff for the club. Letters between them continued, his to her sent care of Agatha, in whom Maddy confided about her warring emotions. He wrote with care and restraint, hardly deigning to register disapproval of her ongoing cohabitation with a man of Harry Loring's sort. Her responses were briefer, more cryptic, yet no doubt tinder of a sort for the torch he carried. And then his letters had stopped, without explanation; an appealing, if not precisely fervent, option in her life was closed, she assumed, nor could she blame the man in view of her studied discouragement.

"You've hit the nail on the head," he said, clasping his arms behind his back like a schoolboy orator. "If you send me to the woodshed for a thrashing I'll gladly take my medicine—but don't send me packing, Maddy dear. Too much has gone into my showing up here. I feel rather like a bad penny."

"Stop the silliness," she said. "It's just that I supposed—not having heard from you—that—"

"Of course. I thought the same." He took her hands, and they melted into a kissless embrace that was nonetheless ardent. He glanced about him as they parted. "Your home is charming."

"Thank you. I've poured myself into it."

"And one would have thought you were sublimely happy—but your letters told me otherwise—without quite conceding as much. Your humor is missing from them."

"Yes, well, one copes—and the house *has* been a joy." She led him to the sofa. "You say you've come from the club?"

"Yes. Quite handsome it is, too—for a gambling hall."

"I would not characterize it that way."

"I'm sure. I meant no offense, only that—"

"You disapprove."

"Not of it—only your connection with it."

"I see." She sat in a wing chair adjacent to him. "You saw Harry?"

"I did—though I doubt he saw me. He seems—very much in his element—more so there than here, if I may say so."

"You needn't."

"But you don't deny it?"

"I don't wish to discuss it, Newell."

"I've come to discuss it."

"Then our reunion will be brief."

"Maddy, it's beneath your dignity to remain in this—I think there is something decidedly perverse in your—"

"I'm familiar with your estimate of Harry. Surely you didn't come here to tell me that."

"*He* is of no interest to me whatever. It's the nature of your bond to him—what is it, Maddy—some misguided, unrequited sense of loyalty that holds you in this—"

"Newell, you're descending into naked jealousy."

"Jealousy? You think that's all it is when I saw the man there tonight, fondling some hoyden in the corner of his own establishment like a—"

"*Stop* it, Newell."

"Why do you go on with him?"

She stood up. "I will *not* listen to this—in my own house—"

"Listen to me," he said. "I've seen other women—any number of them—Boston is not a city lacking in widows and other unattached women of a certain age and charm. But none of them has sustained my interest—has beguiled and disarmed me, has *haunted* me as you have. And yet, despite a real measure of reciprocity you've shown me, despite a frank acknowledgment that your companionship with Loring leaves you well short of happiness, you've kept me at arm's length and beyond. You've built a wall—and I haven't understood why, except that I was simply inadequate to fulfill your needs and that you would discard Loring for no one less. And so I decided to end my pursuit, this pointless pining from afar—I'm not without pride, Maddy." He enclosed her waist with his hands and gently sat her back down on the sofa's edge. "Yet I knew I'd not be able to live with myself if I didn't make one final effort to come to you and speak my mind fully and to offer you the dignity of a proper marriage, and of financial security, and of an adoring and attentive love— if not, perhaps, the intensity of passion, however fleeting, that you have— apparently—become accustomed to." He swallowed heavily. "That's what I came here—barged in here tonight to say to you, dearest Maddy. I ask only that you don't say no to me. Not now—not without thinking hard about what I've said and how I feel."

She eased her head against his shoulder. "Newell," she whispered, "Newell, Newell, Newell—you know so little about me—"

"I know enough, I think."

"Then you should understand my profound reluctance to—'discard,' I believe, was the word you used. I do not discard people I've loved, Newell. I was—it is a dreadful word but apt—I was discarded once myself and know the pain of the victim."

"I regret the word, but if this man dishonors you it appalls me to see you—even if I'm not to be the one to take his place—"

She brought her head close to his and placed a finger on his lips, then kissed them hungrily and sent him away.

Harry tumbled through the door at five before two, looking careworn and depleted. That jocular, lecherous demeanor he displayed at the club, she thought, to give him every benefit of the doubt, was obviously sly a facade for the constant striving and worry that the club demanded of him.

"Somebody threw a big rock through one of the front windows tonight," he told her, "about half an hour before closing. Two of the customers were cut—could've been much worse. Cops haven't a suspicion—just some mindless vandals, they say." But Harry was more skeptical, particularly since two mornings earlier somebody had strewn the club's garbage, waiting to be carted off, all over the sidewalk in front of the place. "I think they're trying to intimidate us, Maddy."

"Who is?"

"I'm not sure exactly—maybe all of them."

"All of who?"

"My distinguished peers in the casino industry. I think they'd like to be rid of us."

Possibly he was right, but to conclude as much from what could have been two unrelated acts struck her as a bit premature. Instead of saying so she stroked his forehead for a moment and then brought him a glass of iced Apollinaris water, his usual nightcap. When he had unwound she remarked as offhandedly as possible, "Newell was here tonight."

"Newell?"

"Forbes."

"Oh, him. Is that old reprobate still panting after you?"

He had decided some time back that her flirtation—or whatever it was—with Forbes had been no more than her way of hitting back at him for his own petty philandering; on reflection, he rather admired her spunk for it and gave it no more thought. "He's not so old," she said with a forced laugh, "and hardly a reprobate."

"But the panting part is true, I take it."

"He's a very discreet gentleman—"

"Oh, I know."

"What do you think I should do about him, Harry?"

It was a more important question than he realized. He addressed his iced water. "Whatever you'd like, I suppose. If you find him such stimulating company perhaps I should have him stuffed and put over the fireplace for your next birthday present—seeing as I'm not around in the evenings."

"Don't be cruel—cynical is bad enough."

"Actually I think you should encourage him."

"*Why?*"

"Isn't he wealthy?"

"He's a man of means, I should say. His bank account doesn't come up."

"The club might need an investor if things don't pick up a bit. Perhaps he'd be attracted to a sound business opportunity—and think he can purchase your favor in the bargain."

"What an interesting notion."

"I thought so."

"Harry," she said, with scarcely a pause for emotional ballast, "will you marry me—tomorrow?"

He sipped at his drink for a moment. "Tomorrow, do you mean, or today? It's past midnight."

"Either. All right, today."

He drained his glass. "If it's just the same to you, I'd rather skip it for today—I've a great many things that need attending to."

"Tomorrow, then."

"And I suppose you'd insist on a wedding trip and all that."

"Well, you haven't had a day off since the club opened. We could close down for a week—and take a little cruise somewhere." Her tone was oddly casual, given the gravity of the subject.

"That would be inconvenient." He handed her the glass with an appreciative nod. Nobody could top Harry Loring for nonchalance.

"Harry," she said, "will you ever marry me?"

He climbed to his feet, slowly wrapped his arms about her and kissed her on the nose. "If I ever marry anyone on this earth, my sweet, it will be none other than thee—or is it thou?"

She stiffened in his grasp. "Does that mean no?" The lightness was gone from her manner.

"Ask me no questions and I'll tell you no lies," he said, tilting her chin up toward his. "And I think you should consider tinting your hair, my darling. Dun is not your most flattering shade."

After that moment, whatever might happen to them, he could never say that she had withheld her full commitment from him. But the evidence was now in that he saw her offer not as her utmost gift to him but as a technicality.

TEN

1903–1905

*T*he harassments intensified.

Twice more, the sidewalk in front of, the steps leading into, and the elaborately carved facade of the Palm Beach Club were adorned with not only its own refuse but that as well from several nearby establishments, including a greengrocer, a carpenter, a butcher shop and, most appallingly, a stable, all producing an odor that took days to dissipate and discouraged the club's clientele from attending. The window pelting also continued in the wee hours, requiring the repeated and costly hiring of a glazier to repair the damage before the club opened for business the following evening. Harry's appeals for protection to the police precinct were greeted with apologies that manpower was lacking for constant vigilance and the suggestion that the club retain watchmen to ward off the vandals. "Then what the hell am I paying you for?" Harry demanded of precinct captain Morrow as he was shown out of the stationhouse.

"I didn't hear that," said the captain, and turned away.

The expensive enlistment of round-the-clock guards prevented new assaults against the club building. But there could be no remaining doubts of the collusive plot against the P.B.C.'s operation when its linen supplier, then its liquor wholesaler and finally its food vendors all advised that their charges would be raised by twenty-five percent and, furthermore, that due to various mechanical or organic disorders afflicting their wagons, drivers and horses they could no longer deliver their merchandise—the club would have to send someone to pick it up. When inquiry of alternate suppliers disclosed that they would impose the same prices and also declined to deliver, Harry understood the reach and power of the forces against him. He saw no immediate alternative, however, but to capitulate, pressing Arthur Timmons into service as a drayman who scurried all over town to keep the club supplied. On one occasion the dutiful youth was assaulted shortly after leaving the Fulton Street fish market. When Harry's complaint to the police was greeted with indifference he had no choice but to hire still another guard to accompany Arthur on his rounds.

Even more troubling were the rumors circulating at the city's other casinos that the Palm Beach Club operated a crooked wheel and engaged in related shady practices. So pervasive and concerted were these reports that Harry was reduced to dark but impotent rage. There was no way to counter such slurs publicly, and to address them on his own premises seemed only to lend substance to the slander. The club's revenues dipped precariously.

Harry would not be daunted. He conducted himself like a beleaguered general, exhorting his hard-pressed troops to persevere. The club's cuisine and service improved, if anything, and to retain old customers and lure new ones Harry prevailed on his theatrical crony Eric Bemis to help him enlist some of the New York theater's most celebrated entertainers to perform at the P.B.C. The price, of course, was steep, and when added to the other unforeseen expenses forced on it by its ruthless competitors, threatened to be ruinous. But Harry countered Maddy's objections by arguing that they had no choice; they could fight back or surrender, losing everything that had been invested.

The star performers soon packed the club, but the gambling take remained lower than what was needed to cover the bloated costs of operation. They would simply have to function at a loss for the time being, Harry said, until their enemies relented and expenses could be slashed without fatal consequence. But the sight of the freshly thronged club prompted a new wave of intimidating tactics, this time in the form of a crackdown by municipal officers nobly protecting the public welfare. The Palm Beach Club had served an alcoholic drink to an under-age male on the previous twenty-third of November, a city detective advised its management four months later, and as a result of this lax conduct was to be penalized by the immediate and indefinite suspension of its liquor license. No appeal against this blatantly confected charge could be lodged without risk of public disclosure of the club's illicit gambling rooms, so Harry hurriedly shuttled from one municipal office to another to determine how much had to be paid and to whom in order to have the license restored. Without it, the club was done. The price, distributed among several grasping hands, came to more than four thousand dollars.

After a week's respite from official intimidation the club's white-jacketed *saucier* came pounding on the door to Harry's office with the news that chef Josef had just hurled a meat cleaver at the retreating figure of a representative from the city health department who had served him with an order to cease and desist operations. Harry found the chef spewing Russian invective in all directions and repeatedly plunging his arms elbow-deep into a flour barrel as if mining the creamy powder for some hidden treasure. "See?" he shouted, shoveling handfuls of flour against the nearest wall. "Not-ting—not-ting at all, them filthy liars!" The *saucier* drew Harry's attention to a sheet of paper pinned to the butcher block by the chef's second-best cleaver, which charged the establishment with the presence of "rodent droppings and/or other excremental filth" in the kitchen's flour supply. The club's food-serving license was suspended until further notice.

This time the extortion came to nearly seven thousand dollars, still further depleting the club's ever more slender bank account. Accordingly, when precinct captain Morrow appeared in Harry's office the following week to advise that the gambling commission was raising his monthly fee to two thousand dollars plus ten percent of the profits, he snarled at the police officer that enough was enough. "Tell them I won't pay a penny more, tell 'em there's no blood left in the turnip—*and* tell 'em if they shut me down I'll expose the whole rotten bunch of you right down to the goddamned precinct level." Harry brought his nose to within six inches of the captain's. "You hear me, Mr. *Law*man?"

"I hear you, Mr. Loring. I'll pass along your message."

Maddy expressed admiration, but wondered if they could stand on principle when surrounded by jackals.

"If we don't take a stand here and now," he said, "they'll tear us to pieces. We're already bleeding badly."

The third letter from Russell Corwin's attorney hinted at his exasperation over her failure to respond in any fashion to his earlier requests for a meeting. It was only because of the silence at her end, Mr. Payson wrote, that he was emboldened to commit to writing the delicate subject matter he would have vastly preferred to discuss in person. Suffice it to say, he went on, that . . .

> it would be to your considerable financial advantage if you were to agree to inform me, as intermediary for Mr. Corwin, as to the identity and whereabouts of your daughter. Mr. Corwin is in a declining state of health, and I therefore beseech you, madam, if you possess a remnant of human compassion (as I most assuredly suspect), not to withhold from this repentent and guilt-ridden man the information he so earnestly seeks.

Had Russell truly fallen ill? Was he perhaps even dying and therefore desperate for expiation? And how much would he pay for it? The very thought struck her as doubly despicable—both in him for supposing that so precious a secret could be purchased at any price, and in herself for even pausing to wonder how much might be in it for her. Who was this Mr. Payson to appeal to her on the ground of compassion when his client had displayed none toward her for so long? But his repeated appeals were nevertheless beginning to wear down her resistance. Perhaps the time was close at hand to disclose to Rachel a full account of her origins; the girl was entitled to know—and once she did, there was no point, none at all really, in withholding her father's name from her or her name from him.

Unlike the first two letters, this one she preserved, slipping it between the blotter and the leather pad on her desk in the corner of the parlor. The matter required more study before her resolving it one way or the other. While the subject lingered in that limbo of indecision her eye was caught one day by a small item on the fourth page of the *Tribune*, one that caused her heart to sink. *"Embezzlement Charged at Corn Exchange Bank,"* read the newspaper heading. The semiannual audit at the bank had disclosed discrepancies in the amount of nearly eleven thousand dollars and led to the arrest of Edwin H. Caldwell, a junior officer, on the charge of purloining that total in small amounts over a period of several months. The accused, identified as a member of a socially prominent New York family, had been released on a twenty-five-thousand-dollar bond pending the outcome of his trial.

Her thoughts went at once toward Rachel and, how the poor child must be suffering at this disclosure. Eddie was apparently as inept a thief as he was unfortunate a gambler. He had started life with every possible advantage, as Rachel had with every imaginable liability, yet he had squandered it all and was bringing her girl down with him. There was not a drop of sympathy in her soul for him. How she wished Rachel rid of him! Yet now it was too late; to abandon him in his degradation would no doubt seem to her as sore a mark against her character as his own sordid career had proved. How could she see the girl again and persuade her otherwise?

At this juncture the lawyer's letter reentered her mind. Perhaps it was a godsend. Whatever the amount of money Russell had placed at Payson's disposal to pry her secret from her, Maddy might contribute to Rachel as a means of liberating herself from Edwin and making a fresh life for herself. And still she hesitated. For in coming in this fashion to the aid of her deeply troubled child, she could not prevent Russell from appearing to be a knight on a white charger, the true source of their love child's rescue—and thereby the unworthy recipient of the girl's gratitude and, very possibly, future devotion. It was too bitter an irony for Maddy to swallow. But to deny Rachel the financial relief necessary to extricate herself seemed an act of supreme selfishness. And so she rationalized. The girl, she told herself, was not strong enough to withstand Edwin's perverse will; the money would quickly fall into his hands, and Rachel would be more surely enslaved to him. If only she could obtain some sense of the girl's innermost feelings at this moment . . .

She addressed a short note of sympathy to her home and offered her the services of a comforting shoulder and receptive ear should Rachel have the need or desire for either. But no response came, not even a line.

All she knew about the precinct captain was what Harry had told her, and so when Ned the bartender showed him into her little office she viewed that grafter with profound distaste. He proved more polite than she had supposed, and what she learned as a result of their curiously cordial interview left Maddy shaken.

Invited to take the chair opposite her desk, the captain said he preferred to remain standing and apologized for troubling her on a matter that he could not avoid bringing to her attention. Perhaps it would be best if he addressed her and Mr. Loring together on the subject.

"He's not at the club just now, I'm afraid," she replied, failing to disclose that she in fact had no idea where Mr. Loring was presently nor where he had slept the previous night. Two weeks earlier Harry had moved into one of the smaller bedrooms in the house, claiming at first that he was doing so in order not to disturb her on his late-night—predawn, actually—home comings. He soon conceded, in view of the abrupt and irrefutable decline in their lovemaking, that he wanted an interlude in their intimacy to allow him time to rethink his feelings and gauge afresh their relationship. Which was not to say he held any rancor, he went on reassuringly, with declarations of his fondness and high regard for her. But since passion was, for the time being, absent from his affections, perhaps abstinence and cool reflection would be therapeutic for them both. When he did not come home at all several nights the next week she understood that it was only she who was abstaining. Her choices were to confront him with an ultimatum that would surely drive him away, possibly for good, or to give him enough tether to exercise his loins in whatever tawdry manner he wished and enough time to come to his senses. She elected the latter, especially in view of his troubles with the club, meanwhile renewing correspondence with Newell Forbes, whose proposal of marriage she had neither accepted nor declined.

"It's just as well he's not here," said Captain Morrow. "I haven't made much headway lately with Mr. Loring."

"You're not likely to do much better with me, Captain. Besides, I leave such matters to him."

"Unfortunately, madam, your position at this establishment requires my informing you of the grave risk you yourself are facing if Mr. Loring persists in ignoring me." The gambling commission had not taken kindly to his defiance of the increased monthly fee it had decreed and the larger slice of the profits it was demanding. Unless the money, in full, was forthcoming during the next two weeks, he said, the owner of the Palm Beach Club could expect to be hauled off to jail for running an illegal enterprise. "And according to our investigation, madam, you are the owner of the club—not Mr. Loring."

"Mr. Loring and I are coproprietors."

"Perhaps by your own agreement, madam, but according to your bank account and lease for these premises—both of which certain sources tell us are in your name solely—you and only you are the responsible party."

"That's a mere technicality—for purely personal reasons."

"Nevertheless, the law views you alone as the proprietor. And Mr. Loring himself contends that he is only a trusted employee."

"Does he . . . ?"

"No doubt he's said that thinking it's a way of evading the commission's reach—and that we'd never bother pursuing you in this matter. I just thought you ought to know that he's wrong about that. If the club's in your name you're the one who'll have to go to jail, madam."

"I see . . ."

The captain gave the hat he was holding a little twirl. "It's not my place to say, madam, but it kind of looks to me as if maybe your partner is hiding behind your skirts."

"You're quite right, captain—it's not your place to say." She kept tight rein on her emotions as she confronted this agent of naked venality. "With regard to your so-called commission's demand for a higher share of our profits, I can tell you truthfully, sir, since I've just been going over our figures this morning, that the club is operating at a loss presently— and has been doing so for several months now." She turned around the ledger on the desk in front of her so that it faced him. "Here, you see—these numbers in red indicate the net results. It's plain to anyone even remotely familiar with accounting practices that we have no profits to share with your—superiors—or anyone else."

The captain's hat was motionless in his hands now. "You can show me numbers in rainbow-colored ink if you'd like, madam, but that's not going to persuade the commissioners that they're wrong about your take here. They can see the size of the crowd and figure from your food and drink prices where you stand. If you think you're really running in the red, Mrs. Memory, I would bet you—if I was a betting man, which I'm not—that your trusted employee is holding something out on you. Maybe a whole lot of something. You might want to have a nice heart-to-heart talk with him sometime real soon." He replaced his hat and tipped its peak toward her with due respect. "I'll be back to you."

Cold dispassion took possession of her senses. She had not, before that moment, conceived of even the possibility that to Harry Loring she had been a dupe to be manipulated—tenderly, to be sure. The facts were that he had set up the club operation with her name on all the documents, and while it may not have been his intention to hide behind her skirts, the device did serve to protect him and expose her. He had said, or implied, that his doing so, as with his granting her sole title to the house, was a way of demonstrating his feelings for her and assuring her that he would not wander off—the sort of security, one might say, that Mary Lily Kenan gained by Henry Flagler's presentation to her of a million-dollar pearl necklace. But why had she supposed he would exclude her from the near-automatic workings of his nature? Because he loved her? In his fashion, yes. But she had, until then, it seemed, blinded herself to the shallowness, the limits, of that love, which served himself first and last—and her when it suited his purposes and needs. He was so gifted in dispensing blandishments, in smiling winningly, in lifting her spirits and her petticoats, that she could not bear to think that however scheming he was where others were concerned, she might, in the end, be no different from the rest to him. Could he have *really* stooped now to pocketing money that was rightfully hers? If she had outlived her other uses to him, why not? Oh, lord . . .

On leaving the club after making her morning bank deposit, she went straight to the Pinkerton Detective Agency offices to learn the truth, however unpleasant it might prove, about Harry's nocturnal pursuits. One week later the neatly typewritten report was delivered to her bound in a discreet gray folder sealed in a large manila envelope. The subject, it said, divided his time between three prime locations—his residence on East 36th Street, the club where he was employed and a flat on Bank Street to which he went at approximately one o'clock nightly, remaining there until noon on two of the days he was under surveillance. The flat was leased to a Miss Mona Geiger, an entertainer in the singing and dancing field, most recently employed at the Palm Beach Club but currently without a known source of income. The monthly rental, according to the landlord, was being paid in cash by the subject.

She had never deluded herself with regard to Harry's fidelity, but before when he wandered, the transgression had always been casual, prompted by a yen for variety, perhaps, or a sudden seizure of lust or a need to reassure himself of his continuing attractiveness to other women. Or he would claim some professional advantage to be gained by servicing a well-placed set of loins. But he had avoided habitual promiscuity, which she would not have tolerated, and never to her knowledge had he been in such constant, such flagrant pursuit of another woman. In keeping a doxie at his disposal under lock and key and *paying* her sustenence he had, she now felt, crossed the line between tolerable inconstancy and intolerable betrayal.

At first her fury was uncontainable. The man she had given herself to was now a lowlife, plain and simple. She broke things in the house, knickknacks they had collected on their travels. She snapped at Ruby Lee whenever the poor girl did anything the least bit clumsy or unthinking. And she did her best to avoid Harry altogether whenever he was in the house, remaining in her room or going off on household errands or attending to her chores at the club. Instead of confronting him with the growing body of damning evidence she smoldered. She would bide her time a bit longer and let the bill of particulars accumulate. She herself paid the precinct captain the increment for police protection and asked him not to disclose the transaction to her coproprietor. And she made it her business to appear at the club nightly to monitor its operations as well as Harry's.

So it was Maddy who first noted the arrival at the club of a visitor she had never expected on the premises—Colonel Edward Bradley. Braced as she was now to guard her own interests, she welcomed Bradley, insisted that he be management's guest for the evening, and merrily confessed her little masquerade as Madame Memphis during her tenure in his employ. Bradley in turn conceded that he had found her alter ego a touch more flamboyant than he preferred a woman to be but nevertheless admired her usefulness to the Beach Club. He was in the city on business matters for several weeks, he said, and could not resist the opportunity to visit their establishment. "Our great pleasure," said Maddy, wondering all the while if he did not suspect the ill-got source of the funds with which the club had in part been founded.

Harry felt a similar anxiety, she could tell at once by the elaborate manner in which he greeted Bradley as he bounded down the steps from the gaming rooms. "We've borrowed more than one leaf from your book at the Beach Club," he said, "but you know the old saw about the sincerest form of flattery." Bradley, smiling, nodded as Harry began to usher him about on a tour of the place, but before long he turned the task over to Maddy and uneasily retired to his upstairs office to wait for the visitor's arrival after he had dined and taken in the entertainment. By evening's end, thanks in part to her careful shepherding, the knowledgeable guest was lavish in his praise of the Palm Beach Club. From the warmth of Mr. Walters' greeting at the front door to the crispness of the waiters' uniforms to the smartness of the table china to the brightness of the electric lights over the gaming tables, Bradley said he saw all the evidence of careful even inspired management. "Harry's learned his lessons well," he said, "and no doubt your assistance has been invaluable." The crowd was, of course, more raffish than his own in Florida, he noted, but this being New York, a more exclusionary policy would likely have played into the hands of their competitors.

"They have not been overly kind to us as it is," she said. "Downright hostile, I should say."

"So I've heard. It's a wonder you've been able to prosper."

"Unfortunately," said Maddy, "that's more illusion than fact. The place is still running at a loss, I'm afraid."

"Odd," said Bradley. "I'd have thought from the volume of play upstairs that you'd be turning a pretty penny."

Maddy alluded to "extraordinary expenses" and then, suddenly uncertain of Bradley's motives in pursuing the subject, dropped it.

When he returned to the club the following night her suspicion was heightened that more than professional curiosity had prompted Bradley's appearance. Over dinner he confessed as much to her. He was there, he said, at Henry Flagler's request. Harry had missed the last quarterly interest payment on his sizable loan, sending along instead a note that said finances were temporarily somewhat tight at the club but he had every expectation that conditions would improve and prosperity was just around the corner. Prudence dictated that someone familiar with the operation of casino clubs pay a visit to the P.B.C. to determine if the Flagler stake was imperiled, and given their long association, Bradley had been recruited for the task.

The news staggered Maddy, though she was at pains not to disclose her feelings. She and Harry had arranged, after opening the club's bank account, for which she was the sole signatory, that in order to protect their benefactor as his attorney had insisted, the check for nearly two thousand dollars to cover the quarterly interest payment would be made out to Harry, who would deposit it in his personal account and issue a check of his own to Flagler, thereby eliminating any traceable link between the financier and the club. Since she had made out the bank draft to Harry for the last interest payment as scheduled—and he had neglected to pay over what was due—there simply could be no mistaking Harry's game.

"What troubles me frankly," said Bradley as he sipped his coffee, "is that from what I saw last night I can't find any reason why Harry wasn't able to meet his obligation. That's why I thought a second visit would be in order—if you don't mind my being candid."

Maddy nodded and, calculating where her own interest now lay, said, "I'm a little concerned myself, so long as we're being honest with each other." She asked if it were possible for Bradley to gauge the approximate scale of the gambling take just by observing the crowd upstairs and its pattern of betting. "I have the sense that we're losing something between the floor cracks—and Harry may not be aware of it."

"Or may not know that you're aware of it—or am I being unkind?"

"I would rather not elaborate just yet . . ."

Bradley agreed to scrutinize the gaming action and reported his findings to her in her office the next morning. Based on the size of the crowd and the average bet that was placed, he said the net take on the night ought to have been somewhere between two thousand and twenty-five hundred dollars—"possibly on the higher side, since Harry no doubt pays his upstairs boys something less than we do our more experienced help."

Maddy blanched. The envelope Harry had left for her in the safe with the previous night's gambling take contained $938. "I see," she said.

He did not need to question her further. "I'm sorry to be the bearer of—"

She raised a hand. "Your visit has been . . . sobering," she said. "Please let Mr. Flagler know that I'll do my best to see that his interests are protected."

"BAIL JUMPER SOUGHT"

Edwin Holcombe Caldwell was a fugitive from justice, declared the two-paragraph story, after his failure to appear for a pretrial hearing scheduled for the previous day at the New York county courthouse. The twenty-five-thousand-dollar bond posted in his behalf following the charge of bank embezzlement was forfeited as police sought the whereabouts of the thirty-one-year-old socialite and closely questioned members of his family. "His attractive wife, Rachel, denied having plans for a clandestine rendezvous with the accused," the article concluded.

Maddy ran upstairs, her breakfast ignored, and reached blindly into her closet for a dress. Any dress. Her mind was a blur. She knew only that she had to see the girl, that she was needed, that the moment was at hand. She ran out the front door in a semi-disheveled state, hurried to Lexington to hail the first empty hack that approached, sailing past a waiting older couple in the process, and absentmindedly ran a comb through her hair on the short ride uptown while she tried to assemble her jangled thoughts.

The girl was doubtless enduring the tortures of the damned. Yet in pitying her, in rushing to her, Maddy realized that she was more relieved than angered by Eddie's flight. It was the ultimate confession of his irresponsibility and selfishness. The girl was infinitely better off without him—and his dreadful parents. And if she felt the world had abandoned her, she would shortly learn otherwise.

There were too many vehicles and people filling Forty-eighth Street for her cab to drive through, so she got out at the corner and soon discovered that the blockage was due to the same cause that had drawn her there. The crowd at Rachel's doorstep, spilling down the steps and into the street, was composed about equally of newspapermen and curiosity seekers. What business had they being here, badgering a young wife and mother in her humiliation?

Maddy elbowed through the offensive clutter, clambered up the steps and, malevolently eyeing those who with the utmost reluctance yielded space for her to squeeze past, grabbed the door knocker. "Won't do you no good, lady," growled one of the gentlemen of the press, his hat pushed to the back of his head. "The missus ain't takin' no callers today."

She rapped hard anyway, drew no response, tried again, earned a round of ridicule and persisted a third time. Nothing. From one of the reporters she begged for a scrap of paper and, rummaging in her purse for the nub of a pencil she had long since learned to carry with her, scratched out a note: *"Please, my dear Rachel, allow me to speak with you. I shall wait by your door all day if need be, and all night and all tomorrow—and forever if you make me. Madeleine Memory."* She slipped the folded scrap under the door and sat down on the top step, determined to do exactly what her note promised.

By noontime the crowd had begun to thin out a little, and as the minutes crept by, more and more of them drifted away, sensing that nothing newsworthy was likely to occur. Finally, when only a few bystanders remained on the sidewalk below, she heard the snap of the door bolt behind her and her name being softly called through the inch-wide opening. She was quickly on her feet and through the swinging door, against which Rachel threw her weight to close and rebolt it. Without a word she led Maddy through the inner door and into the front hallway.

Once there, Maddy's arms instinctively opened, and Rachel fell into them, sobbing against her shoulder. Maddy held her tight, rocking her slightly. "Oh, my dear, my poor, poor dear."

The tears quickly subsided as Rachel, struggling to regain her dignity, separated herself from Maddy. Rachel made a small sound somewhere between a sigh and a hiccup. "That's the first time I've cried this entire awful month. I promised myself I wouldn't—and I didn't—but when I saw you again, something happened. You have the strangest effect on me."

"I know, I know," Maddy said, then looked about her at the untidy house. "Is there anything I can do to help—straighten up or look after the children—make you some tea, perhaps?"

Rachel smiled. "Thank you, but there's no need, really not. Things are a bit of a mess, I'm afraid—I had to let the maid go—but I can do the straightening. I'll have to learn to." She led Maddy down the hall to a small cozy room lined with paneling. "The children are up on the third floor with their nanny—I'd love you to meet them sometime. They don't know a thing about what's happened, of course. I've told them their father's off on a business trip." She invited Maddy to sit. "We call this the library, though there are precious few books. Eddie isn't much of a reader—wasn't—" She looked at the floor for a moment, as if in memory of the lately departed. "He didn't even leave me a note—he just never came home three nights ago—and I knew what it meant." She glanced up, the short, bitter narrative ended. "Now then, can I bring you something? You had a far worse ordeal out there than I did in here—I was looking through the curtains on the second-floor windows—"

"I don't think uninvited guests are entitled to refreshments."

"Uninvited doesn't mean unwelcome."

Maddy smiled and searched her daughter's face. "I expected—you don't look nearly as miserable as I feared. You must be—"

"Stronger than you thought? Yes—I've surprised myself, too. This past year, you see, I've learned a valuable lesson, Mrs. Memory—"

"You must call me Maddy."

"Maddy, then. When I finally realized that I no longer loved Eddie—if I ever did in the first place—he lost the power to hurt me. Everything that's happened—all his broken promises, his abandonment of the children, his callousness toward me, the horrid business at the bank and now his running away—they're all evidence of his childishness, of how utterly self-centered he is. It may sound awful to you but I don't care *where* he's gone—or with whom—"

Maddy nodded, elated at Rachel's newfound strength. "Is there someone else?"

"Lord knows. Lately he'd taken to taunting me, saying he'd found a woman who truly understood him, could give him what he needed—whatever that is—blind indulgence, I suppose. Of course, it could all be a lie, like the rest of his life has become." She ran a hand over the dimpled surface of the leather sofa they were sitting on. "I should be sad for him, I guess—but I'm not. I'm just empty inside." She looked at Maddy. "Do I sound horrible to you?"

"You sound smart and strong—and maybe a little proud."

"Oh, I am—it's the strangest thing. I suppose most women would be scared to death, feel they'd failed and were nobody anymore. But I don't feel that way. I'm still who I am, whoever that is." She smiled ruefully. "Certainly I'm no longer a Caldwell—Eddie's parents have made that abundantly clear, especially after his running away cost them twenty-five thousand dollars."

"They can hardly blame that on you."

"Why not? It's easier than facing up to their son's true character. I'm a sorceress of low birth who cast an evil spell on their innocent darling and lured him into matrimony."

Maddy took her hand. "What will you do now?"

"Do? Lord knows. I'll try to survive as best I can. This house has to be sold—for the most it can fetch—and I'll see what's left after the mortgage has been settled."

"And if and when Eddie reappears?"

"I simply won't have him. Two children are all I can manage."

"Where will you go? How will you get along?"

"I can't say as yet. Nanny will stay for a time—as long as the money holds out. Then I'll have to find work, I suppose—though heaven knows, I'm not suited for much." Her eyes fell on Maddy's coarser hands. "The rewards of a gentle upbringing," she said quietly.

Maddy turned to face her more squarely. "Rachel, I'd like you and the children to come live with me—for the time being—until you can get your bearings and—"

Rachel's eyes lighted pleasurably but dimmed an instant later. "You're a dear, Maddy, but I could never do—"

"Why not? I have plenty of room—the house is too big for me alone, and the neighborhood is pleasant and well suited for the children. Each of them could have a room on the third floor, and their nanny as well. And there's a splendid room for you—"

Rachel's look turned stern. "I don't mean to sound ungrateful to you, but you're forgetting this newfound pride of mine. I simply cannot accept charity—and not from a relative stranger, no matter how—"

"Do I seem a stranger to you?"

"No . . . no, you never have—it's true . . . from the first moment I saw you crouching beside me in that closet. But the fact is—"

"You're not in possession of the facts." Maddy stood and drew Rachel to her feet after her. "Didn't I see a mirror in your front hall?"

"Yes . . . "

Maddy led her quickly to the pier glass. "Pull your hair off your forehead as I'm doing, and tell me what you see."

She watched as Rachel's eyes, so like her own, flicked from one of their images to the other, back and forth, again and again, until they froze on hers for a long, eternally long, moment. "Oh," she whispered, "oh, my God in heaven . . ."

The key rattled around futilely in the lock several times, followed by muttered curses, more useless probes at the lock and finally the sounding of the door chimes. "Who is it?" she called through the door after letting him wait several moments, as if she had been summoned from the second floor.

"It's *me*," Harry growled. "What's wrong with the lock?"

"I changed it."

"Why?"

"To keep you out."

Silence, then more quietly, "Why?"

"Because you don't live here anymore."

"Since when?"

"Since I discovered you've made other arrangements downtown."

She thought she could detect his heavy breathing through the barrier between them. "You're being idiotic, Maddy," he said finally. "She's just a cheeky little tart."

"Leggy, too, if I recall."

"*Maddy.*"

"I know about everything—there's no point in your going on."

"What *everything?* Maddy, let me in. I'll be glad to—"

"The money—your deceit—you treacherous son of a bitch." Her voice was icy.

"Maddy, I'm not going to stand out here debating with you in the middle of the night with the whole neighborhood listening. Let me *in*."

She did, as she knew she would have to for one final, fruitless exchange with him.

"You've twisted it all to make me into a prize villain," he said after she had tolled off the list of indictments against him. It was preposterous for her to claim he was trying to protect himself at her expense by placing the club's lease and bank account in her name. He had had two purposes, he said, the foremost being the one he had stated—it was the next best thing to a wedding band that he could give her for security, like the house: a token of his esteem for her, a reward for her devotion to him, an assurance that he would not abandon her since she held their purse-strings.

"But you *have* abandoned me," she said, momentarily losing control.

"Nonsense. I'll attend to that part of it in a moment." His other reason for omitting his name from the deed to the house and the club's legal documents, he continued, was to insulate them against any claim Flagler might lodge in the event his loan to Harry could not be paid back in full. "I was trying to protect you, Maddy—not hide behind your skirts." As to his skimming off from the nightly gambling profits, it was true enough, but he had good and sufficient reason. "The plain truth is that you've stopped working as hard as I do—you don't really give a damn about the club—you've indulged me, like a little boy slavering over a lollipop. Running a gambling establishment is beneath your damned dignity, so you put in your couple of hours a day and think you're entitled to an equal share of the profits. Well, I don't—and it's my money—I went out and got it—never mind how—and I'm entitled. I was going to tell you sooner or later, but I didn't see the rush—"

"What I didn't know wouldn't hurt me."

"Yes, frankly. As to Flagler's interest payment, he can afford to wait awhile—the man has tens of millions, and I'm struggling to make my little enterprise succeed. And what I tell the city grafters about our profits is one hundred percent excusable. They're nothing but a bunch of vicious thieves—you know it as well as I do. For that bastard of a precinct captain to come in and fill your head with poison about me is the last word in gall—and for you to *believe* him is—is beyond my comprehension."

That left the small matter of Miss Mona Geiger. "Would you have liked it better if I'd told you about it?" he demanded. Surely, he said, it could not have been a secret to her that as she had grown older and colder toward him he was turning elsewhere for emotional relief. Just as he was unable to give her what she most sought from him—his name and the security of a marriage that would have smothered him—so she had proved unable to continue supplying him with the satisfaction he craved *and* was entitled to. And he had never promised her faultless fidelity, had never pretended to a monogamous character and had long since stopped demanding as much from her. "You've wandered as well as I, my dear Madeleine."

"You think the two can be equated?"

"I think my conduct—under all these circumstances—is at least not dishonorable and is understandable. You've made me into some kind of unmitigated cad."

"I see."

"I doubt it."

"Oh, but I do. Everything is my fault—nothing is yours."

"It's not a question of fault. It's human nature—yours and mine. We're just different—and not as complementary as we used to be. I don't see the tragedy—it will just take some getting used to."

His words pursued her across the room as she stood by the parlor window, studying the street lamp and only half-listening now to his contortions of logic and truth. "You know," she said when he had become silent to await the effects on her of his counterattack, "I don't think I've properly appreciated until now the superlative quality of your gift for dissembling. You are without doubt the most consummate confidence artist in the Western hemisphere—possibly the Eastern as well. You're such a habitual liar and schemer that you don't even know, yourself, when you're going into your act." She turned on him. "Three months ago I would have listened to you and accepted every word you've said and honestly believed the shortcoming was mine. But that moment is past, Harry. You really missed your calling—you'd have been masterful on the stage—but your performances can no longer fool me. Glib words are no substitute for the truth—and the truth is that you've discarded me emotionally and are using me for your financial advantage. Well, that's done, Harry—you and I are *over* with."

"Maddy, I know you're going to regret what you're—"

"I want your things out of the house by six o'clock tomorrow night—and I want you out of my life forever." The words had no trace of hysteria to them, only the chill finality of a judge pronouncing sentence. Their love had died, been slain by his mindless greed—whether he was aware of it or not. There was genuine corruption in him that she had at long last tired of explaining away. She had to distance herself from it before it consumed her as it had him.

"Very well," he said, "if that's what you really want—"

"It is."

"Then let me have your key to the club—you can keep the house."

"And the club?"

"You needn't ever set foot in it again."

"But it's half mine—that's our arrangement."

"Thanks to my generosity."

"So you say. Legally we're equal partners. We have an agreement, and if you want it to continue to operate you'll have to buy me out. And if you don't, I'm closing it down."

He was stunned, and the hairline of scar tissue on his temple seemed to throb. "Who the hell do you think you are? You're an ungrateful vicious bitch—"

"*Get out.*" She turned away and headed for the stairway. "I don't have to listen to this."

"Oh, yes, you do. You can't discard me like a piece of refuse just because you take it into your dried-up brain—yes, dried-up is what you are, my dear—because all of a sudden you decide I'm a skunk. That club is my life, whatever you think of it—or me. I've dreamed of it and worked for it and stole for it—and then out of love for you I gave you half—and a splendid house that I could just as well have done without. But none of that's enough for you because you can't possess me utterly—can't stick me under a bell jar or leash me like your little Pomeranian. But you've never given up trying. And now you want *me* to pay *you* for the privilege of getting out of your life. Fat chance."

She advanced two steps up the staircase and paused. "Without me, mister, you wouldn't have had your club. You didn't have the strength of character to persist, or the patience, or the stability. *I* gave you those things—and you've repaid me with worse than betrayal. I don't want your damned money, but I've got to have enough to live on and pay for the mortgage."

"You've got some money stashed away—who do you think you're fooling? And I'll meet the damned mortgage payments. I promise you that much."

"Your promises aren't worth dirt, Harry. You've got three days to make an acceptable offer, or I'm closing the club—and there's not a damned thing you can do to stop me."

But Harry did not come the next day to remove his things from the house. Nor was there any offer from him to buy out her interest in the club.

Plainly he thought she was bluffing in her threat to shut the place down, although no more was required under their agreement than for her to declare the partnership dissolved. No doubt he supposed her incapable of punishing him so severely; and truth to tell, she herself was uncertain of her resolve. If she wanted him out of her life, all she had to do, after all, was to separate herself from him physically and sell him her half of the club for a song. But how would she live? Her savings would dwindle rapidly, leaving nothing for the future unless he agreed to settle with her. And he could afford to—Lord knew how much he had taken out of the gambling receipts. If he chose to toss it all away on some high-stepping tart or in his other dissipations that was too bad for him, but she was entitled to live decently. So she steeled herself and prepared for the worst: if he would not be fair with her, he would have only himself to blame for his own ruin.

She went to the club the third morning following their confrontation, removed the checkbook and ledger from her office and brought them back to the house. After an hour's deliberation she hid them in the attic in the fake bottom drawer of Harry's steamer trunk, thinking he would never look there, of all places, for them. Then she returned to the club to wait for his arrival.

He showed up just before five, jaunty as ever and trading quips with the staff. She heard him ascending the stairs, two at a time and whistling a catchy new popular tune. As he bounded past her door she opened it and motioned to him to join her. "Why, my dear Madeleine," he said, "how nice to see you back with us."

"I'm not back—I've come for the last time."

"This is goodbye, then?" His tone was anything but solemn.

"I meant every word I said to you the other night."

"Oh, I'm sure you did." He sat on the corner of her desk and folded his arms across his chest. "I've been hoping, though, that you'd think better of it with the passing days."

"Nothing has changed, Harry—except my determination."

"Oh, my." He gave his head a shake. "My, oh, my."

"Don't toy with me, you arrogant bastard."

He drew a deep breath. "Must we go in for name-calling again?"

"Just pay me what you owe me, and we'll be done with it."

"I owe you nothing."

"You *owe* me more than all of it—but I'll settle for half."

"I'm not paying you anything. If you want to leave the club then leave—and I'll send Arthur to get my things from the house."

"Until you make me a satisfactory offer I'm not signing a single bank draft in the club account."

"Then we'll just have to operate on a cash basis until you come to your senses."

"There won't be enough—there's a month of bills owing plus the payroll plus the rent—plus a lot else."

"Then I guess I'll have to dip into my personal funds."

"That's fine with me—but I doubt they'll last all that long."

"In that case it would probably be cheaper if I just go to see Mr. Payson tomorrow morning and give him your precious Rachel's name and address."

"What!"

"You wouldn't like that very much, would you?"

"How in the hell do you—"

"I was writing a letter in the parlor about ten days ago, and my ink ran. I didn't want to dirty the clean blotter so I turned it over to use the reverse side, and lo and behold there was a letter beseeching you to reveal your most fervently guarded secret. Naturally, I considered it a most confidential matter—and would never dream of using it against you—except in the most extreme circumstances—"

"You're despicable."

"—which these appear to be."

"I can't believe that even you—"

"If it's you or me, Maddy—yes, even you—I'll do what I have to do."

Her mind was churning. "You really would stoop to anything, wouldn't you? But in this case it won't do you any good. As it happens I've already met with Mr. Payson—"

"No, you haven't."

"Oh, but I have—"

"You can't bluff me, Maddy—bluffing is my business, remember? Telling Corwin about Rachel is the last thing on earth you want to do."

"I—you don't know everything that's—"

"I know you're lying through your teeth."

Her lips pinched tight with frustration. "Well, you're wrong."

"Am I? Then I'm sure Mr. Payson will advise me to that effect when I show up at twenty-six Broadway in the morning."

Her right hand reached out for the glass paperweight on the desk in front of her, and her fingers flexed over its smooth hemispheric surface. For an instant she considered leaping up and bringing the object crashing down on his head. Instead, she said with venom in her throat, "You breathe a word about Rachel to anyone, and I swear, Harry, as God is my witness, I'll go to the authorities and tell them everything I know about you. They'll lock you up and throw away the key."

"And who was my faithful accomplice during all those dastardly adventures? Who used her passkey for me, who lied for me, who fronted for me—and who benefited so much from the results of those thrilling pursuits? Whose diamond bracelet is still there in the little red tin on the pantry shelf—I saw it there the other day. Who has a house of her own from that filthy lucre—and all those lovely clothes—and a maid and lives like an authentic lady? You so much as peep to the law, and you'll wind up in the cell next to mine, my darling."

Less to inflict a wound on Harry than to win the daughter she could not till then proclaim her own, Maddy wrote to the attorney to say she was prepared to disclose the information he wanted from her.

The cost of so doing, of course, was that she could no longer exact her vengeance on Russell Corwin. But that loss was almost precisely balanced in her mind by the gain she would realize in removing from Harry Loring's hands the one weapon with which he could still harm her. Tipping the scales decisively, though, toward giving in to Russell was her abiding stake in the girl. And Rachel had made it plain that Maddy could not have her, that she would not move into her mother's house, unless she was told the whole story of her birth, most emphatically including the name and nature of the man who had fathered and then abandoned her. "You must trust me, Maddy," she said, sensing her mother's fear that on discovering her father's identity she would seek him out and, quite possibly, cling to him. "I understand what you must have gone through bearing a child all alone. But I've loved you from the moment I set eyes on you—and nothing will change that."

She considered fabricating a father to satisfy Rachel's curiosity while still denying Russell the satisfaction of meeting his daughter now in the full bloom of her womanhood. How would Rachel ever be the wiser if told the man who fathered her vanished without a trace? But Maddy did not have it in her, after so many years of estrangement from the girl, to deny her the truth. Nor would a lie have countered Harry's threat against her. Nor would it have gained her the use of whatever money Russell had offered to break her silence. Briefly she weighed the idea of negotiating with Mr. Payson for the maximum price he had been authorized to pay. But that notion was as unseemly as the one of deceiving her own daughter. And so after gathering up various documents that pertained to the complex transaction she had in mind, she appeared at the lawyer's office just off Bowling Green two minutes before nine on the designated morning. The rest of her life, she felt certain, was hanging on the outcome of the interview.

Mr. Payson's appearance and manner hinted at the highest rectitude.

His hair was snow-white and abundant, his suit spotlessly black and without a wrinkle, his rectangular face impassive yet not indifferent, his voice mellow and Olympian. "You are not a woman easy to persuade, Mrs. Memory," he said, taking her hand.

"You must understand the sensitive nature of the information you wish, Mr. Payson."

"If I did not, madam, the silence with which you greeted my earlier initiatives has corrected the failing. But please be assured I have understood from the start."

She clasped her hands on her lap and waited for the attorney to broach the question that had brought her there. But he was too astute to rush to it. A brief, anxious silence lasted until she broke it. "And what, if I may ask, is the nature of Mr. Corwin's illness?"

"You may ask, madam, but I am not at liberty to discuss it."

"Then perhaps I've come under false pretenses."

"You may believe whatever you wish, Mrs. Memory. My instructions, though, are quite clear, and I cannot veer from them."

"Of course. At any rate, I want it understood by Mr. Corwin that I have not been swayed by any consideration for him—only for the girl. And certainly not in the least by the financial arrangement your letter mentioned."

"I understand, madam."

"And you'll convey that?"

"As you've stated it."

There was nothing left then but for her to pronounce Rachel's name. She said it softly yet precisely. Mr. Payson wrote it down without expression. Nothing could have been more matter-of-fact or less ceremonial. But the moment the words left her lips she felt lightened, airborne nearly. Perhaps it was due to a certain astringent quality about the attorney, midway between the ministerial and the surgical, that she experienced so immediate a sense of being cleansed, shriven. The secret she had clutched to herself with such tenacity for so many years was at last exposed to the sunlight; a great weight was lifted from between her shoulders.

"And where," asked Payson, "can Mrs. Caldwell be reached—in the event Mr. Corwin chooses to do so?"

"Where? I believe she intends changing her residence very shortly—in the next several days, perhaps."

"Would you know the new address?"

"Yes—care of my own."

The attorney's face lost a bit of its repose. "Your daughter will be living with you?"

"Yes. Is there something wrong with that?"

"Not in the least, madam. It's only that—well, Mr. Corwin might well fear that you would interpose yourself between him and Mrs. Caldwell should he choose to address any correspondence to her—if you will forgive my stating it so directly."

"That is not my nature, Mr. Payson. And if I were not prepared for the two of them to communicate I should not have appeared in your office, sir, you may rest assured."

"I meant no insult, madam. I was merely anticipating what might—"

"Yes, of course."

The attorney reached into his top desk drawer, withdrew an envelope and passed it into Maddy's hand. "As per my instructions, madam."

"Thank you," she said, and placed it still sealed inside her purse.

"Forgive me, Mrs. Memory, but don't you wish to examine the contents?"

"Not just now."

"Perhaps if there is some question—"

"As I said, the money is beside the point."

"Quite." Payson knitted his fingers together for a moment. "Still, I'm obliged to inform you that the envelope contains a bank draft in the amount of ten thousand dollars."

Her heart jumped. A small fortune. Enough to meet the mortgage payments for some years to come. To assure a fine roof over her own and her daughter's and her grandchildren's heads . . . "I see," she said, revealing no emotion over the size of the number. "And why are you obliged to do so?"

"Mr. Corwin wished to know your response."

She smiled inwardly. "I suggest you advise Mr. Corwin that you were unable to elicit one."

"As you wish, madam."

"And now, Mr. Payson, if there is nothing else you need—"

"Nothing at all, madam," he said, rising.

"Then I require a few additional moments of your time." She reached into her purse for the small packet of documents she had prepared. "I should like to retain your services in connection with an entirely unrelated matter, if you would be willing."

The attorney resumed his seat.

The moments mounted to well over an hour. At the end it was settled that the attorney would immediately direct a letter to Mr. Loring, noting under the terms of his partnership agreement with Mrs. Memory that in the event of an irreconcilable disagreement between them, either party could buy out the other at a fair price or, that failing, the partnership was dissolved. Since Mr. Loring had declined to tender such an offer and Mrs. Memory had no inclination, let alone the means, to do so, the Palm Beach Club would, accordingly, enter a state of suspended operation one week hence, pending an accord between the parties on an equitable distribution of assets. If such an accord was not reached within seven calendar days thereafter, the partnership would be null and void, the club shut and its liabilities discharged. Of the latter, by far the largest was the settlement of a loan from Mr. Henry Flagler, who had advanced a substantial sum to Mr. Loring for the establishment of said club. Absent sufficient assets to retire said loan, all the club's furnishings, equipment and supplies, its lease and its current cash balance at the Corn Exchange Bank would be delivered into the hands of Lionel Teasdale, Esq., counsel to Mr. Flagler, in lieu of any further claims against said club. In consideration of Mr. Loring's acquiescence to said transfer of assets, Mrs. Memory agreed not to bring suit against him to compel the return of certain funds that were removed from the club premises without her knowledge or permission. Resumption of the club's operation would be solely at the discretion of Mr. Flagler, Mr. Loring being free to resume whatever sort of life he chose, excepting only that his services could not be retained by any future proprietor of said club for a period of five years—and that he make no effort to see Mrs. Memory in person for the same period, dealing with her if necessary through the below named counsel.

"The letter will be delivered by hand first thing in the morning, madam," Mr. Payson said, bowing a farewell.

"Please come in, Arthur." She opened the door wide. Her first thought was that he had come to collect Harry's things.

"Miz Mem'ry—" The strapping young man took one step forward and paused on the threshold. "I'm real sorry to bother you, ma'am, but I think you better come quick to the club."

"What is it, Arthur?"

"It's Mr. Loring, ma'am—I never seen him like this."

His wide-eyed concern was contagious. "Like what, Arthur?"

"He's all weepy and woebegone—stays locked up there in his office an' all—won't talk 'cept to say it's your fault, ma'am, and you gonna shut down the club 'cause you angry with him for nothin'."

"I'm angry at him, all right, Arthur, but it's not for nothing—it's for good and plenty. And if the club closes it's more his doing than mine."

He dropped his head. "Yes, ma'am."

"Did he send you for me?"

"No, ma'am—Mr. Walters and the chef, they sent me. They're plenty worried—an' nobody's been paid yet this week. An' when they tell Mr. Loring that, he says you s'posed to do the payin'."

She heard the great gasping sobs above from the second-floor landing. He was either having a severe breakdown or putting on a masterful performance for her benefit. But the sound was wrenched out of him so convulsively that it was impossible for her to believe even he could manage such a sham. And from the looks on the faces of the staff members who gathered behind her as she started her ascent they were persuaded of the authenticity of Harry's upset. On the other hand, if he had been poisoning them all against her they might be serving as unwitting collaborators in his ploy.

She rapped lightly on his door; the sounds inside abruptly ceased. No invitation to enter followed, though, and she tapped a second time. "It's me, Harry—may I come in?"

"No."

"Why not?"

"Your lawyer's done your talking for you—there's nothing more to say. Just go the hell away."

"Is that what you really want?"

There was no response.

"Harry?"

"Harry's dead—you've killed him."

She sighed wearily. "He sounds like a pretty lively corpse."

No comeback. Then, ever so faintly, the sound of fresh crying.

"Harry—let me in."

After a long moment she heard him unlatch the door but not open it. Slowly she turned the knob and eased back the door a few inches. The scene took her breath away. The floor was littered with newspapers, magazines, letters, envelopes, gambling chips and dollar bills in assorted denominations. The lamp on his desk lay shattered on its side and the rest of the surface was piled with food-encrusted dishes, a half-dozen partially emptied liquor bottles, upright and overturned glasses and his heaped evening clothes. The only light in the room filtered in through a slit between the curtains. By it she could make out his form lying face down on the Chesterfield divan and wearing only his union suit. His face, she could tell from the side of it exposed toward her, was grizzled with a three-day growth of beard.

She stepped gingerly over the debris, watching the slow, rhythmic rise and fall of his shoulder blades. After several moments of contemplating his unbathed and unkempt condition, she said quietly, "There's no point in your carrying on this way."

"What way?"

"Like—this."

"I'm not carrying on," he said, swiveling his head to glance upward. "I'm lying down—can't you see that?"

His voice was husky, his eyes vacant. "I—Harry, is something really the matter with you, or is this—business—supposed to break my heart?"

No answer. Finally he asked, "What do you want from me, Maddy?"

"Only what I'm owed."

"I've given you whatever I have to give. You're trying to bleed me to death."

"You know that's not true."

"This is so unlike you, Maddy. You've never been cruel before. You seem—to be relishing my pain."

"Harry, I'm only doing what you're forcing me to. I have to live, too."

"By ruining me? By taking away the one thing I've spent my whole life hoping for and finally getting? And now out of misguided hatred you're—" Real tears seeped from him, flushing grime from his smeared face. He wore a shattered look in the half-light. "Would it help any if I said—I'm sorry? I never meant you harm." He got himself upright and circled his arms around her waist, his head touching her breasts. "Maddy—don't do this to me. Please—"

If there was anything worse than Harry railing at her in self-defense, it was to see him this way—pitiable, pathetic, bearing no resemblance to the masterful, debonaire companion she had so long adored. He had been reduced to a shadow. Was the transformation as much her doing as his? The question stabbed at her. Why had he never before shown her such emotional fragility? Had she mistakenly gauged him as invulnerable to her disapproval, or was it merely that she had not ever had him at such a disadvantage and pressed it to the hilt?

"Harry," she said, her hands involuntarily fondling the nape of his neck, "will you behave yourself if I—just—get out of it?"

His head rubbed up and down against her.

"All right, then. If you'll agree in writing to meet all the mortgage payments on the house I'll forget about everything else," she said.

His head rested against her so still that she was uncertain whether he had heard or understood her. Then it began to bob gently, pressing on her in soft heavy sobs, continuing until she felt her blouse grow warm and moist from him. She stroked his unruly hair till finally his head lay still again. Then he asked in words muffled by her bodice, "Will you still be my partner?"

"I wasn't cut out for the gambling business."

"I need you, Maddy."

But I no longer need you, Harry, she thought, especially not the pain you keep inflicting. And thinking it, she could at least spare him hearing it aloud.

Mr. Walters appeared on her doorstep several mornings later, all dressed up but looking thoroughly dejected. "Forgive me for coming without an appointment, Mrs. Memory," he said, "but things have taken rather a dismal turn at the club."

Harry had dismissed him the previous evening, Mr. Walters revealed as soon as she had seated him in the parlor and asked Ruby Lee to bring them coffee.

"Oh, my," said Maddy. "Over something unpleasant, I take it."

"Over you, madam. I had the temerity to mention to Monsieur Pinay that I thought Mr. Loring had acted in a shabby fashion toward you—perhaps it was none of my business and I shouldn't have spoken, but it was my heartfelt feeling—and at any rate, Raoul mentioned it to Chef Josef and so forth and so on till word somehow got back to Mr. Loring. He pulled me into his office—quite literally by the scruff of the neck—and called me disloyal and then told me to leave."

"Your solicitude is most appreciated, Mr. Walters, but I'm saddened that you should have become the victim of a purely private quarrel."

"That's just the point, though, madam. The situation between you has affected us all at the club. The truth is that without your involvement, it's uncertain that the business can continue. Mr. Loring is—he seems to be acting in most erratic ways—uncontrollable, one might say." Harry, Mr. Walters said, was snapping at the dealers and croupiers for the most minor irregularities, had yelled—actually yelled—at his tempermental chef in front of the kitchen staff about a slightly charred chateaubriand served to a prominent customer and flaunted his relationship with Miss Geiger, whom he had reintroduced to the premises and placed in charge of the entertainment. Bills and salaries, meanwhile, were going unpaid, and worst of all, Harry was drinking—with devastating effects. "Two nights ago, I am forced to tell you, madam, after the customers had gone," Mr. Walters added, his unhappiness growing with each revelation, "Mr. Loring was rather badly off and was boasting in most unattractive language of how he had, well, taken you in and gotten you to relent with an appeal to your sympathies, crying like a baby in your presence, I believe, with the help of some pepper or foreign substance that he'd rubbed into his eyes, and similar carryings-on that apparently convinced you to—"

"Thank you, Mr. Walters. I don't need to hear more."

She presented herself to Mr. Payson the following morning. She had let Harry work at her heartstrings once again, had actually convinced herself that she could achieve her purpose of professional and emotional separation from him without, as he put it, destroying him. It was not, as he had said, her nature to act cruelly, to devise stratagems to do in those who had dealt unkindly with her, but Harry could not resist his own worst impulses, had pressed his luck once too often and succeeded in making an utter fool of her. It really was the last straw.

The arrangements were completed expeditiously through the two attorneys. All the club's assets were turned over to Mr. Teasdale, who thereupon canceled Harry's debt to Flagler and sold the club, lock, stock and wine barrels, to a newly formed partnership consisting of Mr. Walters, Monsieur Pinay, Chef Josef and his brother. Henceforth, the Palm Beach Club was to operate as a deluxe restaurant featuring refined entertainment—no more dancing Bouquet of Sweetheart Roses. Chef Josef and Mr. Walters were to reside in apartments on the third and fourth floors. And Harry—Harry was out in the cold, having escaped without Maddy's suing the pants off him for what he had pocketed.

"I feel real bad, ma'am, how things turned out so—" He shook his head sorrowfully, unable to say the rest.

"I know, Arthur." She placed an appreciative hand on his arm. "Thank you for saying so." She took a breath and then directed him to the stairway. "Mr. Loring's valises are set aside for you in the attic. You'll see them together on the right side. And I've left open the dresser drawers and closet doors where all his clothes are."

"Yes, ma'am."

"If you need my help just ask. But I'd rather you attend to—"

"Yes, ma'am." Arthur reached into his inside jacket pocket. "Mr. Loring asked me to give you this."

She waited until Arthur was midway up the stairs before she tore open the large envelope. It contained a single sheet of notepaper attached to a familiar-looking gray folder. The note said:

Dear Maddy,

The deed is done. I hope you are satisfied.

I wish to add only that I consider your position regarding our mutual friend Flagler to be naive in the extreme. The man has made millions in ways that were in many, if not most, cases unwholesome, to say the least. You should have had no compunctions about a debt of honor to such an exploiter of humanity. You and I were simply members of the victimized portion of society who were able to rise above our assigned places. I regret that you do not choose to share my perspective.

It gives me no pleasure whatever to attach a report I had commissioned by the Pinkerton agency. I do so solely in the hope that, having erred gravely in the assessment of my character, you do not compound the mistake by miscalculating that of your Boston friend.

I leave for England tomorrow. Arthur will accompany me. If you need to reach me for any reason, the Thalia Club will forward my mail. I sincerely hope you find happiness in the rest of your life and pray that you may someday search into your heart and discover which of us is truly the wronged party.

Harrison St. John Loring

The scrollwork under his name was excessive, she decided, considering the nature of the letter, as was the formality in his use of all three names. Plain "Harry" would have served. But his excesses were no longer her concern, she told herself. He would swim or sink without her.

She opened the Pinkerton folder with a rush of apprehension. Its subject, said the report, was Evelyn Newell Forbes. Odd that he had never mentioned his androgynous first name, though she could hardly blame him for having dropped it. The omission, however, proved the least damaging item as her eye skimmed over the two-page indictment. The subject was born, it said, in Boston, attended the Latin Grammar school there and began working for the Penibel Piano Company of Quincy as a salesman and demonstrator. "Although the subject frequently claims that he is a graduate of Harvard University, records there fail to substantiate that any such individual was ever in attendance . . . At age twenty-seven subject married Edith Whitehall . . . children Mary and Peter . . . employed by the Aroostook Paper Company in various capacities from 1879 to 1900 when he was dismissed for reasons unknown. Divorced February 1897 by Edith Whitehall Forbes on the grounds of adultery and naming as corespondents Mrs. Marlene Newfield, Mrs. Iris Untermann, Miss Edith Watson and Mrs. Catherine Spain; uncontested. "Subject appears to derive a living by enticing women best described as 'past the bloom of youth' to turn over a portion of their assets to him in return for certain favors and services of an intimate nature. He generally encounters these women on-board ships and at resorts, wherever widows or single women of means are likely to congregate."

Men.

The whole interior of her being ached, but she had no tears left. Her own sixth sense had steered her away from greater receptivity to Newell's professions of ardor. She had told him that he knew her too little to be so fixed on her, but it was she, of course, who suffered the ignorance. Mrs. Memory she was, and Mrs. Memory, it seemed, she would remain.

Arthur began clattering down the stairs with Harry's belongings. It would take him several trips to carry them all out to the wagon he had parked in front of the house. As he went methodically about the task she hurried to her desk and drew out a sheet of stationery.

> Harry,
>
> You were the one who taught me that a gentleman never welshes on a debt. Whatever Flagler is or isn't did not alter our obligation to him, in my view, and I acted accordingly. If you wish to remain a gentleman in my eyes, whatever else you are or aren't, you must not blame me for my action.
>
> I am in your debt with regard to N.—you see, I cannot even commit his name to paper—and in many other ways. Yet I believe the debt has been more than amply repaid. I wish you health, happiness and a modicum of remorse with regard to the outcome of our friendship and remain
>
> Yours sincerely,
> Madeleine

When Arthur was done she gave him the note for transmittal to his employer. "There's something else," she said, reaching into her desk and withdrawing her once favorite item of jewelry. The string of amethyst and rose-quartz beads had lately become a painful reminder to her of a long chapter in her life from which she earnestly wished now to insulate herself. "I'd like your mother to have these as a gift from me—if you think she'd like them—along with my fondest regards."

His eyes widened and clouded. "She'd surely 'preciate them, ma'am," Arthur said, enclosing them in his large brown hand.

She opened the door for him, and just as he was about to go through, she reached up and gently pulled his head down far enough for her to kiss him on the cheek. Then she closed the door and watched out the window as he drove off.

Harry Loring, she did not doubt, had passed out of her life forever.

*   *   *

It was four weeks to the day since Rachel and the children had left for Paris, and she had had nothing more from the girl than a postal card from Cherbourg, saying that the crossing was mild and they were all safe and sound.

The absence of correspondence was doubly troubling because Rachel knew of Maddy's profound apprehension over her month-long visit with her lately discovered father and had promised to write her all the news regularly. If Maddy could have prevented the trip without seriously endangering her precious but still fragile relationship with Rachel she would have done so, but the girl was determined—and, Maddy consoled herself, understandably so. She was driven, in the first place, by a mounting curiosity to meet the man who had fathered her—a primal urge that needed no defending. Then there was the matter of Russell's illness; the man might be on his deathbed, and if she did not see him promptly it might well be too late. Finally, he had sent the money for their transatlantic passage, along with assurances that she and the children would be comfortably provided for at the Corwins' home in Paris. How in good conscience, Maddy asked herself, could she have posed an obstacle to the visit? "The children and I will be fine," Rachel had reassured her. "We're a strong, healthy lot, I've already been to Paris four times, I know the language adequately—there's nothing at all for you to worry about." She kissed her mother on the cheek. "Still, you're a dear to concern yourself so."

But she had been unable to voice her gravest fear: that the girl would allow herself to be seduced by her father into accepting a life of luxury that he could provide for her, of the sort to which she had grown accustomed during her whole life until the severe troubles with Eddie had begun. Maddy was just getting to know the girl, to understand her turns of mind and mood, to engage her opinions and character. And now Russell was calling her away. How easy it would be for him to suggest that Rachel stay on in Paris another week or two when the planned visit had expired, and the weeks would become months, and the months years, and Rachel would be lost to her forever. Surely, though, the girl could not be so heartless. Her abandonment of her mother could never be so abrupt. Even if it were to prove a more nuanced thing, the thought of it was almost more than Maddy could bear. And Russell had so many material enticements to offer. His Parisian home was no doubt large and lovely, and they probably had another in the country—so good for the children, of course. There had to be a small regiment of servants to look after their every need, and beautiful, expensive clothes would be lavished on them, and excursions to the theater and opera. All kinds of things Rachel had grown up with and come to expect as her due—and now had no prospect of regaining. Because what could her mother offer her beyond emotional sustenance? A house that was modest, for all its charms; a naive and ignorant young woman in Ruby Lee to serve as the children's nanny, sometime cook and maid-of-all-work; and a life of genteel but decidedly reduced circumstances that Maddy would have to scrimp to maintain. Why shouldn't Rachel be drawn to an accommodating father who could afford to spare no expense in the winning away of a daughter he had once abandoned and in the cosseting of grandchildren he had never hoped to know?

When no further word reached her from Paris, Maddy grew more frantic with each passing day. She made up all sorts of excuses to quiet her fears. Perhaps Russell's health had taken a turn for the worse, and in the shadow of death Rachel had forgotten her promise to her mother. Or maybe one of the children had become sick and Rachel was so caught up with the nursing and fatigued from worry that Maddy had slipped her mind. Or possibly the problem was not health at all but Russell's designs on Rachel: he might have instructed the servants to intercept her letters to New York, thereby leaving her emotionally marooned. Was that too farfetched? Yes . . . more likely the whole thing was attributable to unreliable postal service. *Any* explanation was better than the one she feared most: that Rachel had indeed found her father so beguiling, and Thérèse so loving and *sympathetique,* that she wished to remain with them in Paris to enjoy the good life and had simply not steeled herself to writing Maddy to that effect.

Bathed in such morose thoughts, Maddy dimly heard the front doorbell ring. Her gloom momentarily caused her to forget that Ruby Lee was upstairs diligently treadling away at the sewing machine and out of earshot. When the bell rang again several times in succession, as if the caller were impatient, Maddy stirred to life. Probably it was a salesman, one of those young, jaunty fellows working his way through barber college or some other institution and needing his commission on whatever worthless trinket he was peddling. In no mood to be charitable, she would quickly send him on his way.

She opened the door abruptly. "Yes?"

It was Rachel, with Billy and several valises at her sides and a squirming Amanda in her arms. "I left my key home," she said, all smiles, "or we'd have barged right in."

"But how—? Why didn't you—" Maddy was speechless with joy.

"I know—I should have written or cabled but everything was so—well, it's a long story. Let me get the children settled and I'll tell you everything."

"Ruby Lee!" Maddy called over her shoulder, unburdening Rachel of Amanda, kissing them both vigorously and kneeling to include Billy in her overflowing welcome. The maid was swiftly dispatched to the drugstore on Lexington Avenue for a pint of vanilla ice cream while Maddy scurried about the kitchen, fixing jam sandwiches and milk for the children and watching them consume their mid-afternoon snacks with only minimal disfigurement to the spotless oak floor. On her return, Ruby Lee relieved Rachel of her charges, who proceeded to beat their ice cream to death with spoons and help it melt down to soup. Maddy used the opportunity to lead Rachel off into the parlor.

"In the first place, he lied to me," Rachel began. Russell Corwin was no more on his deathbed than President Teddy Roosevelt was at the moment, and other than a touch of the gout his health appeared in no way to be flagging. It was his wife who had been ailing for some time—a problem with one or several of her internal organs that had left her bedridden and testy—so Russell could not have left her home alone while he made an extended trip to New York to become acquainted with his illegitimate daughter. Even if he had been so disposed, Thérèse would not have permitted it. She kept her husband on a very short leash with a very large allowance, and so, not surprisingly, what Thérèse wanted, Thérèse got. "He had the decency, at least, to apologize for misleading me," Rachel added, "but frankly he felt I wouldn't have come otherwise. I know, a lie is a lie, but I felt sorry for him—for having to resort to such trickery. He's not a strong person—his wife thoroughly dominates him." The very fact, Rachel said, that he had reached out to her at all had caused a rift between the couple. Thérèse saw no reason whatever why Russell should have harbored a sentimental attachment to *la bâtarde,* as she had taken to calling his daughter, according to one of the household servants whom Rachel had befriended shortly after her arrival. And the invalid woman found Billy and Amanda, with their messes, their curious probing fingers, their cries and giggles and all their galloping exuberance, to be noisome in the extreme. "She told Russell they were little American savages."

Maddy shook her head. "I feel sorrier for her than for him—she couldn't have any children of her own so she naturally resented you and yours."

"But that was no reason to detest us so vocally. She'd scream at Billy and Amanda from her bedroom every time they made the least little

sound—and you know it's impossible to keep children at this age absolutely quiet."

"So I've seen," Maddy said with a delighted smile.

After twelve days of constantly hushing the children, taking her dinner on a tray next to Russell's at Thérèse's bedside, then talking with
him far into the night after his wife had retired only to wake up at
dawn with the children, Rachel was thoroughly exhausted. "And I was
too depressed to write and tell you it all." She announced to Russell
that she did not feel welcome under the same roof with Thérèse and
booked passage home, reaching the ship only minutes before its departure, with Amanda clutched to her bosom and practically yanking
Billy's little arm off in her haste to make it up the gangplank. "The
whole thing was a disaster—"

"I'm so sorry for you, darling."

"—but I don't think it was a mistake. I had to go, Maddy."

"I know."

"He's pitiable. And yet I don't dislike him."

"Well, I suppose that's only natural since you've had no—"

"Maddy, he's offered to support me and the children."

"What?"

"Yes—and you, too, if you choose not to marry."

"I see."

She saw Maddy's eyes close and her features tighten. "Oh, I know
exactly how you feel, but that doesn't make him any less sincere. As soon
as he heard what happened to me with Eddie—and the Caldwells—and
the van Ruysdales—and you—he said he felt responsible—at least
partly—and wanted to atone for it. And as I could easily see, he said, there
was no question of his being able to afford it."

Maddy fought to keep down what she was feeling. "And what did you
tell him?"

"That I'd think about it and discuss it with you—and then write him
what we've decided."

"We? No, it's your decision, Rachel. I won't have anything more to do
with the man. And it's not even his money—it's that woman's."

"Does that make a difference?"

"Not in the least."

"Then why shouldn't we accept it? He's neglected us for all these years,
and if his conscience bothers him why not let him assuage it? I'd say he
owes it to us."

She took Rachel's hand and clasped it tight. "And I say, my darling
girl, there are some things in this life that can't be purchased—at any

price. You may do as you wish—you have your own and the children's well-being to consider far ahead of anything else."

"Maddy, I'd never do anything to hurt you."

"Then the subject is closed."

Actually, it was not. After the children were tucked away that evening, Rachel begged her mother's forgiveness for raising the topic again. "Oh, Maddy, I feel—I keep wondering—if you haven't shut your mind to reality just to spite Russell. I can understand your feelings toward him, I truly can. But I don't see the point of refusing even to consider his proposition."

"I don't want to see him buy your affections."

"Or your forgiveness?"

"I think that's less likely."

"Then you're underestimating me, Mother."

Rachel had not called her that before. The word melted her. "I'm not, darling. Our grievances toward him are quite different, though."

"But what do you gain by denying him the chance to do penance?"

She had asked herself the same question over and over. It was one thing to have taken his money in exchange for yielding up Rachel's identity to him—if she hadn't, Harry would very likely have carried out his threat to make the disclosure; nothing at all would have been gained that way, she reasoned, and the ten thousand dollars had been put to good use. Now, though, the circumstances were not beyond her control, and by her refusal she would strip Russell of his chief weapon against her. But she could not expect the girl to appreciate the delicate circumstances surrounding the earlier transaction—to understand why her mother had revealed her name and whereabouts to her father only for a steep price. Or to see the distinction between that admittedly rather tawdry bargain and the continued acceptance of his guilt-money. The former was unavoidable; the latter, reprehensible. "I suppose I save my pride," she told Rachel, "and perhaps help strengthen yours."

"At the cost of security and comfort for all of us."

"We'll do all right. I have something put by."

"But how long will it last? It's going to be costly to maintain a home for four. I can't bear the thought of our draining you."

"I can work again—I still have my health, and credentials."

"I won't have that, not at your age. You've worked hard and long enough—you need to preserve your strength."

"I'm not made of gossamer."

"I need you, Maddy—Mother. If anyone is to go to work it should be me. I'm young and strong and—"

"And your children need *you*. What's more, you've never worked a day in your life. What kind of position do you think you could possibly get? You've no training, no experience. If you found anything it would pay a pittance."

Rachel nodded at Maddy's undeniable assessment. "Well, then," she said, after thinking for a moment, "perhaps you could sell the house and we could take a flat and bank the profit and—and have that much more to sustain us until I might be free to—"

"No." Maddy's eyes roved about the parlor. "I love this house. It's the only thing of value I've ever owned. And it's spacious enough for raising a family—*my* family." She patted Rachel's knee. "There are lots of hotels in this city, and all of them are in need of competent head housekeepers. I'm sure I'll find something suitable—for a few years, anyway—and by that time there'll be enough for us to manage on decently."

"Maddy, it's not fair to you."

"I couldn't think of a fairer thing on the whole earth," she said and kissed the girl's forehead. "Now you go along to bed. You've had an ordeal."

The *Times* joined the pile of newspapers at her feet. For some reason there had been few advertisements that day for hotel housekeepers, and all of those were for small places unlikely to offer her a wage commensurate with her experience. Only the *Examiner* was left. She lifted it off her lap with a sigh that turned into a gasp of alarm as a heavy thump upstairs was followed by shrieks. Was that Billy or Amanda? She hadn't yet learned to distinguish the children's voices at that distance. "What is it?" she called out.

"Amanda tripped," came the faint reply. "She'll be fine."

Good Lord. There was always something percussive in the air with the two of them around. Amanda, so seemingly placid and pleasant, had not yet mastered the dignified art of walking and was forever running, little creased legs churning mightily, to keep up with her faster, more nimble brother. Billy, whose head was just high enough to clear most tables, was fascinated by small objects and constantly removed them for detailed examination. When, as frequently happened, the delicate things could not withstand the strain of his intensive (not to mention sticky-fingered) scrutiny, Maddy learned finally to exile all the bric-a-brac to high shelves beyond reach of the insatiably curious child. Rachel, her mother discovered, was not fond of saying "no" to either of her offspring.

She opened the *Examiner* to the "wants." Ahh—there were two for housekeepers. The first was for the head position at the Hiawatha Hotel on West Forty-third, a new place, Maddy supposed, never having heard of it. And the Buckingham needed an assistant housekeeper. Now wouldn't that be irony? It was just over ten years since she had worked there in the same capacity and would likely have succeeded to the top position if Miss Armbruster had prevailed on her to accept the year-round burden. Possibly Mr. Chambers was still the manager—he had held a high opinion of her and might be favorably inclined. So long as she was prepared to return to work, at least for the time being, it would be lovely to be among some familiar faces. She'd get herself over there first thing in the morning . . .

The Buckingham desk clerk, a man she did not know but who seemed gravely affronted by her use of the front door rather than the employees' entrance, advised her that Mr. Chambers was indeed still the manager but would not be available until noon to interview candidates for the housekeeping position. She was free to await him in the lobby, the clerk added frostily, so long as she did not occupy a chair needed for the comfort of the hotel guests.

She had better use of her time than to cool her heels for three hours. Besides, the Hiawatha job was likely to pay better. She walked in no great hurry to the address and glanced up at its ornate facade. The size was just right—perhaps one hundred rooms; it wasn't tall or wide enough for more. But what about the accommodations? She did not wish to associate herself with a tawdry establishment, not after all this time.

The furnishings in the lobby turned out to be overly embellished; perhaps the management had elected to turn it into a showplace but skimped on the rooms themselves. She would see. Her wait was brief; the manager was on hand and interviewing. He was hardly intimidating. The fellow did not look a day older than Rachel. It was hard for her to believe he had had much experience in the lodgings field. Perhaps his father owned the place. He was a polite enough young man who treated her deferentially. After singing the praises of the hotel, which was in its maiden season and had unfortunately lost its housekeeper to illness, he listened attentively as she detailed her professional background and assured him that any of her former employers would gladly supply letters of reference.

"I have no doubt of it, madam. Perhaps if you had brought along one or two—"

"Oh. Yes, well—I'm afraid I've only just decided to return to work. I could obtain them soon enough, I think."

"No need just yet. I wonder, though, if you'd find it impertinent of me to ask your age, madam."

"I—yes—but is that highly pertinent?"

"I think so. The position is arduous."

"My health is very good."

"I'm sure. Still and all, it would be useful if—"

"I am in my forties."

"I don't mean to put too fine a point on it, madam, but how far into your forties have you—progressed?"

"I'm—forty-seven."

"I see."

"As I say, I'm well and have very rarely been sick—"

"Frankly, though, Mrs. Memory, the position of head housekeeper requires someone who is alert and active every minute on the job."

"I'd surely be able to—"

"I don't believe a woman of your age could manage to withstand the constant physical demands that the position would make on her. It's nothing at all personal, madam."

"But I assure you—"

"Thank you for coming by."

Did she actually look as decrepit as all that? She glanced at her reflection in a shop window. So there was gray in her hair—what of it? Lots of people began to go gray in their thirties, some even in their twenties. Her face bore relatively few lines, except for the ones webbing the corners of her eyes and the faint suggestion of several between her eyebrows. The skin beneath her chin was still taut. It was not fair to judge her arbitrarily by the calendar. The Buckingham was a better bet, anyway. Perhaps the assistant's position would be less draining on her. At any rate Mr. Chambers would remember the kind of worker she had been; besides, being older than she, he would be more inclined to value her age than to scorn it.

The manager of the Buckingham proved every bit as delighted at the sight of her as she had hoped. It pleased him to learn that she had retained a social relationship with the former Miss Armbruster—"It's very like a family connection," he said, "this little establishment of ours"—and that she had encountered no difficulties as housekeeper at so grand a hostelry as the Royal Poinciana was said to be. "But mightn't you find it a bit of a—what shall we say?—a comedown to resume your former position at a small place like ours?"

"I shouldn't think so."

"But you're so eminently qualified for a supervisory position."

"Yes, but I think a lesser rank might be well suited to my—current disposition."

"Something a bit less taxing, perhaps?"

"I don't mean to say that I'm not entirely up to—"

"No, of course." Mr. Chambers examined a sheet of paper on his desktop. "Well, I'm not sure we could meet your financial needs. The salary has been set with a somewhat less experienced person in mind."

"My needs are not excessive, sir, and I have scaled my expectations accordingly, although of course I should need a certain—"

"Let's leave that until the end, shall we? The fact is that I could not possibly find a better qualified candidate for the position. The only step that remains is for you to pass muster with our present head housekeeper. Normally that would present no problem for you whatever, but she is a most particular woman when it comes to her assistants and we've had to let go a few people who didn't measure up to her standards."

"Mmm, she sounds formidable."

"But I'm confident that your wonderful record—and my spirited endorsement—will carry a good deal of weight with Miss Sanderson."

"Sanderson?" She felt herself grow suddenly queasy. "Not, by any chance, Bettina Sanderson?"

"Why, yes—the very one. You know her? Why, of course—what's the matter with me? She used to work at the Royal Poinciana as the first assistant housekeeper, wasn't it? Well, this would be turning the tables a bit but I shouldn't think that would in any way—"

"You're most kind, sir," she said, rising, "but I don't think it would be wise for me to submit myself to her."

"Why, is there anything I should know about her? She's too finicky by half, but otherwise she's an exemplary—"

"If she retains your confidence I'll say nothing to undermine it. It was grand to see you again. I'm grateful for your courtesy."

There were plenty of other jobs in the city. She drew herself up to her full height and walked as majestically as she knew how through the lobby, past the supercilious deskman and out the front door. Once on the sidewalk, she relaxed her posture. Her back was beginning to ache again. A sure omen that it would rain the next day.

She had a bite at a nearby tea shop, lingering longer than she realized, and then resumed her search for suitable employment at the two remaining places on her list. At the first, she was too late—the position had been filled an hour earlier; at the second, the line of applicants was too long to justify the wait. She went home, subdued and weary, and took a long nap before supper.

She unfolded the *Tribune* impatiently. The "wants" in the *World,* the *Herald* and the *Times* had yielded nothing. No hotel worth its salt seemed in need of a housekeeper these days. Her patience and stamina were wearing thin from the search. Perhaps a private family might be better to work for than a sizable hotel: fewer responsibilities and less wear-and-tear, but of course the wages would be significantly lower. No, that would not do. She had a family of her own now; working for another was beneath her dignity. She would simply have to keep looking and possibly settle for something in a less dignified hotel than she would like. The expenses of adding Rachel and the children to the household had mounted higher and faster than she had supposed and—

"SHOOTING AT SARATOGA." The heading at the top of page seven caught her eye. The gay times she had spent up there during Augusts past with Harry flashed into her mind. In her memory it was a lovely, peaceful place, not ever a site of violence. Idly she began reading the story:

Saratoga Springs, N.Y.

At 12:30 yesterday morning, Sam Suggs, a card dealer at the Sparkling Spring Casino on Regent Street, suddenly and without warning, according to witnesses, who numbered more than a score, seemed to have taken a look at a man who stepped up to his faro table and then withdrew a pistol from an inside coat pocket. After shouting, "I've got you now, you _____ _____!" he shot the patron of the establishment, Mr. Harrison St. John Loring, in the region of his upper left thorax.

She felt her whole body convulse. Her eye raced on.

Immediately, several witnesses were able to disarm the assailant, who, while muttering incoherently, offered no resistance. Dr. Ansel Harding, a physician living only a few doors from the casino, was called, and he administered medical attention to the victim for the rest of the night and into the morning.

Oh, God in heaven. Her eyes brimmed, forcing her to lean closer to the printed page.

Despite the doctor's persistent ministrations, however, the patient succumbed to his wound at 8:53 in the morning. Mr. Loring's personal servant, Arthur Timmons, advised that there were no immediate survivors.

Mr. Suggs, upon being brought to the Saratoga Springs police station, would say only that his victim had wronged him some years ago while the assailant was employed at a casino in Florida. Funeral plans for Mr. Loring are unknown at this time.

Harry. The tears streamed down her face, but she uttered no sound. Her mind reeled backward. Suggs—who was he? The episode eluded her. There had been so many episodes, so many mischievous smiles, so many feints and bluffs and desperate gambles, that one of them was bound to have caught up with him. Oh Harry, Harry . . .

Her capacity for caring deeply had eroded with the passing months, her rage dwindling to bitterness and then a blank marblelike void. But a pang of longing went through her. He had surely loved her, in his fashion, had charmed her, disarmed her, delighted and enlightened her, opened her to a world she had feared to know, then exploited her and betrayed her—and now he was gone. His virtues inseparably meshed with his vices; he had not hidden that fatal flaw of character from her. To every gambler who had ever played cards with him, every easy mark he had gulled, every woman he had made love to, Harry Loring had brought an incandescent excitement, gaiety and laughter, daring and adventure, and a sense of possibilities where others saw only shadows. But he had been wanting in any sane proportion, in depth and any willingness ever to take the long way around—and it had been his ruination, as she always feared it would be.

She dropped the paper beside her chair. In a little while she would give Billy and Amanda their baths. They and their mother had become her reality.

"Mis Mem'ry, I came to see you today because—" His eyes, she saw, still bore traces of redness and swelling.

"I know, Arthur—it was in the paper. Please, won't you sit down?"

"Thank you, ma'am, but no. There's a train leaving for Florida in about an hour and I mean to be on it."

"Are you going back for good?"

"Maybe. For a while, anyway. Gives me time to catch my breath, see what I can do. I just came here, ma'am, to bring you this." He reached into his pocket and produced a rather rumpled envelope bearing the embossed imprimatur of the Thalia Club. "He—Mr. Loring—had some time before—the end—and he said some things he wanted me to write down and deliver to different people after he—went." He handed her the envelope. "I copied it over on the club stationery when I got back to the city so as it would keep better."

She smiled her appreciation. "What was done about—the arrangements?"

"Ma'am?"

"Mr. Loring's remains, Arthur."

"I took care of all that—up there. Didn't seem much point in bringing him back here."

"I see. And where is his resting place—exactly?"

Arthur seemed slightly flustered. "Well, he didn't hold much for church, you know, ma'am—he told me that night he wanted to be put straight into the ground, just like he was, with no fuss. But I asked around, and the Reverend Mr. Grimes of the Bethany African, he said they couldn't do that—it wasn't holy enough—so we got him a plain coffin, the plainest one they had, and the reverend, he didn't say too many words but they were fine ones, and the choir came and sang real nice. I think he would've liked it."

"I'm sure he would have," she said, taking his hands in hers. "But I didn't hear you say where he's buried."

"He's—in the colored folks' cemetery."

"I see."

"Do you think that would make a difference to him? They told me it could always be changed if—"

She shook her head. "I'm sure he wouldn't care. He might even enjoy it. That's as good a place as any other."

"Thank you, ma'am." Relief was written large on his grave, seamless face. "I've got to go now."

"God bless you, Arthur."

Her fingers trembled as she struggled with the tightly sealed envelope. The handwriting was an awkward imitation of his, but the words were unquestionably Harry's:

Maddy girl,

I have little time left. I want you to know no matter what I may have done, I never loved any woman but you. But I could never measure up. I wasn't good enough for you and always knew it. You deserved better. Perhaps you will yet find it.

A gentleman never welshes on a *real* debt, but what I owe you, I can never truly repay. My attorney will be in touch with you regarding the disposition of my estate.

Take care of yourself, my love. And if you should choose to be laid to rest beside me, you would honor me in death as I ought to have honored you in life—it is my sole regret.

H.

Only then did her sustained grieving for him begin. She dwelled on the ineffable sweetness of the man and the varieties of passionate tenderness he displayed. All the rest she drove from her mind.

* * *

It was several months before the attorney summoned her. In that interval Maddy would frequently stop what she was doing, sometimes in the midst of a sentence, and rush off to her room, closing the door tightly behind her. Her often red-rimmed eyes gave mute testimony to her melancholy, but she declined to disclose the cause of it beyond citing "the loss of an old friend." For while she had no misgivings about her long, bittersweet relationship with her late lover, she was reluctant to divulge its illicit nature to Rachel out of fear that it would lower her regard for her mother.

Meanwhile, she was listless, abandoning her search for employment, and seemed unable to take any nourishment, to the consternation of her daughter and grandchildren. Little Amanda, mirroring her mother's concern, would occasionally climb onto Maddy's lap during dinner and attempt to feed her, picking up morsels of food with her fingers and guiding them gently into her grandmother's mouth while approximating the same locomotive noises—*choo-choo, choo-chew, chew-chew*—that Maddy made as she fed the child. Rachel became increasingly worried about her, attributing her mother's extended malaise to a concern over their worsening financial predicament. But Maddy denied it, and when Rachel ventured that perhaps she ought to write her father in Paris, Maddy's irritability only deepened.

And then Harry's attorney summoned her to his office. "Mr. Loring was a most unusual person, as I hardly need dwell upon," he said to her, "and I suppose it's fitting that his last will and testament includes one unusual feature."

He had named two heirs, Arthur and her, "the only two people on earth who ever truly cared for me." To Arthur he had willed all his personal effects, including several curious antique objects providing their owner assistance in card playing, and ten thousand dollars outright. "Unfortunately, I do not know Mr. Timmons's whereabouts."

"I suspect his mother may know. I have her address at home."

"Excellent." The attorney then sat back a few inches and reached into his desk for a pack of playing cards. "Now with regard to your bequest, madam, I am instructed to advise the following. You and I are each to cut the deck once, you proceeding first, and if the card you turn up is the higher, then the entire balance of Mr. Loring's estate is to be yours. If mine is higher, one-half the balance will be otherwise disposed of." He looked sheepish as he placed the deck before her.

"I—it seems—" Maddy smiled and shook her head.

"I understand your feelings, madam. But I can only do as the will instructs me. He was a sporting gentleman till the end."

It was so like him, gambling with her even from the grave. Carefully she removed her glove and more carefully still reached toward the cards. Her hand hovered over the stack for a long moment, her thoughts more in prayer for his still conniving soul than for her own good fortune in the draw. Her fingers reached midway down and turned over the deck. The nine of diamonds.

"Very good, madam." The attorney unceremoniously replaced the top half of the deck and without delay made his own cut of the cards. It was the ace of spades.

Maddy's eyes widened and then quickly narrowed. "If I didn't know better, I'd say that—"

"And you'd be quite correct. He insisted on training me in the trick, madam, and in my utilizing it on this occasion."

"But why on earth would he—"

"For your amusement and amazement, I believe."

"And perhaps my punishment as well."

The attorney held up his hand. "In accordance with the outcome of our little contest, I hereby present you with a bank-draft drawn on Mr. Loring's estate in the amount of eighty-seven thousand three hundred fifty-four dollars"—he glanced at the financial instrument—"and nine cents."

"Good God."

"And I have here as well a draft in the identical amount"—he handed her both—"made out to Rachel Memory Caldwell."

That afternoon, upon returning from an excursion to the park with the children, Rachel found her mother seated on the sofa in the parlor. Traces of tears were still visible on her cheeks, but her expression was one of deep serenity. Wordlessly, she handed Rachel the piece of blue-green paper on her lap.

Rachel looked at the bank draft dumbly, her brow knitted. "I don't understand, Mother."

"Tonight," she said, "after the little ones are in bed, I will tell you a story with much sadness and even more happiness in it."